Minette Walters is one of the world's bestselling crime writers. She is the author of twelve novels, winning the CWA John Creasey Award for *The Ice House*, the Edgar Allan Poe Award in America for *The Sculptress* and two CWA Gold Daggers for *The Scold's Bridle* and *Fox Evil*. She lives in Dorset with her husband.

MINETTE WALTERS

The
Last Hours

THE OMNIBUS EDITION

ALLEN&UNWIN

The Last Hours first published in Great Britain in 2017 by Allen & Unwin.

The Turn of Midnight first published in Great Britain in 2018 by Allen & Unwin.

This omnibus edition first published in paperback Great Britain in 2021.

Allen & Unwin
c/o Atlantic Books
Ormond House
26–27 Boswell Street
London
WC1N 3JZ

Phone: 020 7269 1610
Fax: 020 7430 0916
Email: UK@allenandunwin.com
Web: www.allenandunwin.com/uk

A CIP catalogue record for this book is available from the British Library.

Paperback ISBN 978 1 91163 065 4
E-book ISBN 978 1 76087 326 4

Maps by Janet Hunt

10 9 8 7 6 5 4 3 2 1

Printed and bound by CPI Group (UK) Ltd, Croydon CR0 4YY

For Madeleine and Martha

With special thanks to The Dorset History Centre
for their help in the making of this book

AND

For my excellent Durham friends in Dorset
Amber, David, Geoffrey, Huw, Isobel, Jill,
Josh, Les, Mike C, Mike W, Richard
and Patrick and Lynden in Australia

Develish, 1348

Mid-Dorsetshire, 1348

N
W E
S

To Shasbury

To Sarum

Blandesforde
Town

River Stour

To Sherborne

Wall

Church
Guard House
Manor House

River Stour

To Develish

To Holcombe

Blandesforde, 1349

In Dorseteshire the plague made the country quite void of inhabitants so that there were almost none left alive. From there it passed into Devonshire and Somersetshire, even unto Bristol, and raged in such sort that the Gloucestershire men would not suffer the Bristol men to have access to them by any means. But at length it came to Gloucester, yea even to Oxford and to London, and finally it spread over all England and so wasted the people that scarce the tenth person of any sort was left alive.

Geoffrey the Baker,
Chronicon Angliae temporibus Edwardi II et Edwardi III

We see death coming into our midst like black smoke, a plague which cuts off the young, a rootless phantom which has no mercy or fair countenance. It is seething, terrible, wherever it may come, a head that gives pain and causes a loud cry, a burden carried under the arms, a painful angry knob, a lump. It is an ugly eruption that comes with unseemly haste. The early ornament of a Black Death.

Jeuan Gethin (d. 1349)

And there were those who were so sparsely covered with earth that the dogs dragged them forth and devoured many bodies throughout the city.

Agnolo di Tura, *Cronica Senese*

Men and women [of Florence] abandoned their dwellings, their relatives, their property . . . as if they thought nobody in the city would remain alive and that its last hour had come.

Giovanni Boccaccio, *The Decameron*

So great a plague has never been heard of from the beginning of the world to the present day ... The sickness befell people everywhere ... and generated such horror that children did not dare to visit their dying parents, nor parents their children, but fled for fear of contagion.

John of Fordun, *Scotichronicon*

Towns once packed with people were emptied of their inhabitants, and the plague spread so thickly that the living were hardly able to bury the dead. In some religious houses not more than two survived out of twenty. It was calculated by several people that barely a tenth of mankind remained alive ... Rents dwindled and land was left untilled for want of tenants (who were nowhere to be found). And so much wretchedness followed these ills that afterwards the world could never return to its former state.

Thomas Walsingham, St Albans Abbey, *Chronicle*

Many villages and hamlets became deserted ... Sheep and cattle went wandering over fields and through crops and there was no one to look after them ... In the autumn [following the pestilence] no one could get a reaper for less than 8d, or a mower for less than 12d. Therefore, many crops perished in the fields for want of someone to gather them.

Henry Knighton, *Chronicle*

The
Last Hours

THIRD DAY OF JULY, 1348

One

THE SUMMER HEAT WAS SUCKING the life from Develish. Leaves wilted on trees, ponies stood heads down, too tired to crop the grass, chickens settled in the dust with their eyes closed and serfs leant heavily on their scythes in the fields. Only blowflies prospered, swarming around the mounds of dung-soiled straw outside the cattle sheds and buzzing annoyingly through every room in the manor house.

It was not a day for travelling, which explained Sir Richard of Develish's ill-humour. His voice rose in anger each time his steward or servants failed to react fast enough to his demands, and since the journey wasn't one he wanted to make, there was a good deal to rage about. Only the calming influence of his wife, Lady Anne, allowed the preparations to go ahead. Quietly, she overruled every decision Sir Richard made and ordered the servants to pack his bags according to her instructions.

Eleanor, their fourteen-year-old daughter, listened to it all from Lady Anne's chamber upstairs. She was as resentful about her father's trip as he was, and wished her mother in Hell for forcing him to take it. The girl should have been working on an embroidered pillow for her trousseau but, instead, she stood at the window, watching a covered wagon being loaded with wooden chests of food and clothes, and money for her dowry.

Eleanor was spoilt and petulant at the best of times, but the heat made her worse. Her eyes were drawn to a serf who was weaving new sapling whips into the wattle fence that surrounded the orchard. He worked deftly, flexing the green wood with strong, sun-browned arms before threading it between the weathered wood of previous years. Only a foolish slave would labour so hard in those temperatures, and a satisfied smile lit Eleanor's face when she recognised him. Nothing pleased her more than to find reasons to belittle Thaddeus Thurkell.

Like all bondsmen, he was dirty and ragged, but he was half a head taller than most Dorset men, and his swarthy skin, long black hair and almond-shaped eyes bore no resemblance to the man he called father—short-limbed, weaselly-faced Will Thurkell. One rumour had it that Eva Thurkell had run away to Melcombe to sleep with a sailor, another that Thaddeus was the result of a snatched coupling with a passing gypsy.

Whatever the truth, the father hated the son and the son hated the father. The boy had been subjected to daily beatings while he was growing up, but these days Will was too afraid of him to lift the stick, for it was said that Thaddeus could bend an iron bar over his knee and fell a grown man with a single punch to the head. He paid lip service to his lowly place in Develish, ducking his head when he had to, but there was no respect in the way he did it. He looked past people as if they weren't there, particularly the man who acknowledged him as a son.

Will Thurkell was lazy and resented the *ad opus* work he was expected to do for the manor in return for his strips of land. Even as a young boy, Thaddeus had had to sweat in his father's place on the threat that his mother would be given the rod if he didn't. A sad and sorry woman without an ounce of spirit, Eva had had more than her share of punishment down the years. Only the dwarfish, pale-skinned children who came after Thaddeus had been spared her husband's wrath.

This wasn't to say that Eleanor had any sympathy for Eva. The harlot had known the rules when she lay in sin with another, and it was her own fault if she couldn't pass her bastard off as Will's. Gossip said she'd tried to claim Thaddeus was the product of rape, but few believed her since she hadn't mentioned violation until the swarthy baby, so different from her husband, arrived. The stain of illegitimacy made Thaddeus as sinful as his mother, though you wouldn't think it to watch him. He carried his head high instead of hanging it in shame.

Eleanor liked the idea of bringing Thaddeus Thurkell to his knees. He was six years older than she was, and she dreamt of humbling him. As the temperature rose, he shed his tunic and laboured on in short hose and a loose-fitting shirt with rolled-up sleeves. It pleased the girl to spy on him; it pleased her even more to think he knew she was doing it. When he tied a piece of cloth around his forehead to keep the sweat from his eyes, he stared directly at her window and her cheeks flushed rosy red from guilty desire.

It was her father's fault for promising her to the ugly, pock-marked son of a neighbouring lord whose demesne, larger than Develish's, was two days' ride away. She faced a joyless future married to Peter of Bradmayne, who was so puny he could barely sit astride a horse. Eleanor's own pony, a pretty little bay jennet with white stockings, was cropping grass in the part of her father's demesne that lay beyond the moat. She was tempted to go outside and demand Thaddeus saddle it and assist her to mount. If he dared to look at her while he was doing it, she would slice his face with her crop.

This amusing fantasy was cut short by the sound of her mother's footsteps on the stairs. Eleanor scurried back to her stool and her embroidery, and pretended industry where there was none. Her feelings for Lady Anne bordered on hatred, because Eleanor knew perfectly well that she had her mother to thank for choosing Peter of Bradmayne as a husband. Lady Anne preferred duty and discipline to love. She had been brought up by nuns and should have taken vows, since her favourite pastime was nagging and lecturing her daughter about her failings.

Eleanor could tell from the silence that Lady Anne was counting how many stitches had been added to the design since last she looked. 'It's too warm,' she declared mutinously. 'My fingers keep slipping on the needle.'

'You don't sew it for me, daughter, you sew it for yourself. If you see no merit in the task, then choose something more rewarding to do.'

'There is nothing.'

Through the open window Lady Anne could hear the shuffle of horses' hooves on the baked mud of the forecourt below as Sir Richard's retinue mustered for the journey. In the fields beyond the moat, she could see the serfs at the back-breaking task of making hay; closer in, Thaddeus Thurkell sweated over the wattle fence. It wasn't difficult to guess what Eleanor had been doing with her time. 'Your father summons you to say goodbye,' she said. 'He will be gone a fortnight.'

The girl rose. 'I shall tell him I don't want him to go.'

'As you please.'

Eleanor stamped her foot. 'It's you who makes him go. You make everyone do things they don't like.'

Lady Anne's eyes creased with amusement. 'Not your father, Eleanor. He may throw tantrums to remind us of the efforts he makes on our behalf, but he wouldn't be going to Bradmayne if it wasn't in his interests to do so.'

'What interests?'

'He's heard rumours that Peter of Bradmayne's childhood sickness has returned. He wants to see the truth for himself before he puts his seal to the marriage contract.' She shook her head at the sudden hope in her daughter's expression. 'Be careful what you wish for, Eleanor. If Peter dies, you may end up with no husband at all.'

'I won't shed tears because of it.'

'You will when your cousin inherits this house. Better by far to be mistress of Bradmayne than a lonely old maid relying on a relative's charity for bed and board.'

'The world is full of men,' the girl said defiantly. 'There are many more pleasing husbands than Peter of Bradmayne.'

'But none that your father can afford,' Lady Anne reminded her. 'Develish is Sir Richard's only demesne, and he has never been granted another. Do you not think he would offer a larger dowry if he could? He spoils you in everything else. Be grateful for Bradmayne and pray that Peter is strong enough to give you sons so that one may become Lord of Develish.'

Eleanor loathed these conversations in which her mother preached and she was forced to listen. 'Perhaps I'll be cursed like you,' she muttered spitefully. 'Father says it's your fault he has no heir.'

'Then you have a sad future ahead of you,' the woman answered. 'I mourn the lack of a son every day, and so should you.'

'I don't see why,' the girl said with a flounce of her long skirts. 'It's not my fault you never had one.'

7

Lady Anne despaired of her daughter's stupidity. Eleanor was an undoubted beauty, with her pale skin, blonde hair and startling blue eyes—a miniature of her father—but despite years of patient teaching, she was incapable of keeping a thought in her head. 'If you had brothers, My Lord of Blandeforde would have granted your father's applications for more lands on their behalf and he could have used the levies from the other estates to ensure your future,' she said quietly. 'As it is, he has been unable to persuade a man of wealth to overlook the paucity of your dowry. We have had many visitors here but none has made an offer for you.'

Eleanor's eyes narrowed. 'They're afraid I'll grow scrawny and ugly like you, Mother. Even Father can't bear to touch you any more.'

'No,' Lady Anne agreed. 'I count it as one of my few blessings, although I dislike the way you encourage him to put his hands on you.'

'You mustn't be so jealous. I'm not to blame if Sir Richard loves me more than he loves you. You should have taken care not to disappoint him.'

Humour glimmered briefly in Lady Anne's eyes. 'Your father loves many women,' she said, 'but you are his only child. If you didn't have his likeness he'd doubt your parentage.'

'You lie.'

The woman eyed her curiously. 'What offends you, Eleanor? That your father can't make sons or that he pretends I'm the only competition you have for his affections? Where do you think he goes when he rides from home of an afternoon? Who do you think he sees? He has as strong a taste for serfs as you do.'

The girl stamped her foot again. 'I *hate* you,' she hissed.

Her mother turned away. 'Then pray that Lord Peter is free of sickness and agrees with Sir Richard that you should be married before summer is out. If your husband can overlook the selfishness of your nature, you should find him easier to tolerate than you do me.'

∽

Thaddeus Thurkell was careful to keep his contempt well hidden as he observed the daughter's farewell to her father out of the corner of his eye. Nothing about it was honest. Sir Richard and Lady Eleanor were too alike—self-satisfied and demanding of attention, each arrayed in brightly embroidered apparel—and the only purpose of their noisy parting was to make everyone aware of it. As always, their behaviour and dress eclipsed the quieter people around them and, as always, Lady Anne stood apart, unloved and unnoticed. She had none of the flamboyance of her husband and daughter, and Thaddeus liked her better for it. He knew that she'd spent time in a nunnery as a child, being educated by the sisters, and he assumed her quiet wisdom and knowledge of medicine came from that experience.

It wasn't Thaddeus's place to feel sorry for Milady—he had no business thinking about her at all—but he couldn't see her in the presence of her husband and daughter without being offended on her behalf. They paid her as little respect as his stepfather paid his mother but, unlike Eva, Lady Anne had too much pride to show she cared. She made it appear that she was standing apart by choice, and looked the other way when Sir Richard ran his ham-like fists over his daughter, pulling her close and planting juicy kisses on her lips before heaving his burly body onto his black charger and calling to his retinue to fall in behind him.

As the convoy set off, Thaddeus kept his head down and continued to weave the green hazel into the wattle fence. The sound of the cart wheels creaking over the rough track wasn't loud enough to mask the swish of Lady Eleanor's embroidered gown as she walked across the forecourt towards him, but Thaddeus refused to give her the satisfaction of turning around and dropping to one knee. His penance would be a kick and a torrent of abuse for impudence, but he preferred that to paying homage to someone he despised. If there was any charity in Lady Eleanor, he had yet to see it.

To prove the point, the girl picked up one of his sapling whips and struck him with it. 'How dare you turn your back on me!' she snapped.

Thaddeus straightened and this time the whip, swung in an upward arc, caught him under the chin.

'Know your station,' Eleanor ordered. 'Lower your head and bend your knee. It's not for you to look at me.'

Thaddeus didn't answer, simply stooped to retrieve another sapling from the ground and began to feed it into the fence, ignoring the blow that landed across his shoulders. He was sure Sir Richard's new steward was watching from the house, and his penalty for breaking off from his work to humour Lady Eleanor would be severe. Gossip said the man had been brought in to raise extra revenue for Sir Richard's extravagances, and Thaddeus was disinclined to oblige him by paying a fine. He held Lady Eleanor and the steward in equal contempt, but he could take a thrashing more easily from a fourteen-year-old girl than his family could afford a pound of grain.

He was spared further punishment by Lady Anne. She caught her daughter's wrist and forced it down, removing the whip while congratulating the serf on the excellence of his work. 'You must excuse my daughter, Thaddeus. She doesn't know the difference between a job done well and a job done badly. You deserve much praise for what you do.'

He turned and bowed to her. 'Thank you, milady. I trust this day finds you well.'

'It does indeed.' She put her hand on Eleanor's arm. 'Come, child. We have things to attend to inside.'

Thaddeus watched them walk away, wondering why so little of the mother was in the daughter. The girl took after her father in everything—even cruelty—with only the neatness of her build resembling Lady Anne's. The woman was dark, the girl blonde like her father. Thaddeus's own situation made him peculiarly sensitive to family likenesses. He looked for differences between generations in the way a hunchback looked for telltale twists in the spines of others. It soothed a man's brain to believe he wasn't alone in his affliction.

As a child, Thaddeus had prayed his hair would change colour or his bones stop growing so that Will would look at him one morning and see something he recognised. But as he grew older and the beatings became worse, he learnt to glory in the fact that he had no relationship with the man. It wasn't by accident that Will's progeny were small and slow-witted, and Thaddeus was not. He couldn't remember the number of times his mother had begged him to play the idiot in front of Will. It was the cleverness of Thaddeus's mind that drove her vicious husband mad, not the darkness of his looks or his tallness. *Cover your gaze, keep silent*, Eva had urged. *Do not provoke him with the slickness of your tongue or the scorn that blazes from your eyes. He has none of your ability, and he knows it. Do it for me if not for yourself.*

Thaddeus had mixed feelings about his mother. She rarely showed him love for fear of Will's jealousy, but her need of him shouted from her pleading eyes and her desperate clutching at his tunic whenever she heard Will approach. She made Thaddeus promise each day that he would not abandon her, but it irked him that she had never found the courage to defend him against Will's physical and verbal assaults.

He had heard his mother being called a whore all his life, and it was hard to think of her as anything else. When he was ten, he'd asked her who his true father was, but she'd refused to tell him. Will would beat it out of him and their situation would become worse. Her husband's rage would be uncontrollable if he had a name to brood on instead of believing that Thaddeus was the result of rape by a stranger.

Her answer had led Thaddeus to think his father must be known to Will. He studied his own face in the beaten metal plate that passed for a mirror in Will's hut and then searched the features of every man in Develish—rich and poor alike—looking for eyes, complexions and noses that resembled his. He didn't find them, and as time passed he came to accept the rumours that his father was a foreign sailor. He even liked the idea. There was more to respect about a man who travelled the seas than one who was bonded to a feudal lord.

Precisely what Thaddeus's status was in Sir Richard's manor had never been defined. As Eva's bastard, he had no right to inherit Will's holdings—several strips of land and the dwelling that went with them—but when Thaddeus asked the priest what would happen to him after Will was dead, the old man had shrugged and told him to work hard and keep improving his skills. As long as Sir Richard valued the quality of his labour, there was no reason for Thaddeus to concern himself with his future. Even slaves were well looked after when they had their master's approval.

It was Will's favourite taunt to call Eva's bastard a slave. He claimed he owned Thaddeus body and soul; that without his patronage the boy would have been left to die in one of the ditches outside Develish. He seemed unaware that serfdom itself was a form of slavery, and that the oath of fealty he'd sworn to Sir Richard—*I will not marry or leave this land without my lord's permission and I bind my children and my children's children to this promise . . .*'—tied him and his legitimate offspring to Develish in a way that it didn't tie Thaddeus.

The person who had explained this to Thaddeus had been Lady Anne. She had drawn him aside on Lady Day in his thirteenth year when he was cleaning out the poultry pens and told him the bailiff was coming for him. 'You must take care he doesn't find you,' she warned. 'This is the day when Sir Richard hears the oaths of bondage. Since you cannot be governed by the pledges Will has made, I urge you to be wary of making any of your own. Without land or dwelling, you will be dependent on my husband's goodwill for your food and board, and that is not a fate I would wish on you, Thaddeus.'

He didn't understand why Lady Anne took an interest in him but he owed her more than he owed anyone else, and she had never once asked for anything in return. 'If I escape the bailiff this year, milady, he will find me the next.'

'My husband's steward is unwell and not likely to live another twelve months,' she told him, 'and it's he who questions your position. Sir Richard will have forgotten the matter inside a week, and a new steward will know nothing of your circumstances. Every year that passes is a year of freedom gained. Remember that.'

Thaddeus thought of the punishment he would receive for leaving his work. When the bailiff had finished with him, Will would take over. Was it worth so much pain just to avoid mouthing a few words of servitude? 'Do freemen endure starvation more easily than slaves, milady?'

Lady Anne smiled. 'You know they do not, Thaddeus, but a slave will always die before his master does. If you value your life, show care not to swear it away too easily, and take even more care to stay silent on the subject. If my husband is warned in advance that you have the right to declare yourself free of him, he will consult the bishop and use Church law to rule against you.'

The thrashings had been as bad as any Thaddeus had received but, as Lady Anne had predicted, the old steward died and his query about whether a bastard was bound by the oath of a man who refused to adopt him as his own was forgotten. It made little difference to Thaddeus's life except that he began to imagine a future outside Develish. His dreams were necessarily limited by his ignorance of what lay beyond the village, but they sparked a hope he'd never had before. He paid more attention to the stories told by the pedlars and merchants who passed through Develish, and listened to what the leading bondsmen said when they drove sheep to other demesnes or nearby markets.

He was most interested in descriptions of the sea which he knew lay to the south. His ambition was to reach it one day and take a ship to a foreign port where he would be known as something other than Eva Thurkell's bastard or Will Thurkell's slave. In winter, when the trees shed their leaves and he climbed the wooded slopes at the end of the valley to collect fallen branches to feed the manor house fires, he could see hills all the way to the horizon. They seemed to rise in height to shimmering purple in the far distance, and he convinced himself that his gateway to another world lay on the other side. But how far away it was, and how long it would take him to walk there, he had no idea.

ΩXΌ

Eleanor wrested her arm from her mother's grasp as they entered the house. 'Don't ever speak to me like that in front of a slave again,' she stormed. 'Thaddeus was insolent. He deserved to be whipped.'

Lady Anne walked away from her. 'You behaved badly, daughter. Be grateful I spared you further shame.'

The girl pursued her. 'It's you who has a taste for serfs not I or Father. Do you think I don't see the way Thaddeus behaves towards you? When he makes a bow to Sir Richard, he does it to avoid a beating, but the ones he makes to you are genuine. Why is that?'

Lady Anne was surprised that her daughter was so perceptive. 'I gave him liniment once or twice for his bruises when he was a child. I expect he remembers.'

'He feels sorry for you. That's why he does it. I can see it in his eyes.'

Lady Anne paused before they reached the kitchen. The room was uncharacteristically silent, as if every servant inside was listening to the conversation. 'Then you see wrongly, Eleanor. Only God knows what is going on inside a person's head.'

The girl smiled. 'Thaddeus makes himself your equal if he dares feel pity for you. What is that if not insolence? Will Father say I behaved badly if I tell him Eva Thurkell's bastard assumes the rights of a freeman?'

Lady Anne studied her for a moment. 'I suggest you worry more about Sir Richard's displeasure when he learns how interested *you* are in Thaddeus Thurkell, Eleanor. There is as much to read in your eyes as there is in anyone else's.'

The third day of July, 1348

*S*ir Richard has left for Bradmayne, accompanied by 10 fighting men and the bailiff, Master Foucault. They take with them the gold I have preserved so carefully for Eleanor's dowry. I wonder if the effort was worth it when she curses me in one breath for not saving enough to purchase a better husband, and blames me in the next for preventing Sir Richard from gambling it away on games of chance. With no dowry, she would be unable to wed at all, and she assures me she would prefer that to being married to Lord Peter.

In my heart, I hope the rumours that the boy is ailing are true, for I see no happiness for Eleanor in Bradmayne. Her father has told her so many lies that she's ill-prepared for what she'll find there. It amuses him to belittle Lord Peter in her eyes for he's jealous of her affections, but he doesn't hesitate to paint Bradmayne as a place of beauty, wealth and wonder.

Such descriptions are quite different from the reports Gyles Startout brings me. If I thought Eleanor would believe me, I would try to advise her, but Sir Richard has made fine work of persuading her that I'm responsible for this match. Everything I say falls on deaf ears, in particular my attempts to portray Lord

Peter in a kinder light. If she succeeds in giving him a son, I fear the baby will be conceived and born in hatred.

I spoke with Gyles in private before Sir Richard left. He is more loyal than I and Develish deserve, tolerating insult from both my husband and the men he rides with in order to bring us news from the world outside. I have asked him to enquire of the Bradmayne servants how Eleanor might best make a friend of My Lady of Bradmayne—even the knowledge that My Lady has a fondness for ribbons would be of use. I fear Eleanor will suffer great loneliness without a confidante.

FOURTEENTH DAY OF JULY, 1348

Two

Bradmayne, Dorseteshire

GYLES STARTOUT QUICKLY LOST INTEREST in whether or not Lady Eleanor's future mother-in-law could be wooed with ribbons. A more pressing concern was how accurately he was interpreting what he was seeing. He knew from previous visits to Bradmayne that the enmity between My Lord and his people was powerful—floggings were frequent, taxes high and distrust a common emotion—but the divide seemed peculiarly wide now.

Since Sir Richard's arrival nine days ago, Gyles had been watching serfs gather in groups about their doors in the village, debating heatedly with each other and looking towards the heavily barred gate in the manor's boundary wall. They appeared restless and angry, though at three hundred paces they were too far away for Gyles to make out their expressions or hear what they said. None attempted to approach the gate.

Only the steward, the bailiff and the priest were permitted to come and go at will. The priest went on foot, giving blessings and receiving courtesy in return; the steward and bailiff rode on horseback, the one shouting orders and the other enforcing them with a bull whip. Once or twice, Gyles saw women gesture towards the church which stood inside the manor enclosure, as if asking the priest why they couldn't visit him there, but the man invariably shook his head. It seemed everything inside the wall was out of bounds to peasants.

Gyles observed all this during the long, tedious hours he was confined with other fighting men in an open-sided barn on the forecourt. Each of My Lord of Bradmayne's guests had brought his own entourage and space was limited. There were some fifty soldiers occupying the barrack and all but Gyles were French. He spoke and understood their language but had little in common with them. They were hired mercenaries who talked of home and showed no interest in Dorseteshire or her people, complaining the soft, unintelligible burr of their dialect deterred conversation.

The intense summer heat—made worse by Sir Richard's injunction that his men wear their heavy woollen livery at all times—sapped energy. To move was to cause a river of sweat to pour down the soldiers' backs. Yet with only two wells inside the manor enclosure, and a crowd of invited lords and their guards camped on the available land, water was becoming a scarce commodity. Gyles was aware of it because he heard and understood what the house servants said, but the French, whose drinks of choice were ale and sour wine, remained ignorant.

They sat in the shade of the barn, tossing dice and mocking Gyles for choosing to stand apart in the lee of the manor house. They called him 'Grandpere' because of his forty-five years and grizzled hair, and jeered at him for playing soldier when he didn't have to. They believed him slow-witted because he was born into bondage, and Gyles did nothing to change their opinion. He'd suffered the jibes of fighting men for as long as he'd been in Sir Richard's retinue.

He was there because Lady Anne had persuaded her husband to elevate a Develish serf to fighting man, and Gyles gained no respect by his low-born status or having a woman plead for him. Even soldiers who were recent additions to Sir Richard's retinue looked down on him, and the tasks he was given were menial. He made no complaint. His loyalty to Lady Anne far outweighed the frustration of acting as stable hand to his colleagues or slop-emptier to his Norman master.

He was Milady's eyes and ears on every journey her husband took, and the information he brought home benefited Develish. Lady Anne was interested in how other demesnes were managed— well or badly—and secretly recorded Gyles's detailed accounts on vellum. In private she used what she learnt to influence Sir Richard's stewards; in public she pretended interest in trifling descriptions of banquets and cockfights, which were all her husband saw fit to bring back from his visits.

In truth, Gyles doubted Sir Richard was capable of describing anything else. His intellect was poor, his appetites carnal and he had so little interest in the management of his own demesne that he was unlikely to see progress in another. He could make his mark on the letters and writs his steward placed in front of him, but his inability to read meant he had no idea what he was signing.

Most of the knowledge Gyles gained came from talking to serfs. Develish born and bred, he was easily recognised by Dorseteshire men as one of their own. They knew of his family and gave him their trust despite his role as soldier to a Norman lord. But Gyles had yet to find a single person in Bradmayne—even those he'd befriended on previous visits—who was willing to speak with him. The house servants shook their heads nervously when he tried to engage them, and the barricaded gate put the field serfs beyond his reach.

On the third day, he approached the guards who manned it. He told them truthfully that he had a cousin who was married to a Bradmayne man and asked permission to walk to the village to spend an hour in her company. They refused, citing orders from My Lord of Bradmayne that guests and their retainers must remain inside the enclosure. When Gyles asked the reason, he was advised that an unexpected levy had caused unrest amongst the bondsmen.

It was a persuasive answer. My Lord's revelries to celebrate the contract of alliance between Bradmayne and Develish were showy and lavish, designed to secure the dowry of gold that Sir Richard had brought with him. If Bradmayne was feeding his guests at the expense of his people, the sense of injustice would be considerable.

Gyles was careful never to show his disapproval of the excesses he witnessed on trips such as these. To watch Sir Richard toss a half-eaten haunch of venison to a pack of hunting dogs or slump to the floor through inebriation offended him when serfs were hungry, but to reveal it in his expression would be to forfeit his position. He knew well that his French colleagues would betray him if they guessed at his contempt for the man he served. Or, indeed, for the whole ruling class.

Lords lived off the labour of peasants, spurring them to greater effort through punishment. No hired French mercenary knew this as well as Gyles, who had toiled many years in Develish's fields. The work of a serf was arduous and unremitting, and starvation came perilously close when crops failed or taxes were raised without warning. Gyles remembered his own anger when his family's small reserves of grain and beans were seized by Sir Richard's stewards to be wasted on days of indulgence such as these. Yet he began to doubt that an unscheduled tax was the root of the villagers' anger when he absented himself to walk around the boundary wall and saw that the peasant strips to the west still had crops to be harvested. Levies were easier to bear in summer when food was plentiful, and My Lord's own virgates to the south were full of ripening wheat and beans. Gyles questioned why he would stir unrest amongst his people when he had abundant grain of his own.

By the sixth day, he noticed that the restlessness in the village had given way to fear. When the women looked towards the house, it was to search for the priest. At the sight of his robed figure passing through the gate, they dropped to their knees, holding out their hands in supplication as he made his way towards them. Their manner suggested they were seeking absolution as a group, and the priest's all-embracing signs of the cross implied that he was giving it.

He carried a leather bag which Gyles guessed contained vials of holy water, unction and medicine. When he entered a dwelling, which he did frequently, he remained inside for a long time, and even the dullest mind could guess he was bringing succour to the sick. Gyles assumed the priest's potions and prayers were effective because no bodies were brought out, and it led him to wonder why the serfs were so afraid. Whatever malady had entered Bradmayne was clearly survivable.

He changed his mind on this morning, the ninth, when his sharp eyes picked out a mound of freshly turned earth on common land to the east. It had the appearance of a grave, yet it was overly large for a single corpse. He had no recollection of its being there the previous day and questioned when it had been dug. Overnight? If so, why the secrecy? And by what right did My Lord of Bradmayne deny his people a Christian burial in consecrated ground?

Sickness had been at the forefront of Sir Richard's mind on the journey here. He'd talked of rumours that Lady Eleanor's future husband was ailing and ordered his men to watch and listen for anything that might confirm the stories. He was convinced Lord Peter would be paraded before him with his face painted with rouge to give the semblance of health. There were advantages to forming an alliance between Bradmayne and Develish, but not if it meant paying a dowry for a doomed marriage that failed to produce heirs.

Predictably, Sir Richard's ability to assess Peter of Bradmayne's health was gone within a few hours of their arrival—in drink, he would have thought a one-legged serf a suitable mate for his daughter—but Gyles could see nothing wrong with the young man. He looked as well as he had on previous visits. He lacked stature and carried the marks of childhood pox on his face, which Sir Richard had been overly keen to convey to his daughter, but his skin was bare of rouge and he feasted and drank as heartily as his father's guests.

It was no secret in Develish that Lady Eleanor wanted out of this marriage, and Gyles felt some pity for Lord Peter. He might come to regret his father's choice of a bride when he experienced Eleanor's mercurial tantrums. There would be little to please her in Bradmayne if even her husband disappointed her. In his more cynical moments, Gyles thought the girl would appreciate serfs being stung by the whip for every little misdemeanour, but he didn't doubt she'd be shocked by the squalor.

Men urinated where they stood, women emptied slops outside their doors, and dogs and vermin scavenged on the excrement. It was no better inside the enclosure, where an open sewer ran beside the house, creating such a stench that even Sir Richard noticed it. On the rare occasions when he was sober enough to stumble from the house, he clutched a clove-scented orange to his nose. Gyles found the evidence of rat infestation more disturbing. Their droppings were in the kitchen and in the grain stores, yet nothing was done to deter them. My Lord of Bradmayne seemed ignorant or careless that human filth was being transferred on fur and feet to his food.

Out of the corner of his eye, Gyles saw the priest present himself at the gate as he did every morning, and he turned from his inspection of the mound of earth to watch what happened. The exchange was different from previous days. The priest, his cowl pulled over his head to hide his face, seemed bowed with fatigue, and the guards drew away from him in alarm. With trembling hands, he blessed them with the sign of the cross then raised the bar himself and walked with unsteady steps towards the village.

There was no sign of the steward and bailiff whose habit was to leave the enclosure at the same time with saddles and bridles on their arms. Their horses, hobbled on pastureland outside the boundary wall along with those of My Lord of Bradmayne's guests, continued to graze peacefully in the sun. Were they still abed after a night spent overseeing the digging and filling of a mass grave? Gyles wondered. Or, worse, weak with sickness like the priest?

He watched and waited until midday, then sought out Pierre de Boulet, Sir Richard's captain of arms. Had he not believed it necessary to speak with the Frenchman, Gyles would have kept his suspicions to himself, for he could guess the response he would receive for daring to voice an opinion. De Boulet, yet to reach thirty and only two years a captain, never hid his annoyance that an English serf was one of Sir Richard's fighting men.

'What do you want?' he demanded in French after Gyles had stood for several minutes in silence, watching him roll dice in the dust of the barn floor with three of his fellow captains.

Gyles answered in the same language. 'A moment of your time, sir.'

'I'm busy.'

'It's important, sir.'

'Speak.'

'In private, if you please, sir. The matter concerns Sir Richard.'

De Boulet, losing money steadily, glared at him. 'You overreach yourself. My Lord's affairs are no concern of yours.'

Gyles made a small bow. 'Would you rather I spoke with Master Foucault, sir? As bailiff to Develish, it is he who has charge of Sir Richard's gold.'

With a sour look, the Frenchman excused himself from the game and stood up. Foucault was another who challenged de Boulet's right to choose who rode in Sir Richard's retinue. The bailiff's place was at home, assisting the steward in enforcing his master's authority; instead he was here, entrusted with the treasure chest until Sir Richard saw fit to pass it to My Lord of Bradmayne. And for what reason? So that Sir Richard's fighting men, absolved of responsibility, could form a guard whenever it pleased him to step outside.

Gyles understood de Boulet's frustrations better than the Frenchman knew. To be captain of arms to Sir Richard was to suffer indignity. There was no ignoring the smirks of amusement that rippled through the open-sided barn each time he and his men were obliged to form a line when their inebriated master emerged onto the forecourt to piss into the sewer. De Boulet's predecessors had never lasted long, preferring to seek employment elsewhere rather than enforce Sir Richard's humbling orders.

'You have no business speaking of My Lord's gold in front of others,' de Boulet snapped, following Gyles outside. 'I'll have you flogged if you do it again. What do you know?'

'I know Sir Richard wants the dowry guarded until he's assured Lord Peter is well, sir.'

De Boulet's eyes narrowed. 'Do you have reason to think he isn't?'

'No, but I believe there's a killing sickness in the village, sir. The priest has been tending the afflicted for days and, overnight, a grave has been dug in one of the fields.'

The Frenchman's scowl deepened. 'You call me from my game to tell me peasants are dying? How is that news? Ten died of fever and running stools in Pedle Hinton last year.'

'But none was refused a Christian burial, sir. If you look east to the common land, you'll see a mound big enough to cover a number of bodies. It was excavated in secret while the rest of us slept. It seems My Lord of Bradmayne wants to close the church to the dead as well as the living.'

De Boulet looked where Gyles had indicated. 'To what end?'

'I don't know, sir. Either he's afraid of the sickness spreading to the enclosure or he wants his guests to remain ignorant that his serfs are dying. Perhaps both. It will not serve his interests if Sir Richard falls ill before the dowry is paid . . . or questions whether to pay it at all.'

'Sir Richard worries for Lord Peter's health, not a handful of peasants.'

Gyles gave a small bow as if in respectful agreement. 'Indeed, sir, but the mound looks some thirty paces in length and two wide—large enough for forty bodies laid side by side. More if the dead are children. That's well above a handful.'

'You can't judge size from such a distance. Who's been filling your head with this nonsense? Who have you been talking to?'

'No one, sir. The field serfs are banished from the enclosure and the house servants won't speak with me. The length of the mound can be estimated by the oaks to the right of it. Felled, such trees stretch to more than sixty paces and the grave is easily half that . . . if not more.'

The Frenchman looked towards the common land again and saw that Gyles was right. 'It matters not. Illness in the village is no threat to us. Our stay will be over in three days.'

Gyles ducked his head again, more to hide his irritation at de Boulet's complacency than to feign respect. 'The priest looks far from well, sir, and the bailiff and steward have not appeared this morning. If all three have the sickness, it is inside the enclosure already. I cannot say what manner of affliction it is, but it seems to spread quickly. The number labouring in the fields today is much reduced from last week. My Lord of Bradmayne has four hundred people bonded to him, yet this morning I have counted a bare ten dozen at work on the strips. The women, children and greybeards remain in the village but their numbers too seem diminished.'

'For a serf, you seem very able with figures.'

Gyles raised his head. 'You will see I am right if you make the count yourself, sir.'

'What if you are? It's a problem for My Lord of Bradmayne, not Sir Richard.'

'Sir Richard would think it a problem if he knew about it, sir. Without workers, a demesne loses value very quickly. Dead men can't bring in the harvest or plant for next year, and My Lord of Bradmayne will struggle to raise taxes if his people are dying. To form an alliance with him in those circumstances would be risky.'

De Boulet was unimpressed. 'You pretend a knowledge you don't have.'

'My worries are as much for Develish as for Bradmayne, sir. We will do our own people no service if we take a sickness home with us. We should leave now while Sir Richard and the eleven who form his entourage are well.'

'Our demesne is in no danger from it. By God's grace and the purity of our air, we're blessed with good health. Sir Richard's piety keeps it so.'

De Boulet was as self-deceiving as Sir Richard if he believed God's grace so easily won, but Gyles saw merit in exploiting his credulity. 'Indeed, sir, and My Lord of Bradmayne must know he cannot match our master's goodness. He wouldn't need to hide what is happening here otherwise. Shouldn't Sir Richard be told this before he hands over his gold? Men of devotion don't willingly tie themselves to those whom God seeks to punish.'

De Boulet turned away, his reluctance to raise such a subject with Sir Richard all too obvious to Gyles. 'I'll make enquiries about the steward and bailiff, though I doubt there's any truth in what you say,' he snapped. 'It's the habit of low-born serfs to scare themselves with fancies.'

Gyles watched him walk towards the door of the manor house and then resumed his place in the lee of the wall. He hoped quite sincerely that de Boulet was right. He would rather be mocked for imagined fears than take a sickness to Develish which could kill upwards of forty in a week. Lady Anne might know of such a malady but not Gyles. Even starvation, the dreaded red pox and the bloody flux took time to create sufferers and weaken them so badly that they succumbed.

☙

As the sun dipped towards the west and the shadows lengthened, a woman made her way up the road from the village. She was wringing her hands and weeping. The guards ordered her to stop when she was still some fifty paces from the gate.

'Faether Jean ha neod a-help,' she cried, sinking to her knees in despair. 'The bweils on en's droat ha burst and 'e be zweemish. My Lord mus' sen men to car en to the church.'

One of the archers raised his bow. 'Cease your prattling and go back,' he said in French. 'You have your orders.'

'But Faether Jean neods en's hwome an en's bed. You must ax My Lord to show en ma'cy.'

Gyles stepped away from the wall and called to the archer. 'She's asking for help,' he said, approaching the gate. 'She's telling you that Father Jean has collapsed and begs that My Lord of Bradmayne send men to carry him to the church.'

'What else did she say?'

'The boils on the Father's neck have burst. He needs his home and his bed. She wants you to ask My Lord to show him mercy.'

The archer looked as if he were about to gag on bile. 'There's no point,' he muttered. 'The priest will be dead by nightfall. He knew it this morning. He used his cowl to hide the pustules on his neck but I saw the signs of death in his face. If you can make this woman understand you, tell her to care for him as best she can.'

Gyles pondered for a moment then raised his voice and spoke in broad Dorset brogue, choosing dialect words no Frenchman would understand. 'Goodhussy, I be Gyles Startout, kin to Aggy Bushrod. Thease Franky gaekies do be too affrighted o' they lord to ax ma'cy vur the preost. I zee a greave on the zummerleaze. How min ha a-deaded? How min ha the cothe?'

The answers she gave shocked him. Three dozen dead and as many again with fevered heads and pus-filled boils on their necks and in their groins. He asked her if she knew what manner of disease it was but she said she didn't. None had seen the like of it before. The blood turned black as the body died, and all who saw it shook with terror.

Gyles asked next how and when the sickness had started, and she told him merchants and pedlars had spoken of it coming to the port of Melcombe on St John the Baptist's day in June. A child had died in Bradmayne twelve days ago—almost certainly of the pox—but My Lord, out of fear for himself and believing it to be the sickness, had ordered his gates barred and the serfs to remain at a distance.

The priest had consoled them by saying they had nothing to fear from a disease in Melcombe, but he was wrong. Within days of the festivities beginning, many were complaining of feverish heads and painful aches in the neck, at the top of the legs and under the arms. The pus-filled boils grew as big as hens' eggs and no one survived beyond three days. The dead had been left to lie amongst the living until the steward persuaded My Lord to allow a grave to be dug. They'd kept their hope while Father Jean stayed well and took their confessions, but now they had none. God had sent this plague to punish them.

The guards grew impatient, warning Gyles that he was endangering the woman's safety by speaking with her so long. My Lord of Bradmayne's instructions were clear: no serf was allowed to approach so close. Gyles called out their words to her, adding a final question of his own. What sins had the villagers committed to deserve such a punishment?

She cried out in anguished tones that she didn't know. They had lived their lives according to the teachings of the Church and had honoured their oaths to their lord however grievously he treated them. He despised them for being English and blamed them for bringing this evil to his demesne. He would condemn them more when he was told that the priest was ill.

Her words became inaudible, muffled by the angry shouts of the guards, and with a look of desperation she rose to her feet and made her way wretchedly down the road.

The archer laid his bow against Gyles's chest, preventing him from leaving. 'You can't speak of what you've learnt here.'

Gyles gave a small shrug. 'The truth will out whether I do or not. The hour of Vespers is close and Father Jean is not in his church. My Lord of Bradmayne's guests will wonder why.'

He observed subsequent events from his chosen post against the manor house wall. It seemed My Lord was ready to adopt any priest, even Father Jean's young acolyte, to keep his visitors from learning that Bradmayne was a place of death. The lad—barely sixteen or seventeen—paraded in his dying teacher's vestments and welcomed My Lord and Lady at the door of the church.

But his boyish face showed a terrible fear.

Perhaps he knew his own end was close.

Three

Night fell but Gyles remained where he was. His mind was too troubled for sleep. Any hopes he'd had that de Boulet would persuade Sir Richard to leave were dashed when the captain re-emerged from the house. Assured by My Lord of Bradmayne's chamberlain that the steward and bailiff had ridden from the demesne on business, he refused to listen to Gyles's account of what the peasant woman had said, claiming he had more sense than to annoy his master with the ignorant ideas of serfs.

Gyles didn't push the matter for there were too many questions he couldn't answer. Why was news of a killing sickness in Melcombe unknown to Sir Richard before he arrived here? It was eleven days since they'd left Develish but, even during their journey, they'd heard no mention of it. Could such a thing really leap from Melcombe to Bradmayne in a single week? Did this explain why My Lord of Bradmayne's guests were also ignorant?

More than anything, Gyles wondered if the peasant woman was right to speak of a plague sent by God. Lady Anne would never countenance such an idea but Gyles could think of no other explanation for blackened blood and boils the size of hens' eggs. Did the Church not teach that such a punishment had been visited on the unbelievers of Egypt?

The sound of a soldier retching and moaning inside the barn chilled Gyles's blood for he feared the cause. He imagined his own neck already swollen and blistered and raised trembling fingers to touch it. When they found nothing, he forced himself to think calmly. Milady had said many times that superstition was the enemy of reason. God gave men brains for a purpose and only the wilfully ignorant refused to use them.

She had come to Develish as a young bride nearly a decade and a half ago. At the time, few saw anything to admire in her. Barely fourteen years old, plain and modestly dressed, no one doubted that Sir Richard had taken her in marriage to secure her dowry. Twenty years her senior and as handsome as any man alive, he made no secret of the fact that he had little affection for her, calling her his chattel and cursing her as freely as he cursed his serfs.

What Lady Anne thought of her situation could only be guessed at, since she rarely spoke and her face lacked expression. Little was known of her history except that she'd been placed in a convent at six years old when her uncle had inherited her father's estates, and her deference to Sir Richard's will said obedience was all she'd been taught. Free of the restraints a more spirited wife might have imposed on him, he continued to indulge his excesses to the detriment of his people as carelessly as he had before.

It was hard to say when and how Milady's influence began to show itself. Gyles's wife, Martha, saw it in the quiet way she took over management of the house, sparing the servants a beating by correcting their mistakes before Sir Richard could learn of them. Gyles saw it in the surprising choice of an English steward— shortly after Lady Eleanor was born—who ordered sewage pits to be dug downwind of the village, and a three-room dwelling to be built away from the houses for the purpose of tending the sick.

When the serfs complained about the added burden this would impose on them at the end of long days labouring in the fields, the steward said it was for their own benefit and displayed a writ with Sir Richard's mark. No one believed their lord had known what he was signing. His carelessness for anyone's welfare but his own, and his ignorance of letters, suggested he'd been duped by his wife, for it was well known that Lady Anne's ability with the quill was as great as her ability to read.

She won no friends by it. The work of digging and building was arduous, and the serfs grumbled bitterly about the foolish notions she'd brought from her convent. Their resistance grew louder when the pits and the hospital were finished and the steward enforced their use with the threat of fines. The women cursed Milady's arrogance for believing she knew better than they how to care for the sick while the men baulked at pissing and defecating into communal holes. It wasn't the place of an unformed girl to tell her elders how to live their lives.

Their resentment lasted barely a season. Of all the advances Develish made in the fourteen years that followed, none was so welcome or immediate as the improvement to health that came from the use of latrines and Lady Anne's curing of illness inside her hospital. When her people tried to praise her for her kindness, she shook her head and urged them to silence. It wasn't wise to draw attention to anything she did in Develish, for Sir Richard's fickle nature took as much pleasure in destroying as building.

Amongst the many wisdoms she passed to her serfs was that disease spread more quickly when the sick mingled with the well, yet as Gyles listened to the muted groans of the soldier, he couldn't recall that the priest, the steward or the bailiff had visited the barn. Only kitchen servants had come, bearing food and drink, and none had shown signs of fever. He sustained a small hope that overindulgence of wine had given the man a sore head, but as the night wore on and others began to cry out, he abandoned the idea.

From his vantage point, he watched torches move to and fro between the village and the common land. He couldn't see who was carrying them or what they were doing, but he guessed that families were taking out their dead. As the processions came and went, the moon travelled three hours of time across the sky and he dreaded to think how many more had been added to the grave. The speed and scale of what was happening bewildered him. He knew of nothing that killed so many in a single day—unless it be war.

Nevertheless, he worried more for Develish and his family than he worried for Bradmayne. Without news of what was happening here, Lady Anne and her people would be defenceless if their lord carried the sickness home. Gyles knew Sir Richard would do it without a care if it gave him access to the corrupt priest who cleansed his black conscience every morning with the body and blood of Christ. Even a man who made sincere penance for his sins would be loath to depart this world without the succour and blessing of the Church, and Sir Richard was not such a man.

In the hour before dawn, Gyles made the decision to ride with the news himself. If he travelled across country, he could do the journey in one day and give Lady Anne another day and a half to prepare. The skin would be flayed from his back if Sir Richard returned to Develish in good health, but he closed his mind to thoughts of future punishment. His single regret was that he hadn't left that night but must wait until the next to make the attempt. To try in daylight would be madness when the horse of every fighting man was hobbled in full view of My Lord of Bradmayne's guards.

෨෬

Gyles had cause to revisit that regret as soon as the sun rose for he knew his chance had gone. Three soldiers, hot with fever, lay insensible upon the floor of the barn and five more were propped against the boundary wall, faces contorted in pain and vomit staining their tunics. The sight disturbed one captain enough to go in search of his lord, and Gyles didn't doubt that others would follow.

Within the house, the voices of women raised a soft lament and, minutes later, a maid ran to the church to summon the priest's apprentice. With skirts flying, he scurried along the path, clutching holy oil in his hands, his fear mirrored in the faces of servants who were gathered in groups on the forecourt. Word spread in whispers that Lord Peter was ailing.

De Boulet seemed much diminished from the angry man of last night who had condemned all serfs to Purgatory when he'd ordered Gyles to keep his fears to himself. He approached across the forecourt, his manner conciliatory. 'Your thoughts seem more credible today,' he said. 'Francois Valennes has been retching all night and complains of pains beneath his arms. Two others—Gerard and Simon—sweat with fever. Is this the sickness of which you spoke?'

'You must ask the chamberlain, sir. His word as a Norman carries more weight than mine.'

'I'm talking to you. Last eve, you tried to tell me of a peasant woman who came from the village. The time was inopportune then but I'm ready to listen now.'

A cynical smile lifted the corners of Gyles's mouth. 'Her ideas will be as ignorant today as they were yesterday, sir . . . and you'll be no keener to repeat them to Sir Richard. Perhaps less, if he asks why you kept the information from him.'

De Boulet clenched his fist. 'I'll not take insolence. Relate what she said.'

Gyles did so.

'The priest is dead?'

'The guards seemed certain he wouldn't last the night. He may have joined others in the common grave. By my estimation another three dozen have been added to it. I watched the torch processions as bodies were carried out. The same is happening in Melcombe. The woman spoke of hundreds dying there.'

De Boulet's shock was tempered with disbelief. 'Not possible,' he protested. 'Such news would have reached Sir Richard before we left Develish.'

'I thought the same until I asked her when the sickness arrived in Melcombe. St John the Baptist's Day, she said . . . a bare three weeks since. My Lord of Bradmayne barred his gate ten days ago, but he deceives himself if he thinks only English serfs will be taken. Inside this enclosure, it's Normans who are suffering.'

De Boulet shuddered. 'We must leave. I'll seek out Sir Richard.'

Gyles glanced past him towards the front door. 'No need,' he murmured as their lord staggered outside, yawning and scratching at his groin before unbuttoning himself to piss in the sewage channel. 'He's here and will notice in a moment that his honour guard is not. I fancy he'll find that more provoking than warnings of an unknown malady.'

A different lord might have asked why the guard was absent, but not Sir Richard. He cursed his captain for a cur and a varlet and demanded the line be there when he made his way to early

Mass. For good measure, he ordered de Boulet to have his men stand to attention all day whether he was on the forecourt or not. He rebuttoned himself and made to go back inside.

Gyles spoke when de Boulet did not. 'There will be no Mass, sire. The church bell is silent and there is no one to hold the service. The priest is dead and his apprentice has been called to the house.'

The back of Sir Richard's hand struck his cheek. 'You dare address me without leave?'

'I took an oath to protect you, sire. It's my duty to speak. My Lord of Bradmayne is keeping from you that some seventy of his people have died of a sickness never seen before. Now three of your own men have it. Francois Valennes, Gerard Dubois and Simon Arcourt. Other soldiers too are afflicted.'

He stared in front of him as Sir Richard struck again.

'If I offend you by trying to save your life, sire, then I apologise. But you put yourself and your gold in peril by staying here. The servants whisper that the priest's apprentice came to the house to anoint Lord Peter, who is ailing. At least discover the truth of that before you seal the marriage bargain.'

He should have made mention of Lord Peter first, he thought, as Sir Richard lowered his hand to rub his knuckles. The boy's health was all that interested him. He turned to de Boulet. 'Does he speak the truth?'

'I believe so, sire.'

'Then why does he address me and not you?'

De Boulet bowed in a showy display of deference. 'His knowledge is greater than mine because he understands the speech of the people, sire. What he knows has come from the serfs—be they villagers or servants. What I know is learnt from observing the soldiers who have fallen sick overnight.'

Sir Richard studied Gyles with suspicion. He'd never hidden his dislike and distrust of the serf who had been imposed on him by his wife. 'Lord Peter looked well enough yesterday. If he ails this morning, it's from a surfeit of wine. He drank with the best of us last night.'

'He did not attend Vespers, sire.'

'Your meaning?'

Gyles braced himself for another blow. 'You hold your drink as well as any man, sire, but your memories of last night may not be accurate. Lord Peter has attended every service since our arrival but he missed Vespers yesterday eve. I ask myself why.'

Sir Richard frowned, thinking back. 'Now you muddle me. What form does this malady take?'

'Fever, pain and boils, sire. As the sufferer dies, the blood turns black. No one survives beyond three days. My Lord of Bradmayne is mortally afraid of it. He looked to keep it out by barring his gates but has not succeeded. His priest, steward and bailiff are dead, and now his guests' fighting men are falling to it.'

The punch to his midriff was vicious, causing him to double up in pain.

Sir Richard smiled in satisfaction. 'Bradmayne assures me his steward and bailiff are away from the demesne on business while the priest sits with a dying greybeard who has been of service to his lord these many years. Shall I take you inside so that you may call My Lord a liar to his face? It would make good sport to see you flogged within an inch of your life.'

Gyles straightened, sucking breath into his lungs. His gaze locked with Sir Richard's, and for once he made no attempt to disguise his own dislike. 'A more profitable sport would be to lay bets on which of My Lord's guests has the good sense to leave first, sire. My guess would be Chaldon. His captain went in search of him a quarter-hour since.'

Sir Richard spat on the ground. 'I'll flay the skin from your back myself if you're leading me false,' he warned. 'It'll make a pretty piece of vellum for Milady when she welcomes me home.'

೧೦

Their departure followed soon afterwards. De Boulet, summoned to the great hall by a frightened servant, returned with orders to ready Sir Richard's wagon immediately. It seemed Lord Peter wasn't alone in being afflicted with fever. An elderly guest, the chamberlain and several of the servants had also succumbed. De Boulet whispered that an unholy row had broken out between My Lord of Bradmayne and his wife. My Lady, overcome with grief for her son, was screaming imprecations at her husband for assuring her his house would be safe. She held nothing back, crying out that God had visited a pestilence upon them in punishment for My Lord's sins.

According to de Boulet, she had revealed that the demesne was encumbered by debt and Eleanor's dowry was all that stood between them and ruin. Every night her wicked husband had plied Sir Richard with mead, urging him to seal the marriage contract before dawn, and every night God had given Sir Richard the wisdom to resist. Develish was blessed in her lord. Bradmayne was cursed in theirs. They would all be dead before the week was out.

De Boulet's shock at what he'd witnessed showed itself in the incompetence of his orders. Sir Richard's wrath had been terrible, and de Boulet feared it would become ungovernable if the covered wagon wasn't standing on the forecourt when he exited the house. He seemed confused about which horses should pull it, and ordered four of his men to round up the mounts outside the wall.

Gyles stepped forward. 'With respect, sir, it would make better sense to catch and saddle our horses once we're outside the enclosure. Sir Richard's charger, the wagon and the two heavy horses that pull it are in the orchard where Master Foucault has been guarding them as closely as he guards the gold. If you organise servants to bring Sir Richard's clothes and possessions to the front door, those of us who are well will ensure the wagon is here to receive them.'

De Boulet seemed overly ready to defer to the serf, perhaps looking to blame him when things went wrong. 'What of Valennes, Dubois and Arcourt?' he asked. 'Will Sir Richard expect them to ride?'

Gyles glanced towards the barn. 'Not unless his wits have gone,' he answered impassively. 'They're beyond help. When we leave, we must leave them behind.'

⚬⚬

With no choice but to pass through Bradmayne village, Sir Richard ordered Master Foucault to drive the covered wagon ahead of him and his men, instructing him to use his whip freely on any serf who came too close. None did. The living cowered behind their doors and only the dead were outside.

For the most part, Gyles averted his eyes from the sad little corpses—many of them children—that were stretched in the dust beside their dwellings, but he felt a terrible sorrow as he passed the Bushrod home and saw his cousin Aggy staring sightlessly at the sky. He knew her by the embroidery on her kirtle—it was the same motif his wife always stitched—but her features were unrecognisable. Blackened blood encrusted her lips, nose and eyes as if the viscous fluid had leaked from every orifice in her body. In the dark interior of her hut, he made out the faces of her children, and shame smote at his heart as he rode on by. A better, braver man would have stopped to offer them comfort.

Sir Richard took his charger to the head of the column once they'd left the village, muttering prayers to himself and making frequent signs of the cross on his face and breast. If he was begging God's indulgence, Gyles doubted it was for anyone but himself. Sir Richard never wasted prayers on serfs and seemed quite careless that three of his men had been abandoned to die in Bradmayne. Master Foucault, sitting astride one of the heavy horses which pulled the wagon, tried several times to catch Gyles's eye, seeking explanations, but Gyles ignored him. He had no better understanding than the bailiff of what they'd seen. He guessed Aggy must have died that morning—she'd have been taken to the grave overnight otherwise—but he was numbed once again by the speed and magnitude of what was happening.

He felt death all around them as they travelled at walking pace through the countryside. Even the birds had fallen silent. The only sound in the summer air was the clop of hooves on the baked mud of the road and the grind of wagon wheels in the ruts. Two hours ahead lay the market town of Dorchester, a sprawling centre of trade and business, where livestock and produce changed hands every day. On their journey out, the highway had been busy with merchants, pedlars and drovers, but now there were none. The road was empty for as far as Gyles's eye could see.

He dreaded to think how many were dead or dying in Dorchester, which stood on the route north from Melcombe—the only road out of the port—and formed the crossing for others, such as the one they were riding now. If Bradmayne had the sickness, Gyles reasoned, then Dorchester must have it also, and the absence of people on the road suggested he was right. In his heart, he hoped he wasn't. There would be no escape for anyone if death was travelling the highways.

ᘓᗝ

A pall of fear hung over the market town as they entered it. Ghostlike figures shrank into shadow as Sir Richard's convoy passed, the lower halves of their faces bound with rags to keep from breathing infected air. Their eyes were wary and suspicious and they avoided each other as assiduously as they avoided the strangers on horseback. Most wore the dress of servants or slaves, and Gyles guessed they'd been turned out by their masters to purchase bread, ale or meat from the few traders who were brave enough to open. Foucault kept his whip to hand but he had no more cause to use it here than in Bradmayne.

They passed doors marked with crosses in blood-red paint, some wedged shut by heavy boulders. Behind those with no markings, they glimpsed frightened faces at half-closed shutters. None spoke. None called out, asking for news. A wooden barrow, piled high with corpses, stood untended at the side of a thoroughfare, and the stench of corruption that rose from the shrouded bodies was so terrible that two of the younger fighting men, ashen-faced, leant to the side to vomit on the ground.

Sir Richard shook his fist at the darkened houses around them. 'Are you heathens that you leave your dead unburied?' he roared.

He rode on, calling down curses on the heads of all sinners, and Gyles wondered that any man could believe himself so righteous. Sir Richard barely glanced at the door of a church on the corner of the highway north which, firmly barred, displayed a cross and the words MAY GOD HAVE MERCY ON US in brilliant red paint. The letters may have been unintelligible to him but he couldn't fail to understand that men of God were dying inside. Was he so secure in his piety that he believed himself more favoured than they?

Gyles had no such illusions. When he died, he would die a sinner, for it was a long time since he'd made confession. He tried to keep faith with the idea that it was possible to escape this pestilence but doubt overwhelmed him.

In twelve days, the world had changed beyond all recognition.

THE SECOND AND THIRD WEEKS
OF JULY, 1348

Four

Develish, Dorseteshire

A WEEK AFTER SIR RICHARD's departure a messenger arrived in Develish from the Bishop of Sarum to announce that a deadly plague was ravaging Melcombe and the villages around the mouth of the River Wey. In the absence of the liege lord, the man delivered the news to Sir Richard's steward, speaking in biblical terms about boils, effusions of blood and communities laid waste. He was so frightened by what he had to say that his tongue stuttered over the words.

Alarmed, the steward escorted him to Lady Anne. 'He comes from the bishop, milady. God has visited a punishment upon us.'

Lady Anne was in her spinning room. Two servants were carding wool while she twisted and turned the combed strands on a hand-held spindle. She laid her work aside and motioned to the girls to leave, frowning at Hugh de Courtesmain to hold his tongue until the door closed behind them. He had been appointed steward only two months previously, and Lady Anne knew little about him except that he had come from the north on the recommendation of Sir Richard's sister. She missed his predecessor, an older man, who had sought and taken her advice more often than he should. Hugh de Courtesmain would never be so obliging. Lady Anne's only conversations with him had been in the presence of her husband, and she'd been unimpressed by the new steward's willingness to follow without question every instruction Sir Richard gave.

'What kind of punishment, sir?'

'A plague which breaks out in bloody pustules on the skin and kills within a week, milady. It's believed to have come off a ship in Melcombe but no one has seen such a sickness before. It moves as fast as a horse can ride.' His voice rose in panic. 'Should I send word to Sir Richard to return home?'

'Be calm,' she told him. 'We'll die of fear before we die of sickness if you rush around the house saying Death is at the door.'

The messenger dropped to one knee. 'He speaks only the truth, milady. His Grace has instructed me to ride from manor to manor, warning of the danger.' He took a rolled parchment from inside his jerkin. 'It's written here for those who can read. I am instructed to give you one hour to copy it before I ride on.'

Lady Anne nodded. 'There is food in the kitchen. Master de Courtesmain will take you there. You may eat as much as you like but do not frighten my servants with talk of a pestilence. I will speak to them myself after you are gone.'

She waited until the men had left then unrolled the parchment. The text, written in French, spoke of a malady which had begun in Melcombe shortly after the feast of St John the Baptist and was now spreading to the east, the west and the north. The sickness took the form of headaches and fever, followed by dark, blood-infused swellings in the neck, the armpits and the groin which turned the body black and caused the sufferer to succumb in under a week. The pain was terrible. There was no cure. All who came in contact with it died. Many hundreds had perished already.

His Grace called it a plague, sent to rid the world of sinners, and the only remedy he could offer was in the last few words of his text.

> *A Black Death has fallen upon our land. Few will be spared. Make atonement for your sins and pray for God's forgiveness when you stand before Him in judgement. Seek mercy to avoid the eternal damnation of Hell. There is no salvation except in the Lord Jesus Christ.*

Lady Anne moved to a desk in the corner of the room and dipped a quill in the inkwell to transcribe the document to a piece of calfskin vellum, but her hand shook so much that the letters she made were illegible. She broke off to compose herself. She didn't doubt the sickness was real, nor that the pain and death it brought were as terrible as His Grace suggested, but was it truly a punishment sent by God?

A Black Death has fallen upon our land.

What did His Grace mean by this? That darkness would shroud the land in eternal night?

Few will be spared.

She reread the symptoms of the disease, trying to remember if the abbess of her convent had ever described such a thing.

There is no cure.

Yet how could that be, when Mother Maria had taught her that even the worst of the poxes and the most debilitating of agues could be survived? The old and the young had fewer defences against illness, but as long as the signs were seen early their fevered heads could be cooled with wet towels and herb infusions given by spoon to dull pain and encourage sleep. *Quiet the mind and the body will heal itself,* Mother Maria had always said.

Lady Anne had proven the worth of this advice many times in Develish, along with the other lessons she'd learnt regarding the importance of cleanliness, separating the sick from the healthy to stop the spread of disease, and the value of education. Sir Richard was the envy of his friends because of the strength and ability of his serfs, but none believed the cause was anything other than God's grace—particularly Sir Richard, who took pride in displaying his devotion before the altar every morning.

Despite her convent education—or perhaps because of it?— Lady Anne had never found belief in God easy; certainly not the God that her husband and the bishop worshipped. She was permanently at war with Him, although it was a secret war, conducted inside her head. She played the pious woman in public, mouthing responses in church and confessing her sins to the parish priest, and never allowing anyone—least of all her husband and daughter—to guess at her doubts. Sir Richard would have had no better excuse to annul their marriage than to argue before the Lords Spiritual that he was married to a heretic.

She picked up the quill again and resumed her task, aware that the hour was passing and the messenger would return before she was ready. But ready for what? To inform her people that God wished them dead and their only hope was to entreat Him on their knees for a place in Heaven? Could it be that Mother Maria had taught her false?

'Do not believe in a vengeful God,' the woman had urged her young pupil. 'Jesus came in love not hate. Bishops preach damnation because they are as greedy for their tithes as the King is for his taxes, and they know that men who fear God's wrath will pay more readily.'

Lady Anne pressed her wrist against the edge of her desk to keep her quill steady.

A Black Death has fallen upon our land.

How could she write this when the sun still shone, the birds still sang, and the sounds of life and laughter drifted up from the rooms below? She looked through the window and saw that the sky was blue and clear all the way to the horizon. Whatever this Black Death was, it wasn't visible in the heavens.

She remembered Mother Maria telling her stories about the tribes of Dogheads and Fishheads—men with human bodies and animal features—who were rumoured to live in the lands at the edge of the world. The Church had believed in these myths for centuries, and it wasn't until a Venetian sailor, Marco Polo, wrote of his travels east to Cathay and his failure to find a single man with the head of a dog that the idea of such people even existing became an embarrassment for the Church.

The abbess's retelling of the tales had entranced Lady Anne, and when she was old enough she had been allowed to read them for herself. The faded manuscript had been entitled *The Travels of Marco Polo*, transcribed from the Italian by the abbess herself, and the cultural ideas contained in it—very different from England's— had unlocked the young girl's mind in a way the Bible never had. Who was to say this Black Death wasn't as mythical as a Doghead or a Fishhead? Or that other favourite of the Church, angels who danced on the heads of pins?

Mother Maria, so willing to debate with Anne while she remained in the convent, had warned her to be careful when she left to be married. The cleverer a woman was the more she had to pretend she wasn't to a man of lesser intellect who owned her as surely as any other piece of property. 'If your father had lived, he would have found a worthier match for you, child, but your uncle has shown little interest in you since he put you in my care. You must choose between Sir Richard, who wants you only for your dowry, or dedicate yourself forever to the Church.'

Lady Anne had chosen the life of a chattel wife in Develish, being too curious about the world to remain cloistered inside a convent, but nothing had prepared her for the torment of being married to a husband as ignorant and brutish as Sir Richard. How often she had wished him dead, and how often she had had to remind herself of Mother Maria's parting words.

'Don't sour your heart with hatred, Anne. Show love to those who need it, for you can be sure it will be returned to you a thousandfold.'

With sudden decision, Lady Anne discarded the first piece of vellum, took up another and wrote a new text in English. If His Grace had received his words from God, and spoke truthfully when he said the only remedy against this pestilence was absolution, then she was committing an irredeemable sin by pretending otherwise; but it seemed to her a greater sin to spread panic through Develish. The lives of the serfs were wretched enough without condemning them to spend their last days in intolerable fear.

ෙ෨

Sarum makes it known that three weeks past a strange sickness entered Melcombe harbour by a foreign ship. It brings headaches and fever and painful swellings under the arms and in the groin. Do not be alarmed. There is solace to be had from herbs and liniment.

Sarum urges his faithful servants to stay within their lord's demesne for fear of the sickness spreading. In charity, leave food at the gate for passing strangers but be

*wary of allowing them inside. God will protect those who
protect themselves.*

*For the sake of all, confess your sins and pray daily
for the sickness to pass. Blessed are the pure in heart when
they beg mercy for others.*

*Your brother in the Lord Jesus Christ,
Sarum*

ОХ

Sir Richard's steward read Milady's copy of the letter twice. He
looked puzzled. 'Is this what was written, milady?' He spoke
in French.

Knowing him for too short a time to trust him, she told a
half-truth. 'Not precisely,' she admitted in the same language.
'His Grace wrote in your tongue, sir, but since Sir Richard finds
English easier to read, I thought it wiser to make a translation
for him.'

Hugh de Courtesmain knew that Sir Richard could barely read
or write, but he hesitated to call this woman a liar. He knew, too,
that Sir Richard's knowledge of English was minimal and only
Lady Anne had fluency in both languages. 'The tone surprises
me,' he said carefully. 'It speaks of a mild sickness which can be
helped with herbs, yet His Grace's messenger led me to believe
the opposite. He warned of a dreadful pestilence that cannot be
cured. Once contracted, the sufferer dies.'

'And did the messenger's words give you comfort, Master de
Courtesmain?'

'No, milady. I found them cause for great alarm.'

'Then His Grace was wise to keep his letter calm and offer good
advice. Whatever form this malady takes, it is surely sensible to

stay at home, close our gates and be wary of strangers. If we can keep the sickness at bay, we will have more chance of avoiding it.'

Hugh moved to look out of the window. He was a similar age to Lady Anne, twenty-nine to her twenty-eight, but his was a Norman ancestry like Sir Richard's and hers a Saxon one. He felt she was unsympathetic to him as a result and suspected her of taking advantage of his absences to go through documents in his office. She was too clever at concealment for him to know how she used the information she gained, but he saw her influence in Develish everywhere, most notably in the high regard that Sir Richard's tenants had for her.

This did not, however, give him any sense that she was an intelligent woman. Despite her ability to read and write, he saw her, as he saw all her sex, as subservient to men and full of the same deceit that Eve had practised on Adam. 'In Sir Richard's absence, the responsibility for his demesne is mine,' he told her coolly. 'Had I thought you would miscopy His Grace's letter, I would have performed the task myself.'

Lady Anne studied his rigid back. How neat he was in his fine wool tunic, fitted britches and sleek dark hair, and how sure of his position here. She had known the first time she met him that he would betray her to Sir Richard if she offered him help in the management of the demesne. His English predecessors had taken it gladly, and the only deceit she had asked of them—a mild one—was to convince Sir Richard that it was more appropriate for his wife to read documents to him than for his stewards to do so. It had never ceased to amaze her that her lazy husband—too idle to learn his letters when there was a chattel wife to perform the task for him—accepted without question that the sentences she spoke aloud were the ones written on the page.

'You offend me, Master de Courtesmain,' she answered lightly. 'I might as easily say you took more from the messenger's words than was there. Do you doubt His Grace's advice is wise?'

'I doubt that it's *his* advice, milady.' He turned with a cynical smile. 'Where's the sense in shutting our gates against a mild affliction that kills no one? For myself, I would rather have news of how the pestilence is affecting our neighbours than refuse them entry for fear of catching a headache.'

'You may change your mind when your head begins to ache in earnest. From my experience, the best cure for a disease is never to catch it.'

'With respect, milady, your views are of no importance. His Grace's messenger spoke of a punishment sent by God to chastise the sinners of Dorseteshire. You will deprive Sir Richard's people of salvation if you persuade them there's nothing to fear.'

He was unprepared for the cool derision in the gaze that met his. 'Perhaps you hope God will spare you because you're a Frenchman, Master de Courtesmain?'

'We speak of Develish, milady.' He pointed to the vellum. 'I have found several of His Grace's letters to Sir Richard in the steward's office and none of them reads like this. On every visit here, he has found enough sin to keep the fires of Hell burning until the end of time. He writes more about Sir Richard's duty to keep his people from eternal damnation than he does about God's love and protection.'

'I expect it amused him to tease Sir Richard for being Develish,' said Lady Anne, rising from her stool and shaking her kirtle hem to the floor. 'Even bishops enjoy humour from time to time.'

'His letters are penned more in anger than fun, milady. He writes that the peasant class in Develish is as base as it can possibly be. Few take absolution and those who do are less than sincere in what they confess.'

Lady Anne scolded herself for not removing His Grace's parchments before this steward arrived. She should have realised how inquisitive he would be about his new surroundings. 'The secrets of the confessional are between a sinner and his priest, Master de Courtesmain. It's not for you and me to discuss them. If you're a God-fearing man, you should know that.'

He made a stiff little bow. 'I am indeed a God-fearing man, milady, which is why I would rather know the true advice His Grace sent.'

Lady Anne smiled slightly. 'If he were with us now, he would remind you of the sacred oath my husband took to protect his people when he inherited these lands. As Sir Richard's steward, you must do your utmost to uphold that pledge since you say, quite rightly, that you stand for him in his absence.'

Hugh had the uncomfortable feeling she was getting the better of him. 'Only against thieves and bandits, milady. There is no mention of pestilence in the pledge.'

'Nor of eternal damnation,' she answered dryly. 'Father Anselm does his best on Sir Richard's behalf to root out the Devil inside us, but he seems to find the task simpler when he's in drink. God's purpose is not always easy to understand.'

Hugh's discomfort grew. On the few occasions when he'd heard this woman speak, her comments had been brief and stilted, and he'd failed to see the sharp mind beneath the tight-fitting wimple and dowdy homespun clothes. Sir Richard's sister had told him before he left Foxcote for Develish that Lady Anne was more suited to the dry, disciplined life of a nun than married to a man as rambunctious as her brother, and Hugh had seen nothing in

eight weeks to contradict that opinion. It hadn't surprised him
that Sir Richard preferred warmer beds to hers.

He glanced down at the letter. 'It must have occurred to
you that friends as well as strangers may carry this infection.
Bradmayne is only a day's ride from Melcombe and less than
three from here. Do you expect me to refuse Sir Richard entry
when he returns?'

'You must do what you think is right, sir. My husband is
certainly selfish enough to bring a sickness back with him. He
will look to me to cure him as he always does, and pay no regard
at all to whether anyone else is afflicted by it.'

Hugh worried he was committing a sin just by listening to
her. 'I have no authority to refuse him.'

'Indeed, but it's of no matter at the moment. For now, our duty
is to inform the servants and the tenants of His Grace's words.
Do you wish to do it yourself or should I?'

The Frenchman shook his head, rolling the calfskin vellum
and handing it to her. 'They are your words, milady. You will
speak them with more honesty than I can.'

A gleam of irony appeared in her eyes. 'If you believe them
false, then you must prevent me saying them at all. You should
tell our people that God has ordained a terrible and painful death
for them and instruct Father Anselm to give continuous absolution for the numerous evils they have committed. They will
die in agony of suppurating boils but at least their sins will be
shriven . . . for as long as Father Anselm remains sober enough
to remember the Sacrament of Penance.'

Hugh was deeply shocked, not just by the sarcasm in her voice
but by the implicit heresy of her last sentence. He believed himself
a devout man because he followed the teachings of the Church

without question. 'He is a priest, milady. He has the power to absolve us whatever state he is in.'

'Then be sure to tell our people that,' she said. 'If they're to die of a plague, at least let them be comforted that, even in stupor, Father Anselm can guarantee them a place in Heaven. He labours harder on his beehives to make mead than he does on rehearsing his catechisms.'

Hugh stared at the floor. He had never heard anyone talk in such belittling terms about a member of the clergy. The system that governed their society depended on serfs believing what their priests told them about reward in the next life. 'He is still a man of God, milady.'

'But not a very good one, Master de Courtesmain. Before I came here, he tried to seduce the female serfs under guise of hearing their confessions, and it was only because they had the sense to tell me about it that I was able to curtail his appetites.' She placed the roll of vellum in the pocket of her kirtle. 'The advice in here is wise. I suggest we follow it.'

He found her calmness strange. Had she not seen the fear in the messenger's face or heard the quiver in his voice? 'Why are you not afraid of this plague, milady? If God seeks to punish us, we cannot escape.'

'I would rather believe He loves us, sir, and gave us reason and wisdom to help us live.'

'Were you being truthful in what you wrote about herbs and liniment?'

'You must hope I was. If you doubt it, at least give optimism to others that a sleeping draught will lessen the pain. The best cure is not to allow the sickness to enter.'

'Would those be Sir Richard's instructions?' he asked.

'You know they would not,' she replied. 'Sir Richard has no care for his people. He would order you to summon his wagon and horses so that he could remove himself as far from the pestilence as possible. The responsibility for what happens here would be yours and mine. As it is now.'

Hugh de Courtesmain was innately duplicitous. It was a trait which had served him well on his last estate, where he had gained the favour of Sir Richard's sister at the expense of her servants. He prided himself on being handsome enough to capture the heart of any woman—servant *or* mistress—and clever enough to twist what they said to his own advantage. He didn't doubt he could do the same in Develish.

He lowered his head in respectful deference. 'Then we must offer our protection to those who have pledged allegiance, milady. It would be churlish to do anything less.'

He noted the smile she gave him and congratulated himself on winning her confidence so easily. By the time Sir Richard returned, he would have Milady eating out of his hand.

ᏋᎧ

An hour passed before the two hundred servants and field serfs—male and female, young and old—were gathered in the great hall. Lady Anne spent the time in the kitchen, tasting broths which the cooks were preparing for the evening meal. Hugh de Courtesmain leant against the far wall, pretending a calm he didn't feel. His powerful distrust of bondsmen caused him to be deeply wary of allowing them too close.

He watched in disbelief as Lady Anne made her way from the kitchen, walking amongst them, taking their hands and greeting them by name. She seemed to have no sense of her position but treated them as equals, listening with courtesy to what they had to say. In a society where peasants were the lowest class, bound to their master and his land for life, Hugh felt it dangerously unwise to allow them a voice.

His disbelief turned to anger when she took her place beside him and beckoned her chambermaid to step forward. 'Will you perform a task for me, Isabella? His Grace, our Lord Bishop, has written to the people of Develish, and I'd like you to read the words aloud so that everyone may hear them and know them to be true.' She took the roll of vellum from inside her kirtle.

Hugh stepped between her and the girl, his back to the room. 'You make a mockery of your authority, milady,' he hissed. 'His Grace's words are not for the eyes of a peasant girl.'

Lady Anne ignored him, moving aside to hand the vellum to the girl. 'Make sure you raise your voice, Isabella. My Lord Bishop's title at the beginning is pronounced "Sairum".' She clapped her hands for silence.

Hugh was shocked by what followed. Isabella's reading was as fluent as any he'd heard. She phrased each sentence with understanding and delivered the words in a sweet, young voice, putting special emphasis on *Blessed are the pure in heart when they beg mercy for others*. He was watching the faces of the crowd, and it seemed to him that none found her prowess unusual, as if the ability of a peasant to read was an accepted skill in this demesne.

His mind raced in confusion, leaping from outrage at this overturning of the social order to anger that so much deceit had been practised on Sir Richard. How had these serfs found time to learn letters when their every waking hour was owned by their lord? Why did they choose to hide their talent except from Lady Anne? What other sedition had she taught them? Who had read the documents in his office? Were these the sins they hid from their priest?

Lady Anne's voice broke into his thoughts. Isabella had finished her reading and the silence in the hall was absolute. There wasn't even a shuffle of feet to cover what Lady Anne said. 'You seem startled, sir, yet Isabella has been reading since she was eight. She is a fine pupil and a fine teacher.' Her gaze rested on him for a moment. 'Perhaps you think literacy so hard that it can only be mastered by stewards and lords?'

'I've never been on a demesne where serfs were educated, milady. The practice is an unusual one. A villein's role in life is to labour for his master, not to steal time in order to learn letters.'

'Have you had reason to complain of the work that is done in Develish? I know you've made enquiries of our neighbours at Funtenel and Pedle Hinton, but I'm not aware that their crops produce greater yields than ours.'

Hugh knew the opposite to be true. An examination of his predecessor's records showed that the yield from Develish land was higher. Hugh hadn't been able to account for it, except to put it down to the composition of the soil, but it meant the amount that was levied in taxes, both for the manor and the Church—one half of everything grown—was greater than the half levied at Funtenel and Pedle Hinton, and Sir Richard's coffers had benefited as a result.

Even so, Sir Richard had been bullying Hugh to increase the levy above one-half when the harvest came in, saying that previous stewards had been too cowardly to face down the serfs. With but one demesne, Sir Richard looked to seize as much as he could from it, reminding Hugh that he had been taken on because his sister had vouched for his harshness in dealing with shirkers and thieves on the Foxcote estate. Sir Richard expected him to be as tough in Develish, yet his demands had put Hugh in a difficult position. There was no comparison between his job as bailiff to an inept steward on a poorly run demesne where the serfs had only enmity for their lord, and this bountiful one of Develish which seemed at peace with itself.

He took note of some words in his predecessor's records—*Sir Richard urges me again to kill the goose that lays the golden eggs. He cannot see the folly of such an action*—and attempted some reasoned arguments to keep the levy where it was. He explained how the harvest would suffer if the serfs were left with too little to feed their families. Ill health and ill will would enter the community and the value of Sir Richard's share would drop.

Such excuses fell on deaf ears. If a slave couldn't pay what was demanded of him, he must be flogged. Even simple mathematics—such as five-tenths of one hundred bushels of wheat was worth more than six-tenths of eighty—failed to change Sir Richard's mind, and Hugh knew it was only a matter of time before he was instructed to seize two-thirds of everything produced.

Looking at the faces in front of him now—all watching closely for his reaction—he wondered if these people had a better grasp of logic and fractions than their master. Could it be they were working for themselves as much as for Sir Richard? Did they understand the advantage of swelling their master's coffers because their own would swell as well? If so, it made sense of some strange figures he'd seen in the records where visiting merchants appeared to have bought more grain from Sir Richard than was recorded in the tax receipts or from his own fields. Were the serfs selling their own produce with his? Was their ambition to buy themselves out of bondage? And who was helping them to do it? There was only one person in Develish who could—and, he now believed, *would*—have taught them such radical ideas.

He turned to Lady Anne. 'I have no complaints about the work done in Develish, milady,' he said, 'unless it be that my fellow stewards at Funtenel and Pedle Hinton bombard me with questions about the secret behind our yields. Being so new to my post, I am sure they hope they can trick me into revealing it . . . but since I don't know the answer, there is nothing I can tell them.'

Lady Anne took the vellum from Isabella and gestured for her to rejoin the servants. 'There is no secret, sir, except that the people of Develish are better workers than most. You will discover the truth of that in the efforts we make to carry out My Lord Bishop's instructions. In charity and hospitality, we will leave food for wayfarers . . . in purity of heart we will beg mercy for others . . . and in the wisdom granted us by His Grace, we will seclude ourselves from this sickness.'

Hugh knew he had been outmanoeuvred. 'I bow to your superior knowledge, milady,' he murmured, 'and I will put on record that you have taken the fate of Develish into your own hands. We must look forward to the time when Sir Richard and His Grace, My Lord Bishop, have cause to thank you for it.'

ജ

If he'd hoped to scare Lady Anne into handing back the reins to her husband's estate, he didn't succeed. In the days that followed, she became the only authority in Develish while he assumed the role of bystander. He looked for a messenger to ride to Bradmayne with a letter for Sir Richard, but no one would make the journey without Lady Anne's permission. And she would not give it. Her orders were clear. No one was to leave the demesne, and no one was to enter it.

To that end, she brought every serf to live on the land inside the moat. Small dwellings were erected beside the path to the church, on the orchard and in the paddocks for the adults to share as best they could, while the graveyard was divided into pens for sheep, pigs and cattle. The centre of the great hall—normally slept in by the servants—was turned into a dormitory for the children and frail elderly, and the four corners became repositories for wheat, corn and preserved meat and vegetables. The female servants were ordered to share Lady Anne's chamber while Hugh and the male servants were spread amongst Sir Richard's.

To explain her insistence on keeping the pestilence out, Lady Anne allowed the rumour to spread that His Grace's messenger had talked of people dying in Melcombe, but she perpetuated the lie that it was curable with medicine. She ordered leaves, roots and flower petals to be gathered from the meadows—St John's wort, toadflax, henbane, foxglove, common hemlock, wild garlic and many others—and set two of her servants to drying and storing them in labelled jars. Even Hugh, who believed her claim to be false, drew confidence from the impressive array of descriptions on public display in the hall. *Lavender and sage: soothes headaches. St John's wort: gives relief to troubled minds. Henbane: gives sleep to the afflicted. Foxglove: gives strength to the heart.*

On several occasions, Hugh came upon small groups of serfs whispering amongst themselves. They moved apart at his approach, greeting him politely enough by ducking their heads in recognition of his position, but none spoke to him. He thought he saw anxiety in some of the faces, and once he heard mention of His Grace's messenger 'riding in as if he had the Devil on his back', but if the bondsmen knew they were being lied to they kept it to themselves.

In three days, the manor house and the land on which it stood was turned into a fortress, and the number of people concentrated within its curtilage was two hundred. Had it been a castle, like Restormel in Cornwall, there would have been room to spare for such a multitude, but the house was a more modest structure on a handful of acres inside a water boundary, and conditions were cramped.

The moat was fed by a tributary of the River Pedle, known as Devil's Brook. It flowed the length of the valley, heading south towards the larger estates of Afpedle and Woodoak, but Sir Richard had seen merit in diverting its course around his demesne in order that Develish would seem grander than it was. He'd set his serfs to labour month after month on the excavation of a mighty trench—ignoring his wife's warnings that they were exhausted after a long day's toil in the fields—claiming My Lord of Develish should stand no less tall than My Lords of Afpedle and Woodoak.

It was some ten years since the moat had been finished but only now did it serve a more useful purpose than bolstering Sir Richard's self-esteem. In a final act of separation from the outside world, Lady Anne ordered the wooden bridge across it to be hacked out and burnt, leaving the serfs' village and the hectares of fields that stretched to the horizon empty and untended. The heat of the bonfire was unbearable in the warm July temperature, but everyone was drawn to watch this symbolic burning of a bridge. Including Hugh de Courtesmain. As the blaze died, he listened to the comments around him. He wasn't alone, it seemed, in understanding the consequences.

'She'll make an enemy of her husband if she means to keep him out . . .'

'Worry more about his anger against us for siding with her . . .'

Hugh knew the names of Sir Richard's bondsmen from the records, but he had yet to learn which face went with which title. Until now, he had sent the bailiff, Foucault, to summon men for *ad opus* work inside the moat, and he regretted not taking the trouble to speak to them himself. He recognised only one of them—a tall, black-haired serf who had been the butt of Lady Eleanor's anger on the day of her father's departure. The incident had made him curious enough to ask one of the servants who the man was, and she had given his name as Thaddeus Thurkell.

Thurkell seemed to have taken charge of the bonfire, either on Lady Anne's orders or through choice. 'Sir Richard will infect us all if he has the sickness,' he said quietly, stooping to pick up a piece of smouldering wood which had fallen away from the fire and tossing it onto the embers. 'Lady Anne shows great courage by keeping him out. His wrath will fall on her before it falls on us, and we will hear every insult he hurls at her across the moat before he tries to bully us into overturning her instructions.'

'Be silent, boy,' another man hissed angrily. 'Your views count for nothing.'

'Let him speak, Will,' called a woman from the back. 'We have more reason to trust Lady Anne than Sir Richard. What else do you have to say, Thaddeus?'

'If Sir Richard is willing to listen, he will be told there is enough food in John Trueblood's cottage to last him and his retinue a fortnight. As long as they remain unaffected during that time, it will be safe to let them in. The bishop's messenger spoke of the sickness running its course in three to four days, so fourteen will be ample to prove Sir Richard and his retinue are free of it.'

There was something compelling about the man, Hugh thought, and not just because he was taller and stronger-built than everyone else. He seemed to have knowledge which the others did not.

'And if he orders his men to storm the moat?' asked someone else.

'We must prevent them crossing.' Thurkell's dark eyes searched the faces in front of him. 'Sir Richard's oath to protect us was as sacred as yours. He will stand in judgement before God if he brings illness and death to his people.'

'You are very bold to speak for God, Thaddeus.'

'I remind you only of what is contained in the oath of fealty. Recall the words you mouthed and remember the conditions on which you bound yourselves and your children to Sir Richard's will—that he would hold to *you* as steadfastly as you hold to him.'

'He's not a reasonable man. He'll have us flogged whatever we do.'

Thaddeus gestured towards a wooden raft on the bank of the moat which Lady Anne had ordered constructed before the bridge was burnt. 'Then use this vessel to return to your cottages now and make obeisance to him when he returns. You'll save yourselves a flogging but you may fall ill of the sickness.'

'Tell us what you know of this sickness, Thaddeus. There's some of us don't believe it's curable by St John's wort nor understand why Lady Anne is so determined to keep it out.'

Another woman raised her voice. 'The servants in the kitchen saw My Lord Bishop's messenger. They said he could hardly eat for trembling over the news he brought. Is Lady Anne lying to us?'

Hugh was as interested in Thaddeus's answer as everyone else, because the serf seemed to be speaking for the mistress. Hugh had seen how angry Lady Anne had been when her daughter had taken a whip to Thaddeus Thurkell, and he had wondered then if there was more to this relationship than villein to mistress.

Thaddeus used a pitchfork to stir the fire. 'She has never lied to us yet,' he answered calmly. 'Every ailment can kill if the body's weak or old. You know that. You all lost children to the pox before Lady Anne came to Develish.'

'It's a big step to bar her husband from crossing the moat for fear we catch a fever.'

'If every little one in Develish falls ill at the same time, twenty may be cured but not fifty. You ask miracles of Lady Anne if you expect her to save them all. What if she develops the fever herself?'

'She must teach us to make the infusions,' said the woman from the back.

'Then ask her for instruction. The more help we give her the more we help ourselves.'

After that, the conversation fragmented. The watchers broke into smaller groups and began to disperse. Only Thurkell remained to tend the dying bonfire. Hugh de Courtesmain approached him. 'You talk like a freeman,' he said in English, 'yet the records show you're a bondsman.'

Thaddeus made a small bow. 'My apologies, sir,' he answered in French. 'I wasn't aware there was a difference in the way men speak . . . except in which tongue they favour.'

It wasn't unusual for serfs to speak French—the language had been in common use since William of Normandy—but Lady Anne had given Hugh the impression that the peasant class in Develish spoke nothing but English. Now, he had an unpleasant feeling that everything he'd said to Sir Richard since he'd arrived had been overheard and understood. 'Only freemen have choices in life,' he said stiffly. 'Bondsmen do not . . . yet you urged your fellows to make decisions for themselves.'

'Our minds are free, sir. No one has devised a law to stop us thinking.'

The steward found himself at a disadvantage, having to look up to a serf. The man must be six feet tall at least, standing a good eight inches over Hugh. 'Who told you I find my own tongue easier to understand? Am I of so much interest to the house servants that they carry the news outside?'

'You have been of interest since the day you arrived, Master de Courtesmain. You know more of England than we do. Only Sir Richard has ever travelled so far north as his brother-in-law's demesne.'

Hugh's displeasure and suspicion grew. He had told the servants nothing about himself since he'd been at Develish—he certainly hadn't advertised that he'd come on the recommendation of Sir Richard's sister—yet the knowledge seemed to be public. 'Who gave you this information?'

'There has been talk of little else these last eight weeks. Any new arrival arouses curiosity.'

'What else do you know?'

Thaddeus looked across the moat to the fields that rose in a gentle slope towards woodland. Most were divided into strips, but the farthest was laid to grazing and contained a handful of ponies, flicking their tails listlessly in the heat. 'That you have no ties to hold you here, Master de Courtesmain, and are obliged to no one. If you choose to take one of those mounts and head north to escape the sickness, no one will think the worse of you.'

Hugh followed his gaze. 'You are wrong. I am pledged to Sir Richard and will need his permission to abandon my post, or face judgement afterwards.'

Thaddeus kicked another timber back onto the bonfire. 'A wise man lives for today and faces tomorrow when it comes.'

'Yet Lady Anne seems anxious enough about how this sickness will affect us. You'd think it was sent to kill us the way she defends against it.' He searched the younger man's face for a reaction but couldn't tell whether Thaddeus knew the bishop had warned of something worse than headaches and fever. 'If God's purpose is to punish us, only a foolish woman—or a devil—would try to thwart Him.'

The serf's eye rested on him for a moment. 'I don't pretend to know God's purpose, Master de Courtesmain,' he said, turning back to the fire, 'but you are as free to ride south to Bradmayne to warn Sir Richard of what is happening here as you are to ride north. If he is well and untouched by the sickness, he will reward you for your loyalty. If he is not, you will have the privilege of dying at his side.'

The sixteenth day of July, 1348

What God gives with one hand He takes with the other. I thank Him most humbly for Thaddeus Thurkell but I am deeply troubled for my friend Gyles Startout. We have planned and achieved so much together and he should be here at my side.

I cannot believe Bradmayne is unaffected by this Black Death, since it lies within a day's ride of Melcombe. No one will mourn if Sir Richard is lost to us but hearts will break if Gyles fails to return—my own included. I pray that he comes back to us safe and well.

Five

Hugh de Courtesmain's loyalty to his master was put to the test sooner than he'd expected. Early on the afternoon after the bridge was burnt, a shout arose that riders were approaching along the dirt road from the south. It was the only highway through the valley, following the contours of Devil's Brook, and anyone who used it was visible from a long distance. There was a footpath east to west which occasionally brought pedlars or minstrels over the hills from Pedle Hinton and Funtenel, but it needed a strong heart and sturdy legs to tackle the steep slopes and dense woodland that covered them.

As he had been doing for several days, Hugh was paying court to Lady Eleanor in her mother's chamber, listening to the miseries of the girl's life and tolerating her tantrums. At fourteen, she was easy prey to a man twice her age who was willing to tell her what she wanted to hear in return for her confidences. She was as indiscreet as Hugh had hoped she would be, repeating everything she knew, or thought she knew, about Develish.

He discovered that Eleanor was as poor at reading and writing as her father, apparently encouraged by Sir Richard to view literacy as the preserve of the Church and men such as Hugh, who were employed to keep records. Her opinion—formed by Sir Richard—was that education was unnecessary when other, lesser people existed to perform the dreary tasks associated with it.

Hugh learnt about Lady Anne's dislike of her husband and her insistence on having a separate bed chamber so that she could refuse him access to her bed. He learnt, too, of the woman's preference for the company of peasants, particularly Thaddeus Thurkell, the bastard product of the harlot Eva and a foreign sailor. In Sir Richard, Eleanor found no fault except that he'd allowed his witch of a wife to pick Peter of Bradmayne as a worthy husband for his daughter.

As the shouts outside were taken up and grew louder, Hugh broke off from listening to Eleanor's complaints to move to the southern window. He narrowed his eyes to focus on the distant riders, and felt a knot of panic in his stomach when he recognised Sir Richard's charger and saw a man slumped in the saddle on its back. One member of the retinue had hold of the reins and was leading the animal at a walk, two others—all that were left of the retinue of eleven who had set out—followed behind. There was no sign of the wagon.

'Who is it?' Eleanor asked from where she was sitting on a stool.

'It's hard to tell at this distance, milady.'

The girl joined him at the window. 'It's my father,' she declared with satisfaction. 'I knew he'd come back. He'll be furious at what my mother has done. I hope he makes her live in the village with the serfs so that she knows what it's like to sleep with people who are beneath her.'

Hugh wondered why she was so unquestioning of what she was looking at. 'Are you sure it's Sir Richard, milady? He had eleven men accompanying him when he departed but I see only four returning.'

'That's his horse,' she said impatiently. 'The black charger. There.'

Eleanor's only charms for Hugh were the prettiness of her face, the blueness of her eyes and the silky blondeness of her hair. Her dullness of mind had no charm at all. 'If it's your father, he can barely stay on his mount,' he pointed out carefully, 'and Lady Anne will not allow him across the moat if he's unwell.'

'She'll have no choice. He'll order the raft to be sent across and no one will dare refuse him.'

Hugh was sure the order would be given and equally sure it would be disobeyed. He moved to the window which overlooked the courtyard and watched Lady Anne walk through the crowd that was gathered there. She said something to Thaddeus Thurkell, who gestured to a group of men, all armed with pitchforks, to take up positions on the bank of the moat. He didn't know whether to admire the woman's courage for easing her slender figure between the serfs in order to stand alone before the incoming riders, or condemn her effrontery in daring to challenge her husband's authority.

He had planned to put himself conveniently out of earshot if and when Sir Richard returned—closeted in the church with Father Anselm, perhaps—but he was compromised by being with Lady Eleanor. He could hardly argue now that he was unaware of his master's arrival. As if to prove the point, the girl declared her intention of going outside to greet her father.

Hugh stepped in front of her to bar her way. 'Your mother has been less than honest about this sickness, milady. There is no cure. If Sir Richard has it, he will spread the infection through Develish and we will all be dead within the week. The only way to prevent that is to keep him out.'

Eleanor's eyes widened. 'I don't believe you. Why are you taking her side when you haven't before?'

'I hoped news of the pestilence was exaggerated and that your father would come back to us in good health . . . but if eight of his men have died already, I fear Bradmayne must have had the infection when he arrived there.'

A tiny smile appeared at the corner of her mouth. 'Does that mean Lord Peter's dead?'

'Very probably, milady.'

'Good.' She turned to the window again.

Over her shoulder, Hugh watched the slow-moving convoy reach the first of the serfs' cottages. The leading rider jumped from his horse and hammered on the door, flinging it wide when he got no answer. His calls as he moved from dwelling to dwelling were loud enough to carry to the manor house, but there was no response from anyone standing on the forecourt. It was as if the crowd beside the moat was holding its collective breath in the hope that silence would persuade the travellers to go away.

Hugh watched the other two retainers dismount and move forward to catch Sir Richard before he fell from the saddle. One cushioned his shoulders while the other freed his feet from the stirrups. They cradled him briefly, casting around for somewhere to put him, before making the decision to lay him on his back on the dusty road and slumping down beside him. To Hugh's eyes, they looked as unable to support themselves as their master, but they were too far away for him to tell whether it was fatigue or sickness that ailed them.

The man who had led the convoy in—the only one who appeared to have any strength—walked the two hundred yards from the village to the manor house. He ran his gaze slowly over the faces on the other side of the moat, as if he were counting them, and then made a bow to Lady Anne.

'I'm pleased to find you and our people well, milady. May I ask the reason for the village being abandoned?' He spoke in a formal English that Hugh could understand.

'Indeed you may, Gyles. We do what His Grace, the Bishop of Sarum, has advised us to do. He sent word of a sickness, spreading from Melcombe, which gives fever and headaches to those unfortunate enough to catch it, and urged us to close our gates and remain inside the demesne until it has passed. The sickness is curable with herbs and liniment but causes pain while it lasts.'

Hugh saw uncertainty in the man's face. He opened his mouth as if to tell Milady she was wrong.

She spoke before he could. 'It gladdens our hearts to see you, Gyles. This eve we will urge the children to dance with joy at your safe return. In their innocence, they question every day why they've had to leave their dwellings. There's so much to frighten them here—not least the shadows in the great hall at night. We try our best to keep them from having nightmares and hope you will also.'

The man pushed a tired smile onto his face. 'God forbid anyone should fear me, milady.' He gestured towards the village. 'What would you have me do for Sir Richard? He's been suffering with fever since he woke this morning.'

'When did you leave Bradmayne?'

'Three days ago, milady, but our progress has been slow. When the fever comes, it comes quickly and robs the body of strength. Of the eight who were well enough to ride with Sir Richard, five have succumbed along the way.'

A shiver of fear ran up Hugh's spine, and he searched the crowd for their reaction. Surely now they would panic? But no.

The serfs who had ranged themselves beside Thurkell—all of whom Hugh recognised as men who had led the building of huts and the herding of animals across the moat before the bridge was burnt—gestured to women behind them to calm their neigh-bours. Lady Anne did the same, placing soothing hands on the shoulders of two children who stood at her side, drawing them close. 'What of you, Gyles?' she asked with unruffled composure. 'Do you have a fever?'

'I am the only one who does not, milady. Captain de Boulet and Master Foucault, the bailiff, suffer as badly as Sir Richard.'

'Then I will send medicine across on the raft and you must administer it to them. John Trueblood's cottage has rush mattresses and food. You may shelter there until all of you are well. We ask only that you wait fourteen days before joining us on this side of the moat.'

'Sir Richard is impatient to cross now, milady. He seeks succour from his priest.'

'Tell him Father Anselm will come to him, Gyles. Meanwhile, he must take henbane and St John's wort to help the fever pass so that his mind is clear when he receives the body and blood of Christ.' She motioned to one of her servants. 'Bring me a basket of vials and I will explain to Gyles how to administer them. Sir Richard has nothing to fear from this fever.'

As Hugh watched the little pantomime unfold, he could only admire Lady Anne's deceit. The crowd, convinced the bottles of yellowish liquid would reverse the sickness, called encourage-ment as the raft, carrying the basket, was run across the moat on a pulley system. They urged Gyles to stay strong and wait for the day when Sir Richard had recovered enough to re-enter the manor. The event took on a festive character—as jolly as a harvest celebration—and Hugh wondered if anyone realised that

Lady Anne was condemning the wretch on the other side to die along with his master.

His gaze settled on Thaddeus Thurkell who, alone, was pulling on the rope that controlled the raft. The serf knew what Gyles's fate was to be, Hugh thought, and he was ready to act as Lady Anne's executioner if the need arose. He held a knife in his right hand while he manipulated the pulley system with his left, and his pitchfork was speared into the bank of the moat. If Gyles took fright and tried to mount the raft, Thaddeus had a dagger and a forked lance to make sure he never reached the other side.

'Why does Thaddeus hold a knife?' Eleanor asked curiously.

'To free the raft if it becomes snagged on reeds.'

It was a poor explanation but Eleanor accepted it. She seemed unable to think about anything that didn't concern herself, and her butterfly brain had already forgotten Hugh's warnings of a virulent infection which killed within the week. 'Why didn't Mother ask if Peter's still alive?' she demanded irritably. 'She's so *mean* to me. It's not fair to make me wait until Father gets better before I find out if I still have to marry into beastly Bradmayne.'

∞

Another two days passed before Lady Anne summoned Hugh de Courtesmain to the steward's office to tell him Sir Richard had died and de Boulet and Foucault wouldn't live through the night. She had taken over Hugh's work space as easily as she had taken over his duties, and Hugh found her at his desk, running through a list of rations, with Thaddeus Thurkell leaning over her shoulder and prompting her from a list of his own. If Hugh had ever doubted that Isabella was alone in being able to read on this demesne, he doubted no longer.

The knowledge added to his shock at the intimate tableau. The woman had removed her wimple, allowing her long, brown hair to hang loosely about her face, and Thurkell was bare-armed with his shirt sleeves rolled up and the tails hanging loose about his britches. It was hard to say which of them was the more senior since, without her head covered, Lady Anne looked younger, and Thurkell, with a week's growth of strong dark stubble, looked older.

Hugh was even more shocked at the matter-of-fact way Lady Anne declared her husband dead. She spoke in French. 'You should know you are no longer obligated to Sir Richard, Master de Courtesmain. He succumbed to his illness yesterday and we expect the captain and the bailiff to follow him tonight. You are free to leave if that is your wish.'

It was a moment before he answered. Had she lost her wits that she spoke so lightly of her husband's death? Could she have forgotten what the bishop's messenger had said about boils and effusions of blood? The village was a mere two hundred paces away and he felt bile rise in his throat at the thought of Sir Richard's corpse so close. How long before the stink of it reached the demesne?

'Why do you persist in this mockery?' he demanded angrily. 'Do you have no fear of retribution? You lead your people false with claims of a cure.'

She raised her dark eyes to his, a small query creasing her brow. 'Is it *you* I've led false, Master de Courtesmain? If so, I most earnestly beg your pardon. I thought you understood that Sir Richard could not live. There would be no reason to keep him from his bed otherwise. Gyles was able to ease his pain with St John's wort and henbane . . . but that is all. He does the same for Captain de Boulet and Master Foucault, but they will die as surely as their master.'

'Then we are all dead,' he said in despair. 'God would not take a lord but spare his serfs.'

Lady Anne shook her head. 'I doubt this malady recognises a man's status, sir. In Bradmayne the field serfs died first, but the household began to suffer soon afterwards. Lord Peter was receiving the last rites even as Sir Richard left.'

Hugh stared at her in shock. 'How can you know this? Gyles has not been near the moat since you sent over the medicine.'

'Thaddeus crossed to the village when everyone was asleep and spoke to Gyles in private. There's no point alarming our people unnecessarily, and we need Gyles to bury the bodies so they won't become a source of infection to others.'

The steward took a hasty step backwards, holding the sleeve of his tunic to his mouth and nose. 'What was to stop Thurkell carrying the malady back with him?'

It was the serf who answered, using French as Milady had. 'I stood at a distance from him. We're lucky it's Gyles Startout who came back in good health. He's one of our older people, a man of almost half a century with experience of the world. He has a wife and children and he's clever enough to understand the sense of isolating the well from the sick. He saw how quickly the pestilence spread through Bradmayne and has no wish to see the same happen here.'

'Is he afflicted?'

'Not yet.'

'How can that be?' Hugh asked Lady Anne.

She treated the question seriously. 'I learnt in the convent that diseases work differently on different people,' she said. 'If they did not—if they worked on each of us the same way—we would break out in a rash every time our children had the pox. Yet that's not what happens. If we catch the pox when we're young, we don't catch it when we're grown. The nuns had no explanation for it, and neither do I, but my own experience shows it to be true.' She paused. 'It may be that Gyles is lucky or that he has some inner strength which is stopping the sickness from invading his body.'

'But this is a deadly pestilence with putrid boils, milady, not a mild rash on the skin. The bishop's messenger called it a Black Death.'

'Then give me the benefit of your advice, Master de Courtesmain. If we are destined to die anyway, what would you have me do?'

'Tell your people to make their peace with God. Remind them that confession and absolution are the only routes to salvation. Urge them to beg for mercy.'

She eyed him for a moment. 'And what sins should I tell them they've committed to merit this death? What prayers would you have them say that might change their Creator's mind about their fate? Do you not think my husband begged for mercy even as his life ebbed away?'

'You promised him the priest, milady.'

'The priest declined to go. He made himself insensible with drink rather than put his life in peril.'

Hugh's lips thinned at the blasphemy of her words. 'That's heresy, milady. It's no wonder God seeks to punish you and your demesne.'

Lady Anne smiled slightly. 'His punishments are very arbitrary, sir. If my sins have brought this illness to Dorseteshire, God was cruel to ravage Melcombe and Bradmayne first. From what Gyles told Thaddeus, there is little chance that anyone is left alive in either place.'

Thaddeus raised his head. 'It makes no sense that confession will ward off the pestilence,' he said reasonably. 'The household at Bradmayne sought absolution every day—Sir Richard likewise—and they all became ill. Yet Gyles, who saw the priest only at a distance, remains well.'

The interruption offended Hugh, suggesting as it did that Thurkell was on an equal footing with his mistress and his master's steward. 'This man's arrogance and lack of respect for his superiors is reason enough to attract God's displeasure,' he told Lady Anne. 'He should learn his place. It is not for a slave to give advice.'

She smiled slightly. 'I have made Master Thurkell my steward, sir, and I value the help he gives me. We have known each other these many years and he is as educated as you and I. I do not seek to diminish you in the eyes of Develish by giving your position to Thaddeus, but you were Sir Richard's choice, not mine, and his death has freed us of any debt to each other.'

Hugh's heart lurched with dread. He sought for a suitable response, as afraid of being pushed out of the demesne as he was of staying. He made a bow. 'I'm willing to switch my allegiance to you, milady.'

'You would be wrong to do so if you believe me a heretic, sir. If God seeks to punish Develish for my sins, He will punish you also.' She went on when he didn't answer: 'Is your heart so pure of intrigue and deceit that you feel confident of accusing others? Lady Eleanor tells me you are her only friend, but I question why a man of your age would find my fourteen-year-old daughter so interesting.'

Hugh's face flushed a dull red. 'She was worried for her father, milady. I sought only to comfort her.'

'My chambermaid, Isabella, is worried for hers. Will you comfort her similarly?'

'I don't know Isabella's father.'

'Indeed you do, sir. His name is Gyles Startout, and far from being a sinful man he has shown courage and generosity, first by caring for Sir Richard and now for Captain de Boulet and Master Foucault. Gyles will bury them deep in the ground beyond the village, and say prayers for their eternal souls as he does so, but he knows that if *he* is fated to die, he will suffer alone and his body will rot above ground until his bones are clean and dry.'

The thought of such a death terrified Hugh. He had been watching the village intermittently for the last forty-eight hours and had seen Gyles emerge several times from John Trueblood's cottage to squat in the dust and turn his face to the sun. On each occasion, he had searched for signs of the pestilence on the man, but the distance was too great. The previous afternoon a rider had approached along the highway, and Gyles had run out, waving his arms in warning. Hugh couldn't tell if any words were exchanged, but the stranger left immediately. 'Where did the visitor come from yesterday?' he asked. 'Did he bring news?'

'From Afpedle,' said Thaddeus. 'The pestilence has killed over fifty there and a hundred in Woodoak. Gyles said the man was mortally afraid when he heard there were sufferers here.'

'Where is he headed?'

'North. Nowhere in the south is safe. Gyles said they heard news as they journeyed home that every village twenty miles to the east and west of Dorchester is affected.'

Hugh marvelled at the calm way both Lady Anne and Thaddeus spoke, as if the content of their speech were no more alarming than a prediction of rain. Did they lack imagination? Had they no fear of pain or death? His own terrors—rooted in the Church's nightmare visions of Hell which had been drummed into him since childhood—had his heart beating inside his chest like a caged bird.

He ran his tongue across his lips to moisten them. 'Why are you not afraid?' he asked the serf. 'Do you believe so much in Lady Anne that you think you'll live?'

Thaddeus reached for a piece of vellum on the desk. 'This is a record, made by your predecessor, of how we dealt with a killing disease which affected our sheep five years ago.' He turned the skin towards the steward. 'Had we not separated the healthy from the sick, we would have lost them all. The method has been practised in monasteries for many years. Do you wish me to translate it from the English?'

Hugh's hatred for the serf was very great. 'There will be no need if it's written in the English that nobles speak,' he answered stiffly.

Thaddeus smiled slightly. 'It is, sir. Dorset brogue is hard to write but even harder to read and understand.'

April 24. Another 3 ewes fell sick today, making 12 in total. The 5 purchased from Pedle Hinton died on Tuesday. I have ordered the sick animals to be slaughtered and burnt, and the healthy ones to be placed on the clean grass of Short Halves.

May 6. Word came from Pedle Hinton that their entire flock has succumbed. It is clear their 5 ewes brought the disease into Develish. I have instructed that new animals must always be held apart until we are satisfied of their well-being.

June 3. 120 animals continue in good health, and I am hopeful we are through the worst. The total loss is 12 ewes, 2 rams and 8 lambs. I have given the order that sick animals must be destroyed immediately in the future. The flock is too valuable to allow infection to spread.

Hugh couldn't accept there was any equivalence between men and animals. He gave a dismissive flick of his fingers. 'What lessons do you take from this?' he asked sarcastically. 'That a sick man must be treated the same as a sick sheep? Do you plan to kill anyone in Develish who complains of a headache?'

Thaddeus lowered his gaze, but not before Hugh saw the derision in his eyes. 'The lesson of the text is how to deal with disease through isolation,' he said. 'It makes no mention of murdering men. If you have read your Bible, you will know that God instructed Moses to prevent the spread of sickness by separating the well from the ill.'

'How so?' Hugh demanded of Lady Anne. 'I know of no such instruction.'

'You will find it in Numbers,' she said. 'A leper must live alone, away from his people. There was no instruction to kill him, only to keep him separate so that the plague of leprosy could be contained.'

Was she telling the truth? Hugh wondered. 'But what if you can't keep the pestilence out, milady? There's not enough room to separate the sick from the healthy inside the moat.'

She nodded. 'If that happens, we will send the sick to the village and ask for volunteers to care for them. We can only do our best, Master de Courtesmain.'

'It's for God to decide what is best, milady.'

'Indeed, and you're a good Christian to keep reminding me of it. Your humble acceptance of God's design for you will set a fine example to others when the time comes to call for volunteers.'

There was a short silence.

'I will be of no use in the village, milady,' said Hugh, uncomfortably aware that he was painting himself as a hypocrite. 'I know nothing about medicine.'

'Then you must think seriously about whether you wish to remain in Develish,' she said with amusement. 'If you find no virtue in us, and can make no contribution to our welfare, it would be sensible to leave, would it not? Our rations will last longer if we have one less mouth to feed—and you'll be more comfortable back in Foxcote, where the people are less sinful than here.'

Hugh cursed himself for giving her the opportunity to laugh at him. He didn't doubt she'd read the letter from Sir Richard's sister, detailing how Hugh dealt with brawls, adultery and thieving on My Lord of Foxcote's demesne. Hugh had found the missive neatly filed on one of the shelves in this office, and could remember the words.

> You can rely on Hugh de Courtesmain, brother. He is a
> fine bailiff and will make a finer steward. He uses his
> whip on wrongdoers with the righteous energy of a zealot.
> Would there were more like him, ready and willing to
> tell their masters who the malefactors are. He is my only
> source of information and I shall miss him.

Hugh had interpreted this as unstinting praise and had been flattered by it. Sir Richard, too, had seen only merit in what his sister wrote, promising his new steward great reward if he brought tales of wrongdoing to his master's ears. But faced with a woman who found no fault in her serfs, Hugh was less certain of his righteousness in flogging a starving peasant for hiding a small sack of flour to feed his children, or in telling the bad-tempered wife of a brutal lord that the transgression had happened.

He was in something of a quandary. He had no desire to return to Foxcote—having managed to escape it once—nor to journey alone through villages raging with sickness, but he couldn't see a future for himself in Develish either. What role could he play if Lady Anne had passed the position of steward to Thaddeus Thurkell? Was she planning to reduce Hugh to the level of a hated serf?

He bent his knee. 'May I think about it, milady?'

She nodded. 'Indeed you may, Master de Courtesmain, although I suggest you reach a decision quickly. There will be desperate people on the road once the pestilence spreads north.'

❧

Outside the room, Hugh had the uncomfortable feeling he'd made a fool of himself by misunderstanding the purpose of the conversation. Why had Lady Anne told him he was no longer obligated to remain on the demesne and then asked for his advice? Why give him the choice to leave instead of ordering him to go? Had she been testing his willingness to think for himself instead of mouthing the sort of responses Sir Richard would have expected?

Ahead, at the end of the great hall, he saw one of the house servants showing a group of women how to prepare and infuse dried herbs. Some were grey-haired, far older than any of the serfs in Foxcote, but they still looked strong. To his right, mothers sat nursing babies, watching thirteen-year-old Isabella teach letters to their older children; and in the kitchen to his left, seen through the open door, cooks were preparing a meal for two hundred. The fragrant smell of stewing mutton scented the air, and Hugh tried to imagine a similar scene in Foxcote. It would never happen, he thought, and it wouldn't be happening here if Sir Richard had returned in good health.

His pulse beat erratically as he contemplated his future. He would be without position or status if he remained—at the mercy of serfs—but he knew for certain he would die if he left. It frightened him badly that the only Englishman to travel with Sir Richard was alive while every Frenchman was dead.

Six

DEVELISH'S CHURCH WAS A PRETTY little stone building with a tower, a vaulted ceiling, an altar carved from solid oak and a rush-strewn floor. A mural of the Annunciation—with the Archangel Gabriel bearing the face of a previous lord, and the Holy Mother the face of his wife—lent vibrant colour to the north wall, while mullioned windows in the south wall allowed sunshine to pour in and dapple the painting with gold.

The smell of burning candle wax was powerful, but not powerful enough to mask the smell of drink on Father Anselm's breath nor the stink of urine on his cassock. He slept in a chamber in the tower and, had Lady Anne not insisted on her servants cleaning it daily, the church would have reeked of his odours. He was not a man who espoused cleanliness in the way that most of the serfs did, being too lazy to fetch water from the well himself.

Hugh hesitated inside the door, seeing the priest suddenly through Lady Anne's eyes. He even made the leap of imagination to wonder if Father Anselm numbed his mind with alcohol because he understood his own deficiencies. All that elevated him above his fellows was a smattering of Latin, a small facility with a quill and the blessing of a bishop. Was it wise of Hugh to offer his secrets to such a person?

He had come to make confession but his instinctive reluctance to go through with it was strengthened when he saw that Lady Eleanor had reached the church before him. She stood by the altar, her small body shaking with grief, and Hugh quailed at performing the role of friend and comforter.

It was too late to retreat. Father Anselm greeted his arrival with inebriated relief and beckoned him forward. 'I have told this child that My Lord Bishop will hear of her mother's wickedness,' he breathed into Hugh's ear.

'What wickedness, Father?'

The old man looked blearily at Eleanor as if he couldn't remember what she'd been saying, and the girl stamped her foot, anger overcoming emotion. 'She refuses to let my father's body across the moat for burial. She says it's for the good of all, but she lies. She does it out of hatred for Sir Richard.'

Hugh glanced at the priest, wondering if he knew how deadly the pestilence was. 'I am deeply sorry for your loss, milady,' he said with a small bow. 'The news of his death upset me greatly.'

'Then make my mother listen to reason,' she begged. 'My father's soul cannot depart unless the proper rites are said and his sins forgiven.' A terrible dread showed in her eyes. 'I can't bear to think of him in Limbo.'

There was a brief uncomfortable silence before Father Anselm reached for her hand and gave it a clumsy pat. 'No man had a purer spirit,' he said. 'He came here every morning to confess his sins. He is with God now.'

Eleanor shook him off. 'There's no certainty of that unless his eyes and lips are anointed,' she cried. 'You must ride to His Grace of Sarum and demand an edict ordering Lady Anne to bring his body inside the moat.'

The priest turned to Hugh, a calculating gleam in his rheumy eyes. 'Perhaps Master de Courtesmain will go? You are still liegeman to Sir Richard, are you not, and have pledged your support to his daughter? She tells me her only happiness is speaking with you.'

He wasn't as drunk as he was pretending, Hugh thought, cursing the man for trying to push the responsibility onto him. 'I am at Lady Eleanor's service,' he murmured, 'but I fear the journey to Sarum and back will take too long to allow her father to be buried in the graveyard. In this heat, and with so many flies—' he gave an apologetic shrug—'he cannot be left above ground for more than a day.'

'He speaks the truth,' sighed Father Anselm. 'You must resign yourself, child. There's nothing to be done now. When the time is right, we will inter the bones with all the ceremony you desire.'

'It'll be too late.' Tears streamed down her cheeks. 'At least take holy oil to his body so that his soul can find rest.'

Hugh kept his eyes on the ground, wondering how the priest would answer when he had declined to give unction to Sir Richard while he lived.

'His Grace would not permit it,' Father Anselm said sorrowfully, washing his hands in front of his bloated belly. 'I am shepherd to every soul in Develish. If I cross the moat, Lady Anne will prevent my return and all will be denied absolution, including yourself, milady. Am I not right, Master de Courtesmain?'

How tempted the Frenchman was to say no and expose the priest for the hypocrite he was. A true man of God would have been at Sir Richard's side from the moment he returned, with or without his mistress's blessing, but Hugh saw too many problems for himself if Eleanor believed he was willing to be her champion. 'Yes, Father, you are. The demesne cannot be left without a priest.'

Eleanor clenched her hands into fists at her side. 'I don't care. My mother breaks God's laws in what she's doing.' She searched their faces. 'Will you not condemn her for it?'

'We would be wasting our breath, milady,' Hugh answered. 'Her people support her in whatever she does.'

Eleanor's eyes flared angrily. 'They're not her people,' she stormed. 'They're Sir Richard's.' She rounded on Father Anselm. 'You know full well she's without rights or property in Develish, for she was never pleasing enough to be granted any. Sir Richard called her his chattel wife for good reason and it's your duty to denounce her as such.'

'And who will run the demesne if the serfs heed what I say and take her authority from her?' he asked reasonably. 'Would you rather be governed by Thaddeus Thurkell?'

Hugh looked past her as she declared her contempt for the whole peasant class, staring through the window behind the altar which overlooked a stretch of the moat to the east. Several men were working on the wall lining the bank, using wet clay to bind flints and large stones into the structure. They sang as they worked—a lilting Dorseteshire folk tune—and their voices were strong enough to carry into the church. The wooden cross on the altar partially obscured Hugh's view, and out of habit, he touched his fingers to his forehead and his chest.

'It may be that Lady Anne's refusal to allow Sir Richard's remains into the demesne is a lesser sin than endangering the people he pledged to protect,' he said carefully. 'The sickness is worse than anyone thought. The rider who came yesterday reported whole villages being lost for miles around. He said a pestilence is sweeping the land. The people are calling it a Black Death.'

He had forgotten that Eleanor had been beside him when he watched Gyles speak with the rider. She stamped her foot in fury. 'You lie for your own purposes,' she hissed. 'You can't know what he said. Only Gyles Startout heard him.'

Hugh gestured towards the window. 'Why do you think the men are fortifying the walls, milady? They sing to persuade their children there's nothing to worry about, but they know there'll be no one left alive if the pestilence enters. Last night, I watched Thurkell post guards to the north and the south. I believe their plan is to stop anyone entering.'

'Then my mother lied when she said it was curable.'

He had told her as much two days ago. 'Her reasons were honourable, Lady Eleanor. She made the pretence to stop fear taking hold, though I doubt there are many who still believe it. They will know by your father's death that the fever kills.' He gestured towards the window. 'These men out here show courage by remaining calm—as does your mother. Each understands that a terrible death awaits us if the pestilence enters.'

Father Anselm nodded. 'Master de Courtesmain speaks wisely, my daughter. It will endanger us all to allow your father's body across the moat.'

Eleanor looked from one to the other, her expression resentful. 'You would rather take her side than mine.'

Beneath lowered lids, Hugh studied her face, wondering where this dislike of her mother came from. At times, when he'd listened through the litany of Eleanor's miseries, he'd wondered if it wasn't an intense love she felt for the woman, warped and twisted by her inability to win praise from Lady Anne. She was certainly jealous of those who could—most especially Thurkell.

It was an emotion Hugh was willing to exploit since he felt the same himself. 'It's not a question of sides, milady. There's nothing to be done while Thaddeus Thurkell guards the moat and upholds your mother's rule to prevent anyone crossing.'

A look of calculation entered Eleanor's eyes. 'He's a base-born slave. He can't prevent *me* crossing . . . or you either, Master de Courtesmain.' She drew close to Hugh and plucked at his tunic. 'Will you take me to Foxcote so that I can lay my grievances before my uncle? He will not stand idly by when he learns of the sacrilege my mother commits against his wife's brother.'

Hugh disengaged her hands and stepped backwards, made uneasy by the press of her young body against his. 'You know that's impossible, milady. Your mother has freed me from my obligations so that I may return north if I choose, but she won't allow you to travel with me. It would be unseemly, and the roads are dangerous.'

Eleanor assessed him through narrowed eyes. 'Is that the truth or are you finding excuses for why she doesn't want you as her steward? It must gall you to see Eva Thurkell's bastard in your place.'

'It's the truth, milady.'

'Good,' she said with satisfaction. 'Then you must ride for Foxcote immediately. When my uncle learns of Sir Richard's death, he'll send soldiers to ensure my father's burial and a wagon to carry me away from the pestilence. Even my mother will hesitate to refuse My Lord of Foxcote's orders if they're backed by fighting men.'

Hugh sketched a small bow as if to signify agreement. He hadn't the will or the energy to argue with her, but she was sadly deluded if she thought her uncle would spend money on her rescue or that her aunt, Lady Beatrix, would view the arrival of a pretty, young niece with favour. Even more deluded if she thought all demesnes were like Develish. Eleanor had no reason to fear the serfs here, but she would if they harboured as much hatred for the ruling class as the people of Foxcote did.

He excused himself, leaving Eleanor to take absolution, and made his way to where latrines were being dug at the rear of the orchard. The idea was novel to him. The practice in Foxcote and other demesnes he'd visited was to empty slops into the nearest river or to defecate in the fields. The air of Develish was the sweeter for this clean disposal of waste—Hugh had noticed it on the day of his arrival—but he wondered now why he had accepted so easily that Sir Richard's piety was the reason.

One pit—for the use of the house servants—had been there for years, but it was too small and inadequate for the needs of two hundred. The excavation of four new pits seemed to serve a double purpose, since the clay soil was promptly removed to reinforce the moat wall. He stood watching the labourers work for several minutes before one tossed a wooden spade onto the ground in front of him. 'Do you wish to make yourself useful, Master de Courtesmain, or are you here to admire us?'

The man had a cheerful grin on his face, but Hugh's nerves reacted in the way they always did when a bondsman did something unexpected: they tightened in fear. He stooped to retrieve the spade. 'Who am I speaking to?'

'Alleyn Startout, brother to Gyles and cousin to John Trueblood.' He put his hand on the man next to him. 'This be Adam Catchpole, cousin to Clara Trueblood, and next to him be James Buckler, cousin to Will Thurkell. You'll be mighty welcome in this hole with us if you have the heart for a little digging, sir.'

He spoke in the same clear English that his brother had used. 'Are all Dorset men so easy to understand?' Hugh asked. 'On my last demesne the dialect was unintelligible.'

'Ours too if we choose to use it.'

'Why do you not?'

'Out of deference to Milady. When she came here, Dorset words meant as little to her as they do to you, and there wasn't one amongst us who wanted her to think we were keeping secrets from her. Our children barely know the brogue now.'

Hugh rested the spade against his knee and began to roll up the sleeves of his woollen tunic. 'Perhaps they've learnt the King's English from the lessons she gives them in reading?'

Alleyn Startout eyed him with amusement but didn't answer the question. 'You should remove your tunic, sir. Your britches, too. It's hot, dirty work in here and it would be a shame to spoil good cloth. You'll be freer and cooler in just your undershirt. There are some rags by the heap of spoil. You'll want to wrap them round your hands to prevent blisters.'

Hugh wondered afterwards why he hadn't refused the invitation and walked away. What had he been trying to prove? That he had something to offer? That he wasn't afraid of these people?

They were bigger and stronger than their equivalents in Foxcote, and their hearty laughs and teasing banter sounded like mockery. He recognised them as the men who had stood beside Thurkell at the moat and knew they were leaders amongst the serfs. He had to force himself to jump into the pit with them, but, once there, they gave him room and showed him how to find a rhythm in chopping out the heavy clods and flicking them onto the spoil heap. He worked at only a quarter their speed, and by the time the sun had reached its zenith he was exhausted.

He lowered his spade to the ground and bent double, panting for breath. 'I can't do any more,' he said.

'No shame in that, Master de Courtesmain,' said Alleyn Startout. 'You've done well despite those soft hands of yours.

You'll feel the pain tomorrow, I wager, but you can be proud of the work you've done this morning.'

He brought his palm down in a friendly pat on Hugh's shoulder, and the steward ducked away from it, raising his arm in involuntary defence.

Startout stepped back. 'I beg your pardon, sir, but you've no need to fear us. There's not a man here wishes you ill.'

Hugh took a breath to calm himself. He was ashamed that he'd made himself so transparent. 'We should all wish we had your brother's courage, Master Startout.'

'There's no sense wishing the impossible, sir. Only Milady can claim to be as brave as Gyles. If we live, we'll know who to thank.'

'Will you not be thanking God, Master Startout?'

Hugh thought he detected a small hesitation before the man answered. 'Indeed I will, sir. I thank him every day for giving me and my family life. We are peculiarly blessed in Develish. Death from illness is rare, even amongst the children.'

Hugh had read this in the demesne's records. In the graveyard, too, the dates on the tombstones had shown longer lives than in Foxcote. There, a man could expect to die before he reached thirty-five, but here some lived to fifty and beyond. He couldn't account for it any more than he could account for the higher crop yields. He searched the faces of each man in turn. 'What makes you so blessed? Only the strongest of children survived beyond five years on the estate I came from.'

'It'll be because their serfs lack learning,' said James Buckler, as if the fact were common knowledge. 'When a man's taught to prize a healthy child and a woman's taught how to care for herself, the little ones thrive.'

'And what form does this care take?'

'A proper distribution of food. Mothers need nourishment to produce healthy offspring, and youngsters need it to strengthen their bones. The rewards come when they're old enough to help their fathers in the fields. More hands produce higher yields for everyone.'

The idea of serfs looking beyond the day was alien to Hugh. He had grown up with the Church's teaching that the only reward for hunger and pain on Earth was the promise of bliss in Heaven. 'How can a man work if he doesn't take the lion's share? His family will die if he's too weak to till his plot.'

'That's where the teaching comes in. A wise man learns to curb his appetites. Four healthy youngsters are more valuable to him than eight in their graves.'

Hugh wasn't sure he'd understood correctly. 'His appetite for food?'

The three men laughed. 'His *carnal* appetites,' said Startout. 'A man who is reckless in his demands for intimacy will wear his wife out and give himself too many mouths to feed.'

'Like Buckler's cousin Will Thurkell,' murmured Catchpole. 'If it wasn't for young Thaddeus putting food on the table, the whole brood would be dead.'

'Will's no example to anyone,' said Buckler dismissively. 'He'd cut off his nose to spite his face if he thought it would punish Eva and Thaddeus more.'

Hugh recalled the uncontrolled appetites of the men of Foxcote, who took their wives whenever they felt like it, sometimes their daughters too. 'By what means does a man curb his desire for intimacy when even monks find abstinence difficult?' he asked.

His question was greeted with another laugh. 'There are many ways a wife can pleasure her husband without falling with child,' said Catchpole. 'A man can spill his seed on the ground if he chooses.'

Hugh's shock showed in his face. 'But such actions are sinful. It is against the Church's teachings for a man to satisfy himself.'

There was a brief silence before Alleyn Startout responded. 'Must a serf behave differently from a priest or a monk, sir? It's well known that Father Anselm pleasures himself. He leaves the evidence in his piss-pot.'

Hugh's shock deepened. 'It's not for the peasant class to question the clergy. You challenge God with such views and bring this pestilence upon Develish.'

Adam Catchpole studied him for a moment before resuming his digging. 'It's no wonder you've been too timid to talk to us, Master de Courtesmain. You must have thought yourself in a Godless Hell these last few weeks.'

With a small shrug at Hugh's expression, Alleyn Startout laced his hands and bent down to form a step. 'You'll be happier elsewhere,' he said, encouraging the steward to accept the hoist.

Hugh shook his head in frustration. 'Why are you not afraid of God's anger? Sir Richard is dead and your brother likely to follow within the week. Do you feel no responsibility for that?'

'I do not, sir. If my brother dies it will be because he caught the disease in Bradmayne . . . as did Sir Richard. Do you want to blame the poor dead folk of Bradmayne for visiting their sin on *us*?'

James Buckler flicked a clod towards the soil pile, narrowly missing Hugh's head. 'I see more anger in you than I see in God,' he said. 'You should return to your demesne in the north. Alleyn speaks the truth when he says you'll be happier somewhere else.'

ഇൾ

There was no solitude anywhere. With so many crammed into such a confined space, Hugh couldn't move fifty yards without encountering serfs. He felt they were laughing at him behind their hands, willing him to be gone and careless if he died along the way. The thought of a lonely death terrified him. Who would bury him? Who would mourn his passing? To add to his woes, he had the beginnings of a headache, and his heart beat with fear because of it.

Eva Thurkell discovered him hiding behind the northern end of the manor house where it abutted the water. She'd come searching for him at the request of her son, but it had taken her a good half-hour to find him. There was barely room for him to stand on the narrow strip of grass between the wall and the water, and she guessed correctly that he'd chosen this place because he didn't want to be observed.

He was rocking to and fro, his slim fingers pressed to his temples and his lips forming words that were inaudible. She guessed he was praying and retreated around the corner so that he wouldn't see her. She knew nothing about Hugh de Courtesmain except what she'd heard through gossip several weeks ago. *Sir Richard brings a steward from Foxcote to increase our taxes.*

Eva had asked Thaddeus if it was true, but he'd shaken his head and said he didn't know. It was the same answer he gave to all her questions. *Why couldn't the bailiff find you today, son?* I don't know. *How does Lady Anne guess when you need liniment?* I don't know. *Is it right that some of the house servants can read?* I don't know. *What do you hear when you're doing* ad opus work *at the house?* Nothing . . .

She knew now that Thaddeus had been lying to her for years, and she felt deeply betrayed by it. She had sacrificed so much for him and it hurt her deeply to be repaid with distrust and hidden secrets. He hadn't thought even to tell her that Lady Anne had raised him to steward but had left her to discover it for herself. Did he expect her to be pleased to see him at the woman's side, or to have to learn from the likes of Clara Trueblood and Rosa Catchpole that her son had more education than any man in Develish?

For a woman who chose to blame others for her ills, Eva had little difficulty finding a focus for her grievance. She had always known Thaddeus was clever but it hadn't occurred to her that his cleverness came from teaching or that his teacher was Lady Anne. She saw the looks of respect he gave Milady and felt a terrible jealousy because of it. The only emotion he ever showed his mother was exhausted irritation when she made him promise yet again not to leave her.

She heard Hugh de Courtesmain cry out in pain, and moved away from the corner to look at him. He must have sensed her presence, because he turned towards her with a startled expression. 'Who's there?'

'Eva Thurkell, sir, mother to Thaddeus. He asked me to bring you to him.'

Hugh frowned, wondering how so small and fair a woman could have produced a man as tall and dark as Thaddeus. There was no similarity between them, or none that he could see. He held up his hand to keep her away. 'You mustn't approach. My head is pounding. I think I have Sir Richard's fever.'

Eva took a hasty step backwards. 'I'll fetch Lady Anne.'

Hugh shook his head. 'Fetch your son,' he told her.

But Eva didn't take kindly to orders, and certainly not from a man who had lost his standing in Develish. 'Thaddeus knows nothing of medicine.'

'It matters not. Medicine is useless against the fever. I need someone strong enough to operate the raft. I beg you to do as I say, Mistress Thurkell. If you do not the infection may spread through the compound.'

Eva obeyed him out of fear, but her mind was full of mutiny as she returned to the house. Was truth absent from Develish? Had Lady Anne lied too? *Medicine is useless against the fever . . .*

She found Thaddeus alone in the steward's office. He was using an abacus to calculate how long the rations would last, and Eva felt renewed resentment at this further ability he'd hidden from her. 'You could have taught your brothers to do the same,' she said.

'I could,' Thaddeus agreed, 'if I'd been willing to take a beating from your husband for having a skill he lacked. They will learn to do it now if they have the mind for it. Isabella Startout is teaching them letters and Amelia Buckler the abacus.' He raised his head. 'Did you find Master de Courtesmain?'

Eva's anger grew. 'You've become so cold, Thaddeus. Should I blame Lady Anne for that? Has she turned you against me?'

He sighed, his face expressing the irritation she knew so well. 'You are my mother. I feel the same for you as I have always done.'

'How can you when you keep so many secrets from me?' she cried. 'Why must I learn from others that Lady Anne singled you out for an education?'

'You would have told your husband and he would have found a way to prevent it.'

A spark of viciousness burnt in Eva's soul. 'You have only yourself to blame for Will's treatment of you. If you'd been less arrogant towards him, we would all have been spared the rod.'

Thaddeus ignored her to resume his counting, and Eva's resentment boiled over.

'It's your fault I'm despised by everyone,' she went on. 'You should have died and let me live my life in peace. Instead I gave up my happiness for you—and this is my reward: to be ousted from your affections by a woman who can't make sons herself.'

Thaddeus had heard these words all his life. Eva used them as effectively and frequently as Will had used his cudgel, and with the same intention—to get her own way. 'You gave up nothing,' he said. 'With Will for a husband, you would have lived a life of misery whether I was born or not. Be grateful he took out more of his anger on me than he ever did on you.'

Eva's lips thinned. 'And who persuaded him to give you a home? Without my pleading, you would have been cast into a ditch and left to die.'

'And for that I thank you,' said Thaddeus quietly. He dipped his quill into the ink and wrote a figure on the vellum in front of him. 'Why is Master de Courtesmain not with you?'

Her face grew harder. 'You are Eva Thurkell's bastard,' she snapped. 'He has no more respect for your orders than anyone else in Develish.'

Thaddeus assessed her for a moment. 'You have other children, madam,' he said, rising to his feet. 'I suggest you seek succour from them in future and forget any claims you think you have on me. I am not a Thurkell—which is, and always has been, a source of great happiness to me.'

꙰

The steward was a sorry sight when Thaddeus found him. He was some twenty feet from the corner of the wall, supporting himself against a stone buttress.

'What ails you, Master de Courtesmain?' Thaddeus called.

Hugh turned frightened eyes towards him. 'I have all the symptoms of the pestilence,' he rasped from a dry mouth. 'You must keep your distance, Thurkell.'

The man's fear was so powerful that Thaddeus was not immune from it. He felt the beginnings of panic churn in his gut as he racked his brains for what to do next. It was one thing to prevent the pestilence crossing the moat, quite another to have it inside the compound. But why should Hugh de Courtesmain have been infected before anyone else? The steward had barely left the house this last week, preferring to watch others work from an upstairs window.

'It makes no sense,' he said, voicing his thoughts aloud. 'If the pestilence is carried on the wind, the men guarding the walls would have sickened first. As would I from crossing the moat to talk to Gyles Startout.'

'God makes an example of me for others to learn,' Hugh answered tearfully.

Thaddeus shook his head impatiently. 'Do you think yourself more important than Sir Richard? Was a lord's death not example enough for us?' He stared at the ground, searching for answers. 'Have you been to the village against Lady Anne's command? Did you try to see to Sir Richard when he first returned?'

The man didn't answer.

'You need to speak to me, Master de Courtesmain. If I can't understand why you have the pestilence, then everyone here is at risk. Did you make contact with Sir Richard or any of his retinue?'

'No.'

'Then how do you account for the ague that is shaking your body?'

'My sins have found me out.'

Thaddeus gave a dry laugh. 'The only way your sins will kill you, sir, is if you're hanged by the neck for theft or murder. If it were otherwise, God would have struck you dead the first time you told a falsehood.'

Anger gave the steward energy. 'If anyone deserves to die, it's you,' he hissed. 'You're the product of lust, and your mockery is offensive.'

'Yet I am well, and you are sick. How do you explain that?'

'The Devil favours you.'

'Then you are doubly unfortunate, sir. It would seem your sins are bad enough for God to strike you dead, but not so bad that Satan chooses to let you live.'

Hugh lowered his head, nausea welling in his throat. He had convinced himself he was the most God-fearing man in Develish, and the injustice of his position struck him hard. 'What should I do?' he whispered.

Thaddeus stripped off his shirt and knelt to soak it in the moat. 'Coolness will bring some relief. If you move a yard towards me, the bank is wide enough for you to sit with your legs in the water. When you are settled, I will throw this shirt towards you so that you may cover your head and shoulders with it.'

'What then?'

'Remain where you are until I return with Lady Anne. It may be that some of her medicine can help you.'

The man looked at him in despair. 'I have not received absolution. Lady Eleanor was in the church when I went to speak with Father Anselm.'

Thaddeus rose to his feet, bundling the wet shirt into a ball. 'There is time for everything,' he said calmly, throwing it to the Frenchman. 'Even Sir Richard didn't die immediately . . . much as he deserved to.'

ᘓᗕᘐ

Hugh had no belief in God's love, only in His vengeance, and his thoughts grew turbulent at the prospect of judgement. It wasn't fair that he should have to account for himself ahead of baser men like Thurkell. Despite the icy cool of the serf's shirt against his skin, he felt himself on fire—like a foretaste of Hell—and he cursed his Creator for inflicting this punishment on him. What had he, a pious man, done that the heretical mistress and the lying bondsmen of Develish had not?

His heated brain looked for reasons. Was he being asked to atone for the acts he'd performed in Foxcote? Was it a sin to flog a starving man in public with his hollow-eyed wife and children watching? Yet how was Hugh to blame? A bailiff was as bound to obey the orders of a sworn lord as serfs were. If the priest and the bishop had spoken against the whippings, Hugh might have searched his conscience, but the Church endorsed and encouraged the chastisement of wrongdoers. With so much hatred for the ruling class in Foxcote, harsh punishment had been the only way to exact the levies, and the bishop had been as demanding of his tithe as the King was of his.

Hugh had lived his life according to the rules—enshrined in the oaths of allegiance made before God—that each class was subservient to the one above. But Sir Richard had died before his bondsmen, and Thaddeus Thurkell, the lowest of the low, had risen so high that he was performing the duties of steward. Thurkell was little better than a slave—a bastard without property or rights of inheritance—yet he stood now at Lady Anne's side. How was this possible in a social order blessed by God? The disturbing idea that the Church's teachings might be wrong—even a source of evil—took root in Hugh's mind.

With a groan of despair, he folded his arms around his covered head, pressing Thurkell's damp shirt against his feverish skin. The reek of sweat in the cloth was powerful, and Hugh was reminded of the terrible stench of fear and filth that had come off the naked bodies of the men he'd whipped. In remorse for those past deeds, he murmured *mea culpas* before whispering the Creed in Latin. '*Credo in unum Deum, Patrem omnipotentem, factorem caeli et terrae, visibilium omnium et invisibilium . . .*'

Was that the moment when his head ceased throbbing? Or had the pain been absent for some time? He couldn't remember. His only awareness was that his declaration of belief in one God, the Father Almighty, Maker of Heaven and Earth and All Things Visible and Invisible, had eased his anguish. And in his confused and overly superstitious mind, he came to believe he'd been saved by a miracle.

Seven

THAT NIGHT, LIT BY A bright moon, Thaddeus slipped into the dark waters of the moat beneath Alleyn Startout's northern guard position and swam in long, slow strokes to keep ripples to a minimum. He pulled himself out on the other side and lay still in the grass until Alleyn raised a hand to confirm that his departure had been unobserved. Even so, he moved at a crouch through the peasant strips, taking cover where he could behind unharvested wheat and rye. The fewer who knew of his nighttime visits to Gyles the better. There'd be no holding anyone to Lady Anne's rules if it became known that Thaddeus was breaking them at her command.

Once inside the shelter of the dwellings in the village, he stripped off his sodden shirt and wrung out the water. It was all he was wearing. Even his boots remained under Alleyn's watchful guard for fear Eva's hostile eyes would notice their dampness tomorrow. She was ready to use anything to vent her spite on Lady Anne, and it wouldn't worry her if she brought down her son in the process. She could tolerate her husband's scorn more easily than she could Thaddeus's.

The door of John Trueblood's hut stood open and Thaddeus could see into the interior. Gyles had been burning candles to illuminate it since Sir Richard, delirious with fever, had cried out for the light of God to shine on his face. Perhaps he believed the guttering flames were indeed divine, for Gyles said he became easier in his mind afterwards. Thaddeus thought it more likely that Lady Anne's medicines had dulled his pain but, whatever the cause, Sir Richard seemed to die peacefully enough.

The previous night, Thaddeus had dug a grave in the far corner of the common pasture and watched at a distance as Gyles placed Sir Richard's body across the black charger and walked the animal up the highway from the village. He marvelled at how gently Gyles lifted the dead weight from the horse's back and how reverentially he laid his master in the earth, saying a prayer as he did so. Perhaps Gyles thought Thaddeus would find such kindness strange, for he had called out an explanation as he shovelled dirt over the corpse. 'If I deny this man forgiveness, I cannot ask it for myself.'

'You won't need it, sir,' Thaddeus answered. 'We expect you to return to us in good health. Lady Anne believes you have an inner strength that defies this sickness.'

Gyles gave a hollow laugh. 'If she's so confident, why does she keep sending you to pick my brains? Are fourteen days too long to wait for answers?'

'It depends who comes up the road, sir. Single riders don't worry her but an army of frightened people will. We can't hold off a hundred if they encircle the moat and enter at the same time. The more you tell us now the better prepared we will be.'

Gyles shovelled a last spadeful of earth over Sir Richard and reached for the charger's reins. 'You must paint red crosses around the boundary walls to make strangers afraid of what's inside.

I will do the same on the doors in the village if you bring me the means.' He left the spade on the ground at a distance from Sir Richard's grave. 'Have you the energy to dig another pit tonight, large enough for two? The captain and the bailiff will not last through tomorrow, I think.'

He had been right about Foucault, whose body now lay shrouded on the ground outside John Trueblood's dwelling, but de Boulet still clung to life. The captain sat propped against a pile of rushes, naked from the waist up, drawing loud, rasping breaths through his open mouth. Every detail of his suffering was visible to Thaddeus. Grotesque misshapen swellings, livid with poisoned blood, clung like a cluster of apples to his neck, while smaller boils, some oozing pus, had erupted across his chest and arms. More terrible than anything, his right hand, resting in his lap, was black to the wrist as if it had been dipped in tar.

Even at thirty paces, Thaddeus could smell the poor man's stench and he wondered how Gyles could tolerate being so close. He knelt at de Boulet's side, cooling his brow with a moistened cloth which he dipped from time to time in a bowl of water. His movements were clumsy and rough, but the compassion behind the gestures caused tears to flow freely down de Boulet's face.

'You should leave,' he whispered. 'You will die if you don't.'

'I said I would not, sir. Would you have me break my word?'

'You owe me nothing. It troubles me to think how badly I've treated you in the past. We might all have lived if I'd listened to you.'

'Be at peace, sir. Nothing you could have said to the master would have persuaded him I was right. We left because Lord Peter was ailing. Had he remained well, we would still be in Bradmayne.'

A long silence followed, punctuated by de Boulet's rattling breaths. After several minutes, he spoke again. 'I have little time left. Will you hear my confession? God may judge me less harshly if I acknowledge my faults.'

'Say what is in your heart, sir, but do not fear God's judgement. He created you in love, not hate or anger.'

Thaddeus stepped away, unwilling to intrude further. Whatever sins the captain carried on his conscience were for Gyles's ears only. Even without the authority to absolve, there was no better man to ease another's passing.

He made his way behind the dwellings to Will and Eva's hut, pushing open the door and waiting for his eyes to adjust to the darkness. He had slept here all his life but had never thought of it as home. From the time Will set him to work, it had been a place to lay his head and nothing more. He had even taken his meals outside, preferring to eat and think in solitude rather than witness the rancour inside. Now, when he watched his younger half-siblings learn their alphabets with Isabella in the great hall, he realised he barely knew them. Even the youngest, a tiny replica of her mother, had called him 'slave' from the moment she could speak, and Thaddeus had closed his mind to her as firmly as he'd closed it to Will and Eva.

Did he have regrets? Perhaps. His childhood had taught him to shun people rather than allow them close, and he envied Gyles his compassion and the love so many in Develish had for him. If Gyles survived the next fourteen days, Lady Anne would make him steward and Thaddeus would have little to do. The prospect depressed him. In an unconscious echo of Hugh de Courtesmain's fears, he knew he would fare badly without work to distract him, for he lacked the ability to live in idle communion with others.

With a sigh, he blanked such worries from his mind and set to searching his mother's chest. Like every woman in Develish, she had received gifts of dye from Lady Anne over the years—blue woad, yellow ochre and red madder—but since Eva had a dislike of red, she had hidden the madder away, choosing to criticise Lady Anne for giving her something she couldn't use rather than barter it for something she could. As Thaddeus's fingers located the jar beneath a pile of rabbit skins, he had reason to be grateful for his mother's stubborn foolishness.

He went next to Alleyn Startout's hut, where the man had assured him he would find a pitcher of limewash and another of flaxseed oil. Thaddeus showed no respect by taking the cooking pot and ladle from the ashes of the fire to use as a vessel for the liquids, but he made a silent vow to Alleyn's wife that he would replace them if they all came through the pestilence alive.

He heard Gyles call to him as he began to mix the oil and the madder into a thick paste. 'Are you there, Thaddeus?'

'I am, sir—making the means for you to paint red crosses on the doors. Is the captain still with us?'

'No. He's gone, Master Foucault too. I mourn their passing. Each bore his suffering with more fortitude than I would have shown.'

Thaddeus doubted that. 'The grave is dug. Are you ready to take them to it?'

'Not yet. I need to find myself again.'

Thaddeus paused in his stirring. 'What troubles you?'

'De Boulet was young and I am old. I should have died before him.'

'God isn't ready for you, sir.'

There was a short silence. 'You've no need to honour me with a title, Thaddeus. We are as base born as each other. Gyles will do well enough. The company of a friend is welcome, particularly one who has Lady Anne's respect. You tell me she's appointed you steward. Does the work sit easily with you?'

'Not as easily as it will sit with you when you return. There are many who think me too young for such a position.'

'Only the foolish ones,' said Gyles. 'Milady told me two years ago that my daughter Isabella's fluency in reading and writing was exceeded only by yours. Her hope has always been that you would one day become steward to Develish.'

His words surprised Thaddeus as much because Lady Anne had discussed his future with Gyles as because she had plans for him. 'She has never said so.'

'She was too wise to fill your head with dreams of something that might never happen. Sir Richard would have needed powerful persuasion to take a serf for his steward. He'd have ordered you flogged for being able to read before he allowed you the title of master.'

Thaddeus resumed his work, diluting the paste with limewash. 'Then I have the pestilence to thank for my good fortune, if only for a short time,' he answered lightly. 'Every man and woman in Develish expects you to be steward in fourteen days, Gyles. It would be wrong if you do not lead us at Lady Anne's side when you command more respect than anyone else.'

There was another silence, longer this time. 'God may have other plans for me. I've been on this Earth too long and confessed too little to avoid being punished. If the captain's trifling sins merited a terrible death, mine will be worse.'

Thaddeus heard the tremor in his voice and felt at a loss as to what to do or say. He was young enough to be Gyles's son, had seen but a fraction of what the other had seen, and had no words of comfort. Despair and loneliness could not be dispelled with meaningless talk. He pushed the cooking pot aside and rose to his feet, stepping outside and closing the door of Alleyn's dwelling behind him.

'I will walk with you to the grave,' he said. 'The burial of the dead is not a duty that any man should have to do alone.'

೧೮

Alleyn Startout gestured angrily to the eastern sky as Thaddeus pulled himself from the moat and leapt for the top of the wall. 'You're a damned fool,' he snarled, seizing Thaddeus's arm and hauling him over. 'Dawn's almost upon us. You'd better have a good reason for making me shit my britches these last three hours.'

Thaddeus stripped off his sodden shirt a second time and wrung it between his hands. 'Your brother was in need of company,' he said through teeth that chattered with cold. 'He suffers greatly by what he does for us.'

'Does he have the sickness?'

'Not yet, but he fears he can't escape it.' He began to dress himself again.

'Did you tell him how much his family loves him?'

'He knows the affection you have for him.'

Alleyn eyed him with disfavour. 'You're a cold fish, Thaddeus. I should have gone in your place. Gyles needs words of hope and kindness at a time like this.'

Thaddeus stooped to pull his boots over his frozen feet. 'I don't doubt your face would have been more welcome than mine, but I question what hope you could have given him. He knows better than you how this sickness kills. He's witnessed its fickle cruelty for two weeks now.'

Alleyn took his flippancy for disrespect. 'There's always hope,' he hissed. 'Lady Anne's favour has made you arrogant. You would rather see Gyles dead than lose your place as steward. I will make the crossing tomorrow and attempt to raise his spirits where you have lowered them.'

Thaddeus straightened. 'You will not. I've given him my word no Startout will cross the moat. He would rather die believing his family safe than be the means by which they catch the pestilence. He doubts any of you will keep your distance.'

'You mean *you* doubt it and pretend the request is his. You have no trouble keeping away from him yourself, I imagine. Your heart's too cold to offer a hand in friendship.'

Thaddeus's gaze rested on him for a moment. 'Gyles wouldn't take it even if I offered it. He has too much care for Develish.'

'Then there's no reason for me not to go.'

'There is, and I say again that you will not.'

Alleyn raised a fist as if to strike. 'I take my orders from Lady Anne not a stripling half my age. Do you think I'd be standing guard for you if she hadn't asked me?'

Thaddeus folded a huge palm over the fist and forced Alleyn's arm to his side. 'If you care for your brother, you'll do as I say,' he murmured. 'Gyles is too weary and troubled to feign gladness. His mind is full of guilt.'

Alleyn wrestled free. 'You talk in Greek. What does he have to feel guilty about?'

'He's alive and all others who went to Bradmayne are dead. He left eight along the way and acted as priest and confessor to the three he brought home. Every death weighs heavily on him, for he sees no reason why they have suffered and he has not.'

'He should be grateful that God is smiling on him.'

'And you would tell him so?'

'Of course. Did you not?'

'I thought it better to learn what his feelings are than instruct him on what they ought to be.'

Alleyn frowned. 'At least say you tried to comfort him.'

'He spoke and I listened. If he dies, he has given me leave to repeat everything he said to you and his family. If he lives, he will embrace you with all the gratitude you desire.' Thaddeus checked that his damp shirt was hidden beneath his tunic. 'I'm sorry your guard duty frightened you. Next time I'll ask James Buckler to take this post.' His dark eyes, showing more scorn than sympathy, rested on Alleyn for a moment before he set off across the forecourt.

෨෬

Alleyn took his grievances to the other leading serfs. He found ready allies in James Buckler and Adam Catchpole, his companions of the latrine pit the day before, but John Trueblood shook his head. 'Thaddeus can't do right in any of your eyes,' he said. 'You find fault with everything he does.'

James Buckler spoke. 'He likes his role too well. Alleyn's right to say Lady Anne's favour has made him arrogant.'

John Trueblood smiled cynically. 'You've been listening to Eva. She'd have all Develish spurn him if she could. And for why? Because he did what he should have done years ago and has broken all ties with her.'

'It's cruel to do it now.'

'Since when did you have a fondness for your cousin's wife, James? Or your cousin either, for that matter? Will Thurkell's a brute and Eva's lazy. You've said it yourself many times. Between them, they'd have broken Thaddeus if Milady hadn't taken an interest in him.'

'That's no reason to make him steward,' Adam Catchpole retorted. 'One of us should have been given the position until Gyles returned. We've been her leading serfs for years.'

John Trueblood gave a grunt of amusement. 'And which amongst you fancies yourself as a scribe? Not I. My hands are more used to handling tools than quills. It's a skill that only the young seem able to master easily. Even Gyles, with his daughter Isabella as teacher, takes time to fashion his letters.'

Adam Catchpole frowned. 'Are you saying Milady will keep Thaddeus as steward whether Gyles returns or not?'

'She'd be foolish not to. Gyles will serve her better as captain of her guard than sitting at a desk, scratching in a ledger and using the abacus to calculate rations.' Trueblood looked towards Alleyn. 'Your brother has no ambition to be a clerk. You know that as well as I. Why stir up trouble by pretending he does?'

'The trouble is of Thaddeus's making. The position of steward is higher than any other and he uses the power it gives him to belittle others. Many resent him for it. They remember the circumstances of his birth better than he does.'

ౘౘ

The door to the steward's office stood open, showing Lady Anne sitting alone at the desk with her back to the window. The sun had been up several hours and the light, shafting through the leaded panes, tinged her hair an auburn red and threw her face into shadow. As John Trueblood tapped on the doorframe, he thought he saw exasperation in her eyes.

The impression was fleeting, for she smiled as she looked up from her work. 'Do you seek me or Thaddeus?' she asked, laying down her quill and looking from one man to the other.

'You, milady,' said Alleyn Startout. 'The matter concerns Thaddeus.'

She invited them in, watching Adam Catchpole close the door behind him and stand before it as if on guard. She could guess what the nature of their complaint was going to be but chose to begin with flattery in the hope of diverting their ill humour. 'Master de Courtesmain speaks well of all of you,' she said warmly. 'He praised you as hard workers and said you showed him friendship yesterday when he helped with the latrine. I thank you for your kindness.'

It seemed Alleyn had been nominated spokesman. 'We did what we thought you'd want, milady,' he answered stiffly. 'If the Frenchman cannot be steward, he must be given other ways to occupy his time. Thaddeus serves you ill by not setting him tasks. His idleness allows him to whisper against you.'

The family resemblance between Alleyn and Gyles was strong but that was as far as the similarity went. Alleyn had none of his older brother's cleverness. Lady Anne flattered him further. 'Your advice is good, Alleyn. I shall ask Thaddeus to do as you say.'

'He should have thought of it himself, milady.'

'If you have ideas on what work Master de Courtesmain might be willing to do, I will gladly hear them. At present, he seems undecided on the role he wishes to play in our community.'

'Then he must be ordered to leave, milady.'

She folded her hands beneath her chin. 'Master de Courtesmain must have offended you badly to merit such a punishment. May I ask what he said?'

James Buckler answered. 'He called us sinners, milady—accused us of bringing the pestilence to Develish.'

Lady Anne's eyes creased with amusement. 'Are your shoulders not broad enough to take the imaginings of a frightened man, James? I stand accused of bringing the pestilence to all of Dorseteshire, but I wouldn't send Master de Courtesmain to his death for it. He'd collapse through fear as soon as we forced him onto the raft.'

John Trueblood gave an involuntary laugh. 'He's a poor creature, milady. My wife says he mistook sunburn for the pestilence and babbles constantly about miracles since your salve calmed the throbbing.'

'Maybe so, but I think we owe him charity before punishment.' She turned her attention to Alleyn, whose grim expression spoke of other grudges. 'You have more to talk about than Master de Courtesmain.'

'I do, milady. Thaddeus Thurkell will have told you about our argument this morning. I wish to put my side.'

She eyed him thoughtfully for a moment. 'Can I persuade you against such a course by saying that Thaddeus has made no mention of you, Alleyn?'

'No, milady. If he's held his tongue, it'll be through shame, and you should know the reason.'

John Trueblood placed a hand on his arm. 'Think twice before you speak, my friend. I warned you outside. Milady has no more desire to hear your imaginings than Master de Courtesmain's.'

Alleyn pushed him away. 'The truth should be heard. Thaddeus likes the position of steward too well to let it go to my brother, milady. He looks for Gyles to die.'

Lady Anne's surprise was genuine, not least because she had no plans to make Gyles steward. 'Is Thaddeus expecting to lose his place?'

'Everyone expects it, milady. Gyles is the most admired man in Develish.'

She nodded. 'Continue.'

The list of Thaddeus's faults was long, ranging from his bastard birth to his lack of respect for Alleyn that dawn. 'He mocked me when I took him to task for his coldness, milady. My brother needs comfort but Thaddeus denies it. He fails even to tell him how sorely his family misses him.'

Lady Anne lowered her gaze to the ledger so that he wouldn't see what was in her eyes. 'At least you don't accuse Thaddeus of wanting to kill your brother,' she said lightly. 'From the sombreness of your expression, I expected stories of murder.'

'His heart is hard enough.'

She ran her finger down what Thaddeus had written that morning. 'Are you proficient enough in letters to read these words, Alleyn?'

'I doubt it, milady. Gyles's daughter, Isabella, was a better teacher to him than mine to me.'

'It's a difficult skill to master unless you're young. Gyles can make out words when they're written but he finds it near impossible to inscribe them.' She raised her head to look at Adam Catchpole. 'Do you read well? James? John?'

All three shook their heads.

'Then I will read aloud. The text is Thaddeus's. *Now that his companions are gone, Gyles has no reason to stay in the village. I have urged him to avoid further contact with travellers by sleeping in the forest land to the west. He has agreed to make himself visible to us at noon each day. His family will worry less if they see that he continues well.*' She paused. 'Is that the coldness you refer to, Alleyn?'

'What else has he written, milady?'

'Nothing you will like.'

'Then it's about me.'

Lady Anne shook her head. 'Your name does not appear. He records the symptoms of the sickness. *This Black Death begins with a sore head and fever. Within three days the sufferer is too weak to stand, walk or ride a horse. The boils that grow on the neck, beneath the arms and in the groin cause unbearable agony.*

So large were Captain de Boulet's—the size of apples—that some burst, causing a terrible stench as pus and putrid blood leaked out. Smaller, suppurating boils had erupted on his chest and arms, but there were too many to count. The flesh of his hand was black to his wrist.' She raised her head. 'There is more if you wish to hear it. He talks of Captain de Boulet's courage and Gyles's compassion, and writes of how he walked with your brother to the grave and gave him company for the rest of the night.'

James Buckler spoke when Alleyn didn't. 'Do all die in the same way, milady?'

'I fear so. There are many pages about what Gyles witnessed in Bradmayne and the journey home. If Gyles had a facility with the quill, Thaddeus would have given him vellum and ink so that he could write the account himself, for he believes as I do that a record of what is happening here should survive even if all in Develish die.' She paused. 'It will be as if we never existed if our history cannot be read.'

When her remarks were greeted with an uneasy silence, she began to sort through a pile of vellum.

'Should we leave, milady?' John Trueblood asked.

'Not yet, John. I'm searching for a writ that Thaddeus prepared . . . and, since it concerns my leading serfs, you should read it first. It troubles me greatly that Alleyn saw reason to criticise Thaddeus when no one—not even Gyles—is able to perform the role of steward so well.'

The men fidgeted awkwardly, fearing public humiliation. Alleyn was particularly discomfited, sensing he'd lost the sympathy of his friends as well as Milady's. John had been right. He should have held his tongue. Far from bringing Thaddeus down, he had succeeded only in confirming his right to stand at Lady Anne's side.

Lady Anne found the page she'd been looking for. She handed it to John Trueblood. 'Will you see that this is displayed, John? Thaddeus has been urging me to post it these last few days, but I've spent more time settling trivial disputes than acting in ways that will profit Develish.'

John Trueblood pulled a wry smile, glancing towards Alleyn. 'There's so little free space, milady,' he said by way of excuse. 'It's all too easy for people to get on each other's nerves.'

She nodded, bending her head to her work in dismissal.

Lady Anne makes it known that henceforth John
Trueblood, Alleyn Startout, James Buckler and Adam
Catchpole will advise her on behalf of the serfs of Develish.
She looks to them for wisdom and counsel and urges
her people to do the same. She empowers them to settle
grievances with fairness and justice, holding due regard
for the good of all.

In nomine Patris et Filii et Spiritus Sancti
Thaddeus Thurkell, Steward

AUGUST, 1348

Eight

Develish, Dorseteshire

ELEANOR'S LIFE HAD BECOME A dreary round of watching events unfold from the windows in her mother's chamber. The dissatisfaction she had witnessed amongst the serfs when Lady Anne made Thaddeus Thurkell her steward seemed to have abated, although Eleanor didn't understand why. His behaviour hadn't changed except that he talked more frequently with four of the older men. Their names were unknown to her, but they seemed to enjoy the attention Thaddeus paid them.

Gyles Startout no longer inhabited the village but was camped in woodland beside Devil's Brook. When the sun was at its highest each day, he swam the river to stand on the pastureland and wave to his family, but the sight gave Eleanor no pleasure, for it galled her that a Develish serf still lived when her father was dead. Before Gyles left, she watched him paint red crosses on the doors of the serfs' cottages, but it wasn't until passing travellers swathed their mouths in cloth and hastened by, refusing even to draw water from the well, that she guessed the signs were a warning.

In the first days after Sir Richard's death, there had been many walkers and riders on the highway north—sometimes alone, sometimes in twos, sometimes in groups—but now the traffic had ceased altogether. Eleanor chose not to dwell too long on why that should be, preferring to blame her mother for Develish's sudden and frightening isolation. What would become of her if her life must be lived forever with only hated serfs for company?

In a world of separation, she chose separation for herself, turning her back whenever her mother or the servants entered the room, refusing to speak and taking her meals alone. She took to wearing the expensive gowns her father had bought for her in order to point out the difference between herself and the common people, and her only entertainment was to spend hours in front of a tiny looking glass, braiding her hair and pinching colour into her cheeks.

She convinced herself she was keeping the memory of her father alive, better still reminding everyone of the sacrilege committed against him, but the truth was she had no other way of attracting attention to herself. When Sir Richard was alive, he would summon her to his side when the mood took him, praising her beauty and making sure she was noticed; now that he was dead, she was of interest to no one. Even Hugh de Courtesmain had deserted her, defecting to Lady Anne with the zeal of a convert.

Through the whispered gossip of the servants who slept in her mother's chamber, Eleanor learnt that the steward had suffered sunstroke while digging the latrines. The soft little Frenchman had laboured too long in the noonday heat with his head and arms uncovered, and had mistaken the symptoms of sunstroke for the pestilence. The women found his ignorance amusing, even more amusing his refusal to accept that a cold, damp shirt and treatment with lavender oil and rosehip salve had cured him. It seemed he preferred the idea of a miracle, which he took as a sign from God that he should remain in Develish, and threw himself into the work of the demesne by way of penance and gratitude.

It wasn't in Eleanor's nature to seek Hugh out. She waited impatiently for him to come to her as a servant should. Had he not spent days assuring her of his loyalty and friendship? When he didn't come, and she watched from the window as he performed tasks for Lady Anne and Thaddeus Thurkell, her grudge against him festered and grew. Like Lady Anne, he had adopted homespun clothes, making himself indistinguishable from the base creatures who treated Sir Richard's home as their own.

Nothing pleased Eleanor, and she frightened herself with the powerful rages that came from nowhere and set her pounding her fists against the wall. On occasion, Father Anselm inserted his fat little body into the room—almost certainly on the instructions of her mother—but he was as ineffectual as Lady Anne in persuading Eleanor out of her self-imposed solitude. The priest bleated about the need to forgive her mother for refusing entry to Sir Richard; Lady Anne talked of responsibility.

After days of unbearable lecturing, Eleanor was provoked into a response. 'Why do you hate me so much?' she cried to the woman. 'If you had any love for me, you'd have ordered Master de Courtesmain to escort me north to my aunt.'

'I have a great deal of love for you, Eleanor, which is why I won't let you leave. How far do you think you'd travel before you decided the roads were too dangerous and the riding too arduous? There would be no coming back even if you changed your mind half a mile up the road. You would have to do as Gyles is doing—sleep in woodland for fourteen days.'

'I'm not so poor-spirited. I would ride as far as my uncle's estate.'

'Your aunt would not welcome you. She has five daughters of her own, and only the three elder are likely to find husbands.

There's no place in her household for an unmarried girl of fourteen without dowry or prospects.'

'You squander my dowry on these serfs,' said Eleanor, gesturing angrily towards the windows. 'I have more entitlement to Sir Richard's wealth than they.'

'Your father took what gold we had to Bradmayne and it has not come back. We must wait for Gyles to return if we're to find out where the wagon was abandoned and whether the chest is safe.' She knew these facts already, but she wasn't prepared to share them with Eleanor for fear of how the girl would react if she learnt that Thaddeus had crossed the moat to speak with Gyles.

'Then let me have the grain so that my uncle can sell it on my behalf.'

Lady Anne bit back the cutting retort that sprang to her lips. She was growing increasingly weary of Eleanor's selfishness, but wearier still of taking her to task for it. 'Which grain, daughter?'

'The sacks in the great hall.'

'Few belong to us. I ordered Sir Richard's bushels to be turned into bread and eaten first. Of those that are left, half are destined to pay taxes and the other half are the property of the serfs. If you go downstairs, you'll see sacks marked with the names of the families who've donated them. They've agreed to share everything they have for the good of all . . . yourself included.'

Eleanor frowned. 'You lie. My father owned everything in Develish.'

Lady Anne smiled slightly. 'Is that what he told you?' She watched the girl for a moment. 'How do you think serfs live if they can't grow food for themselves as well as for their lord, Eleanor?'

'I don't care enough to find out. You should have taught me better if you'd wanted me to understand.'

Lady Anne thought of how often she'd tried and how often her husband had wrecked the lessons by taking his daughter away to teach her how to throw dice and fill her head with promises of gowns. In time, she had come to realise that Eleanor's determined refusal to learn suited Develish better. Eleanor would have had even more cause to run to her father with tales of wrongdoing if she'd known the extent of her mother's involvement in the running of his demesne. It was one thing to cure illness and encourage the quiet spread of literacy, quite another to talk freely with bondsmen about the ways and means of buying themselves out of serfdom.

'It's of no matter,' she said, preparing to leave. 'Even if we had grain to spare—which we don't—there's no wagon to carry it and no one willing to accompany you. You imagine falsely if you think Master de Courtesmain would have put himself in peril on your behalf.'

The girl gave a bitter laugh. 'You've turned him against me, just like you turn everyone. He was ready to escort me after my father died.'

'I don't think so,' answered Lady Anne dryly. 'The road north is dangerous and he prizes his own life too much to take responsibility for yours.' She paused. 'He has no liking for Foxcote, Eleanor, and neither would you if I was careless enough to let you make the journey.'

'My aunt will make it pleasant for me.'

Lady Anne shook her head. 'Lady Beatrix is jealous of her own daughters' prettiness. What makes you think she would tolerate yours?'

Eleanor took the implied compliment as her due. 'I'm her brother's only child. She will love me as she loved Sir Richard.'

'Your father filled your head with some strange fantasies, Eleanor. Be grateful I've denied you the chance to test them. I wouldn't have wanted you to embarrass yourself.'

Eleanor brought her foot down in the familiar, petulant stamp. 'It's you who's the embarrassment. Look at you. You're no better than a peasant woman. You shame us both in the way you dress and behave.'

With a sigh, Lady Anne walked to the door. 'And you behave foolishly, daughter. Your gowns will be so soiled and tattered by the time we receive visitors again that you'll be taken for a strumpet in cast-off clothes rather than Sir Richard's daughter.'

Consumed with frustration, Eleanor listened to her mother's footsteps disappear down the stairs. She barely understood herself what she was trying to achieve with her sulks and silences, but Lady Anne's cool response to them pushed her beyond endurance. She wanted the woman to lose her temper, scream, shout and hit her daughter in anger so that everyone in Develish would know their mistress wasn't a saint. Instead, Lady Anne delivered her little barbs with reason and logic, and left Eleanor feeling cheated.

She stared down at the front of her gold-embroidered gown. Was her mother right? Was it silly to wear her finest clothes when there was no one to see them? With sudden decision, she flung off her trailing surcoat and reached for the laces at the back of her close-fitting bodice. Without help, she had only managed to secure the few that held the garment tight against her waist, and in her impatience to undo them she converted the bows to knots.

There was too much childish rage in Eleanor to react calmly to fastenings that wouldn't loosen. She tore at them, ripping them out of the gown and fulfilling her mother's prediction of tatters. With a howl of fury, she embarked on a feral rampage through Lady Anne's chamber, wrenching the tapestries from the wall, breaking the stools and tossing as much of the servants' bedding straw onto her mother's bed as she could. She was standing quivering in the middle of the room, still hot with her tantrum, when thirteen-year-old Isabella Startout appeared in the doorway with a bowl of spiced beans and cabbage for her young mistress's lunch.

The little maid had grown used to leaving the food on a stool behind Eleanor's frigid back, but this time she stood in the doorway, looking around the room in disbelief. 'Who did this?' she asked in amazement. 'Has someone attacked you, Lady Eleanor? Are you hurt?'

Eleanor didn't answer.

'I'll fetch Thaddeus,' the girl said. 'He'll know better than I what to do.'

Eleanor balled her hands into tight little fists. 'Don't you dare,' she snapped. 'Clean it up yourself and leave.'

Isabella's astonishment grew. She had been on the receiving end of her young mistress's bad temper many times—usually in the form of a slap—but she had never known Eleanor to wreak destruction on a room before. It looked more like the work of a madwoman than a lady of quality, and she wondered if Eleanor's wits had become unseated by the solitude she'd imposed on herself. The girl certainly looked mad enough, standing amidst the debris, her gold-embroidered gown on the floor, her shift half undone and stuck with pieces of straw, her face red and blotchy with rage.

Isabella stepped warily into the chamber, placing the bowl of spiced vegetables on the windowsill before moving well out of Eleanor's reach. 'I cannot do it on my own, milady. I'm not tall enough to rehang the tapestries and not skilled enough in carpentry to repair the stools.'

'Get one of the male servants to help you.'

Isabella may have been younger than Eleanor by a year, but she was a great deal older in wisdom. 'It would be better if you and I did it, Lady Eleanor. Another servant might talk, and gossip about you will spread through Develish.'

'I don't care.'

'But it would not be wise to let a man see you like this, milady. At least let me help you to dress yourself modestly.'

Eleanor's eyes narrowed. 'Who are you to preach at me?'

Isabella lowered her gaze, knowing better than to seem to challenge the girl. She felt more pity than fear, doubting Eleanor realised how absurd she looked with her breasts exposed and her feet buried amongst rush matting. The maid had little liking for her young mistress—few did—but pity made her wonder if it was grief that had caused Eleanor's tantrum. It must be hard to mourn a father alone, she thought, knowing your sorrow wasn't shared by anyone else.

Yet she had never believed that Eleanor's love for Sir Richard was as deep as she pretended, nor his for her. They had put on shows of affection in public but, to Isabella's eyes, the emotion was contrived, and she had wondered many times if Eleanor engaged in a false and shallow intimacy with her father to make her mother jealous. She had seen the sly glances Eleanor cast in Lady Anne's direction as she kissed her father's face, and witnessed her frustration afterwards when Milady showed only indifference.

Isabella had no idea what Eleanor had hoped to achieve through these strange little dramas but she'd always sensed that the girl's professed hatred for her mother was as false as the love she declared for her father. 'I don't mean to preach, milady,' she said now, 'only to remind you that Lady Anne cares for you and would not want scandalous whispers to circulate about her daughter.'

Eleanor stared at the girl for a moment, then ran for the bowl of food and threw it at her head. 'If you ever speak to me like that again, you filthy creature, I'll have you flogged. Now bring a male servant to clean up this mess.'

She was back at the window, sneering at Hugh de Courtesmain for aping the mannerisms of a serf, when the door opened behind her. But it wasn't until a man's voice gave an order that she knew Isabella had disobeyed her. She swung around, clutching her shift to her chest, eyes blazing, to find Thaddeus and half a dozen servants in the chamber. She stamped her feet and shouted at them to leave, but no one paid attention. They took their orders from Thaddeus and held her off with their brooms when she tried to kick them.

The only notice Thaddeus took of her was to throw a homespun kirtle in her direction and tell her to cover herself. Otherwise, he spoke to the servants and, inch by inch, Eleanor found herself backed into a corner as the straw was swept into bundles and the tapestries rehung. When the chamber was restored to neatness, Thaddeus handed the broken stools to one of the men for repair and told them all to leave, shutting the door behind them.

'Why didn't you order them to keep their beastly mouths shut?' Eleanor demanded. 'You don't want my mother shamed by me, do you?'

Dishevelled though she was, the heightened colour in her cheeks added to her beauty, and Thaddeus wasn't immune to it. If her nature had matched her looks, every red-blooded male in Develish would kneel before her. 'It's too late for that,' he said, crossing his arms. 'Everyone in the hall saw Isabella come down the stairs with blood on her face and food on her clothes.'

'She tripped and fell. If she says differently, she's lying.'

'She had no need to say anything. You're known for your bad temper as assuredly as the irritating midge is known for his bite.' He nodded to the kirtle which was lying on the floor where he'd thrown it. 'Cover yourself, milady, because you will no longer be sleeping in this chamber. When you are suitably clothed, I will escort you to your new apartment.'

For the first time in her life, Eleanor had nothing to say. In every fantasy she'd ever had about this man, it was she who gave the orders and he who obeyed. She cringed against the wall, quite unaware of how ridiculous she looked with her shift hanging off her shoulders and her mouth dropped open in surprise.

'The choice is yours,' Thaddeus said. 'I am just as happy to take you out half-dressed. I don't care to look at your bare breasts myself, but it may give pleasure to the young bucks clustered in the forecourt. I will count to ten. If you are still without an over garment, we will leave anyway. One . . . two . . . three . . .'

'You overstep yourself,' she said angrily.

'Four . . . five . . . six . . .'

'I *hate* you,' she stormed.

'Seven . . . eight . . .'

She scurried across the floor to pick up the kirtle and pull it over her head. 'Stay away from me,' she ordered, pointing a trembling finger at him. 'I'm not going with you.'

Thaddeus opened the door. 'But you are, Lady Eleanor, and you can either go of your own free will or under restraint. Your mother has done her best to reason with you, but your antics this noon have made you my responsibility.' He gestured towards the stairs. 'Will you walk or shall I summon John Trueblood and Adam Catchpole to carry you? Your exit will be witnessed by the children at their lessons in the hall, so I suggest you conduct yourself in as dignified a manner as possible.'

Eleanor looked for softness in his face but found none. 'How am I your responsibility?'

'I am steward and your selfishness is affecting the lives of others.'

She stamped her foot. 'And I am Lady Eleanor, daughter to Sir Richard of Develish. You have no right to take me anywhere. My mother won't allow it.'

'Sir Richard is dead and Lady Anne has more to worry about than a spoilt miss.' He gestured towards the stairs again. 'Will you walk or do you insist on making more of a fool of yourself than you have already?'

'When this is over, you'll still be a low-born bastard and I shall still be a high-born lady,' she said angrily. 'You might wish you'd remembered that when I lay charges against you with the High Sheriff.'

'If that day comes, milady, you must hope the sheriff believes you are who you say you are.'

She frowned. 'My mother will tell him. Everyone in Develish will tell him.'

'Only if they're alive and choose to do so.'

ତ୍ତ

Father Anselm protested strongly at having Eleanor wished on him by a stern-faced Thaddeus Thurkell, who tossed some straw onto the floor of the church and told the girl to make the best of it. He ordered her to keep her space clean, use the same latrines that the serfs used, and join the queues for meals if she wanted to be fed.

The priest, terrified at the prospect of Eleanor's temper, blocked Thaddeus's exit and pleaded with him to consider the impropriety of what he was doing. 'This is not a suitable place for Sir Richard's daughter, my son.'

'I can think of no better,' answered Thaddeus. 'What harm can come to her in a house of God?'

'She will be alone and unattended.'

'Except for you and the servants who come to clean your chamber, Father. I will instruct the women to honour any reasonable requests that Lady Eleanor makes of them. They will bring her fresh clothing each day and I trust you will permit her, out of modesty, to dress in your chamber.'

Father Anselm flicked an unfriendly glance in the girl's direction, clearly disinclined to permit any such thing. 'His Grace would never allow it—nor, I am sure, would Lady Anne. A priest's rooms are for male use only.'

Eleanor gave a derisive laugh at his reluctance. 'You needn't worry, Father. I have no more desire to be here than you to have me. I shall leave as soon as this—' she made a dismissive gesture with her hand—'*bastard* has gone.'

'You'll sleep in full view of everyone if you do,' said Thaddeus mildly. 'At least here, you can have some privacy.'

'I shall refuse to stay wherever you put me.'

'As you choose, milady.' He made a small bow. 'Just don't complain afterwards that you weren't warned.'

Eleanor stood at the door, watching Thaddeus walk away. A tiny doubt niggled in her brain. 'What did he mean?' she asked the priest. 'How can he make me sleep in full view of everyone if I don't want to?'

Father Anselm shook his head. 'You should return to the house and ask your mother these questions.'

'He's a slave. I shall have him hanged when this sickness has passed.'

'Indeed. Lady Anne was wrong to make him her steward. He is not a Godly person.' The priest placed a clumsy hand on her shoulder. 'The church is no place for you, Lady Eleanor. It's not fitting for a young girl to share sleeping arrangements with her confessor.'

She smacked his hand away. 'Stop telling me things I already know. If I'm forced to sleep here, then you must find room in one of the serfs' huts. You have more in common with them than I do.'

But Father Anselm wasn't so easily browbeaten. He enjoyed his priestly privileges too much to give them away on the command of a fatherless fourteen-year-old. An inebriate he might be, but he wasn't without cunning. He wouldn't have maintained his position in Develish all these years if he hadn't learnt to recognise where the authority lay. He'd always known that Lady Anne held the reins of power and that the only reason she tolerated him was because he took his duties lightly. A priest who inspired fear in her serfs would have been removed long since, with or without Sir Richard's permission.

Giving a small nod which Eleanor could take for agreement if she liked, and a muttered excuse about preparing himself for None—the mid-afternoon prayer hour—Father Anselm retreated to his tower and bolted the door quietly behind him. He was a past master at avoiding trouble by remaining closeted in his chambers with an empty flagon for a piss-pot and a cask of mead to keep him company. Like most men of God, he had more affection for his bees than he did for his congregation.

Disinclined to test Thaddeus's patience immediately, Eleanor marched about the church, cursing him under her breath, but it was a short time before her anger turned on her mother for allowing a bastard slave into a position of power in Develish. Her rage against them both, so all-consuming, frightened her, and with a sudden onset of panic, she dropped to her knees before the cross and begged God to protect her. Whatever happened to others on this demesne, let nothing untoward occur to the beloved daughter of His faithful servant, Sir Richard of Develish.

Shouts and calls from outside drew her back to the doorway. She stared past the graveyard and the serfs' huts to the court-yard in front of the house where a band of people were standing at the edge of the moat. She looked for Thaddeus's tall figure amongst them, and spotted him when he rose from his knees beside the tethered raft and spoke to an urchin beside him. The boy nodded vigorously before spinning around and running towards the church.

Eleanor's first thought was that he'd been sent to check on her, and she stepped into the shadows behind the door, ready to slap his dirty face if he came too close. But he wasn't interested in her. He darted through the entrance, took a quick look towards the altar and then ran to the door of the priest's chambers. 'Father! Father!' he shouted, hammering on the wood. 'An army approaches. You must ring the bell to alert Gyles. He is in the village, searching out supplies, and they'll be upon him before he knows they're there.'

'Who speaks?'

'Robert Startout, son of Alleyn and nephew to Gyles. Please hurry, Father. My uncle is free of the pestilence but these strangers may bring it to him.'

'Who gave the order?'

Eleanor was watching the boy's face, saw the calculation in his eyes as he assessed how honest to be. 'Lady Anne commands you,' he called. 'Pull twenty chimes. If we need more, I'll come back.'

He rested his ear against the door, listening to the sound of the priest muttering to himself as he shuffled across the floor. As the first peal rang out, the lad turned to leave and found Eleanor between him and the entrance. 'You lied,' she said coldly. 'It was Thaddeus Thurkell who gave the order.'

The boy ducked his head. 'I didn't know you were there, milady.'

From his height, she judged him to be ten or eleven. He should have been quaking in his shoes to be talking with the daughter of the manor, but he wasn't. 'You took my mother's name in vain. She'll punish you when I tell her.'

He kept his eyes on the floor, sidling around the far wall until he was opposite the entrance. 'I do it only to save my uncle, milady. Father Anselm wouldn't dare refuse an order from Lady Anne, however drunk he is.'

'You can't speak about a priest like that.'

'I just did.' He took to his heels so fast he was through the door before she knew it, and she heard his laughter between the chimes as he ran through the graveyard, quite careless that Eleanor knew his name and would repeat what he'd said to her mother and the priest.

The seeds of doubt that Thaddeus had sown in her mind took root and grew. *If that day comes, you must hope the sheriff believes you are who you say you are.* But would a boy like Robert Startout dare deny she was Lady Eleanor of Develish? Didn't he fear her anger? Didn't he fear her *mother's* anger? Eleanor watched the child skid to a halt in front of Thaddeus, saw Thaddeus stoop to ruffle his hair with appreciation as the peals continued to ring out. The boy's hero-worship of the man was obvious even to Eleanor's bitter eyes, as was the camaraderie amongst the band of men beside the moat.

They clapped each other on the back when the figure of Gyles Startout, a distant dot to Eleanor, emerged from John Trueblood's cottage and gave a wave to show he was alive. Thaddeus, so much taller than the rest, lifted his arms above his head and pointed both index fingers towards the north before turning his hands to beckon the man towards the moat. Why was he doing that? Eleanor wondered. Was he planning to let Gyles return to the compound?

She was too curious not to find out and, as the bell fell silent, she made her way towards the courtyard, standing half hidden in the lee of the archway to the vegetable garden. She could see Gyles Startout approaching from the village and, in the distance beyond, a covered wagon and ten riders moving slowly down the highway. The covering looked like leather and Eleanor thought she could make out a crest painted on the side. If so, it must contain someone of nobility.

'Are you well?' Thaddeus called as Gyles Startout came within earshot.

'I am. Thirteen days and still no signs of fever. What do you wish me to do with these visitors?'

'Nothing, my friend. There are too many of them and you've done more than enough for us already. Are you strong enough to swim the moat?'

'I am.'

'Then leave your clothes beside the way for anyone who wants them and cover yourself with this when you reach our side.' Thaddeus stripped off his tunic. 'It'll stop the ladies swooning when you rise from the water.'

Eleanor couldn't account for why there was so much joy over Gyles's return, nor the laughter that greeted Thaddeus's last remark. Where was the mystery in a fuzz of dark hair about the groin or a fold of pink flesh between the legs? And how bad could the sickness be if a serf was able to remain free of it? She jumped when Hugh de Courtesmain's voice spoke at her shoulder. 'You should show your pleasure, Lady Eleanor. Gyles is proof that it's possible to survive this pestilence. It means your mother was right to say that God does not intend us all to die.'

'Perhaps you speak too soon,' she said. 'Perhaps Gyles is not as well as he claims. Perhaps Thaddeus Thurkell was foolish to believe him. Will you praise my mother when you fall sick in earnest, Master de Courtesmain?'

'You shouldn't hate her so much, milady. It does you no good with the serfs.'

Eleanor stepped away from him angrily. 'Your views are nothing to me,' she snapped. 'You give your allegiance as it suits you, whispering words that people want to hear. I've watched you pretend to be one of them and I despise you for it.'

His eyes held hers for a moment. 'I do what I do to survive, milady. While we live inside this moat, the serfs hold the power. Four of them serve as counsellors to your mother, and this man who returns will lead her guard. The most powerful is Thurkell. You would be wise to do as I do and make allegiances where you can.'

'I will not.'

De Courtesmain shrugged. 'When the pestilence has passed, authority will go to whoever is strong enough and clever enough to seize it, milady, and a young girl without friends will be weak.' He shifted his attention to the wagon and riders who were emerging from the village. 'These men prove my point.'

Eleanor followed his gaze. 'How so?'

'With the driver there are eleven of them and they carry longbows. If they choose to pick us off one at a time in order to storm the moat, they are free to do so. We have no defence against arrows.'

'Why would they want to?'

Hugh wondered if she even knew that men were guarding their walls to prevent the sick and hungry entering. 'We have food, milady. If they come from a demesne where people are starving, they may try to steal ours. Ask yourself why they've brought a wagon if not to fill it.'

☙❧

The same thoughts were running through Lady Anne's and Thaddeus's minds. They had been confident about repelling unarmed peasants, but they hadn't bargained on trained soldiers with bows. Sir Richard had taken his experienced fighting men to Bradmayne as protection along the way, and their weaponry had gone with them. What remained in Develish—some short bows and a handful of rudimentary crossbows—were no match for the range and killing power of the longbow.

'You were right to call Gyles back,' said Lady Anne. 'They were never going to be frightened off by the crosses on the cottage doors.'

'Do you recognise the emblem on their tunics, milady?' Thaddeus asked.

Lady Anne shook her head. 'They must have come a distance. I know all the crests for twenty miles around.' She raised her hand to shield her eyes from the sun, studying the faces of the riders. They looked very determined, she thought, as if they knew that entry to Develish would be denied them. 'We cannot let them take our stores,' she said.

'Then we'll have to negotiate, milady. They'll discover very quickly that we have nothing to threaten them with from this side.'

She eyed him for a moment. 'Except more fear than they feel already,' she said slowly. 'Are you willing to put your soul in jeopardy again, Thaddeus?'

He answered with a laugh. 'If it keeps us alive. I can repent tomorrow as long as I don't die today with an arrow through my heart.'

Nine

THE BANK OF THE MOAT was almost deserted by the time the leading riders reached it. They had seen the crowd of people who had thronged the forecourt scatter as the convoy drew near, retreating into the house or into makeshift shelters on the demesne. Now only a small woman and a tall man remained to greet them. From their dress—humble, homespun cloth—the armed men took them for serfs and their captain addressed them as such.

'Where is your lord?' he demanded.

Lady Anne dropped a deep curtsey. 'He is dead, sir. His blood turned black and burst from huge boils on his neck two weeks ago. We have never seen the like. Milady followed him within days, and many more have died since.'

The captain turned with a startled look towards the house as a howl of grief cut through the air. The sound was taken up by the ululation of women's voices as they cried a lamentation for the dead. 'Who do they weep for?' he asked.

'A child,' said Lady Anne, wringing her hands in despair. 'We have so few left. We lose them in a day once the pestilence invades their little bodies.' She raised her kirtle hem to her eyes, wiping away tears. 'It is a plague of terrible ferocity, sir.'

'Where do you bury your dead?'

'There are too many for burial,' said Thaddeus, his voice breaking with distress. 'We dug a pit at the beginning but the stench of corruption became so terrible, we had to fill it in. Now we lower the bodies into the moat behind the church. The water covers them and disguises the smell.'

'The dead have poisoned our well,' said Lady Anne, dropping to her knees. 'The air, too.'

The captain raised his hand involuntarily to his mouth as Thaddeus dropped to one knee beside Lady Anne and held out cupped palms in a pleading gesture. 'We beg your assistance, sir. Those of us who are still alive are desperate. We need food and drink if we are to live another day.'

The captain nodded to the raft which Thaddeus had released to float idly in the middle of the moat. 'Why do you not retrieve this and use it to draw water from the village well and collect the harvest from your fields?'

'No one dares enter the moat,' said Lady Anne. 'Our priest, God rest his soul—' she crossed herself—'had the courage to try and became infected immediately. His death was terrible to behold. His eyes bled and his tongue swelled and burst in his mouth.'

The man nudged his charger away from the water's edge. 'Why is there no bridge?'

'Sir Richard ordered it destroyed to prevent the pestilence getting worse,' Thaddeus told him. 'But it was too late. Death was already inside and the corrupted bodies spread the infection. We are gravely in need of your help. If the sickness does not kill us, starvation will.'

The captain stared at them for a moment and then turned to ride back to the wagon. He leant across the animal's withers to listen to someone inside the wagon. 'My Lord of Bourne wants to know why there was such a crowd on the forecourt if so many have died already,' he called.

'Sir Richard took in serfs from the neighbouring demesnes,' Lady Anne called back. 'We numbered over four hundred two weeks ago but, so terrible is this pestilence, we are barely half that number and many are dying. The healthy stay in the open air as long as possible to avoid the stink of suppurating boils.'

'Why did they run inside as we approached?'

'Out of fear, sir. You carry bows. If you choose to kill us, you may.'

'Are you and this man not afraid?'

Lady Anne wrung her hands again, praying that the sheep in the graveyard wouldn't choose this moment to bleat or the cockerels in the vegetable garden to crow. 'We are more afraid of starvation,' she cried. 'By your charity, give us some grain or meat so that we might live another day.'

The captain listened again to the man inside the wagon. 'My Lord asks what good another day will do when God has already forsaken you.'

'Even one hour of life offers hope, sir,' Thaddeus called. 'Our dead perish without absolution or burial, and we are deeply fearful of what awaits us.'

A gnarled hand parted the leather covering that hung over the wagon, and the face of an elderly man appeared in the opening. He stared hard at the two people kneeling on the ground and then scanned the façade of the manor house. They could still hear the keening lamentations of the women, but the voices had quietened, as if sorrow were exhausting. 'God has judged this county harshly,' he said. 'Death consumes the land from Melcombe in the south to Shafbury in the north, leaving villages empty of people for miles around. What evil has Dorseteshire done that this plague has been visited upon you?'

'We know not, sire,' said Lady Anne, clasping her hands together and holding them out in entreaty. 'Sir Richard was a good man, yet he was taken first.' She studied Lord Bourne through half-closed lids, and wondered if she'd ever seen such coldness in a face. His lips were as thin as threads and his eyes as pitiless and unforgiving as glass.

'Then you must pray to the Lord for guidance on your sins and make what repentance you can before He judges you,' he answered. 'You will receive no assistance from me. If God saw fit to punish you, then so be it. All I can do is protect others from the taint of your wickedness.' He beckoned to the captain. 'Use fire arrows to burn the raft, and set torches to the village and the crops as we leave. It will be a warning to pilgrims that these people have been condemned.'

He remained to watch as the soldiers wrapped tallow-soaked hemp around their arrow heads and set them alight with flint on char cloth. With ten flaming arrows thudding into the surface timbers of the raft, dry from the summer heat, the vessel burnt rather better than Thaddeus thought it would. Certainly My Lord of Bourne found the results pleasing. His thin lips parted in an ugly smile before, with a last look at the two people kneeling on the ground, he ordered his driver to turn the wagon.

The torching of the village lasted well into the afternoon but Bourne's enthusiasm for burning what was left of the crops seemed to desert him. Instead of moving on to the land after the thatch on the last cottage blazed into life, the soldiers mounted their horses and followed the wagon north along the highway. Most of Develish had crowded onto the forecourt to witness the destruction of their homes, and Gyles Startout suggested to Thaddeus that enough men with enough buckets might be able to salvage something from the ruins.

The black-haired giant shook his head. 'We need it to keep burning in case My Lord decides to camp up for the night,' he said. 'The glow will be visible for miles. Better he thinks we're beaten than that we sold him a bagful of lies.'

'He'll be in Hell quicker than any of us,' said Gyles. 'What manner of man takes it upon himself to deliver God's judgement on a whole community?'

'One who believes himself blessed with righteousness,' Thaddeus answered.

Gyles watched sparks shoot towards the sky from the thatch on John Trueblood's cottage. 'At least fire is a cleanser,' he observed. 'If infection lingers in the walls, it will be gone by the morning.'

๛

Eleanor had run with everyone else into the house when Thaddeus gave the order to vacate the forecourt, slipping up to her mother's chamber and closing the door behind her. From the window, she had a good view of the inside of the wagon and saw more of the occupant than anyone else. Despite the warmth of the day, he was dressed in a rich, red robe with ermine trimmings, and his fingers were encrusted with rings. A small dog nestled on his lap and beside him on the seat was an iron-bound chest which almost certainly contained gold.

Her reaction to My Lord of Bourne was quite different from her mother's. She saw him as an ally, God's answer to her prayer for protection, a man who would take pity on her and remove her from Develish if she could only inform him that serfs had taken control of her father's demesne. In a frenzy of activity, she drew her gowns from the coffer by the wall, trying to decide which would impress an elderly lord while, through the casement, she listened in disbelief as Lady Anne told lie after lie, cowering on her knees and pretending to be no better than Thaddeus Thurkell.

She was pulling on a blue silk surcoat, shot with silver, when she heard My Lord instruct his men to burn the raft. Hastily fastening the hooks at the front, she ran to the door and trod lightly down the stairs to the great hall. Every back in the room was turned towards her, every eye trained on the windows. Even the lament that the women had been keening died to nothing as the soldiers coated their arrows with tallow and struck their flints. Unnoticed—or so she thought—she tiptoed along the floor.

'Where are you going in all your finery?' asked a round-faced woman, trapping the girl's train under her rough wooden clog. Wife to John Trueblood, she knew Eleanor well, having been a house servant since the time of the girl's birth. 'Do you think to denounce your mother as a liar to that vile old creature out there?'

Eleanor turned to look at her, lashing out her hand for a slap. 'How dare you question me?'

But Clara Trueblood caught the girl's wrist and twisted it painfully. 'I'd slap you back if you weren't your mother's daughter. She deserved better than you, Miss Eleanor.'

The girl wrenched at her train. 'It's *Lady* Eleanor.'

'In your own mind, perhaps, but not in anyone else's. Do you think a noble will treat you as a lady if you throw yourself on his mercy? You'll be lucky to travel a mile before he forces himself on you as reward for his kindness.'

'That's how slaves behave,' Eleanor hissed, 'not men of quality.'

Clara's eyes lit with humour. 'It's a pity you didn't tell your father that. He might have restrained his appetites if he'd known you disapproved.' She blocked Eleanor's other hand with her forearm. 'I'm almost tempted to let you go. It might do you some good to learn the facts of life the hard way.'

'Then why don't you?' the girl demanded with glittering eyes. 'No one wants me here.' She tried to rip the hooks on the bodice of her surcoat. 'I'll go in my shift if I have to.'

'And have My Lord take you for an idiot peasant girl? He'll think you mad with the pestilence if you run out half naked and try to swim the moat to reach him . . . though I doubt you have the ability. He'll take you for a witch if you sink.'

The sound of the burning arrows thumping into the raft reached them through the open front door, followed by a muted gasp from the throng of people around the windows as the timbers caught alight and flames leapt into the air. With a violent shove, Eleanor pushed Clara backwards and ran towards the entrance, thrusting the door wide. But she was too late to attract Bourne's attention. The wagon was already leaving, the aperture in its side closed.

She would have cried out to him if her mother hadn't chosen that moment to rise from her knees and look towards the house. Lady Anne said something to Thaddeus and he, too, rose and turned. They were so close to each other, like people who shared a deep intimacy, that Eleanor was taken aback. She recognised, as Hugh de Courtesmain had done, that neither looked their age. She could see that, without her austere wimple, and with her soft brown hair falling loosely about her face, her mother was beautiful; and with a shock so powerful that it took her breath away, she knew the intimacy was real.

ᘯᘓ

Night was falling by the time Lady Anne sought out her daughter. The blaze from the village lit the darkening sky with orange light, and Eleanor was watching it from the tiny porch in front of the church door. She was alone. The priest had been too drunk or too stubborn to respond to her cries and entreaties to come out of his chamber and console her.

'Where is Father Anselm?' Lady Anne asked.

Eleanor didn't answer, and her mother walked into the church to find it shrouded in gloom without even the altar candles lit. A dull glow showed beneath the door to the tower, and she guessed the old man had locked himself in to avoid the dramas outside. It was a good thing he had. Another priest might have advanced across the forecourt towards the soldiers, bearing the altar cross and giving lie to her claim that he was dead.

She walked back to her daughter. 'Clara tells me you wanted to leave with My Lord of Bourne,' she said. 'But do you think he would have taken you, Eleanor? Have you not asked yourself where his own family was and why he was travelling with only fighting men for company?'

The girl remained obstinately silent. She looked paler than usual, as if the emotions of the day were finally taking their toll.

'He saves himself, not others,' Lady Anne went on gently. 'Sir Richard would have done the same.'

Eleanor was stung into defending her father. 'He would have taken *me*.'

'There wouldn't have been room after he'd packed the wagon with food and water for the journey. More likely, he would have promised to send the wagon back for you when he reached his destination . . . and you would have waited in vain for a ride that never came.'

Eleanor remembered the chests and boxes in My Lord of Bourne's wagon. 'You wouldn't have let me go anyway.'

'No,' Lady Anne agreed. 'I would never have entrusted you to your father's care. Your presence would have become a burden to him within a mile of this house if you'd dared to complain about the hardness of the seat or the slowness of the journey.'

'I wouldn't have complained.'

Her mother's eyes filled with teasing laughter. 'You complain about everything, daughter,' she said, touching a finger to the girl's cheek. 'Not a day passes when you don't have some new grudge to hold.'

Eleanor smacked the finger away. 'I never complained to Sir Richard.'

Lady Anne tucked her hands into her kirtle. She'd been naive to think Eleanor would ever accept she had come out of affection. 'You didn't need to. He purchased your good humour with baubles and gowns and gave you an hour of his time when it amused him. Would you have loved him so much if he'd given you no presents at all?'

There was a roar of sound as the walls of John Trueblood's cottage collapsed in a shower of sparks, and both women turned towards the village. Every cottage had now been reduced to glowing embers, and the light dimmed perceptibly as the flames died away. What had once been a thriving community existed no more.

'Evil man,' Lady Anne murmured. 'He did this to demonstrate his puny authority.' With a sigh, she re-entered the church. 'Shall we light some candles? Shall I help prepare your bed?'

The girl gave an indifferent shrug. 'There's no point. I shan't be sleeping here.'

'Where then?'

'In your chamber.'

But Lady Anne shook her head. 'You will draw unwelcome attention to yourself if you try to return to the house tonight, Eleanor. You can hammer on the door as loudly as you like, but it won't be opened to you. Your only choice will be to sleep in the open air if you refuse to make your bed here.'

The girl's eyes narrowed as her resentment of earlier rose to the surface again. 'On whose orders?' she spat. 'Thaddeus Thurkell's? Do you want me out of your chamber so that he can share your bed? Does he plan to move in for good now that Sir Richard is dead?'

Lady Anne ignored her. 'I doubt Father Anselm will trouble you, but if you hear the bolt on his door being drawn, run to the first hut on the path. John Trueblood will protect you.'

The girl clenched her fists in frustration. 'I will not ask help from serfs. They may have power over you, but they have none over me. I will always be above them.'

Briefly, Lady Anne closed her eyes. 'By what measure, Eleanor? You have none of their skills—you lack even the skill to be pleasant—yet you insist on thinking yourself superior. How so?'

'By virtue of my birth,' the girl snapped. 'I don't forget who I am, even if you do.'

'You might be happier if you did,' said Lady Anne, walking towards the door. 'You are one and they are two hundred, and your birth will count for nothing if they decide to range themselves against you. You can stamp your foot and claim to be Sir Richard's daughter as often as you like, but you will gain no power by it, only ridicule.'

'I am *your* daughter, too.'

Lady Anne paused. 'Are you sure? You change your mind so frequently it's hard to keep up. This morning I was a peasant woman, two minutes ago I was Thaddeus Thurkell's whore, and now I'm your mother. Should I be flattered by this sudden willingness to acknowledge me?'

'You don't have to mock,' the girl said tearfully.

'But you're too old to be hiding behind my skirts, Eleanor. If you want to be respected, you must learn to stand on your own two feet. You can't keep living in idleness just because an accident of birth gave you a title.'

The girl used her toe to draw semicircles on the floor. 'How can my birth have been an accident? God *intended* me to be Lady Eleanor of Develish.'

Lady Anne glanced towards the orange glow of the village. 'But for how long?' she murmured. 'Not a person here is known outside these boundaries. Our names and faces will vanish from history if we die of the pestilence. Only the foundations of the houses will remain to show that we ever existed.'

ᏋᎯᏬ

Eleanor lacked the intelligence to see beneath the surface of her mother's words. She took them literally and lay awake on the rush matting, arguing against them in her mind. As ever, she interpreted what she'd heard in terms of herself.

It was absurd to say that Lady Eleanor of Develish was unknown beyond these boundaries. Her father had introduced her to many people. His friends who had visited the demesne . . . My Lord of Blandeforde . . . His Grace the bishop. Sir Richard's sister in Foxcote knew of her, as did the household at Bradmayne and perhaps others beyond, if Peter's father had spread news of her betrothal to his son far and wide.

But would any of them know her if she stood before them?

Hard as she tried to fight the doubts, they grew as the night wore on and sleep eluded her. She came to recognise that, though her aunt knew her name, Lady Beatrix would not know her face. Eleanor had never been to Foxcote, and no one from Foxcote had ever visited Develish. She remembered the cursory attention her father's friends had paid her before joining him at the dicing table or urging him to set up a cock fight on the forecourt; remembered, too, that none had offered their sons in exchange for her paltry dowry. She recalled her one and only meeting with His Grace, when the bishop had ignored her to speak to her mother; and her one and only meeting with My Lord of Blandeforde, when he ran bored eyes over her extravagant gown and curtly refused to grant Sir Richard extra lands because 'a daughter' was of no account.

By the time dawn broke on the eastern side of the valley, fingering light through the altar window, Eleanor knew that her mother and Thaddeus Thurkell were right. The only people who could swear on oath that she was who she said she was were the people of Develish.

She recalled Hugh de Courtesmain's words.

You would be wise to make allegiances where you can . . .

The thirteenth day of August, 1348

*T*he demesne seems more settled since My Lord of Bourne's visit. Perhaps our people needed evidence of the dangers that lie outside our boundaries to understand why I have chosen to confine them. To hear My Lord say that Death consumes the land from south to north of Dorseteshire made us all afraid, as did his burning of our village. Was he acting on the orders of the High Sheriff? Or, worse, the King? Do men of power plan to destroy every community that has been visited by the sickness?

Gyles's return has raised all our spirits because it seems this dreadful pestilence can be avoided. He does his best to help us discover how and why he managed to stay healthy, but we're no nearer finding an answer. Thaddeus argues that it cannot be in the touch or on the breath of sufferers, for Gyles would surely have succumbed; but I wonder still if Gyles has something within him that resists the infection. I've seen so many times that some fall to the pox while others do not.

Gyles talks much about the filth of Bradmayne. He describes open sewers, men defecating outside their dwellings and rodent infestation in the grain stores. He urges me to believe *that all or any of these were the cause of the sickness, but I find it hard to agree with him. Develish was as filthy when I came here but no one died of boils and blackened blood.*

Nevertheless, Gyles's advice to maintain our cleanliness is good. With so many packed into so small a space, it's more important than ever to keep the lice and the vermin at bay. We can afford the flux as little as we can afford the pestilence.

In nomine Patris et Filii et Spiritus Sancti
Anne of Develish

Ten

THADDEUS SAW A CHANGE IN Eleanor over the next two weeks, but he didn't believe it was genuine. Her nature was too like her father's to capitulate so easily. Dressing in homespun, taking her place demurely in the meal queues and even offering to stir cauldrons of potage, frumenty and broth might persuade others she'd mended her ways, but not Thaddeus. After three days of sleeping in the church, he'd allowed her back into her mother's chamber on condition she kept a rein on her temper. She gave the promise readily, even apologised for her previous behaviour, but the look in her eyes told a different story. Any pledge Eleanor made would not be honoured, he thought.

On one occasion, she came to the steward's office when he was alone, closing the door behind her and walking around the desk to press her warm, young body against his. She made a pretence of reading what he was writing in the ledger, but since her knowledge of letters was as poor as her father's he guessed her reason was to draw attention to herself. He gave her no satisfaction, continuing with his work as if her presence meant nothing to him.

'Do you not see me?' she asked, leaning in such a way that her right breast brushed his arm. 'Am I not beautiful, Thaddeus?'

'You are what you are, Lady Eleanor. Most would say the wolf's bane flower was beautiful until the root poisoned them.'

Her voice filled with tears. 'Why are you so cruel to me? I do all that you demand of me, do I not?'

He stood up and moved away from her. There was no dampness in her eyes, only calculation. 'Wearing homespun and eating with the serfs doesn't mean you should forget yourself, milady. As you pointed out so well in your mother's chamber, I am a base-born bastard and you are Sir Richard's daughter. I suggest you do nothing to bring shame on your father's name.'

The promised curb on her temper was as false as the tears in her voice. In fury, she seized the inkwell and poured the black liquid over the ledger. 'I would never demean myself with you,' she cried.

'Then we're in agreement, milady.' He opened the door. 'I'm sure you can find more congenial company elsewhere.'

She flounced past him with a look of pure hatred. 'I'll make you pay for your arrogance,' she hissed.

Thaddeus didn't doubt she meant her words but he had more to worry about than Eleanor. The boredom of life inside the enclosure was taking its toll on everyone, particularly the men. Once the latrines were dug and the walls raised and fortified, there was little for them to do except take their turns on the guard steps at night; and with no exercise and too much time to sit and think, they were beginning to question what the future held for them.

The idea that Develish was unique in surviving the pestilence gathered momentum—as did a dread that only Dorseteshire had been afflicted by it. Would anyone from outside the county be brave enough to enter to see if people still lived? Who would send messengers to tell them when the pestilence was over? Was their safety guaranteed only so long as they remained inside the moat? How would they live when their food ran out?

Thaddeus knew these fears and uncertainties would quickly have turned to superstitious panic if Gyles Startout hadn't survived. Father Anselm hadn't preached Hellfire and damnation all these years for serfs to reject easily the idea of divine vengeance. Will Thurkell, for one, was fond of warning that God intended to punish Develish anyway, if not through slow starvation then by encouraging neighbour to turn on neighbour. Yet Gyles stood as proof that a Dorseteshire man could come into contact with the Black Death and live to tell the tale; and since he refused to believe he had a greater right to God's mercy than others in Sir Richard's retinue—and said so bluntly to anyone who asked— most adopted his level-headed approach and refused to listen to Will's scaremongering.

Thaddeus knew his stepfather well enough to know that Will's only interest was in stirring up trouble for Eva's bastard. If he could undermine Thaddeus's position as steward, he would, for it galled Will as much as it galled Eva to discover how many secrets had been kept from him. He wore his resentment openly, but never with such malice as when Thaddeus summoned Lady Anne's counsellors to speak with her in private.

'Why do you ignore *me*, boy?' he demanded on one such occasion, planting himself squarely before the assembled group. 'Am I not good enough for your precious mistress?'

Thaddeus gestured towards the door of the house. 'You're as free as anyone to talk with Lady Anne,' he said. 'Go ahead of us and put your grievances to her. We'll wait here until you're done.'

'I'm talking to *you*, boy. Answer the questions I put to you.'

Gyles Startout frowned. 'You overstep your mark, Will,' he said severely. 'If you cannot show respect, at least behave with courtesy. It was Lady Anne who chose her council, not Thaddeus.'

But Will was in no mood to back down. 'Do you take me for a fool? She keeps you at her side because you tell her what she wants to hear . . . never mind there's many of us who question the wisdom of what she's doing.'

John Trueblood eyed him with amusement. 'No one's keeping you here, Will. We'll help you leave if you think you'll be better off outside the moat. God forbid you should have to tolerate a regime you despise, never mind you gobble the food you're given and shirk every task you're asked to perform.'

Adam Catchpole's face split in a wide grin. 'We'll do better. We'll send the other malcontents after you, if you give us their names. I can think of at least one—your ill-tempered wife. She'll welcome your leadership if you say you'll take her somewhere better.'

Thaddeus stepped in before the baiting grew worse. It might entertain him to watch his stepfather being teased, but he knew Will would take out his frustrations on Eva afterwards.

'If there's something you wish us to say to Lady Anne on your behalf, tell us what it is and we will repeat it. Today she seeks advice on what to do when the stores run low. Our plan is to find men brave enough to leave the demesne in search of supplies.' He gestured around the group. 'These five have put their names forward, knowing the risks and knowing they may not come back. Gyles has offered to go first because he's survived the pestilence once and hopes to do so again. May we ask you to go second if he doesn't return?'

Will's expression was comical. 'I've never left the demesne,' he blustered. 'I wouldn't know where to go.'

'And you think the rest of us do? If My Lord of Bourne is to be believed, every village for miles around is dead or dying of the pestilence. None of us knows which place is safe—not even Gyles—so whoever makes the journey will be riding into peril.'

Will seized on the one fact he could answer. 'I can't ride. You know this. My back is too weak even to mount a horse.'

Thaddeus made a small, ironic bow. 'Indeed. It's well known you're too crippled to do anything arduous.'

James Buckler watched his cousin slink away. 'He'll put a knife between your ribs if you're not careful,' he warned Thaddeus in an undertone. 'Whatever jealousy he felt for you before is nothing compared to what he feels now. Your destiny was to be a slave, my young friend, not a steward.'

John Trueblood nodded. 'He has a powerful envy of you, Thaddeus, and your mother a powerful dislike of Lady Anne. They'll incite rebellion if they can.'

ତ୨୦

As August lengthened, Thaddeus wondered if John Trueblood's words were coming to pass. The weather continued to be unseasonably warm and fights erupted over the smallest slight. The young bucks were the worst—boys aged between fourteen and fifteen who fell out with increasing regularity. Tired of pulling them apart, Thaddeus joined Gyles Startout on the western wall, and asked his advice on how to keep them occupied.

Despite the difference in their ages, the two had become close friends since Thaddeus's secret trips across the moat. Gyles had been unstinting in his support of the young steward, brooking no argument from anyone about Lady Anne's right to appoint Thaddeus to act as her right hand. Since Thaddeus could read and write as well as Hugh de Courtesmain, he said it made good sense to give him the Frenchman's job.

He had warned Thaddeus frequently against Hugh, and did so again now. 'You'd do better to keep the Norman occupied,' he advised. 'De Courtesmain's adept at sewing discord between the families. Isabella said she heard him telling young Catchpole that his father stood in lower regard with Lady Anne than young Buckler's father, and you don't need more than that to set two lads at each other's throats.'

'Your twins are as bad,' Thaddeus answered. 'They fight each other as often as they fight the others. We need to find a way to exhaust their energy if it's not to get worse. At the moment, every little sneer is taken as an insult, whether fed by de Courtesmain or not.'

The older man pondered for a moment. 'I could put them through sword training . . . though it might make the problem worse. They're likely to kill each other if they have a weapon in their hands.'

'They'll kill each other anyway if we can't wear them out,' said Thaddeus dryly. 'Your Olyver and the Trueblood boy were going at it hammer and tongs all morning.'

Gyles scanned the western horizon where the footpath disappeared into dense woodland. 'It'll be a useful skill for others to learn,' he said. 'When I go looking for new supplies of food, I'd rather have men beside me who can fight than men who can't.'

Thaddeus nodded. 'Do we have swords?' he asked.

'Not here. I left the weapons we brought back with the saddles and bridles near my camp in the woodland—but they'd be no good for training anyway. We need carpenters to make wooden ones. When the time comes for real swords, we'll forge them from iron.'

'What iron?'

'Hinges and barrel hoops. You'll make enemies of the women if you steal their cauldrons.'

Gyles's lessons became so popular that the adult men joined in as well. They stood in lines across the orchard, thrusting and parrying with exuberance, and it wasn't long before Thaddeus realised the exercise attracted them as much as the swordplay. The life of a serf was intensely physical, sixteen hours of hard labour on the land in the summer with the odd break for food, followed by eight hours of sleep. They weren't used to being inactive.

He ran the idea of exercise for exercise's sake past Lady Anne. 'They haven't fallen out so much since Gyles started training them, milady, but he can't tutor them all at the same time. If we divided them into groups and kept rotating them, they wouldn't get so bored.'

'What would they be doing?'

Thaddeus's dark face twisted in a wry smile. 'That's what I'm trying to work out, milady. The best I've come up with so far is a daily race: running from one side of the compound to the other.'

She steepled her hands in front of her face, her eyes far away in thought. 'I remember Marco Polo writing about the tedium of long sea voyages,' she murmured. 'I believe the sailors sang and danced to pass the time.' She paused, searching her memory for further information.

Thaddeus let the silence drift, knowing she would continue and that what she said would be interesting. He had listened to so many of her stories about Marco Polo, and they had fired his imagination in the same way they had fired hers.

'Mother Maria talked of an arena in Rome where they fed Christians to lions and compelled slaves to fight to the death for the amusement of the people. I imagine that was to keep tedium at bay also.' She smiled at Thaddeus's expression. 'It wasn't all about death and punishment. They had chariot races and foot races and wrestling, and competitions to see how far each man could jump or throw a spear. They called them "games", and whoever won became the champion and had to defend his crown against new challengers. The crown was made of laurel leaves.'

'And men practised for this?'

Lady Anne nodded. 'They must have done. It was a great honour to be a champion.'

'Will our people think a crown of laurel leaves worth striving for?'

'Why would they not if we say the games will happen on St Edward the Confessor's Day and the champions will be carried shoulder high before the dancing begins? If we can't promise a little fun, they may begin to question why it's necessary to keep living in this confined space.'

Thaddeus was relieved at how eagerly the idea of competition was taken up. With the help of James Buckler, he devised and set up arenas for six different games: a marked path for a foot race of ten circuits around the perimeter of the forecourt; a target for archery in the orchard; a roped-in track of twenty yards, with a line in the grass marking the take-off point for the longest jump; another roped-in track to test how far a man could throw a wooden spear; an enclosed space in the middle of the forecourt for wrestling matches; and another space, with boulders graded by weight, to test a man's strength in lifting.

Some of the apple trees in the orchard had to be sacrificed, and a few of the temporary dwellings taken down and rebuilt else-where, but the idea of games seemed to appeal to everyone. Sword and archery practice continued in the mornings and athletic training occupied the afternoons. The women took their breaks from preparing food to watch their husbands, sons and brothers test themselves against each other, calling encouragement and laughing out loud when they ended up on their backs. And when it became obvious that the younger boys couldn't compete with the adult men in lifting or wrestling, and the men couldn't keep up with the youngsters on the running track, James Buckler proposed the idea of two champions—a senior and a junior.

'Is it true that you've had to up the men's rations?' he asked Thaddeus one evening as they stood beside the wrestling ring, watching Alleyn Startout grapple with his brother.

Thaddeus nodded. 'We can either sit in idleness all day, eating less but fighting amongst ourselves, or occupy our minds and bodies and eat more.'

'What difference will it make to how long the stores can last?'

'Two weeks . . . maybe three. We'll be looking at empty plates by Christmas is my guess.'

'Has Milady advanced Gyles's departure date?'

'Not yet. She clings to the hope that messengers will come.'

Buckler studied Thaddeus's face, still undecided whether Eva's black-haired bastard was worthy of the respect Gyles gave him. James had never condoned his cousin's brutality towards the boy, oft times stepping in to save Thaddeus from a beating so severe he might have died, but he'd always understood Will's resentment. Who wouldn't be angry to have another man's child foisted on him, particularly one as different as Thaddeus? The only mystery was who the sire was.

To look at Eva now, it was hard to remember how much jealousy she'd inspired when she first came to Develish. She'd been too aware of herself, too willing to excite attention, too ready to have men look at her. Even James had watched her covetously, wondering why God had smiled so kindly on his lazy, good-for-nothing cousin. The betrothal had been arranged through Sir Richard's steward with Will's eager agreement—his temper was too uncertain to attract a Develish maid—and he counted himself a fortunate man when his handsome bride arrived from a demesne near Melcombe. All might have been well if she hadn't played the innocent, assuring Will with demurely lowered lashes that she was as clean and pure as snow.

It was being taken for a gullible fool that had angered Will. He had strutted so proudly for seven months, confident that Eva's growing belly contained his son, and he had no answer to the knowing grins of the women and the sympathetic looks of the men when Thaddeus was born eight weeks early. Her cries of rape afterwards were always going to fall on deaf ears, since it was clear to everyone she had hoped to pass the child off as Will's. Most believed she had lain with several men and didn't know herself who the father was.

Whoever he was, he had left his imprint strongly on this unknown son. It was hard to see anything of Eva in the olive skin, dark eyes and black hair. But was he to be trusted when his father was so clearly not from Dorseteshire—or even from England?

'Milady could be right,' James said. 'Does it never occur to you that the pestilence has passed, and we're worrying about whether it's safe to return to our fields while the rest of the country is celebrating?'

In different ways, the same question was put to Thaddeus every day. How would Develish know when the sickness was over? Who would tell them when it was safe to return to the village and rebuild their houses? When would life return to normal? He had no answer except the one he gave James now. 'We would have seen beacons on the hills. The King would not leave us in ignorance for want of a signal.'

With a nod of farewell, he made his way towards the graveyard to check on the livestock. Dusk was falling rapidly but two of the sows were in litter, and he wanted to make sure all was well with them before he retired for the night. They lay on their sides in the straw, fast asleep and showing no signs of imminent delivery, and he leant into the pen to scratch the bristles on their heads. They were fine animals who wouldn't reach the end of their breeding lives for another three or four years, but he knew he would have to slaughter them if messengers hadn't come by the middle of December. Everything would be thrown into the stewpot when Develish began to starve, including the three cows in a corner of the herb garden which supplied them with milk.

As his soothing fingers brought grunts of approval from the sows, he heard a girl laugh inside the church, and his immediate thought was that Father Anselm was up to his old tricks. The man hardly left his chambers these days, appearing only on Sundays; but since no one complained to Thaddeus that their priest was unavailable, he had left him to his own devices. He looked towards the church door and saw that it was closed, but the glimmer of a candle flickered in the window of the chancel. He might have gone in to check if another voice hadn't responded to the girl's laugh—the rougher chords of a youth—which certainly wasn't Father Anselm's.

Thaddeus didn't feel it was his place to monitor what happened in the church. If the priest was happy to let youngsters use it to steal moments together, then that was his choice. Half of him wanted to applaud Father Anselm for his generosity—there was nowhere else for secret assignations in the compound—but the other half knew the old man would be rewarding himself by spying through peepholes in his door. He had been caught so many times looking through doors in the village that Lady Anne always referred to him as a 'voyeur'. 'He likes to watch young girls,' she had told Thaddeus many years ago. 'You should warn your sisters to be wary of him.'

After a quick check of the other animals in the graveyard, he decided to walk around the perimeter of the moat wall before the light faded completely. The bondsmen took it in turns to stand six-hour shifts at the four points of the compass, scanning the horizon for signs of movement. They watched in pairs, usually an older man with his son, so that the lad could run to alert others that people were approaching. For the most part, strangers had come along the dirt road from the south, with a few travelling east to west along the footpath, but both routes had been empty since My Lord of Bourne had set fire to the village.

Some of the men complained that it was pointless standing guard when the sky was overcast and darkness obscured their view, but Gyles kept them to their marks. Even if a warning came only when marauders were fording the moat, it would be better than no warning at all. Complacency was as much an enemy as boredom, and, as Gyles pointed out, the best time to storm a fortress was in the dead of night. Nevertheless, with no traffic on the highway, it had become harder and harder to persuade the men to take their duties seriously.

Thaddeus, too, had his doubts. Every time he looked at the crops of beans, peas and vetch going to rot in the fields, and thought of how a failure to plant in the autumn would result in no crops at all next spring, he wondered if Lady Anne had been right to impose a strict isolation. Thaddeus had so much respect for her knowledge he'd agreed with her at the beginning, but he hadn't understood then how urgent the problem of hunger would become.

Where was the harm in crossing the moat to retrieve the harvest and plant for the next season, as long as there was a good enough alarm system—the church bell—to recall their people in a hurry?

Lady Anne shook her head firmly when he put the suggestion to her. Both the bishop's and Gyles's warnings of a quick and terrible death could not have been clearer. Was Thaddeus willing to risk the lives of his family and neighbours on a pestilence that killed in under a week?

'We've seen no sufferers since Sir Richard's return, milady, and he's been dead nearly two months now.'

Lady Anne rested her cheeks in her hands and massaged her tired eyes. 'But we don't even know how the malady passes from person to person,' she pointed out. 'Perhaps the infection is already in our land. Perhaps every man who has ridden up the highway has carried it on his clothes or on his horse.'

'Then it will never be safe to cross the moat,' Thaddeus said reasonably, forbearing to remind her that he'd done it himself several times. 'We are destined to die as soon as we set foot on contaminated ground.'

She sighed but didn't answer, and he let the subject drop. He guessed she was as undecided as he was, and he didn't want to force decisions on her that she wasn't ready to make. There was a limit to how many worries one person could carry before the weight became intolerable. Privately, he made up his mind to accompany Gyles on his scouting trip and leave Hugh de Courtesmain to act as steward during his absence. They needed information. Without it, every choice they made could be wrong.

He began his walk around the moat wall with the south-facing guard point which stood behind the church. It was nothing more than a three-foot-high step which allowed a man to look over the parapet, but it was empty. Whoever was supposed to be there had either deserted his post or never arrived. Annoyed—because he had a good idea who the absentee was—Thaddeus hoisted himself up and stared into the darkness ahead. The light was so dim that all he could look for were signs of movement. A hundred stationary figures could be crouched around the borders of the meadows and he wouldn't know they were there unless a shadow shifted.

His presence disturbed the sheep in the fenced-off areas of the graveyard between the church and the moat wall, and they bleated an alarm to each other. Thaddeus was as certain as he could be that Will Thurkell should have been manning this position, and he knew his stepfather well enough to know that the noise of the animals would have tested his nerves very quickly. He guessed Will had left his eldest son, Jacob, to do the job in his stead; guessed, too, that the girl in the church had seduced Jacob away. It wouldn't have been hard. Jacob, at sixteen, was as lustful as any of the young bucks on the demesne, but too small and uninviting to attract a girl's eye. As he had done almost every day of his life, Thaddeus cursed Will for his laziness and his stupidity. If the man hoped Thaddeus would turn a blind eye to this, he was even more of a fool than Thaddeus thought him.

He lingered at the guard post for a long time in order to give Jacob a chance to return, if only because he held him less culpable than Will. He had no fondness for his half-brother. Jacob had been so adept at deflecting his father's anger on to Thaddeus's broader shoulders that, at ten, Thaddeus had been whipped for every one of six-year-old Jacob's crimes. He would have come to hate the boy in earnest if Lady Anne hadn't taught him that misdirected anger was a waste of time.

Smoothing ointment onto his bruised ribs, she said, 'Your father would beat you whether Jacob told lies or not, Thaddeus.

He teaches his own son nothing by doing it, but you, at least, are learning that cruelty breeds hatred.'

'Is that a good thing?' Thaddeus had asked in puzzlement.

'Yes, if it persuades you that injustice and unkindness give rise to all the evils in the world.'

He liked the feel of her soft fingers on his throbbing skin. They spoke of love in a way that his mother's whining demands never did. 'Are you telling me to do what Jesus said? Turn the other cheek and let Will thrash me as often as he likes?'

'I'm telling you to remember what it's like to be treated unfairly, Thaddeus. You'll grow up to be as vicious as Will if you allow his cruelty to fill you with hatred.'

'I'll never love him.'

'Then find a way not to hate him.' She pulled his shirt over his head and helped him ease his arms into the sleeves. 'A clever person sets his own path in life and travels forward. A man who wastes his life on vengeance stands still.'

'How do you learn not to hate a person?'

'By understanding how little he matters to you,' said Lady Anne. 'Why expend emotion on someone who is of such low account? Will Thurkell can teach you nothing and give you nothing. His cudgel may hurt at the moment, and his whip may sting, but in four years, when you over-top him by six inches, he will be too frightened even to lift his hand against you. Live for *that* day, Thaddeus.'

'What if I want to kill him when that day comes?'

She wrapped the pot of ointment in a sacking bag and tied the corners. 'You will have chosen the path he wants you to take. Nothing would please him more than to prove you sprang from the Devil.' She placed the bag in his hands. 'Use this salve morning and night to ease the pain but don't let Will see you do it. He'll resent you even more if he knows you've been speaking to me.'

He studied her gentle face for a moment, wondering how someone so young could have so much wisdom. 'Do you think my real father was a good man, Lady Anne?'

She gave a small laugh and pinched his chin between her thumb and forefinger. 'He must have been,' she said. 'You wouldn't be so brave otherwise.'

After half an hour, Thaddeus gave up his vigil and retraced his steps around the church to haul Jacob outside. He was too late. The light in the chancel window had been extinguished and, when he entered the church, it was empty. With a curse of frustration, he strode to the door of the tower and thumped on it loudly. 'Father Anselm! It's Thaddeus Thurkell. There were a couple of youngsters in here a while back. Do you know who they were?'

If the man was awake, he wasn't answering, and Thaddeus returned outside to walk around the western end of the church. He couldn't believe Jacob would have taken the longer route to the step, but he glanced across the graveyard as he rounded the building, looking for the boy's silhouette above the moat wall. His eyes were well adjusted to the darkness but he would have missed the figure sprawled face down on the grass in front of the nearest sheep pen if the moon hadn't been on the rise. There was just enough light to show the colour of the tunic—saffron yellow—the same Thaddeus had worn when he was twelve.

He stepped around a couple of gravestones and brought the sole of his boot down heavily on his half-brother's back. 'I'll have your hide if you've been stealing Father Anselm's mead, you little weasel,' he growled. 'I gave you fair warning to stop your thieving ways.' When there was no response, he used his foot to rock the body from side to side. 'Come on, Jacob. Wake up!'

He wondered afterwards why it took him so long to realise the boy was dead. Even a couple of kicks didn't bring a reaction, yet the idea that death was the reason for Jacob's stillness never occurred to him. It was only when he rolled the body over and saw the open, staring eyes that he knew he was looking at a corpse. The shock was tremendous. It was only a matter of hours since he'd watched Jacob practise the long jump in the orchard. Had he been ill then? Had he been hiding symptoms of the pestilence out of fear?

With a feeling of dread, Thaddeus knelt beside the limp form— even smaller in death than in life—and felt for lumps under the skin of the neck before slipping his hands inside the boy's tunic to probe under Jacob's arms and around his groin. The skin was warm and moist to the touch, and Thaddeus jerked away, wiping his fingers with revulsion on his shirt sleeves. He'd never been so intimate with his brother in life, and it made him retch to be doing it now. Yet he had to find out how Jacob had died.

He slipped his arms under the boy's neck and knees and, with a grunt of effort, rose to his feet and walked back around the church with Jacob's dead weight cradled against his chest. He couldn't think of anywhere else to put him except on the chancel floor in front of the altar. He needed more light than the moon offered to examine the body properly, but he baulked at making Jacob a public exhibit by doing it in front of an audience. In any case, if the boy had died of the pestilence, it would make things worse to carry his infected body through the compound.

His hands were trembling so much, it took him longer than it should have done to locate Father Anselm's tinderbox at the back of the altar and coax a spark onto the char cloth from which to light a wooden splint. Though not superstitious like Hugh de Courtesmain, Thaddeus found himself turning at every creak of a wood joint to search the darkness behind him. A barely discernible glimmer of light showed under Father Anselm's door but the priest remained as still and silent as Jacob's corpse.

Thaddeus couldn't avoid the cross as he lit the candles on the altar. 'Is Hell any worse than the misery you inflict on us in this world?' he asked aloud, his voice echoing around the empty church. 'Is Satan's fire more terrible than this pestilence you've sent to kill us?' As the wicks sprang into flame, dispelling the shadows around him, he heard the bolt being drawn on the tower door.

'Who lights the Holy Table without permission?' demanded Father Anselm in a querulous voice.

Thaddeus blew out the splint. 'Thaddeus Thurkell,' he said. 'You didn't answer when I knocked, Father. I thought you were asleep.' He turned to look down the length of the church at the shadowy figure behind the half-open door. 'You would be wise to shut yourself in again. If I have need of you, I will call.'

But the old man was not to be put off so easily. With the candles well aflame on the altar, he could see Thaddeus far better than Thaddeus could see him. 'You have blood on your clothes,' he said accusingly. 'What have you been doing? Who is that on the floor in front of you?'

'My brother Jacob.' With a frown, Thaddeus glanced down at his pale woollen shirt, saw the red stain where he'd held his brother's body close and the smears on his sleeves where he'd wiped his hands. 'I thought it was sweat,' he said in sudden confusion, dropping to his knees and moving Jacob's arm to disclose the blood on the boy's yellow tunic. He undid the cord that was tied around Jacob's waist and pushed up the tunic to look for the source of the bleeding. There was so much blood—most of it still wet—that it was hard to see where it was coming from until a bubble of escaping air formed around a wound between two of the ribs.

The priest shuffled towards him. 'Is he dead?'

'I believed he was when I found him, yet there seems to be breath in him still.' Thaddeus pushed the body to stir it back to life. 'There. Do you see?'

Father Anselm shook his head. 'I've known corpses to exhale fetid air from dead lungs even as the lid is hammered on their coffins.' He lowered himself painfully to kneel beside the body. 'Jacob sees no more, Thaddeus. His eyes are already glazing. Fetch the oil from the altar. It's too late for him to receive absolution, but his restless soul may find peace if I anoint him.'

Thaddeus watched the little ceremony with mixed emotions. There was something reassuring about Father Anselm's careful application of holy oil to Jacob's forehead, eyelids, nostrils, lips, ears, breast, hands and feet, as if unction could indeed bring rest. Thaddeus even fancied that Jacob was sleeping once the priest's fingers had closed the staring eyes and crossed the wrists above the sunken chest. Nevertheless, he was so troubled by the manner of his brother's death that he made few responses to the chanted Latin prayers.

He tried to persuade himself the wound had happened accidentally, but reason told him that couldn't be true. The puncture must be deep to have robbed Jacob of life. In the candlelight, Thaddeus could see other marks on the boy—scratches on his face; a slash across his right palm, suggesting he'd caught a blade in his fist; another across his forearm, suggesting he'd tried to deflect it. They all spoke of a fight, ending in a final thrust of the blade between the ribs.

Father Anselm crossed himself as he came to the end of his prayers. 'Was this your doing, Thaddeus?' he asked. 'You have his blood all over you.'

Thaddeus shook his head. 'I found him by the sheep pens behind the church. I thought he was drunk until I turned him over.'

He eased the cord from under the body to see if Jacob had been carrying the knife he used for splitting saplings. Like most bondsmen, Jacob wore his tools knotted into loops at his side, but while his awl was there, his oak-handled blade was not, and Thaddeus wondered if that could be the knife that had killed him.

'Did you hear a fight outside?' he asked the priest. 'There must have been a serious argument for this to have happened.'

The priest wouldn't look at him. 'I hear nothing in my chambers.'

Thaddeus didn't believe him. He pushed himself to his feet and walked to the window which overlooked the sheep pens. The altar candles made the darkness of the graveyard impenetrable, although he could make out the faint sheen of white fleeces here and there. He remembered how much lighter it had been when he mounted the step to scan the woodland to the south. 'Someone may have seen the altercation from this window,' he said, 'or at least seen Jacob sprawled on the grass. I heard a girl laugh as if something amused her. Do you know who she was, Father?'

The priest didn't answer immediately and Thaddeus turned to look at him. He was still kneeling beside the body, his hands writhing frantically in front of him as if a conflict in his mind was finding expression in physical activity. 'It's a bad, bad business whatever the reason,' he muttered.

It was a strange choice of words, Thaddeus thought. He hadn't asked why Jacob had been in a fight, only who might have witnessed it. He frowned. 'Are you saying the girl had something to do with this?' he asked. 'Was she the cause of the disagreement?'

But Father Anselm gave another shake of his head. 'I am as ignorant as you, Thaddeus,' he said. 'I saw nothing and heard nothing. Lady Anne must send for the High Sheriff and charge him with finding the culprit. It's not for you or I to decide a person's guilt.'

'Even if she was willing to send a messenger from the demesne, what makes you think the sheriff will come—assuming he's alive? Why take an interest in one death when hundreds are dying of the pestilence?' Thaddeus walked back to help the priest to his feet. 'It may be that Jacob pulled his knife first and his opponent sought only to defend himself. I need the girl's name in case she saw something, Father.'

The old man headed towards his chambers. 'You must blame yourself for this, Thaddeus,' he said over his shoulder.

'How so? It's not I who put a knife through my brother's ribs.'

'I warned you not to bring that young woman into my church.'

⚬⚬

Thaddeus left a single candle burning for Jacob on the stone sill of the altar window and returned to the step in the moat wall. He wanted space and time to think, and the guard post on the southern boundary offered solitude. He was hesitant to fetch Lady Anne from her bed when there was nothing she could do in darkness that couldn't more easily be done in daylight. Nor did he want to wake his mother to tell her that one of her children was dead. Her anguished weeping would rouse the compound to action, and common sense told Thaddeus he had a better prospect of uncovering the truth if he could prevent a hue and cry until he was ready.

He needed to examine the ground where he'd found Jacob to see if the boy had dropped his knife into the grass. If it wasn't there, the chances were good that Jacob's opponent had taken it, and a search of every youngster might reveal it, along with bloodstains on clothes and cuts on hands and arms. To look for such things in darkness was foolish. A crafty culprit would take advantage of the night to slip away unnoticed and drop a knife or a blood-spattered tunic into the sewage at the bottom of the latrines.

Thaddeus dwelt increasingly on what Father Anselm had said. He'd pressed the priest to explain his words but the old man had refused. 'It's not something I would wish Lady Anne to hear,' he muttered, closing and bolting his door behind him.

It took little imagination for Thaddeus to knit what he already knew into a plausible scenario. Eleanor's sudden willingness to consort with serfs . . . the increase in fighting amongst the young bucks . . . secret assignations in the church. If she wasn't setting the boys against each other deliberately, she was doing it for fun.

∽∅∽

Eleanor was awakened by Isabella's tiny, callused hand on her mouth. 'Hush, milady,' the girl whispered in her ear. 'Stay silent for fear of rousing your mother. You would not want her to hear the message I bring.'

In the thinning gloom of pre-dawn light, Eleanor could just make out Isabella's face. The little maid was kneeling on the floor beside her, staring hard into Eleanor's eyes to see if she understood. When Eleanor gave a small nod, she removed her hand and leant forward to whisper again.

'Terrible things are being said about you by some of the serf boys, milady. They speak of what you do with them in the church. You must come to the steward's office now if you don't want your mother to know.'

Isabella took satisfaction from the sudden fear in her young mistress's eyes. It meant Thaddeus was right in what he'd said about Eleanor. He had woken Isabella from her place in the hall amongst the children—to whom she acted as nurse and comforter during the nights—and explained what he wanted her to say to her young mistress. Another girl might have questioned the words, but not Isabella. She had seen the way her twin brothers looked at Lady Eleanor.

Holding a finger to her lips, she assisted Eleanor to her feet and led her by the hand past the many sleepers towards the door. Occasionally, their feet brushed against the straw mattresses, but any sound they made was buried beneath the snores of the older women. Most worked in the kitchen and slept in Lady Anne's chamber to be on hand for meal preparation. Each would complain of a dry mouth when the sun was high enough to wake them, but all knew they slept better and more deeply, undisturbed on Lady Anne's floor, than in their husbands' beds.

Eleanor began to resist the tug of Isabella's hand as they reached the bottom of the stairs, but the maid would have none of it, gripping her more firmly and forcing her towards the steward's office. Nevertheless, Isabella wouldn't have succeeded if Thaddeus hadn't seen what was happening and come out to meet them. He gripped Eleanor's arms and frogmarched her inside, ushering Isabella in behind her and closing the door. 'I do this for your mother, not for you,' he said coldly. 'For myself, I would prefer the truth of your character to be known.'

The room was lit by a single candle on the desk. By its light, both Eleanor and Isabella could see the dark stains on Thaddeus's shirt, although he couldn't tell whether either of them guessed it was dried blood. For his part, he looked at the two girls with their tumbled hair, pale woollen night shifts and bare feet, and thought how alike they were. Strangers would be unable to say which was the mistress and which the maid unless they knew Eleanor was blonde. He stood with his back to the door to prevent her leaving.

'Who was with you in the church yesterday evening?' he demanded curtly. 'Give me his name.'

Eleanor dropped her gaze. 'I haven't been to the church for days.'

'There are plenty who will say you have, including Father Anselm.'

'There's no law against praying.'

'You don't go there to pray. At best, you delight in teasing young men to a frenzy; at worst, you lie down with them. No other girl on this demesne would dare to use the church for such purposes. They'd be afraid of Father Anselm denouncing them.' He gave an ironic bow. 'But that doesn't apply to you, does it . . . *milady*? Even a priest can't bring himself to tell Lady Anne that her daughter's a common whore.'

Eleanor raised her head, a look of pure hatred on her face. 'Who accuses me? Who dares suggest that I would cheapen myself with peasants?'

Thaddeus nodded to a piece of vellum on the desk. 'The list is there. Read it and tell me if any of the names are wrong.'

Isabella was close enough to see what was written and she raised a hand to her mouth to hide her smile. *Bushels of wheat—25 . . . Barrels of salt beef—6 . . . Sacks of turnips—23 . . .* The only pity was that Lady Eleanor had no idea what a mockery Thaddeus was making of her.

'You know I cannot,' the girl said with a spark of anger. 'Tell Isabella to read it to me.'

But Thaddeus shook his head. 'You should have applied yourself to your lessons instead of preening in your looking glass. It's not for Isabella to make you a free gift of your accusers. You're quite sly enough to say they forced themselves on you if you think Lady Anne will believe you.'

Eleanor was all too predictable. 'My mother will believe it because it's true,' she said. 'She knows I have too much dislike of serfs to allow them to put their hands on me.'

A faint smile lifted Thaddeus's mouth. 'You found it amusing enough last night,' he said. 'Amidst all the laughter, you found time to light a candle in the chancel window. How so, Lady Eleanor, if you were dragged into the church by force?'

She didn't answer, and in the silence that followed they heard the sound of treble voices in the great hall.

'The children are stirring,' Thaddeus said. 'If you don't want questions asked about why you're away from your bed, give me the name of your companion last night. Otherwise I shall keep you here until your mother wakes, and you can make your explanations to her.'

Nervously, Eleanor ran her tongue across her lips. 'Why do you need it? What will you do if I tell you?'

Thaddeus folded his arms over the bloodstains on his shirt. 'Ask instead what I will do if you don't,' he murmured. 'I have no regard for you at all, Lady Eleanor, and it matters little to me if I have to summon every man to a public meeting on the forecourt to ask what they know of you. Be sure I shall join in the laughter if you're branded a harlot like my mother.'

He spoke with such contempt that Isabella felt a small measure of compassion for Eleanor. She knew her young mistress harboured a secret desire for Thaddeus, for there wasn't a maid in Develish who did not. He was so different from other men, both in looks and manner, that every girl of marriageable age vied for his attention, becoming jealous if he favoured a rival with a smile. Serfs and servants yearned for him as a husband; Eleanor looked to make him her fool, a lovelorn slave who worshipped her from a distance. All were disappointed. He searched the horizon more often than the faces of Develish's daughters.

Isabella's mother said it was the cruelty of his upbringing that had made him cold, and warned her daughter against losing her heart to him. *Handsome is as handsome does*, she told Isabella. *Choose a boy of your own age who craves your love, not one so much older who does not.* It was advice more easily given than taken. For all her willingness to obey her mother's wishes, Isabella felt a fluttering in her heart whenever Thaddeus sought her out to perform a task for him or Lady Anne. The respect he showed her when making these requests had led her to think of him as a kind and gentle person but, seeing the hardness in him now, she realised he was very different from her imaginings.

Eleven

A COUPLE OF MEN STOOD stretching outside their open doors when Thaddeus walked across the orchard to the line of serfs' huts in front of the moat wall, but most were yet to wake. He gave a light knock on the rough wooden planking of the Startouts' lean-to and pushed it open. Gyles opened his eyes with a yawn but rolled over happily when Thaddeus shook his head. 'You have ten minutes yet,' Thaddeus told him. 'It's Olyver I'm after.' He stooped over the boy and shook him roughly. 'Up!' he commanded. 'I have a job for you.'

'Why can't Ian do it?' Olyver muttered mutinously, kicking his twin brother who slept beside him.

Thaddeus hauled him to his feet and dragged him towards the door. 'Because I want you.'

The lad stumbled outside, bleary-eyed and dishevelled. He was fourteen, but in the morning light, with spindly legs protruding from beneath his inadequate nightshirt, he looked younger. Thaddeus pinched one of his ears between his thumb and forefinger and, deaf to his protests, led him unceremoniously towards the church. 'Be grateful it's me that's doing this and not your father,' he said. 'If Gyles hears what you were up to last night with Lady Eleanor, he'll flay the skin off your back.'

He marched Olyver around the church and brought him to a halt some ten yards from where he'd found Jacob. The red light of the rising sun was turning to gold and it would be a matter of minutes only before every detail of the scene sprang to life. It wouldn't be long either before James Buckler took up his shift on the southern guard step.

Thaddeus gave Olyver's ear a final, painful twist before releasing him. 'There was a fight out here yesterday evening. I think you know the names of the two boys involved. Give them to me.'

Olyver clutched his hand to the side of his head. He would have denied knowing anything if Thaddeus's tone hadn't been so grim. 'Jacob Thurkell and Edmund Trueblood,' he muttered.

'What were they fighting about?'

The boy didn't answer.

'Jacob should have been on guard duty on the step. What did Edmund say or do to make him abandon his post?'

Olyver looked around wildly to see if there was an escape from Thaddeus's questioning. 'You'll have to ask Edmund.'

Without warning, Thaddeus used his superior height and strength to hook a foot around the back of one of the youth's knees and upend him, winded, to the ground. 'Give me some answers,' he ordered, grinding his heel into Olyver's solar plexus, 'or you'll wish you hadn't been born. What were you doing with Lady Eleanor inside the church?'

'You're hurting me.'

'I haven't even begun,' said Thaddeus indifferently. 'My brother was killed last night, and I'd as soon hang you for it as anyone. If you don't tell me what Jacob and Edmund were fighting about, I'll charge you with murder. You know full well that Lady Eleanor won't step forward to defend you. She'll deny ever being in the church.'

The boy's eyes widened in alarm. 'I know nothing about a killing,' he gasped. 'I swear to God.'

Thaddeus eased the pressure of his heel, and told the boy to sit up. 'Tell me what you do know.'

It was a grubby little story, akin to what Thaddeus had worked out for himself during the night—adolescent youths competing for Eleanor's favours. Olyver talked about touching and kissing, and spilling his seed on the church floor, but from the way he stuttered and stammered through the details Thaddeus guessed things had gone further than that.

He asked bluntly if Olyver had put his cock in the girl's hole. 'You're a damn fool if you have,' he said. 'If you're not hanged for murder, you'll be hanged for rape.'

'I didn't,' the boy protested. 'I may have told the others I did, but—' He broke off. 'That doesn't make it rape, does it?'

'It'll be whatever Lady Eleanor says it was, and she's already told me you forced yourself on her.' Thaddeus eyed him with derision. 'What the Hell did you think you were playing at?'

'It wasn't just me.'

'Who else?'

The boy squirmed unhappily. 'Anyone who could take a whipping.'

Thaddeus frowned at him. 'A whipping? From whom?'

'Eleanor,' came the barely heard answer. 'You earned a reward if you didn't flinch.'

Thaddeus recalled how the girl had struck him with a hazel sapling the day Sir Richard had left for Bradmayne, and how her delight in what she was doing had turned to fury when her mother stayed her hand. 'Where did she hit you?'

'Across the back.'

'Show me.'

Reluctantly, the boy twisted around and raised his shirt. 'It doesn't hurt,' he said.

Thaddeus doubted that, more so when he pressed a finger against a newer-looking weal—probably inflicted the previous evening—and heard the boy's intake of breath. How twisted did a girl have to be to inflict pain one moment and offer sexual favours the next? And what did she hope to achieve by it? Humiliation? Obedience? Dominance? 'What was she testing?' he asked. 'Your willingness to be her slave?'

Olyver looked confused, as if such an interpretation had never occurred to him. 'It was just a game,' he said naively. 'You didn't have to play if you didn't want to.'

Thaddeus wondered if the lad had genuine feelings for the girl. Her beauty and the sweet scent of her hair made her a great deal more attractive than a weather-toughened peasant girl. Hard work hadn't raised calluses on her fingers or roughened her skin.

'Who else was willing to play this game?'

Reluctantly Olyver named four, including his own twin brother. Ill-feeling had developed between them, and when they weren't vying to prove themselves to Eleanor, they were fighting for dominance amongst themselves. Olyver admitted to lying about how far he had gone with the girl, but claimed the others had lied as well. It was all about posturing and boasting. Thaddeus found it interesting that Eleanor had targeted only the adolescent sons of the leading serfs—Startout, Trueblood, Catchpole and Buckler—and wondered why. Was it their fathers' influence within the demesne that attracted her?

'Was Jacob involved?' he asked.

Olyver stared at his hands. 'Not really.'

'What does that mean?'

'He used to watch. He was always hanging around the church with his nose pressed to the window, fiddling with his cock and getting himself excited.'

'Did Eleanor know?'

The boy nodded. 'She lit the candle on purpose so that he'd be able to see us. She thought it was funny. He got a whipping if we caught him with his britches down.'

'From Eleanor?'

'Yes.'

A cynical smile lifted the corner of Thaddeus's mouth. 'And who held him while she did it? You?'

Olyver didn't answer, and Thaddeus pictured his brother alone on the guard step night after night, waiting for a light to appear in the church. It wasn't hard to imagine the turbulence of emotion that Jacob must have experienced. He was more used to rejection than he was to love.

'Why was Edmund here last evening?'

'He came to see if I was with Eleanor . . . and fight me if I was.'

'So how did he end up fighting with Jacob?'

'He came round this side to make sure we were in the church— you can't see so well through the window where the candle is—and caught Jacob with his nose to the glass. He gave him a slapping for being a peeping Tom and Jacob started hollering. Me and Eleanor went outside to see what the row was about.' Olyver gave a shrug of embarrassment. 'I know he's your brother, Thaddeus, but none of us likes him much. He's always stealing off us.'

'*Was*,' corrected Thaddeus. 'He's dead.' He watched the grass in front of them turn from pink-tinged grey to pastel green as the sun appeared above the eastern horizon. He could see the flattened area in front of the sheep pen where Jacob had been lying, but not the oak-handled knife. 'Was it Edmund who killed him?'

Olyver shook his head in genuine bewilderment. 'He can't have done. Jacob was still on his feet when me and Eleanor came round that corner.' He nodded to the western end of the church. 'We started laughing and Edmund gave a ruddy great roar and came charging across the grass towards us. Last I saw of Jacob he was standing over there—' he pointed towards the sheep pen—'cursing and whining about Edmund boxing his ears.'

'Where did you and Edmund fight?'

'Round the other side near the pigs.' The boy's eyes glittered briefly with remembered triumph. 'Edmund got the worst of it. He left with his tail between his legs.'

'What time was it?'

'A half-hour before sundown. It was still light when Edmund's nose started bleeding.'

'Did Eleanor watch the fight?'

'Must have done. She pulled me off when Edmund started spewing blood all over the place and then gave him her kerchief to stop the flow so he wouldn't feel badly about losing.'

'What happened then?'

'Edmund left, and me and Eleanor went back inside the church.'

'Did you look out of the window to see if Jacob was still outside?'

'Eleanor did. I sat on the chancel step to get my breath back.'

'What did she say?'

'That he'd gone.' He rocked forward, clasping his knees to his chest. 'I don't see how he can be dead. He didn't take nearly the pummelling off Edmund that I got.'

Thaddeus walked the few yards to the sheep pen and knelt by the flattened grass, feeling around for Jacob's knife. He located it almost immediately, half buried in the earth near where the body had been lying. Had Jacob dropped it, he wondered, or had someone else flung it to the ground before he fell? There was no way of knowing. He withdrew it carefully and examined the blade for blood, but all he could see were streaks of mud. He couldn't even prove that this was the weapon that had killed his brother.

He turned to look at Olyver. 'I found Jacob here some quarter-hour after you left the church. He'd been stabbed in the chest and he'd been dead for some time.'

The boy looked scared. 'How do you know?'

'Because I arrived at the pig pens not long after you say Edmund left. You and Lady Eleanor were still inside. I heard her laughing and saw the candle in the window. There wasn't time for Jacob to leave and come back . . . and even if he had, I'd have heard the fight which led to his stabbing. Jacob would have cried out. He had slash marks on his arms where he tried to defend himself.'

Olyver stared in fascination at the knife in Thaddeus's hand, struggling to make sense of what he was saying. 'I swear to God it wasn't me, Thaddeus. I never got near him—and Edmund just gave him a slapping. Ask Eleanor if you don't believe me.'

Thaddeus rose to his feet. 'You're a fool, Olyver,' he said coldly. 'Your sister has more sense in her little finger than you will ever have.' He gestured towards the path. 'Return to your father's hut. Tell him some of the sheep got out and I needed your help to round them up, then go about your day as normal. You're to speak to no one of this, including Edmund and Eleanor. If I find you have—and their stories differ from yours as a result—I'll have no choice but to ask Lady Anne to try you for murder. Do I make myself clear?'

The boy's ashen face told him he did.

൦ൽ

The Truebloods' dwelling was on the path leading to the church. John was already outside, and he watched curiously as Olyver Startout hurtled past him in his nightshirt. Thaddeus, following some few yards behind, nodded to James Buckler, who was making his way to the guard step, then paused with a lazy smile outside the Truebloods' lean-to, staring after Olyver. 'He lent me a hand with the sheep,' he told John by way of explanation, 'and now he's embarrassed to be seen half naked. I have a job for Edmund. Is he dressed?'

John stooped to look through the door. 'You're wanted for work, boy. Shift yourself.'

The youth emerged with a scowl, nostrils caked with dried blood and one eye swollen. 'I don't reckon I'm fit,' he muttered. 'I got the worst of it in a wrestling match yesterday.'

His father tut-tutted at the sight of him. 'You're taking these games too far, Thaddeus. This isn't the first time he's come back with a bloody nose.'

'It's Edmund's choice, John. No one's forcing him to fight. If he can't take a beating, he shouldn't go looking for one.' He clapped a friendly arm across the boy's shoulders, turning him towards the graveyard and urging him along the path. 'He'll be back within the hour.'

Edmund tried to pull away. 'I've got bruises all over,' he complained, easing his sore muscles as Thaddeus brought his weight to bear on them. 'It's not fair to make me work.'

Thaddeus took no notice, propelling him past the pig pens and into the lee of the tower, where he slammed Edmund against the wall. He gripped the youth's neck between an iron thumb and forefinger. 'Tell me what happened here yesterday evening, and keep your voice down if you don't want Father Anselm or James Buckler to hear. If you lie to me, I'll know.'

Edmund's wide-eyed alarm was even greater than Olyver's, perhaps because he'd seen the other boy running from the church as if the hounds of Hell were after him. It didn't take a great thinker to work out that it must have been Thaddeus who'd frightened him, or that the information Olyver revealed had worsened Thaddeus's temper. Unsure of exactly what he had to account for, Edmund stammered and stumbled through his story, but it became clear to Thaddeus very quickly that he had no idea Jacob was dead.

Edmund's version differed little from Olyver's, except that he seemed more ashamed of himself. He showed none of Olyver's bravado when he spoke of his assignations with Eleanor, perhaps realising belatedly how squalid they sounded when described in detail to someone else. Indeed, he wouldn't have mentioned Eleanor at all if Thaddeus's grip on his throat hadn't tightened when he tried to pretend his fights with Jacob and Olyver had been about 'nothing much'.

He told Thaddeus how he'd found Jacob at the window, and dragged him towards the sheep pen to 'give him a good slapping' for being a peeping Tom. He guessed it was Jacob's howls that brought Eleanor and Olyver outside. They came around the corner of the church, pointing their fingers and laughing at Jacob's whining and Edmund's red-faced fury. He remembered charging at Olyver, remembered Olyver side-stepping and the pair of them ending up in a rolling wrestling match amongst the gravestones at the front of the church, but he didn't recall seeing Eleanor again until she ordered Olyver to stop hitting Edmund's head on the ground.

'She was kind,' he muttered, as if he felt she needed defending. 'She knelt down and wiped my face with her handkerchief then gave it to me to hold against my nose.'

'Only because it suited her,' Thaddeus said, releasing the boy and watching him slump against the church wall. 'What were these assignations about? Apart from Lady Eleanor's pleasure at being able to whip a serf and watch him beg for his cock to be rubbed by way of reward?'

The boy stared at the ground, a dull flush staining his cheeks.

'What did she want you to do for her, Edmund?'

'Prove my worth . . . prove I can take a beating . . . prove I'd make a good champion.'

'Against whom?'

There was a long hesitation. 'You,' he answered. 'She doesn't like you at all, Thaddeus.'

ॐ

The noise of the compound stirring to life was becoming louder and more insistent, and Thaddeus knew he couldn't keep Jacob's death secret much longer. Without explanation, he ordered Edmund to stand on guard in front of the church door while he went inside to check that the scene was unchanged from the previous night. He knelt beside Jacob again, rearranging the yellow tunic to make the bloodstains less visible and pressing his hands over the boy's folded ones in a vain attempt to bring some colour and warmth into them. But they were as white and cold as marble. It might have been a statue lying there.

There was no sign of Father Anselm. Thaddeus considered trying to rouse him, but decided it wouldn't be wise to give the priest time to order his thoughts. He was more valuable to Thaddeus confused and incoherent from being woken out of a stupor, than thinking of ways to excuse his inaction. He pulled the door closed behind him as he left, making sure the latch was firmly engaged, then warned Edmund not to go inside or allow anyone else to enter. He showed no sympathy when the boy asked what reason he could give, saying only that Edmund would be up to his neck in trouble if he disobeyed.

He returned to the house and sought out Alleyn's son, young Robert Startout, ruffling his hair and asking him to run to the Thurkells' hut with a request that Will and Eva attend Lady Anne in the steward's office. Then he made his way to Sir Richard's chambers, pulled on a woollen tunic and a leather jerkin to hide his bloodstained shirt, and asked Hugh de Courtesmain to accompany him downstairs.

The Frenchman was on his knees, tying his straw mattress into a tight bundle. He sat back on his heels and studied Thaddeus's dark face curiously. 'Has something happened?' he asked. 'You've been absent from your bed all night.'

Thaddeus let the question pass. 'Lady Anne may need your support,' was all he said, reaching down to help the man to his feet.

Hugh's curiosity deepened as he followed Thaddeus towards the steward's office. The serf's expression was quite unreadable, although his steps faltered as they approached the open door, and it seemed to Hugh that he had to force himself to enter. Yet why, since there was nothing unusual about the smile or the greeting that Lady Anne gave him?

'Good morning, Thaddeus. Good morning, Master de Courtesmain.'

'Good morning, milady,' the men said in unison, bending their necks.

If Thaddeus had needed confirmation that the decision he'd reached was the right one, he found it in Lady Anne's face. It was as pleasing and kind to him as it had always been, and he wanted it to stay that way. Nothing he'd learnt from Olyver and Edmund had persuaded him to alter his decision in the dark hours before dawn that Jacob's death must be deemed an accident. Indeed, his resolution had been strengthened by what the boys had told him.

The harmony of Develish was too fragile to survive a trial for murder, and no one would be more damaged by it than Lady Anne. In lieu of the High Sheriff and My Lord of Blandeforde, it would fall to her to put her people to the question in order to uncover the truth, and, worse, pass a sentence of death on the culprit.

'You look worried, Thaddeus,' she said. 'Is something wrong?'

'I was thinking about my brother Jacob, milady, and wishing I'd been more of a friend to him when he was growing. He's always known better how to find trouble than escape it.'

She held his gaze for a moment, wondering what Jacob had done that meant the problem had to be brought to her. Caught red-handed thieving, she guessed, and her heart sank at the prospect of having to order him flogged if his victim demanded it. She felt a momentary annoyance that Thaddeus hadn't dealt with it himself, and might have said so if Robert Startout hadn't sidled into the room to pluck at the tall serf's tunic and whisper that Will and Eva were waiting outside.

Thaddeus touched his head in gratitude then sent him on his way. 'I asked Will and Eva to come here, milady. Do they have your permission to enter?'

There was such bleakness in his expression that Lady Anne's heart sank even more. Had the whole family been caught thieving? she wondered, as she gave a reluctant nod. Thaddeus beckoned the couple inside. It was obvious that neither of them wanted to be there. Will's face was screwed into a scowl of annoyance, as if being summoned to the house was beneath his dignity, and Eva wore her dislike of Lady Anne in the slant of her eyes and the aggressive jut of her chin.

'What do you want with us?' Will demanded of their mistress. 'We have things to do.'

'You must address your questions to Thaddeus,' she said. 'It was he who summoned you.'

Will took up a stance of defiance, chest thrust out and fists clenched at his side. 'Well, boy?'

Thaddeus pulled a stool forward from the corner of the room. 'Would you allow my mother to sit, milady? What I have to say will cause her distress.' He took Lady Anne's silence for agreement and pressed Eva onto the seat, lowering himself to his knees in front of her and clasping both her hands between his. 'Jacob is dead,' he said quietly. 'I laid his body in the church during the night and Father Anselm gave him unction so that his sins would be shriven. A candle is burning for him in the altar window and Edmund Trueblood guards the entrance so that no one can disturb his rest until you have said your prayers over him.'

Eva stared at him in puzzlement. 'How can he be dead? He was well yesterday. Do you tease me with such a story?'

Thaddeus shook his head. 'I found him beside the sheep pens when I went to check the guard step. He was lying on his front and seemed to have been dead for some time.' He turned to Lady Anne. 'I thought he must have perished of the pestilence, though I couldn't see how. It wasn't until I carried him into the church and lit the candles that I discovered he had a wound in his chest.'

She was as puzzled as Eva. 'What kind of wound?'

Wearily, Thaddeus released his mother's hands and rose to his feet. 'A pierce wound in the chest . . . but I believe he did it to himself by accident. There's no sign of anyone else being there. My guess is he grew bored of his guard duty and started practising sword thrusts with his knife. If he was standing on the step in the dark, he'd have lost his balance very easily.'

'Then why did you find him beside the sheep pens?'

'I believe he was going in search of help, milady, not realising how badly he was hurt. It looks to me as if he pulled the knife from his chest and collapsed on top of it. I found it this morning in the flattened grass where he'd been lying.' He ran a tired hand around his jawline. 'He couldn't have been saved even if someone had been with him. He would have bled to death whatever happened.'

Eva rose unsteadily to her feet. 'It's your fault,' she cried, rushing at her husband and pummelling her fists against his chest. 'You were too lazy to do your job, just as you've always been.'

Thaddeus pulled her off before Will could retaliate. 'You need to mourn your son not fight with each other,' he said, placing his body between them. 'If anyone's to blame, it's me. If I hadn't tried to turn farm workers into soldiers, Jacob would still be alive.'

'I'll see you hanged if it was you who killed him,' Will snarled, his eyes full of hate. 'You're too slick with your guesses, boy. I say you're a liar.'

Thaddeus stared him down. 'There's many will point the finger at you, Will. The roster says you were with him last night—the *only* person with him—and you're known to be a violent man.'

Will flicked a nervous glance at Lady Anne. 'I didn't go. The wife will vouch for me. I stayed in our hut all night.'

'Then don't accuse others of lying,' Lady Anne said. 'If you hadn't shirked your responsibility, your son would still be alive.' She turned her attention to Thaddeus. 'Why did you not come for me as soon as you found Jacob? Or fetch his parents to say prayers over him?'

'I was afraid it was the pestilence, milady. Until I found the wound in his chest, I thought the blood had come from a burst boil in his armpit. I was planning to take his body across the moat and bury him beside Sir Richard.'

'And exclude yourself from returning?'

He nodded.

'I would not have wanted that, Thaddeus.' She rose from her stool and moved around the desk to stand before Eva. 'I grieve for your loss,' she said with sincerity. 'I hoped everyone would live through this terrible ordeal, and it saddens me greatly that Jacob has not. When you have paid your respects to him, you may choose where you'd like him to lie and Thaddeus will have the grave dug. All of Develish will attend his funeral to say prayers for his soul.'

Thaddeus watched his mother's eyes well with tears, and knew it wouldn't be long before her grief became inconsolable. He made a small bow to Lady Anne. 'Does Master de Courtesmain have your permission to take over my duties, milady? He is more than able, and I cannot serve you as well as I should while this sorrow afflicts my family.'

She gave the permission readily but a tiny flutter of alarm beat in her breast as Thaddeus ushered Eva and Will from the room. There was something very final about the way her trusted friend had handed his responsibilities to the Frenchman.

Twelve

EVA'S HYSTERICAL WAILING BEAT UPON Thaddeus's ears as he half carried, half led her towards the church. Bondsmen and women stood back to let them pass, trying to catch Thaddeus's eye for an explanation. He ignored them, keeping his gaze lowered to hide his dislike of the way his mother was forcing him to hold her tight. It seemed to Thaddeus she was more intent on proving he still cared for her than expressing genuine anguish for Jacob.

Angry at being snubbed by his wife, Will pulled his other children from the crowd and shooed them in front of him, cuffing their heads when they showed signs of dawdling. In a detached way, Thaddeus viewed the absurd little procession for what it was: a piece of mummery. They were all just actors in a play whose only design was to obscure the truth.

He watched Edmund shake with terror as they approached, guessing the boy thought Eva's screaming had something to do with him; yet unless he'd disobeyed Thaddeus and opened the door, he was still unaware that Jacob was dead. It was the nature of youth to challenge the boundaries of behaviour but dread the shame of their behaviour being made public. Thaddeus gestured him aside. 'Wait here until I come out,' he murmured, raising the latch on the door. 'This family may enter but no one else.'

While his half-siblings dropped to their knees beside Jacob's body, and Eva flung herself on top of it, kissing the cold, white face, Thaddeus knocked on Father Anselm's door and called to the priest that he was needed. To his surprise, the old man appeared almost immediately, properly attired in his alb and embroidered cope, and with a linen stole about his neck. He beckoned Thaddeus to stoop. 'Does your mother weep because her son was murdered?' he whispered in the serf's ear.

'No, Father. She believes he died in an accidental fall and sheds tears for her loss.'

'Then God has given you wisdom. I prayed all night that you would see sense.'

He moved past Thaddeus to walk the length of the church, and Thaddeus could only admire the performance he put on as priest to a bereaving family. It seemed even God preferred lies to the truth if Father Anselm felt absolved of being party to a falsehood. Thaddeus remained where he was for a few minutes, head bowed in silent farewell to his brother, then slipped quietly outside and ordered Edmund to follow him.

He stopped outside the archway into the vegetable garden. 'Find Peter Catchpole and Joshua Buckler and bring them here,' he said. 'If they ask why, say only that I will explain when I return. Do you understand?'

The youth was quite clever enough to recognise that he was being sent to round up two of his rivals. 'What about Olyver and Ian Startout?'

'No questions, Edmund. Just do as you're bid.'

Once again, Thaddeus sought out Robert Startout to act as his messenger, ordering him to bring his cousins, Olyver and

Ian, to where the rebuilt raft was sitting on the moat bank by the corner of the house. He made a last visit to Sir Richard's chamber, stuffing his few possessions—his tools, his wooden bowl and spoon, the square of cloth he used for washing—into the leather bag that Lady Anne had given him when he was fourteen. He stood in the doorway for a moment, looking around the room, and then abandoned his home of the last two months without a backward glance.

The Startout twins were waiting for him when he re-emerged from the house. He slung his bag into the middle of the raft, made sure the ropes at either end were attached to stakes in the bank, then ordered the boys to help him push it down the mud bank into the water. Only the timbers riding above the surface had been burnt by the fire arrows. The submerged beams had remained intact, and it had been a simple task for Thaddeus and Gyles to enter the water, attach ropes and heave the structure onto dry land. Since that made it easier to carry the raft out of sight of men like Lord Bourne and since there wasn't enough planking in the compound to make such repairs again, Thaddeus had chosen to keep it out of the water after the rebuilding was complete.

Even dried out, it was heavy, and Ian grumbled when it failed to budge. 'We need more men,' he said, standing back and looking around. 'Where is everyone? And why are we doing this anyway? Does Lady Anne know you're planning to cross, Thaddeus?'

Thaddeus ignored him, using his own strength to set the structure moving and needing only Olyver's help to keep the momentum going. He slipped the ropes from the stakes and walked the raft to where Hugh de Courtesmain had sat between the north-west wall of the house and the water, kneeling down to thrust the chisel from his belt into the narrow strip of grass as a temporary mooring post. He kept hold of both ropes and ordered the boys to join him. They came reluctantly.

Ian, in the lead as usual, challenged Thaddeus again. 'You'll lose my father's respect when I tell him you made us do something wrong. He won't lick your arse so much after this . . . and neither will Lady Anne.'

Thaddeus whipped out a hand. 'Don't ever question me again,' he said, grabbing the boy by the back of the neck and forcing him to his knees. 'When I want your opinion, I'll ask for it.'

Ian tried to wrestle himself free. 'You can't tell me what to do,' he growled. 'A Startout's above a Thurkell bastard any day. You're only where you are because Lady Anne has a soft spot for you. Everyone knows it.'

Thaddeus moved so fast that the boy was in the water before he knew it. 'Can he swim?' he asked Olyver, watching Ian's thrashing arms.

'No.'

'Get on the raft.' He waited until Olyver had scrambled aboard then loosened the ropes between his fingers. 'Keep his head above water. If you can't haul him out yourself, support him while I pull you back in again.'

Heart in mouth, Olyver flung himself flat on the planking and reached for his twin's flailing hands. He wanted to call out that he couldn't swim either, and that if Ian pulled him in, they'd both be in trouble, but he was too afraid. Any care or kinship Thaddeus had ever felt for either of them seemed to have gone. His face had been without expression when he'd lifted Ian bodily from the ground and thrown him into the water as if he were discarding a piece of rubbish and not another human being.

He cupped his brother's head in his hands, but when he turned towards Thaddeus to urge him to pull them to the bank, there was no sign of the tall serf anywhere. He had left them stranded in the middle of the moat, moored only to a single chisel and drifting out of sight of anyone in the courtyard, quite careless of whether Ian was saved or not.

ɕ૦ઝ

Peter Catchpole and Joshua Buckler were bombarding Edmund with questions in the herb garden, bored with his muttered refusals to give answers.

'Maybe it has something to do with the Thurkells,' Peter said. 'Why did they all troop off to the church like that? What was Eva wailing about?'

'I don't know,' said Edmund grimly. 'You'll have to wait for Thaddeus.' He looked up in relief as footsteps approached and Thaddeus appeared in the archway. 'He's here. You can ask him.'

But they were disappointed. No explanations were forthcoming, only orders to collect their possessions from their parents' huts and bring them to the front door of the house. Joshua Buckler, a ginger-headed youth with a face full of freckles, was about to ask why, but he changed his mind when Thaddeus fixed him with an unfriendly gaze. He'd always thought Thaddeus had a soft spot for him—they were cousins of a sort through his father's relationship to Will—but there was no liking in Thaddeus's eyes now.

'You have the time it takes you to put your things together and run to the house,' he told them. 'No more. Whoever is last will not eat today.'

Edmund, who had good reason to believe that Thaddeus meant what he said, took to his heels immediately, and the other two, spurred by his example, weren't far behind. Thaddeus followed them into the courtyard, paused to make sure the raft was still obscured by the house, then entered the great hall and headed towards the kitchen. He stood out of sight of those inside, watching the bustle of preparation for the first meal of the day at noon. Some women slapped and kneaded dough, others were plucking chickens or filling cauldrons with water from the well.

Thaddeus satisfied himself that Lady Anne was amongst them before walking to the steward's office. As he'd hoped, Hugh de Courtesmain was inside, acquainting himself with the day's rosters. He looked up when Thaddeus entered. 'Is all well at the church?' he asked.

'As well as it can be,' Thaddeus answered. He spoke in French so that Hugh would fully understand what he said. 'I have a message for Lady Eleanor before she and her mother attend Jacob's funeral. Will you deliver it in case I'm too busy to do it myself?'

Hugh nodded. 'What do you want me to say?'

'"Allow my brother to rest in peace."' He shook his head at the look of enquiry on the other man's face. 'Lady Eleanor will understand the meaning if you tell her it comes from me. I have a message for Lady Anne also.' He paused, thinking of all the things he'd like to say but couldn't. '"Light a candle for each of us when you light one for Jacob."'

Hugh frowned. 'You can't ask such a thing, Thurkell. We're all sorry about your brother's death, but Lady Anne would be profligate to sacrifice two hundred candles to his memory.'

Thaddeus stood with his head bowed. 'You're right,' he said. 'It's a waste to burn a flame unless it shows the way home. Please tell Lady Anne I'm sorry to have made the request.'

'You talk in riddles,' said Hugh tartly. 'There'll be no need for me to say anything. I won't pass on the message.'

The tall serf smiled slightly before moving to the door. 'The first sow should farrow tomorrow so make sure Adam Catchpole is on hand. He's the best pig man we have.'

Before he left the great hall, he walked to the area where the children slept and looked for the slate Isabella used to teach them their letters. It lay on top of her neat roll of straw with the chalk she used to mark it. He bent to slip two small squares of sealed parchment beneath it then turned on his heel and made for the door.

∽

The three youths were waiting for him outside, each accusing the others of being last to return. Thaddeus ordered them to silence and, with a glance behind to see if anyone was watching, shepherded them ahead of him around the corner of the house. Peter Catchpole and Joshua Buckler grinned at the sight of Olyver and Ian Startout sitting in cross-legged misery on the raft, but Edmund Trueblood felt a chill run up his spine. None of the fears he'd experienced that morning was as bad as his new conviction that Thaddeus intended to exile him and his erstwhile friends from the demesne, and in such a way that no one would see it happening.

His anxiety was mirrored in Olyver Startout's face. 'Thaddeus means to get rid of us,' he muttered to his twin.

Ian, white-faced and sodden from his immersion, peered at the group on the bank through half-closed lids. Frozen to the bone from the wind blowing down the valley, he was filled with regret after Olyver told him Jacob had been murdered. Most of all, he wished he could take back his angry words to Thaddeus, which he'd repeated parrot-fashion from listening to Eleanor. It was she who had filled his head with jealousy of Thaddeus and she who referred to the serf as 'the Thurkell bastard'.

He watched Thaddeus pull his chisel from the bank and wrap the mooring ropes around his fist. 'If he is, he's coming with us,' he muttered, his throat gravelly from coughing up water. 'He left his bag on the raft.'

'He can't make us go if we don't want to,' Olyver said urgently. 'Each of our fathers is more important than he is. We need to call out, alert them to what he's doing.'

'You'll take a ducking if you do.'

'Then we'll jump him. He's not strong enough to fight us all at the same time.'

Ian felt the raft begin to move as Thaddeus pulled on the ropes. '*You* jump him,' he snarled. 'It wasn't me who blabbed his mouth off . . . and it sure as Hell wasn't me who killed Jacob.'

They heard Thaddeus's dry laugh from the bank. 'We can hear you. The wind carries your voices. If you must fight, fight each other. It matters little to me if you drown in the moat. I imagine your father will fish your bodies out eventually.' He let the raft drift again. 'What's your pleasure?'

There was a short silence before Ian spoke. 'Is this punishment for Jacob?' he croaked. 'I swear to God I never laid a hand on him, Thaddeus. I didn't even know he was dead till Olyver told me.'

Out of the corner of his eye, Thaddeus saw a shocked Peter Catchpole take a step to the side as if he were about to flee. He caught hold of the boy's shirt and jerked him back. 'Are you another who's going to swear you had nothing to do with my brother's murder?' he demanded coldly.

Peter stared at him wildly. 'I don't—I didn't—' he stuttered. 'Is that why your mother was crying?'

Thaddeus turned to Joshua Buckler. 'What about you? How guilty are you of last night's events?'

Joshua's face paled beneath his freckles, his shock as apparent as Peter's. He shook his head vigorously, his mouth too dry to form any words.

'Who amongst you dares test his word against Lady Eleanor's?' Thaddeus asked, releasing Peter abruptly and bending to the task of pulling the raft towards the bank again. 'She will have invented a story of her own by now and it won't serve any of you well. If you're lucky, she'll claim she's never spoken to any of you and knows nothing about the fights you've been having. If you're not, she'll say she was dragged to the graveyard by Olyver and forced to watch Jacob being killed by Edmund to prevent him speaking of the rapes he'd witnessed.'

'That's not what happened,' protested Edmund.

Thaddeus gave an indifferent shrug. 'It's how she'll portray it if she's asked, and her word will carry more weight than yours. Father Anselm won't defend you. He has more chance of keeping his benefice if he says one of you killed Jacob.'

Edmund ran his tongue across his lips. 'He'll be lying.'

'He always does. You should have remembered that before you used his church as a bawdy house and passed Sir Richard's daughter from hand to hand like a common harlot.'

As if on cue, the bell began to toll behind them, signalling a death.

༅

Eleanor watched the raft cross the moat from the window in the end wall of her mother's chamber. She recognised the five youths accompanying Thaddeus but was quite ignorant of what this sudden departure meant. Having been too afraid to leave the room since Thaddeus had ordered her to return to it, all she knew was what she had been able to see and hear from the upper storey: Eva's loud wailing as Thaddeus led the Thurkells towards the church; his return with Edmund; the rounding-up of the other four boys; Ian's near drowning and the tolling of the bell.

When the raft reached the far side of the moat, all six disembarked and Thaddeus gave it a push to send it back to the middle. He looked briefly towards the demesne then headed through the peasant strips towards the village, beckoning to the others to follow. Eleanor would have remained watching if she hadn't heard her mother's footsteps on the stairs. Heart beating erratically, she flung herself on her straw mattress and pretended sleep.

'You must dress yourself, daughter,' Lady Anne said from the doorway. 'Father Anselm summons us to the funeral of a young bondsman. If you fail to attend, it will be noticed.'

Eleanor remained as she was with her back to her mother. Was there more? she wondered.

'Answer me, daughter. Do you not hear the bell? Do you not ask why it rings?'

'The death of a serf is no business of mine. I won't have known him.'

'Maybe not, but you will know his name. It's Thaddeus's half-brother, Jacob Thurkell. You will pay respect to the family alongside the rest of Develish.'

'What clothes should I wear?'

'Something plain.' Lady Anne paused. 'Does the death of a young man trouble you so little that you don't ask how he died, Eleanor?'

The girl took a small piece of straw between her thumb and forefinger. 'How did he die, Mother?' she asked, poking the reed between two floorboards and snapping it in two.

'In a fall from the southern guard step.'

There was a brief hesitation before Eleanor spoke again. 'Who told you of it?'

But Lady Anne wasn't inclined to answer. 'Make haste,' she said. 'It would be impolite to keep Jacob's family waiting.'

ઉન્જ

Lady Anne was puzzled by her daughter's choice of clothing when Eleanor presented herself downstairs in an embroidered gown, her forehead adorned by the gold circlet her father had given her. Gone, it seemed, was her recent affection for homespun kirtles; in its place was the sort of ill-judged flamboyance Sir Richard would have displayed at a serf's funeral. But why?

'At least keep your eyes lowered,' Lady Anne said. 'Jacob's death may mean nothing to you but it matters to his parents.'

'You shouldn't care so much, Mother,' the girl said dismissively. 'Neither of us will be welcome. Eva hates you for taking Thaddeus from her. She'll hate you even more when she finds he's left Develish.'

Lady Anne frowned. 'What are you talking about?'

Eleanor hid her triumph. 'Did you not know? I saw him cross the moat with five serf boys before you came to fetch me. I thought he did it with your permission but it seems strange to me now.' She examined her mother's face with feigned curiosity. 'Why would he not wait to see his brother buried?'

'Which five boys went with him?'

'I don't know,' said Eleanor with a careless shrug. 'They all look the same to me.' She shifted her attention to Hugh, who stepped through the open door as the tolling bell fell silent and made a bow to her mother. 'Perhaps you should ask Master de Courtesmain.'

Hugh ignored her to address Lady Anne. 'Father Anselm requests your presence in the church, milady.'

'Of course. Has a plot been chosen and a grave dug?'

The steward nodded. 'I oversaw the task myself.'

'Why did Thaddeus not do it?'

'I don't know, milady. It may have escaped his mind. It's an hour since I saw him.' He glanced at Eleanor. 'He asked me to give you a message before the funeral, Lady Eleanor, in case he was too busy to deliver it himself.'

The girl looked uncomfortable suddenly, a fact that didn't escape either Hugh's or Lady Anne's notice. 'I will hear it later in private.'

'There was no instruction about privacy, milady, only that you should receive it before the service. The message runs: "Allow my brother to rest in peace." Thaddeus said you would understand the meaning if you knew it came from him.'

ର୍ଦ୍ଧ

The church was too small to take the whole of Develish at one time so half the bondsmen were gathered around the graves and pig pens at the front. They stepped back to let Lady Anne pass before bowing their heads in preparation for prayer. Inside it was the same. All eyes were fixed on the floor, showing deference to the hastily made coffin in front of the altar. If anyone was aware that Thaddeus was absent, it wasn't obvious. Even Eva seemed too sunk in misery to look for him, perhaps believing he was waiting outside to lower his brother into the ground.

Lady Anne knelt in her prayer stall at the side of the chancel, grateful that she had an excuse to close her eyes and think. She was at a loss for what to do. Every instinct told her to send Gyles Startout in pursuit of Thaddeus and demand explanations, but a horrible fear held her back. She listened to the rustle of Eleanor's gown as the girl knelt beside her, heard the purity of her voice as she chanted her responses to Father Anselm more loudly than anyone else. And she wondered if a woman had ever had so much cause to distrust a child as she distrusted hers.

Allow my brother to rest in peace . . .

She remembered the troubled look she'd seen on Thaddeus's face that morning, and the qualms she'd felt when he'd handed his duties to Hugh de Courtesmain. He knew then he was going to leave, she thought, relying on the shock and confusion of Jacob's death to cover his departure. But why, and why take five young serfs with him?

So much of her suspicion was focused on Eleanor. If the girl had seen Thaddeus leave, why had she not mentioned it when Lady Anne went to rouse her? Why wait until she came downstairs? And what had prompted Eleanor to dress in all her finery? Was it Jacob's death that gave her cause for celebration? Or Thaddeus's departure?

At some point during the liturgy, perhaps when Father Anselm intoned the commandments, Lady Anne recognised that Thaddeus must have lied about the events of the previous night. It wouldn't have taken him long to discover that Jacob had died of a stab wound once he'd carried the body into the church and lit the candles. So why pretend he was worried about the pestilence? And why wait until daylight to make the death known to Lady Anne and his parents? Even stranger, why had Father Anselm agreed to the delay? Why anoint the body but not insist on Eva being present while it was done?

Her mind struggled for answers, but they all led to one conclusion: that Jacob had not died by accident and Thaddeus knew it. He was well enough versed in English law to know that responsibility for crime and punishment lay with the liege lord, or in serious felonies with the High Sheriff and the Courts of Assize; but since those authorities were beyond his reach—and the liege lord was dead—the burden of trial and sentencing would have fallen on Lady Anne. And what sentence could she have passed on a murderer except death by hanging?

She recognised, as both Thaddeus and Father Anselm had done, that even to look for the perpetrator would divide and destroy the community. Suspicion would fall on everyone. Fingers would be pointed as old animosities surfaced, and the harmony so many had worked to create would be replaced by discord. But how much more damaging that discord would become, Lady Anne thought, if the killer was found and punished. Jacob's reputation for thieving and his parents' laziness made them widely disliked. To order the taking of another life to appease the Thurkells would not go down well.

Lady Anne didn't want to believe that Thaddeus was his brother's killer, but his departure made her doubt him. Why had he left the demesne if he had nothing to answer for? She wouldn't be questioning Jacob's death at all if Thaddeus had stayed—and nor would anyone else—but his actions seemed likely to spark the very distrust he had wanted to avoid when he claimed the death was an accident.

Her brain grew tired of trying to understand. She had too many questions and too few solutions, and the pain she felt in her heart at Thaddeus's desertion without explanation or farewell was overwhelming. She shied away from the reasons why, telling herself she had come to rely on him more than she realised.

As the long service finally ended, she performed the rites demanded of a liege lord, offering thanks for Jacob's short life as his coffin was lowered into the ground, giving a shilling on behalf of his soul to Father Anselm and dispensing pennies in Jacob's name to every bondsman in Develish as she passed amongst them on her way out of the graveyard. She was thanked by all, particularly Will and Eva Thurkell, to whom she gave sixpence, but she had no illusions that her generosity would prevent tongues from wagging when the news became known that Thaddeus and five young serfs had left the demesne.

'You shouldn't have wasted our money like that,' Eleanor hissed in her ear as they walked back to the house. 'It's not as if anyone liked Jacob. He was always stealing.'

Lady Anne's step slowed. 'I didn't know that,' she lied.

Eleanor's response was scathing. '*Everyone* knows it, Mother. They must have thought you mad to give him a funeral fit for a lord. You didn't make offerings for my father but you showered them out for Thaddeus's thieving brother.'

'It seemed the right thing to do.' Lady Anne stopped to look across the moat towards the highway, wondering if Thaddeus had already left the valley. 'How do you know so much about Jacob, daughter? It's barely three hours since you told me all serfs look the same.'

'The servants talk. I can't help overhearing what they say. They'll be laughing at you behind their hands for giving sixpence to the harlot.'

Her mother glanced at her. 'And at you for mistaking a funeral for a wedding, Eleanor. What is it that gives you reason to rejoice?'

Eleanor was spared having to answer by Isabella's quiet arrival at Lady Anne's side. She saw the girl before her mother did, and this sudden reminder that Isabella existed brought a look of disquiet to her face. The expression was fleeting but it was seen by Lady Anne.

She smiled at her maid. 'Did you want me?' she asked.

'I found this under my slate, milady. The inscription on the front says "For Lady Anne".' She handed over a square of parchment.

Lady Anne recognised the writing as Thaddeus's. She was quite sure Isabella had, too, since she showed no curiosity about who had left it for her to find. She broke the wax seal and cast her eyes over the letter before looking at Eleanor. 'You seem anxious,' she said. 'Why so, daughter? Do you want to know what is written here?'

The girl made no reply.

'It's from Thaddeus. He lists the five youths who have left the demesne with him—Edmund Trueblood, Olyver and Ian Startout, Peter Catchpole and Joshua Buckler—and apologises that they didn't take leave of their families.' She looked enquiringly at Isabella. 'Did your brothers tell your parents they were going, child?'

'I don't believe so, milady. My mother was asking for Ian only moments ago.'

'And what about you? Were you told?'

There was the tiniest of hesitations. 'No, milady.'

Lady Anne knew she was lying, but not Eleanor. Eleanor felt emboldened enough to raise her head. 'Is that all?' she asked.

'What more would you expect, daughter?'

'An excuse for why they've absconded. If my father were alive, he'd send soldiers after them.'

Lady Anne glanced again at Thaddeus's note. The words he'd written were so reasonable that she would have had no grounds for suspicion over Jacob's death if this was the first she'd learnt of his departure. It was Eleanor's sly pleasure at telling her something she didn't know that had caused her doubts.

'Why do you accuse them of absconding?' she asked mildly. 'It seems a strange interpretation to put on their actions.'

'They left without your permission. What is that if it's not absconding?'

'It depends what you understand by the word. I have only known serfs to run away in the hope of avoiding justice or persecution.' She studied her daughter's face. 'Can you think of a reason why Thaddeus and his companions should have feared such thing—so much that they'd rather risk their lives on the pestilence than stay within the safety of the demesne?'

Eleanor looked away. 'Who knows why serfs do what they do? Father said the only thing they understand is the whip.' She nodded to the parchment in Lady Anne's hand. 'Blame Thaddeus for refusing you an explanation. It shows how arrogant he is and how little he respects you.'

'But he gives a *fine* explanation, daughter,' Lady Anne answered with a feigned lightness of tone. 'He describes qualities in his companions that Sir Richard would not have recognised since he had none of them. Courage . . . thoughtfulness . . . self-sacrifice . . . generosity of spirit. Thaddeus writes that they go in search of supplies so that the rest of us may live.' She paused. 'Perhaps you're unaware that our stores will be gone by late December and brave men are needed to find more? We'll starve otherwise.'

'It's not my business to count sacks of grain. That's for you to do.'

'And every serf here. They understand hunger better than you do, Eleanor. You should be thanking Thaddeus, not accusing him of arrogance.' Lady Anne placed a hand on Isabella's shoulder. 'This child's twin brothers go for their father Gyles, who was first on the list to leave.'

Eleanor stared at Isabella with dislike. 'Only because Thaddeus forced them,' she said spitefully. 'They didn't go willingly.'

Isabella ran her tongue across her lips. She addressed Lady Anne. 'I'm sure they did, milady. They told me several times they'd go in Father's place if they could.'

'You lie,' sneered Eleanor contemptuously. 'Thaddeus threw Ian into the moat because he refused to get on the raft, and he'd have drowned if Olyver hadn't saved him. Neither of them wanted to go . . . and nor did the others.'

Lady Anne tucked the parchment inside her kirtle. 'What interesting stories you tell, daughter,' she murmured. 'You change your mind so frequently I'm at a loss to know what to believe. This morning you couldn't tell one serf from another yet now you seem able to differentiate between identical twins. I wasn't aware you knew the names of Isabella's brothers; you take so little interest in bondsmen.'

Eleanor hunched her shoulders, fixing menacing eyes on the maid. 'Ask this girl how I know. She bores me stiff with the way she prattles on about her stupid family.'

There was only the briefest of hesitations before Isabella answered. 'It's quite easy to tell the twins apart, milady. They've never wanted to look the same so Mama dyes Ian's tunics red with madder and Olyver's blue with woad.' She forced a smile to her lips. 'Ian lets his hair touch his shoulders because he thinks it makes him handsome, but Olyver cuts his short.'

'There!' said Eleanor. 'Now do you believe me? All I told you was what I saw from the window, and it's not my fault if it's different from what Thaddeus pretends. You shouldn't have favoured him so much if you'd wanted to keep his obedience. He does as he pleases because he thinks himself your equal.'

Lady Anne tried to imagine shy Isabella ever 'prattling on' to Eleanor, but the wretchedness in the maid's face made her realise how frightened she must be for her brothers. Whatever the truth behind this sudden departure, Thaddeus had placed himself and five young boys in terrible peril. And for that she cursed him. He asked too much of her to bear the burden of their families' grief while begging her to praise their courage and give their ill-starred venture her blessing.

She had placed all her trust in him, yet this sudden departure said the trust was not returned. Nevertheless . . .

She reached for Isabella's hand. 'You mustn't worry for Ian and Olyver, child. Thaddeus promises to return with them inside a fortnight and I have every confidence they will come back to us in good health. He has more knowledge than most about how disease is spread and will not endanger their lives unnecessarily.'

The firm certainty of the girl's reply surprised her and she wondered why the words Isabella used were so similar to those in Thaddeus's letter.

'Indeed he will not, milady. He is wise as you, and would not have allowed these boys to accompany him if he thought they would come to harm. They are the sons of your leading serfs and will acquit themselves bravely.' In an unexpected gesture of appeal, Isabella dropped a deep curtsey. 'They will have left in secret because they knew their mothers would stop them otherwise. Please have faith in Thaddeus, milady. He has proven his allegiance to everyone in Develish these last few months . . . but to you most of all.'

For Lady Anne

My Most Revered Lady,
I have departed the demesne this morning with Edmund
Trueblood, Olyver and Ian Startout, Peter Catchpole and
Joshua Buckler. They have offered to travel with me for
the good of Develish, but I beg you to accept my sincere
apologies for leaving without the permission of you or
their parents.

I know how reluctant you are that anyone should
make this journey—particularly the leading serfs on
whom you depend—but the need to replenish our stores
grows stronger by the day. It is the sons of these men who
have volunteered in their place, and they have chosen to
leave in secret while my brother is buried to spare their
mothers the pain of parting.

My own mother is already destroyed by the loss
of Jacob and would prevent my departure if she could.
I believe you would too, Dear Lady, even though you
understand better than she how urgently we need news
of the world outside. Please tell our families to expect us
again within two weeks. I pray there will be reason to
rejoice when that day comes.

My young companions have good hearts and
undertake this venture out of love for you and the people
of Develish. Please find it in your heart to think well of
them and praise their courage to their families. We beg
your forgiveness for leaving, but we go in the hope that we
have your blessing.

Your obedient servant,
Thaddeus Thurkell

For Isabella

My Good Friend,
I have never needed your kindness and wisdom more.
Give the second parchment to Lady Anne and lend your
support to the story I have given her that your brothers
and their friends have chosen to take their fathers' places
in the search for supplies.

I have asked Lady Anne to praise their courage and
give us her blessing but do not be offended on our behalf
if she feels unable to do so. I've begged her to believe that
we go in secret to spare our mothers' grief, but she may be
persuaded otherwise if Lady Eleanor uses our absence to
speak against us.

Dear Friend, please believe that I do what I do to
free your brothers and their friends from intrigue, not to
ensnare them in more. As far as it is in my power, I will
keep them safe. If our venture is successful, the reasons
I have given for our departure will be accepted on our
return even if they are questioned now.

Protect yourself by saying nothing of what you
witnessed this morning with Lady Eleanor. It is better for
all if Develish remains ignorant of the conversation. You
may have your own ideas of what happened last night
but do not speak of them to anyone, particularly Lady
Eleanor, who cannot be trusted.

Your brothers are free of any grave sin, as are their
friends and I. Believe in us and pray for our safe return.

Your obedient servant,
Thaddeus Thurkell

Would I could show my distress as openly as Eva Thurkell. She howls for Thaddeus even more loudly than she howled for Jacob. The death of her younger son was quickly forgotten once she learnt of her firstborn's departure. Poor Jacob. His thieving made him greatly disliked. Whether he died by accident, as Thaddeus wants me to believe, or through malice at the hand of another, his passing is barely mourned.

I can't decide who deserves my curses more—Eleanor or Thaddeus. I fear the one was responsible for Jacob's death and the other, knowing it, has chosen to leave rather than have the truth prised from him. But why, oh why, did Thaddeus not share his concerns with me before departing? Does he believe Eleanor took Jacob's life deliberately and wanted to spare me the pain of sitting in judgement on her? I fear so. Yet I struggle to accept she would kill another without reason. For all her raging against me and our people since her father's death, she is surely not so lost that she would commit murder?

I don't begin to understand why Thaddeus has taken 5 serf boys with him but it cannot be chance that they are the sons of my leading serfs. Thaddeus has spoken often of his admiration for these men, and I believe he would spare them shame if he could. But shame for what? Were their sons participants in

Jacob's death? Surely not. It may be that one was involved—but not all 5.

The letter Thaddeus left for me asked that I promote a fable that he and his companions had my blessing to leave Develish in search of supplies. For the sake of their parents, I have done so. Perhaps Thaddeus knows my daughter better than I because praise for the boys has reduced Eleanor to silence. All her earlier joy at their departure has vanished.

Yet she was very intent on maligning them at the outset. Did she hope accusations against runaway serfs would go unchallenged? If so, she clearly hadn't expected Isabella to counter with such a moving defence of Thaddeus's loyalty and her twin brothers' courage.

Thirteen

NONE OF THE BOYS SPOKE as Thaddeus pulled the raft across the moat and ordered them to jump off on the other side. Edmund Trueblood, Peter Catchpole and Joshua Buckler were still rocked by the news that Jacob was dead—worse, murdered—while Ian Startout was sunk in cold, wet misery and Olyver was wondering how he and his twin would survive without tools or food. At least the others had been given time to pack, judging by the bags they were carrying. He wanted to say Thaddeus was being unfair, but he didn't dare. The sound of the bell tolling for Jacob's funeral was a grim warning not to test the man's patience too far.

Once ashore, Thaddeus cut the ropes and released the raft to drift back into the middle of the moat. He didn't want Gyles coming after them while they were still in the valley or marauders gaining easy access to the demesne while everyone was at prayer. Perhaps the boys hoped for a pursuit, because they stood in melancholy despair, staring towards the house, only rousing themselves when Thaddeus set off at a loping run through the peasant strips, ordering them to keep pace with him or fend for themselves. They ran smartly to catch up. Each might feel he'd done nothing wrong—or nothing that merited exile—but they all feared being abandoned to the pestilence. Not one doubted that Thaddeus meant what he said. He'd always been withdrawn—a boy of secrets grown into a man of secrets—but this callous indifference to his companions was new, and it made him a persuasive leader. They were afraid of incurring his displeasure and being left to die by the wayside of putrid pustules and blackened blood.

When they reached the burnt-out remains of Develish village, Thaddeus led them to his own family's hut. Parts of the clay walls still stood, but the timbers and thatch had been reduced to ash and charcoal. Thaddeus used his feet to clear the debris from one corner of the earthen floor, and ordered the Startout twins to start digging. 'Your father wasn't idle after Sir Richard died,' he told them. 'He buried stores from John Trueblood's cottage in here so that scouts would have rations to begin their journey. Dig up what you can.'

'We have no tools,' protested Olyver. 'You let Edmund, Peter and Joshua fetch theirs but not me and Ian. We haven't even got spoons or bowls. What are we supposed to use?'

'Your hands.' Thaddeus took his chisel from his belt. 'You can break the clods with this. The rest of you search through the other buildings.' He gestured around the village. 'Look for anything useful that escaped the flames—metal pots, clay jars, tools and blades. Bring what you find to the well, and await my return.'

'Where are you going?' Edmund asked nervously.

Thaddeus nodded towards a far field. 'To round up the pack ponies and horses that came back with Sir Richard,' he said. 'We won't get far on foot.'

It was a reasonable explanation, but the five boys watched in disquiet as he set off. They could see he had no ropes or halters, and their anxiety grew when he abandoned the path to the field where the animals grazed and headed towards the western woods. He kept low, using the rows of beans and vetch in the peasant strips to hide his progress from watchers behind the moat. They waited until he forded Devil's Brook and disappeared amongst the trees, and then rounded on each other in recrimination.

'What if he plans to leave us here?' Olyver demanded. 'Someone should have gone with him.'

'No one held you back,' retorted his twin acidly. 'Why didn't you go? It was your big mouth that got us into this mess in the first place.'

'Stop arguing!' snapped Peter Catchpole. 'I don't understand what this is all about. Why are we here?'

'Jacob was murdered last night,' said Ian. 'Thaddeus found him dead in the graveyard with a stab wound in his side . . . assuming what Olyver told me is true.'

Olyver clenched his fists. 'Why would I lie?'

Peter glared from one to the other. 'Who cares if Jacob's dead? It's not my bloody fault. *I* didn't kill him. I was with my father on the western step all night.' He jerked his head towards the demesne. 'I say we return to the raft and get back across the moat before anyone misses us.'

'We can't. Thaddeus cast it adrift. Do you know how to swim? Joshua? Edmund?'

They shook their heads.

'It's a bad idea, anyway,' said Edmund, hunching his shoulders. 'Everyone's going to know the truth by now. Think of the questions we'll be asked.'

'Well, I'm damned if I'll be held guilty,' said Joshua angrily. 'I didn't know anything bad had happened until Ian started whining that *he* hadn't done it.'

'Don't point the finger at me,' snarled Ian with equal anger. 'Edmund's the only one who had a fight with Jacob last night.'

Edmund shook his head. 'It wasn't a fight,' he said. 'I boxed the silly churl's ears and he backed away before I could hit him again.'

'So who gave you the black eye?' demanded Peter, pointing at Edmund's battered face.

'Olyver.' Edmund glanced at his opponent. 'If I find you told Thaddeus I killed his brother, I'll have your guts for lying. He damn near strangled me this morning because he thought I'd done it, and it's only because he realised I didn't know Jacob was dead that he let me go. How come you knew if the rest of us didn't?'

Olyver kicked at a stone. 'Thaddeus told me. He dragged me out of bed before it was light and took me to the graveyard. He knew I'd been in the church last night . . . though I don't know how. He showed me where he'd found Jacob near the sheep pens and said he'd been stabbed. There was a knife lying in the grass.'

'Whose knife?'

'It looked like Jacob's, but I swore it wasn't you or me who used it on him. It had to be someone who came along afterwards.'

The silence that followed was finally broken by Peter Catchpole. 'It doesn't make sense. If none of us is guilty, why did we have to leave the demesne?'

Edmund rubbed the bruised muscles on his arms. 'Because of Eleanor,' he said. 'She was in the church last night and Thaddeus was furious about it. I expect he's hoping that if we're not around to talk—and Eleanor stays silent—Lady Anne won't find out about the other stuff.'

'I wouldn't have talked anyway,' retorted Joshua indignantly. 'I only went with her a couple of times and I sure as blazes didn't know she was in the church last night.'

'Me neither,' said Peter. 'It's unfair to include us.'

'That's the right of it,' agreed Ian, tugging his wet shirt away from his skin. 'We get sent out to catch the pestilence and scutty Eleanor gets to go on pretending butter won't melt in her mouth.'

'You were happy enough to set your cock crowing for her two days ago,' said Edmund sarcastically.

Ian ignored him. 'I called Thaddeus a bastard because of her. That's all she ever talks about—the Thurkell bastard. It gets into your brain after a while. She'll do the same to us, call us anything she likes—murderers, rapists, thieves—and the whole of Develish will believe her if she whispers it into their ears often enough.'

Olyver turned on him angrily. 'Eleanor's not to blame for this. It's Thaddeus who forced us to leave . . . and we all know why. He'll see off anyone he thinks is competition.'

Peter eyed him scornfully. 'He can't stand Eleanor. It's Lady Anne he admires.'

'It's more than admiration,' Olyver retorted. 'He's looking to make himself master of Develish.'

Perhaps Ian's near-drowning experience had given him a little wisdom, because he was quick to recognise the voice of Eleanor in his twin's words. 'Don't you think the rest of us were given the same story every time she gave us a peek at her skinny little teats, brother? You've got your brains in your rod if you imagine differently.' He jumped back smartly as Olyver balled his hands into fists.

Edmund stepped between them. 'There's no point fighting,' he told Olyver. 'At least recognise that Thaddeus has made himself as much of an exile as he's made us.'

'He'll have his reasons,' the other boy said sullenly.

'Maybe so, but he can't be master of Develish if he's not at Lady Anne's side. He's losing more than us by leaving. There aren't many serfs who're clever enough to be steward of a demesne. It'll be Master de Courtesmain performing the task now. He's the only one can read and write as well as Thaddeus.'

'And you can bet Eleanor will switch her favours to him,' said Ian. 'If Lady Anne's wise, she'll make one of our fathers her steward. She'll never be able to trust the Frenchman the way she trusted Thaddeus.'

'Do you think he told her he was leaving?' asked Joshua.

Ian shook his head. 'We wouldn't have had to go in secret if he had.' He paused, working through thoughts in his mind. 'Olyver said Thaddeus threatened to put him on trial for murder if Edmund's story didn't tally with his own. I think that's what this is about.'

'But our stories *were* the same,' protested Edmund. 'We both told him we didn't kill Jacob. He could have put us to the question in front of Lady Anne, and we wouldn't have said any different.'

'Right . . . but someone stabbed Jacob—and according to Olyver, the only other person at the church was Eleanor. Would you have wanted to say *that* to Lady Anne? Do you think she'd take the word of a couple of serfs over her own daughter's? Thaddeus warned you as much.'

There was a short, startled silence.

'Are you saying Eleanor killed Jacob?' asked Edmund.

'She must have done, if it wasn't you or Twin . . . unless you want to accuse the priest.' Ian glanced towards the demesne. 'That's why we're here and Eleanor's in there. Thaddeus is saving Lady Anne from having to condemn her own daughter as a murderess. There's no one left who knows—or can guess—what really happened.'

∞

Thaddeus saw relief on the faces of the five youths when he rode into the village on Sir Richard of Develish's charger with three horses and three ponies in tow. He noticed that a pecking order had been established, with Ian at the top. He had no quarrel with that. The lad had a quick mind and a strong character, and he was a natural leader whether he chose to obey orders or not. Indeed, if anything had surprised Thaddeus that morning it was to hear Olyver Startout name his twin as one of Lady Eleanor's acolytes. He found it as hard to picture Ian demeaning himself before Sir Richard's daughter as he did to picture their younger, but much wiser, sister Isabella doing it.

Thaddeus didn't doubt their blood ran hot to be noticed by Eleanor—there was no questioning her beauty—but he had yet to understand her reasons for encouraging them. He dismissed as naive Edmund's belief that she'd wanted a champion, for no girl, however foolish, would think a half-grown boy would dare challenge a member of Lady Anne's council. He'd racked his brain most of the night, trying to work out her purpose, but the best he could come up with was that she'd wanted to destroy the harmony her mother had worked so hard to create. There would be no surer way to split the community than to make accusations of rape against the sons of the leading serfs and force Milady to sit in judgement on them. Even in the strange times they lived in, and even if Lady Anne suspected Eleanor of lying, she could not take the word of a bonded man against Sir Richard of Develish's daughter.

Thaddeus had cursed the youths roundly for making him party to their sordid games, but he felt a weight of responsibility now when he saw how young they looked. Edmund Trueblood was the tallest, brown-haired and square-faced, but he was growing too fast and his hands hung from his wrists like paddles. Peter

Catchpole, almost as tall with dark down growing on his cheeks, was scowling like a two-year-old who'd had his favourite toy removed; and Joshua Buckler, the smallest and slightest with ginger hair and freckled skin, looked ready to cry with nervousness. As for the twins, their belligerent desire to prove themselves different from each other showed in the way they were standing as far from each other as they could.

It was clear that some sort of argument had been raging, but Thaddeus gave no sign of being aware of it as he handed the rope halters of the other animals to Ian before jumping down from the charger. Whatever disputes they had must be settled between themselves. All four horses, including the charger, were saddled and bridled, but the three ponies—one of them Lady Eleanor's bay jennet—wore no harness at all. 'Two of us will have to ride bareback,' he said. 'There are no saddles this side of the moat except those which came home with Sir Richard.'

'Where were they?' Ian asked.

'Your father left them near his camp in the woodland. He used the time after Sir Richard died to hide everything of a value from passing thieves.'

'What if he'd succumbed to the pestilence himself? You wouldn't have known where to look.'

Thaddeus thought of the times he'd crossed the moat at night to speak with Gyles in secret. 'He showed me when I came out here to speak with him. I learnt a great deal from your father—as you would have done, if you'd bothered to listen to him on his return.' He eased a sacking bag from the charger's saddle and laid it on the ground to open it. 'He hid these weapons along with the saddles. Four swords, three short bows and twenty arrows. Be wise in what you select. You know your strengths and weaknesses from the training Gyles gave you. Sir Richard's sword is the longest and heaviest. Whoever chooses it will need to practise hard in order to find its reach and balance.' He glanced around their worried faces. 'If none of you is ready to fight, then say so now. I'd as soon travel alone as take frightened boys in need of protection.'

There was a brief silence before the other four looked to Ian to speak for them. 'Who do you want us to fight?'

'Anyone who threatens us.'

'Where are we going?'

Thaddeus jerked his chin towards the southern horizon. 'Out there, in search of supplies and news. Your fathers expected to go but I've volunteered you instead. You can behave like men or you can behave like children. I'm not your nurse and I'm not your keeper. If you'd rather crawl back on your hands and knees to pay court to Lady Eleanor and answer questions about my brother's death, feel free to do so. Otherwise, choose your weapons.'

'Sir Richard's sword should be yours.'

Thaddeus shook his head. 'You've all had more training than I have. Edmund's the most proficient with a wooden blade so I suggest he takes it. The others select from the rest . . . but recognise that what you choose must be carried across your backs. Understood?'

They nodded.

'The sack is for food and anything else you've managed to salvage from the ashes. We'll strap that to the spare pony.' He assessed the five boys. 'You two look the lightest,' he said, pointing to Peter and Joshua, 'so you'll ride the jennet and the other pony. It means you'll be the first to go bareback, but we'll switch the saddles around after a couple of hours. If you're confident of controlling your mounts with just a rope halter, then do so; if not, we'll lead you.'

The boys shifted uncomfortably, afraid the others would laugh if they asked to be led.

'You'd do well to be honest,' said Thaddeus unemotionally. 'If you're thrown and your animals bolt, you'll be left behind.' He glanced around the group. 'The same is true for the rest of you. You'll prove your worth through wisdom, not false bravado. Do I make myself clear?'

They nodded.

'Good.' He handed the reins of the charger to Olyver and ordered him and Edmund to take over care of the other animals from Ian. 'Show me what you've found,' he said.

Ian took him to the well, where a sack of dried beans, another of dried plums and a crock of salted pork stood amongst an assortment of beaten metal dishes and a handful of wide-necked earthenware flagons. 'There were only four that weren't broken,' Ian said, indicating the flagons. 'We've washed them out and filled them with water but there's nothing to use for stoppers. They'll be empty within a hundred yards if we carry them on horseback.'

Thaddeus nodded, wishing he knew more about the country beyond Develish. It was one thing to gaze towards a purple horizon as a child, dreaming of taking a ship across an ocean, quite another to know what lay between the demesne and the coast when he'd never once travelled out of the valley. It made no difference which vantage point he had chosen on the surrounding hills; all he had seen were further hills. It had led him to picture Dorseteshire as a lady's gown dropped upon the ground, with intricate folds running in different directions—though whether each valley had a watercourse, he didn't know.

He had wrung what information he could out of Gyles Startout during the many conversations he'd had with him, but, despite the numerous journeys Gyles had made as part of Sir Richard's retinue, his knowledge of watercourses was limited to the estates that lay along the roads. He knew that Devil's Brook followed the highway to a larger river which ran through Afpedle and was crossed by a ford at Athelhelm, but nothing about streams or springs elsewhere. 'We replenished our pitchers at the manors we visited,' he had explained. 'Sir Richard never slept in the open air. He expected to be fed good food and ale every night from whichever lord he descended upon.'

'Did you never see ponds or lakes in the open countryside?'

Gyles shook his head. 'Only in villages where the ground has been cleared and cultivated. The rest is woodland and you can't tell what's hidden amongst trees from the road. I saw a flood at Winterburn once when the rains fell and the brook overflowed. The land stood under water for days.'

'Where's Winterburn?'

'North-west of Melcombe.'

'How did you find your way there?'

Gyles smiled at Thaddeus's ignorance of journey-making. 'The same way a man finds his way anywhere—we followed the road. It's hard to go wrong. Merchants, pedlars and drovers travel them every day.'

'How do you know you're on the right one?'

'You ask.'

'But what if everyone's dead of the pestilence? How would a man find his way then?'

Gyles eyed him curiously. 'Are you planning to leave us, Thaddeus?'

Thaddeus shook his head. 'Not yet, but I may come with you when it's time to look for new supplies. We'll have more success if two of us go.'

He memorised the names of the places Gyles mentioned, along with compass directions, but he had no idea how far they were from each other or from Develish. Gyles measured journeys in days, not miles, and Sir Richard's speed had been governed by the time it took his heavily packed wagon to travel.

Sarum—north-east
Melcombe—south-west
Blandeforde—north-east
Bradmayne—south
Athelhelm—south
Afpedle—south
Pedle Hinton—west
Winterburn—north-west of Melcombe
Dorchester—north of Melcombe

Even as he recorded the details, Thaddeus questioned what value they had. Knowing the name of a place didn't tell a man if it was safe to enter. Whether he and Gyles travelled together or went in separate directions to increase their chances, the dangers would be huge. Only a fool or a martyr would enter a village where infected corpses lay unburied on the road.

He recalled that thought as he and Ian looked at the flagons. Without the means to carry water—or knowledge of streams— they would need access to a well, but Thaddeus wasn't keen to enter any kind of settlement that day. They needed time to toughen their muscles, grow used to foraging food from the countryside and practise with their weapons before they ventured anywhere near people.

With sudden decision, he stripped off his leather jerkin. 'We need discs to tie over the tops of the jugs. Cloth won't work but leather should.' He took his knife from his belt and handed it to Ian. 'Cut what you need from the sleeves.' He returned to the horses, took Edmund's blade, and sliced two feet of rope from one of the halters, handing it to Peter to unravel. 'Make me seven pieces of string,' he told him. 'They need to be strong, so keep as many fibres together as you can. Bring them to me when you're finished.'

'What do you want me to do?' Joshua asked.

Thaddeus rolled the weapons out of the sack. 'Find owners for these, and come up with an easy method for us to carry them across our shoulders.'

He went back to the well and tested the beans and the dried plums against the crock of salted pork, working out how best to distribute their weight across the spare pony. The boys had collected eight dishes made of tin and pewter, battered and twisted from use, and one heavy iron cauldron. He abandoned the cauldron and sorted the rest into two even piles.

He closed his mind to how unprepared they were for this journey, determinedly pushing his fears and doubts away. There was no going back on the decision he'd reached at dawn when he recognised that he couldn't stay in Develish if he lied about Jacob's death. He might persuade everyone else that the boy had met with a tragic accident but Eleanor knew differently, and Thaddeus couldn't have stomached her triumph if he'd remained on as steward and turned a blind eye to what she'd done. Either she'd have thought him too dim-witted to see what had really happened, or she'd have believed that the bastard son of a harlot took it for granted that Lady Anne's daughter was above the law.

He had toyed briefly with the idea of making it clear to Eleanor that he knew the truth, threatening her with exposure if she put a foot out of place, but the plan was so weak he abandoned it immediately. There was precious little evidence now to show she'd killed Jacob, and there would be none at all when memories of the incident faded. And who would believe Thaddeus's second story if he was forced to admit the first was a lie? His honesty would be as compromised as Eleanor's; and Eleanor would have the advantage of working on Edmund and Olyver to support whatever tale she chose to tell.

He watched Ian cut patches from the sleeves of the jerkin and wondered if he'd been right to play God with these boys' lives. Perhaps they had more sense than he thought, and would have understood the need to keep their mouths shut and avoid all further contact with Eleanor.

Ian seemed to read his mind. 'You shouldn't look so worried,' he said. 'We won't let you down.'

'Worry more that I'll let you down.'

'You haven't so far,' the boy said gruffly. 'You could have ordered us out on our own, but instead you came with us.'

'I had no choice. What explanation would I have given for sending you away?'

Peter Catchpole appeared at Thaddeus's side and laid a handful of strings on the low wall around the well. 'You'd have thought of something if you had a mind to it,' he said matter-of-factly. 'You're giving up more than we are by leaving.'

'Why do you say that?'

Peter shrugged. 'Lady Anne made you her steward. That's a high position for a serf. You could have won your freedom if you'd stayed.'

Thaddeus picked up three of the strings and nodded to one of his piles. 'Hand me the crock and the five dishes,' he said, kneeling beside the sack and pulling it open. He arranged the items neatly across the bottom then pulled the sacking tight around them and bound it with one of the cords. He created a strap for the pony's back by tying another cord some twelve inches from the first, then packed the second pile of foodstuffs and plates into the space that was left. 'Use the last string around the bottom,' he instructed Peter, 'and make the knots good and strong. We don't want to lose anything.'

He moved to help Ian, clamping the leather discs around the necks of the flagons so that the boy could use the remaining cords to create a firm seal. 'We'll have to find a way to carry them upright,' he said. 'Any ideas?'

'How much rope do we have?'

'Only three spare halters ... but we'll have to use one to tie the sack to the pack pony, and I'm not keen to cut the others any shorter. We need as much length as possible if we're to hobble the horses tonight.'

Ian glanced towards the well. 'We could take that one,' he said, nodding to the coils on the crankshaft. 'The bucket, too. No one's drawn water here for weeks.'

Thaddeus followed his gaze. 'It's a hanging offence to pollute or destroy a community well,' he murmured, 'and very uncharitable. Water is given by God to sustain life. Supposing wayfarers come by, out of their minds from thirst?'

Ian shifted uneasily. 'It was just an idea.'

Thaddeus gave a grunt of amusement. 'And a good one.' He flicked the ratchet on the wheel and started to lower the bucket. 'But we should fill our bellies first, and the animals' too. It might be a while before we find water again.'

It was on the tip of Ian's tongue to ask when they might see food but second thoughts prevailed. He'd rather earn compliments from Thaddeus than disapproval. A warrior fought on an empty stomach. Only children cared about where their next meal was coming from. 'If we take the bucket, we can balance the cauldron against it across the pony's back,' he pointed out. 'We'll struggle to cook anything on tin plates.'

Fourteen

LADY ANNE CLOSED THE OFFICE door and walked to the window, searching the farthest field for signs of her husband's charger and the other horses and ponies which had been left to fend for themselves after Sir Richard's death. She couldn't see them there, nor could she see them on the highway north when she shifted her attention to the land beyond the village.

What to believe? Who to trust?

With a sigh, she took up her quill and recorded the names of those who had left in the steward's ledger, recalling the honesty in Isabella's eyes when she'd begged her mistress to have faith in Thaddeus's allegiance. What did Isabella know? Had Olyver and Ian confided in her that one or both had had a fight with Jacob? Had she told Thaddeus and asked for his help? Lady Anne frowned in perplexity. But why had six gone if only two were responsible? It made no sense.

She would have summoned Isabella to the room if Hugh de Courtesmain hadn't chosen that moment to enter. He sketched an extravagant bow which set Lady Anne's teeth on edge, being so different from the shy courtesy Thaddeus always displayed. 'My apologies, milady. I hadn't realised you were here.'

'Now you are steward again, the office is as much yours as mine, Master de Courtesmain. I was merely bringing the ledger up to date, though I have yet to write the sad details of Jacob's death. I can't find the words to express it without seeming to blame him. "Died by accident from a self-inflicted wound" suggests foolishness or suicide. Wouldn't you agree?'

'I would, milady.'

She held her quill above the page. 'Can you think of a better phrase? One that means his family can remember him with honour?' She studied his face, but if the Frenchman had any suspicions about Jacob's death, they were well hidden.

'Perhaps "Died in a fall while bravely guarding the southern step" would serve the purpose, milady.'

'It would indeed. Thank you, Master de Courtesmain.' She smiled her gratitude before bending her head to inscribe Jacob's memorial. 'Your skill with words can serve me well in another task, sir, but I fear it's a difficult one. If I felt able to do it myself, I would, but I lack your abilities.' Was he deluded enough to believe such nonsensical flattery? she wondered.

It seemed so. He made another bow. 'You have but to ask, milady.'

She turned the ledger towards him. 'If you read what is written here, you will see that Thaddeus Thurkell and five of our serfs left the demesne this morning while everyone's attention was on the funeral. They went in secret without my permission and without taking leave of their families.'

Had Hugh de Courtesmain not shown delight so clearly in his dark eyes, masked immediately by a feigned look of puzzlement, Lady Anne might have been tempted to trust him. But she couldn't. Any answer he gave would be tainted by his ambition.

With Thaddeus departed, he could hope for permanent reinstatement as her steward.

'I would not have thought Thurkell so irresponsible in his obligation to you, milady,' he said carefully. 'It must trouble you greatly.'

'I certainly worry for his life and the lives of his companions,' she answered, 'but I can only admire their bravery, Master de Courtesmain.' She took Thaddeus's letter from her kirtle and passed it across the desk. 'You have my permission to read this and make the details known around the demesne. I myself will take on the task of speaking to the parents of all those who have gone, stressing my praise for their courage and my faith in Thaddeus's promise to return in two weeks—but your talent with words is so persuasive, sir, that I give you the task of calming the fears of others. Perhaps a notice, posted on the front door, will serve the purpose just as well? Enough of our serfs can read to make my sentiments known to their neighbours.'

Hugh read the parchment without expression, and Lady Anne wondered if he would accept her endorsement of what it said. 'Was it necessary to deprive Gyles Startout of both his sons?' he asked.

'Thaddeus would have had no decision in it,' she answered. 'Their twinship would not have allowed one to go without the other.'

Did he believe her? She couldn't tell.

He remained silent for a moment or two. 'But why take youngsters at all? Surely the fathers of all these boys would have been a better choice? Each is older and more experienced than Thurkell. What use can their sons be to him in such a perilous venture?'

'Ask rather how dire our situation would be if we lost all our leading serfs in one fell swoop, Master de Courtesmain. Thaddeus has taken the burden for now, but if he fails, Gyles will command the next scouting party and John Trueblood the one after that. Will you volunteer when your time comes, sir? Death from the pestilence will be quicker than death from starvation, I think.'

Hugh gave a twisted smile. 'I am always at your service, milady.'

'And I thank you for it. I shall pray each day that Thaddeus and his brave young companions succeed in their quest and the time never comes when you have to leave us.'

There was a short hesitation and she wondered if she'd been too effusive. 'Thurkell asked me to give you a message, milady,' Hugh said then. 'I understand now what it means but it seemed overly extravagant at the time. "Light a candle for each of us when you light one for Jacob." I thought he was talking about the whole of Develish and told him we couldn't afford to squander two hundred candles in his brother's memory.'

It was her turn to hesitate. 'What was his response?' she asked.

'That I was right—it would be a waste to burn a flame unless it showed the way home. I accused him of talking in riddles, and he reminded me the sows are due to farrow tomorrow.'

Lady Anne lowered her eyes to the ledger, turning it around and dipping her quill in the ink as if to continue with the day's formal record. 'You've read his letter,' she said calmly. 'He expects to return within a fortnight. Give that message of hope to everyone and say that Lady Anne will light six candles in her window every night to guide them in. I shall value your support in helping to dispel any fears our people may have, Master de Courtesmain. If we keep reminding them that our best young men have set out on this journey, they will have more faith in their success.'

Hugh gave his promises gladly, flattered by her need of him, but he had seen the emotion in her face when he told her he had a message from Thaddeus, and it made him wonder if there was more to the story than she'd told him.

౭౦

Martha Startout sought out her daughter in Lady Anne's spinning room to pass on the news that Olyver and Ian had left the demesne. Isabella expressed appropriate shock, but her mother's response was not what she'd expected. However often Martha dabbed at her eyes with the hem of her apron, she couldn't hide the pride she felt in her boys, and for that Isabella sent a silent prayer to God to bless her beloved Lady Anne. 'Someone had to go,' Martha explained, 'and Thaddeus chose your brothers. He wanted the best, you see.'

'For what, Mama?'

'To discover what's happening with this Black Death before our stores run out. Your father has been talking of nothing else for weeks. He expected to have to go himself, and he never thought Thaddeus would take his sons in his place, nor that they would go in secret to avoid others having to draw lots.'

'Is Papa cross with Olyver and Ian?'

Martha shook her head. 'He's unhappy that they left without his blessing—' a small smile lifted the corners of her mouth—'but he's strutting like a peacock at their courage and taking every plaudit that comes his way.'

'Then I shall strut as well,' said Isabella, jumping from her stool to wrap her arms tightly around her mother. 'I know they'll come back, Mama, because Thaddeus will make sure of it. If Father was able to survive the pestilence, then so will our twins.'

'I hope you're right, child. Our hearts will be broken otherwise.'

Isabella waited until her mother left before resuming her carding of the wool in preparation for spinning. She knew the job so well that her actions were mechanical, leaving her mind free to think. It seemed the story she had wanted Lady Anne to tell was being told, and Thaddeus and his companions had been elevated to the status of heroes. How easily Isabella could go along with that. Lies didn't come naturally to her but praise for Thaddeus did. She was even willing to laud her brothers—however stupid she thought them—if it meant she could avoid questions about what she knew.

Her heart leapt with alarm as Eleanor's voice broke into her thoughts from the doorway. 'You're such a good little girl, aren't you, Isabella? Always busy, always working, always ready to do what's asked of you.'

The maid stood up, forcing a smile to her face as she bobbed a curtsey. She had hidden away in the spinning room in the hope that Eleanor wouldn't find her, but her mind had been working overtime on the warnings in Thaddeus's letter. *Protect yourself by saying nothing of what you witnessed this morning with Lady Eleanor . . . It is better for all if Develish remains ignorant of the conversation . . .* 'Do you require something, milady?'

Eleanor moved around the room, swishing her train across the floor and treading petulantly on any servant's bedroll that was in her way. She paused by Lady Anne's sewing tray and picked up a large iron bodkin which was used to create the hanging loops for embroidered tapestries. She tested the point against her fingertip. 'Do you really think Jacob was stupid enough to fall on his own knife?' she asked slyly.

Isabella kept her eyes on the needle. 'He was always clumsy, milady. My father had to rescue him once from the moat when he lost his footing and fell in.'

'I say Thaddeus killed him and has run away to avoid being found out. We both saw the blood on his shirt this morning.'

Isabella moistened the inside of her mouth. 'The stains will have come from when he carried Jacob into the church, milady.'

Eleanor jabbed the bodkin into the wooden tray and pulled it out again. 'Is that the story he told you?'

'He told me nothing, milady. I know only what you and the rest of Develish knows.'

'But we can all make guesses, can we not? Do you think I'm alone in wondering if Thaddeus murdered his brother? Why would he leave the demesne in secret if not out of fear of discovery?'

'For the reasons he gave your mother, milady. He has no need to fear discovery. No one doubts Jacob's death was an accident.'

Eleanor looked at her out of the corner of her eye. 'You're very quick with your answers. How so? Have you been working them out since you hid yourself away inside this room?'

Isabella took a step to the side so that the spinning wheel was between her and her young mistress. 'I speak only the truth, milady. You will find no sympathisers if you accuse Thaddeus of murder without good cause.'

'Do you dare to tell me what I can and cannot do?'

Isabella hesitated. Her fear of the girl advocated silence but her resistance to letting Eleanor believe she could accuse whomever she pleased overcame caution. 'People will say there's no smoke without fire if you act out of spite, milady. They will ask how you know so much about Jacob's death . . . and why you accuse Thaddeus when he's but one of six who has left the demesne in search of food for the rest of us.'

'If they do, it's for their own purposes. My mother turns them into saints rather than admit they've absconded.'

Not for the first time, Isabella wondered if there was something wrong with Eleanor. Had she forgotten what had been said in the steward's office at dawn? Could she not see that the only person to benefit from Thaddeus's decisions was herself? 'You know the purpose,' she answered carefully. 'It's to keep Lady Anne from learning you were in the church last night with a peasant boy. My parents would be no happier to know that it was Olyver who was with you.'

Eleanor set to jabbing the needle into the tray again. 'They should be pleased that I singled out their son for favour. It sets him above the rest.'

Once again, Isabella hesitated before she spoke, but Eleanor's arrogance lit a flame of rebellion in her heart. 'Your father said the same when he singled out serf girls for favours,' she said quietly. 'He was hated for it by every person on this demesne. Lady Anne put a stop to it when it was made known to her, and any respect she had for him was lost. She has no trust in Father Anselm either, because he stayed quiet about what he knew rather than attract Sir Richard's displeasure. It would shame and infuriate her to learn that the same has happened again.'

Eleanor stared at her for a moment, a strange look in her eyes—*anxiety?*—but when she spoke her voice was cruel. 'If we survive this pestilence, I'll have you barred forever from Develish. I hate the sight of your coarse, ugly face. It makes me sick just to look at you.'

Isabella stared at the ground to hide her expression. 'As milady pleases.'

Eleanor gave a sneer of derision. 'As milady pleases,' she echoed in imitation of Isabella's gentle voice. 'Why are you so spineless? Even Jacob showed more spark. At least he *tried* to fight.'

She was unprepared for the look of horror that Isabella suddenly fixed on her, and the change in the girl's expression as her eyes were drawn to the doorway.

'I apologise if my daughter keeps you from your work, Isabella,' said Lady Anne, entering the chamber. 'She has so few skills herself that it galls her to see them in others.'

Quietly and carefully, Eleanor replaced the bodkin in the sewing tray before turning around. 'We were having a little fun together, that is all. Did you need me for something, Mother?'

Lady Anne nodded. 'You will join me in the church to say prayers with Father Anselm for the safe return of Thaddeus and his five companions.' But she didn't look at Eleanor. Instead her dark eyes searched Isabella's face. As Thaddeus had earlier, she saw how fine the little maid's features were and how well her dark prettiness compared with Eleanor's blonde beauty. 'If my daughter had spoken the truth, she would have said it's the loveliness of your face that offends her, child. She knows how beautiful you would look in one of her gowns, and the idea frightens her. It's jealousy that makes her cruel.'

Isabella dropped a curtsey as the two women left, unsure what to make of Lady Anne's angry chastisement of Eleanor. It was rare for her to take anyone to task in front of others, not even serfs, for she preferred to correct mistakes in private, and Isabella couldn't recall Eleanor ever being faulted so openly. Her mother always said this was a pity, since the girl's behaviour grew worse through lack of public admonishment, but her father believed Lady Anne was wise not to give the girl reasons to hate her more. He blamed himself for Eleanor's hostility towards her mother. Had Lady Anne not taken the side of the Startout family against her husband, Sir Richard would not have punished her by estranging her from her daughter.

⚬⚬⚬

Eleanor had the sense to stay silent as she and her mother made their way through the demesne, smiling sweetly whenever a peasant bowed to Lady Anne, hoping her mother's irritation would pass more quickly if she played the role of dutiful daughter. She wished she knew how long Lady Anne had been in the doorway and what she had seen and heard, but, as ever, it was impossible to read what the woman was thinking.

Even Sir Richard's bad temper, his violent slaps and kicks whenever his wife annoyed him, had failed to bring passion to Lady Anne's face. Eleanor had come to despise her because of it, and had accepted her father's view that her mother was a cold and barren woman who made her husband's life intolerable.

She found herself trying to recall what Sir Richard had looked like and was disturbed that she could not. It was as if his death had robbed her of memory, though in truth she hadn't seen much of him when he was alive. Her mother had been right to say he rationed his daughter to an hour of his time on the days when he wasn't hunting or travelling abroad to carouse with friends. Her recollections were confusing. She clung to the belief that he'd loved her, but Isabella's talk of serf girls had awakened an unpleasant memory.

It was from a time barely remembered, when Eleanor was four or five. Lady Anne had moved out of Sir Richard's chamber forever, her face suffused with a blazing anger which her daughter had never seen before or since. She had ordered an iron bolt to be put on her door, and had taken Eleanor and every young maid to sleep in her room, refusing entry to Sir Richard however hard he kicked and hammered on the panels.

Eleanor wasn't told what had caused the schism, but she recalled her mother nursing a young girl who lay close to death for several days. Much blood had come from between her legs, and her face had grown paler as Lady Anne tried to stem the flow with napkins. Which maid was it? Eleanor couldn't remember, but she recalled her feelings of jealousy as Lady Anne pushed her away in order to devote herself to a slave.

Somewhere at the back of Eleanor's mind was an image of her mother slamming the door in Father Anselm's face when he came to the chamber, begging to say prayers for the girl's recovery. Eleanor wished she could recollect more of the details, but she'd been a child herself and had quickly forgotten the incident. Her father had given her a pony shortly afterwards and the maid had become an anonymous servant again. But who was she? Did she still live in Develish?

Eleanor remembered how everything had changed afterwards. Only male servants were allowed in Sir Richard's chamber, and only the married female servants were permitted to serve him at table. Her mother had become secretive, removing herself from her husband's presence unless visitors were in the house, and her father's travels had become more frequent and of longer duration. When he was at home, no one smiled; when he left, the servants and bondsmen talked and laughed freely, showing respect to Lady Anne and treating the demesne as their own.

How Eleanor had hated them for it and how often she had tried to tell Sir Richard that his serfs had more loyalty to his wife than to him. On occasion, he had questioned his various stewards about it—particularly his daughter's stories of merchants pausing in the village to load produce onto their wagons—but the stewards had shaken their heads and shown him the tax receipts. No lord in Dorseteshire had more loyal or more productive labourers than Sir Richard of Develish.

The sound of Lady Anne raising the latch on the church door brought Eleanor back to the present, reminding her that she must make a show of caring that Thaddeus and his companions fared well on their journey, when in truth she hoped they were gone forever. How much easier it would be to malign them if they weren't there to contradict her, and how sweet if Thaddeus died of the pestilence and her mother was left broken-hearted. With her pretty lips forming a pious smile, she bent her head in deference to God and stepped inside.

'There's no audience for your play-acting,' said Lady Anne, closing the door behind them. 'The place is quite empty.' The smell of incense lingered on the air from Jacob's funeral. 'Perhaps you hope God is impressed by false smiles and demurely lowered lashes, for be assured I am not, Eleanor.'

Eleanor watched her warily, seeing that her attempts to mollify Lady Anne hadn't worked. 'I thought we came to say prayers for Thaddeus and his companions.'

'If we do, we'll say them alone.' Lady Anne ran her eyes over Eleanor's gown. 'Will the words you speak be the same as the feelings in your heart? You seem to be celebrating Thaddeus's departure, so I question whether your pleas for his safe return will be sincere.'

Eleanor didn't answer and, with sudden decision, Lady Anne gripped her arm and marched her towards the altar. She didn't know what she wanted to achieve except to remove the insufferable smirk from the girl's face. The candles which Thaddeus had lit the night before remained in place, melted pools of wax lying on the rough wooden surface around them, and in the rushes on the floor was a flattened depression where Jacob's coffin had rested.

Eleanor, alarmed by the expression on her mother's face, pulled herself free in the middle of the chancel.

'Why are you so angry with me?' she cried. 'I'm not to blame for Thaddeus leaving.'

Lady Anne bit back an immediate expression of disbelief. The truth would never be had from Eleanor. 'I'm angry about many things, daughter, but mostly Jacob's death.' She stirred the flattened rushes with her foot. 'He was too young to lose his life needlessly.'

'What if he was? It has nothing to do with me.'

'I thought otherwise when I heard what you said to Isabella.'

Eleanor forced a careless shrug. 'I can't remember anything of the conversation now.'

'You said, "At least Jacob *tried* to fight."'

'Oh, that.' The girl stared at the ground, pretending to think about it. 'One of the servants told me Jacob fell off the guard step while practising swordplay, and Isabella mocked the silly boy for killing himself by accident. I said she should at least commend him for trying.'

Lady Anne marvelled at how easily the falsehood slipped from Eleanor's tongue. Did she think her mother would believe that Isabella was capable of such unkindness? 'How strongly your father's blood runs in your veins,' she murmured. 'He couldn't tell the truth either.'

Eleanor was relieved to be on familiar ground. 'You wouldn't have believed him whatever he said. You hated him too much.'

Her mother ignored her. 'Sir Richard didn't think anyone could see through him, not even God.' She reached for the cross. 'It used to make me laugh when he clasped this crucifix to his breast, drank the holy wine and cried tears of joy as the degenerate priest pronounced him clean.'

Eleanor was as shocked as Hugh de Courtesmain had been to hear a priest denounced in such blasphemous terms. 'You can't speak of Father Anselm like that.'

'Why not? God's no more in him than in this piece of wood. He absolved your father of his crimes to keep his benefice, not because Sir Richard showed contrition. A life of sin is easy when a priest can be bought as cheaply as Father Anselm.'

Eleanor glanced nervously towards the tower door. 'He'll hear you,' she whispered.

'Be sure he does, daughter. He sees and hears everything in and around his church. I expect he knew Jacob was dead before Thaddeus did.' She ran her finger over the crucifix. 'He may even have watched him die, though he wouldn't have gone to his aid. He learnt long ago that pretending to be deaf or drunk makes his life easier . . . even in the confessional. He can better excuse his failings as a priest if he can blame them on mead.'

A knot of fear tightened in the girl's belly. She had never heard her mother speak like this, and it frightened her. 'Why do you say these things? This is God's house. Aren't you afraid of His anger?'

'Should I be?' Lady Anne glanced around the room. 'Where is He? I don't see Him.' She shook her head at her daughter's shocked expression. 'What do you fear? That the walls will run with blood because I dare speak the truth aloud? God has known these many years that I see Him more easily in an act of kindness than I do in the hypocrisy of the Church.'

The concept was too complex for Eleanor, and she fixed on what she understood. 'There's no greater sin than heresy. You'll go to Hell if you continue.'

'Perhaps so, but not for questioning whether God forgives as easily as the Church pretends. Bishops grow fat on the indulgences they sell while knowing the promises they offer are false. Redemption can't be bought with a bag of gold. God judges us by our deeds not by the number of *mea culpas* we say.'

'You can't know that. Forgiveness is open to everyone.'

Lady Anne replaced the cross on the altar, wishing she'd fought harder for Eleanor. She'd resigned herself too early to taking second place in the girl's life, wearied by the conflicts between them and overly ready to accept that Eleanor had more of a bond with her father than she could ever have with her mother. 'Not in this world it isn't. Gyles Startout said a prayer as he interred Sir Richard in unconsecrated ground, but he might as easily have cursed him. No man was more wronged by Sir Richard than Isabella's father.'

Eleanor's fear became dread as the memory of the young servant rose in her mind again. 'I won't listen any more,' she cried. 'You want me to hate Sir Richard as much as you do, but I can't. He was my father and I loved him.'

'But you *will* listen,' said Lady Anne, moving to cut off any attempt Eleanor made at escape. 'I'm tired of how you treat our people. There's not one deserves the ill manners and cruelty you display towards them. Are you so blind, or so lacking in feeling, that you can't see it for yourself but must ape the ignorant behaviour of your father?'

'He wasn't ignorant.'

'Indeed he was. Can you not guess why he told you the only thing a serf understood was the whip?' She searched the girl's face for intelligence. 'It was the only thing *he* understood. It gave him a paltry sense of power to threaten a man with a beating. He felt bigger and more important with a whip in his hand—rather as you do, daughter.'

Eleanor turned away, but not before Lady Anne saw fresh shock in her eyes. She was tempted to ask if Eleanor had threatened Jacob with a beating the night before, but she held her tongue, recognising that the only answer she would believe was 'yes'. Every instinct told her the girl had some guilt in Jacob's death, yet to know it for sure would be intolerable, since to learn the truth would mean becoming complicit with Eleanor in hiding it.

'If I'd wanted you to hate your father, I'd have filled your head with poison from the day you were born,' she went on. 'It wouldn't have been hard. You accepted his lies readily enough.' She paused, studying the girl's rigid back. 'It worries me that he taught you to have so little care for the hurt and pain your words and actions cause others. Do you think God smiled when you threatened to banish Isabella from the demesne? What bad turn has she ever done you to deserve such a punishment?'

'You always take her side,' the girl muttered.

'With reason. You should have asked Sir Richard why Isabella's father was the only Develish serf in his retinue when all the others were Normans. It was the recompense I demanded for the crime Sir Richard committed against Isabella's sister. Sir Richard took it for granted that Gyles's oath of fealty would keep him loyal and that a rise in status was reasonable restitution for a daughter's violation and death.'

Eleanor clapped her hands to her ears. 'I'm not listening.'

Lady Anne ignored her. 'Her name was Abigail. She was a tiny little thing, barely ten years old, and it was five days before I could stop the bleeding. She wasn't grown enough to withstand your father's lust.' She watched Eleanor press her palms harder over her ears in a vain attempt to block her mother out. 'I asked Father Anselm to send a messenger to My Lord Bishop, begging His Grace's presence here, but the priest refused, saying no crime had been committed. Sir Richard claimed the girl was a wanton who had sought him out for favour, and Father Anselm absolved him of any wrongdoing. God knows he'd done it often enough in the past.'

Eleanor screwed her eyes tightly closed as if blindness could bring deafness.

'Both men claimed it was common knowledge that Abigail was fourteen, and even Gyles and Martha couldn't contradict them because they didn't know for certain how old she was. Four months later, when I demanded the parish ledger to record her death, I discovered her birth had been inscribed by Father Anselm ten years previously. He lied quite shamelessly to uphold the story that she was through puberty and already experienced.' She looked towards the tower door. 'If ever I had a spur to teach our serfs to read and understand numbers, it was the anger I felt at how easy it was for a dissolute priest and a corrupt lord to twist the truth. Abigail lived just long enough to see the Christmas before her eleventh birthday, too frail from loss of blood to survive longer, and I never allowed the priest to record a birth or death on this demesne again.'

She waited through a short silence to see if the girl would respond. 'Gyles wanted to kill your father, but I urged him not to forfeit his own life so recklessly. He was of no use to Martha and his other children on the gallows.' She paused. 'I was able to persuade him that Sir Richard was more useful to us alive. There would be no controlling a new lord the way I was able to control your father after I inscribed the details of Abigail's deflowering and death on parchment and threatened to hand it to My Lord of Blandeforde if Sir Richard ever laid a finger on one of our people again. He knew I meant what I said, and he knew My Lord of Blandeforde would not excuse his brutality even if the priest did. Blandeforde takes oaths of fealty more seriously than the Church does.'

Eleanor dropped her hands, fearful to speak but more afraid to keep listening. What would be left to her if everything she believed in was shown to be false? 'You can make Sir Richard sound as horrible as you like now that he's dead,' she wept, keeping her back to her mother. 'There's no one to say if it's true except Father Anselm . . . and you want me to hate him as well.'

Lady Anne tucked her hands inside her kirtle with a weary shake of her head. 'You're not so foolish or so childish that that's all you take from what I've told you. God demands more of you than the priest would have you believe. If it doesn't trouble your conscience that a serf was buried today—and six others are risking their lives on the pestilence—at least recognise that God is no more deceived by your false smiles and loudly chanted responses than the people of Develish are.'

Eleanor wished the priest would emerge from his chamber to cast her mother down for lies and blasphemy. She wanted to scream that everything was Lady Anne's fault, that her coldness towards Sir Richard had made him angry. If he looked to hurt his people, it was because of the love they showed his wife. At least they took notice of him when he threatened to have them flogged. But Eleanor knew that, once started, she wouldn't be able to stop, and her own anguished jealousy would pour from her mouth.

She looked around eventually because the silence went on for so long, but the church was empty and a surge of sudden and terrible abandonment ripped through her heart. Not even the lifting of the latch on the door or the rustle of reeds on the floor had betrayed her mother's departure. Lady Anne might have vanished into thin air for all the evidence there was that she had ever been there.

Notice

*Lady Anne makes it known that 6 brave sons of Develish
have left the demesne this morning with her blessing. They
show great courage by making this journey on behalf of their
people. Lady Anne asks that prayers be said daily for their
safe return. She will light candles in her chamber window
each night to guide them home.*

In nomine Patris et Filii et Spiritus Sancti
Hugh de Courtesmain, Steward

Fifteen

South of Develish, Dorseteshire

THADDEUS WAS AT THE REAR of the column, leading the pack pony, as they headed down the highway. Ian and Olyver were at the head, with Joshua on a halter between them, closely followed by Edmund and Peter. He had instructed those with reins to keep their mounts to a walk in order to give the group time to get used to riding again, but the animals were skittish from lack of exercise, and Joshua and Peter clung to their ponies' manes for dear life in order not to be thrown.

Joshua had asked why they were heading south towards the pestilence instead of away from it. 'Do you want us all to die?' he'd muttered gloomily.

'If we go north where there is no sickness, we'll have to pay for the food we need,' Thaddeus had answered matter-of-factly. 'If we go south, where whole villages have perished, we can steal it along with a cart to carry it in. It's easier to rob the dead than the living.'

'What if the infection's on the stuff we touch?' Edmund had demanded in alarm.

'You'll have it already,' was Thaddeus's unsympathetic response. 'The sword you're carrying was Sir Richard's.'

His most urgent concern had been to reach the woodland at the end of the valley before Jacob's body was brought out for burial and people crowded the graveyard at the back of the church. From what he knew of Father Anselm, the priest would stretch the funeral service till kingdom come if it meant avoiding difficult questions about Jacob's death, since a congregation bored and exhausted by prayer would make haste to leave rather than linger for conversation. But the priest's fondness for mead made him unpredictable. In drink, he was as likely to let slip that Jacob was murdered as to follow his own urgings to Thaddeus to keep the manner of the death secret.

The only person responsible enough to maintain guard on the southern step was Gyles Startout but, even if he saw the departing convoy and recognised his sons amongst the riders, Thaddeus doubted he'd do anything without speaking to Lady Anne first. Nevertheless, Thaddeus couldn't rely on that, and he had felt the weight of suspicious eyes all the way to Develish's southern boundary. His nerves were stretched to breaking point by the time the demesne had disappeared from sight.

'What were you worried about?' asked Ian.

'That the alarm bell would ring. We need Jacob to be buried before anyone knows we're missing. If the coffin's still above ground when Lady Anne is told of our departure, she'll become suspicious and order it opened.'

'Why does that matter?'

'She'll see the cuts on his arms and hands where he tried to defend himself, and she'll know he didn't die by accident.'

'Is that what you told her?'

Thaddeus nodded. 'She seemed to accept it, but she may change her mind when she discovers we've left. It depends what Lady Eleanor says.'

There was a short, unhappy silence.

'I think the bell would have rung by now if anyone saw us leave,' Thaddeus went on, 'and I've done what I can to make our motives appear good. We have a friend in Isabella. She knows some of the truth and will find a way to defend us if the need arises. She has more wisdom than all five of you put together, and hasn't forgotten how her sister died—' he cast a critical gaze over Olyver and Ian—'even if her brothers have.'

Ian's face reddened in shame but Olyver spoke defiantly. 'You can't blame Eleanor for that. She's not responsible for what her father did.'

It was clear to Thaddeus that Olyver's feelings for Eleanor were stronger than the others. Even Edmund, who'd tried to excuse the girl when Thaddeus had had his hands around his throat, seemed to have cooled towards her. Every so often he mouthed oaths to himself as if he were picturing his parents' reaction when they learnt how he'd tugged at his rod for Eleanor's amusement.

'Maybe not,' Thaddeus answered coolly, 'but I can blame her for following in his footsteps, and *you* for doing the same. If you want to know how a man of honour behaves, then look to your father—not the grunting hog who sired the vixen you so admire.' His dark eyes raked the other boys with disdain. 'The rest of you needn't look so smug. Your mothers were all subjected to Sir Richard's lust before Lady Anne came to the demesne. None was as young as ten-year-old Abigail Startout, but he raped them just the same. Be grateful his seed was so weak that you weren't looking to impregnate your own half-sister when you played your games in the church.'

It was hard to tell if this was news to them because they turned their faces forward and adopted silence. Those who had chosen swords—Ian, Olyver and Edmund—had buckled the scabbards onto belts which they'd looped over their heads and under one arm, allowing the weapons to be carried diagonally across their backs. Joshua and Peter had done the same with their short bows, bending the yew and attaching the strings before passing the D shapes over their heads. It gave them the rakish look of bandits but not the ability to draw their weapons in a hurry. Nor was there any point in Joshua and Peter trying, since the arrows were tied in a bundle and secured to the pack pony.

They were a motley crew indeed, dressed in crumpled woollen tunics and peasant britches, quite unready to fight or even outpace pursuers. Thaddeus was carrying both a sword and a bow, but they might have been ornaments for all the use he'd be able to make of them. Every step the charger took caused them to jolt against his shoulder, while the stirrup straps which Joshua had manufactured from strands of rope were rubbing relentlessly against his calves.

Even at full extension, Sir Richard's stirrup leathers had been too short for Thaddeus to ride in comfort. When Joshua pointed this out, saying Ian and Olyver could more profitably use the straps as halters for their weapons since neither had come with belts, Thaddeus had agreed to take hemp instead. He was regretting it already, knowing they'd all have blisters by the evening, particularly Joshua and Peter, who were unable to prevent themselves sliding to and fro across their mounts' withers.

At least the pack pony was doing its job. The rope from the well had allowed them to create a workable harness, and Thaddeus had more confidence now that the load would stay on the animal's back rather than slip beneath its belly. They had secured the flagons two by two on either side, and the jerkin patches seemed to be working. With luck and no accidents, he hoped to keep everything intact until they made camp that evening.

His plan—all too reliant on the meagre snippets of information he'd learnt from Gyles—was to follow the highway south until he judged it sensible to move across country in search of an unpopulated part of the river that ran through Athelhelm and Afpedle. Reason told him such stretches must exist but, with only the sun to guide them once they left the road, he wasn't confident of finding any. Nor would he recognise when it was 'sensible' to leave the route, since he had no means of knowing how far they could travel in a single hour or how long it took a horse, moving at walking pace, to reach the ford at Athelhelm.

His greatest fear was to meet other travellers, for he wanted to avoid the company of people. He scanned the road ahead constantly, but the dips and rises of the undulating terrain meant he couldn't see far. If riders or walkers were on the highway, he and his band would be upon them almost before they knew it. Every so often he paused in a gap in the hedgerows which lined the road to try to make out what lay beyond them, but all he could see was dense green woodland rising towards the horizon. He was beginning to understand why Gyles had been so ignorant of the countryside beyond the roads. Even Devil's Brook was invisible behind the thick vegetation that grew along its banks. Thaddeus knew it was there because he could hear the constant trickle of water, but it was an early warning that to find suitable areas to camp beside a river might not be easy.

The boys began to flag as the sun reached its zenith and their bellies rumbled with hunger. The dusty highway seemed to stretch interminably in front of them, and the horses' gaits, no faster than a man's, persuaded Joshua and Peter to take to their legs rather than endure the pain of travelling bareback. Thaddeus made no protest except to warn them that walking would do nothing to harden their thighs and calves for riding.

'Then give me your saddle,' said Peter grumpily. 'Try it yourself and see what it's like. You said we'd swap every two hours.'

'We haven't done two hours.'

'How do you know? It feels like two hours to me.'

Thaddeus ignored him, his attention drawn to thinning vegetation to their left. For whatever reason—poor soil or a forest fire in the past—the ground was becoming more open with fewer trees and stunted plant life. He reined in the charger and called to the boys to stop, shielding the sun from his eyes with his hand and looking south-east over scrubland towards an undulating roll of hills in the distance. Was the Pedle valley on the other side? he wondered. Was this the right place to leave the road?

'Did your father ever talk about the hunting trips Sir Richard took?' he asked Ian.

'Sometimes.'

'Did he say where they went, whose land they rode across? They were always back by nightfall, so they can't have gone far.'

The boy shook his head.

'I remember him telling us once that everything for miles around is the fiefdom of My Lord of Blandeforde,' offered Olyver. 'You get flogged if you're caught trespassing and hanged if you're caught stealing venison.'

'But who's going to catch you?' asked Joshua, his freckled face full of awe. 'I always thought Develish was big—' he waved his hand at the horizon—'but this is *huge*. Where do you suppose it ends?'

'At the sea,' answered Thaddeus, while realising how meaningless the answer was. His mind was as naive as Joshua's at coming to terms with size. In twenty years, his imagination had never taken him beyond the valley he lived in. Lady Anne had told him of Marco Polo's travels to Cathay but, try as he might, he had been unable to picture the people of the east or the magnificence of their palaces. He related everything to life in Develish, unable even to grasp what a journey of twenty miles represented.

'Where does the sea end?' asked Edmund.

'I don't know.' Thaddeus narrowed his eyes to examine the distant slopes, wondering if there were any tracks through the trees. Would they arrive to find the vegetation so thick they'd have to turn back? 'We'll head in that direction,' he said with sudden decision. 'It'll be safer than staying on the road.'

'What if we're caught trespassing?' demanded Peter.

'You'll find out what it's like to ride bareback at full gallop,' Thaddeus said dryly, jumping from his saddle. He passed his reins to Joshua, unhitched his sword and used it to chop a pathway to Devil's Brook. 'Bring me the bucket from the pack pony,' he told Peter. 'We can live without food but not without water.'

ര∞

The sun was behind the ridge by the time they reached the fringes of the woodland, although Thaddeus estimated they had another three hours of daylight before it set. The lie of the land had been deceptive, taking them up and down a series of smaller hills to reach the higher one; once they had crossed what seemed to be a sunken bridleway. Thaddeus recalled Gyles speaking of drovers' roads, trodden down by herds and flocks, and wondered if that was what it was. They had all taken to their feet by then, no one able to bear the pain of bareback riding or the chafing of saddles and stirrup leathers. Walking through gorse and brambles was no better, but jabbing thorns took their minds off their blisters.

As they drew close, Thaddeus could see that the trees on the slope were beeches, growing in tall stands, their dense green canopies blocking out the sun and plunging the forest into shade. It meant there was little vegetation underneath to impede their passage, but he feared getting lost amongst the serried rows of trunks if they couldn't take their bearings.

Suddenly the problems they faced seemed insurmountable. The horses were as tired and hungry as their riders. At least out here on the edge of the forest, there was grass for the animals, even if the water would be gone by the morning. What joy would they have if they continued through the trees and pitch-darkness fell before they reached the other side? Perhaps there was no other side . . .

With a sigh, he came to a stop. 'I've led you false,' he said. 'If we enter this woodland and become lost, we'll have no grazing for the animals and little hope of finding the river tomorrow.'

'Where do you expect it to be?' asked Ian.

'In the valley beyond this hill. Your father told me of one that runs through Afpedle. I hoped to make camp beside it tonight, well away from demesnes and people.' He leant back to draw air into his tired lungs. 'But the truth is I don't know where we are or how far this forest stretches. If we go back the way we've come, we at least know we can take water from Devil's Brook.'

Peter Catchpole, always the quickest to give up, sank to his knees. 'I'm done,' he said. 'The rest of you can do what you like, but I'm happy to die here.'

Ian saw the same resistance on the other boys' faces. 'Couldn't we camp here for the night and return to the highway at dawn?' he asked Thaddeus.

'It'll be much harder. We'll be stiff as boards by the morning, and you'll get nothing to eat. There's not enough water to soak and cook beans and pork as well as wet your throats. If we're going to go back, we need to do it now.'

Ian glanced towards the forest. 'Why are you afraid of getting lost?'

Thaddeus followed his gaze. 'There's no way of seeing the sun, let alone the moon. We could end up travelling in circles.'

'Not to mention bumping into every tree when night falls,' added Edmund morosely. 'I say we camp here even if we do end up stiff and hungry in the morning.'

A mutter of agreement rippled through Peter, Olyver and Joshua, with only Ian dissenting. 'But it's a slope,' he pointed out. 'We don't need the sun. We just keep heading up till we reach the top, then down the other side till we reach the river.' He flinched at the look of impatience in Thaddeus's eyes. 'Sorry. I shouldn't have spoken. It's a bad idea.'

The tall serf pulled a wry smile. 'Quite the contrary. I wish I'd thought of it myself.' He stood for a while, staring towards the trees. 'Right,' he said at last, 'this is what we're going to do: Peter, Olyver and Edmund will take charge of the horses and make camp here; Ian, Joshua and I will use what's left of the daylight to find a path up this hill.'

'What if we can't find our way back?' Joshua asked nervously.

'We will.' He lifted the bow from his shoulder and handed it to Olyver for safekeeping, urging Joshua to do the same. 'Take a sword instead. We'll use the blades to mark the trees along our trail, and you—' he pointed to Peter—'will light a fire at dusk to guide us in. Edmund will have authority in my absence. Make sure the animals are properly hobbled before you set them loose to graze,' he warned, giving the boy the reins of the charger and the pack pony halter.

'Should I give them any water?'

Thaddeus unhitched the flagons from the pack pony's harness and set them carefully on the ground away from careless feet and hooves before slipping the knot on the bucket. 'We'll pour two of the flagons into this. We'll each take a mouthful but the rest must go to the horses. The empty flagons will come with us in case we find water and the others will remain untouched until we return. Understood?'

Edmund nodded. 'What about food?'

Thaddeus gestured to the open land around them. 'There's a good three hours of daylight left. Find what you can. If we see any mushrooms on the forest floor, we'll bring them back in this.' He tapped the leather knapsack which was looped into his belt at the front.

'What if bailiffs come?'

'Ride as if the Devil were after you.'

☙❧

The climb was steeper than anything they'd encountered so far, but the trees were less densely packed than Thaddeus had feared from a distance. Their smooth grey trunks soared to about twenty feet before producing branches, making it easy to navigate a path between them, and he showed the boys how to slash strips of bark from either side of a tree at fifty-pace intervals so that a trail was blazed in both directions. Looking back, the pale green stripes flickered like candles in the gloom, and Joshua's anxiety lessened.

The ground underfoot was soft and springy from moss, and they made good speed, although Thaddeus stopped at regular intervals to pick the frilled yellow fungi that grew in clusters around the roots of the beeches. He called them by the French name Lady Anne had taught him—chanterelles—but Joshua and Ian knew them only as egg mushrooms. Both asked how he planned to cook them without bacon fat or water.

'You're the experts, I suppose,' Thaddeus murmured. 'When was the last time either of you took a turn in the kitchen?'

'I've watched the women do it,' said Ian.

'They shrivel to nothing if all you have is a hot pan,' Joshua added helpfully. 'You have to put them in a stew or fry them in lard.'

'What are they like raw?'

'Not nice. My father eats them dried but he's the only one who likes them.'

Thaddeus stooped to pick another handful. 'You'll be grateful for anything by the time we get back. It'll be a rare miracle if Peter's managed to get a fire going so I wouldn't pin your hopes on eating even shrivelled remains.'

It was the season for fruits and he told them to keep their eyes open for berries, but though they came across brambles here and there, the plants were leggy and undernourished in the deep shade, and any fruit had long since been taken by predators. Whenever they paused to mark a tree, they heard the rustle of small rodents in the undergrowth and the songs of birds in the trees and, once, a larger animal—possibly a fallow deer—darted away from them as they approached. They caught a glimpse of a white scut as it vanished from sight.

'We should have brought a bow,' Ian said.

'We'd never have hit it,' Joshua retorted. 'It was gone before we even saw it.'

Thaddeus halted. 'I think we must be near the top,' he murmured, breathing deeply from the exertion of the climb. He hadn't eaten for twenty-four hours, hadn't slept for thirty-six, and his mouth was as dry as a bone. 'It disappeared too fast. We'd still be able to see it if it was running uphill.' He made a couple of nicks on the trunk nearest him. 'It might be safer to mark the bark at twenty paces from now on. We can't afford to go wrong and miss the trail down.'

The trees became noticeably thinner as they continued—as if the soil were too poor to sustain them—and it was a matter of minutes only before they reached a ridge where nothing grew at all except moss and straggly grass. Thaddeus stared around him in amazement. From the highway, he had assumed the woodland continued unbroken from one side of the hill to the other, obscuring any view of what lay beyond, but instead they could see for miles.

The valley below them, much wider and longer than Develish, stretched from east to west with a sparkling river meandering along its bottom and wooded slopes rising to the horizon on the other side. The water was only visible where trees weren't overhanging the riverbanks, but in two places well apart from each other on the farther side great tracts of land had been cleared for cultivation and grazing. They weren't close enough to make out buildings or people, but Thaddeus recognised them as manors from the patchwork of peasant strips, common land and meadows. He guessed the nearest, which was almost directly ahead of them, must be Afpedle, but he couldn't name the other which was many miles to the west.

Joshua pointed to the sun which was barely an hour from setting. 'We need to turn back,' he urged.

Thaddeus nodded, lowering his gaze to see if there was anything to indicate a settlement on this side of the river. It made sense that there should be—water was a prized commodity—but the woodland dropping away in front of them hid everything except the odd sweep of grass to right and left where the river's course took a sharp bend. The tree canopy seemed to undulate as if the slope was a series of folds rather than a single incline—much like they'd crossed from the highway—and while it appeared that the forest must reach the water's edge, he was cautious enough to suspect that an even larger estate than Afpedle was hidden by the trick of the rolling hills.

He drew Ian's attention to a particularly long loop in the river to the west. 'Do you see any sheep on the grass over there?' he asked.

The boy narrowed his eyes. 'It's miles away,' he protested. 'No one could see anything on it from this distance. Why do you want to know?'

'I'm wondering if the land's been cleared for grazing. Your father mentioned a village called Athelhelm where they forded the river to reach Afpedle.' He squinted into the sun. 'Can you make out the highway? Or the end of Devil's Brook?'

'I expect we'll be able to see it if we walk along the ridge,' said Ian. 'These hills seem to slope in every direction.'

'What about over there?' Thaddeus indicated the demesne that he thought was Afpedle.

'What am I looking for?'

'People . . . animals . . . signs of life.'

Ian shook his head. 'I can make out a manor house and a church, but that's about it.'

'Joshua?'

The other boy was too nervous even to try. 'We need to go back,' he pleaded. 'The forest will be dark long before the sun sets.'

Thaddeus hesitated for a moment then placed his sword on the ground, lifted his belt over his head and unbuckled it to release his knapsack. 'Do you think the pair of you can make it down successfully and lead the others and the horses up tomorrow morning?'

'Where are you going?' Ian demanded.

'To fill the flagons at the river. I'll meet you at this spot before noon. The more water we have the better.' He handed his bag to Joshua and relieved the boys of the empty pitchers. 'Do your best with the chanterelles but don't be stupid about how you cook them. The animals will need to drink before the climb as well as you.'

'What if you're not here when we arrive?' Joshua asked anxiously.

'I will be.'

'You can't know that. Anything could happen.'

Thaddeus responded impatiently. 'Just make sure *you're* here,' he warned. 'I don't plan to sit on this ridge all day while the five of you lie abed, complaining about bruises and blisters.' He nodded towards the trail they'd blazed. 'Be on your way, and remember the saying *more haste less speed*. Make sure you know which tree you're heading for before you leave the one you're at.'

He watched until they dropped out of sight then attached the flagons to his belt, looped it over his head again and stooped to pick up his sword. His earlier crisis of confidence had gone. He had found the river—a cause for elation rather than fear—and his curiosity was greater than his fatigue. The only concern he had was that his blade was now so blunt he would struggle to make the necessary slashes to find his way back to this part of the hill, and by way of precaution he built a small cairn from the chalky white stones that lay amongst the grass. It was a matter of pride to be where he'd said he would be, even though seven horses would be hard to miss once they breasted the ridge.

His stubbornness kept him going even when the night became so impenetrable that he fulfilled Edmund's prophecy of walking into trees. His face and arms were whipped and lacerated by every unseen bramble, dog rose and branch in the last quarter-mile of his descent, and he hardly dared believe it when his weary legs carried him into another grassy clearing and he heard the sound of running water.

Sixteen

THE UNMISTAKEABLE SIGHT OF THADDEUS'S tall figure silhou-
etted against the sky came as a relief to all the boys, but to none
more than Ian. He and Joshua were ahead of the others, leading
two horses each, and the resentment they felt against their
companions was evident in the tightness of their lips and the
battle scars on Ian's knuckles. His only method of persuading
Olyver, Edmund and Peter to make the climb had been to pummel
them into submission, taking a beating himself in the process,
and the bramble scratches on Thaddeus's face paled to insigni-
ficance beside the bruised eyes and split lips that emerged from
the woodland a good two hours later than they should have done.

'I see you've been enjoying yourselves,' Thaddeus murmured,
inspecting the horses and ponies whose heads were drooping
with exhaustion. 'Have these poor beasts had anything to drink?'

'One of the flagons was empty by the time Joshua and I got
back,' said Ian.

'You didn't have to take the rest,' grumbled Peter. 'You could
have left some.'

'So could you.'

Thaddeus unknotted the cord that tied the bucket to the pack pony. 'At least this harness has been rigged properly. Who do I have to thank for that?'

'No one,' said Ian. 'It was never taken off. These lazy churls did nothing while we were away except tie the horses to trees at the edge of the woodland and go to sleep. By the time me and Joshua got back it was too dark to see what we were doing. Peter hadn't even tried to make a fire.'

'So you haven't had anything to eat?'

'No.'

'And the animals haven't grazed?'

'No.'

Thaddeus carried the wooden pail to where he'd left his two flagons in the shade. He said nothing as he emptied both of them into the pail and moved from horse to horse, allowing each to drink. When every last drop had gone, he reattached the bucket and flagons to the pack harness. 'There are clearings on the way down where the grass is richer than up here,' he said, taking the halters of the pony and the charger. 'We'll pause at each to give them a chance to crop.'

'How long will it take us to get to the river?' Peter asked, looking out over the valley.

'Twice as long as it would have taken if the horses had been able to feed overnight.'

'You can't blame me and Olyver for that. It was Edmund's job to hobble them.'

Edmund glared at him. 'I couldn't do it on my own. You and Olyver were supposed to help.'

'At least I found some berries to eat,' Olyver snapped. 'You'd have had nothing at all if it hadn't been for me.'

Thaddeus glanced from one to the other. 'So you have full stomachs, and Joshua, Ian and I have empty ones, despite having less sleep and expending more energy than any of you?'

'Hardly *full*,' replied Peter. 'We had a handful of berries each, that's all.'

Thaddeus shook his head. 'I told you I didn't want children on this journey. Which of those words did you not understand?'

They looked away.

He nodded towards the woodland on the southern slope. 'Ian and Joshua will come with me,' he told the other three, 'and when the shadows of the trees have lengthened by two yards you may follow us or return to Develish with your tails between your legs. If I hear your voices or catch sight of your faces before I'm ready to tolerate them again, you will forfeit water and food for another twenty-four hours. Are there any words *there* that you don't understand?'

They shook their heads.

'Then pass charge of your mounts to me.' He took the reins of their three horses. 'If you lose your way and fail to make rendezvous with us before nightfall, no one will come looking for you. I'm not here to play nursemaid to spoilt brats.' He set off along the ridge with his three animals in tow, looking for the second cairn he'd built, calling to Ian and Joshua to follow.

'You can't leave us here,' Olyver whispered to his twin.

Ian shook his head. 'I can and I will. You're the one who made bad choices, brother.' He clicked his tongue to encourage his own two charges forward. 'If the three of you can't manage to spot a track made by seven horses, you'll prove to be as useless as Thaddeus thinks you.'

But as the boys discovered when they finally plucked up the courage to set off, the trail was marked by chalk crosses.

Overnight, Thaddeus had come up with a better solution than blunting the blades of his sword or his knife on bark. The water of the River Pedle was so clear that when dawn broke he could see the gravel along its bottom and the fish that teemed in its depths. He didn't know that the clarity of the water depended on filtration through limestone but he couldn't miss the chalky outcrops that shone white in the grass around him.

His route back up had brought him out some two hundred yards from his original cairn, which was why he'd built a second one, and Edmund, Olyver and Peter had the sense to recognise it for what it was—a pointer to the trail down.

Olyver was the first to spot the chalk crosses on the bark of the trees. 'Maybe Thaddeus isn't as angry with us as he seemed,' he said in relief.

'We'd be fools to count on it,' said Edmund. 'He made the marks for himself not us.'

While they'd waited for the shadows to lengthen, they'd made the decision to stick together whatever happened, recognising they were stronger as a group than on their own. 'Just because he's made it easy for us doesn't change anything,' said Peter. 'It's still us against him.'

Olyver, troubled by his twin's desertion, frowned. 'That's not what I agreed to. We've been trembling like rabbits about getting lost and dying of thirst—you more than any of us. We need to apologise for being idiots or we'll go another twenty-four hours without water.'

'He's not God. He can't stop us drinking if he's camped near the river.'

Edmund, whose innate pugnacity wasn't improved by hunger or dehydration, clenched his fists. 'But you won't go first, will you?' he snarled at Peter. 'You'll whine and moan until me or

Olyver takes a drink then pretend innocence yourself. I never took you for a two-faced swine before but it's *really* getting on my nerves now.'

'You're no different,' Peter snarled in response. 'An hour ago, you wanted to punch Thaddeus in the face for abandoning us, now you want to kiss his arse for putting crosses on trees. You're so frightened of him, it's pathetic.'

'Take that back.'

'I will not.'

Olyver moved between them and thrust them apart angrily. 'If all you can do is fight, then I'll go on my own. Twin was right. We made bad choices yesterday and I, for one, don't want to make any more. We need to start proving our worth the way Ian and Joshua have done.'

Peter favoured him with a sarcastic smile. 'How? There's no challenge to walking down a marked trail. Even my little sister could do it.'

'Right,' said Olyver curtly. 'It's shaming that Thaddeus rates us no higher than a four-year-old. He couldn't even trust us to lead our mounts down this slope because he knew we'd skimp on the grazing.'

'We weren't given the chance,' protested Edmund.

'We wouldn't have taken it—we'd have complained about the time it was wasting and brought our animals down half dead—and if you can't see that, you should head back to Develish now.' He punched the nearest tree. 'Our hearts haven't been in this venture from the start. We've been looking on it as punishment instead of a chance to make something of ourselves.'

'You more than anyone,' said Peter. 'It's you who blabbed and you who still holds a candle for Eleanor. You'd have stayed in Develish and lied for her if Thaddeus had let you.'

For once Olyver didn't rise. 'I've had time to think about it. Twin spoke a lot of sense yesterday.'

'Yeah, well, I don't plan to take another beating off him,' said Peter harshly. 'Thaddeus left Edmund in charge, not Ian. Your brother takes liberties when he thinks he's above us.'

Edmund stirred the leaves on the forest floor with the toe of his boot. 'We'd still be asleep if Ian hadn't forced us up—you know it and I know it—so maybe you should show him some gratitude. Thaddeus wouldn't have wasted water coming back to where we were camped if the other two had made it up the slope alone with the horses. I'm with Olyver. We do this right or we don't do it at all.'

ତ୍ରତ

A mist greeted them the lower they went, drifting in wisps amongst the trees, but it was damper and thicker by the time they reached the grassy bank beside the river. Even so, they had no trouble finding Ian and Joshua, dead to the world beside the saddles and tack, and the seven hobbled horses, grazing peacefully on the grass. Desperate for water, they dropped to the ground and pushed their faces into the cool stream, only glancing around for Thaddeus when they finally raised their heads.

The green sward, clothed in fog, showed the ghostly shapes of alders and bulrushes growing along the riverbank for two hundred yards in either direction, but there was no sign of the tall, imposing figure of Thaddeus. The boys didn't know whether to be relieved or disappointed. Having primed themselves to admit their faults and apologise, they felt strangely cheated to be denied the opportunity.

Olyver glanced back towards the woodland which was some thirty yards behind them, but the fog was closing in fast on the trees. It gave an eerie feeling to the place, and he shivered suddenly in the rapidly cooling air. 'Perhaps we should have checked that Twin and Joshua are alive,' he whispered. 'They could be dead for all we know.'

'Shut your mouth!' snapped Peter. 'I'm not in the mood for stupid jokes.'

Edmund propped himself on his elbows and nodded to a break in the bank where animals had trodden out a path to reach the water. 'We're in a meadow. There are sheep droppings everywhere.'

'So?'

'It means we're near a demesne. Do you suppose that's where Thaddeus has gone?'

'Probably,' said Olyver.

'I thought he wanted to avoid people.'

'He'll be looking to see how close the nearest house is. He won't light a fire if he thinks it'll be spotted.'

'Meaning we're going to go another night without food,' said Peter gloomily, preparing to push himself to his knees. 'If we've any sense, we'll take a flagon of water and some of the dried plums, and hoof it up the hill before he returns.'

He gave a howl of shock and fear as a boot thudded down on his back and squeezed every last drop of air from his lungs. 'You're a miserable creature, Peter Catchpole,' said Thaddeus's voice. 'You'd steal from your own mother if it meant you didn't have to work.'

Olyver and Edmund scrambled to their feet, stuttering out the apologies they'd prepared. 'We didn't know you were here,' Olyver finished weakly. 'We looked for you but didn't see you.'

'You should have looked a bit harder. Anyone could be hiding in this mist.' He jerked his chin towards the east. 'Edmund's right. There's a village about a mile in that direction, and I'm guessing they use this grassy swathe along the bank as common land.

It becomes wider the closer you get to the houses.' He pointed towards the west. 'The woodland encroaches on the river after about a hundred paces this way but there seems to be a footpath which may lead to another demesne. It'll be a fair distance, I think. I walked a good thousand paces but didn't see any sign of one.'

Warily, Edmund nodded to Peter. 'He can't breathe,' he said carefully. 'His lips are turning blue.'

'Is that right?' Thaddeus lifted his foot indifferently and watched the boy's shoulders heave as he gulped down air. 'My mistake. I thought you were strong like your father, Peter . . . not weak and puny like your baby sister.'

'I didn't mean it,' the boy gasped out.

'What didn't you mean?'

'About taking food. It was a joke, that's all.'

'Yet I distinctly heard you tell Olyver you weren't in the mood for stupid jokes. You seem to think you can set rules for others and decide in your own good time whether you want to follow them yourself. How so? What greatness of mind sets you apart from the rest of us?'

The boy struggled to his knees. 'None.'

Thaddeus nodded, letting the issue go as easily as he had abandoned the boys on the ridge. He indicated a small clearing on the fringe of the woodland which was sheltered by low-growing alders and hawthorns. 'We'll make camp there. It offers more protection than the open grass. Bring me as much dry kindling as you can. The quicker we build a fire, the quicker we'll be able to eat.'

'Should we wake Ian and Joshua?'

'No. If they sleep now, they can take the first guard shift tonight. I didn't see any people in the village to the east, but that doesn't mean they aren't there.' He turned towards the west, trying to locate the sun through the swirling mist. 'I don't know how much light is left and I don't know how cold it's going to become, so work as fast as you can. Bring me enough firewood to last till dawn then start looking for bracken to make our beds.' He glanced from one to the other when they didn't move. 'Are we agreed . . . or do you want to fight about it?'

'We're agreed,' all three said in immediate unison.

'Then stay alert while you do it. You'll get more than a boot between your shoulder blades if a bailiff catches you.'

⁊ʘ

However hard he tried, Thaddeus couldn't follow his own advice. He stayed awake long enough to light the fire but, without food or proper sleep for forty-eight hours, and wet through from the damp mist that had penetrated his clothes, the warmth of the blaze brought oblivion as soon as he lowered himself to the ground. The boys found him slumped on his side, as dead to the world as Ian and Joshua. With his eyes closed and his body relaxed in sleep, he looked younger and less formidable, despite the thick, dark stubble around his jaw, and even Peter couldn't bring himself to carp or criticise.

'He's only six years older than we are,' he reminded the others before setting off without complaint to collect more wood.

It was hard to believe, Olyver thought. Thaddeus's height and strength had made him an adult before his time. From the day he'd over-topped his stepfather, he'd been thrust into the company of men and forced to do the *ad opus* work around the demesne that was Will Thurkell's responsibility. It had distanced him from his peers because his days were longer and more arduous than theirs, and distanced him also from the adults because his fear of being laughed at meant he rarely spoke.

Olyver recalled his mother saying that Thaddeus had never had a childhood, which was why he didn't know how to smile, show emotion or share confidences. It was a warning to Isabella not to lose her heart to a man who preferred his own company and avoided close friendships, but Olyver thought now that Isabella's response had been more accurate. 'You shouldn't judge so harshly, Mama. Thaddeus has more kindness in him than anyone I know— apart from Lady Anne—and he proves it in what he does, not in false smiles.'

Martha had dismissed her daughter's fancies, reminding her that Thaddeus was Eva's son and the acorn never dropped far from the tree. Eva was selfish, satisfying her own needs before anyone else's, and Isabella would do well to remember it. She would do well to remember, too, that Thaddeus's father must have been a bad penny or Eva wouldn't have kept his name a secret all these years. The same sentiment had been echoed repeatedly by Eleanor whenever she described Thaddeus as the sinful product of Eva's lust. A bastard. A mongrel. A slave.

Yet Lady Anne thought well of him, as did Olyver's father, Gyles, who refused to listen to Martha's old wives' tales about acorns and bad pennies. 'Deeds speak louder than words,' was all he ever said, in endorsement of his daughter Isabella's view.

Like many before him, Olyver found himself wondering just who Thaddeus was. Where had Eva met the man who fathered her son? And why was Thaddeus so dark when she was so fair? He looked nothing like Eva, nor like any man Olyver had ever seen, with his almost black eyes and brown skin. More than anything, Olyver wondered where Thaddeus's cleverness of mind had come from when Eva's was so dull. Could his father really have been the base-born pedlar or foreign sailor that gossip said he was?

These thoughts ran through his head as he took it upon himself to prepare a meal. His own belly writhed with hunger pangs, as did Edmund's and Peter's, and he knew that Ian and Joshua would be desperate for food when they awoke. He had watched his mother soak beans numerous times overnight before cooking them, in order to soften and swell the flesh, but he gave up any idea of doing the same. What did it matter if his weren't as good as Martha's?

He wasn't prepared to soak the preserved pork too long either, although he washed the surface salt from the belly strips in the flowing water of the river. The meat, cut into thick, fatty slices, had been packed in layers inside the container, and he was tempted to cook every last morsel. But he closed his mind to the demands of his empty stomach, knowing they would all regret their greed today when there was nothing to eat tomorrow.

As darkness fell, Peter and Edmund abandoned their search for any more bracken and squatted beside Olyver, sniffing the aromas that came from the steaming cauldron which sat atop the fire, flames licking up its side. Every so often, Olyver added more water as the liquid evaporated, stirring the stew with a wooden stick.

'What's in it?' Edmund asked.

'Beans, pork and the egg mushrooms from Thaddeus's bag.'

'What does it taste like?'

'Suck the twig and you'll find out.'

Edmund gave a stir of his own and caught the drippings on his tongue. 'I've had worse,' he said.

Peter did the same. 'Me, too,' he agreed, 'though I can't remember when.' He handed the stick back to Olyver with a grin. 'Are you sure you've put enough salt in it?'

'Why do you think I keep adding water? It's getting worse the longer it cooks. If we weren't so hungry, I'd have soaked the pork properly.'

'We could try sweetening it with some dried plums,' Edmund suggested. 'They can't make it taste any worse.'

Olyver nodded. 'Good idea. Throw in a couple of handfuls. I remember Mother telling me once that the King's favourite dish is suckling pig stuffed with figs, and if a king can eat sweet and salt then so can we.'

'I could do with one of them right now,' said Peter.

'A king?'

'A suckling pig . . . all to myself. I saw one cooked for Sir Richard once. It was crackly and crunchy on the outside, juicy on the inside, and served with a great hunk of bread for all the drippings in the platter.' He closed his eyes. 'I'd suck the bones till they squeaked and even eat the figs if I had to.'

'I'd have a whole deer,' said Edmund dreamily, 'then a goat . . . then a lamb . . . then a chicken or two . . . all with crispy skin.'

The arrival of Ian and Joshua, yawning as they slumped beside the fire to warm themselves, disturbed Thaddeus from sleep, although he didn't advertise the fact, preferring to listen to their chatter and marvel at how quickly Eleanor was forgotten and their friendships restored. Edmund still bore the marks of the thumping Olyver had given him two nights previously, and they all sported split lips from their fight that morning, but their humour was healthier than Thaddeus had known it for weeks.

It was a mystery to him why they had ever allowed Eleanor to divide them. Did she have a side he had never seen or was the urge to copulate so strong in juvenile males that even Sir Richard's daughter became desirable? He had never been tempted to lie with a girl himself, having struggled too long and hard with the random nature of his own birth to wish the same fate on another child. Nor had he dreamt of freedom all these years only to jeopardise it by making a bondsman's daughter pregnant. He had higher ambitions than to settle for the life of a married serf in Develish.

He roused himself when it became obvious that hunger had killed all thoughts of keeping guard. 'Time to eat,' he said, sitting up and brushing his long hair from his eyes. 'The chances are we'll die from Olyver's cooking, but that's marginally better than dying of starvation. Where are the tin platters? Who has a spoon?'

Edmund, Joshua and Peter produced theirs but neither of the twins had any implements at all. Thaddeus gave Olyver his own spoon to use as a ladle. 'I'll need a knife, too,' the boy said. 'There are only three pieces of meat in here. I left the rest in the crock for the days that follow.'

'Very wise,' said Thaddeus solemnly, slipping his blade from its sheath and passing it over.

He hid a smile as every eye focused on the withered strips of belly pork that emerged from the pot, each one carefully cut in half so that no piece was larger than the next, and watched the boys mouth the numbers as Olyver counted out identical spoon-fuls of beans and plums and gravy. Nevertheless, he was taken by surprise when the lad handed the first plate to him and the others sat patiently, awaiting his verdict. 'Eat,' he ordered. 'I'm not your patriarch.'

'You're our leader,' said Ian. 'It amounts to the same thing.'

Perhaps it was fatigue that caused a surge of unexpected emotion to rip through the reticent, black-haired giant. 'Just get on with it,' he said gruffly. 'I'm damned if I'll be the only one who dies of salt poisoning.'

FIRST TWO WEEKS OF
SEPTEMBER, 1348

Seventeen

Develish, Dorseteshire

THE MOOD IN DEVELISH CHANGED after the departure of Thaddeus and his companions. A new uncertainty gripped the people, as if something they'd come to rely on had been lost. Yet their doubts seemed to centre more on themselves than the six who had gone, and, in her mind, Lady Anne likened the demesne to a house. With all the elements in place, a well-built structure stood firm; with a handful of supports missing, it began to waver.

Isabella noticed it also, but she put it differently. 'Thaddeus would never believe how much he's missed, milady. He's too shy to think he could matter so much.'

'In what way does he matter, Isabella?'

'In the same way you do, milady. He makes people feel important by listening when they speak. My father says his rearing would have turned him sour if you hadn't taught him that everyone—even the humblest—should be heard.'

Lady Anne buried her own feelings deep, but she was less able to quell her anger against Eleanor. The girl's behaviour worsened as the days went by. She raged against any serf who did something she didn't like, and her temper became so uncertain

Lady Anne ordered her to remain in her chamber. The servants were instructed to leave food outside the door, but as often as not it remained untouched.

A rumour spread that Eleanor was lovesick for Thaddeus, and Eva Thurkell played on the story to cause embarrassment for Lady Anne and her council. She claimed that Thaddeus had advised Lady Anne to send Eleanor away when news of the pestilence first reached them, cautioning against confining a girl so beautiful with boys of her own age. Foolishly, Lady Anne had refused, only to regret the decision later when her leading serfs, each eager for power, encouraged their sons to vie for Lady Eleanor's favour. Pressured to succeed, the boys had introduced animosity to their sword-fighting and wrestling, wounding and bruising each other for all to see.

These facts were true. No one could deny them. Eva's second son, Jacob, would still be alive if he hadn't feared being hurt in the arena. To say that Thaddeus had encouraged the games—and had indirectly caused the death of his brother—was false, for, alone amongst the adult men, Thaddeus had not taken part. The same could not be said of Gyles and Alleyn Startout, John Trueblood, Adam Catchpole and James Buckler, whose aggressive vying with each other had not gone unnoticed.

Fearful of losing her authority, Lady Anne had ordered Thaddeus to remove the sons of these ambitious men. By doing so, she had killed two birds with one stone, for all Develish knew that Eva's tall, handsome firstborn was Lady Eleanor's true love. The distress the girl had shown since Thaddeus's departure proved it; but if doubts remained, Eva reminded her neighbours of the warning Milady had given her daughter in front of the kitchen servants.

Worry more about Sir Richard's displeasure when he learns how interested you are in Thaddeus Thurkell . . .

Lady Anne's leading serfs urged her to quell the rumour. They were loyal to a man and resented Eva's slurs. She showed them Thaddeus's letter and gave permission for it to be nailed to the front door, asking them to draw particular attention to the fact that Thaddeus had left without her permission but promised to return within a fortnight. She found an unexpected ally in Isabella, who confessed shyly to her parents that her twin brothers, Ian and Olyver, had told her of their secret plans before they left. It was a small but necessary deceit, she felt, if it helped Thaddeus free her brothers from further intrigue.

'They wanted to make you proud,' she told Gyles and Martha. 'Please don't think badly of them because Eva is angry with Thaddeus for leaving. Lady Eleanor's distress is shared by all the young girls in the demesne. I've seen a thousand tears shed for Thaddeus. There's many dream secretly of becoming his wife.'

Martha stroked her daughter's cheek. 'Are you one of them, my sweet?'

'Not any more, Mama, for he will never be content in Develish now that he's travelled outside it. But I do yearn for his safe return with our twins. They swore to me they would not stay away beyond a fortnight . . . and that gives the lie to Eva's story. They would not be coming back if Milady had banished them.'

With the help of Gyles and Martha, common sense prevailed and Eva's jealous tongue found fewer listeners. Mothers shook their heads when their daughters sought to ape Lady Eleanor's distress, warning they had no patience with such nonsense. Thaddeus had never shown interest in Develish girls. He searched the horizon too often to take a homebody for a mate. Better to stop fretting and look elsewhere for a husband.

Lady Anne's feelings remained hidden. To outward appearances, she was as composed as she had always been, yet she could barely tolerate other people's company. Master de Courtesmain's exaggerated deference set her nerves on edge while the five leading serfs who made up her council treated her with such grave formality during their meetings that it was hard to be open with them. It seemed they were as much in need of Thaddeus's quietly voiced opinions as she was.

Thaddeus had understood when to be silent and when to offer advice. If he had something to impart that he didn't want others to hear, he wrote it down. Lady Anne did the same. So rarely did she have to explain what she was thinking that, at times, she believed he could read her mind. He foresaw problems as quickly as she did and offered solutions before she asked for them.

The same could not be said of Master de Courtesmain and her leading serfs, who looked to their mistress to provide answers for everything. Once or twice, Lady Anne found herself wishing her husband were still alive. Life had been simpler when she'd managed the demesne behind Sir Richard's back. The serfs had been patient and forbearing of mistakes when he was the enemy and she their secret friend. Now there was no room for error. She had taken the role of liege lord and must be wise all the time, and the burden weighed heavily on her, for she doubted her ability. She governed through the goodwill of her people, and a single poor judgement would lose their support.

Five days after Thaddeus's departure, Martha Startout brought her a jug of warm water, spiced with chamomile, apples and cloves. 'You look tired, milady. This tonic might help.' Martha poured the infusion into an earthenware beaker, pretending ignorance of the sudden rush of tears in Lady Anne's eyes. 'You work too hard, my dear. There's never a moment in the day which you can call your own. You should take an hour for yourself now and then.'

Lady Anne pressed a thumb and forefinger to the bridge of her nose. 'I doubt it's possible, Martha. There's nowhere for any of us to be alone.' She took the beaker, thanking the woman for her kindness. 'You mustn't waste concern on me when you have more pressing anxieties. Your sons do a fine thing for Develish and I pray for them each day.'

'I know, milady, and I thank you for it.' The woman took a step towards the door, but changed her mind and turned around. 'The mothers of all the boys give each other solace, milady. Clara Trueblood saw that Rosa Catchpole and Jenny Buckler were upset and begged me to join her in comforting them. She says worry and loss are better understood by people who share the same feelings.'

'Clara has a wise head.'

'Indeed, milady. So wise that she knows you are in pain also. She says it isn't our place to talk to you about it, as you keep your feelings so private, but—' She broke off as Lady Anne lowered her head and touched her fingertips to her eyes. 'Should I stop? Do I offend you with my blunt ways? Gyles tells me constantly that I must learn to keep my mouth shut.'

'No, Martha. I like to hear you speak.'

'It troubles us that you carry so many burdens alone, milady. Our husbands do their best to advise you, but they've become shy without Thaddeus to prompt them—and Master de Courtesmain is not to be trusted.' She paused. 'At times like these, your best and closest confidante should be your daughter . . . yet Lady Eleanor seems more determined than ever to find fault with you.'

Lady Anne made a gesture of apology, as if to take the blame for Eleanor's hostility upon herself. 'The error's mine. Our ways and interests are so opposite that she believes me indifferent, and nothing I say or do changes her mind. She misses her father's love.'

'Only because she imagines it to be greater than it was, milady. You have been the only constant in her life. There was a time when she wouldn't leave your side. I recall her as a small child, skipping from house to house in the village as you moved amongst us. She was never happier than to be in your company and the company of serfs.'

Lady Anne remembered. 'I should have tried harder to keep it so.'

'You weren't given the chance, milady. Sir Richard punished you harshly for banishing him from your chamber after what he did to my Abigail, and Lady Eleanor was so young her affections were easily stolen. The justice you gave my family caused unhappiness in yours, and for that Gyles and I feel responsible.'

'Without reason,' said Lady Anne sincerely. 'Eleanor was too like Sir Richard not to become close to him. The burden that weighs on me is that Abigail died. I would have saved your daughter if I could, Martha.'

'I know that, milady, and I thank you most humbly for trying. But I worried when you defied Sir Richard to do it. I feared you hadn't foreseen how lonely you would become if you made an enemy of your husband.'

A fresh dampness appeared in Lady Anne's eyes. 'I lost nothing except the unwelcome attention of a man I disliked.'

'You lost a great deal, milady. For all the loyalty you've shown Sir Richard's people, and they you, your position sets you apart. You deny yourself close friendships for fear of how they'll be interpreted.'

Lady Anne lowered her gaze. 'What would you have me do differently?'

The woman reached across the desk to place her palm against her mistress's cheek, smoothing her thumb across the soft skin. 'Worry less about how you are viewed and allow yourself to be loved in the way your people want to love you. You will not lose respect by accepting embraces from those who wish to comfort you.'

Lady Anne thought of the mother who had died giving her birth and the father who had fallen mortally sick before she reached her sixth year. She had never felt their loss as deeply as she did in Martha's tender touch. Not even the abbess of her convent had expressed her affection for Anne so openly. She placed her hand over Martha's by way of gratitude, but her mind told her she would be wrong to let her guard down too easily. Some burdens—those that had been sworn to secrecy—could never be shared.

ℰℐℐ

Hugh de Courtesmain was gone from outside the door by the time Martha left, but he'd heard enough to pique his curiosity. Later, when Lady Anne was overseeing the noonday meal, he consulted the ledger that recorded Develish's births and deaths.

Abigail Startout, daughter to Gyles and Martha
Born summer, 1328—died winter, 1338.

No cause was given for the death, even though the passing of a child was a rarity in the demesne. He found the steward's ledger of 1338 and searched through the entries in November and December. He read that the winter had been unduly wet, and footrot had been common amongst the sheep, but the only mention of a Startout was on Christmas Day.

There was quiet celebration in the village when Sir Richard let it be known that Gyles Startout will ride in his retinue. Such honour is usually reserved for free men.

Hugh began randomly selecting archived scrolls from the shelves around the room, unrolling parchments to examine the dates beneath the seals. Lady Anne watched him for several minutes from the open doorway before she made her presence known. He seemed most engrossed by a letter from Sir Richard's sister, dated some fifteen years previously.

She moved into his line of sight, giving silent thanks that she'd had the sense to hide the documents she didn't want him to find beneath her gowns in the coffer in her chamber. 'What do you seek?' she asked.

His face flushed a guilty red. 'Understanding, milady. I know so little of the history of Develish.'

'You won't find it in Lady Beatrix's letters, sir. I believe she and My Lord of Foxcote visited once when Sir Richard's father first purchased the demesne for his son, but they haven't been since. What is it you wish to know?'

'I wondered why Sir Richard was in Dorseteshire when his family estates are in the north, milady. I presume Develish was the only demesne his father was able to acquire for him?'

'It was the most distant.'

'I don't understand, milady.'

'Sir Richard incurred debts that his family could barely afford. The price for paying them off was to renounce any claims he might have on land in the north and make his way as well as he could down here.' She smiled at de Courtesmain's expression. 'I imagine your next question will be why Develish is not encumbered with debt if Sir Richard was so profligate?'

'Yes, milady.'

'My dowry made it solvent again . . . as that letter from Lady Beatrix makes clear. If I remember correctly, she congratulates her brother on a betrothal that would solve his problems but spare him the annoyance of a demanding wife. She thought a youthful heiress who'd been trained in obedience was a good choice for her feckless brother.'

Hugh was as disconcerted as ever by the directness of her speech. 'Lady Beatrix will not have written this herself, milady. She has no learning.'

'Indeed. Her brother had the same failing. One of my first tasks as his bride was to read his sister's words to him. He thought it amusing to make me say aloud what she thought of me.' Her smile reached her eyes. 'I thought it amusing also.'

'The words are hardly complimentary, milady.'

'But I learnt so much from them, Master de Courtesmain. Lady Beatrix was merely agreeing with what Sir Richard had already told her about me. I could have wasted five years trying to discover how to please my husband . . . instead I found the information I needed in a single letter. Obedience and meekness are far more easily feigned than love and admiration.'

Hugh wondered why Sir Richard had been so blind to his wife's deceits. Had he thought education such a poor skill that it needn't be feared? 'He can't have thought you meek when you barred him from your chamber, milady. That wasn't the act of an obedient wife.'

Lady Anne eyed him thoughtfully. 'You've been listening at too many doors, Master de Courtesmain.'

'Indeed I have not, milady. I learnt the story from your daughter. She said her father was very distressed by your determination to keep him from your bed.'

'She led you false,' Lady Anne lied. 'The separation was Sir Richard's choice. He grew bored with my inability to make heirs— as I'm sure Lady Eleanor took pleasure in telling you.' She glanced at the ledger of births and deaths which was open on the desk at the entry for Abigail Startout. 'Is there other history I can help you with?'

Hugh hesitated. He wished he could read this woman's thoughts as easily as she read his. 'There is, milady. I'm curious to know why some of Lady Beatrix's letters are missing.' He proffered the parchment he was holding. 'This letter is dated Midsummer, 1333, while the next in order is Lady Day, 1335.'

'Why does that trouble you?'

'Lady Beatrix told me she'd written to her brother every quarter day since he became lord of Develish—' he gestured towards the shelves—'and that would seem to be true. There are four scrolls a year, dating back two decades, except for the six that are absent from the latter half of thirty-three and the whole of thirty-four. I find that strange, since the period covers your marriage and the birth of Lady Eleanor.'

Lady Anne gave a small laugh. 'I expect Sir Richard ordered his steward to burn them. He grew tired of his sister's teasing that he hadn't managed to produce an heir.' She moved to the shelves. 'Shall we search a little harder? It may be they've become lost amongst My Lord Bishop's parchments about Hell and damnation.'

A look of annoyance flickered in the Frenchman's eyes. 'Now *you* tease *me*, milady.'

'I do, Master de Courtesmain. You deceive yourself if you think you can find truth and enlightenment in Lady Beatrix's letters.'

☙❧

The night found Eleanor standing at the window of the spinning room, watching the passage of a watery, cloud-covered moon across the sky. Barefoot and dressed only in her night shift, she shook with rage against her mother for banishing her here to sleep alone. So much fuss had been caused by moving the servants to other quarters that all were reminded of when Sir Richard had been barred from his wife's chamber a decade ago, and Eleanor guessed that tongues were wagging about why her daughter had received a similar punishment.

As her fevered eyes stared into the darkness, it wasn't long before her rage turned on Thaddeus and his companions. Unable to blame herself for her mother's cold abandonment, she blamed them for leaving Develish. The demesne had lost its gaiety since their departure, as if fear for their survival had become a drain on everyone's spirits. Lady Anne had ordered the games postponed until their return but, far from accusing their mistress or Thaddeus for the sudden spoiling of their fun, Eleanor felt the serfs blamed her. She saw dislike and accusation in every face, and her hatred for Isabella grew as each day passed. There was only one person likely and able to spread stories about her behind her back, and that was the sly little chambermaid who was always at Lady Anne's side.

With a cry of fury, Eleanor beat her forehead against the wall. There were times when she feared she was going mad, so hot was her head and so chaotic her thoughts, for the only insight she could bring to what was happening to her was that it was her father's fault for dying.

The first she learnt of her banishment to the spinning room was when she returned that afternoon from trying yet again to persuade Father Anselm to hear her confession. The priest infuriated her by remaining closeted in his tower, pretending not to hear her, never mind how loudly she beat on his door and screamed at him to come out. She glared angrily at Hugh de Courtesmain as she mounted the stairs in her silver gown and saw him standing outside her mother's chamber. She was as suspicious of his whispering tongue as she was of Isabella's.

'What do you want?' she demanded.

He made a small bow. 'I'm the bearer of good news, milady. Your mother has agreed to allow you some privacy. I have had your clothes and possessions moved to the spinning room. You may sleep in there from now on, free of annoyance.'

Eleanor frowned. 'What annoyance?'

'The presence of servants, milady. You have told me many times how demeaning you find it to share accommodation with the lower orders. The women who were sleeping in the spinning room have been moved downstairs.'

He expected to see pleasure in her face. Instead her frown deepened. 'Are you telling me you made this request on my behalf? Why did you not ask my permission first?'

Hugh avoided the question. 'I hoped you'd be pleased.'

'Perhaps so . . . but why would Lady Anne allow me a privacy she doesn't enjoy herself?'

'Because she enjoys the company of servants, and always has. You are more like your father.'

He could see he'd used the wrong phrase when her eyes narrowed with mistrust. She made to push past him. 'You take too much upon yourself when you claim to know my thoughts,' she snapped. 'I don't choose to be alone. Bring my possessions back immediately and reinstate me at my mother's side.'

With a sigh, Hugh placed himself firmly between her and the door. 'I cannot, milady. This chamber is barred to you henceforth.

Your mother has ordered it. I sought only to make the situation more acceptable to you.'

Eleanor's face paled suddenly. 'What explanation did she give?'

'She said it would be better if you slept alone and asked me to arrange it.'

The fear in the girl's face was unmistakeable, but Hugh watched her hide it behind a forced smile. 'Then you were right in what you said at the start,' she declared. 'I'm to be allowed some privacy at last . . . as befits the daughter of a lord.'

Hugh bent his head in deference. 'Indeed, milady. I assumed that was the reason.' He watched her walk unsteadily towards the spinning room, noticing for the first time how thin she was becoming. There was something very wrong with her, he thought.

It was two hours before Eleanor found the courage to seek out her mother. She changed from her gown into one of the hated kirtles and presented herself demurely at the door of the steward's office. It stood half open and she watched Lady Anne for several seconds before she announced herself. The woman was by the window, reading from a piece of parchment, her back to the room.

'What do you want of me, daughter?' she asked without turning around.

Sir Richard had always said his wife was a witch with eyes in the back of her head, and Eleanor wondered if he was right. 'How did you know it was me?'

'The same way I always know,' said Lady Anne, moving to the desk and tucking the parchment into her ledger. 'You walk as impatiently as your father.' She studied the girl for a moment. 'What's so important that you had to change into homespun to impress me?'

Eleanor stepped into the room and closed the door behind her. 'Why have you banished me from your chamber, Mother? You will make me the subject of gossip by doing so.'

'You are that already, Eleanor, and through your own fault. Your voice is too shrill. You should have lowered your tone if you didn't want your need for absolution to be known around Develish.'

The girl's shock showed in her face. It hadn't occurred to her that her screaming rants against Father Anselm would be heard outside the church. 'He won't speak to me,' she said, her eyes growing damp with tears. 'He heard your heresy and believes I share it.'

Lady Anne was unmoved. 'Blame yourself, daughter. Even Sir Richard had more sense than to threaten the priest with a flogging if he didn't hear his confession. I warned you to find some wisdom. People are wondering what you've done that makes you so desperate.'

Eleanor clenched her fists. 'They'll wonder even more if you bar me from your room.'

'Yes.'

'Then why are you doing it?'

'Because you give me no choice. Your refusal to take responsibility for what you do worries me. Your behaviour gets worse each time you scream at the priest to free you from guilt. You can barely contain your fury against everyone, particularly Isabella, and I'm afraid that what you did once you'll do again.'

'But I haven't done *anything*,' the girl cried. 'You believe ill of me because you hate me.'

Lady Anne walked to a chest at the side of the room and stooped to lift the lid. 'You should have burnt these if you didn't want them found,' she said, removing a couple of folded garments.

'Trying to hide them amongst your gowns was foolish when you're too lazy to care for your clothes yourself. A servant was bound to discover them eventually.' She shook out a gown and shift, and laid them on the desk. Both were stained with blood. 'It was Jenny Buckler who brought them to me. She came out of kindness because she's worried you're having trouble with your monthly bleeds.'

Eleanor seized on the excuse as her mother knew she would. 'I was embarrassed,' she whispered. 'I didn't know it was happening and I had to clean myself as best I could.'

Lady Anne shook her head. 'The blood is in quite the wrong place. The back of the shift would be marked, not the front and sleeves of the gown.' She refolded the clothes and replaced them in the chest. 'I intend to let Jacob rest in peace because Thaddeus wished it, but I can't protect you from gossip, Eleanor. You must deal with that yourself.'

Spots of anger mottled Eleanor's face. She knew of only one way to excuse herself. 'It was your precious Thaddeus who killed Jacob,' she hissed. 'All I did was cradle the poor boy against my breast as he lay dying. The youths who accompanied Thaddeus would say the same if they were here. They watched it happen. Why do you think he took them with him if not to remove witnesses to his crime?'

Lady Anne studied her thoughtfully. 'Why did you not speak of this sooner?'

'You wouldn't have believed me after Thaddeus persuaded you it was an accident. I've tried to persuade Father Anselm to say the words for me, but he's as deaf to my entreaties as you are.' Tears welled in Eleanor's eyes. 'You would rather blame me for Jacob's death than your precious Thaddeus.'

Lady Anne moved to the desk to open the ledger and pick up her quill. 'Have you spoken the truth, Eleanor? If so, I should record it here.'

Eleanor painted a cross over her chest. 'I've spoken the truth.'

Her mother dipped the quill in the ink and began to write. 'Then you will make these same accusations before the people of Develish in one hour's time,' she said calmly. 'If Jacob was murdered, it should be known to all, as should the name of the criminal who committed the act and the accomplices who watched him do it. I shall order Jacob's coffin to be raised from the ground so that all may see the wound in his side, and you will produce your clothes as evidence that you witnessed his death and that what you say is true.'

Eleanor retreated to the door, her eyes wide with fear. 'I will not.'

'No,' Lady Anne murmured, laying the quill aside. 'I didn't think you would. Lies are never so easy when you know they'll be challenged. I asked the fathers of all the boys if they knew where their sons were that night, and only two—Edmund Trueblood and Olyver Startout—are unaccounted for. They may have been at the church with you, but not the others.' She watched the girl fumble with the latch in her haste to be gone. 'If it helps you mend your conscience, I'm willing to believe that Jacob tried to press himself on you. It's about all his father taught him, that violence will force a woman to submit.'

But Eleanor rejected this better chance to excuse herself. Convinced her mother was setting yet another trap, she raised the latch and ran into the hall, intent on hiding away from the twin devils of persecution and mockery that leered at her from every face she passed.

ের

The following morning, Father Anselm gave a start of alarm as a shadowy figure peeled away from the wall inside the church and moved to prevent him entering his chamber. With the sun too low in the sky to dispel the dimness inside the building, he had no idea what or who was confronting him.

'You're ruled by your belly, Father,' said Hugh de Courtesmain's voice. 'I guessed you'd go looking for something to break your fast if I prevented a servant bringing you supper here last night.'

He'd had to use guile to lure the priest from his tower, since no amount of knocking or calling the day before had elicited a response. He'd waited all night in the lee of the porch, unseen by the guard on the southern step, and his patience had been rewarded when the church door opened at dawn and Father Anselm had made his unsteady way along the path to the house. He watched the old man press his nose to a window of the great hall in order to satisfy himself it was safe to enter, and Hugh guessed the person he wanted to avoid was Lady Eleanor.

He would have found these antics humorous if he hadn't been so curious about Father Anselm's reluctance to speak with the girl. He'd put it down to laziness until Eleanor was banished from her mother's chamber, implying Lady Anne was equally disinclined to converse with her. Gossip was rife that Lady Eleanor was lovesick for Thaddeus Thurkell, causing her to pine and lose her appetite. To the servants it made perfect sense—the tall serf was the only man who'd ever stood up to her—but Hugh found it hard to believe. He couldn't count the number of times the girl had expressed hatred for the base-born slave, accusing him of turning her mother against her.

Sure that Isabella would know the truth, Hugh had asked the maid directly the previous evening why her young mistress had been banished to the spinning room, but Isabella had claimed ignorance, staring back at him with eyes empty of guile. He didn't doubt she was lying—she was too close to both Lady Anne and Eleanor not to know the reason—and he wondered who had ordered her to secrecy and why. It made him all the keener to uncover the truth.

He was tired of being a cipher in Develish, tired of Lady Anne's unwillingness to confide in him, tired of the way her distrust influenced how the serfs perceived him. Each was courteous enough, but none showed him the respect he felt was his due. Though Hugh might hold the nominal title of steward, he wielded no authority except as mouthpiece for Lady Anne when it suited her to use him as a messenger.

He resented her for it, believing he'd proven his worth and loyalty many times in the weeks since Sir Richard's death. In his own mind, she had an obligation to treat him with the same respect she showed Thurkell—sharing her thoughts and seeking his advice—and instead she belittled him. He saw amusement in the faces of men like John Trueblood and Adam Catchpole when he repeated her instructions to them. They knew as well as he that any small boy could have memorised her words and performed the task as easily.

What was the point of a steward without power? Why reinstate him if she couldn't trust him? On the rare occasions when Hugh searched his heart for blame, he recalled how he'd bowed and scraped to Sir Richard while turning his back quite openly on the insignificant wife in her homespun clothes and nun's wimple. But what could he have done differently when he owed his position to the husband? The fault was Lady Anne's. She kept her secrets too well. How could a newcomer have guessed that it was the reserved little woman who wielded influence in Develish and not the flamboyant liege lord?

If Hugh understood anything, it was that knowledge bestowed power—he'd learnt it in Foxcote—yet, search the demesne ledgers and the steward's office as he might, he'd discovered nothing he could use to enhance his influence. He had a suspicion Milady kept a private journal, since the reports she wrote in the public ledgers could not account for the hours she spent at the steward's desk. Yet he could find no evidence of it. Nor could he locate the edicts and letters that were clearly missing from the shelves, where obvious gaps suggested scrolls had been removed. It seemed Lady Anne had distrusted him even before she saw him, almost certainly because he'd come on the recommendation of Sir Richard's sister.

Hugh resisted the priest's attempt to push past him, folding his arms and pressing his feet solidly into the ground. He would have preferred Father Anselm drunk and uninhibited in what he chose to confide, but after a night's sleep the man appeared in command of his wits and deeply annoyed to be prised from his tower on false pretences.

'You're wasting your time if you hope to persuade me to hear Lady Eleanor's confession,' he snapped. 'Her mind is unseated. Only a mad girl would threaten to whip a priest in order to receive absolution.'

This was the first Hugh had heard of a whipping, but it hardly explained the priest's reluctance. 'You shouldn't take it to heart, Father. Lady Eleanor threatens us all when she's in a temper. It's the only way she knows how to get what she wants. Surely her words speak more of her need for your comfort than any serious wish to harm you?'

The old man's eyes glittered angrily. 'Do you come at Lady Anne's behest? Are these the words she's told you to say? Does she dare accuse the Church of hypocrisy then turn to a priest to rid her daughter of demons? You do yourself no favours with me or God by allowing her to use you in this way, Master de Courtesmain.'

Hugh kept his surprise well hidden. *Hypocrisy? Demons?* 'If Lady Anne has caused offence, I was unaware of it,' he said carefully. 'Please accept my apologies if I've done the same in error. I am a man of faith, as you know, and would not wish to trespass even by accident against my Maker.'

But Father Anselm was in no mood for false words. 'Return to Milady and instruct her to soothe her daughter's madness with herbs before she asks the Church to intervene. There's nothing I can do for Lady Eleanor while she remains in this frenzied state. The girl swoons each time her brain grows hot with anger.'

'You talk as if she's possessed.'

'And well she may be with a heretic for a mother and a father buried in unconsecrated ground. The fault is Lady Anne's, so let her cure it. She brought this madness on her daughter with her blasphemies against God and her mockery of the Church and Sir Richard.'

Hugh took what he could from these statements. 'You believe God punishes Lady Eleanor because her mother has blasphemed? When did this happen, Father?'

The priest wasn't inclined to answer. With a sudden thrust, he used his larger bulk to knock the Frenchman aside. 'Develish has been well-named since Sir Richard brought her here as a young bride,' he muttered, raising the latch on his door and pushing it open. 'Only Satan would deride God's laws by teaching serfs to believe themselves on a par with lords. Milady has destroyed her daughter by it and must take the consequences.'

He stepped inside and made to shut the door behind him, but Hugh thrust his foot against the jamb. 'Are you saying serfs are responsible for Lady Eleanor's troubles? Which ones and what harm have they done her? Is it Thaddeus Thurkell? She's had a particular loathing for him since Lady Anne raised him to stand at her side.'

'With reason,' the old man said curtly, signalling his intention of slamming the door against the soft leather of Hugh's boot. 'What place does Lady Eleanor have in this world if even a slave is encouraged to consider himself her equal?'

Eighteen

Thaddeus's camp on the River Pedle

IN THE WEEK THAT FOLLOWED the setting up of their camp, the boys took on the tasks of looking after the horses and trapping rabbits and squirrels for the cooking pot while Thaddeus vanished for hours on end to learn what he could about the villages around them. With no desire to enter a demesne or reveal his presence before he was ready, he went on foot and chose to watch each settlement from a distance, hidden within the shelter of woodland. He walked many miles, both to study the demesnes from different vantage points and to create a map in his mind of the highways and footpaths that linked them. Each night he refused the boys' pleas to go with him the next morning, saying it would be foolish to put every life in danger from the pestilence before it was necessary.

The truth was different. They hadn't the stomach to see what he was seeing and he asked himself why he'd ever thought half-grown boys could take the place of their fathers. Even Gyles, who'd tended Sir Richard while he was dying, would baulk at the half-eaten corpse lying in the dust of a road that headed south-east from the River Pedle. Thaddeus was alerted to it by its smell, but his hasty retreat hadn't saved him from the gut-wrenching sight of disembowelled innards. Where humans were dying, scavengers were thriving.

In eight days, he saw just one living person: a mendicant friar on his knees before a door in Athelhelm, retching blood and bile into the dust of the ground. His face beneath his cowl was drawn with pain and Thaddeus guessed he was as badly afflicted as the people he was tending. Yet he pulled himself upright to answer the voices that cried to him from inside the houses. Knowing he could never do the same, Thaddeus was left to wonder why so saintly a man merited so terrible a death.

At one hundred paces, the sweet, sickly smell of corruption that blew from Athelhelm village was powerful. It was the same in Afpedle. Thaddeus estimated the village had once housed upwards of four hundred field serfs, but the only evidence of them now was in the all-pervading stench of death. Hard as he tried to shut his mind to the atrocities he witnessed, they resurfaced in his dreams. The most haunting was an image of an infant being torn apart by dogs, for he couldn't say if it was dead when it was pulled from its cradle. The movement of its tiny arms as it was shaken in powerful jaws had had the semblance of life.

He returned through the mist each evening, his knapsack stuffed with herbs, vetch and beans for the cooking pot. He never said where he acquired the produce, but the boys guessed he was stealing from peasant strips. It was their first inkling that the demesnes around them must be empty of people, for theft of food by a stranger would have been impossible if serfs were working their fields. A hue and cry would have followed Thaddeus back to the camp and he and his companions would have been taken in charge.

To keep the boys occupied while he was away, he ordered them to practise their archery on the stretch of green sward beside the river, urging them to fire their arrows in longer and longer flights. It was left to Ian to maintain order, and as often as not he had to use his fists to achieve it. By the end of the week, when frustrations were at boiling point, the boys pleaded with Thaddeus to give them something worthwhile to do.

'We're going mad with boredom,' Ian said. 'How are we supposed to help you find supplies for Develish if we never leave this camp?'

Thaddeus nodded, while wondering how well they'd keep their sanity when he explained the first task he wanted them to perform. There were many worse madnesses than boredom.

He called them together around the fire, yet to be lit, and began by describing each of the settlements around them. The largest demesne was the one he believed to be Afpedle, standing on the other side of the river a mile to the south-west. The meadows and grazing pastures held some three hundred sheep, but the village was deserted. The same was true of the one to the east, the name of which he didn't know. It was quite different from Develish and Afpedle, with two-storey buildings amongst the wattle-and-daub huts, and padlocks on most of the doors. Not one was recognisable as a manor house, although great tracts of land around the dwellings had been cleared and cultivated. The meadows beside the river must once have grazed stock, for their manure was everywhere, but now the village was as empty of animals as it was of people. Thaddeus described it as a place without life, since not even vermin were visible. Yet a mile to the north was a recognisable demesne with a grand stone house, a church, a handful of serfs' cottages and a plague of rats.

Edmund gave a shudder of disgust. 'I *hate* rats.'

'Well, you'd better get used to them because they're everywhere,' said Thaddeus unsympathetically. 'I've never seen so many—or such bold ones. They're feeding on the grain left behind by fleeing or dying peasants.' He nodded towards the west. 'There's another settlement about a mile that way. I believe it's Athelhelm because it stands at the end of Devil's Brook and there's a ford where the highway crosses the river, leading to Afpedle. There are people in it but most seem to be dying.'

'How do you know?' asked Ian.

'I spent a day watching a monk going from habitation to habitation. He remained a long time in each, offering comfort to whoever lives there. Several times I heard cries from inside the dwellings.'

'Did you speak to the monk?'

Thaddeus shook his head. 'He could barely hold himself upright. I'm guessing he has the pestilence himself.'

'Did he have pustules?' Peter asked, his eyes alight with morbid curiosity.

'If he does they were hidden beneath his cowl. It's a lesson to avoid anyone who covers his head. It may be that the people of Athelhelm were free of the disease until they showed charity to a mendicant friar.'

'What if he continues on to Develish?' Joshua asked.

'He won't make it that far,' said Thaddeus. 'He'll die by the roadside like a corpse I saw to the east.' He smiled grimly at the boys' expressions. 'Death is all around us. The monk is the only living person I've seen, and he's more of a problem to us than he is to Develish. The whole of Athelhelm is.'

'Why?' asked Ian.

'We can't avoid it if we want to drive sheep or a wagon of grain from Afpedle to Develish.' He ran his boot over the cold ash of last night's campfire to smooth it. 'This is what the country around here looks like. I've studied it from each end of the ridge behind us and walked some miles up and down each highway.' He took up a stick and used the point to make a dip in the ash. 'Here's Develish—' he drew a straight line to another dip—'and here is the ford at Athelhelm. The river runs from west to east—' he drew another line at right angles to the first—'with Afpedle here and the highway out of it continuing to the south.'

'What about the village to the east?' asked Olyver. 'Doesn't that have a ford we could use? Where does that highway go?'

Thaddeus made another dip and drew a line above and below it. 'Both to north and south the road curves towards the east. I can't say where it leads to in the south, but I would guess it goes to Blandeforde in the north.'

The boys looked at the geometric shapes he was making. 'Perhaps all routes lead to Blandeforde . . . ours, too,' Edmund suggested. 'It must be an important place if the lord owns the land for miles around.'

Joshua's natural anxiety showed in his face. 'We'd be mad to go anywhere near it with a stolen wagon and stolen sheep,' he objected. 'There'll be bailiffs everywhere.'

Thaddeus eyed him with amusement. 'First steal a wagon. At the moment, I can't see how to do that, let alone steal livestock.'

'You said Afpedle was deserted.'

'It looks it,' Thaddeus agreed, 'but that doesn't mean it is. The household may have retreated behind the manor house walls, pulling their carts and their stores behind them.' He paused, picturing the demesne in his mind. 'There's a good three hundred sheep grazing the common lands, but the only way to drive them out is through the village.'

'Does that matter?' asked Ian. 'If everyone's behind the manor walls, they won't come out for fear of catching the pestilence. We can take what we like.'

Thaddeus thought of the visit he'd made to Afpedle that day. He'd hoped to find the dogs gone, their interest in the place sated. 'My Lord of Afpedle didn't make the same preparations we did. He may have closed his doors to save himself against the pestilence, but he didn't try to save his field serfs.'

'How do you know?'

'Dogs are fighting over corpses inside the huts. The stench of death is terrible. In some places, where the doors are wide open, clothes have been torn apart and left in blood-soaked rags on the ground. Ravens and rats are everywhere and, come night, I imagine there are foxes and badgers as well.'

There was an alarmed silence.

Thaddeus stared at the ash. 'I can't account for it. When Gyles was nursing Sir Richard, a rider on the highway called to him that the pestilence had killed fifty in Afpedle, yet there must have been people living in those huts until recently. The stench wouldn't be so bad otherwise.'

Olyver was the first to find his voice. 'What is it you don't understand?' he asked.

'Why all in Afpedle didn't die at the same time.'

'Maybe some were strong like Gyles and managed to survive,' said Edmund.

'Then what caused them to fall to it two months later?' asked Thaddeus. 'There must be some other way of catching it than breathing the air of an infected person.'

'Perhaps they died of something else,' Ian offered. 'Perhaps marauders killed them.'

'For what?'

The boy shrugged. 'Grain?'

Thaddeus shook his head. 'Serfs wouldn't give up their lives for a sack of corn when there's food in the fields around them. None of the strips have been fully harvested.'

Joshua raised a tentative hand. 'You made Gyles take off his clothes and swim the moat naked in case he carried the sickness on his skin or hair,' he reminded Thaddeus.

'Only to persuade the rest of you he was well. Some might have thought he was hiding the marks of the pestilence otherwise.'

'The water could have worked, though. Lady Anne always says washing is good for us.'

Thaddeus stared across the river, a deep frown creasing his brow. He remembered how Gyles had immersed himself in Devil's Brook after burying Sir Richard and the two others who'd died shortly afterwards. He'd asked Thaddeus for a fresh set of clothes, saying he couldn't rid himself of the feeling that the men's dirt was still upon him. He'd burnt his livery, tunic and britches on a fire, and had only professed himself clean once he'd scraped off his beard and cut his hair short enough to cleanse with potash and soda.

Thaddeus wished he'd had the sense to ask what form the 'dirt' took instead of keeping his distance from Gyles and muttering words of sympathy. Many times he'd asked how the pestilence had entered Bradmayne, but all the twins' father could tell him was that, while there was no sign of sickness when they arrived, upwards of seventy were dead by the time they left nine days later. The serfs in the village were the first to be afflicted, but the malady soon gained a hold inside My Lord of Bradmayne's house.

Lady Anne had put her own questions to Gyles once he was back inside the moat. Had Sir Richard heard nothing of the disease during his two-day journey to Bradmayne? Was My Lord of Bradmayne unaware of it?

Gyles couldn't answer for Sir Richard or My Lord of Bradmayne, but for himself he'd heard nothing of a killing disease along the way. He realised within a week that something was wrong in Bradmayne village, but his warnings to Sir Richard's captain of arms had gone unheeded. Sir Richard's days were filled with banqueting and gambling, and as long as the wine and ale kept flowing, the deaths of peasants were ignored.

'What caused Sir Richard to sober up and leave?' Lady Anne had asked dryly.

'Lady Eleanor's future husband was the first in the household to be afflicted, milady. Sir Richard wasn't inclined to hand over the dowry when he discovered it. We left within the hour, taking the gold with us.'

'Was Sir Richard sick by then?'

'I can't say, milady. He complained of a sore head after a night spent at Steynsford to break the journey, but he put it down to drinking into the early hours. Most of his fighting men had fevers. Three never left Bradmayne and another five were too weak to sit on their horses by the second evening.'

'What happened to them?'

'We left them with the wagon outside Pedle Hinton, milady. Sir Richard doubted he'd be given a bed for the night if he had sick men in his entourage.'

'But he had no qualms about pretending to be well himself?'

'None, milady. He'd have done the same here if you hadn't refused him entry. In truth, it made no difference to Pedle Hinton. The pestilence was already upon them before we arrived.' Gyles gave a weary shake of his head. 'I wish I could be of more help to you, but I have no explanation for why the sickness spreads and kills so quickly. When we rode through Dorchester town on the journey out, the streets were thronged with people, trading their wares in the markets. Eleven days later, doors were barred and windows shuttered, and the few frightened serfs we saw ran away. In all my life, I've never known such devastation occur in so short a time.'

There was nothing in what Gyles said to make Lady Anne or Thaddeus believe the pestilence was different from any other malady, except in its virulence and killing power. Lady Anne had learnt in her convent that poxes and fevers were caught through contact with the sick, and she had proven many times that isolating sufferers, be they sheep or men, slowed the spread of disease. Even so, her mind had remained troubled. Like Gyles, she knew of no sickness that could travel the highways so quickly or kill so many at the same time. If Melcombe hadn't been to the south-west of Develish, and if the warm summer breezes hadn't blown from that direction, she and Thaddeus would have believed the wind was responsible. But as the days passed, and no one in Develish fell to the pestilence, that fear left them. Thaddeus suggested Gyles might have miscalculated the number of dead.

'Barred doors and shuttered windows were as likely to be hiding the living, milady. Only fools would venture out with a killing sickness abroad.'

Lady Anne shook her head. 'His Grace's messenger spoke of hundreds dead in Melcombe. If I thought it possible, I'd say it must be healthy people carrying the disease from demesne to demesne—merchants and pedlars selling their wares, perhaps— but how can they infect others unless they have the ailment themselves?'

'Sir Richard rode two days before his body was overwhelmed,' Thaddeus reminded her. 'A merchant may be strong enough to journey for a week before he drops.'

'While knowing himself to be ill? How selfish does a man have to be to care so little for the lives of others, Thaddeus?'

'I doubt merchants or pedlars have your learning, milady,' he answered. 'Most will believe what the Church tells them: that the gift of life or death is in God's hands, not in their own.'

Nevertheless, the more he thought about it afterwards, the more Thaddeus began to wonder if Lady Anne was right. He had watched the passage of people along the road in the early days of the pestilence, expecting some to fall by the wayside from weakness as the sickness took hold. To his relief, none had, and he had assumed that only the healthy were travelling towards safety until he asked Gyles where Shafbury was, being one of the wasted places named by My Lord of Bourne. Two days' ride to the north, Gyles had told him, on the same highway that ran through Develish.

Thaddeus gave up on the puzzle eventually. It made no sense that a man could be well yet carry the disease upon him. How could he do so? Where would it be? What would it look like? Once in a while, he found himself harbouring the treacherous idea that the most reasonable explanation was the Church's— God was deciding who to afflict—and he might have come to believe it if anyone in Develish had succumbed. Yet days turned into weeks and no one sickened. It was as if their self-imposed exclusion from the world was thwarting every disease, and not just the pestilence.

He recalled these thoughts as he listened to Joshua remind him of Lady Anne's views on washing. She had become even more insistent that her people maintain a good standard of cleanliness once everyone was inside the moat, arguing that to have so many crammed into so confined a space was to invite trouble. Some had found her ideas amusing when she first arrived in Develish as a fourteen-year-old bride. She had urged mothers to pick lice from their children's hair and fathers to forbid their families from urinating and defecating wherever they felt like it. Many had resented her high-handed approach, questioning why a young maid with no experience of life felt bold enough to instruct her elders.

As time passed and her commitment to the welfare of her husband's people—so much greater than Sir Richard's—became apparent to all, they started to see merit in what she said. There was no denying that the health of their children improved under her tutelage, and that the digging of a public latrine away from the village brought an end to the bouts of sickness and loose stools which had plagued the demesne so often in the past. Thaddeus had asked her once why she had such a fear of human waste that she wouldn't even allow it to be thrown into Devil's Brook. Wasn't that what everyone did?

'It is,' she agreed, 'yet few would drink from a pitcher that contained another man's excrement. The Bible tells how Moses taught the Israelites to keep themselves clean in body and mind, instructing them to bury their waste in the ground at a distance from their camps. The rules served them well during their long wanderings in the wilderness. They remained strong as a people and found their way to the Promised Land. We would be wise to learn from them.'

Thaddeus lost count of the number of times Lady Anne quoted from Scripture to prove she had right on her side. It seemed strange to him when she argued so strongly against the teachings of the Church. As he grew older, he realised she made a distinction between what she read on the page and what was spoken in the pulpit. When his reading was fluent enough, she inscribed the parables of Jesus in English and asked him to read them carefully and make up his own mind whether God had intended the poor to suffer so that the rich might live in luxury.

He found himself picturing her face now, wishing she was at his side to give him the benefit of her wisdom. 'There's human filth everywhere in Afpedle,' he told the boys. 'The loudest noise is the buzzing of flies. The dogs feed on excrement outside the houses. For all I know they carry the pestilence on their teeth.'

The silence that followed was very long. Each boy was regretting his expression of discontent about being confined to the camp. It was one thing to grow weary of archery practice, quite another to venture into a world of unimaginable horror.

'So what shall we do?' asked Ian eventually. 'Go back to Develish empty-handed?'

'It depends how brutal you're willing to be,' said Thaddeus. 'The quickest way to cleanse these villages is to do what My Lord of Bourne did to ours and burn them to the ground. The scavengers will leave once everything is reduced to a cinder.'

Peter's alarm showed in his face. 'But you said there were people still alive in Athelhelm,' he protested.

'I did,' Thaddeus agreed unemotionally, 'and we must hope they're too sick to rise from their beds when we set light to their thatch.' He reached for some kindling to start a new fire on last night's ash. 'They'll die outside on the highway otherwise and there'll be no driving sheep through Athelhelm then.'

ໜ

He took himself along the riverbank, downstream from the camp, and removed his boots to enter the water. He could hear the raised voices of the boys in the distance, but he blocked his ears deliberately to the argument that was raging between them. He didn't want to know what was being said or who was saying it. He needed them to reach a decision for themselves, free of his influence, so that they couldn't accuse him afterwards of forcing their hands.

The mist which descended every evening as the air cooled in the valley drifted like smoke along the surface of the water. The river, so much wider than Devil's Brook, teemed with fish, although the boys had had no success catching them during the day. As twilight fell, Thaddeus hoped for better luck. Tickling trout and lulling them to sleep was one of the few skills his stepfather Will had taught him down the years. Sir Richard, wanting the sweet pink flesh for himself, had made it a flogging offence to steal fish from Devil's Brook, but few had taken any notice. When food was scarce, the promise of a meal far outweighed the pain of a whipping.

Will had been particularly adept at running his fingers delicately from tail to gills, although Thaddeus had never understood why. It took stealth to locate a fish beneath overhanging plant cover, and patience to soothe it into a trance, yet Will had neither of these qualities in everyday life. He could wade through water like a spectre, making no ripples at all, or lie for hours on the riverbank waiting for a trout to rise, but he couldn't keep his temper for half a minute anywhere else. It was strange.

The water was warmer than the air, which accounted for the mist. At the edge, it was only deep enough to reach above Thaddeus's knees, and he stood for several minutes, allowing the silt stirred up by his feet to settle again. The fear that water might carry the pestilence had left him. They were downstream of Athelhelm and had been drinking from the river for days, yet nothing was amiss with any of them.

Close by, he heard the plop of a water vole diving from its nest, apparently unconcerned or unaware of a human presence. Will had taught him that trout always face upstream when they rest under the cover of the riverbank, and he began to move slowly towards the camp, feeling with his fingers for the stir of a tail and a silky soft underbelly. He lost three through clumsiness before he caught one, hooking it out by its gills and tossing it far enough onto the bank so that it wouldn't flap back into the water. But as he waited for peace to settle again, he found it harder to block out the boys' insistent voices.

'It seems pretty clear to me,' said Ian. 'If the only way to drive sheep from Afpedle to Develish is to burn the sick in Athelhelm, then that's what we have to do.'

'I don't care what you say,' snapped Joshua angrily. 'It's murder and I won't do it.'

'They'll die anyway,' said Edmund.

'You don't know that,' Peter told him. 'You don't know anything about the pestilence. None of us does. Maybe it's possible to catch it and live.'

'And maybe it's not.'

'Then we should wait until everyone's dead before we do anything.'

'How will we know?' Olyver asked reasonably. 'Are you and Joshua planning to search each house to make sure it's only corpses we reduce to ashes?'

'We shouldn't even do that,' said Peter. 'The Church forbids the burning of bodies.'

'We'll go to Hell whatever we do,' Joshua cried wretchedly.

'Not if we return to Develish and starve with everyone else,' said Ian. 'God will think us fine fellows if we sacrifice ourselves and our families instead of some dog-chewed corpses.'

'You shouldn't talk like that.'

'Why not? Do you think God's listening to me?' There was the sound of a log being thrown on to the fire. 'Thaddeus seems sure there's no one alive in Afpedle. I say we start there to see if it works. If it doesn't, if the dogs and vermin stay and we can't steal the sheep, there'll be no point burning Athelhelm.'

'What if there are people alive in the manor house? They'll see us doing it.'

'They'll be grateful to us. It can't be much fun watching dogs tear into bodies. Imagine if we'd had to do it. You'd recognise your mother's clothes being dragged out of your house, wouldn't you?'

'You've a sick mind,' said Joshua.

'And you're walking around with your eyes closed,' Olyver retorted on his twin's behalf. 'You're in Hell already, you just can't see it.'

'Let it rest,' said Edmund. 'You, me and Ian can go with Thaddeus, and Joshua and Peter can stay behind. Someone has to watch the horses and guard the camp.'

Thaddeus's fingertips brushed gently against a flank. He lowered them to the fish's belly and used soft little strokes to work his way towards the gills. The creature was long and fat, and Thaddeus brought his other hand around to grapple him from the water. There was a lot of fight in him. He was a granddaddy of trouts who didn't want to die, and Thaddeus felt a moment of regret as he ripped the creature's gills and flung him to the bank to gasp out his life on the grass. It seemed a shame to add another death to the death that was all around them.

Nineteen

AFTER TWO DAYS, A SHOUT arose that a rider was coming down the road from the north. He travelled alone, and hope ran through the demesne that he was a messenger from My Lord of Blandeforde. Lady Anne, showing caution, urged her people to remain in the house and chose only Gyles Startout to stand beside her as the rider approached.

He wore a livery she recognised although, even from a distance, the tabard looked more lived-in than previously, suggesting it hadn't been removed or brushed since the last time she saw it. On that occasion, the rider had been clean-shaven in the Norman style; now, his jaw and cheeks were covered with thick stubble in the manner of English serfs who trimmed their beards with shears rather than blades.

'It's My Lord of Bourne's captain of arms,' Gyles murmured. 'What brings him back? Was it not enough to burn our village?'

'He's been camping rough unless I miss my guess,' Lady Anne answered. 'We should be wary of him, Gyles. If he's parted company with his master and his fellow soldiers, it will be because they've succumbed to the pestilence.'

'He will notice that the raft has been rebuilt, milady. I should have ordered it moved from sight.'

Lady Anne placed a comforting hand on his arm. 'There was no time. Six strong men are needed to lift it . . . and this devil would have wondered why anyone here was still well enough to perform such a task.'

Gyles tapped the bow that was slung across his shoulder. 'If you give the order I can topple him quite easily. He'll be within range in another twenty paces.'

She shook her head. 'Not until we know what fate has befallen My Lord of Bourne. I'd rather not invite trouble before I have to. We must use guile as Thaddeus and I did last time.'

'I haven't Thaddeus's skill with words, milady.'

Lady Anne's fingers squeezed his arm reassuringly before she dropped her hand to her side. 'Then say nothing. I will speak for both of us.'

They waited in silence as the charger covered the last thirty yards to the edge of the moat. What the captain made of the neat little woman and the grizzled-haired serf beside her was anyone's guess, but Lady Anne was conscious that their well-fed appearance was greatly at odds with the picture she'd painted last time of a demesne beset by pestilence and starvation. A powerful stench of sweat and unwashed body drifted towards them as the man and his mount came to a halt.

He ducked his head in mocking salute and spoke in French. 'My Lord of Bourne sends his respects, My Lady of Develish, and offers condolences for the loss of your husband.'

'What makes you think my husband is dead, sir?'

'You would not have needed to use subterfuge the last time we came, milady.' His eyes raked her from head to toe. 'It will gladden My Lord's heart to know you are still free of the pestilence. He admires you greatly for trying to protect Sir Richard's people against a death that has killed so many.'

Lady Anne wondered how he had come by so much information, and a painful dread gripped her heart. 'You seem more knowledgeable than at our previous meeting, sir. How so?'

'Men speak of your demesne, milady. It's well known for its pure air and bounteous produce.'

It was hardly an answer. 'Which men? We long for news of the outside world. Do our neighbours fare well in this time of pestilence? Has My Lord of Bourne visited Pedle Hinton and Funtenel?'

'He has visited all the demesnes in this region, milady.'

'But not been granted admittance if your unkempt appearance is any guide. It puzzles me therefore that you know so much about us.'

'Travellers have eyes, milady. The wiser amongst them move across country to avoid habitations, and several have reported in Blandeforde that they've seen people alive behind your walls. The hills that surround you are high and give good vantage points. From our camp amongst the trees on your northern slope, we've seen a great deal of activity here. So much so that My Lord of Bourne doubts any have died since you withdrew behind your moat.'

Lady Anne hid her relief that Thaddeus and his companions hadn't had secrets forced from them. 'My serfs will be happy to learn that My Lord of Blandeforde knows of our survival, sir. They worry that messengers might never be sent to announce that the pestilence has passed.'

'And they should continue to worry, milady. My Lord of Blandeforde and his household left Dorseteshire for their estates in the west several weeks ago, as did most of his vassal lords.' He glanced from her to Gyles. 'Only widows and peasants remain, and they become fewer in number as each day passes.'

Lady Anne took the words for a threat. 'Yet My Lord of Bourne is still with us,' she said lightly. 'Why, sir? A man so righteous, and so afraid of sin, would surely have found sanctuary in another county?'

'He rides for the King, milady. He is here to take inventory of all the estates in Dorseteshire.'

She studied him curiously. 'You tease me.'

'No, milady. I speak the truth.'

'Does the King not know that a pestilence rages here?'

'I can't say, milady. I take my orders from My Lord of Bourne and he takes his from the King. Each of us does as we are instructed.'

'Perhaps so, but what use is an inventory when a worker who is alive one day may be dead the next? The wealth of a demesne rests in its people. Does your master not understand that? His errand is a foolish one. His time would be better spent returning to the King with news of Dorseteshire's plight.'

The captain looked amused. 'Do you expect me to repeat that to him?'

'Why wouldn't you?'

'He'll not take advice from a woman, milady.'

Lady Anne smiled faintly. 'Then at least persuade him that he wastes his time in Develish. An inventory was taken here last Lady Day by My Lord of Blandeforde's steward. Your master will find the record in My Lord of Blandeforde's treasury—or, if you prefer, I can send across the copy our own steward made. Which is your pleasure?'

A look of unease crossed the man's face. 'I have no authority in these matters, milady. I'm instructed to tell you that, however difficult your situation, you are not exempt from the payment of taxes. You will assemble your people on the forecourt at noon tomorrow so that a head count may be taken and your dues calculated. If your husband were alive, My Lord of Bourne would look to him for payment, but since he is not, the responsibility is yours.'

Lady Anne felt Gyles stir beside her and knew he understood the intention behind the words as surely as she did. To be certain, she dropped her head in a respectful bow. 'In which coinage should this payment be made, sir? Gold or grain?'

'Gold, milady. We will leave you your grain to feed your people.'

Lady Anne kept her gaze lowered to hide her anger. In a county where vassal lords were absent or dead, and only ill-educated widows and peasants had been left to guard demesnes, who would dare oppose a lord with an army at his side? If his claim to ride for the King was disbelieved, he had soldiers with longbows to threaten death. 'What should I do for the best?' she whispered to Gyles in English. 'Present a challenge or feign obedience?'

'Present a challenge, milady. Your cleverness unsettles him.'

She raised her head. 'Are you not ashamed to serve such a man as your master, Captain? I saw that he was steeped in evil the last time he came, but I hadn't guessed he was a common thief and murderer. What ransom does he demand in order that the lives of my people may be spared your arrows?'

The charger became skittish, as if the animal felt its rider's discomfort. 'You speak from ignorance, milady,' the captain snarled, wrestling with the reins. 'The collection of taxes is lawful.'

'Indeed, but only My Lord of Blandeford has authority to collect them here. Your master uses his absence to steal what he can, and looks to the pestilence to destroy all witnesses to his crimes. If everyone dies, there will be no one to accuse him.'

'You would be wise to watch your words, milady.'

'You also, sir. You condemn your master out of your own mouth when you pretend he rides for the King. There's not a man or woman here who doesn't know how and when taxes are collected, and all will give testimony to My Lord of Bourne's treachery when the pestilence has passed. You and your men will be tried with him, for I don't doubt you've murdered innocent widows and peasants on his order.'

The captain's eyes narrowed. 'The word of a serf means nothing against a lord's. It needs only for you to die to free us from any suspicion of wrongdoing. Think on that before you malign My Lord further. Your house will burn as brightly as your village if he commands it.'

Gyles unslung his short bow and fed an arrow on to the string. 'This is but one of many that is trained on you,' he said, raising the weapon to his cheek. 'Think on *that* before you make threats against Milady.'

The captain turned towards him with contempt. 'Do you try to scare me, serf?'

The words had barely left his mouth before he gave a howl and clapped a hand to a bleeding ear. 'Be grateful my aim is as good as it is,' Gyles said impassively, feeding another arrow on to his string. 'When I go for your heart, you'll not have time for fear.' He raised the bow again but this time twanged the string, whistling through his teeth in imitation of an arrow's flight. He smiled to see the captain flinch. 'I never did meet a Norman with courage. From the stench of you, you've been shitting yourself for weeks.'

'Enough!' the captain cried. 'Order him to lower his weapon, milady!'

'Does he frighten you?' she asked with amusement. 'He should. He's been captain of arms to Sir Richard of Develish these last ten years, and now commands Sir Richard's people. There are twenty more who can aim an arrow as well as he does. If you doubt me, I will ask them to step from their hiding places and take that handsome charger from between your legs. He will make a good meal for us.'

The captain nudged his mount backwards. 'I came in peace. You offend against the laws of hospitality by attacking me.'

'A man is known by his deeds, sir. We've been more hospitable than you deserve. In the spirit of justice, we would be within our rights to return you to your master with your clothes ablaze. Tell him that Lady Anne requests he depart this valley and leave us in peace. There will be no reason for us to accuse him of perfidy unless further crimes are committed here.'

The captain shortened his reins with a derisory laugh. 'You think he'll allow a chattel wife to best him? He'll take your gold and more besides if you defy him.' He turned the charger and spurred it to a gallop.

Gyles tensed his arm to loose the second arrow, but Lady Anne reached for his wrist to deflect his aim. 'His death won't achieve anything. Alive, he may persuade his master to see sense.'

Reluctantly, Gyles lowered his bow. 'I hope you're right, milady. There's more than gold to attract them here now they know our women are free of the pestilence.'

The sixth day of September, 1348

*T*his entry may be the last I ever make. If so, let it stand as an accusation of murder against My Lord of Bourne and his fighting men. My Lord, who is a stranger in these parts (his crest being unknown to me), has issued threats against me and my people if I do not release to him the little gold that remains in Develish.

He claims to be in Dorseteshire on the King's authority, tasked with collecting taxes in the form of coin. I believe this claim to be false. For his own benefit, My Lord of Bourne seeks to exploit bereft widows who are sadly ignorant about how taxes are counted and rendered. I am not such a one. Sir Richard was vassal knight to Blandeforde, and I, as Sir Richard's widow, have inherited the obligation. All dues owed to the King from Develish are faithfully passed to My Lord of Blandeforde, who stands as the King's treasurer in this region of Dorseteshire.

By transgressing against this lawful order, My Lord of Bourne shows himself to be a common thief. He has already committed one crime against Develish by ordering his archers to fire our village some two months ago. On that occasion, *he claimed to act on behalf of God, assuming the rights of a virtuous judge to destroy my people's homes as an example to others that Develish harboured sinners. Today, he has given warning that the manor house will burn likewise if I do not satisfy his greed for gold.*

I have refused, and my people prepare to defend Develish against him. Should we die in the attempt, I beg anyone who finds this document to deliver it to My Lord of Blandeforde and beg justice on our behalf.

My Lord of Bourne is a man of great evil who should be condemned for the iniquity he perpetrates in the King's name against the suffering widows and peasants of Dorseteshire.

In nomine Patris et Filii et Spiritus Sancti
Anne of Develish

Twenty

To the youths' shocked eyes the next morning, the violent chaos in Afpedle was a thousand times worse than Thaddeus had described. Gore-stained clothes and possessions had been dragged from every house, and the stench of death was unbearable. None of them had seen so many rats nor heard so many fighting dogs. Guttural growling rumbled around the village, interspersed with screams of pain as teeth ripped into the cheek of an adversary.

Thaddeus had led them to the edge of some woodland, two hundred yards downwind of the first cottage, and they didn't need his words of warning to keep their voices low and make as few movements as possible. All understood the danger of attracting the attention of the dogs. Ian counted three nosing around the detritus on the ground—a hound and two mastiffs—but he guessed there were more inside the huts. 'They look like hunting dogs,' he whispered. 'Where do you suppose they've come from?'

'The manor house,' Thaddeus murmured. 'I imagine the lord ordered their release to preserve his stores. He probably expected them to go for the sheep.'

'Why aren't they interested in the rats?'

'There are easier pickings inside the huts.'

'I can see a baby's cradle on its side in the road,' said Olyver, his face grey with nausea. 'Do you think it had a child in it?'

'Ignore it,' Thaddeus told him firmly. 'Concentrate on what we need to do, not on what's been and gone and can't be mended.'

'We must kill the dogs,' Edmund said. 'We'll never get close enough to fire the thatch otherwise.' He was beginning to understand why Thaddeus had urged them to practise hitting targets at a distance. 'Only longbows have the range to shoot from here.'

'What if we were upwind?' suggested Thaddeus. 'Would the breeze carry the arrows farther?'

'The dogs would scent us,' said Ian, 'and I don't fancy trying to kill them if they come at us in a pack. None of us is quick enough on the draw for that.'

'We'll have to pick them off one at a time,' said Olyver, 'and we can't do it from here. Edmund's right. We need longbows. Even then, we'd probably only wound them.'

Thaddeus watched the two mastiffs square up to each other, lips drawn back in snarls, teeth bared in anger. Their jaws were wide enough to break a man's leg, and they'd be twice as dangerous if they were thrashing around with a barb in their shoulder. 'We have twenty arrows,' he reminded the boys, 'and that's not enough to do what we need to do unless you're confident of hitting your target each time. I suggest we think of a way to contain the dogs. We can decide how to kill them once the village is burnt.'

It was a plan more easily proposed than performed. Olyver spotted some sheep pens in one of the fields, but they weren't sturdy enough to contain a pack of hounds; and wattle fencing, the only secure way to corral animals, took too long to construct. Nor, as Edmund pointed out, would dogs act like sheep. 'There's no way to herd them in a flock. They might enter a trap if we bait it with a carcass, but they won't all go in at the same time.'

'Maybe we don't need to contain them,' Ian suggested. 'Maybe all we have to do is keep them away from the village long enough to set the thatch ablaze. If someone—' He broke off abruptly.

'Go on,' encouraged Thaddeus.

The boy shook his head with a wry smile and gave his usual answer. 'It's a bad idea.'

'Tell me anyway.'

'I was just thinking that hunting dogs follow a scent, and if one of us could lay a trail and stay ahead of them—' He broke off again at Thaddeus's expression. 'I told you it was a bad idea.'

'I've heard better,' Thaddeus agreed before ordering the boys to gather wood for a fire. 'Only dry kindling,' he warned. 'We need it to burn fast and furiously when the time comes.' He picked up his sword. 'Take it in turns to stand watch until I come back.'

'Where are you going?' asked Olyver.

Thaddeus jerked his chin at the bundle of arrows on the ground. 'To find something to make these blaze. They won't burn thatch on their own.'

⁑

Ian estimated three hours went by before he heard the crack of a twig, and Thaddeus's tall figure appeared amongst the trees. The boy had an arrow in his bow, levelled at Thaddeus's heart, and the tall serf gave a nod of approval. 'Good,' he murmured laconically, easing a sheaf of plants from his shoulders. He stooped to undo the rope that bound it. 'I found a field of flax on the other side of the manor. It should have been harvested a couple of months ago.'

'Will it work?'

'Ought to . . . the seeds still have oil in them.' He pulled the sheaf apart to reveal a roll of greasy strands of wool. 'If we use these to bind the stems to the arrows, the fat in the wool should keep smouldering after the flax has burnt out.'

'Will they fly straight?' asked Olyver.

'We won't know until we start. The one I threw in the field worked well enough, but it wasn't burning.' He began pulling and twisting the fleece into thin strings. 'Where's Edmund?'

'Watching to see the dogs don't come this way.'

'That's wise. Separate the plants into groups of ten. As long as the stems are bound tightly to the shafts, it doesn't seem to affect the flight too badly.'

Both boys set to work, although neither saw the point of what they were doing. Even if the flax burnt bright and strong, and even if the arrows flew straight, what use would they be if the targets were too far away? 'We've counted seven dogs in all,' said Ian at last. 'Five wolfhounds and two mastiffs. When they aren't fighting, they're sleeping. The only other place that interests them is the manor house. They nose around the walls and whine as if they want to be let in.'

Thaddeus tied off the last arrow. 'You'll need every one of these when the time comes, but keep some in reserve until you see how well the blaze spreads. Start by firing into alternate roofs at the beginning.'

Olyver frowned uneasily. 'Won't you be with us?'

Thaddeus shook his head. 'You're all better bowmen then I am. My task is to lure the dogs away.' He looked at the pile of firewood the youths had collected. 'You'll need to move this as soon as they leave and build your fire within range of the village. Are you confident of being able to light it in a hurry?'

Neither boy answered.

'This isn't a game,' he warned. 'I'll string you from the nearest tree if I come back and find you haven't even managed the easy bit.'

'What if you *don't* come back?' Ian asked, his unease as great as his twin's. 'What if the dogs catch you?'

'They won't.' Thaddeus pointed to the surplus flax stems. 'You can use these to set the blaze going. Which of you has the tinderbox?'

'Me,' said Olyver, adding in a rush, 'You can't just say they *won't*. What if they *do*?'

Thaddeus cuffed him lightly across the back of the head. 'I haven't come this far to die of a dog bite. Worry about your own responsibilities and not about mine.'

He took them to where Edmund was standing beside an oak at the edge of the wood and made all three repeat what they had to do several times. He refused to name a leader, saying it would be the fault of all and not the fault of one if they were unsuccessful. Their only excuse for not performing their task would be if he failed to draw the dogs off, although he wouldn't tell them how he planned to do that.

He didn't want them any more scared than they were already.

☙❧

His idea involved Sir Richard's charger and the long coil of rope he'd cut from the Develish well. He'd returned to the camp to retrieve them. Peter and Joshua had been agog with curiosity to see him again so soon, but Thaddeus had been no keener to satisfy their curiosity than he was Ian's, Olyver's or Edmund's. After buckling on the best saddle, the longest stirrups and the strongest reins, he had ridden the animal along the northern bank of the river towards Athelhelm.

The route took him past Afpedle, which stretched away on the other side, and he had a better view of the demesne's layout from horseback than he'd had on foot. Clumps of alders and high-growing bulrushes obscured most of the land at eye-level, and only the manor house, church and village, being on higher ground, had been visible when he walked the path. He paused for several minutes to study the highway to the south. It ran straight and true on a shallow incline for a good three miles before losing itself in woodland on the next set of hills, but even on horseback he was too far away to see how badly rutted it was. He searched the road for people or animals, but couldn't see any.

He crossed the river some five hundred paces short of the ford at Athelhelm, spurring the charger up the far bank before dismounting to continue on foot. This part of the highway, linking Afpedle to Athelhelm, was completely hidden behind trees and he was wary of emerging onto it without knowing what was there. He led the animal quietly through the alders, stopping every so often to listen, watching the horse closely to see if it sensed the presence of dogs.

It was a peculiarly docile creature and had probably been chosen by Sir Richard for that reason. The man would have whipped mercilessly any horse that tried to unseat him, though Thaddeus doubted this one had enough spirit to do anything so daring. He questioned whether it could even achieve a gallop, since it was clearly used to ambling along at Sir Richard's speed, and he cursed himself for not choosing Lady Eleanor's skittish bay jennet as he swung into the saddle to nudge the lumbering creature out of the trees and onto a road that was empty in both directions. He turned its head towards Afpedle, and drove his heels sharply into its flanks, calling to it to gallop.

The beast took off at such speed that he lost his stirrups immediately and stayed in the saddle only by virtue of having legs long enough to clamp around the animal's belly and a quick enough reflex to grab its mane with both hands. He clung on, desperately working the reins through his fingers in order to bring the creature to a halt before they reached Afpedle. It wasn't part of his plan to career into a village full of dogs, unprepared and unprotected, knowing he could be thrown at any minute.

Sir Richard had called his charger Edward, after the King, but Thaddeus renamed it Killer when he finally wrestled it to a halt. 'Are you trying to break my neck?' he demanded between laboured breaths as he slid from its back. 'Is that all you do? Walk or bolt? Weren't you taught anything in between?' He ran his palm down the animal's sweaty neck. 'How the Hell am I going to stay on your back when you have a pack of hounds snapping at your heels?'

That question was still unresolved when he returned from helping the twins prepare the arrows for firing. He'd tied Killer to a tree in the woods to the west of the demesne, and the animal's nostrils flared in alarm at his approach. With reason. Thaddeus made a strange silhouette with a dead sheep across his shoulders, its head lolling from side to side and gory mucus dripping from its nose. He had separated it from the herd earlier, confining it to a pen so that he could slaughter it when he came back. He needed it fresh and warm and able to leave a trail of blood in its wake. To that end, he had driven his knife through the cord at the back of its neck to prevent it bleeding from a slit throat before he was ready.

He spoke soothing apologies to the horse as he lowered the sheep to the ground. 'You'll like me even less when I release its entrails,' he warned, removing the coil of rope from Killer's saddle and tying one end tightly around the sheep's neck, adding a loop about the horns for good measure. He secured the other to the pommel then placed the limp body across Killer's withers and hoisted himself up behind it.

'I'm the only one who can free you of this weight when the dogs are upon you,' he murmured into Killer's ear as he leant forward to loosen the reins from the tree. 'Try to remember that when you think about ditching me at the roadside. We'll get on a lot better if you do.'

∾

Ian had moved away from Olyver and Edmund to concentrate on the far side of the village, where the highway continued towards the south. Wood-covered slopes, turning russet and gold as the leaves prepared to fall, rose towards the horizon and he wondered what lay beyond. Another valley? The sea? If Thaddeus was going to lead the dogs anywhere, it would surely be that way. Yet nothing seemed to be happening. Olyver and Edmund were complaining of boredom and hunger pangs, and Ian was becoming more and more convinced that Thaddeus had failed.

He opened his mouth in a wide yawn, his mind filled briefly with visions of the sea. His father had described it to him once as 'endless blue water', but Ian had been quite unable to picture such a thing, since no water he'd ever seen was blue. There was so much he didn't know, he thought, turning to look towards the strips of peasant land that crisscrossed the land to the west of the village. He picked out what he thought was a deer. It was a good four hundred yards away and he watched it for several minutes, narrowing his eyes to sharpen his focus, before he realised it was Thaddeus on horseback, heading for a point on the highway some twenty yards from the southern end of the village.

His heart gave an almighty lurch. 'Oh my *God*!' he groaned. 'What the *Hell* does he think he's doing?' He beckoned frantically to Olyver and Edmund to join him. 'Thaddeus is using himself as bait,' he whispered.

They all felt his fear as the horse reached the end of a strip and stepped out onto the road. 'Why is he going so slowly?' Olyver asked.

'Maybe he's waiting for the dogs to spot him.'

Edmund, who had the longest sight, shook his head. 'He's using his knife on something. I think it's a sheep. There!' He pointed excitedly as Thaddeus tossed the now bleeding carcass onto the ground and gave out a high ululation which was loud enough to carry to the boys.

If it was a signal to them to start their fire, none responded. They froze in terror as a storm of barks rose from inside the village and a wolfhound emerged from behind the last house, questing the air for the source of the new scent. Thaddeus nudged the charger into a walk so that the carcass began to move along the ground behind it, spilling blood and entrails in the dirt.

'He should be going faster,' said Olyver in an agony of nerves.

And his words seemed prophetic when the hound loped into a trot and another three ran into view behind it. To the watching boys, whose perspective was skewed by distance, the next few seconds were a frightening blur. The leading pack seemed to be on Thaddeus before, with a crescendo of wolf-like howls, the mastiffs and the remaining hound raced from the village and bounded after them.

'Oh my *God*!' Ian blurted again, taking a step forward. 'We need to do something.'

Edmund put a hand on his arm to hold him back. 'They've reached the tail end of the guts, that's all. Look. He's moving now. Jesus!'

'He'll never stay on,' said Olyver morosely. 'Not at that speed.'

☙☞

Thaddeus's only memory of the ride was a feeling of exhilaration. Even while the dogs were bounding from the village, he felt a gambler's thrill at waiting until the last moment to set Killer running. It was as if a drug entered his mind to tell him he was invincible, and that whatever he did would work. Forgotten were his worries that Killer would put his foot in a rabbit hole or lose his balance on a rut; forgotten, too, were his fears that his own lack of riding ability would catapult him from the saddle.

As the horse leapt forward at his kick, he bent forward to lie along the animal's back, hooking his feet firmly into the stirrups and slackening the reins so that Killer would have his head. If the weight of the sheep made a difference to their speed, it wasn't noticeable. The charger thundered south, ears flat against his head, the pack in hot pursuit. Perhaps it was the baying of the hounds that acted as a spur because it wasn't necessary for Thaddeus to kick him on again. He ran at full pelt towards the forest-covered inclines ahead, and slowly but surely the dogs began to tire.

His plan had been to cut the sheep carcass loose when the pack caught up with them, but as the dogs began to fall back he saw merit in keeping their interest. Clearing them from the village long enough for the boys to fire the thatch was one thing; disorienting them by leading them well away from scents they knew and recognised would be even better. As the woodland closed in and the slope of the hill steepened, he pulled gently on the reins, willing the horse to drop to a canter, but when the mad career continued, he called, 'Who-oa, boy, who-oa!' into Killer's ear.

Thaddeus would come to learn the secret of controlling the charger—drawling commands in the lazily pronounced French that Sir Richard had used—*ahl-lez . . . trah-thez . . . gahlop-ez . . .*

who-oa—but he didn't know it then. The halt was so abrupt that he slid out of the saddle onto the animal's neck and would have gone over its head if his boots hadn't become tangled in his stirrups. 'Godstruth!' he roared. 'I meant slow *down*, you stupid oaf, not *stop!*' He thrust himself backwards, wrestling to free his feet while looking over his shoulder to see how close the pack was.

He reached for his knife, ready to cut the carcass free, but miraculously the dogs, too, had halted, dropping to the ground some thirty yards behind him with their tongues lolling out of their mouths. He could feel Killer's chest heaving between his knees, and his own lungs working like bellows to pull in air. And he laughed because the tableau was so unreal. The hounds looked completely amiable, hunkered down on all fours with their eyes half closed and their tongues dripping saliva into the dust.

He turned Killer broadside to the road so that he could lean on the pommel and keep his eyes on them. There was no reason to move as long as they remained where they were, but he placed his blade on the rope so that he could cut it in an instant. Looking back towards Afpedle, he wondered if he'd overestimated the distance from the demesne to this woodland. How long had he been in the saddle? Two minutes? Five minutes?

It must have been more than that, he thought, as a thread of smoke rose in the air above the village. Even on a good day it was hard to get a fire going in under five minutes. He found himself speaking aloud. 'Are you trained to stop when a horse stops?' he asked the dogs. 'Do you get a reward for it? Does your lord throw you venison to keep you sweet?'

One of the mastiffs tilted its head to the side, ears pricked as if it were listening, and Thaddeus wished he knew more about what happened during a chase. What role did the dogs have other than to stalk the deer? And why didn't they kill it and maul it themselves instead of leaving it to be shot by an arrow? All he could remember about Sir Richard's hunting trips was that the man was flamboyantly dressed in fur-lined mantles and smart leather boots and returned, as often as not, empty-handed. He'd had no hounds of his own—claiming a dislike of the animals—and rarely went hunting in the woods around Develish.

The only dogs Thaddeus had known were the handful of tatty mongrels that kept the rats down in the village and begged for titbits from the serfs' tables. They were underfed and mangy, more prone to cowering than attacking, and because of the need to ration food they had all been quietly disposed of when Lady Anne ordered her people inside the moat. There had been tears from the children, but every adult had understood the necessity, the men taking it upon themselves to slit the wretched creatures' throats. Such a method of killing would not be possible on the sleek beasts in front of him with their huge jaws and pestilence-poisoned teeth.

'Your lord gave no thought to anyone when he set you free,' he told them. 'Did he love you so much that he couldn't bring himself to order your deaths? Or were his people too afraid of you to do it?' Three of the dogs yawned, offering proof, if Thaddeus needed it, that their bite would break an arm.

He looked beyond them to where the thread of smoke had become a rapidly expanding plume above the rooftops. But as the thrill of the ride diminished, he began to see how pointless this exercise was. Even if he continued along the highway, and even if the dogs followed, there was no guarantee they wouldn't find their way back to Afpedle and form a barrier yet again to the stealing of sheep. In all probability, with the corpses burnt, they'd ravage the entire flock in the next two days and there'd be nothing to steal anyway.

Depressed, and with no better idea of what to do than take the pack over the hill into the next valley, he readied himself to spur Killer into motion again. It meant turning the animal's head towards the slope, but when he pulled on the rein the horse reacted by dancing sideways and setting the sheep carcass in motion. All seven dogs leapt to their feet, moving forward purposefully, heads lowered for an attack, and taken by surprise, Thaddeus left it too late to cut the rope and release the carcass.

ᗧᗣ

Once the roofs were ablaze, Olyver, Ian and Edmund returned to the shelter of the trees, reluctant to see corpses revealed as the walls and doors burnt away. They were sickened enough by the number of rats that dropped from the thatch to run helter-skelter about the road in search of hiding places. Edmund threw a stone at one that was heading in their direction. 'I hate the little bastards. If anything carries disease, they do. I've seen them in the latrines.'

Even three hundred yards away, the sound of the inferno was loud. Dry timbers roared and popped as the flames took hold, and sparks leapt from house to house, setting fire to everything, including dead plants in the small cottage gardens. Had they been standing closer, the heat would have been unbearable.

'Do you think the flames will do for them?' Edmund went on, throwing another stone for good measure.

'It'll burn their babies,' said Ian, 'stop them breeding so fast.'

Olyver stared towards the distant hills. 'Do you suppose Thaddeus can see the smoke and knows we've done our bit?'

'He's not blind. I expect Peter and Joshua can see it as well. It's rising high enough.'

Edmund followed Olyver's gaze. 'What if Thaddeus isn't back by dusk? We can't wait until dark to find our way to the camp.'

Neither of the twins answered.

Edmund persisted. 'We need to make a decision now.' He searched their faces. 'We can't stay here all night. I'm starving—and I don't want to share my bed with rats.'

Olyver rounded on him angrily. 'Will you stop with the rat talk!' he snapped. 'It's getting on my nerves. They'll be the least of our problems if Thaddeus is dead.'

Twenty-one

Develish, Dorseteshire

THE FIRST ELEANOR KNEW THAT the demesne was in danger
was when Clara Trueblood entered the spinning room shortly
before dawn and told her that Lady Anne desired her presence
in the church. She spoke impatiently, annoyed at having to thrust
against the coffer that Eleanor had placed behind the door to keep
servants at bay. Being a large-boned woman, it had presented little
difficulty, but she tut-tutted over the effort. 'Make haste, milady.
Every woman and child in Develish is there. Only you are missing.'

'I don't choose to go.'

Clara took no notice. 'I'll help you dress.' She picked up a kirtle
which lay in a heap on the floor and shook it out.

Eleanor backed away. 'Where's Isabella? I'll not let anyone
dress me but her.'

'She's in the church with the children, milady. You must allow
me to do it or come in your undershift.'

'I will do neither.'

With a frustrated sigh, Clara laid the kirtle over a stool. 'There's
no time to argue. Gyles expects an attack at any moment.'

Eleanor stared at her. 'What attack?'

Clara clicked her tongue again. 'Are you ignorant of what is happening here? Have you not seen how our people guard the walls and draw water from the moat to fight fire? Were you deaf to the industry last night when every room was cleared of furniture?'

'Nothing was done in here.'

Clara looked about her and saw that the girl was telling the truth. The chamber was untouched and she felt a momentary guilt. Was Eleanor so disliked that no one had cared to enter and speak with her? Certainly Clara wouldn't be here now if Lady Anne hadn't asked why her daughter was not in the church.

She busied herself moving coffers, stools and rushes away from the window. 'A messenger came from My Lord of Bourne yesterday,' she explained. 'He gave notice of My Lord's intent to steal all the gold that remains in Develish. Our men prepare to fight while your mother looks to keep the women and girls safe. Does that persuade you to come with me?'

She could see from the sudden hope in Eleanor's eyes that it did not.

'My Lord isn't here to rescue you, child. If his soldiers cross the moat, you'll be treated no differently from a peasant girl. They'll have licence to rape as many women as they want, knowing we're free of the pestilence. Is your mind too closed to comprehend that?'

'What I think is none of your business.'

Clara straightened. 'Indeed . . . though I wonder sometimes if you think at all. God demands more of those He blesses with good fortune than tantrums and ill temper.' She moved to the door. 'The messenger warned that My Lord would return at noon, but Gyles believes he'll come earlier. You must make your decision now. Will you come or will you stay?' She paused. 'If you stay, you must defend yourself as best you can. When fire arrows come through the roof or the window, stamp out the flames on the floor. The smoke will kill you before you can leave the room if you let the fires take hold. Do you understand?'

'I understand that such tasks should be done by servants. Find three to help you and bring them here.'

Clara shook her head. 'They're behind the walls or in the church.'

Eleanor's face flushed with anger. 'Do you refuse my order?'

Clara lifted the latch and pulled the door wide. 'I do. I've given my pledge to stand with your mother in defence of all the daughters of Develish—not just one.' She watched the girl for a moment. 'If you choose to stand with us, you'll be welcome. If not, you must fight alone.'

There was a time, long ago, when Clara had been nurse and carer to Eleanor, and Eleanor remembered her smiling more often than she frowned. Now, any kindness she'd felt for Lady Anne's daughter was gone. She gave a small shrug when Eleanor didn't answer and hurried away down the corridor. Eleanor told herself she didn't care, but the pit of emptiness in her stomach and the hot tears that poured from her eyes said the opposite.

ꙮ

The previous evening, Gyles had stationed all the adult men and youths at narrow intervals around the boundary wall, instructing them to stay seated and get what sleep they could. He was fearful that Bourne would use the cover of darkness to send in his soldiers and he preferred to keep his men out of sight until that happened. A few were armed with swords and short bows which they'd crafted for themselves, but most had only knives or pitchforks. Lady Anne's vaunt to the captain that twenty archers had arrows trained on his chest had been sadly false.

Nevertheless, surprise was as powerful in defence as it was in attack, and Gyles hoped the sight of men appearing at the wall when the alarm was sounded would deter invasion. He chose youngsters with good eyesight to stand on the steps of the compass points, urging them to cry out if even the smallest of shadows moved. He would rather they roused their fathers for no reason than allow My Lord's soldiers to ford the moat.

Conscious that any activity would be seen within the enclosure once dawn broke, he and Lady Anne had set every hand to work through the night on the protection of the house. The shutters at the downstairs window were closed and barred, and the sacks of food in the great hall were moved to the centre of the room, together with rushes, tapestries and furniture. The same was done in the steward's office, the kitchen, the storerooms and anterooms, and the chambers upstairs. Only the spinning room was left untouched, because the servant girls who were sent to attend to it were too fearful of Lady Eleanor's temper to push against the coffer that she'd placed in front of the door.

Their hope was to prevent too many fires taking hold and, to that end, Lady Anne ordered water to be brought from the moat for the purpose of saturating as many of the structure's timbers as possible. Women formed a relay to the house, passing buckets and cauldrons from hand to hand in darkness so that doors, shutters, beams and window frames could be drenched, along with the wooden flooring inside. It would be luck or the Devil that allowed a flaming arrow to find a gap and fly far enough to lodge amongst the rushes and furniture.

Five eleven-year-olds whom Gyles deemed too young to fight volunteered to stay in the house and smother flames before they gathered strength. They were led by Alleyn Startout's son, Robert, and he swore on his heart to Lady Anne that he and his friends would leave if the task became too big for them. She took his face in her hands. 'Make sure you do,' she said. 'I can't afford to lose any of Develish's sons.'

Gyles reasoned that Bourne's soldiers would have a limited supply of arrows and he saw advantage in persuading them to fire on the house. The more they wasted on trying to set it ablaze the more depleted their stock would become. To convince Bourne and his captain that the house should be their target, he gave orders that no one should be abroad within the enclosure once dawn broke. My Lord must be persuaded that fear had driven every man, woman and child in Develish to take shelter inside the building.

'They will look to create turmoil with fire arrows,' he told Lady Anne and the other leading serfs. 'Once the timbers are alight, they will expect all inside to run to the forecourt, making easy targets. We can't fight them that way.'

'How then?' James Buckler asked.

'By hiding elsewhere and waiting until their store of arrows is expended. If the house fails to burn because of its drenching, they'll keep trying until it does—or that is my hope.' He paused to order his thoughts. 'Once their longbows are rendered useless for lack of arrows, we'll have a better chance. There are ten of us to every one of My Lord's men. If we can draw them to the moat the odds will be in our favour.'

'What will bring them?'

'Curiosity . . . arrogance . . . disbelief. They may think we've fled the demesne during the night if they see no evidence of us. Serfs are supposed to run in fear, not stand and fight.'

John Trueblood looked doubtful. 'The house is the only structure large enough to hold two hundred. Where else can we hide?'

'The men will stay where they are—out of sight behind the wall. The women and children will go to the church with

Lady Anne.' He turned to his mistress. 'You must make sure that all are inside before the sun rises, milady. My Lord won't hesitate to burn it if he sees women and children enter—house of God though it be—and our men won't fight if that happens. There's no quicker way to break a man's spirit than to threaten his family.'

Before they went, Lady Anne and the women took parcels of bread and cheese to the men and youths who guarded the wall, offering them comfort and support for what lay ahead. Many tears were spilt as wives and mothers hugged their husbands and sons. None doubted that what they were doing was right, but all feared the outcome. Their only real skill was farming. Even Gyles had never had to kill a man.

Lady Anne folded the grizzled serf's hands in hers after she'd dispatched the women and children to the church with their own parcels of food. So much weight rested on his shoulders, and so many lives. 'There's still time to fill a chest with the gold that remains and take it across on the raft,' she said. 'It may content My Lord and his soldiers.'

Gyles shook his head. 'I don't think so, milady. The captain won't let you live and bear witness against him. I saw it in his eyes. He means to kill you even if his master doesn't . . . and he'll have his pleasure of you first.'

She turned her wrist to show him the sheathed dagger bound to her arm. 'Not without a fight, he won't.'

Gyles's broad face split in a smile. 'I expected no less, milady. As long as you resist, we all will. Now go. Join our women and children in the church while it's still dark. Our plans will come to nothing if My Lord sees you enter.'

✆

Eleanor dressed herself in the gown she'd worn for Jacob's funeral and adorned her hair, throat and wrists with the gold her father had given her. Satisfied that she could not be taken for a serf girl, and had gold to bargain with, she moved to her mother's chamber, where the view across the demesne was better than from the spinning room. Nothing moved. Nothing stirred. Only the sound of birdsong outside broke the silence that wrapped the house. Had she been unable to see the men who crouched beneath the boundary wall in the orchard, she would have believed that everyone had gone.

As time passed, and the road remained empty, she convinced herself that Clara had lied. The story of My Lord of Bourne was an elaborate trick, designed to make a mockery of Eleanor. She felt the eyes of every man in the orchard upon her, guessed they knew what she was hoping for and would speak of it afterwards. They would say Sir Richard's daughter had arrayed herself like a queen to impress My Lord of Bourne, and the women of Develish would laugh to know she had stood at this window all day, looking and longing for kindness from a stranger.

She dragged the stools and rushes from her mother's bed and flung herself upon it. A fear that the serfs had gained control of the demesne took hold of her mind. She tried to remember if she'd seen Lady Anne since she'd run from her presence two days ago. In her imaginings, she pictured her mother venturing from the demesne to seek help from My Lord of Bourne. Why else would Develish men be hiding behind the boundary wall, sharpening their knives?

The weariness of long, sleepless nights caught up with her and she drifted in and out of consciousness. Each time she woke, she had no recollection of why she was lying on her mother's bed. Her fears and anxieties were so numerous it was hard to remember which had driven her there. In rare moments of clarity, she knew there was something wrong with her for, try as she might, she could not escape the dark visions of Hell that inhabited her mind. When the sound of breaking glass dragged her from sleep and she saw flames burst from the rushes that she'd kicked from the bed, she believed the Devil had come for her.

She watched Him dance in the fire for several long seconds before, with a cry of despair, she rose from the bed and beat Him to the ground with her fists.

෨෮

Inside the church, those women who stood by the chancel window watched a rain of fire fall from the sky and each prayed that the timbers were still wet enough to resist. A blazing arrow found its mark in the front door and they held their collective breath as the burning tallow licked at the wood. 'May God be praised,' whispered several as the flames hissed and died.

The shutters on the ground floor withstood the onslaught, but not the unshuttered windows of the upper storey. Lady Anne watched an arrow break through a lattice into her chamber and another into Sir Richard's. She placed her arm around the shoulders of Alleyn Startout's wife and drew her close. 'Don't be afraid, Susan. Robert is as wise as any boy on this demesne. He'll not put himself or his friends in peril for the sake of bravado. He knows to leave through the kitchen if fires take hold.'

Susan Startout was less sure. 'He wants to be as brave as his cousins, milady. He would have gone with Thaddeus had Ian and Olyver shared the secret with him.'

'There's nothing braver than what he does now. I worry less for Eleanor, knowing she's not alone.'

She would have gone to fetch the girl herself had the wives of the leading serfs not stopped her. Clara Trueblood blocked her way with a gesture of apology. 'You'll be lost to us if you leave now, milady. Lady Eleanor will do everything she can to keep you in the house. There's no reasoning with her.'

Jenny Buckler nodded. 'We need you here, milady. Without your guidance, the women and children will take fright and run outside.'

'Gyles looks to you for strength, milady,' Martha begged, pointing to the window above the altar. 'The sun is already above the horizon. You cannot leave or return without being seen, and his plan will fail if we're forced from the church by fire. There is no protection from the arrows of longbows.'

☙❧

Robert Startout caught Eleanor's hair and dragged her backwards, hooking a foot around her ankle and causing her to fall. 'Wantwit! Clod-brain! Numbskull!' he shouted, straddling her midriff and pummelling her face and chest with his fists. He used his foot to nudge the boy on the floor. 'Get up, Walter! Get up!'

The other pushed himself to his knees with a groan. 'I didn't do nothing wrong, Robert.'

Eleanor began to squirm and Robert pushed the heel of his palm against her nostrils. 'We must tie her up. She'll be the death of us otherwise.' He jerked his chin towards a skein of raffia amongst the rushes on the floor. 'Bring me that and make haste before another arrow comes.'

Walter Catchpole handed it to him. 'Why did she hit me?'

'Who knows? Maybe she wants the house to burn. Maybe she likes the idea of soldiers ramming their cocks up her cunt. She's stupid enough.' Robert looped fibres about Eleanor's left wrist before dragging her right hand across his knees to bind the two together in a tight figure of eight. 'Now do the same with her feet or she'll kick me when I get off.'

When he was satisfied that Eleanor couldn't move, he stood up and wrapped a double strand of the rough raffia around her neck. He used her hair to drag her to the bed and made a slip knot for the noose before attaching the end to one of the legs. 'Raffia's strong and it'll tighten if you struggle,' he said, staring down into her tearful eyes. 'You'll be dead before the fibres break.'

'And you'll be punished,' she whispered through thickening lips.

'Not if I let you burn and say it was an accident.' Robert turned towards the window as another pane shattered. This time the arrow lodged against a lead strip and he used his boot to kick it to the ground outside. He stooped to gather up the rushes and toss them onto Lady Anne's bed, careless if they fell on Eleanor. 'You have to be the stupidest scut in Develish,' he said in disgust, retrieving the tallow-covered shaft that Walter had extinguished. 'Why would you hit someone who was trying to save you?'

He dropped the object onto her chest and shepherded Walter ahead of him into the corridor. After that he took no further notice of her. He reappeared each time he heard breaking glass, sometimes stamping at flames, but more often covering them with wet rags. The smell of sodden cloth clogged Eleanor's nostrils as did the vile odour of half-burnt mutton fat from the arrow head; but each time she thought about raising her bound hands to fling it from her, she was too afraid of the rough rasp of raffia against her throat to do it.

When the hail of arrows finally finished, Robert brought Walter and three other boys to crouch beneath the windows and watch events unfold. Walter suggested that Robert should release Lady Eleanor but Robert refused. If he was going to be punished for tying her up, he'd rather take a beating from his father than from her. At least he'd be allowed to explain himself first.

'Her face is all messed from where you punched her,' said Walter. 'How will you explain that?'

Robert grinned. 'I'll say I did her a favour. She's so pissing ugly now only a blind man would want to rape her.'

༄

Gyles had hidden himself inside the stone archway to the orchard, from where he could see the highway north and the road to the village. As he'd predicted, My Lord came early, and it was clear he had no intention of discovering whether Lady Anne was willing to comply with his demands. He halted his wagon two hundred yards from the moat, keeping his driver and a fighting man to guard him while the captain and a troop of eight rode west and south across the peasant strips.

Gyles moved from tree to tree within the orchard to watch their progress. They came to a halt when they had the front of the manor house within their sights, ranging themselves some three hundred paces from the boundary wall, directly facing the front façade. Even Gyles's short bow, the best of those found in the storerooms, lacked the draw to send an arrow so far. Thereafter, the fire fusillade began.

It seemed My Lord's men were ill-trained in the use of the longbow, since as many arrows dropped into the moat or onto the forecourt as lodged in the timbers of the house. Gyles began to worry that the tinder-dry wood of the serfs' huts, the animal fodder, straw and foliage inside the enclosure would catch fire, forcing his people into the open to smother the flames. But it seemed God was smiling on Develish. Even when an arrow landed three paces from Gyles's feet, the blazing tallow petered and died within seconds, leaving only a charred circle in the grass.

When the onslaught came to an end, the captain sent a rider to My Lord's wagon. A quarter-hour passed before the rider returned and the captain ordered his men to remount. Gyles watched him lead them back in the direction they'd come and then ran at a crouch to the boundary wall, sending a message from person to person to stay out of sight until he gave the order to stand. 'Surprise is our most powerful weapon,' he urged. 'If we cannot lure them in, we cannot defeat them.'

'Do you look to kill them all?' John Trueblood asked. 'Is that possible? Surely My Lord will never come close enough.'

'I look to deter him from ever coming back,' Gyles answered. 'We'll not be so ready another time. Pass the word along the line that every man with a bow should make his way towards the entrance. Tell them to keep low.'

Another hour passed before the captain brought nine soldiers in a tight phalanx down the road from the village. He halted them thirty paces from the moat and shouted to all inside the house to come out.

Gyles glanced around the small group of bowmen who crouched beside him. 'You have your instructions,' he whispered. 'Aim for the horse and not the man. The target is larger and the confusion will be greater. Move when I do.'

He waited until the captain's cry came again then stepped from behind the shelter of the wall. He left the broad chests of the leading horses to his fellows, aiming his own arrows at the flanks of those behind. One after another, the poor beasts bucked and reared, throwing their riders and whinnying piteously. When Gyles saw that the captain, well protected inside the phalanx, was still astride his mount, he aimed at the man and not the animal.

He wanted the captain's heart but found only the sleeve of his loose-fitting shirt as the charger leapt from the midst of the melee and bolted back down the road. Three others fled with him, as did two loose horses with shafts hanging from their rumps and bellies. Six of the soldiers lay curled on the ground admidst the death throes of the remaining four chargers.

'Lie still,' Gyles called in French, 'or I shall order my archers to kill you.'

One man kicked another from his legs and struggled to a kneeling position, only to slump forward again with an arrow lodged in his shoulder.

'You were warned,' Gyles cried, giving the piercing whistle which was the signal for every Develish man to reveal himself. 'Your lord and your captain have abandoned you, and you are now at the mercy of people you've wronged. Your only chance is to do as I tell you. Do you accept my terms?'

'What are they?'

'Death or life—which do you choose?'

'Life.'

'Then stand. Remove your weapons, tabards and boots and place them on the ground in front of you. If I think you're hiding anything from me, I'll return you to your lord as naked as the day you were born.'

Five did as he asked.

'Auguste can't rise,' their spokesman said. 'He's dying from the injury you inflicted.'

'I doubt it . . . but, if he is, break off the shaft and strip him of everything. Without clothes, his corpse will be easier for vermin to scavenge. We don't want his stink blowing over us longer than necessary.'

Auguste rose to his feet, pulling the shaft from his shoulder without even a grunt to show it pained him. 'My Lord will make you pay for this, serf.'

Gyles gave an abrupt laugh. 'He'll be a fool if he tries. God is on our side. It's no accident that Develish lives while all around are dying.' He raised his bow again. 'Remove your tabard and weapons. There's an army of one hundred Englishmen ranged against you and each is ready to cross the moat and cut your thieving heart from your body.'

Angrily, the man dropped his sword and removed his livery. 'Your boast is an idle one,' he snapped. 'I count only nine archers.'

'You count wrong,' roared James Buckler, seizing a pitch-fork from his neighbour and bounding on to the northern step. He balanced the weapon on his palm before launching it like a spear. A cheer rose in the air as it thudded into the ground at the Norman's feet. 'The next will take your throat.'

'And mine the throat of the thieving scum behind you,' shouted Alleyn Startout, stepping out from behind a buttress. 'There's no love for Normans here. We'd as soon turn you into carrion for crows as let you leave with your lives.'

Cries of agreement ran like wildfire along the wall. Pitchfork handles were pounded on the hard earth. A youth threw a stone and others, keen to show their hostility, followed suit.

Bleeding and battered, the French turned and ran, hopping and skipping to avoid the sharp stones of the road.

'Will they come back?' Adam Catchpole asked at Gyles's shoulder.

A gleam of triumph lit Gyles's eyes. 'They'll have to replace their weapons and horses first.'

෧෨

Robert squatted beside Eleanor. 'I wouldn't have hit you if you hadn't hit Walter,' he told her. 'You had no call, since he was only trying to keep you from burning. Me, I'd probably have let it happen, since I don't like you and I'm not kind-hearted like Walter. He saves pigeons with broken wings. I eat them.' He searched her eyes. 'You truly are a numbskull, aren't you? Isabella says you can't write your name or count numbers properly. That's pretty shameful. My sister can do both and she's only five years old.' He took his knife from his belt. 'If you had a little learning, you'd know that something big happened here today. But since you haven't, you'll weep and wail and wish you'd been rescued.' He sawed through the noose at her neck. 'It wouldn't have happened, you know. Wearing gold doesn't prove you're important. Your mother wears none and she's the only lady My Lord of Bourne would have taken. She's clever and beautiful and a man can tell in a second that she's high-born. When you open your mouth, you show yourself for what you are—a brainless, bad-tempered scut.' He sat back on his heels. 'I'll give you another black eye if you try to hit me when I cut the bonds at your wrists. It won't make any difference to my punishment. If I'm going to be beat, I'll be given the same number of lashes how ever many bruises you have.'

Eleanor ran her tongue across her swollen lips. 'I won't hit you.'

'You'd better not. You look like a piebald pig already. You'll look worse if I give you another pummelling. The whole of Develish will laugh when you stand in front of them to accuse me.'

When she didn't answer, Robert ran the blade between her ankles then split the raffia at her wrists and jumped away. 'You'll wait a long time for a maid to help you,' he warned, heading for the door. 'They're running about the enclosure, looking for their fathers and brothers.'

'Tell Isabella to come,' she whispered.

He shook his head. 'I will not. It wouldn't be fair to make her miserable when everyone else is celebrating. Her place is at her father's side. If it wasn't for my Uncle Gyles, we'd all be dead.'

Twenty-two

Thaddeus's camp on the River Pedle

DARKNESS WAS FALLING BY THE time Ian, Olyver and Edmund reached the river. They stripped off their clothes and boots to wade across, holding the bundles above their heads, and the cold water lapping about their chests did nothing to alleviate their misery. They had waited in vain for Thaddeus to return, or at least show himself on the highway to the south of Afpedle, and their mood was sombre and withdrawn.

Joshua had the sense to hold his tongue as they slumped beside the campfire to pull on their tunics and britches, but Peter was agog with curiosity. What was Afpedle like? Was everyone dead? Had they seen corpses? Was the smell as bad as Thaddeus claimed? Why had he come back for a horse and some rope? Had they succeeded in burning the village?

He grew irritable as each question was greeted with silence. 'What's the matter with you?' he demanded at last. 'At least tell us where Thaddeus is.'

'We don't know,' muttered Ian.

Peter frowned. 'Why not?'

'You wouldn't have to ask if you'd come with us,' retorted Edmund.

There were enough frustrations on both sides for the makings of a fight but Joshua intervened before they boiled over. 'I caught some squirrels and I've been soaking the last of the beans,' he said. 'I'll cook them now. If Thaddeus isn't back by the time they're done, we'll leave his share in the pot.'

For his part, Peter distanced himself to stand watch by the river, both to cool his temper and to demonstrate to Edmund that guarding the camp was as important as burning villages. He peered hard into the gathering darkness and rising mist to prove it. He wouldn't have seen the shapes if he hadn't—two black shadows, darker than the night, that slithered out of the trees on the far bank.

Dry-mouthed, he began a hasty retreat, drawing his knife from his belt and holding it in front of him. 'Intruders to the south!' he grated, desperately trying to produce saliva. 'Intruders to the south!'

For a few dreadful seconds, he was afraid his friends would think he was teasing, but to his relief he heard swearing and their running feet on the grass. 'Over there,' he whispered, pointing with his blade as all four youths ranged themselves beside him. 'Do you see them?'

Ian nodded. 'What do we do? We've used up all the arrows.'

'Call a warning,' murmured Olyver.

Ian raised his voice. 'This is an armed encampment!' he shouted. 'Guarded by soldiers! Return the way you came if you value your lives! Any attempt to enter the water will be taken as an act of war and met by death!'

A strange susurration—a low rumble of sound—drifted towards them through the mist. Joshua shivered with dread as he imagined the jaws of Hell yawning open to unleash the Black

Death. And perhaps he wasn't alone in this fear; there was a marked tremor in Ian's voice as he tried again. 'Come no closer! We have longbows and will loose our arrows if you continue forward! Do you hear me?'

'I hear you,' answered Thaddeus's laughing voice. 'And I see you. You make fine silhouettes against the fire.' He muttered something that clearly wasn't intended for the boys. 'Before I cross, you'd be wise to put yourselves behind it. I'm not expecting trouble but I don't want to invite it either. Keep quiet and don't make any sudden movements.'

Whatever the boys anticipated during the minutes that followed it wasn't that Thaddeus, naked and dripping with water from head to toe, would surface from the river with Sir Richard's charger in tow and seven saturated dogs at his heels. He moved well away from them, waited while they shook themselves then ordered them to drop before taking his clothes from Killer's back. He pulled them on, tied a loose hobble around the animal's front legs and unbuckled the girths. 'You're a fine fellow,' he told him, removing a strange-looking pack from his withers then slipping off the saddle and the bridle and lowering them to the ground. 'You have my permission to take a well-earned rest.' He tapped him lightly on the rump and sent him to find the other horses, all the while keeping a close eye on the dogs.

To Peter and Joshua the scene was a great deal less alarming than it was to Ian, Edmund and Olyver. 'Why did he expect trouble?' Joshua whispered. 'They seem tame enough.'

'Not in Afpedle, they didn't,' answered Olyver. 'We thought they'd killed him.'

The boys watched as Thaddeus knelt on the grass and fiddled with the pack. They couldn't see what it was because the light from the fire didn't reach far enough, but there was no mistaking the dogs' interest. They inched forward on their bellies, barely able to contain their excitement, giving sharp yaps to prompt the kneeling man to work faster. 'One at a time,' he told them. 'You first.' He pointed to a mastiff and lobbed something towards it. 'Good boy. Now you.' He repeated the action with each dog in turn.

'Is he feeding them the dead sheep?' Olyver asked his brother.

'Either that or a plague-ridden corpse,' said Ian. 'Let's hope it's the sheep.'

Edmund shifted unhappily. 'It's not funny,' he muttered. 'He shouldn't have brought them here. If they don't bite him, they'll bite us.'

'Well, at least he's not dead. An hour ago, you wanted him back with rats in his beard . . . now you're quibbling over a few dogs.'

'What if they have the pestilence on their teeth?'

Ian was spared having to answer by Thaddeus. 'It's safe to come out now,' he called, picking up the saddle and bridle and walking towards them. 'They seem quite content as long as I feed them.' He dropped the tack and the rest of the sheep's carcass to the ground and squatted beside the fire, rubbing his hands and looking to see if there was any food in the pot. 'Let's eat,' he said cheerfully. 'I've never been so hungry in my life.'

Or smiled so much, Ian thought, wondering what had happened to raise his spirits so high. He felt a small jealousy that Thaddeus had had fun on his adventure while he, Olyver and Edmund had not. 'We thought you were dead,' he said accusingly.

'I can't think why.'

'The last time we saw you the pack was almost upon you.'

'You saw wrong. I told you I hadn't come all this way to die of a dog bite.' He accepted a plate of stew from Joshua. 'You three seem to have done a good job. The village was still burning when I led my new-found friends across the peasant strips.'

'But we didn't *enjoy* it,' said Olyver severely, sensing the same emotions in Thaddeus as Ian had. 'What happened that's made you so—' he cast around for a word—'*jolly*?'

Thaddeus's eyes gleamed with mischief as he chewed on a squirrel leg. 'I feel alive,' he said. 'Maybe I'll order each of you to ride a bolting horse up a highway with ravening hounds at its heels. It's good to embrace fear.'

He could see from the boys' uncomprehending expressions that his words made no sense to them. But he had no other explanation. All he knew was that he'd lived more intensely in the last few hours than in the twenty years that had gone before.

He replied to their questions eventually, but in such an understated way that they were left believing the whole escapade had been rather dull. 'It was all quite easy once I realised the dogs were trained to respond to voice commands,' he told them. 'Sir Richard's horse has only two speeds—fast and slow—so we did most of the journey at a walk.'

'Where did you go?'

'Over the hill into the next valley. I was hoping to lose the dogs along the way but it didn't happen. Even when a deer jumped out in front of us, they stayed glued to Killer's heels . . . probably because I'd hauled the sheep back onto the saddle. They seem ready to adopt anyone who'll feed them.'

'Couldn't you have left them to fight over the carcass and ridden off at high speed?'

'I could,' Thaddeus agreed, 'but when the moment came to do it, Killer started dancing around like a prize idiot and I couldn't get my knife free. The dogs moved forward to attack us, and all I could think to do was to shout "Stop!"—and they did. They're very well mannered.'

'You could have tried again later.'

'There wasn't enough highway. The next village to the south is barely a mile and a half from the top of the hill, and if I'd turned round I'd have led the dogs straight back to Afpedle. I thought I'd have more luck shaking them off if I took them through woodland to the river, but the trees were too dense to escape them. A slow walk was the best we could manage.'

He described what he'd seen when he breasted the hill: another wide meandering river with streams running off it to form lakes; dense, lush forests on the slopes and valley floor, and a demesne within hailing distance, twice the size of Afpedle. 'The manor house stands beside a lake. It's very beautiful.'

'Did you see any people?'

Thaddeus shook his head. 'I didn't want to go too close. The place looked rich enough to have soldiers with longbows and I didn't fancy an arrow between the eyes. I worked my way through the woodland instead, and gave the dogs a dunking in the water. Myself and Killer, too.'

'The horse is called Edward,' said Joshua.

'Not any more he isn't. He damn near broke my neck the first time he bolted.'

'What names have you given the dogs?' asked Ian.

'None individually, but they seem to answer collectively to Deadly Sins. *Up*, Deadly Sins, *down*, Deadly Sins. It works a treat.'

Edmund glanced nervously towards the pack. 'Why did you bring them here? You were scared enough of them this morning. What if they bite us? How do you know they haven't got the disease?'

'I don't . . . and if you're worried about being bitten, keep your fear of them hidden. At least their fur's clean. I took Joshua's advice. They've swum through five different stretches of water, including this one.' Thaddeus smiled slightly. 'The truth is, I couldn't get rid of them. They wouldn't let me out of their sight. In the end, I saw merit in keeping them.'

'Why?'

Thaddeus shrugged. 'They'll be easier to kill if they're not running wild.'

Shortly afterwards, he stoked up the fire, ordered the boys to make their bracken beds behind it, and propped himself against the saddle so that he could watch the dogs. For once, he didn't feel the need to set guards, sure the pack would sense strangers long before human eyes or ears could, but he had no such certainty the animals wouldn't turn on him during the night. He told the boys their best defence was fire and, for himself, kept his knife and the remains of the sheep close.

'Get what rest you can,' he murmured. 'Tomorrow you'll be gathering hazel whips to make new arrows.'

At some point during the night, Joshua crept around the fire to join him. 'I'm not afraid of dogs,' he whispered. 'I taught the mongrels in Develish to catch squirrels and rabbits. They became so good at it, my father complained about the number of rodents we were eating.'

Thaddeus smiled. 'How did you teach them?'

'With food . . . the same way you persuaded this pack to follow you. You can train a dog to do anything as long as you reward it afterwards.'

'Except these aren't cowering mongrels,' Thaddeus told him. 'They're hunting hounds with a taste for human corpses. How long will they obey me when the mutton runs out?'

'They won't. You'll have to get some more. They give their loyalty to the person who feeds them. That's how it works. I'll show you tomorrow, if you like.'

'Mm. Well, at their rate of consumption, loyalty comes expensive. They've eaten half a sheep in one day—that's more than we've had in a week. We'd be better off without them.'

Joshua hesitated before he answered. 'At least give them a chance to prove how useful they can be,' he urged. 'If I was able to teach a cur to catch rabbits, I ought to be able to coax a trained hound to bring down a deer. They could be a source of more food rather than less.'

Thaddeus didn't say anything.

Joshua ploughed on determinedly. 'Lady Anne was wrong to have the mongrels slaughtered. We wouldn't have needed the guard steps if she'd let them live. They'd have patrolled the compound all night and barked at the first sign of trouble.' The boy paused for a reaction, and went on when he didn't get one, 'Look how well these dogs are protecting us now. Look how alert the mastiffs are.'

'You're too soft-hearted, Joshua. You'd feel differently if you'd seen them this morning. They're not so pretty when their teeth are bared.'

'But that's a good thing,' the boy pointed out. 'You'd feel a lot safer riding into a village if you had a pack of ferocious dogs around you. You'll be able to do anything you like—steal anything you like. No one will challenge you.'

He couldn't tell if Thaddeus was persuaded because the man's expression was impossible to read even in daylight, but he drew hope from the fact that Thaddeus let the subject drop.

It was true that Joshua had a soft heart when it came to dogs. He still yearned for the dead mongrels, one in particular—Red— whose fur had been as ginger as Joshua's hair. He had slept at Joshua's side every night of his life, and Joshua had begged his father not to kill him. But James Buckler had done it anyway.

His son had hated him for it, and the rift between them had not been mended before Joshua left. He had hated Lady Anne, too, for ordering the slaughter, and it had soothed his anger to listen to Eleanor's poison about her mother. 'Do you miss Develish?' he asked Thaddeus suddenly.

'No.'

'Not even Lady Anne?'

Thaddeus glanced at him. 'What prompted that question?'

'Everyone knows you like her.'

'Why would I not? She's been a better teacher to me than my mother ever was.'

Joshua flicked him a mischievous smile. 'You can't compare her with your mother. She's barely eight years older than you.'

Thaddeus adjusted his position against the saddle, wondering if it was Eleanor who'd pointed that out to the boy. 'I'm more interested in our lack of arrows than in the age of your doxy's mother,' he said. 'We need to start gathering hazel whips tomorrow. Did your father teach you how to splice them?'

But Joshua wasn't so easily diverted. 'Do you think Lady Anne knows the truth by now?'

'It depends what Eleanor's told her.'

The lad leant forward to clamp his hands between his knees. 'She started it, you know. We wouldn't have had the nerve to make advances ourselves.'

Thaddeus had worked that out for himself, but he wasn't ready to let Joshua off so easily. 'Is that supposed to make me feel better about you?'

'We were bored and she was there. That's all it was.'

'I could say the same about your older sisters,' Thaddeus murmured. 'There's many a time they've come flaunting themselves at me. Should I have shown them my cock because I had nothing better to do?'

Joshua wriggled his shoulders in embarrassment. He knew full well that both his sisters yearned for Thaddeus as a husband. 'No.'

'Then don't blame Lady Eleanor for your behaviour. Take responsibility for your own actions and live with the consequences afterwards.'

'You shouldn't try to find good in her,' the boy warned. 'She has only hatred for you. I expect that's why she killed Jacob—because he was your brother.'

'Then her conscience will weigh the heavier for it,' Thaddeus answered. 'There's no sillier reason to kill a person than because you hate someone else.'

☙

Ten miles away, in Develish, Eleanor stood at the window of her mother's spinning room, drawing the point of a six-inch bodkin across her arm. Careless of the pestilence, men had crossed on the raft to butcher the dead horses and bring them into the enclosure, and now the choicest parts were roasting over an open fire in the middle of the forecourt. As the night lengthened and their bellies filled, the peasants sang and cavorted, their faces glowing in the heat of the flames; and in their midst, her dark hair tumbling about her shoulders, danced Lady Anne.

Such a sickness overcame Eleanor to see her mother's joy that she took up the bodkin to paint brilliant red stripes on her pale skin. Each stinging cut brought a momentary respite from the visions of Hell that bedevilled her mind. In her troubled imagination, she fancied her mother and every serf in Develish had become a demon sent to torment her. It pleased her to hurt herself.

God would take pity on her when He saw that her blood flowed as freely as Christ's.

She was much in need of His pity. She was her father's daughter—Sir Richard lived through her—yet her certainty that her place in Develish was safeguarded by the privilege of her Norman birth was gone. My Lord of Develish was dead of the pestilence and My Lord of Bourne defeated. Only Lady Anne, who claimed a Saxon heritage, remained; and she had more love and care for her serfs than she did for her daughter.

Eleanor watched as Lady Anne stooped to hear something Robert Startout was saying. She could tell from the way Robert gestured towards the spinning room window that he was talking about her, and guessed that what he said would not be kind. Her heart fluttered anxiously until he nodded gravely when Lady Anne dropped to one knee and placed a finger over his lips to urge him to silence. Shortly afterwards he moved to speak with Walter Catchpole and the boys laughed and clapped each other on the back. What pleased them more? Eleanor wondered. That Robert would escape punishment for beating her? Or that the bruises he'd inflicted meant she was too ashamed to be seen?

Warring emotions of loneliness and jealousy raged in Eleanor's heart as she stared at the happiness below. She had pleaded with her mother to say nothing of what had happened and keep her hidden until her beauty returned, but now she condemned Lady Anne for agreeing so readily to forgive Robert his crime. It was no accident that her touch on Robert's Saxon lips had been sweeter than the cold, unfeeling way she'd smoothed ointment around her Norman daughter's eyes. She would always choose to exclude Eleanor from a celebration before a brutal serf boy.

In anger, Eleanor dug the point of the bodkin into her arm, and the pain brought a moment of clarity. She had loved her father so much and had scorned her mother to please him, but she trembled to think that everything he'd told her was false. Lady Anne's voice echoed in her mind.

Sir Richard couldn't tell the truth either . . . It used to make me laugh when he clasped the crucifix to his breast, drank the holy wine and wept tears of joy as the degenerate priest pronounced him clean . . . God judges us by our deeds not by the number of mea culpas *we say . . .*

Twenty-three

WHEN THE SUN WAS HIGH enough above the horizon to lift the gloom from the valley, and the dogs began to yawn and stretch with the new day, Thaddeus gave in to Joshua's pleading and agreed to let the boy show what he could do. He had no idea if it was a wise decision, and armed himself with his sword in case things went wrong, but Joshua seemed confident. He first cut titbit-sized pieces from the sheep's carcass, stowed most of them in his knapsack, which he slung from his belt, then walked to within ten yards of the pack with the rest of the meat in his hand.

Before long, Edmund, Olyver, Ian and Peter crawled from their beds to stand beside Thaddeus. 'He's mad,' groaned Edmund, watching Joshua stroke the dogs' ears and feed them from his palm. 'The minute one takes a bite out of him, they'll all be on him.'

Thaddeus shook his head. 'They were hackles and teeth when he started. Now look at them.'

'How do you know they don't carry the pestilence in their saliva?'

'I don't—nor do I know if it's carried in the water we drink or on the air we breathe. The only thing I'm sure of is that the horses don't have it, otherwise we'd be dead by now.' He gave an abrupt laugh. 'It's a good day, Edmund. Enjoy it. We're alive, we're free and Joshua has yesterday's savage dogs eating out of his hand.'

'Maybe so, but you've given up any chance you ever had of killing them,' Peter warned. 'Joshua hasn't forgiven his father for slitting Red's throat, and he won't forgive you either if you do the same to these.'

Thaddeus watched Joshua walk the pack to heel, using arm gestures to show them which way he wanted them to turn. 'We need to make arrows,' he told the others, changing the subject. 'Does anyone know how to splice a hazel whip to give it strength and make it straight?'

All four held up their hands.

'We'll need string to bind the two halves together,' Ian pointed out.

'And feathers for flight,' said Edmund. 'The arrows won't run true without them.'

'And iron to forge the heads,' added Olyver.

'And a whetstone,' said Peter. 'My knife's so blunt I can't tell which side of the blade is supposed to be sharp.'

'Anything else?' Thaddeus asked sarcastically. 'What about a comfortable chair to sit on while you work? Or lanolin to keep your hands soft?' He began to kick the fire out. 'We must do the best we can with what we find. I need enough arrows to burn Athelhelm in four days' time. Or earlier, if we see rain clouds building in the west. One thing's for sure: our luck can't hold forever.'

He tasked himself and Joshua with finding iron and feathers, and sent the other four boys towards the village in the east, where he'd seen several well-established hazel copses on the fringes of the common land. He urged them to keep careful watch while they harvested the whips, since contact with people remained his

greatest fear. Even a healthy-looking man might have the seeds
of the pestilence on his skin or ready to break out inside him. He
decided against leaving anyone to guard the camp. It would be
unlucky chance if a traveller stumbled upon it that day when no
one had approached it in all the time they'd been there.

He told Joshua he wanted to return to Afpedle. 'Will the pack
become restive if we do?' he asked. 'Will you be able to control
them?'

Joshua, who had persuaded the dogs to sit patiently on the
grass, threw him a nervous glance. 'I don't know. Why do we
need to go there?'

'Because there are arrowheads in the ashes of the cottages. We
may not find them all, but it's worth a try. It's also the easiest
place to catch and slaughter another sheep.' He stooped to pick
up Killer's saddle. 'We'll have to ride. There were ducks on the
lake in the next valley, which will give us the feathers we need.'

'I can teach the dogs better if I keep them here.'

Thaddeus flipped the stirrups over the leather. 'You'll be
putting them in jeopardy if you do,' he said. 'I'll not slaughter a
sheep for them and I'll not show them sympathy this evening if
I've had to do all the work. I'm willing to feed an animal that pulls
its weight but not one that's a burden.'

Joshua's heart sank. He had no confidence the dogs would
perform in a way that would impress Thaddeus, but he
wasn't prepared to risk the other man's displeasure by saying so.
'I'll have more control if I start out on foot,' he answered. 'You'll
have to saddle a horse for me and lead it on a halter until I'm
ready to mount.'

As they crossed the river and entered the woodland on the
other side, Thaddeus wondered why Joshua had so little belief
in himself. The lad could perform any task he was given, yet he

was racked with anxiety while doing it. Perhaps his father criticised everything he did instead of setting him a challenge and allowing him to learn from his mistakes? Certainly his skill with the hounds was exceptional. Once or twice, he excused them for straying from the path—'I expect they've been trained to follow deer scent'—but for the most part he kept them firmly at his side. It was only when Thaddeus said Afpedle would come into view shortly that he grew worried.

'It won't be the dogs' fault if they run off,' he warned. 'Everything they've ever known is here. You do understand that, don't you?'

Thaddeus drew Killer to a halt and watched the pack mill amiably around the horse's legs. 'The fault won't be mine either,' he said. 'It's you who's taken responsibility for them. I want results, Joshua, not a string of excuses every time we encounter a problem.'

'What if you don't get them?'

Thaddeus drew his finger across his throat.

The boy set off again, snapping his fingers to bring the pack in behind him. 'You'll rot in Hell if you even try,' he muttered. 'I'll make sure of it.'

Thaddeus smiled to himself and allowed some distance to develop before he nudged Killer into a walk and took up the slack on the second horse's halter. As the forest thinned, he scanned the blackened ruins of the houses, looking for movement or anything he didn't recognise from yesterday. But the village was burnt out and deserted, and only the cloying odours of ash and soot lingered in the air.

The timbers had still been blazing when Thaddeus led the dogs across the common land the previous evening. He had put their lack of interest in their home demesne down to their fear of the flames, but they showed no more recognition of their surroundings now as they padded quietly beside Joshua and dropped, panting, into the dust of the highway when he ordered them to stop. The romantic in Thaddeus sent them a silent 'thank you' for doing what the boy wanted; the cynic made a mental note that anyone with a handful of meat would be able to lure them away in an instant.

He left the horses tied to trees on the edge of the clearing, and moved on foot to join Joshua. 'You did well,' he said, forcing himself to stoop to fondle one of the mastiff's ears. He shared Edmund's view that large hounds with yellow teeth which had recently feasted on corpses were best viewed from afar, but all fears had to be faced eventually and he had softer feelings for this mastiff, which seemed to listen to what he said, than for any of the others.

'You need to stroke them all,' said Joshua. 'You'll make them jealous otherwise. And run your hands around their muzzles so that your scent is as familiar to them as mine. At the moment, the stench of burning is masking smells they might recognise, but it'll be different when we move upwind of the village. They need to fix on you as well as me if you want them to follow us to the next demesne.'

Thaddeus didn't believe a word of it. 'Are you hoping this will persuade me to like them?' he asked as he allowed a hound to lick his hand.

'Not yet—but it might stop you being afraid of them.'

Thaddeus glanced at him with amusement. 'What makes you think I'm afraid?'

'You flinch every time one of them yawns.'

'Mm . . . well, they were a great deal more frightening yesterday than they are today.' Thaddeus straightened, looking along the highway. 'This whole place was more frightening.'

Embers still glowed in the debris of some of the cottages, and with only boots to kick them away, Thaddeus decided to leave the search for arrowheads until the afternoon. He spent half an hour moving around the burnt-out remains, looking for anything that had survived the flames, but the ash was too thick even to make out the shape of an iron cooking pot or a stone pitcher. Without a rake, there was precious little hope of finding arrowheads, but he wondered what else would be uncovered if they had one. He doubted Joshua had an appetite for pulling half-burnt skulls from the ruins of these houses.

Once or twice he was startled by the skitter of small animals in the singed and brittle foliage of the cottage gardens, but the plague of rats which had infested the village previously seemed to have vanished. As had the ravens. With everything cleansed by fire, they had nothing to feed on, and like starving populations everywhere they had moved on.

Thaddeus stood for several minutes staring towards the manor house. It was a solid structure, built of stone, with two outside staircases to access the upper floor. But was anyone alive in there, he wondered, or had the place become home to vermin? On his previous visits, he'd never spotted so much as the whisk of a gown at a window or the hasty retreat of a guard behind a buttress. A wall enclosed an area of about two acres, containing a church, but being only chest height it offered little protection against invaders.

He returned to where Joshua was standing and told him he'd decided to head on to the next demesne. 'We need a rake,' he said. 'We'll never get anything out of the ashes otherwise.' He set off towards the horses.

Joshua pursued him. 'What do you mean we need a rake?' he demanded, calling to the dogs to follow. 'You said you wanted ducks.'

'Those too.'

'Well, I'm not going into a strange demesne to steal a rake. You said you saw guards with longbows.'

Thaddeus shook his head. 'I said I *feared* guards with longbows.'

'I don't care. I'm not risking my life for a rake.'

Thaddeus gave a dry laugh. 'But you think I would, eh? You're a strange fellow, Joshua.' He unhitched Killer and swung up into the saddle. 'Mount up. You'll be riding from now on.'

He led him out across the peasant strips towards where the sheep were grazing on the common land, telling him to veer left when they came to a natural fork. 'Take the dogs to the highway south of the manor house and wait for me there. If they show signs of wanting to return to the village, keep travelling along the road and I'll catch up with you later.'

'What are you going to do?'

'Pen a couple of ewes so that we can slaughter them this evening. They won't be so easy to catch when the light starts to fade.'

Joshua wasn't sure he believed him, and kept checking over his shoulder to make sure Thaddeus was doing what he said. It meant he wasn't watching when two of the hounds peeled away from their fellows and raced towards the manor house, and he only realised he'd lost control when the other dogs decided to follow. Cursing himself for his stupidity, he turned his horse and went after them. As a result, he came at the building from an angle that allowed him to see the south-facing façade and, because he was on horseback, the ground behind the chest-high boundary wall was clearly visible.

His eyes were drawn to a great bank of earth between the church and the forecourt, some ten yards long by four yards wide. He thought it strange until the truth of what it must be dawned on him. A grave. But how many bodies were contained inside it, he wondered, and who had filled it in and banked the earth above it? A shudder of dread ran through him as he searched the windows for signs of life. Could anyone stay alive—*or sane*—after performing such a task?

The dogs ran to and fro along the wall, sniffing the air, and but for the cobbled path which ran beneath the solid oak gate at the entrance, Joshua guessed they would long since have tunnelled their way inside. Yet it was hard to say what was drawing them to the place, since death was the least of what he could smell. Close up, the stench of urine and faeces was powerful—he could see raw sewage on the ground where slops had been emptied out of upstairs windows—and, instinctively, he placed a hand over his mouth and nose to filter what he breathed.

So strong had been Lady Anne's training on cleanliness that Joshua was filled with disgust for the people who lived here and, quite unconsciously, adopted Edmund's fear of rats. They were everywhere, even atop the wall, and he found himself hurling abuse at them as he leant from the saddle and sought to tempt the dogs away with the remaining meat in his knapsack. He told Thaddeus afterwards that he thought the dogs must have been able to hear something from inside the house—a voice, perhaps, that suddenly fell silent—because he found it strange how quickly they lost interest in what they were doing and raced back to his side.

'You think people are still alive in there?' Thaddeus asked as they made their way up the highway.

'They must be. The slops wouldn't be stinking so badly if they were weeks old, and even the burial pit looked recent. There was no grass or weeds on the earth.' Joshua pulled a face. 'The only things moving were rats. I don't blame Edmund for being scared of them. They were squatting in the excrement and you wouldn't want them near you after that.'

He fell silent as his mount reached the top of the hill. The landscape below was as Thaddeus had described—a long, wide valley full of rivers and lakes—but Joshua's ever-anxious mind saw a worse danger than longbows when he took in the size of the demesne ahead of them. 'There'll be bailiffs,' he whispered. 'We'll be flogged if they catch us.'

Thaddeus laughed. 'I thought you said no one would challenge us as long as we had ferocious dogs at our side. Are you telling me I've nursed these wretches all this way for nothing?'

'Of course not, but what if the bailiffs have a hunting pack of their own?'

'You'd better hope yours fight harder than theirs.' Thaddeus pointed to a track leading off to the right halfway down the slope. 'Follow that, and it'll take you to the lake. I'll join you in an hour or so.' He shook his head at Joshua's immediate resistance to the idea. 'Have I let you down so far?'

The boy shook his head.

'Then stop seeing danger around every corner.' He gestured for Joshua to move on. 'Keep going. I'll ride behind you until you've left the highway.'

Thaddeus fulfilled his promise in so far as he followed Joshua to the turning, but he steered Killer into the woodland on the other side of the road almost immediately. Joshua twisted in his saddle to watch, guessing Thaddeus was planning to work his way around to the eastern edge of the demesne in order to spy on it without being seen, and, out of fear for himself if something untoward happened, he cursed Thaddeus angrily under his breath for being an idiot.

☙❧

Thaddeus allowed Killer to pick his own way through the trees—mostly oaks and ash—only correcting him occasionally when he felt they were drifting off course. Their route took them across a well-trodden path which seemed to be heading towards the manor house, but Thaddeus ignored it to remain within the cover of the trees. After half a mile or so, he saw open ground through the trunks ahead of him and slid from the saddle. Tying Killer to a tree, he continued on foot.

He found himself on the edge of a wide expanse of peasant strips. The house was some four hundred yards to his right with the lake visible beyond it, but his attention was entirely focused on a man toiling on a piece of land in front of him. He was barely thirty yards away, dressed in the clothes of a serf, and using a small wooden trowel to dig what looked to be turnips from the earth. Thaddeus couldn't see his face because he was stooping to his work, but the whiteness of his hair and the thinness of his legs suggested he was old.

Careful not to give himself away through any sudden movement, Thaddeus turned his head to look for signs of life on the other strips. He counted twelve people, seven to his left and five to his right, but they were all too far away to judge age or gender. He went back to watching the turnip-digger, debating with himself whether to speak or stay silent. He'd warned the boys strongly against contact with people, but it didn't seem sensible to continue in ignorance when a chance presented itself to learn. At the very least he could find out what this demesne was called and what lay beyond the hills on the other side of the valley.

With sudden decision, he stepped from the trees and showed himself. 'Don't be afraid, sir,' he called. 'I wish you no harm and will keep my distance to show my good faith. My name is Thaddeus. I have travelled from another Dorseteshire demesne called Develish. I seek information only, and will give you what I know in return.'

The man started back in shock, crossing trembling hands above his heart in a futile attempt to defend himself. 'God save me!' he cried.

He was even older than Thaddeus had thought, a venerable ancient with shrunken cheeks and skin so weathered and creased it had the shade and texture of walnuts. But his thinness was terrible to behold. The flesh on his hands was transparent and his legs no thicker than sticks. 'Please forgive me, sir,' Thaddeus cried. 'I did not mean to startle you. I believe myself free of the pestilence but will leave immediately if that is your fear.'

There was a long pause while Thaddeus was subjected to an intense scrutiny. 'How can you be from Develish? You seem overly tall and dark for a Dorseteshire man.'

A truthful answer seemed unnecessary. Thaddeus knew better than anyone that his jet-black hair and olive skin suggested he was a foreigner. 'I was passing through when news of the pestilence reached the demesne. We learnt shortly afterwards that Sir Richard had died and I stayed to assist his widow, Lady Anne, in the administering of the estate. I come at her bidding now to discover news of what is happening elsewhere in our county.'

'Are you a lord yourself, sire?'

Thaddeus smiled. 'Do I look like one?'

'Not in dress, perhaps, but you have the bearing of an important man, and we are sorely in need of help.'

'How many are you?'

'Thirty-seven, sire. Fifteen children under ten, four greybeards too weak to work, the thirteen you see in these fields, and five who have gone foraging for nuts and berries.'

Thaddeus glanced towards the manor house. 'What of your lord and his household? What number are they?'

'The master and his family travelled north when news of the plague first reached us.' His rheumy eyes followed Thaddeus's gaze. 'After that the household servants barred the door to the rest of us and set to feasting on the taxes taken from us last quarter day. There were some sixty at the beginning but we don't know their number now.'

'How many bondsmen have died?'

The old fellow sighed. 'We've buried more than two hundred, but there's been many an absconder since the master left. They thought it better to die upon the road than fall prey to the pestilence or starvation here. One year ago, there were over six hundred souls in Woodoak . . . now there's a bare hundred. Is it the same in Develish?'

Thaddeus shook his head. 'Everyone still lives—apart from Sir Richard and his fighting men, who fell sick in Bradmayne.' He gestured to the land around them. 'Is Woodoak the name of this demesne?'

'It is.'

'And what is your name, sir?'

'Thomas Breakspear,' the ancient replied, with the glisten of tears on his faded lashes. 'I have watched my whole family pass away before my eyes, yet God sees fit to keep me alive . . . though to what purpose, I cannot say. Why should a sinful old man be spared when innocent children are not? Does that make sense to you, sire?'

'What does your priest say?'

'He was amongst the first to perish. No one has had absolution for months. We die as he did, unshriven and unblessed.' Breakspear's gaze held Thaddeus's for a moment. 'Is it because Develish is a pious place that God has allowed them to live?'

Thaddeus wondered if the truth would please him or be a cause for regret that Woodoak hadn't followed Develish's example. Yet he baulked at pretending a piety he didn't have. 'Far from it,' he answered. 'It's because they put their faith in themselves that they have survived.' He described the measures Develish had taken to keep the pestilence at bay, finishing with how Gyles Startout had survived despite Sir Richard and the rest of his entourage dying. 'You and the others working in these fields would seem to be the same, Master Breakspear. Everyone around you has fallen to the pestilence but you have not. Can you account for that—apart from believing in God's mercy?'

'A merciful God would not have taken my children and grandchildren, sire,' the old man said, head bowed, staring at the ground. 'My neighbours should hear your story. Are you courageous enough to follow me to the village and speak to them?'

'Are you unable to tell it yourself?'

A dry chuckle issued from the wrinkled mouth. 'What would you have me say? That I met a black-bearded giant in the woods who claimed to come from Develish where everyone still lives? I'll be sooner believed if I say I saw a unicorn.'

჻

The children playing in the dust of the road scattered as Thaddeus approached, running for the shelter of their houses and closing their doors. A couple of old women, crouched over a cooking pot in the lee of a wall, remained where they were, but the way they canted their heads—intent on listening rather than looking— suggested to Thaddeus they were blind. He sat astride Killer with a dead sheep slung across the horse's withers, his unsheathed sword clearly visible in his hand, following thirty yards behind Thomas Breakspear and the other twelve serfs who had been working in the fields. Seven were women and they called to the children not to be afraid.

'This man is a friend; you do not need to hide from him,' cried one.

'He comes in peace to tell us what he knows,' called another. 'He has slaughtered a sheep so that we can eat.'

Thomas Breakspear raised his voice. 'He is a visiting lord from Develish. He asks only that we keep our distance. He intends us no harm but is ready to defend himself if anyone tries to rush him. Come out of your homes and listen to what he has to say.'

His companions took up the cry, urging the children to be brave, and slowly but surely the doors began to open. One little girl, as insubstantial as a wraith, watched Thaddeus from the shadows before taking off at a run towards a copse of alders growing beside the lake, shouting to people unseen to return to the village. Seconds later a handful of adolescent youths emerged from between the trees, their bodies painfully thin under their tunics.

With narrowed eyes, Thaddeus examined the walls of the manor house, wondering if the clamour of voices had carried to the servants inside. He was willing to give what succour he could to this ragtag group of weak and starving peasants but not to those who had abandoned them; yet the villagers' cries were so loud and clear in the still autumn air that it was hard to believe they weren't being heard. He may have imagined that he saw windows crack open and the flash of faces in the gloom behind, but he didn't think so.

Twenty-four

Woodoak, Dorseteshire

TWO HUNDRED YARDS AWAY, WHERE Joshua was standing at the lake's edge, the dogs leapt to their feet, growls in their throats, ears pricked and muzzles pointing towards the source of the sound. Alarmed, the boy spun around, and stared in disbelief towards the village. There was no mistaking the figure of Thaddeus on the back of Killer, nor the sword in his hand, and to Joshua he appeared to be defending himself against a mob. In desperation, convinced that Thaddeus's luck had finally run out, he did the only thing he could think of. He ran along the grassy bank of the lake with the baying pack in hot pursuit, waving and hollering to deflect the villagers' attention to himself.

Perhaps the people of Woodoak thought the demonic howls of the dogs came from the belly of Hell, because they froze in fear, and Thaddeus had time to wonder if he'd ever seen such an abandonment of hope in human faces. Was acceptance of death so ingrained they had no fight left? For himself, he assumed Joshua was running away from danger and heaved the sheep's carcass from Killer's back to lighten the animal's load. With no safe route through the crowd of serfs, he turned the charger towards the common land between the village and the manor house and gave him his head.

For once the horse decided to do what Thaddeus wanted, moving smoothly from one gait to another and taking directions through the bit, but there was no logic to it unless he enjoyed showing off in front of strangers. Thaddeus smoothed his neck in appreciation as they slowed to a walk at the head of the lake, but he muttered into Killer's ear that he still considered him a contrary brute.

Joshua had stopped some fifty yards down the bank with the dogs gathered around his legs. 'Are you all right?' he called.

'Never better,' answered Thaddeus, drawing close and scanning the trees along the shoreline. 'What did you see? What were you running from?'

The boy glared at him. 'Nothing. I came to rescue you.'

'From what?'

Joshua gestured indignantly towards the village. 'You've been drumming into us that we should keep away from places like this then you ride straight into one. I saw you waving your sword. I thought you were being attacked.'

'You saw wrong.'

'They could have been soldiers with longbows.'

'They weren't.' Thaddeus studied the youngster's angry expression for a moment. 'Do you know the adage "the brave man faces his fears, the coward runs away"?'

'What if I do?' Joshua snapped. 'We can't all be like you.'

Thaddeus gave a bark of laughter. It betrayed the excitement he felt to be dicing with danger again. 'I was paying you a compliment, you obstinate oaf. You should have thought about longbows yourself before you came charging to my aid.' Resting his forearms on the pommel of the saddle, he described his meeting with

Thomas Breakspear and explained why he'd agreed to follow the old man to the village. 'The serfs who've survived the pestilence are starving because they're too afraid to take their lord's sheep or the fish from his lake for fear of being flogged upon his return.'

'Who would accuse them?'

'If Thomas is to be believed, the sixty servants who've barricaded themselves inside the house.' Thaddeus shook his head. 'It seems a wretched place beside Develish. The house servants think themselves above the field serfs and take pleasure in informing on them to their lord. Those who do are rewarded, and those who are named have the skin flayed from their backs.'

Joshua glanced towards the manor house, a deep reluctance to have anything to do with this place welling inside him. 'But it's not our business, Thaddeus. We came for feathers and arrowheads, nothing else.'

'They're looking to me for help. Would you have me turn my back on them?'

'Yes. I'd have you turn your back on anyone who's too foolish to help himself. Why do they not take fish from the water at night as we do, or hunt for venison in these forests where they can't be seen?'

'I don't know,' said Thaddeus, 'but there are youths of your age who seem readier to die than risk a flogging from an absent lord who may never come back.' He turned Killer around. 'I promised Thomas I'd speak to them and that's what I'm going to do. I'll find you when I'm finished.'

With an inward sigh, Joshua watched the horse pick its way delicately across the grass. 'If their lord's as bad as they say, you'll do them no favours by turning them against him,' he called. 'They'll be given the whip anyway.'

The ghost of a laugh floated back to him. 'At least they'll be alive to feel it.'

Joshua followed at a distance to watch and listen. Human nature wouldn't allow him to do anything else, but, even so, he clung to the cover of the woodland and kept a wary eye on the house for archers.

This time Thaddeus approached the village from the lake and halted on the highway thirty yards short of the first two houses. To Joshua, the scene was as disturbing as any he'd witnessed. So thin were the people in front of Thaddeus that their eyes looked huge in their faces and their legs barely able to support them. Joshua, who was accustomed to the hearty, well-fed look of the Develish serfs, was shocked to the core by these timid, pale shadows, yet he felt more anger towards them than sympathy. By what idiocy were they denying themselves when there was meat and fish in abundance?

He found himself urging Thaddeus to put that question to them. Why bother with courtesies when their stupidity was plain to see? But Thaddeus chose a subtler way to uncover the truth, speaking loudly and clearly so that his words might carry to the manor house. He began by repeating what he had told Thomas Breakspear of the measures Lady Anne had taken to keep her serfs alive, describing how the food was rationed and distributed in equal portions to everyone. 'Lady Anne strives to protect all her people,' he said. 'There will be no future for anyone otherwise. If the field serfs die, famine will take the place of the pestilence and everyone will starve—including My Lord of Woodoak, should he ever return.'

'There will be sheep in his fields and pike in his lake,' said Thomas. 'He bound us through our oath of fealty to ensure it.'

'On what penalty?'

'Our lives. Any theft of stock will be punishable by death. The sheep were counted before he left, including predicted births in the spring. If he finds fewer lambs than were promised or a lake less teeming with fish, we will all be forfeit. That is the reason so many of our fellows have left to seek food elsewhere.'

'What if bandits steal carcasses? Will you still be held responsible even though there are too few of you to prevent it?'

The old man nodded. 'We will be at fault if any of My Lord's stock is missing.'

'Including the sheep I slaughtered one hour ago?'

'Not if we leave it lying in the road and the house servants are honest enough to say a stranger killed it.'

'Meaning you can't be accused of theft if you don't eat it?'

'Yes.'

Thaddeus pondered for a moment then looked towards the house and raised his voice again. 'Hear my words and mark them well,' he called. 'I, Lord of Foxcote, vassal knight to the King and cousin to Lady Anne of Develish, have used the authority vested in me to provide food for these starving peasants. By fleeing to safety, My Lord of Woodoak has broken his sacred oath to protect and succour those who have sworn fealty to him, and he will answer for his perjury before the Church and the King. I make this promise in the name of Lady Anne of Develish, who has sworn to seek justice for the poor and needy of Dorseteshire once the sickness has passed. Any lord who dares to put a greater value on the life of a single sheep in his fields than on the lives of his serfs will have his lands and chattels confiscated and his household servants reduced to bondage.'

There was a second or two of silence before a cry came back from the house. 'Where is Foxcote?'

'To the north.'

'Then you are not from these parts and you overstep your authority by being here. The power to reclaim this demesne resides in My Lord of Blandeforde, not in you or Lady Anne of Develish.' The tone of the voice was hard, designed to intimidate.

'You are misguided,' Thaddeus called back. 'This land belongs to the King, as does all the land of England. When I bear witness to what I have seen here today, Lady Anne will take the cause of these starving peasants to our Sovereign Lord and beg justice for them. They have the same right to protection from their lord as you do.'

'No blame can be attached to us. We do only what we were instructed to do.'

'Then your testimony will condemn your master. I will have you summoned to the Court of Assizes so that you may repeat the instructions he gave you. Repeat them for us now so that these serfs may know how little My Lord of Woodoak values their lives.'

His words were met with silence, although Joshua, who was closer to the house, thought he heard an argument break out inside one of the rooms. He half expected shouts of 'imposter' to follow, together with demands that Thaddeus prove he was who he said he was. Surely no one could believe that an ill-dressed serf, with the sleeves cut from his jerkin and mud stains on his britches, was lord of a distant demesne and cousin to Lady Anne of Develish?

'Your refusal to answer says it all,' Thaddeus continued. 'You are as complicit as My Lord of Woodoak in the abandonment of your brothers in the village. Perhaps it suits you to watch them die. Do you wait for the day when you can steal sheep from the fields to fill your own bellies and blame the theft on them? Dead men will make fine scapegoats for your crimes when My Lord returns and finds his stocks depleted.'

'You accuse us of things we haven't done.'

'Not yet, perhaps, but you will. I hear deceit in every word you speak. You have malicious minds and malicious tongues. I have seen the scars on Thomas Breakspear's back where one of you accused him falsely of stealing bread, and I will swear to that on oath before the High Sheriff if Thomas is not alive to do it himself.'

There was a brief pause before another voice spoke. 'You cannot know the accusation was false, nor that what Thomas Breakspear tells you is the truth.'

'I find it easier to believe a man who is starving than one who grows fat on the field serfs' tithes and taxes,' Thaddeus replied. 'You will discover for yourselves how arduous the lives of these people are when you are set to work on the land. There will be no need for soft-handed beard-trimmers when the earth needs ploughing and the wheat sowing. Are you all so foolish that you haven't worked this out for yourselves? How do you expect your lord to keep you when there are no skilled men to plant the fields and reap the harvest?'

Such a silence followed Thaddeus's question that it was clear to Joshua no such considerations had crossed the servants' minds. In truth, they hadn't crossed Joshua's either until Thaddeus had talked about the future as they ate their meals around the fire each night. To live through the pestilence should be the least of their ambitions, he told them. The Black Death promised freedom to anyone who survived it. With so many dead, serfs skilled in farming would be prized once lords became desperate to have their fields ploughed and planted; and their need would give men and women the chance to bargain themselves out of bondage and demand payment for their work.

Thaddeus was amused by the boys' astonishment when he told them that such ideas were discussed frequently by Lady Anne and their fathers. What did they think her council talked about if not to make plans for when the pestilence passed? Did the boys not understand for themselves how different the world might look when that happened? From being the most despised of people, peasants would become the most valued, for without their labour no lord would be able to keep and govern his demesne.

Looking at the emaciated people in front of Thaddeus, Joshua saw the truth of this prediction. My Lord of Woodoak and his household would have nothing if they had to rely on this tiny handful of greybeards and children to grow their food. He felt a sudden admiration for Lady Anne and Thaddeus—his father also—that they'd had the cleverness to foresee these events when Woodoak servants seemed unable even to recognise the disaster that was unfolding before them.

'You speak as if decisions are easy when they are not,' the second voice called again. 'We have not abandoned the villagers out of unkindness. We are too afraid of the pestilence to step outside and share our food with them.'

'Has no servant died of it?'

'We've lost a quarter of our number and those who remain live in fear of each other. We study our fellows for signs of sickness—but we watch the villagers more. So many have perished that we are certain they carry the plague upon them.'

Thaddeus turned to Thomas. 'Who was the last bondsman to die of the disease?'

'Mary Hynd,' the old man answered, looking to his companions for verification. 'She acted as nurse to all who fell sick then succumbed herself at the end.'

'How long ago?'

'Some weeks now. She died alone because she wouldn't allow anyone to tend her for fear of passing the disease to another.'

A woman nodded. 'She showed mercy to all, yet God showed her none. She died in terrible pain, but with the priest long dead there was no one to give her absolution.'

'Where did you bury her?'

Thomas gestured towards a mound of earth to the east of the village. 'In the pit with the others.'

'Were you not afraid to touch her?'

'Indeed. We were afraid to touch any who died, but we couldn't have stayed here if we'd left the bodies to rot. The stench would have driven us out before the carrion-seekers arrived.'

'Yet the sickness has passed you by. Do you not find that strange?'

His question was greeted with weary shrugs, as if the subject had been discussed many times. 'God wills it,' said one of the men.

Thaddeus shook his head. 'A loving God wouldn't save you from a pestilence only to kill you with famine,' he answered. 'There must be a different way of catching the disease than breathing the air of the sick or touching their corpses.' He looked towards the lake. 'Did you wash after each burial?'

'Mary Hynd insisted on it,' said the woman. 'Full immersion, she told us, to take away the uncleanness.'

Thaddeus thought of Gyles. 'What kind of uncleanness?'

The woman frowned as if the question were a foolish one. 'The dead turned black,' she said, 'and all had open sores. Our flesh crawled even to be close to them.'

'But was it not enough to wash your hands? Why did the rest of your body feel unclean?' He shifted his attention to Thomas when she didn't answer. 'Gyles Startout, the Develish man who avoided the sickness, spoke of feeling dirty, but I never asked what form the dirt took. He had to immerse himself in the brook several times and burn his clothes before he felt free of it.'

The old man looked thoughtful. 'Everything felt unclean: the air, the earth, our clothes, our skin . . . My daughter complained of terrible itching before she succumbed. She made her arms red with scratching before the boils appeared in her neck.' He laid a hand on the woman's arm. 'Suzanna described it well when she said our flesh crawled. To take a plunge in the lake gave some relief, even though most of us did it only to humour Mary. She lost her wits towards the end—tried to burn her cottage with herself inside it after she fell sick, and it was only because the lake was so close that we were able to douse the flames.'

'Did she say why she did that?'

'She hoped the fire would spread through the village. She said it was the only way to rid ourselves of the pestilence.'

Thaddeus caught a movement out of the corner of his eye and turned towards a youth who was standing at the edge of the group. The lad had half raised his hand but dropped it again out of nervousness when the black-bearded giant's attention fell upon him. 'Don't be afraid to speak,' Thaddeus told him. 'I'm willing to hear what anyone has to say.'

The boy's response was so mumbled that Thaddeus had to prompt him to repeat it. 'Mistress Hynd believed it was rats that carried the pestilence,' he managed. 'She urged the elders to burn them out of the thatch and out of the walls. Kill the rats, kill the plague, she said . . . but they wouldn't listen to her.'

One of the male serfs who had accompanied Thaddeus and Thomas from the peasant strips stirred impatiently. 'And you know why, young Catstock. There'd have been no shelter for any of us if we'd done as Mary wanted. Every home would have been destroyed. And to what purpose when the pestilence has gone away of its own accord?'

Another youth spoke. 'You haven't slept in your house for weeks, Master Blount. None of us has.'

'Not for much longer. Soon the rains will come and it will be so bitter we will need the shelter of walls and thatch.'

There was a short silence before the first boy raised his hand again and stepped forward to address Thaddeus. 'While she still lived, Mistress Hynd begged us five—' he gestured to the four adolescents ranged behind him—'to build a fire every night beside the lake so that the little ones could sleep outside with us. We began to do it when she first fell sick. The older people joined us one night later and since that time no one has died.'

Thaddeus ran a thoughtful hand around his jaw. 'I've encountered rats everywhere I've been,' he said. 'Some are so bold they come out during the day.' He glanced down the row of houses. 'But I see none here.'

'There've been fewer since our food ran out,' the boy said, 'but we think they still nest in the roofs. We hear rustling sometimes. Me and my friends think Mistress Hynd was right. We want to burn the houses and build new ones away from the village.'

Thaddeus saw the pleading in his face, guessed he wanted this stranger to take his side against Thomas Breakspear and the other elders. 'None of the servants has perished recently either,' he reminded the boy gently, 'yet they remain behind closed doors. How would Mistress Hynd account for that, young Catstock?'

'I don't know, sire, but if she was alive, she would have an answer. She had more wisdom than I do.'

'She sounds wise,' Thaddeus agreed. He looked towards the house and raised his voice again. 'Do you have a reason for why a quarter of your number died but the rest still live?' he called. 'I will not believe you if you tell me it's by God's mercy. Only an arrogant man would claim to have a purer heart than a babe in arms who has had to suffer the pain of this terrible death.'

'It's not for any of us to question God's purpose.'

'Then you must think yourselves peculiarly blessed if He has chosen you for life. It makes me wonder why you eye each other with suspicion and refuse to leave the house for fear of catching the pestilence from these villagers. What is there to dread if you wear God's protective shield?'

There was another period of silence before a woman's voice spoke. Her voice seemed to come from the other end of the house and Thaddeus guessed she was in a different room from the men. 'You talk as if you know why this plague has fallen on us, sire. Will you share that knowledge with us?'

'I know that it began in the port of Melcombe around the Feast of St John the Baptist and has spread far and wide across the county. I know, too, that it cannot be carried on the wind or Develish would have lost as many of her people to it as Woodoak has. I would guess that it was brought to our shores by foreign sailors, but I am ignorant of how it travels so quickly across land, or why some—such as you—have been spared even though your fellows have died.'

'We watch the villagers make a fire each night by the lake. Why do they do that?'

'To enable them to sleep outside and avoid the rats that nest in the walls and thatch of their cottages. Mistress Hynd believed they carried the pestilence. It may be true, since no one has fallen sick from the time they left their homes.' He paused. 'Are there rats in the rooms you inhabit?'

'Not since Mary told us of her concerns. She was a good soul who bore no hatred towards us. She approached the wall one day to urge us to rid ourselves of vermin. The men forced the women to do it by—' Her words were cut off abruptly as if a hand had been placed over her mouth.

This time the clamour of angry voices inside the house was audible to everyone. There was a cry of, 'Leave her alone!' before a girl's voice screamed out, 'The men hold us prisoner, sir. They abuse us terribly. Even the youngest are made objects of their lust. We need your help as sorely as the vill—'

There was the sound of a slap followed by the harsh, grating tone of the man who had spoken first. Perhaps it was the aggression in his guttural sounds or the fact that Joshua took a step forward to see better what was happening, but the seven dogs reacted with rumbling, throaty growls which erupted into barks as Thaddeus shouted for the girl to be allowed to speak. When no one answered, he rounded on Thomas Breakspear.

'Whose voice spoke first? Who is in charge in there?' he demanded.

'My Lord of Woodoak's chamberlain—Gregory de Joulet. He's been steward of the house these last five years and our lives have been the worse for it.'

'I give you fair warning, Master de Joulet!' Thaddeus roared. 'Send the female servants to the front door now or pay the price of refusal. You have the time it takes for my horse to cross the ground between us. Do I make myself clear?'

'You'll get an arrow between your eyes if you try.'

Thaddeus assured Joshua afterwards that he risked nothing by riding Killer towards the house. If there were fighting men inside, they would have shown themselves at the windows as soon as he declared his intent, and no servant would have the accuracy to hit a moving target. But the truth was simpler. The grating harshness in de Joulet's tone reminded him too much of his stepfather Will, and the whimpering cries of the women of his mother Eva. He set off blindly without any thought for the consequences.

He steered Killer at a fast canter along the edge of the lake before turning through an arc to bring him into the shelter of a stone staircase at the western corner of the house. There was no boundary wall to add protection but, close to, Thaddeus could see it was unnecessary. Even astride a horse, none of the windows was low enough to allow an enemy easy entry and each was protected by solid oak shutters, fastened on the inside. Only the windows of the upper storey were open to let in light and air.

Cautiously, keeping Killer close to the façade in order to create an impossible angle for an archer to fire on him from above, he walked the animal along the front until he reached the arched entrance way. The door, seemingly as unyielding as the shutters, was firmly closed, and more in annoyance than because he thought it would achieve anything, he took his foot from the stirrup and stamped the heel of his boot against the middle plank. It was arguable which surprised him more: the sudden arrival of Joshua and the hounds, or the screech of splitting timber as his heel made contact.

Joshua worked the tale into a fine story of heroism for his friends afterwards, but he left out that the dogs took off of their own accord and, with only one stirrup, Thaddeus barely remained in the saddle when the excited hounds caused Killer to become skittish.

'What the Hell are you doing here?' he snapped. 'Move away before this brute throws me!'

Joshua opened his knapsack and backed off, hugging the wall and luring the dogs with a handful of meat. Once he had them around him, he rolled his eyes towards the upper storey to warn Thaddeus that his words could be heard. 'My apologies, sire,' he said with an extravagant bow. 'The pack is overeager to commence the search.'

A gleam of humour appeared on Thaddeus's face. 'All in good time, Buckler. Stand fast till I have this door breached. It's not as sturdy as it looks.'

He manoeuvred Killer broadside once again and smashed his heel twice more against the planking before leaning down to peer through the foot-long splintered crack he'd made. The light was poor because every shutter in the great hall was closed, and his nose told him what he was looking at before his vision did. The smell of burning was powerful but not so strong that it could disguise the stench of corruption. As his eyes adjusted, he made out a pyramid of blackened remains in the centre of the room, with the recognisable shapes of skulls and bones amidst the debris. It was a charnel house of cremated bodies and the reek of death told him the flames had not burnt long nor hotly enough to reduce the flesh to ash.

He wondered what sort of madness had persuaded the servants to attempt such a thing. While the corpses may not have burnt, the fire had spread to everything else. All the doors, including this one, were charred and singed—some so badly that they leant drunkenly off their hinges—and here and there he could make out the ruins of what had once been chests and tables. Tattered remnants of tapestries, black with soot, still hung in places at head height, but the fact that none of the shutters was burnt suggested someone had had the sense to quench the flames before they could climb to the floor above.

He straightened, shaking his head at Joshua. 'A vision of Hell is behind this door,' he said loudly. 'All is destroyed by fire except for half-burnt corpses in the middle of the floor. Were it not for the stone walls, the whole edifice would have collapsed.'

Joshua ran his tongue nervously over his lips, wondering if Thaddeus was speaking the truth or embroidering it to scare the servants upstairs. This time he rolled his eyes towards the dogs. 'We—cannot—let—them—in,' he mouthed.

Thaddeus nodded to show he understood. 'Mark me well, Master de Joulet,' he called. 'The Hell you have created in this hall will be as nothing compared to the one I can create by forcing this door and allowing the vermin of Woodoak to enter. We have watched ravens and foxes feast on the dead in Athelhelm and Afpedle . . . seen rats, filthy with faeces and vomit, scale stone walls in search of food . . . felt the bile rise in our throats as they spread their squalor amongst the living. Do you wish the same to happen here?'

'The fire was not of my making. One of the menservants went mad and set the hall ablaze while the rest of us slept.'

'And what caused him to go mad? The smell of rotting corpses inside the house? Are you a demon or an imbecile, sir, that you refused to bury them outside?'

'Blame the lower servants before you blame me,' de Joulet answered angrily. 'None was willing to go near the pit after the gravedigger died. They preferred a flogging to certain death.'

Joshua saw the contempt on Thaddeus's face, and he put his hands together in a plea to him to act with wisdom. The dogs were becoming restless, their muzzles scenting the air as the smell of corruption leaked through the splintered timbers of the door, and Joshua doubted his ability to hold them much longer. It wasn't as if Thaddeus hadn't burnt corpses himself. 'You came for the women, sire,' he reminded him. 'They'll be safe enough if they leave by the staircase on the western wall.'

'Would you deprive me of my fun, Master Buckler?' Thaddeus asked with a mischievous wink. 'My dogs will make small work of this devil of a steward if I give them leave to enter. The mastiffs will have his throat even before he hits the ground.'

'And every other male servant too, sire. Your hounds are trained to treat men as enemies when you give the command to attack. It's only the women they'll spare.'

'Then we have nothing to lose by forcing the door.'

'We don't know that all the men are as guilty as Master de Joulet, sire.'

Thaddeus used the hilt of his sword to thunder another blow against the wood panelling. 'If that be true, then those amongst you who truly repent of your actions, release the women now—or by God's will accept death at the jaws of my mastiffs.'

ᘒᘖ

Joshua had no need to embroider the later parts of the tale. Thaddeus wore the mantle of lord as easily as he had assumed the role of steward to Lady Anne, and no one in Woodoak thought to challenge him on it despite the raggedness of his clothing or the unkempt appearance of his hair and beard.

By association, Joshua acquired respect as his squire, and for the first time in his life the boy felt able to hold his head high without fear of being pilloried. He even believed it necessary to show confidence if Thaddeus was to maintain his authority. It was all mummery, of course. From beginning to end, Joshua saw problems everywhere, particularly at the beginning when near on twenty female servants—many of them young girls—fled down the stone staircase, faces drawn with terror. He was so anxious the dogs would leap at them that he shouted a command to 'stand', and was mortified when the women obeyed with as much speed as the animals.

They huddled together at the bottom of the steps, bedraggled and dirty, as terrified of what was in front of them as what they had left behind. One of the older women held out her hands to Thaddeus and begged him to protect them.

'The dogs won't hurt you,' he said.

'But we fear everything, sire,' she cried. 'We are as afraid of the villagers as we are of the servants in the house.'

He recognised her voice as the woman who had asked him how the plague had begun. The others seemed to look to her as their leader. 'You have no need to be. Thomas Breakspear is a good man. No harm will come to you from him and his fellows.'

'They will turn us away, sire, and we will have no shelter anywhere.' She laid a hand on the head of the smallest of the maids. 'Even this little one has been defiled by the lust of the male servants. More of our sisters have died of shame than of sickness.'

Joshua had never seen such distress in human faces before. Tears coursed freely down their cheeks, and if Thaddeus had been a priest, they would have flung themselves in front of him, begging forgiveness for the sins that had been committed against them. And perhaps it was their good fortune that he wasn't, for no man of the cloth would have dealt with them as gently as Thaddeus did, nor understood their situation so well.

'The villagers are barely alive, mistress,' he said. 'They have neither the will nor the energy to stand in judgement on you . . . and if they try, they will have me to answer to. No fault attaches to any of you, only to the men who treated you so vilely.' His eyes softened as he watched her, seeing how she used her arms to shield the younger girls. 'Regret nothing,' he urged. 'Live for today so that you may seek justice tomorrow.'

'There'll be no justice for the likes of us, sire. There never is.'

'There are many kinds of justice, mistress, and some are more satisfying than others. For myself, I count it enough to see fear in the face of my enemy when he knows I've grown powerful enough to harm him. Your best revenge will be to survive this pestilence with your strength and wits intact so that your tormentors will live in dread of your anger.'

She didn't say anything, and Joshua wondered if her spirit was so broken that she was beyond helping herself and the others. If so, Thaddeus had taken on a great responsibility by charging to their rescue, and Joshua sent him a silent prayer not to offer any more sympathy. He felt his body itch all over at the thought of these filthy, unwashed women throwing themselves at his and Thaddeus's feet in a desperate plea for protection. Who knew what diseases they carried? Could the man not remember, even for an hour, his own injunction to stay as far from people as possible?

It seemed not. He liked playing a lord too much.

'Tell me how I can help you,' Thaddeus urged the woman. 'No problem is so difficult that it cannot be resolved.'

'We cannot ask the villagers to accept us looking as we do, sire. Our clothes are melted into tatters from putting out the fire and we have not bathed since Master de Joulet left the bodies in the hall. The only well was in the kitchen and it took all our courage to go downstairs to draw water for drinking.'

'Have you no spare shifts or kirtles?'

'They were in the chests that were set ablaze.'

'What about My Lady of Woodoak? Did she leave no gowns behind in her chamber?'

'None that we can use, sire.'

'Why not?'

'They don't belong to us.'

'Nor to me,' said Thaddeus, 'but I'll have them anyway.' He shouted to the male servants to throw down every gown, kirtle and shift they could find. 'When My Lady of Woodoak returns, tell her that Foxcote promises to pay twice their value in restitution on condition that none of these women is branded a thief.'

'What guarantees do we have that you'll do as you say?'

'Are you questioning my word, Master de Joulet? Think rather how you will answer when I bring the High Sheriff to Woodoak and accuse you before My Lord and Milady of mistreating these women so badly that you refused them even the benefit of modesty when they begged to be cleansed of your fetid stench.'

Joshua could only marvel as a score of silk gowns, embroidered kirtles and shifts fluttered from the windows. But he kept his face expressionless. If he learnt anything that day, it was to ape Thaddeus's trick of hiding his emotions. Of course, he worried that the tall serf was overplaying his hand through thrill and bravado, and his courage faltered every time he thought of what could go wrong. His eyes flickered constantly between the highway north and the highway south, certain that soldiers would ride into view when they least expected it.

Nevertheless, he felt more hurt than relieved when Thaddeus ordered him to go back down to the lake to where he'd left his horse and renew the hunt for ducks. 'Do you have no job for me here, sire?' he asked.

Thaddeus shook his head. 'Not unless these gentle souls want an audience while they bathe, Buckler. We'll do them more kindness by taking ourselves off, I think.' He sheathed his sword and turned to the woman again. 'You must discard every piece of clothing,' he told her, 'and immerse yourselves completely in the water. It was the advice Mary Hynd gave the bondsmen and it seems to have worked. When you feel that your hair and bodies are cleansed, dress yourselves in these gowns, and make your way to the village. I will wait for you there.'

'And then you will leave us,' she said flatly.

'I can do no else,' he answered. 'I have people of my own to look after.' He studied her face for a moment, saw the anxiety in her eyes. 'What is your name, mistress?'

'Sarah Standfast, My Lord.'

'It's a good name and a strong one, Sarah. Do you think you can live up to it now? These little maids need you to be fearless . . . and so do I.'

Weary tears rolled from the corners of her eyes. 'I will do my best, sire.'

ळ्ळ

Joshua watched subsequent events from a distance. He couldn't hear anything that was said and had to interpret what he saw through Thaddeus's gestures and the actions of the serfs. Overcoming their resistance to skinning and butchering the dead sheep looked easy enough—the five youths ran to retrieve the carcass as soon as Thaddeus pointed to it—but persuading them to burn their homes took longer. There was much discussion before the women, children and greybeards moved to the place where they lit a bonfire by the lake each night, and the task of setting the village ablaze was given to the youths.

They did it much as Ian, Olyver and Edmund had done at Afpedle, by building a fire at the southern end of the village and then running up the road to toss flaming logs onto one thatched roof after another. Even two hundred yards away, Joshua could see the pleasure it gave them as they turned cartwheels in the dust and punched each other on the arms. He guessed their joy had more to do with winning the argument than the destruction of their homes, but he doubted the older men would put up with such cockiness once Thaddeus was gone.

Thaddeus disagreed when Joshua asked him about it later. 'The youths are the only ones with any spirit,' he said. 'The older men had theirs broken long ago. If I'm any judge, young Catstock will be their leader by Christmas. He's already marked out where the new village should be and decided which trees to fell for wall posts.'

Joshua heard the admiration in Thaddeus's tone, and a knot of jealousy twisted in his gut. 'If he's that clever, he'd be their leader already and they wouldn't be starving.'

'He needed permission to steal. They all did.'

'So you gave it to them?'

They were riding side by side up the highway to Afpedle, six ducks strung on a string around Joshua's neck and a rake secured diagonally across Thaddeus's back. 'Not exactly. I urged them to give themselves permission. There's a difference.'

'How?'

'They need to find a common purpose if they're to survive. Each of them has thought about killing a sheep or taking a trout from the lake, but none had the courage to do it on his own. If they act in agreement, My Lord of Woodoak will have to flog them all . . . or spare them all. My guess is he'll spare them. He'll be too short of field hands to do anything else.'

'Did you tell them they should bargain for their freedom the way you keep telling us?'

Thaddeus nodded. 'I did—though only young Catstock seemed to see merit in the idea. The rest were frightened by it.'

'Why?'

Thaddeus shrugged. 'Perhaps they've lived too long in slavery. Perhaps they don't know how to work for themselves. Perhaps their ignorance of the world beyond Woodoak causes them to fear a life outside a lord's protection. Develish would be the same if Lady Anne hadn't shared her learning with us.'

'Do you think My Lord of Woodoak will listen if his serfs ask for freedom? Sir Richard wouldn't have done. He'd have had us all flogged just for thinking about it.'

'If he has any sense he will.'

Joshua was less certain. From all he'd seen and heard in the village, he thought it likely My Lord was as vicious and unreasonable as his chamberlain. 'I saw some men leave the house by the outside staircase and follow the female servants to the village,' he said then. 'Was Master de Joulet one of them?'

He'd worried that he was the only person to see the group emerge from the upper storey to creep furtively after the women, now clad in brightly coloured gowns and kirtles. They'd looked like exotic birds, picking their way beside the lake and holding their skirts out at the sides to avoid tripping over the hems, but they seemed oblivious to the men behind them. Joshua had breathed a sigh of relief when Thaddeus had unsheathed his sword and nudged Killer forward to confront them. They appeared to have no evil intent, because they fell to their knees before him, but, even so, Thaddeus wouldn't allow them to pass. He gestured for them to go back the way they'd come, and the last Joshua saw of them was when they disappeared into woodland to the west of the house.

'Not unless he's still wet behind the ears,' said Thaddeus. 'They were your age, claiming to be terrified of de Joulet and racked with remorse and regret for what they'd done. They asked to be allowed to join the villagers.'

'Why did you refuse them?'

'It wasn't my decision to make. For all I know they were the worst of the abusers. It's up to Sarah Standfast and the other maids to give them entry, not me.'

'So why didn't they call out to Sarah?'

'Because I told them to scrub themselves clean for three days before they even thought about begging forgiveness,' said Thaddeus with a laugh. 'They'll be a lot more penitent if they have to freeze in sodden clothes for a couple of nights. They didn't just rape the poor wretches, they forced them to search out every rat nest and destroy it before locking them in a room for five days without food.'

'Why would they do that?'

'To be sure the rats hadn't given them the pestilence. I'd have flogged every one of those youths if I'd thought debasing women was their idea and not the chamberlain's. If anyone deserves to die a painful death, he does.'

Perhaps it was fortunate they were almost at Afpedle again and the subject changed to the tasks that lay ahead, because Joshua had a nasty feeling that Thaddeus saw little difference between what de Joulet had done to the maids in Woodoak and what he and his friends had done with Eleanor. If he'd thought another attempt to justify himself would work, he might have tried, but in retrospect he was glad he didn't.

As Thaddeus drew Killer to a halt and unbuckled the rake before dismounting, he turned to Joshua with a smile. 'It was Thomas Breakspear who gave me this. He didn't ask why I wanted it, just said it was the least he could do by way of a thank you.'

'You deserve it. You showed them kindness.'

'Mm.' He swung out of the saddle and reached down lazily to fondle the mastiff's head, showing the boy that the dogs had won his approval. 'He also told me my squire was braver than any of My Lord of Woodoak's fighting men. You did well, Joshua.'

He pretended not to see the flush that stained the boy's freckled face a rosy red. Joshua gave his affection too easily—to dogs as well as humans—and Thaddeus wasn't inclined to take the place of an absent father. He hadn't the skills or the patience to nurture petulant boys to adulthood.

The eighth day of September, 1348

*J*t is three days since My Lord of Bourne and his Norman
soldiers were routed by English peasants and I can still scarce
believe it. How wonderfully my people worked together to defeat
them. Master de Courtesmain urges me to say it was by God's
Grace that Develish has emerged the victor, but in honesty I
cannot. The credit must go to Gyles Startout. I wager My Lord
and his captain of arms will hesitate to undervalue a serf as
brave and fine again.

Once they had departed the valley, Alleyn Startout, John
Trueblood, James Buckler and Adam Catchpole crossed on the
raft to butcher the four dead horses and retrieve everything of
value. John Trueblood claimed the tabards and boots reeked too
much of Norman sweat for self-respecting Englishmen to wear
and tossed them into the moat on the tines of James Buckler's
pitchfork, but the rest came across on the raft. 6 longbows,
6 short bows, 6 swords; also a collection of arrows, and saddles
and bridles for 4 horses. It was a good reward for a battle won.
With half his fighting men deprived of weapons, My Lord will
struggle to mount another attack against us.

We lit a bonfire to celebrate our glorious victory with freshly
roasted horse meat; and the joy we had in feasting and dancing

was wonderful to behold. The rest of the meat has been salted and stored, and the weapons oiled. The house has been restored to some sort of order although many of the inside timbers are still wet from the drenching we gave them. The saddest losses are the latticed window panes in Sir Richard's and my chambers which shattered when they were struck by arrowheads for we cannot replace them without the knowledge or ability to make glass.

It matters not. Boards will do just as well and I would rather lose glass, how ever costly, than the life of one of my people. My single regret is that Thaddeus and the sons of my leading serfs weren't here to share in the glory. They would have laughed out loud, I think, to see My Lord of Bourne's fighting men hop and jump in fear of Englishmen.

I pray most earnestly for their safe return.

Twenty-five

Thaddeus's camp on the River Pedle

PETER CATCHPOLE BECAME INCREASINGLY WITHDRAWN as Joshua bandied acts of heroism with Ian, Olyver and Edmund. Thaddeus, who was turning ducks on a spit, intervened occasionally to bring their stories back to reality, but their boisterous good humour grew louder as the night lengthened. Edmund insisted he'd been right about rats all along. Ian and Olyver said the only right way to burn a house was to fire a flaming arrow. And Joshua claimed the sleeping dogs, replete with half a slaughtered ewe, were the key to success on every level.

They drew breath when their teeth were tearing at roasted duck, but once their appetites were satisfied they began again. This time Joshua—always the object of Peter's teasing in the past for his ginger hair and freckles—set to boasting about how easy it had been for him and Thaddeus to pass themselves off as a lord and his squire. Even dressed as they were in peasant tunics which were wearing dangerously thin, the serfs of Woodoak had accepted them as men of standing.

'Only because I was riding a knight's charger and had a sword in my hand, and you were in command of a pack of hunting dogs,' Thaddeus murmured. 'We wouldn't have got away with it otherwise.'

'Maybe you should have ordered the chamberlain to throw down some of his master's clothes,' Olyver said. 'You'd look every inch a lord if you had an embroidered jerkin and a fur-lined cloak.'

'I was tempted,' Thaddeus admitted, 'but I couldn't come up with a good enough reason to do it. Even Thomas Breakspear would have questioned why I needed to steal his lord's finery when by rights I should have a chest of my own in Develish.'

'We all need new clothes,' said Edmund, holding up his arms to show the holes around the elbows. 'We're living in stinking rags. How long before we can go home to collect some clean ones?'

'As long as it takes,' said Thaddeus with a yawn.

'To do what?'

'Splice these whips into shafts—' he nodded to the pile of thin hazel branches beside the saddles—'sharpen the ends to points and attach the feathers properly. Even then we'll be lucky if they shoot straight. It'll be the Devil's own job setting fire to Athelhelm if they don't, and I'm not driving sheep across the ford until I'm certain the village is cleansed.'

'You mean of rats?' said Edmund with satisfaction.

'Corpses, too.'

There was a short, thoughtful silence before Ian spoke. 'The arrows would shoot straight if they had metal tips. How come you only found three in the ashes of Afpedle?'

'The teeth of the rake were too far apart.' Thaddeus kept to himself the fact that he gave up on the task after hooking a blackened skull from the debris. It was small enough to be a baby's and he'd stamped it back into the ash to avoid Joshua seeing it, splintering it into fragments as he did so. He glanced at the silent Peter. 'You seem down. Why so?'

Edmund answered for him. 'He skived off work for a couple of hours and says he saw soldiers. He's been in a sulk ever since because we didn't believe him.'

'We moved everything out of sight amongst the trees after he came haring back, babbling about an army on the road,' Ian said. 'It was wasted effort. No one passed.'

Peter stared at the ground. 'I never said they were coming this way.'

'You gave a good indication of it when you ran into the woodland to hide,' Olyver growled. 'It was me, Twin and Edmund who rounded up the horses and got them under cover. You're always absent when there's work to be done.'

Thaddeus studied Peter's bent head. 'What were the soldiers doing?'

'I don't know. They were in that demesne you spoke of.'

'The one to the north?'

'Yes . . . and they were the same ones who burnt Develish. I recognised the crest on their tabards.' He clenched his fists. 'It's not my fault they didn't come this way. They *could* have done.'

Edmund aimed a kick at his ankle. 'You're a two-faced toad,' he said angrily. 'You need something to brag about because you're the only one who hasn't done anything brave. If it was me inventing an army, I'd at least pretend it was My Lord of Blandeforde's. You only picked My Lord of Bourne because his was the first name you thought of.'

ᗢᗒ

Thaddeus had to rely on a niggardly moon to show him the way. The dogs had stirred when he stole from the camp but, thankfully, made no sound as his soft tread vanished along the sward. He followed the river east to the highway and then turned left onto the dirt road, moving from dwelling to dwelling in the deserted village, ready to duck out of sight behind the nearest wall if he saw or heard anything.

He paused to listen at doors for a sound that might indicate human presence. To move at night through Develish was to hear a multitude of noises—the snores of men, the cries of babies, the soothing tones of women—but there was only silence in this abandoned place. He could hear the hooting of owls from the woodland and the odd bark of a fox, but there was nothing to suggest people. Even the smell of death was absent.

Once through the houses, he abandoned the road and walked the next thousand paces in the deep shadow of the trees. When the woodland thinned and a flat expanse of pasture opened up in front of him, he came to a halt. A week ago, he'd watched this demesne for several hours in daylight and he recalled its layout easily even though he could barely see it now with the moon obscured. A manor house, a church and a handful of serfs' huts stood to his left, and a dirt track led to the highway on his right. At the time, he'd been struck by how much smaller the acreage of cleared land was than in Develish. Thaddeus had doubted it could support more than sixty people, yet the house was much grander than Lady Anne's, and would require that many servants to manage it. He'd puzzled over how the lord and his household could grow enough to feed themselves and pay taxes until he realised the deserted village to the south, with its own areas of cleared land, must also be part of the estate. He couldn't be certain of the precise relationship between the two communities, but he dared to hope it was an exemplar of what Lady Anne and the people of Develish aspired to become: a demesne where free men paid rent for their land and property, and were at liberty to earn their living in any way they chose. The lord still grew rich on the work of his tenants but, with the price of the tenancy fixed, a free man could sell the fruits of his labour and lay money aside for his and his family's future.

Even in daylight it had been hard to tell if anyone remained in the house. Thaddeus had seen rats around the serfs' huts but no people, and since only some twenty sheep grazed the pasture-land—too few to serve Develish's needs for long—he'd decided to concentrate his efforts on the larger flock at Afpedle. There seemed to be no good pickings at all in this demesne unless food was stored inside the padlocked buildings in the deserted village to the south.

He was beginning to think the manor house as deserted as the village when a flicker burnt briefly at one of the downstairs windows in the house. Shortly afterwards, a rectangle of light opened in the darkness and a man stood inside the front door, holding a lantern above his head. He made no attempt to step outside or call a challenge, merely moved the beam from side to side of the large forecourt. Enough of the light fell on him to show Thaddeus that he was dressed as a peasant, while the trembling of the beam suggested fear. It was a strange little scene, repeated twice more in the hour that followed, and Thaddeus wondered if the man was seeking reassurance that the forecourt remained empty rather than searching for something real.

But empty of what? he wondered. Soldiers armed with fire arrows?

He followed the edge of the pastureland until he came to the track that led from the house to the highway. He stood beneath a tree for a good quarter-hour, listening for sounds, particularly the rustling of rodents in the undergrowth. He heard none. Perhaps his presence had been enough to scare rats away.

When he was satisfied that no one else was abroad, he stepped onto the road. His eyes picked out the horse dung easily because he was looking for it, and when he stooped to gather some between his fingers, the smell and moisture told him it was fresh. He turned up the highway towards Blandeforde and, after two hundred paces, came across another pile. Then another. Caution prevented him going farther, but he was satisfied that riders had indeed been inside this demesne; and since Edmund, Ian and Olyver hadn't seen them, they must have come from the north and returned towards it.

Was Peter right to say they were My Lord of Bourne's men? It made little sense to Thaddeus that a noble without estates in this part of Dorseteshire would linger long in the area where a killing sickness raged. What reasons could he have for remaining? Was he so convinced of his own virtue that he believed the pestilence couldn't touch him? Did he think God had appointed him the cleanser of sinners? If so, he was strangely selective in the demesnes he chose to burn. As Thaddeus made his way back to the camp, passing again through the deserted village, he questioned cynically why this one had been spared.

Were men who were free to lock their doors and run from the Black Death less wicked than serfs who were forced by their oaths of fealty to stand and face it?

∞

Shadows hurtled out of the darkness towards Thaddeus when he was still fifty paces from the camp. He stood stock still as the dogs circled around him, their hackles raised and growls rumbling in their throats.

'I told you they'd earn their keep,' said Joshua with satisfaction, appearing out of the gloom behind them. 'They'd have ripped you to pieces if you'd been a stranger.'

'They seem intent on doing that anyway,' said Thaddeus. 'They've got their muzzles rammed into my crotch and I can feel the heat of their breath through my britches.'

'Only because they like you. They'd be showing their teeth otherwise.'

'Call them off before I wring your neck.'

Joshua snapped his fingers and the pack ranged themselves beside him. 'You've been gone hours,' he said severely. 'Where have you been?'

'Looking for horse dung.' Thaddeus followed him back to the dying fire, only lowering himself to the ground when the dogs looked settled. The other four boys were awake, sitting cross-legged on their bracken mattresses, eyes alight with curiosity. Ian took up a log to toss on the embers, but Thaddeus stayed his hand. 'We'll be safer without flames. Peter was right to say riders came this way recently. I believe they've headed north up the highway but we shouldn't rely on it.' He described what he'd seen. 'Are you certain it was My Lord of Bourne's crest on the soldiers' tabards?' he asked Peter.

The boy nodded. 'I watched from a window in the great hall when he came to Develish. It was on his wagon. I memorised it so I'd know it again.'

'But how were you in a position to see them today? It's a good mile to the manor house, and my orders were that the four of you stay together and not go wandering about on your own. Why did you disobey me?'

'I didn't. I went into the woods for a shit. I was still squatting when I heard voices. I thought it was the others come to spy on me until I realised they were speaking French. It scared the Hell out of me. There were two of them. They were walking down a track behind the houses in the village.'

Thaddeus doubted him immediately. 'You said you saw them in the demesne to the north.'

'It's where they'd come from . . . at least I think so. They called it Holcombe and said it was a good thing it had horses and saddles to requisition.' Peter looked uneasy, as if he knew his story was unconvincing. 'Only one of them was wearing a tabard. The other was in peasant clothes, and he was wearing clogs not boots. I recognised him, though. He was in the first rank of the column behind My Lord of Bourne's captain of arms when they came to Develish.'

'Go on.'

'They complained about being sent to this part of the demesne while their friends had the easy task of putting fear into peasants. The taller one said the demesne looked rich enough to keep My Lord happy, and the other that they were lucky the steward had fled north with the freemen, since serfs were ignorant about taxes.'

'Which taxes?'

'I don't know. I only understood about half of what they said. The one in clogs talked about getting boots if My Lord was feeling generous.'

'What were they doing in the woods?'

'Looking for meat. The one in the tabard said if sheep were anywhere, they'd be on meadowland by the river.'

Thaddeus was sceptical. 'There are sheep in the pasture near the manor house. Why wouldn't they take those?'

Peter shook his head. 'Maybe they didn't want the serfs to see them doing it. They talked about being able to steal at will from this village because there's no one here.'

Thaddeus had thought the same as he'd passed the deserted houses. He eyed Peter curiously. 'Where were you hiding to hear so much? By rights you should have an arrow in your chest.'

'Behind some brambles about twenty paces from the track. They stopped quite near me because the one in clogs was moaning about his blisters.' A wry smile twitched the corners of his mouth. 'I'd have shat myself if I hadn't rid myself of a turd already.' He debated with himself whether to continue. 'They weren't armed. The short one had a knife, but that was all. I was going to take to my heels if they saw me. I knew I could outrun them if they didn't have bows.'

Thaddeus wondered if such an improbable story could be true. Peter was a more fluent liar than any of the others, and Thaddeus wouldn't have given his story credence but for the horse dung. 'So why didn't they continue on to the river and see Edmund and the twins?' he asked. 'Or did they, and you forget to tell us because you did nothing to prevent it?'

The boy's expression closed immediately. 'I knew you wouldn't believe me. I should have kept my mouth shut and pretended it never happened. It would have served the others right if they *had* been seen. They've been boasting all day about how brave they are.'

'Persuade me. I'm listening. What caused the soldiers to turn around?'

The question was greeted with silence and it was on the tip of Thaddeus's tongue to lambast the boy for being a sullen churl when a deep growl cleaved the air, rising to a crescendo of snarls and snaps. A second, lighter growl followed and then a cry of pain, half-animal half-human. The sounds sent Joshua's pack into a froth of alarm. They leapt to their feet, teeth bared, squaring up to each other as if unsure where or who their adversary was.

'I learnt if off the mongrels in Develish,' Peter said unemotionally. 'They were always fighting.'

'Only because you made them,' Joshua countered angrily. To Thaddeus he said, 'He's an idiot. He thinks it's a joke to tease animals, but we'll none of us be laughing if this lot turn on each other. There'll be blood everywhere.'

Thaddeus hid a smile. 'What else can you do?' he asked Peter.

The boy cupped his hands over his mouth and the sweet song of a blackbird trilled in the night, followed by the rattle of a grasshopper and the scream of a hawk. 'Pretty much anything really. I didn't expect the soldiers to be so frightened though. I've never seen two people run so fast. I think there must be wild dogs everywhere.'

☙

With sleep eluding all of them and enough light from the embers of the fire to see by, Thaddeus began splicing a hazel whip into an arrow shaft. 'I asked young Catstock if Mary Hynd saw bites from rats on the people who fell sick, but he said all she talked about was faeces and dirt, and for the life of me I can't see how either can carry a killing disease. Develish lived with rats for years before Milady came but no one died of the pestilence.'

'It doesn't make sense that it's in rats,' said Edmund. 'Humans don't catch illnesses from animals. If we did, we'd fall sick every time a sheep or chicken did.'

'Mm.'

'But?' Peter prompted.

'I can't account for why the pestilence is so different from other sicknesses. Gyles estimated that some seventy died of it within a week at Bradmayne, yet none of the known diseases spreads or kills as quickly. Lady Anne has knowledge of all, but she's never heard of a plague that grows boils and turns the blood black. I doubt Mary Hynd had either, yet she seems to have been as skilled in medicine as Milady—and if she said rats were the cause of the sickness, should we not listen to her?'

'Lady Anne has learning,' said Edmund. 'I'd believe it more if she said it.'

Joshua raised his hand. 'Thomas Breakspear said his daughter kept scratching her arms before the boils appeared in her neck.'

'I remember.'

'I did the same when Red gave me fleas. All the curs had them.'

'What's that got to do with the pestilence?' asked Peter.

'Nothing,' said Joshua with a shrug. 'I'm just making the point that Edmund's wrong to say humans don't catch things from animals.'

Olyver sorted through the pile of whips, looking for any that were naturally straight. 'There were plenty of rats in Bradmayne. Father said it was the filthiest demesne he'd ever visited. Even Sir Richard didn't like it. He kept questioning whether Eleanor would be happy there.'

'It *must* have been bad then,' Thaddeus murmured dryly.

The jibe passed Olyver by. It was days since he'd risen to Eleanor's defence. 'Maybe it's caught by touch.'

Thaddeus shook his head. 'It can't be. Your father spent near a week tending the sick in John Trueblood's cottage, and as often as not clasped their hands between his to comfort them.'

Ian took Peter's knife and set to splicing a whip himself. 'Mother thinks he knows God has spared him but doesn't want to speak of it out of modesty,' he said. 'Do you think she's right?'

'Have you asked him?'

'Only once. He said the question was stupid.'

Thaddeus smiled. He'd been on the receiving end of Gyles's gruff tongue himself once or twice. 'You wouldn't like him so much if he boasted of his goodness.'

'He never boasts about anything. Maybe that's why God let him live.'

'And why Sir Richard had to die,' Edmund suggested. 'He liked nothing better than to flaunt his piety.'

Thaddeus moistened a water reed with his tongue before using it to bind his splice. 'That's not how Gyles sees it.'

'How then?' asked Ian.

'He feels guilty to be alive.' Thaddeus recalled the long night he'd spent with the twins' father after Gyles had buried the last man to die—Pierre de Boulet, Sir Richard's captain of arms. 'He's troubled by the dislike he had for his companions while they were alive, and his failure to help them when they were suffering. He believes there was more he should have done, and the thought weighs on his conscience.'

'What else could he have done?' asked Olyver.

'Nothing that I know of. He never left the sides of the three who came back, even hearing their confessions at the end. I watched while he blessed Captain de Boulet. He said the poor man's sins were small compared with his.'

'Is that true?'

'I have too many flaws of my own to want to count another's. Your father knows his own, which is why he feels he's cheated death through chance and not by God's design.'

Peter leant forward. 'Is that what you feel also?'

Thaddeus nodded. 'Gyles and Captain de Boulet made the same journey, slept in the same quarters, breathed the same air and came into contact with the same people. By any reasoning they should have died together.'

'Unless God needs Gyles for some future purpose,' Peter responded. 'Father Anselm says man can never understand His mind.'

Thaddeus's lips twitched. 'I'd agree with him if he's speaking for himself.'

Joshua reached out a hand to stroke a sleeping mastiff. 'Do you even believe God exists, Thaddeus?'

'Why do you ask?'

'You don't fear Hell. If you did, you wouldn't lie about being a lord or urge serfs to break their oaths of fealty.'

Thaddeus eyed him with amusement. 'I was destined for Hell from the day I came into the world. Would you have me fear damnation all my life because I was conceived and born in sin?'

Peter heard the teasing note in his voice even if Joshua didn't. 'You know that's not true,' he chided. 'None of us goes to Hell for things that aren't our fault.'

'There'll be many a pestilence sufferer longing for such certainty. If you're told by men of authority like My Lord of Bourne that God has sent a punishment to kill you in this life, you'd have little hope that your sins would be forgiven in the next.'

There was a short silence before Edmund spoke. 'Do you think My Lord knows he's wrong?'

Thaddeus shook his head. 'He'd have to question everything else if he believed himself in error on that.'

'Such as his right to be a lord?'

'Such as that,' Thaddeus agreed.

He made few contributions afterwards, preferring to listen as the boys argued the same deep issues that he had debated with Lady Anne these many years. Once or twice he chastised himself for encouraging their thoughts to roam so widely, doubting their parents would sanction heresy, but he did nothing to stop them. Their minds would be the healthier for asking if a life of bondage was all a serf could expect.

∽

With the first grey light of dawn, Thaddeus walked to the river to splash his face with water and rid himself of sleep. He stretched to his full height, loosening the sinews in his neck and shoulders. The night had been clear and cold, but for once he'd slept well, thanks to a stomach full of duck and the ever-alert dogs that lay at Joshua's side to the right of the fire.

He stood watching them for several minutes, recalling a warning which Edmund had given Joshua that Thaddeus wouldn't be the only one wanting rid of them if they harboured fleas. It was bad enough having clothes that were falling apart of their own accord without shredding them further by scratching at pesky insects. Joshua swore the dogs were clean. If they'd ever had fleas, Thaddeus had washed them away by leading the pack through lakes and rivers on his way back to the camp. As a pledge of good faith, Joshua promised to immerse them in the Pedle each morning.

For himself, Thaddeus was never troubled by fleas. The fair skin of his family attracted them while his darker skin seemed to keep them at bay. Will had used it as yet another stick with which to beat him—even parasites knew a worthless bastard when they saw one—but Thaddeus had gloried in his difference after Lady Anne said a person was known by the fleas on his body and the lice in his hair. Only the lazy and dirty were willing to tolerate them, and Will Thurkell was both, although he never blamed himself when his slovenly habits caused his wife and children to become infected.

Thaddeus glanced towards the deserted village to the east. Edmund was right to say they needed a change of clothing. They woke most mornings with their tunics and britches damp from mist and dew, and the autumn sunshine wasn't strong enough to dry them out completely. Spare sets would make life more comfortable.

He returned to the camp and stirred the pile of unfinished shafts with his foot. 'How long do you think it'll take to fletch and sharpen these?' he asked Ian, who was sitting up on the other side of the fire, stroking downy whiskers on his chin as if to encourage them to grow faster and stronger.

'A day?' the boy suggested. 'They'll work better if we go back to Afpedle and find the other arrow heads.'

Thaddeus nodded. 'Did your father ever complain of fleas?'

The question was so unexpected that Ian took a moment or two to process it. 'Why do you want to know?'

'Just interested. Some people attract them and others don't. I wondered what type Gyles was.'

Ian groaned. 'Please don't say you believe that rubbish Joshua was babbling.'

'I keep an open mind. Only simpletons have closed ones.'

'All I know is Father laughs whenever me and Olyver get them, and says if we work harder our skin will turn to leather like his. It drives our mother mad. She says fleas are the Devil's creation.'

'Have you ever seen them on a horse?'

'No . . . but dogs bloody well have them. And there were so many rats in Afpedle, this lot would have boils bursting out all over them if Joshua's right.'

Thaddeus eyed the pack thoughtfully. 'Perhaps they have tough skin like your father.' He turned the subject to the tasks that had to be done, nudging the other boys to wakefulness with his toe. 'Ian, Olyver and Edmund will work on the shafts. Peter and Joshua will come with me. Joshua will be on foot, commanding the dogs, and you and I will be on horseback, Peter. You need to look like a fighting man so wear a bow across your back and carry a sword in your hand.'

'Where are we going?' asked Joshua.

'You'll find out soon enough.' He stooped to pick a piece of charcoal from the fire and beckoned Peter towards him. 'You have more of a beard than the others but you'll look older if you let me darken it. I want a soldier riding at my side not another squire.'

Peter hung back, a look of trepidation on his face. 'I'll let you down. I'm not much good with a sword.'

'You think I'm any better? The idea is to frighten people into keeping their distance not invite them to challenge us.' Thaddeus gave a low laugh. 'If that happens, we'll turn tail and run and hope the dogs are braver than we are. Come. Let's see how fearsome a little soot can make you.'

Ian, observing the mummery from the other side of the fire, wondered if Thaddeus realised how much less guarded he'd become since they'd left Develish. He couldn't remember ever seeing the tall serf touch another person's face—not even his mother's—yet here he was, blacking his fingers to rub them around Peter's jaw in order to give the silly churl some courage.

Twenty-six

Holcombe, Dorseteshire

THADDEUS HALTED AT THE EDGE of the common land that bordered the highway. To their right, the track crossed a ford and continued south; to their left, it ran between the houses of the deserted village, heading north. He pointed to deep ruts in the earth. 'More traffic travels this road than the one between Afpedle and Woodoak.'

'Not recently,' said Joshua. 'There's grass growing in the furrows.'

'Maybe so, but carts and wagons have moved along it regularly in the past.'

Peter looked towards the south. 'Do you think it goes to Melcombe?'

Thaddeus shook his head. 'Wrong direction. The road curves towards the east. I followed it for three miles until I came across the corpse and turned back. There must be another port farther along the coast.' He turned towards the village again and pointed to lumps of stone that stood outside many of the buildings. 'I'm guessing those are mounting blocks and that the craftsmen and merchants who lived here wanted to make life easy for men on horseback because they had wares to sell to travellers on their way to Blandeforde.' He gestured to a large two-storey building which had a barred and gated archway in the middle of its façade. Though built in wood, with wattle-and-daub panels, the timbers were twice the size and strength of anything a peasant would use, and the number of shuttered windows suggested it was divided into rooms. 'That's an inn. Gyles told me some of them have courtyards so that coaches can be driven off the street and up to the door.'

'Why would they need to?' Peter asked.

'Lords object to getting their feet dirty.'

'Are you sure it's not a manor house? It looks big enough.'

Thaddeus shook his head. 'There'd be no reason to have two on the same demesne.' He turned his attention to the first dwelling on the right-hand side of the highway with a pile of cinders beside its wall and a forged metal bar across its double doors. 'I'll wager that's a smithy.'

'What if it is?' asked Joshua.

'It might have tools inside.'

'We can't break in. Someone might hear us.'

'The village is deserted.'

'There could be a hundred people hiding behind the shutters. Maybe My Lord of Bourne and his soldiers crept in overnight.'

'Leaving all the padlocks in place outside?' Thaddeus murmured. 'That's a trick I'd like to learn.'

'We can see only a few from here.'

Thaddeus gathered up Killer's reins. 'I'll check the rest. You two wait with the dogs.' He bared his teeth in a wolfish grin. 'If I run into trouble you can rescue me.'

As he moved away the boys bleated their reluctance to steal, but Thaddeus had no sympathy with them. It was past time they did something to trouble their consciences if they wanted a share of the plaudits on their return to Develish. Even so, he found himself wishing he had his stepfather at his side. Theft came as naturally to Will as it had to Jacob, and Thaddeus didn't doubt both would have known the best way into these barricaded properties.

He walked Killer to the end of the village and back again, stooping in his saddle to examine the padlocks on the doors and pausing by shutters to peer through cracks. He spent longer outside the inn, examining each of the windows and using the height Killer gave him to look over the gate into the courtyard beyond. When he was satisfied, he used the hilt of his sword to hammer loudly on the timbers, announcing himself as Lord of Foxcote.

'Give me entry,' he roared. 'I ride with an army. We're free of the pestilence but we're in need of food and shelter.' He nudged Killer into the centre of the highway and raised his eyes to the upper windows. 'If anyone hears me show yourself now or my soldiers will force the door and we'll take what we need without permission.'

Joshua closed his eyes with a groan. 'He'll have us all dead by the time this is over. If we don't die of the pestilence, we'll be hanged for stealing.'

✂

Thaddeus decided to rob the smithy first. Tools were heavy and there was a good chance the blacksmith had left an axe or a hammer behind rather than carry it with him on his journey north. He warned the boys it wouldn't be easy, since there were no windows in the building and the double doors had the strongest bar and largest padlock. The only way in would be through one of the wattle-and-daub panels.

Their resistance was immediate.

'What if we're caught?' demanded Joshua. 'Anyone could come along the road and see us.'

'I'll not be punished for something I don't want to do,' protested Peter. 'You should have brought Edmund. He doesn't care how many crimes he commits.'

'The twins too,' agreed Joshua. 'They say they're in Hell already so it doesn't matter what they do.'

Thaddeus kicked their legs out from under them so fast they were on their backs in the dust before they knew it. The dogs, unsure how to react, milled around excitedly, reacting with growls when Thaddeus placed his boot on Joshua's chest.

'They'll bite you,' Joshua gasped.

Thaddeus leant down to tug the knapsack from around the boy's neck. He reached inside for a handful of diced mutton and tossed it towards the smithy, watching impassively as the pack raced after it. 'They know even less about loyalty than you do,' he murmured, turning to look from one to the other. 'You look to save your own souls but care nothing for your friends'.'

Peter ran a nervous tongue across his lips. There was no telling what mood Thaddeus would be in from one second to the next. 'Is this because we didn't help burn Afpedle?'

'Amongst other things.'

'Edmund and the twins said we didn't have to.'

'Only because they knew you lacked courage. Joshua can't even bring himself to steal a sheep for fear of being caught. He expects to win the dogs' affection on the back of my efforts, never his own.'

'You said I did well yesterday,' Joshua stuttered.

'When you weren't looking for bailiffs and soldiers around every corner.' Thaddeus shook his head. 'Peter's no different. The pair of you would abandon every serf to die of starvation—including those in Develish—rather than muddy your consciences. You'll shame your fathers when they learn of it.' He lifted his boot from Joshua's chest and stepped away. 'I'm wearied of you. Be gone. Send your friends in your places.'

Peter was the first to scramble to his feet, the thought of how his actions might be viewed in Develish foremost in his mind. 'I want to stay,' he pleaded. 'I'm not afraid of danger, only of doing things badly. Almost everyone does stuff better than me—even Joshua.'

Thaddeus wondered how often Peter had used the same weaselly words to his father in order to avoid work. He gestured towards an alder on the riverbank. 'You have until the shadow of that tree touches the edge of the highway to prove yourself. If you fail, you go back to Develish alone.' He stared into the boy's eyes. 'I'll not accept excuses. Are you sure you want to stay?'

The dark gaze was as cold as Peter had ever seen it, quite different from the warmth of an hour ago when Thaddeus had been rubbing charcoal into his cheek, and any ideas he might have had of pleading nausea or weariness when the task became too hard vanished. 'Yes.'

Thaddeus turned to Joshua. 'What about you?'

'If I go, can I take the dogs?'

'No. I want their eyes and ears in case My Lord of Bourne or the serfs of Holcombe come this way.'

Joshua held out his hand for his knapsack, a stubborn look in his eyes. 'Then I'll stay.'

Thaddeus turned away. 'On the same conditions as Peter,' he warned, dropping the bag to the ground. 'Prove your worth or return to Develish alone. The dogs accepted me as their master before I gave them to you, and they'll do so again. Remember that.'

He led them towards the smithy and stood at one corner for several minutes, assessing the structure for flaws. Serfs learnt the skill of building early, and all were adept at weaving withies around the staves to form the wattle base before mixing clay and dung to press against the wooden mesh. Once dried, the panels were tough and sturdy, and even with a heavy hammer or a sharp axe to crack the clay and split the wattle timbers, the process of destruction was long and arduous.

Hoping this building was close enough to the river to cause problems from damp, Thaddeus knelt to examine the bottom of the upright timber in the middle of the side wall. He took out his knife and pushed it into the wood. With little force, the blade sank in a couple of inches. He pulled it out and tried again a foot higher. 'Our blacksmith's a lazy fellow,' he said with satisfaction. 'He's like Will; doesn't believe in protecting his posts. This one's half rotten.'

Helped by Peter, he cut away at the soft wood until they reached a hard inner core. Because the daub around the post had also absorbed water, it was relatively soft and easy to dig out in order to create fist-sized holes on either side of what was left of the upright. 'Your turn,' Thaddeus told Joshua, rising to his feet and straightening his back. 'See how much of the earth you can shift in front of it. The chances are the wood will have rotted through twelve inches down.'

He walked to where the horses were tied to a rail outside the inn, listening to Joshua's muttered scepticism as he chopped at the clods with his knife, and Peter's worried hushing in case Thaddeus heard. At least one of them was taking his threats seriously, he thought, lifting a coil of rope from Killer's saddle.

Whether the blacksmith had erected the shelter himself or paid someone else to do it, he'd done as Will Thurkell always did and skimped on rubble footings. With the post in contact with damp earth, it fell away as Joshua dug deeper, but instead of being pleased the boy saw further problems. 'I suppose you realise the whole structure will come down if we pull this out,' he warned, sitting back on his heels. 'There'll be nothing to hold the roof up if the corner timbers are as bad.'

'They won't be,' said Thaddeus. 'They're twice as thick and set in crushed stone.' He handed Joshua one end of the rope and wrapped the other around his waist. 'Pass it through the holes and make a decent knot. I'll have your guts if I end up on my back because you haven't tied it off properly.'

'Why don't you let the horses do it? We could attach the rope to the saddle pommels.'

'We could,' Thaddeus agreed, taking up the slack to test the tightness of the knot as Joshua pushed himself to his feet, 'but the girth buckles will break long before the wall does.' He motioned Peter to stand in front of him. 'Take a grip. Joshua, go to the other side of the road and keep the dogs clear.'

Peter was never sure how much he added to the long and tremendous heave that followed. The blisters on his hands afterwards suggested his grip had slipped more often than it held, but the aching muscles in his shoulders and thighs told a different story. He was on the point of calling out that he couldn't continue when, with a loud ripping sound, the timber tore itself free of the ground and the wattle-and-daub panels collapsed on either side of it.

'Enough,' called Thaddeus, dropping the rope and putting out a steadying hand to keep Peter on his feet. 'It's still attached to the upper beam. If we pull any more, we'll prove Joshua right.' He pressed the hem of his tunic to his mouth to filter the dust that was swirling around them, and dragged Peter back ten yards to where they could breathe freely.

As the dust settled, they could make out the contents of the building. The forge and its foot-operated bellows stood at waist height in front of the double doors to allow the insufferable heat and toxic fumes of burning wood and molten metal to dissipate when the frontage was open; and to its side, mounted on a solid wooden block, was an impressive anvil with a flattened surface and rounded edges. Neither looked anything like the simple hearth and small iron wedge that Adam Catchpole used when he was called upon to create a horseshoe or a hinge, but as the objects at the back of the room became clearer, Thaddeus saw that this blacksmith was far more skilled than Peter's father.

There was every manner of tool on a table—knives, hammers, axes, scythes, sickles—as well as an iron ploughshare on the ground, chains hanging from the rafters and two cart wheels with metal rims leaning against a wall. Yet Thaddeus wondered why so much had been left behind. Wouldn't a sensible man have taken the smaller tools to sell along the way? He put the question to Peter.

'They won't belong to him,' Peter answered. 'People bring stuff to my father for sharpening and mending all the time and he keeps it for weeks sometimes. It depends how badly the owner needs it and whether he's able to pay.' He shook his head in wonder. 'That's one monster of a forge.'

Joshua, joining them, stooped for a better view. 'We should send the dogs in,' he told Thaddeus. 'They'll scare out any rats that might be hiding in the clutter.'

'Good idea.'

The boy had to walk right up to the collapsed wall to persuade the hounds inside, but the interior seemed to hold little interest for them. They sniffed lethargically around the forge and anvil but showed no curiosity about anything else. Emboldened, the boy followed them inside. 'There's a barrow here,' he called to Thaddeus. 'Should I put the tools in it?'

'Yes.'

'What about swords and stirrups?'

'Yes.'

'And arrow heads? There's a whole boxful.'

'Certainly,' Thaddeus answered patiently. 'I doubt the three I managed to rake from the ashes in Afpedle will suffice.'

'What about a whetstone for sharpening knives?'

Thaddeus took a deep breath before gesturing Peter towards the fallen wall. 'Get me an axe so we can start on the inn,' he begged. 'We'll be here all day otherwise.'

Twenty-seven

THADDEUS PATTED THE DUST FROM his clothes, looking up and down the highway to see if anything had changed. Nothing stirred. If people were hiding in the village, the sound of the smithy wall coming down hadn't brought them to their doors. He left Peter to collect an axe while he unhitched the horses from the beam across the arched gate of the inn and walked them across to a rail at the side of a two-storey building opposite. It was smaller and more compact than the inn, with inside shutters to the windows on the upper floor, and heavily barred and padlocked ones on the lower.

Thaddeus wondered briefly what it contained before returning to the inn and examining the massive oak gates that filled the archway. They were solidly built, and the beam across them was supported and held in place by slotted wooden brackets. Two were attached to the gates and another two protruded from the walls on either side. The only way to remove the beam was to lift it from the slots, but padlocked chains, wrapped in figure-of-eight loops around the base of the wall brackets, made that impossible.

He tested the links to see if there was any give, but they were too tight for the bar to be dislodged.

'Any ideas?' he asked Peter as the boy handed him a heavy axe.

'Chop through the beam?'

'The grain runs the wrong way and it's a good six inches thick. We'll have to cut in at an angle and it's at a bad height for both of us.'

Peter raised his voice. 'Hey, Joshua! Is there a saw in the smithy?'

'No.' There was a grunt of effort. 'You'll have to give me a hand getting the barrow out. It's too heavy to push over the rubble.'

Peter went to help him, leaving Thaddeus to ponder the conundrum of how to break into a property that so evidently didn't want thieves. Was there another entrance at the back which was less protected than this one? he wondered. Was the intention to persuade thieves to concentrate on the front when the weakness was elsewhere? He walked around the building, testing the tightness of the window shutters and looking for an alternative way in, but the place appeared impregnable. When he emerged onto the road again, he found Joshua and Peter waiting for him with a barrow full of boxes and tools.

'Any luck?' Peter asked.

Thaddeus shook his head. 'It's a fortress.' He eyed the beam again. 'We'll have to do it the hard way.'

'Can't we just be grateful for what's in the barrow?' Joshua pleaded. 'All we wanted was arrow heads.'

'Not me. I came for anything I can find.'

'But what's the point? The barrow's full. We can't carry anything else.'

Thaddeus glanced towards the alder. 'You're very quick to give up on your dogs,' he said. 'A bare hour's passed since you chose to stay with them.'

Joshua bridled. 'I'm not giving up—just questioning why you want to spend all day breaking into this place when it's probably empty anyway.'

Thaddeus turned away, stationing himself in front of the centre of the beam and resting the axe blade flat on top of it to judge his distance. He spread his legs to give himself balance and then swung the haft to the right before bringing it back again with the head tilted at a slight angle. His intention was to cut a V-shaped nick into the surface of the wood, but he misjudged the stroke and the cutting edge glanced away without causing any damage. He pulled the chisel from his belt and asked Joshua to pass him one of the hammers from the barrow.

Grudgingly, the boy handed him a solid-looking mallet. 'It'll take forever if you use a chisel,' he scolded. 'I bet the blade's not even sharp any more.'

'Nothing takes forever.'

'But you keep changing your mind about what's important. Where's the sense in forcing the others to work with rubbish tools to make useless arrows when there's everything here to make good ones?'

'None at all,' Thaddeus agreed, 'so take the barrow and its contents back to the camp. You'll be of more help to Ian, Olyver and Edmund than you'll be to me and Peter.'

Joshua's neck turned an angry red. 'You'll keep the dogs.'

'Indeed.'

'That's not fair. I've done everything you asked.'

Thaddeus ignored him to line up the chisel, and Peter, sensing Joshua's growing animosity, put a hand on his friend's arm to warn him that Thaddeus meant what he said. But Joshua shook him off angrily. 'Why do you always have to do this?' he demanded.

'What?'

'Pay no heed to the rest of us so that you can prove you're bigger and better than we are. You can try anything . . . *do* anything . . . *steal* anything . . . be a *lord* if you want to.'

'All that and more,' Thaddeus agreed, drawing back the mallet and thudding it against the handle. 'I didn't leave Develish to cower before every challenge.'

The blade bit into the wood, but not as much as he would have expected from the way the chisel moved to the left. Puzzled, he repositioned himself and struck it again, and this time it was obvious that the beam had moved along with the blade. He lowered his arms to his side and looked at the chain and padlock around the left-hand wall bracket. 'It's really quite clever,' he murmured.

'What is?' asked Peter.

'How the eye deceives the mind.' Thaddeus moved to the right of the gates. 'We only thought to lift the bar because that's what we always do.' He hit the end of the beam hard with the mallet and watched it slide a couple of inches. 'Remind me not to be impressed by chains again. The only purpose these are serving is to stop the beam being raised.' It took a couple of minutes to knock the bar through one bracket after another, and he gave a grunt of satisfaction when the gates, finally freed of their restraint, swung open in front of him. He turned to Joshua. 'Do you still say we should be grateful for a few tools and some arrow heads?' he asked.

The boy looked at the abandoned wagon in the courtyard. 'No . . . but you have the Devil's own luck. You couldn't have known it was here.'

'There was a gap between the top of the gates and the archway. I saw the cart when I was astride Killer.'

'You should have told me,' said Joshua angrily. 'I wouldn't have argued if I'd known.'

Thaddeus propped the heavy beam against the wall. He was in no mood to placate Joshua, who seemed to think his exploits in Woodoak had set him above the others. 'When I want your advice I'll ask for it,' he said. 'Meanwhile, I suggest you keep a still tongue in your head.'

Joshua clenched his fists. 'I'll be glad when we're back in Develish,' he hissed. 'Our parents know you for what you are. They'll not let you speak to us like this.'

'It makes no matter whether they do or not. You'll be on one side of the moat, and I on the other. I've obligated myself to return to the demesne with supplies of grain and livestock, but nothing more. When my debt is honoured, I'll leave again.'

'You won't be allowed. You're more of a slave than we are. Milady will post you as an absconder.'

Thaddeus shook his head. 'She knows my status better than anyone, for it was she who explained it to me. There's an advantage to being a hated bastard. If Will had wanted to bind me through his oath of allegiance, he should have acknowledged me as his son. By not doing so, he gave me a freedom his own children don't have.'

He gave a small shrug at Joshua's expression. If he hadn't thought his eyes were deceiving him, he'd have said there were tears of anguish on the silly churl's lashes.

✄

Peter rounded on Joshua in fury when his friend muttered for the third time that power had gone to Thaddeus's head. 'Will you *stop!*' he snapped. 'I'm sick of listening to you. You shouldn't have behaved like a spoilt brat if you hadn't wanted a tongue-lashing.'

They were moving cautiously from room to room on the upper floor of the inn, sending the dogs ahead of them to search every nook and cranny for signs of vermin. The animals flushed out cockroaches from under some straw matting but neither boy saw anything large enough or black enough to be a rat. Thaddeus had told them to open any chests they found, looking for clothes, but warned them to be careful as they did so because fabric made good nesting material.

They'd searched four chambers already but there was little to see, apart from bundles of rushes against the walls, some low wooden beds and the odd three-legged stool. Peter was intensely curious about how many people slept to a room and whether they were strangers to each other. It seemed an uncongenial way to live. A man would have to guard his property carefully for fear of sharing his bed with a thief. He spoke his thoughts aloud, but Joshua was more interested in finding fault with Thaddeus.

Peter flicked him a curious glance. 'What's goading you? You were all over Thaddeus last night. Why are you so against him now?'

'We hadn't found a wagon then.'

'So?'

'I don't want to go back to Develish.'

'None of us does. Freedom's better by far than being stuck on a demesne, doing the same things and seeing the same people day after day.'

'But if Thaddeus leaves, he won't take us with him,' said Joshua unhappily. 'He believes we'll hold him back.'

Peter paused before the last door. 'And he'd be right,' he said matter-of-factly. 'I expect he'd be in France by now if he didn't have us hanging like millstones round his neck.'

'Why France?'

'He can say he's Sir Richard of Develish if he feels like it. No Frenchman's going to know different.'

☙❧

Downstairs, Thaddeus was prowling from room to room with as much wariness as Joshua and Peter upstairs. He was sure there must be rats or mice, but he saw no evidence of them, not even droppings. It was strange, and he had no explanation for it other than that the people who lived here had fled before the pestilence arrived, leaving little behind for vermin to feed on. His immediate concern was to find a yoke to pull the wagon or the wherewithal to make one. There could be treasures beyond compare in this village, but none would have any value without the means to carry them to Develish.

Never having been inside an inn, Thaddeus was as curious as Peter. The entrance hall, which smelt strongly of ale, ran along the back of the courtyard and was furnished with oak tables and benches, all heavily stained with spilt liquids and candle wax. He tried to imagine it full of travellers, drinking and carousing through the night, but the light was too dim from the shuttered windows, and the atmosphere too stale and dead, for a picture to come.

Even dingier were the rooms that opened off the hall at each end. They stood at right angles to the body of the building, forming the sides of the courtyard. Thaddeus began on the left, easing the door open gently and listening for sounds as his eyes adjusted to the darkness. He saw row upon row of wooden ale casks along the back wall and a table in the middle of the room laden with earthenware jugs and tankards. Cautiously, he stepped inside and rocked one of the kegs from side to side to see if it contained anything. By its weight, it was clearly full, although he guessed the contents had turned bad long ago. He twisted the screw on an already broached cask next to it, and wrinkled his nose at the sour odour of the liquid that poured onto the ground.

Ahead of him was another door which, once opened, introduced daylight from the ill-fitting shutters across the window that overlooked the road. From the wooden bed against the right-hand wall and the two chairs—one larger than the other—Thaddeus guessed this was the chamber of the man and wife who ran the inn. Who were they? he wondered. And how would they feel upon their return to find they'd been robbed of their wagon?

They'd left nothing of themselves behind. No clothes, no trinkets, no boxes, no chests. The only items of use were a candle and a tinderbox on a stool in the corner. As Thaddeus struck the flint and blew on the char to create a flame, he wondered how the couple had travelled. Were they so rich in carts that they could afford to leave one behind? Or was it horses they lacked? His ignorance of how the world worked outside Develish was huge. Perhaps they were mere tenants of a lord, owners of nothing, who had left on foot, carrying their possessions on their backs.

He made his way across the hall to the rooms on the other side, holding the candle high as he lifted the latch on the first door to reveal the interior of the chamber. He guessed it was an anteroom to a kitchen, for here was yet another table piled with wooden plates and cooking pots. A leather horse collar and harness on the floor seemed to have been tossed in as an afterthought, perhaps to protect them from the weather when winter set in. There were two doors, and he was sure the one to his right must open into a kitchen. On his tour of the outside of the building, he had passed a single-storey addition with a chimney, a heavily fortified door and a well just paces away. Fires were too frequent where cooking was done to risk them spreading easily through a house built of wood.

He decided against trying that door—if rats were anywhere, they'd be close to a food source—and moved instead to the one ahead of him. He expected to find another bed chamber for the use of servants, not a floor covered with yet more wooden casks, standing upright. How much ale was consumed in these places? Was drunkenness a way of life for travellers?

He was about to leave again when the candlelight glinted on something bright in the darkness of the far corner. For a beat of time Thaddeus found himself staring into two disembodied eyes—as strange and demonic as he'd ever seen—before a long, lithe shadow slid along the floor towards him. With a shout of alarm, he dropped the candle and started backwards, stumbling over the horse collar and slamming against the table, causing pots and plates to crash to the floor.

The flame guttered for an instant before it went out, and he caught a glimpse of a large black creature leaping past him into the hall. *Mother of God!* What manner of being was it? All he could think of was demons and, in a rush of religious fear, he crossed himself instinctively.

He was still trying to calm his breathing when Peter and Joshua, alerted by the noise, crept carefully down the corner staircase with the hounds behind them. 'What's wrong?' Peter whispered from the bottom step, seeing Thaddeus in the open doorway.

The tall man gestured behind him. 'Something moved in one of these rooms. It leapt past me into this hall.'

The boys exchanged nervous glances. 'What did it look like?' Joshua asked.

'Nothing I've ever seen. Long and black with slanting green eyes ... about the size of a fox.' He scanned above and below the tables for signs of movement. 'Let the dogs by you. They'll sniff it out.'

Joshua resisted. 'What if it's dangerous?'

'Better they die than we do,' Thaddeus said unfeelingly, nodding at Peter to step off the bottom tread. 'It's time they earned their keep.'

Released, the animals headed straight for the door into the courtyard and within seconds a snarling, spitting frenzy erupted. The dogs' growls were recognisable but not the hissing screeches of whatever they'd cornered. There was something half-human about the cries, and Thaddeus and the boys stood frozen in horror, quite undecided about what to do. They might have remained so if one of the mastiffs hadn't given a howl of pain and come running into the hall, whining and pawing at a bloody gash on its muzzle.

Joshua at least wasn't prepared to have his beloved pets massacred and, with a groan of pure terror, he reached for the sword Peter had tucked into his belt, stepped off the stairs and walked determinedly towards the door.

Never in his life had he seen such a creature as was crouched on the back of the wagon in the middle of the courtyard, swiping and spitting at any dog brave enough to raise its head above the tailboard.

'Even the wolfhounds are afraid of it,' he whispered as Thaddeus and Peter appeared at his side. 'What can it be?'

Thaddeus could only guess, since he'd never seen the like of this animal either. It was as black as night with a tail that lashed from side to side and fangs and claws as sharp as razors. 'I think it's a cat,' he murmured.

It was Peter's turn to paint a cross on his chest. 'We should never have come here,' he moaned. 'That's why everyone's left. It's the home of the Devil.'

Thaddeus remembered Lady Anne telling him once that the Church's persecution of cats was as nonsensical as their belief that a man like Sir Richard had been selected by God to have dominion over serfs. The abbess of her convent had kept a cat in secret—'she would have been branded a witch if the nuns had betrayed her'—and it was a sweet and loving creature without an ounce of wickedness. Cats were animals like any others, she explained, yet the Church had deemed them familiars of the Devil and ordered them killed wherever they were found.

Thaddeus had asked her how their evil manifested itself and she'd shaken her head with a sigh. 'They go out at night to hunt for food,' she said, 'and anything linked with the night is feared. It's when Satan walks abroad.'

Thaddeus had been ten or eleven at the time. 'Is that true?' he'd asked nervously.

Her eyes had danced with a mischievous smile. 'You should know better than I, Thaddeus. Does Satan stand beside you when you steal my husband's fish from Devil's Brook?'

'Only Will,' he'd answered naively.

He remembered the lightness of her laugh, the touch of her fingers on his cheek. 'Then you've nothing to fear,' she'd said. 'Even Will's not ugly enough to be a demon.'

'Are cats ugly?'

'I've only seen the abbess's but it was beautiful to me—rather more beautiful than the ignorant priests who teach us to hate them. If God made the world and every creature in it, then cats are His creation and not the Devil's. It makes no sense to fear them.'

Thaddeus wondered if Lady Anne was right as he watched the ferocious animal draw blood from a hound. 'Call the dogs off,' he instructed Joshua. 'We've nothing to treat them with if their wounds turn bad. Take them into the inn and fetch me the horse collar from the room to the right. Did you find anything useful upstairs?'

Joshua shook his head.

'Are you going to kill the cat?' Peter asked.

'I don't know yet. There's a candle on the floor near the horse collar and a tinderbox in the bedroom on the other side of the hall. See if you can find holes in the walls or the doors which would have allowed it to move around. I'd like to know how any animal can still be alive so long after the inn was abandoned. It should be dead if it was confined to a single room in pitch-darkness.'

'What if I don't find any holes?'

Thaddeus grinned. 'I'll take it for a demon and cut off its head with my sword.'

He closed the door once the boys and the dogs were inside and retreated to the darkest corner of the courtyard, standing immobile in the shadows. He expected the cat to jump from the wagon and disappear into the village, but it remained where it was, as quiet and immobile as the man who was watching it. When two or three minutes had passed, its claws retracted inside its paws and the bristly black fur on its back and tail began to flatten and sleeken.

It became a different animal as Thaddeus watched, slimmer and lither, arching its spine with a yawn, stretching its front legs and settling down in a seated position to wipe its paws over its ears and across its face. Thaddeus wondered if there were any more cats in this village, and whether their presence accounted for the absence of rats. Lady Anne had been very clear that it was rodents they hunted.

He was certain that if he approached, it would take fright and leap away, but he was too curious not to try. Of all the gifts he could take back to Develish, a rat killer would be the most valuable. He moved forward on soft feet and spoke in a quiet voice to alert the cat to his presence. 'I wish you no harm,' he said. 'Are you wild or do you know what it is to live with people?'

The creature took no notice of him, barely glancing in his direction before lowering its head to lick the fur on its flank. Thaddeus talked on for several minutes but the cat seemed unimpressed, showing neither fear nor interest, more intent on cleaning itself than paying attention to a human. Only when its toilet was complete did it rise to its feet and, with a careless flick of its tail, drop from the tailboard and walk through the gate. Thaddeus followed and watched it swagger along the highway towards the river.

He had never seen an animal behave with such confidence. It had had the measure of the dogs and the measure of the man, and it trod the road quite openly, as if it knew it was a match for anything it met. Was this why the Church feared such beasts? he wondered. Because they had minds of their own? The Bible said God had created people in His own image and given them dominion over every living creature on Earth, but the cat seemed unwilling to recognise its subservient position.

The thought brought a smile to Thaddeus's face. He had the same feelings himself and could only admire this Devil's familiar for its wisdom.

Peter came out to drag him back to the inn to see what he'd found. 'There are holes all over the place,' he said, 'but this is the best.' He nudged the bottom of the middle plank in the front door and a six-inch panel swung away from his foot. 'It moves both ways but you wouldn't know it was there unless you looked for it.'

'What's holding it in place?'

'Thin metal rings, but they're so fiddly my father couldn't make them. If you squat down, you can see them.'

Thaddeus did so. The metal was as fine as string and just as pliable, being threaded through tiny apertures in both the panel and the door and twisted together at the back to form a loop. He tapped the pane with his finger and watched it swing to and fro. 'I don't know who's the cleverer,' he said, 'the blacksmith or the cat. One has manufactured metal string and the other has worked out how to use it. How dull-witted we are in Develish by comparison.'

Peter took the comment as a criticism. 'If my father saw these rings, he might be able to copy them,' he said defensively.

Thaddeus nodded. 'I don't doubt that for a moment,' he answered, 'and I'm not blaming Adam or anyone else on the demesne for our lack of knowledge. We do well with the learning we have, but our understanding would be greater if we were free to travel and talk to others.' With sudden decision, he gripped the square of wood and gave it a long, slow tug, causing the rings to unravel. He used his fingers to twist the threads together along the top of the panel then rose to his feet and handed it to Peter. 'Keep this safe,' he told him. 'If Adam can't come here to see it for himself, we can take it to him.'

As Peter nodded in response, an excited shout came from Joshua at the end of the hall. 'Thaddeus! Thaddeus! You need to come here! You'll not believe what's in that room where the cat was . . . A barrel of flour!'

⚮

There were twelve barrels in total, each stoppered with wide round wooden plugs to keep the contents dry and free from vermin. Some were filled with grain, and Thaddeus made the decision to use the wagon to move them three at a time back to the camp. With only one horse collar, he doubted a single animal could pull the vehicle fully laden. Peter's shoulders slumped at the thought of the work involved and suggested they leave the wagon in the courtyard until they were ready to return to Develish.

'It's a mile to the camp,' he said. 'Are you *seriously* saying we have to make that journey *eight* times when we could just as safely leave all this stuff here?'

'I haven't gone to all this trouble to have it stolen from under my nose.'

'Who's going to steal it?' Peter protested. 'The only thieves around here are us—and if we can't move the beastly things, how's a passing bandit going to do it?'

'He won't bother. He'll split the kegs open by toppling them to the ground then fill a couple of sacks with flour and barley. We'll come back tomorrow to find birds feeding on whatever's left.' Thaddeus gave an amused shrug. 'But you're welcome to stay here and guard it, Peter. I'm no keener to break my back on eight journeys than you are. I'll send your friends to join you, if you like. I expect they'll find the shelter of an inn preferable to the dampness of the riverbank.'

'What will you do?'

'Remain in the camp. The horses need pasture for grazing and I'll not leave them unprotected. They're too important to us.' He gestured to the cart. 'What's your pleasure?'

Peter looked enquiringly at Joshua, but the other boy shook his head. 'I'm with Thaddeus. We should move it to the camp. There'll be no escape if riders come along the highway and trap us inside this building, and I don't want to be killing people over food. I wouldn't know how to do it . . . and neither would you.'

Peter suspected Joshua was more afraid that, freed of his companions, Thaddeus would decide to leave, but he was honest enough to admit his friend was right. He doubted any of them could pierce a man with a sword. Not even Thaddeus. 'All right,' he agreed. 'Where do we start? Will Killer take the horse collar?'

Thaddeus looked across the road at the charger. 'Not without some patient training. He's only ever been ridden, Eleanor's jennet also.' He stood for several moments in thought and then ordered both boys back to the camp with the wheelbarrow. 'Joshua, swap places with Edmund and tell him to join me here. Peter, collect the dappled pack pony and bring it back with you. If memory serves me right, it's been used to pull a plough in the past.'

Joshua made a small gesture of protest. 'I can do anything Edmund can do.'

'I'm not criticising you, Joshua. I need the two tallest to help me lift the barrels onto the wagon, and that's Peter and Edmund.' Thaddeus saw a look of anxiety on the boy's face. 'Take the dogs with you. I've better things to do than wear a knapsack of rotting meat around my neck. Killer's ears are as good as theirs. He'll tell me if anyone approaches.'

He watched the youths set off, taking turns to push the barrow, and wondered if he'd made a rod for his own back by demanding more from them than their fathers ever had. With growing belief in themselves, they'd not settle easily to life in Develish again.

Twenty-eight

Develish, Dorseteshire

With a glance behind him to make sure he wasn't observed, Hugh de Courtesmain tapped lightly on the spinning room door. 'May I be of assistance to you, Lady Eleanor?' he murmured. 'I come as a friend. The women in the kitchen tell me you're not eating and I'm concerned for your welfare.'

In truth, he'd had no words with the kitchen staff and was relying only on what he'd witnessed. A new hatred of Normans had entered Develish in the five days since the victory against My Lord of Bourne. There was much talk of filthy, cowardly Frenchmen as rooms were returned to their previous order and patches made for broken windows. Few bothered to lower their voices when Hugh de Courtesmain was near, and he felt himself implicated in My Lord of Bourne's guilt. Eleanor also.

Her refusal to join the other women in the church had been noted, and Hugh heard many a snide comment that Sir Richard's daughter had wanted the Normans to win. Did she not have her father's blood in her? And was blood not thicker than water? One rumour said she'd attacked young Walter Catchpole when he was putting out flames to save the house, but Walter's father,

Adam, said there was no truth in it. As did the other leading serfs when the rumours were put to them. Lady Eleanor had remained in the spinning room on Clara Trueblood's advice, they said, and the boys hadn't seen her.

Hugh found Lady Anne's attitude the strangest. She seemed unconcerned that her daughter had been barricaded inside a chamber for five days, refusing to allow anyone to enter. 'She'll starve to death if she's not given food, milady,' Hugh said.

'You fret unnecessarily, Master de Courtesmain. I took her a loaf of bread, some cheese and pickled eggs during our celebration of Gyles's victory. She'll come out when she's ready.'

'She may be too afraid of your people's hatred, milady. They talk of her Norman blood and say she attacked one of the boys because she wanted the house to burn.'

Lady Anne returned a scroll to its place on the shelves. 'And I hear whispers that you were too frightened to show yourself to your fellow countrymen when Gyles gave the signal, Master de Courtesmain. Is that any truer than the stories about Lady Eleanor?'

'No, milady,' Hugh lied. 'I was as ready to attack as any man in Develish.'

'I imagined no less of you, sir.' She turned to him with a smile. 'Please believe I know my people better than you do. Whatever dislike they may feel towards Normans does not include those who live amongst us. You and my daughter have nothing to fear.'

'Are you sure, milady? They had no love for your husband.'

'Through his own fault. He abused his privilege more often than he honoured it . . . as did My Lord of Bourne when he threatened us with force.' She held his gaze for a moment and he had an uncomfortable feeling she was reading his mind. Her words confirmed it. 'Don't waste your time trying to make an ally of Eleanor, Master de Courtesmain. She knows nothing of France or Normandy, and has only the barest understanding of English history. She'll tell you she's proud of her Norman blood today . . . and tomorrow rebuff you. Look for friends amongst my leading serfs. Once you have their respect, you'll have the respect of all.'

Hugh made an extravagant bow. 'I seek only yours, milady.'

Lady Anne gave the faintest of smiles. 'You have it already, sir.'

Standing outside the spinning room door, listening to the silence inside, Hugh wondered if he was being wise. Lady Anne hadn't ordered him to stay away from Eleanor, but he didn't doubt her words had been a warning. Yet why? Were Father Anselm's stories of demons true? Hugh's superstitious nature might have embraced the idea—he certainly believed Lady Anne's heresy might cause the Devil to come—but the tedious conversations he'd had with Eleanor following her father's death had spoken of selfishness rather than possession.

Hugh believed there were more obvious reasons why Lady Anne had become disenchanted with her daughter and why the girl had threatened to whip the priest. Jacob Thurkell's death outside the church, Thaddeus's secret departure and Father Anselm's refusal to give Eleanor absolution were too coincidental to be unrelated. Hugh hadn't forgotten Thaddeus's message for Eleanor—*Allow my brother to rest in peace*—and he guessed there was more to Jacob's death than had been revealed. It was those details he wanted. If Thurkell honoured his promise to return within a fortnight, his arrival was close, and Hugh disliked the prospect of being reduced once again to the level of hated serf. He needed a hold over Lady Anne—better still, a hold over both her and Thaddeus Thurkell—and the only person who might give him one was Eleanor. Hugh had welcomed Father Anselm's suggestion that the girl was mad. The more disturbed her mind, the more likely she was to reveal secrets.

He knocked again. 'Do you hear me, Lady Eleanor?' he whispered. 'I worry that your isolation keeps you in ignorance of what is happening here. The serfs have taken control of the demesne and watch for Thurkell's return. Your position will be made worse when that happens, I think.'

He heard her breathing on the other side of the door.

'Gyles Startout stands in high esteem for defeating Normans, milady, but Thurkell will be raised higher if he succeeds in bringing food. The people look for a leader and Thurkell will be their choice. He'll take your dead father's place, and every leading serf will stand with him out of gratitude to see their sons again.'

Her response was so low, Hugh barely heard it. 'They should have died of the pestilence.'

'They may have done, milady, but you would be unwise to rely on it. If you're unprepared for what Thurkell might do, you'll become lower than the maid Isabella. There's a great hatred of Normans since My Lord of Bourne came. The serfs denounce everyone with French blood as a thief or a murderer ... even your father.'

'Sir Richard is dead, Master de Courtesmain.'

'And his people will never do right by him unless they are forced, milady. The location of his grave is known only to Isabella's father, and he keeps the knowledge to himself. I've heard him boast several times that he will not allow Sir Richard's soul to find peace.'

Hugh mouthed the deceit deliberately, wagering that Eleanor's love for her father would unlock her tongue. He had no conscience about it. The details of the grave were recorded in the steward's ledger in Thaddeus's handwriting, and Eleanor could have read the words herself if she'd ever found a commitment to learning.

De Boulet and Foucault are buried beside Sir Richard in a far corner of the northern pasture. I dug as deep as I was able but the summer heat has baked the ground hard, and Gyles Startout fears foxes and badgers will scent the corruption through the loose earth. Lady Anne begs me to stay silent on where the graves are, since a man with good eyesight will make them out easily if he knows where to look. Better that Lady Eleanor remains ignorant of her father's resting place than to learn through gossip that scavengers have been at the mounds. As of this evening, Gyles Startout remains well.

It mattered nothing to Hugh that Lady Anne's motives were good. He smarted each time he thought of the secrets she'd kept from him.

'Are you truly my friend, Master de Courtesmain?' Eleanor whispered from the other side of the door.

'Indeed, milady,' Hugh murmured against the panels. 'I'm here to serve you in any way I can. You have but to ask.'

'What should I do?'

'Allow me to enter so that I may talk to you in private, milady. The advice I give you should not be overheard by serfs.'

There was a long silence before Eleanor answered. 'I'm ashamed to have you see me, Master de Courtesmain. I've soiled my shift, and my hair has become entangled in my comb—' She broke off on a sob. 'I'm in desperate need of a friend, sir, but I'd rather starve than have you know how ugly I've become.'

'I won't judge you, milady.'

'I judge myself, sir. Without the help of a servant, I cannot let you in.'

'I will fetch one for you, milady.'

A flicker of hope entered her voice. 'Then let it be Isabella. She has been my maid a long time and will not betray me to the other serfs. I beg you to ask her in secret, for I will surely die if I become a figure of fun.' A sigh whispered against the panels. 'Can I trust you, Master de Courtesmain?'

'You can, milady.'

'Then I will speak with you gladly once Isabella has made me pretty again.'

Hugh came to regret his complacency later, but as he went in search of Isabella, he congratulated himself on the ease with which he'd won his way back into Eleanor's favour. He even felt sympathy for her. His own worst dread was to be laughed at by peasants.

രസ

Isabella frowned unhappily when Hugh drew her from the lesson she was giving the children and instructed her in an undertone to take a bowl of water and some cleaning flannels to Lady Eleanor in the spinning room. 'She has soiled herself and is too ashamed to leave her chamber,' he murmured. 'She begs your help but asks that you don't mention her distress to anyone else.'

'Was it Lady Eleanor who told you to summon me, sir?' she asked. 'If so, I shall have to ask Lady Anne's permission first. She may not be willing to let me perform such a task.'

It was irritation at having a maid question a steward's right to give orders that prompted Hugh to lie. 'The instruction comes from Lady Anne,' he said sharply. 'Do you think she cares so little for her daughter that she would force Lady Eleanor to walk from the house to clean herself at the well? She asked that you help your young mistress because you have a kinder heart and more discretion than others . . . but perhaps she's wrong.'

၈၆

Isabella knelt outside the spinning room door and placed the heavy bowl of water, flannels and towels on the floor. From inside she could hear smothered sobbing which was quite different from the noisy cries Eleanor usually indulged in when she wanted attention. For once the girl's distress sounded real, and with a surge of relief Isabella accepted that Lady Anne might indeed have sent Master de Courtesmain to ask her to help her young mistress. Nevertheless, she found it strange. Milady's instructions that Isabella was no longer to act as maid to Lady Eleanor after she was moved to the spinning room had been very clear. Isabella would have sought her out for confirmation had Master de Courtesmain not insisted on escorting her while she collected what she needed.

He had stayed behind at the bottom of the stairs, for which she was grateful. There was so much about the Frenchman she didn't like. The way he stood in the corner of the hall, watching her teach the children, ready to pounce on any mistake; the way he came up behind her on quiet feet to ask questions about Lady Eleanor; the disdain with which he spoke to her father and the other leading serfs; the extravagant bows he made to Lady Anne, as if flattery was all that was needed to earn her trust. Isabella believed him to be false and self-serving and could not understand why her beloved mistress allowed him to play the role of steward in Thaddeus's absence.

With a deep breath, Isabella tapped lightly on the spinning room door. 'I have come to help you, milady.'

There was a brief silence. 'Is that you, Isabella?'

'Yes, milady. I have flannels and water. If you open the door, I can bring them in. Should I also fetch food from the kitchen? Clara will give me a bowl of warm frumenty if I tell her it's for you.'

'No.' There was the sound of something being dragged away from the entrance. 'Are you alone?' Eleanor whispered. 'I'll only open the door if there's no one else to see me like this.'

'I'm alone, milady.'

☙☙

It was mid-afternoon when Clara Trueblood sought out Lady Anne in the steward's office and asked her if she knew where Isabella was. 'It's unlike her to absent herself without permission, milady. The children grow bored and restless without her.'

Lady Anne laid down her quill. 'I haven't seen her since this morning. Do the children not know where she is?'

'They said Master de Courtesmain called her away, but when I asked him if he knew what had happened to her he told me he didn't.'

Lady Anne frowned. 'What did he want with her?'

'He was looking for Gyles. He assumed she'd returned to her lessons after he spoke with her.'

'How strange. Where could she be?'

'I don't know, milady. I can't find anyone who's seen her. I'm wondering if she's with Lady Eleanor. I thought I heard voices inside the spinning room—but when I knocked, no one answered.'

Lady Anne frowned. 'Isabella would have no reason to be there. It's more than a week since I relieved her of duties to act as maid to Eleanor.'

'She's very biddable, milady. If she thought an order to attend Lady Eleanor came from you, she would have gone.' Clara paused. 'The last person to see Isabella was Master de Courtesmain.'

'You think Eleanor sent him to fetch Isabella?'

Clara nodded. 'He's quite foolish enough to have obliged her, milady. Your daughter's strong-willed and knows of your fondness for Isabella. If she can't get your attention through tantrums, she's sly enough to win it by other means.'

ତ⊙ର

Hugh de Courtesmain came to an abrupt halt when he entered the front door and saw Lady Anne and Clara Trueblood questioning the children in the middle of the great hall. His first thought was to make a stealthy retreat, and he might have succeeded if Lady Anne hadn't been drawn to look at him when the youngest Thurkell daughter pointed in his direction. 'She went with him, milady,' the child piped. 'He helped her carry a bowl of water to the bottom of the stairs.'

Lady Anne caressed the little girl's head. 'We seem to have lost Isabella, sir,' she told Hugh. 'Do you know where she is?'

'I don't, milady,' he answered. 'I haven't seen her since before noon. Could it be she went to the church? Would you like me to look?'

Lady Anne shook her head. 'Clara and the children will do that. What was her reason for taking a bowl of water upstairs?'

Hugh gave a small shrug to express ignorance. 'I assumed it was for some need of her own. She fetched it from the well after I asked her where her father was. It was heavy and I carried it for her through the hall.'

Did Milady believe him? He thought so from the way she instructed Clara to take the children outside and search every inch of the compound. 'But keep them away from the moat,' she murmured in an undertone. 'If we don't find her soon, I shall send the men to walk the walls. It may be she missed her footing and fell in.'

Hugh stepped forward with a small bow. 'Allow me to perform that task, milady.'

Lady Anne shook her head. 'I hope it won't come to that, Master de Courtesmain. You and I will search the house.' She gestured to Clara to take her group outside and invited Hugh to accompany her upstairs. 'We'll begin with the upper storey.'

She led the steward into her chamber and closed the door behind her, standing irresolute for several seconds. Hugh kept his expression neutral, ready to plead ignorance again. He'd guessed something was wrong when the maid didn't reappear, recognising too late that there must have been a reason for her reluctance to attend Eleanor, but he couldn't return to the spinning room without compromising himself. He had no cause to look for Isabella there when he'd told Clara Trueblood he was ignorant of where she was.

Lady Anne raised her head. 'I'm unsure how to proceed, Master de Courtesmain. My fear is that Isabella is in the spinning room with my daughter and that some harm has come to her . . . yet I hesitate to demand entry for the greater fear of making the situation worse. You became a confidant of Eleanor after her father died. Does that friendship still exist, and will she listen to you with more sympathy than she will to me?'

Hugh was uncertain what to say. Was the woman talking from knowledge or guesswork? 'I don't understand, milady. Are you saying Lady Eleanor would cause deliberate injury to Isabella?'

Lady Anne nodded. 'That is what I'm afraid of. She has a great dislike of the maid. I urged Isabella to keep her distance, but perhaps I didn't make my warning strong enough. It worries me that she came upstairs with a bowl of water.'

Hugh pretended puzzlement. 'What has caused this dislike? It's true that Lady Eleanor expresses hatred for serfs, but I don't remember her singling out Isabella. Has the girl done something recently to offend her?'

The question was a fair one, but Lady Anne couldn't answer truthfully without allowing this man into her confidence. And she wasn't prepared to do that. Nor was she certain her response would be right if she did. She could guess that Isabella knew Jacob's death was no accident, even that Thaddeus had told her about it before he left, but it disturbed her that he would leave Isabella in such a vulnerable position. She chose a more artful reply. 'It may be that Thaddeus's departure has upset them,' she suggested. 'My daughter pretends an indifference to him that she doesn't feel, and Isabella is quite pretty enough to have attracted his attention. The girls are of a similar age and jealousy is a powerful divider.'

Feeling on safer ground, Hugh shook his head. 'You are misinformed, milady. If jealousy divides them, then the cause lies elsewhere. Lady Eleanor expresses nothing but hatred for Thurkell. She calls him a bastard and resents most deeply his place in your affections.'

'Yet she finds his coldness towards her intolerable and would make him her slave if she could. The pity is the pestilence came and destroyed her chances of marriage. She would have forgotten Thaddeus soon enough had she gone to live in Bradmayne.'

'He's base born,' Hugh protested. 'There could never be anything between them.'

Lady Anne seemed to find his certainty amusing, because a smile twitched at the corner of her mouth. 'Indeed.' She studied him. 'Does Eleanor trust you enough to open the spinning room door? I'd rather you be honest than pretend a friendship that no longer exists.'

Hugh seized on the excuse. 'Then honesty compels me to admit the friendship is over, milady. She trusted me while I owed allegiance to Sir Richard, but she sees my loyalty to you as betrayal.' He paused. 'What is to prevent us opening the door and walking in?'

'She uses a chest to wedge it closed.'

'Two of the male servants should be able to force their way in.'

'And further harm may come to Isabella while they do so.' She held his gaze for a moment. 'I hope I'm wrong, sir, but I don't believe I am. My daughter acts impulsively, just as her father did, and if it suits her to strike at Isabella in anger, she will.'

'The damage will be limited if she has no weapon.'

'There are bodkins as large and sharp as knives inside that room. Isabella could lose her sight if not her life. Will you at least try to intercede, Master de Courtesmain? Eleanor will count it a victory if it's my voice she hears. I believe she looks to govern me by threatening Isabella, and I cannot allow her to do that.'

Hugh saw pitfalls in whatever answer he gave, but he recognised he'd win more respect from Lady Anne by agreeing than refusing. 'I'll persuade her more easily with falsehoods, milady, but I fear you'll be offended by what I say. Will you let me talk to her in private?'

'I can't, sir. If you annoy her and she decides to hurt Isabella, I shall have to step in.'

'But Lady Eleanor's as likely to speak false as I am, milady, and my own position will be jeopardised if you believe her. I am ignorant about all of this—most particularly your daughter's hostility to you. What if I provoke her to greater anger by saying the wrong thing?'

'Say whatever you think might persuade her to let you in, Master de Courtesmain. Isabella is Gyles and Martha Startout's only surviving daughter. I cannot, and *will* not, protect Eleanor from their wrath if anything untoward happens to her. The whole of Develish will demand retribution.'

For a clever man, Hugh had been slower than Thaddeus to realise how Eleanor's actions might impact on the demesne. Perhaps he'd become so inured to the casual brutality of Foxcote that he'd learnt to discount the feelings of serfs when one of their own was treated cruelly. Yet he saw now how dire the consequences would be if Eleanor killed or wounded Isabella. There would be no acceptance here that a lord's daughter could act with impunity.

He gave a small bow. 'I can but try, milady.' For all his worries about ensnaring himself in Eleanor's web, he was already counting the rewards he could expect from Lady Anne if he gave her what she wanted.

For herself, Lady Anne could only admire the silken net Hugh wove for Eleanor. He was so practised in deceit that lies fell from his tongue as easily as moonshine on a clear night. 'I know Isabella is with you, Lady Eleanor,' he murmured against the panels. 'At the moment I am alone in that belief, but it won't be long before Clara Trueblood returns. As I speak, she leads a hue and cry around the demesne but she will realise soon enough that the only place the maid can be is here.'

They both heard the rustle of rushes as someone's feet stirred against them.

'I watched Clara climb the stairs to speak to you earlier, saw her come away without an answer,' Hugh continued. 'She won't allow you to refuse her next time. The serfs make decisions for themselves now, milady, so if you're hoping that your mother will come to beg for Isabella's release, I must tell you she won't. No one has told her the girl is missing. As usual, she stands at the window of the office, staring north along the highway in the hopes of sighting messengers . . . or, better still, Thaddeus Thurkell.'

He canted his head to one side, listening.

'Lady Anne has lost her authority, milady. I tried to tell you this some weeks ago, but perhaps you didn't understand my meaning. While Thurkell was here, he held the power, but, with his departure, it has gone to the leading serfs and their wives. The foremost man is Isabella's father Gyles Startout, and he will certainly demand retribution for any harm done to his daughter.' He paused. 'If you release her to me now, no one need know she was here. She is wise enough to keep it to herself and you can be sure I will, too.'

Lady Anne heard a giggle from the other side of the door. 'Isabella's silence would suit you, wouldn't it, Master de Courtesmain?'

Hugh kept his face firmly turned from Lady Anne. 'My advice is good, Lady Eleanor. Your mother can't protect you from the serfs' anger if you do something foolish. She governs in name only.'

There was a short silence before the girl spoke again. 'You're quite wrong, Master de Courtesmain. My mother's power is as strong as it ever was.' Her voice grew louder suddenly, as if she'd pressed her mouth to the door. 'Isn't that right, Mother? I know you're there. I can hear the Frenchman's nervousness each time he speaks for fear of what you might learn.'

Hugh glanced over his shoulder to see if the woman would answer, but Lady Anne shook her head and raised a finger to her lips.

'It ought to annoy you to hear him speak so many lies. He longs to know our secrets. He came whispering at my door earlier in the hope I would divulge them. I promised I would if he brought me Isabella. Everyone knows how much you care for her and how desperate you would feel if Gyles's second daughter was lost to him.' Eleanor's voice sounded farther away when she spoke again. 'The silly little miss tries to pretend the needle doesn't hurt when I prick her, but her eyes fill with tears every time.' Both Hugh and Lady Anne heard a whimper of pain. 'There! Do you see how it stings when I press it into her tiny tit? Tell me you're listening, Mother, or I shall do it again. You must fear me very much now.'

Lady Anne stared at the ground for a moment then gestured Hugh to move aside. 'I am here, my daughter—and yes, I fear you.'

'Is that all?'

'What more do you expect? That my fear of you is matched by my fear for Isabella? Be sure that it is.'

'Then ask me what I want from you in order to spare her further pain.'

'I would if I thought you would honour your promise, Eleanor, but we both know you won't. The more I beg the more you will hurt her just to prove you can. You tore the wings off flies as a child for the same reason. Beg rather for your own life, for I will not save you again.'

The girl laughed. 'You will if you don't want Isabella to bleed like her sister. The serfs can't stand in judgement on me. I am Sir Richard of Develish's daughter and none but a liege lord can decide my guilt.' She moved back to the door, and her tone became harsh. 'You love to preach to me about responsibility, so take responsibility for Isabella. I care nothing for the mewling creature, but I know you do.'

'What are you asking of me? Forgiveness?'

The question seemed to wrong-foot the girl, because it was a moment before she answered. 'I want every serf to swear allegiance to me as they did to my father so that none can deny I am Lady

Eleanor of Develish when the pestilence has passed. I am more fitted to run this demesne than a chattel wife who allows slaves to decide how she should govern.'

Lady Anne considered for a moment then turned to Hugh, speaking clearly enough for Eleanor to hear. 'Master de Courtesmain, you will find John Trueblood and Gyles Startout milling corn in the anteroom. Send them here with axes and order young Robert Startout to summon our people to the forecourt. If we find Isabella dead or too injured to live when this door is forced, Eleanor will be dragged outside—in whatever state she is in—to face those she has wronged. Do I make myself clear?'

'Indeed, milady,' said Hugh, questioning with his eyes whether she wanted him to follow through. 'It will take a matter of minutes only to summon the men, but do you think it wise to put an axe in Gyles's hands if his daughter has come to harm? He'll want vengeance if his blood runs hot with anger.'

'And no one will blame him,' Lady Anne answered. 'Certainly not I. Eleanor must accept whatever fate comes to her. Go, sir. Do as I've bid. We've delayed long enough.'

Hugh never doubted afterwards that she would have allowed events to unfold in precisely the way she'd ordered if Eleanor hadn't cried out that she was opening the door. They heard the sound of the chest being pulled away and the latch being lifted. Hugh took in the sorry sight of the girl in the doorway. If madness could be painted, he thought, the picture would look as Eleanor did now—wild-haired, barely dressed, fading yellow bruises about her eyes, a bodkin in her hand and bloody slashes on her arms.

He expected Lady Anne to react as he did—with concern— but she barely glanced at Eleanor as she pushed her way inside and dropped to her knees beside Isabella, who sat immobile in the corner, arms clasped tightly about her knees. She smoothed the hair from the maid's brow and smiled into her tear-filled eyes. 'Are you able to stand?' she asked.

Isabella nodded. 'I think so, milady.'

Lady Anne put a hand under her arm to help her up, shielding her from Eleanor with her own body as she escorted her to the door. 'Master de Courtesmain will take you to my chamber. You must bolt yourself in and wait for your mother.' She turned to Hugh. 'Once the bolt is firm, go in search of Martha and take her to Isabella. Tell her the child has been hurt but do not explain the circumstances. I will talk with them both later.'

Hugh looked past her to Eleanor. 'What of your own daughter, milady? She looks as badly hurt as the maid.'

Lady Anne turned back into the room. 'You have your orders, Master de Courtesmain. Execute them precisely or I'll have you expelled from the demesne. Your determination to advance yourself at the expense of others wearies me.'

Twenty-nine

LADY ANNE DIDN'T SPEAK AS she took the bodkin from Eleanor's hand and placed it in the sewing tray before leading the girl to a stool and pressing her onto it. Arnica had reduced the swellings around Eleanor's eyes from where Robert Startout had punched her, but the discolouration would take another day to fade completely.

She dipped a cloth in a bowl of water on a table near the window and began to clean the blood from Eleanor's arms. It was hard to know if Isabella had caused the wounds by fighting back or Eleanor had done them to herself. Certainly some of the hardened scabs suggested they'd been made two or three days earlier. They ran in parallel stripes across her forearms, apparently scored with measured precision by the point of a needle.

Lady Anne couldn't think why Eleanor would do such a thing unless, like a flagellant, she wanted to make penance for her sins. Had she accepted Robert's beating in the same spirit? She'd been so reluctant to see him punished that she'd begged her mother to swear him and his friends to silence, and Lady Anne had done so.

Yet it was a strangely disturbed mind that was willing to forgive the boy but vented its rage on an innocent girl.

She didn't doubt Eleanor's vanity had had something to do with her refusal to accuse Robert—her face had taken time to regain its prettiness—but there had seemed to be a recognition that Robert was justified in what he did. Eleanor came as close to an apology as she was able, saying she hadn't understood why the boys were in the house or what they'd been tasked to do. She had clutched her mother's hands, pleading to be believed, and Lady Anne had bathed her face with cooling liniment, calmed her fears and promised to ask Robert and Walter to keep the details of what had happened to themselves.

She'd hoped so much that Eleanor had learnt to put herself in another's shoes, but she saw now how misplaced that hope had been. Whatever the girl's reasons for sparing Robert, they did not apply to Isabella. Nor, it seemed, to herself, for it was hard to interpret the cuts on Eleanor's arms as anything other than self-inflicted punishment. Were the marks a visible sign of atonement for Jacob's death? Did she hurt herself to earn God's forgiveness? If so, why invite His wrath by attacking Isabella?

It was easier to believe that Eleanor had lost her mind completely than look for reason in her actions. Her demeanour suggested madness. She stared ahead with vacant eyes and showed no interest when Lady Anne wiped her face and hands before taking a hairbrush and pulling it gently through the tangled blonde curls. 'How am I to help you when the only world you want is the one your father gave you?' she murmured. 'Is it really so hard to see that a serf is as much a person as you are, as loved by God and as deserving of happiness?'

She laid down the brush and stepped to a coffer against the far wall, lifting the lid to remove a clean shift. She would have chosen a homespun kirtle to go over it but changed her mind and took a gown with long sleeves instead. Eleanor put up no resistance to being raised from the stool and dressed, though she turned her back on her mother rather than subject herself to the woman's searching gaze as Lady Anne removed her stained and tattered undergarments to replace them with clean ones. From behind, her naked body was so thin it looked more like a child's than a young woman's.

Once finished, Lady Anne lowered her to the stool again and set to tidying the room. The evidence of what had happened was obvious in the discarded flannels and the overturned bowl and spilt water which Isabella had brought from the well, but there was little to indicate that a fight had taken place. The spinning wheels stood upright, the carded wool was neatly stacked and Eleanor's washing water was where it should be. Only the rushes had been disturbed, showing a trail where Eleanor had dragged Isabella into the corner.

It wasn't hard for Lady Anne to guess that Eleanor had struck the maid with something heavy when she entered the room before dragging the limp body from one side of the room to the other. Lady Anne could only guess at Isabella's terror when she came to and saw the wildness in Eleanor's eyes and the six-inch needle in her hand.

She leant wearily against the wall and stared out of the window, voicing her thoughts aloud. 'What's to be done with you? You harm yourself when you're alone and others when you're not. I begin to wish your father had come home alive. There was always a chance he might have taken you with him.' She hadn't expected an answer and was surprised when one came.

'You should have let me go to Foxcote when I asked,' said Eleanor in a voice devoid of emotion. 'We still had horses in the fields and Master de Courtesmain would have taken me if you'd ordered him.'

Lady Anne continued to watch the highway, wondering at how easily the girl moved from madness to reason. 'Your uncle would have refused you entry as he refused it to your father these many years. He allowed his wife to write to her brother but that's as far as his tolerance went. He's not a forgiving man.'

'I'm not in need of his forgiveness. I've done nothing to offend him.'

'No,' Lady Anne agreed, 'the fault was Sir Richard's . . . but it makes no difference. My Lord of Foxcote will never allow you to live under his roof.'

It was a few moments before Eleanor spoke again. 'Do you lie to me now or did you lie before when you said it was my aunt's jealousy that would make me unwelcome?'

Lady Anne turned to look at her. 'I spoke the truth both times. Your aunt is as vain as your uncle is harsh. There is little to admire in either of them. It makes Foxcote a wretched place to live.'

'How can you know that? You've never been there.'

'Your father took me for a visit shortly after we were wed. It's not a place I wish to see again.'

A gleam of triumph shone in Eleanor's eyes. 'Then it was you who caused the offence and not Sir Richard. Are you blaming him for something you did?'

'Sir Richard was not permitted to enter so I was obliged to stay there on my own. I formed a poor opinion of the demesne during my stay and my feelings will have shown in my face. You may blame me for that but not for anything else.'

'How long did your visit last?'

'A month short of half a year. It seemed an eternity.'

Eleanor stared at her, more confused now than triumphant. 'What did they want from you?'

Lady Anne turned to the window again. The first blush of russet on the woods that lined the valley slopes made the hills as beautiful as she'd ever seen them, but there was no knowing what ugliness the trees were hiding. How much life was dying in their shade? she wondered. Rabbits ripped apart by foxes . . . hedgehogs disembowelled by badgers? It was the necessary cycle of nature—destructive and bloody—but must size and strength always conquer? Had the innocent little sparrow no value except to satisfy the appetite of the predatory hawk?

'Your uncle wanted me for my nursing skills. I cared for his half-sister, who was confined to her chamber. She was a frail child, a year younger than you are now, and her hold on life was slender. My Lord of Foxcote had little care if she lived or died, but he gave me permission to help her if I could. When she was fit again, he committed her to a nunnery and dispatched me home to Develish. I have no knowledge of what happened to her after that. Her fate was never included in any of the messages Lady Beatrix sent your father.'

'What was her name?'

'Mathilde. I would have called you after her if Sir Richard had allowed it. We became friends in the time we spent together.'

'It's a poor name. I would not have wanted it.'

'I thought it pretty . . . perhaps because Mathilde herself was so pretty. She was as blonde and blue-eyed as you are.'

'Was my aunt jealous of her?'

'More than jealous. She was consumed by hatred for her. She believed Mathilde evil and blamed her for every ill that befell Foxcote, even accusing her of causing the crops to fail. She was too stupid to see where the fault really lay.'

A long silence followed and Lady Anne let it drift. She had wished so many times that Sir Richard's steward had not been absent from the house when the parchment arrived from Foxcote four months into her marriage. She would never have known what it said if her husband hadn't tossed it to her and asked her to read it. Even a man as coarse and ignorant as Sir Richard would have hesitated to share such information with a young wife.

It would be wrong to say the letter destroyed any feelings Lady Anne had for Sir Richard—she had none—but it gave rise to the contempt she felt ever after. There was no honour in him. He blustered and roared, claiming some other man must have deflowered the little strumpet, then drowned himself in ale and wept maudlin tears. It was everyone's fault but his—even Lady Anne's for continuing to read aloud from the parchment after he ordered her to stop.

Yet what would have become of Mathilde and Eleanor if she hadn't seen what was written? My Lord of Foxcote's angry words suggested his thirteen-year-old half-sister was as responsible for her condition as Sir Richard was. He demanded reparation for himself but not for the child who'd been entrusted to his care on the death of her mother. There was no future for Mathilde. Any chance she'd ever had of making a marriage was over. He was praying for her death and the death of the incubus inside her.

'What illness did she have?'

'None that couldn't be cured with St John's wort and a little kindness. She cried herself to sleep each night believing her life to be over.'

'Did she thank you for saving her?'

'Yes.'

'I wouldn't have done. I'd rather die than go to a nunnery.'

Lady Anne's breath misted a pane of glass and she watched the tiny droplets fade as quickly as they'd formed. 'It was what she wanted. Her greatest fear was that she would be forced to stay in Foxcote with a brother who loathed and despised her. She found the demesne even more wretched than I did.'

'She sounds sadly poor-spirited.'

'Perhaps so, but her adversities were greater than anything you will ever face. I think of her often and hope she found peace in her convent.'

'How old will she be if she's still alive?'

'Twenty-seven.'

Out of the corner of her eye she watched Eleanor count on her fingers. 'You must have been carrying me while you were nursing her. Was I born in Foxcote?'

Lady Anne nodded. 'I brought you home when you were two weeks old.'

The girl stared at her. 'Why did my father allow it? What if the sickness had been catching? You could have died and I along with you.'

'He hoped to restore himself in My Lord of Foxcote's esteem by offering me as a nurse. He was a frequent visitor to the demesne before his marriage. We travelled north some three weeks after we were informed of Mathilde's condition.'

It was the only reparation Sir Richard could make unless he was willing to impoverish himself by relinquishing Lady Anne's dowry by way of compensation. Her money was all that stood between him and ruin, and he had no desire to give it up. Nor did he have enough regard for his wife to care if another woman's son inherited his estate, as long as the child was his.

As his chattel, Lady Anne had no choice but to do as he bid, but in truth she was as disinclined to see Develish lost as he was.

She knew her marriage would become intolerable if she had to spend it closeted with Sir Richard in the corner of some relative's house. More importantly, she understood the value of secrets. She might have been half her husband's age, but she was clever enough to recognise a lever of power when she saw it. And little Mathilde—so desperate for love—was as willing as Lady Anne could have wished to relate the story of her infant's conception and sign her name to it once Lady Anne had inscribed it on parchment.

As time passed, Lady Anne had come to realise the document was worthless unless she was prepared to reveal that Eleanor was born out of wedlock. She might have used it if the child had been born a boy, and Lady Anne had been blessed with an heir herself, but there was nothing to be gained by proving a daughter illegitimate except heartache for Eleanor. She remembered the day she'd consigned the page to flames—when Isabella had told her with pride that the house servants were becoming so proficient at their letters that most could read quite well.

'Condition's a strange word for a sickness,' said Eleanor into the silence. 'Was she with child?'

'Yes.'

'Am I her daughter?'

'Yes.'

There was a short hesitation. 'Was Sir Richard my father?'

Lady Anne turned towards her. 'It was never in doubt,' she said. 'You looked like him when you were born and you've become more like him as you've grown. I still see your mother in you from time to time, but not often. She was too shy to display herself as you do. You have her features when you're asleep but not otherwise.'

Eleanor stared at her hands. 'Why didn't you tell me sooner?'

'Your father wouldn't allow it. He swore an oath to My Lord of Foxcote that the truth would stay hidden. It was the only way he could avoid paying reparation and being reduced to penury. There was so much—' she sought for a word—'*hostility* surrounding your birth, Eleanor. Had I refused to travel north and bring you home with me, your future would have been very uncertain.'

The girl's face twisted. 'So would yours. You wouldn't have been mistress of Develish all these years if my father had been forced to pay. You paint yourself in the best light but you served your own interests as much as mine.'

'It would certainly have angered me to see my dowry go in recompense to a vicious brute like Foxcote. You were allowed to live because I agreed to raise you as my own. If Mathilde had been left to her brother's mercy, he would have ordered you smothered before you drew your first breath and spent the reparation on a new horse.' She shook her head at Eleanor's expression. 'Try not to be naive, Eleanor. Your father was no keener to acknowledge you than My Lord of Foxcote or Lady Beatrix. He came to love you later but not when you were a baby.'

'I wonder *you* didn't smother me? I've always been a disappointment to you.'

Lady Anne made no answer, for a denial would fall on deaf ears. Eleanor would believe what she wanted to believe, as she always had. Several times in the last two years Lady Anne had tried to persuade Sir Richard to break his oath and be honest with his daughter, but he'd always refused. He feared Eleanor's rages, feared she'd destroy her chances of marriage by disclosing the secret in anger one day. If even one serf learnt the truth, the story of his daughter's illegitimacy would become common knowledge.

Eleanor watched Lady Anne from beneath lowered lids. 'Why do you tell me this now? You could have done it the day my father died, or in the church after Thaddeus left, or in the steward's office. Does Isabella matter so much to you that you only disown me when she cries?'

'It's not in my power to disown you. Only Sir Richard could have done that. You may declare yourself free of me at any time of your choosing, but I cannot do the same. I am bound by the promises I made to Mathilde both before and after you were born.' She spread her hands in regret. 'I'm at a loss what to do with you, Eleanor. I thought it might help if you knew I wasn't your mother, that it might explain why you felt more attachment to your father than to me. The ties of blood between you were very strong. He could capture your affection in a way I could not.'

Eleanor laced and unlaced her fingers through the ribbons of her gown. 'You never tried. You were happy to win the serfs' love, but you didn't care enough to win mine.'

Lady Anne hid a sigh. There were so few words that Eleanor seemed to understand. 'Do you even know what love is?' she asked. 'You seem unable to recognise it unless it's showy and noisy and comes with baubles and trinkets.'

'I saw the worry in your face when you went to Isabella. You never look at me like that. Even when you were wiping my arms just now, there was no concern . . . only anger.'

Lady Anne doubted that was true—she had been trying to soothe the girl not chastise her—but she saw no reason to disagree. It was past time Eleanor faced the reality of her situation. 'Of course I'm angry,' she agreed quietly. 'You clearly understand enough of the law to know that, as liege lord, I must sit in judgement on you. But what do you expect me to do? Pretend you didn't push a bodkin into Isabella's breast? Try to persuade two hundred serfs it was a harmless prank and you needn't be punished for it? Are you *really* so foolish?'

'It makes no difference what they think. You're their lord. They have to accept what you say.'

'As must you. I warned you I wouldn't protect you a second time. As soon as Isabella is strong enough to give her evidence, you will stand accused before our people in the great hall.' She watched the girl for a moment. 'If you're wise, you'll admit your fault and beg Isabella's pardon without obliging her to speak. There's many will be reminded of Jacob's death if you force her to describe how cruelly you wounded her. If I can, I will try to blame your actions on madness.'

Eleanor's eyes flared, but more in rage than fear, Lady Anne thought. 'I am not mad and I will *never* beg pardon of a serf. If you try to make me, I shall take Develish from you. As Sir Richard's only heir, I have more right to it than you. You were his chattel when he was alive, and you have no standing at all now that he's dead.'

Lady Anne turned to the window again. 'Neither of us can lay claim to Develish, Eleanor,' she answered calmly. 'You know this. I've explained to you many times that, upon Sir Richard's death, you will become dependent on a new lord's charity. If Sir Richard's cousin is alive when the pestilence has passed, the demesne will go to him. If he is dead, My Lord of Blandeforde will impose a stranger here.'

'I will not accept that.'

'Then you must hope My Lord believes you appealing enough to find a wealthy widower willing to marry you and pay the fees and taxes of inheritance. If you're lucky, the man he selects won't be above forty.'

'You won't allow it. You'll take him for yourself in order to remain mistress here.'

Lady Anne stared towards the distant horizon. 'You're quite wrong,' she murmured. 'I've always known there would be no future for me in Develish once your father died. When the danger has passed, I shall leave the demesne to make my own future. I prefer to live by the talents I have than be dependent on a man I cannot respect.'

'What about me?' Eleanor demanded mutinously. 'I'll not go with you and play daughter to a woman without status.'

Lady Anne lowered herself to a stool and took up a carding comb and a hank of raw wool. 'I wouldn't expect you to. You must choose a course for yourself.' She pulled the comb across the tangled fibres, drawing them into fine threads.

'I wish to be mistress here.'

'Then present yourself as an obedient servant to My Lord of Blandeforde and beg for a husband. There will be no place for tantrums or anger, Eleanor. My Lord will be more inclined to favour you if he believes you meek and submissive.'

'He won't know who I am. You must make the request for me.'

Lady Anne shook her head. 'It will not serve you well if I do. As the widow of one of his vassal knights, I am as much his property as I was Sir Richard's. There will be no escape for either of us if he forces me into marriage instead. You must allow me to leave and make the request yourself.'

Eleanor's expression was bitter. 'Will you forsake our serfs as easily?'

'Not if they choose to come with me.'

'They can't. My Lord of Blandeforde will hold them to their oaths.'

Lady Anne smiled slightly. 'How? Where is he? Where are his bailiffs? Where are his messengers? Are he and his household even alive?'

Eleanor felt a flutter of fear in her belly. Her imaginings of the future had always centred on her worries about not being recognised for who she was, never that the man she needed to persuade might be dead. 'Someone will come.'

'And what will they find? A deserted house, cottages burnt to the ground and fields untended for months. They'll believe we've suffered the same wretched death as every other demesne in the region.' When the girl made no response, Lady Anne raised her head. 'Our people long for freedom as much as I do, Eleanor. With so many dead, there will be chances aplenty for skilled men and women to earn a good living in the towns, particularly those who are able to read and write. If they take new names and create new histories for themselves, no one will recognise them as Develish serfs.'

Anger rose in Eleanor like a roaring flame. 'They gave allegiance to my father. I'll tell My Lord of Blandeforde they've absconded and demand he hunts them down.'

Lady Anne eyed her for a moment before bending her head once more to her work. 'You won't be believed,' she murmured. 'His bailiffs will think you truly mad if they find you in an empty house with your gown unfastened and your hair unkempt. It's not normal for young ladies of quality to roam around a deserted house without a chaperone or a maid. They'll take you for a slattern.'

'Not every serf will leave.'

'You must pray that's true. You won't be able to feed yourself otherwise.'

The girl's eyes narrowed. 'If you're trying to frighten me into begging Isabella's pardon, you're wasting your breath. No one will brave the pestilence unless Thaddeus returns. They'll be too frightened.'

'Most fear hunger more. We may be able to delay our departure until spring if Thaddeus succeeds in finding food, but if he doesn't, the choice of whether to die of starvation or make a bid for freedom by carrying our rations on our backs will have to be made by Christmas. Some may feel they can't manage such a journey, but Gyles and John Trueblood believe all will want to try.'

Eleanor looked at her in disbelief. 'You would travel on foot with serfs? Have you no pride?'

'None that you would recognise. Mine is in our people's achievements, and I will walk happily with them if it gives them hope. You will do the same without complaint if you choose to come with us.'

The girl stared at her with disdain. 'I will not. It shames me the way you crawl before serfs.'

'Then you must fend for yourself. I will leave the same rations for you that each of us will have, but the job of preparing and cooking the food will be yours. Winter wheat and turnips have been planted in the vegetable garden, and if you tend the shoots properly, they should produce food in the spring.'

'I will not do serfs' work.'

'You will starve if you don't.'

'You must order the servants to remain behind.'

Lady Anne shook her head. 'Each person here will make his own choice for his future . . . as will you. You've a few weeks yet before you need make a decision, but if you're wise, you'll start to think about it now.'

Eleanor stared at her, brittle-eyed. She clung to the belief that none of this was true, and Lady Anne said it only to frighten her into an apology. 'I'll be glad when you go,' she said spitefully, looking to provoke through hurt. 'I never wanted you for a mother.'

'I know—and if I could have found a better way to help you, I would have taken it. It was never my intention to pretend to be something I'm not.'

The girl took these statements for indifference. 'I choose to declare myself free of you now. You can't command me to appear before the serfs if I'm not your daughter.'

'Indeed I can,' said Lady Anne mildly. 'You will answer to Isabella's accusations in one hour's time. If necessary, I shall send Gyles Startout and John Trueblood to bring you downstairs between them.'

'I dare you to try,' the girl warned. 'Do you think I'll let you humble me when your crimes are so much worse?'

'What crimes have I committed?'

'Heresy . . . blasphemy . . . sacrilege . . . false witness. I'll reveal how you've deceived our people all these years about being my mother in order to keep Develish for yourself.'

Lady Anne studied her for a moment. 'You would say those things rather than beg Isabella's pardon?'

'I would and I will.'

'I urge you not to.'

'I will do it nonetheless,' said Eleanor, with a curl of satisfaction on her lips. 'And you must blame yourself when your precious serfs see you for the liar you are.'

With a sigh, Lady Anne laid aside the wool and the carding comb. 'So be it,' she said quietly, standing up and shaking out her skirts. 'I shall ask Master de Courtesmain to summon them to the hall. And since I have every intention of forcing you to acknowledge the harm you've done Isabella, you may say your piece before any accusations are made against you.' She moved to the door. 'Use the next hour to reflect, Eleanor. At the moment, you and I are the only ones who know you're not my daughter. You would be wise to keep it that way.'

☙

Hugh de Courtesmain was hovering uncertainly outside Lady Anne's chamber when he saw her emerge alone from the spinning room. 'Is everything all right, milady?' he asked as she approached.

'Only if Isabella is well,' she answered. 'Is Martha with her?'

He nodded. 'I have sworn them both to secrecy.'

'On whose behalf, Master de Courtesmain?'

'Yours, milady. I didn't think you'd wish your daughter to become the subject of common gossip.'

'And how does Martha feel about her daughter, sir? Is she happy to stay silent to protect mine?'

He gave a small bow. 'She's a serf, milady. She will do whatever she's ordered to do.'

'Indeed. She's a generous woman. One way or another she has given all her children in service to Develish. I look to the day when Thaddeus brings her sons home. She grieved enough for her daughter Abigail. She'll not survive the loss of Ian and Olyver.'

'I pray for the twins each day, milady.'

'I'm sure of it, Master de Courtesmain,' she answered, careful to keep her tone free of sarcasm. 'Will you perform another task for me?'

'Of course, milady.'

'Will you ask our people to assemble in the great hall in one hour? Give no reason, but reassure them that Isabella has been found alive. I fear Clara Trueblood may have spread more alarm than was necessary about the child's safety.' She raised her hand to tap lightly on the door. 'It's Lady Anne, Martha, come to help you. May I enter?'

The door opened a crack and Hugh caught a glimpse of Martha's scared face before Lady Anne slipped inside and closed the room to his view again. After a quick glance to left and right, he pressed his ear to the wooden panels, but whatever conversation was being conducted inside was muted, and he remained in ignorance of why the serfs must be summoned to the great hall or what Lady Anne intended to say to them when they came.

┘┐

Such is human nature that the Frenchman had worked himself into a state of deep resentment by the time the hall was filled with the two hundred serfs. Even the children were present. His anger at his inability to give reasons for the meeting was intensified by the sight of Martha moving freely amongst the crowd, whispering her confidences into ready ears. He watched the faces of the people she spoke to, saw the surprise and disbelief in their eyes, knew she was disobeying his injunction to stay silent.

Had Lady Anne lost leave of her senses? he wondered. Did she think she could control a mob whipped to fury by Martha? He assumed she planned to apologise for Eleanor's behaviour but, if so, she had allowed arrogance to cloud her judgement. Was she really so deluded about these people's love for her that she thought she could persuade them to forgive and forget her daughter's piercing of the maid's breast? They might listen to her pleas today, but her voice would be drowned out by their clamour for justice tomorrow.

He cursed Lady Anne's foolishness in creating a society where peasants considered themselves the equal of lords, cursed his own for swearing Martha to secrecy. He saw accusation in the looks that were directed his way, and fancied Martha was saying the Frenchman hadn't wanted Eleanor to answer for what she'd done. He would have drawn back into the deepest shadows of the corner, fearful of being asked to account for himself, had a sudden silence not fallen on the hall.

Lady Anne had appeared at the top of the stairs, her arm encircling Isabella's waist to support her. The girl looked composed, if a little pale, and smiled when she saw her father at the front of the crowd. Lady Anne asked her if she'd like to join him, but Isabella shook her head. 'I'd rather stay with you, milady.'

They made an agreeable tableau, Hugh thought: each with a face that pleased because of its sweetness. And perhaps Lady Anne wasn't so foolish after all. Who would dare criticise her while Isabella remained at her side?

The woman's soft brown eyes searched the upturned faces. 'You have placed much trust in me,' she said. 'Together, we worked hard to build Develish into a fine demesne, and our shared ambition was always that one day you would be able to buy your way out of serfdom and work your land as free men and women. I regret so much that I didn't try harder to achieve it while Sir Richard was alive. It was a mistake to think we had time on our side.'

'Don't blame yourself, milady,' called a voice from the crowd. 'No one could have predicted the pestilence.'

A murmur of agreement rose from every throat. 'We are only alive because of you,' said John Trueblood from the front.

Lady Anne shook her head. 'You're alive because you've helped each other, John, and you didn't need orders from me to do that. The people of Develish have long understood the value of sharing their effort to promote the good of all.'

'It was you who taught us, milady,' said Gyles Startout. 'Before you came, we had little to look forward to except ill health and hardship . . . not to mention the priest's threats of Hell if we dared complain of our conditions.'

'And I fear that may happen again when the pestilence is over, Gyles. On the day that riders come to discover how we are placed in Develish, there will be nothing I can do to prevent your lives being determined by My Lord of Blandeforde.'

'What will become of us?' asked a woman.

'You must decide that for yourselves. If your choice is to stay in Develish, you have only to give your oath of fealty to a new lord and obey whatever demands he makes of you.'

'But they'll be onerous,' warned John Trueblood. 'We're likely to go hungry for two years if a new lord expects us to replenish his own stores and coffers before we fill ours.'

'What of you, milady?' called a man's voice. 'Will My Lord of Blandeforde determine your future also?'

'Most certainly . . . as long as I'm willing to fall to my knees and beg his charity.' Her eyes danced with sudden humour. 'Who knows? He may even be generous enough to find me another husband like Sir Richard.' She smiled at the laughter that greeted the remark. 'We're not so different, you and I. Our futures will depend on how well or badly My Lord of Blandeforde has digested his food on the day he chooses a new master for us.'

'Will you take this husband, milady?' asked Clara Trueblood.

'No, Clara, I will not. I would sooner be destitute than married to a second Sir Richard. Nor do I wish to enter a convent. The chains of the Church are as strong as those that bind chattels and serfs, and I seek freedom, not further bondage.' She drew Isabella closer. 'As does this child . . . yet if she is found here by My Lord of Blandeforde's men when the pestilence is over, she will be recorded as a Develish serf and her fate set forever. It will be the same for all of you.'

'What alternative do we have?'

'To leave the demesne and forge new lives for ourselves else-where. I have discussed this with your leaders and we are all agreed that if My Lord of Bourne spoke the truth before he fired your cottages, every village for miles around has been laid waste. Why should Develish be different? When riders find it empty they will believe we perished from the sickness. We may go where we please and use our wits to support ourselves. No one will come looking for us.'

Hugh had to brace himself to hide his shock. This was a worse sacrilege than anything he'd heard from the woman before. Far from excusing her daughter, she was inciting her people to insur-rection. Did she know the penalty for such talk? Did her serfs understand what it meant to break their oaths of fealty? Were they all so misguided that they'd do it on her say-so?

John Trueblood turned to address the crowd. 'Those of us who have discussed our choices have taken the time to think about what we want to do, and the rest of you must do the same. It was Thaddeus's view that all must go, or none. To leave some behind will be dangerous. However willing that handful may be to swear that the rest of us have died, My Lord of Blandeforde will use hot irons to extract the truth if he disbelieves what they say.'

'John is right,' said Lady Anne. 'You must talk amongst yourselves and find unanimity before you reach a decision. My earnest prayer is that Thaddeus and his young companions will return before too long to tell us what the countryside is like beyond our boundaries. When you hear what they have to say, you will be better able to decide if the plan is a good one.'

James Buckler spoke up from the far side of the hall. 'As you consider, remember that time is running out,' he said. 'If we tighten our belts, we may be able to stretch our stores beyond Christmas, but without fresh supplies from Thaddeus, we must choose to die here of starvation or brave the dangers of an unknown journey.'

Mutters rippled through the crowd as neighbour turned to neighbour with excited comments and questions. Was this what Martha had prepared them for? Hugh wondered. Talk of freedom rather than condemnation of Lady Eleanor?

Lady Anne raised her hand for silence. 'There's something else you should know,' she said. 'Lady Eleanor intends to remain behind and name you as absconders if you choose to leave. She claims Develish as her own and will do whatever is needed to take her father's place—and she may succeed if she tells My Lord of Blandeforde I acted criminally by refusing Sir Richard entry when he returned from Bradmayne.'

'You did what was right, milady,' said Gyles from the front. 'Does Lady Eleanor not understand that?'

'You may ask her yourself, Gyles.' She glanced along the gallery towards the spinning room. 'I have given her leave to say what is in her heart before she answers to Isabella.'

Thirty

Holcombe on the River Pedle

THADDEUS WAITED UNTIL PETER AND Joshua were out of sight and then carried the axe and hammer across the road to the building opposite the inn. He ran his hand down Killer's neck, encouraging him to stay alert before moving to examine the wide door to the right of the shuttered window. His eyes were drawn immediately to a round aperture beneath the latch. It was similar to one in the church door at Develish, and Thaddeus guessed it served the same purpose: to permit a key to be inserted into a wooden lock on the other side.

Develish's was a hefty thing, carved from solid oak into the shape of a roughly hewn box. No one knew who'd made it—a travelling craftsman, perhaps—but Thaddeus had always been fascinated by the mechanism. A key with square teeth was pushed through the hole into an opening at the bottom of the box and, with careful manipulation, three oak staves inside the box could be moved two inches sideways—in either direction—to slot in and out of carved holes in the stone architrave around the door.

Father Anselm had claimed it was impossible to break until Thaddeus pointed out that the weakness of the design was not in the staves but in how the box was attached to the door. Since it was held in place by wooden dowels, a well-aimed strike from an axe blade on the outside might split the planking enough to loosen the dowels in their holes. More by luck than good judgement, his first blow, sited close to the left-hand edge of the door, hit its mark and he felt a quiet satisfaction as he pushed his knife through the gap and felt a peg move under the pressure. It took several more strikes to locate the other end of the lock—the box was a good three inches wider than Develish's—but by the time Edmund and Peter arrived, he was using a hammer and chisel to tap each dowel from its socket.

The boys came noisily, breaking his concentration.

'Is it true you're a freeman?' Edmund demanded. 'Joshua's weeping his heart out because he says you're going to France and taking the dogs with you.'

Thaddeus paused. 'Do you want to say that again in words I understand?'

'None of us wants to go back to Develish. We like being free. If you're planning to leave, we'd rather go with you.'

'And what does France have to do with any of that?'

Peter wriggled his shoulders in embarrassment. 'I told Joshua you'd be there by now if you didn't have us hanging like millstones round your neck. He really likes you, Thaddeus. It'll break his heart if you go without him.'

'We all like you,' said Edmund. 'Our fathers never let us talk about things that matter.'

'We can be your retinue in France,' Peter urged. 'You can call yourself Sir Richard of Develish. No one will know the difference.'

A whisper of a laugh escaped Thaddeus's mouth. 'You'd saddle me with the name of a short, fat, ignorant man who couldn't read or write, was too insignificant to own more than one demesne, and sired a monstrous daughter who killed my brother and whipped boys for fun? I'd sooner remain a slave.'

'Then call yourself Lord of Foxcote,' said Peter. 'No one doubted you yesterday.'

'You wouldn't want to be him either,' countered Edmund. 'My mother says he's worse than Sir Richard. Even his own family fear him.'

Thaddeus dislodged another dowel. 'How would Clara know? My Lord of Foxcote's never been to Develish.'

'She spoke with the wet nurse who suckled Eleanor after she was born.'

Thaddeus glanced at the boy. 'What would a wet nurse know of Foxcote?'

'Everything,' said Edmund. 'She lived there.' He paused uneasily before Thaddeus's frown, perhaps realising he'd let his tongue run away with him. 'My father said he'd beat me black and blue if I ever repeated the story.'

'You'll get a thrashing off the rest of us if you don't,' Peter retorted. 'You can't stop there. Why would Lady Anne send for a wet nurse from Foxcote? Didn't she think the women of Develish good enough?'

It seemed Edmund needed little encouragement. Perhaps every secret becomes unbearable after a while.

'She didn't send for her. Eleanor was born in Foxcote, and Lady Anne brought the wet nurse back to suckle the baby during the journey because she didn't have milk of her own. Mother said it was because she was never pregnant and didn't give birth to Eleanor.'

The chisel jolted in Thaddeus's hand as he moved it down the split to find the next dowel and he placed his other hand over it to keep it steady. 'I had no idea your mother was so imaginative,' he murmured, picturing practical, down-to-earth Clara Trueblood in his mind. 'Who does she say the father was?'

'Sir Richard, of course. Eleanor looks just like him. It's Lady Anne she doesn't resemble. If you didn't know they were supposed to be mother and daughter, you'd never believe it.'

Peter gave a snort of derision. 'You've got it the wrong way round, stupid. It's wives who foist bastards onto husbands, not husbands who foist them onto wives.' Then, realising what he'd said, he screwed his face into an apology. 'I meant no offence, Thaddeus.'

'None taken.' Thaddeus gave a satisfied grunt as the last of the dowels gave up its purchase on the door and he heard the wooden lock drop with a thud. He straightened and glanced towards Edmund. 'Who does Clara say gave birth to Eleanor if not Lady Anne?'

'Most of it's guesswork. She only told us a short while ago, and Father said she was probably mixing things up in her mind. It's hard to remember what happened two years ago, let alone fourteen.'

'Why did she tell you at all?' Thaddeus asked.

Edmund pulled a wry expression. 'She saw me looking at Eleanor on the forecourt one day and gave me a slapping for it. She called her a changeling and said I'd regret every day of my life if I ever looked at her in that way again. It was why I was pretty keen to leave, as a matter of fact. She'd have drawn my innards if she found out what we'd been doing in the church.'

'It would have served you right if she had,' said Thaddeus unsympathetically. 'What else did she say?'

'I'm not sure I believed it, and even if I did—' He broke off. 'I mean, how's it fair to blame Eleanor? It's not *her* fault if her father was a swine.'

Peter punched him on the arm. 'Give!' he ordered.

'All right, all right! According to Mother, Sir Richard drove Lady Anne to Foxcote at the request of My Lord of Foxcote when she was four months gone with child . . . or claimed she was. The wet nurse said My Lord of Foxcote had summoned Lady Anne to tend his younger sister, who was too ill to leave her room. Lady Anne spent all her time with the girl and twenty weeks after she arrived the baby was born. A week later, My Lord of Foxcote's sister was sent to a convent and Lady Anne took on the wet nurse to feed the infant.'

'It's an intriguing tale,' said Thaddeus slowly. 'How come Clara's the only one who knows it?'

'Lady Anne asked her to suckle Eleanor because she was still in milk for me. The wet nurse had become homesick for her family and kept crying all the time. She whispered the story to Mother before she went home, but Mother kept it to herself for the sake of Lady Anne and the baby.'

Peter was sceptical. 'It can't be true. Why would Lady Anne agree to such a thing? She was young when she married Sir Richard and could have had children of her own. Why burden herself with someone else's child when she might just as easily have played the part of guardian?'

'Mother says she made a promise to Eleanor's mother,' answered Edmund. 'The wet nurse said My Lord of Foxcote would have had the baby smothered at birth if Lady Anne hadn't agreed to take it on. He's not a nice man. She said he kept punching his sister in the belly to bring on a miscarriage until Milady rescued her.'

'How old was the sister?' Thaddeus asked.

'Younger than Eleanor is now,' answered Edmund. 'Mother said it was rape—the same way Sir Richard raped Abigail Startout.'

With sudden savagery, Thaddeus kicked the door open with his foot. 'There's your answer,' he told Peter, stepping inside. 'Lady Anne saved two little girls by what she did . . . though I doubt she's ever been thanked for it.'

❧

The air inside the building was heavy with the stale odours of urine, used in the softening of hides, but they weren't unpleasant enough to force a retreat. Thaddeus and Edmund said the smell of corpses in Afpedle was worse. They moved around the upright barrels on the floor, lifting lids to examine the contents. Most were empty, but the fumes that came out of the two or three that were full made their eyes sting.

They all recognised the place for what it was—a tannery—but none had seen a commercial one before. Thaddeus used his chisel to stir the fluid inside one of the barrels and pulled up the corner of a skin. It had been immersed so long that the leather was beginning to dissolve, and the metal blade tore through the slimy fabric. He moved to the end wall where a series of looms stood in a line, some with half-finished fabric woven into the warp threads. 'It's not just a tannery,' he said. 'They have weavers here too.'

'How do they stand the smell?' asked Edmund, stooping to examine a stretching frame.

'The same way we do, by getting used to it . . . but I expect the vats are kept outside when there are people here.' Thaddeus glanced towards some rickety stairs in the corner, barely more than a ladder leading to a trapdoor in the ceiling. 'Do you want to see if there's anything on the floor above?' he asked Edmund. 'There's nothing for us here.'

The boy looked towards the ladder with a reluctant expression. 'What if there are rats? I won't be able to see them.'

'You could try lighting this,' said Peter, lifting a torch from a pile in the corner and touching the resin-soaked rope around its top to see if it was still sticky.

'We should take them back to the camp,' Edmund said. 'They'll be of more use to us there. I wonder why they needed so many?'

'Because the workers toiled at night as well as day,' Thaddeus answered, nodding to the brackets around the walls. 'I'm guessing these steps lead to a dormitory.' He ordered Peter to hold the torch steady while he coaxed a flame from the inn's tinderbox.

'You're mad,' Edmund protested. 'What will you find anyway? People don't leave things where they sleep.'

'Don't you have any curiosity about the world outside Develish?'

Edmund moved towards the open doorway. 'Not if rats are involved.'

Thaddeus used a spill to warm the resin enough to take a small flame and then left Peter to blow it into life while he mounted the steps to examine the trapdoor. He half expected to find another complicated lock, but a simple heave lifted the panel clear of its frame and he was able to slide it backwards across the floor. He was surprised to feel a draught of air ruffle his hair and he raised his head cautiously to peer through the hole, turning to look the length of the room.

An opening in the centre of the roof, overgrown with green shoots from the live wheat straw that had been used as thatch, allowed dappled daylight to filter inside. It created a confusing scene of strange-looking shadows, and a shiver of shock ran through Thaddeus as his eyes picked out a man standing beside the left-hand wall. He would have leapt from the ladder if Peter hadn't squeezed up beside him and raised the torch above his head.

They both laughed as the flames showed the 'man' to be a fur-trimmed, leather coat hanging on a wooden frame with a conical beaver hat perched atop it. 'Godalmighty!' Thaddeus growled, seizing the torch and climbing out onto the floor. 'I thought it was Sir Richard come back from the dead.'

Peter scrambled up after him. 'Pretty dandy, eh?' He ran a finger down the fur. 'Even my mother doesn't sew this well and she's the best seamstress in Develish.'

Thaddeus opened the lid of a coffer and sniffed the rue and lavender which had been sprinkled over the woollen tunics inside to keep them free of moths. A second coffer held britches, a third jerkins. 'I don't know what we've done right,' he murmured, 'but God seems to be on our side.'

'There are saddles and bridles here,' called Peter from the far end of the room. 'Look!' He dangled some reins from his hand.

Thaddeus placed the torch in a bracket on the wall and cast his eye around the room. It was an artisan's workshop, he realised. Tanners and weavers below, a tailor at this end of the upper storey, a leather worker at the other, and all manner of craftsmen in between. He thought of their anguish when they returned to find that robbers had stolen what they'd laboured months to make, but his sympathy was short-lived. He seemed to have discovered as strong a taste for thieving as his stepfather.

'We'll take the lot,' he said. 'Empty every coffer and throw the contents down to Edmund. We can discard anything we don't want when we're back at the camp.'

☙

The watery sun, obscured by clouds, was two hours from setting by the time their tasks were finished. Thaddeus, who had borne the brunt of the heavy lifting, looked weary as he shouldered the last of the kegs onto the wagon for the final journey, and the boys put his introspection down to fatigue. By then, the twins had joined them, leaving only Joshua to work on the arrows, but despite breaking into other smaller dwellings, little else of value had been found. Apart from cats.

Olyver claimed to have seen a dozen but, since they were all black, Ian said he'd probably counted the same ones twice. Two or three were tame enough to handle, and the boys quickly lost their fear of them as they ran their hands across the silky fur, delighting in the way the animals arched their backs and rumbled sweet purrs from their mouths. Thaddeus, watching, thought they'd be easy to capture when the time came to return to Develish; and if rats were truly the source of the pestilence, these incubi of Satan might prove the best gift of all.

∽

All the boys, even Joshua and Peter, viewed new clothes and tools as reason to celebrate, turning cartwheels on the sward and punching each other's arms in playful fighting. Thaddeus endured their boisterous high spirits for a quarter-hour before walking west along the riverbank towards Athelhelm. He halted when he drew opposite Afpedle and leant against the trunk of an alder to gaze on the deserted demesne. It would please him to see My Lord of Afpedle ride through his gate with a phalanx of soldiers if it meant he could stop thinking, even for a moment, of Lady Anne. All afternoon he had been pushing thoughts of her from his mind, but it wasn't a battle he could win. There was too much heaviness in his heart to dismiss his feeling of loss as easily as he dismissed other emotions.

He tried to concentrate on the problems that remained. By dividing the load across several trips, his fears that the wagon would become bogged down in the sward hadn't materialised, but it was clear that three horses would be needed to pull it fully laden. Yet where to find extra horse collars? And what route should they follow from here to Develish? Without knowledge of the roads, they would be travelling blind.

Worry piled upon worry. The wind had strengthened and he had only to shift his gaze to the western sky to see that angry clouds were forming. With luck the rain would hold off until tomorrow, but it seemed that what God gave with one hand he took away with the other, because their efforts of the day would come to nothing when the heavens opened. The kegs of grain and flour would be saturated, and weeks might pass before Athelhelm was dry enough to burn. He told himself he should return to the camp and set about building a shelter, but he lingered on, his thoughts overwhelmed with doubt and uncertainty.

Lady Anne owed him nothing, and yet it wounded him deeply to think she'd lied to him. He was what he was because of her kindness to him—and he thanked her for it—but he found it hard to accept that she'd allowed Sir Richard's bastard to be treated so differently from Eva's. Why protect Eleanor but do nothing to stop Thaddeus being beaten raw because his 'whore' of a mother had given him birth? Why claim that all men were born equal only to prove by her actions that she didn't believe it? Were the sins of fornication and illegitimacy worse in serfs than in lords?

He couldn't bring himself to acknowledge that his sense of betrayal had more to do with his own feelings than Lady Anne's. In the past few months he'd dared to believe that his love for her was returned. Why else would she express her trust and confidence in him so openly when she raised him from slave to steward on the death of her husband, or speak so freely about her ambition to escape the bonds of chattel marriage to live the life she

chose? Why release her hair from its wimple in his presence or
lean her small body into his when they were reading the ledgers
or keeping count of the rations? Had he imagined these moments
of intimacy? Thaddeus had never sought to exploit the affection
she showed him—he was too shy and too careful of her reputation
to cause gossiping tongues to wag—but in his heart he'd dared to
believe the affection was real.

Yet, if Edmund had spoken the truth, she'd feigned the
emotions of a mother for a decade and a half with such ease
that none had doubted her. Certainly not Thaddeus. A bitterness
entered his heart as he thought how easily he'd been beguiled.
He'd accepted everything Milady had told him from the moment
she'd found him when he was six years old, hiding behind the
church, nursing bruises from one of Will's beatings. She'd smiled
into his eyes, smoothed liniment onto his skin and urged him to
say nothing of their meeting to his parents. It will be our secret,
she had said.

But what had possessed him to think he was alone in sharing
a confidence with her? How many others had been sworn to
silence? He recalled the deceits she'd practised on Sir Richard to
keep him from learning that it was she who managed the demesne,
and the deceits she'd taught her people to hide the sedition and
heresy she preached to them. Was this how she'd earned their
love? Through pretence and lies?

Thaddeus longed to think Edmund's story was the product of
two women gossiping over a mewling infant, but it explained so
much if Eleanor wasn't Lady Anne's daughter. Thaddeus couldn't
recall the number of times he'd wondered why there was so little of
the mother in the child. In every respect Eleanor was the image
of her father, yet if Thaddeus was clear about anything, it was that
Eleanor neither knew nor had guessed that another woman had

given her birth. She was too fond of calling Thaddeus a bastard to be hiding the same knowledge about herself. Even a girl as stupid as Eleanor would hesitate to cast a slur that she knew might come back to haunt her if her secret was revealed.

Thaddeus's thoughts turned to Jacob's death, and he cursed himself for sparing Eleanor to protect Lady Anne. It seemed to him now that he had sacrificed justice for his brother on a lie, leaving Jacob's premature death unchallenged in order to save a mother from the heartache of learning the truth about her daughter. But how hollow that sacrifice was if the girl bore no relationship to the woman.

And how angry would Thaddeus be if his decision to remove the boys had encouraged Eleanor to accuse them in her place? He was a fool to have placed himself and the sons of men he respected in peril for the sake of a vicious changeling who was no better than he was.

෧෮

The light was fading fast by the time Thaddeus returned to the camp, and his simmering frustrations came to the boil when he found the boys mincing about the sward in the stolen finery, waving swords at each other and pretending to be lords and fighting men. Weighed down as he was by regret and responsibility, such childish pranks stole the last of his patience.

He wanted to scream his resentments to the sky. Rail against the demands his mother and Will had placed on him from childhood. Curse his foolish brother for giving Eleanor reason to kill him. Condemn Lady Anne for her lies, and these boys for their immaturity. Must his life always be lived for other people? Must he always rein in his emotions for fear of the anger that raged inside him?

He knocked the beaver hat from Edmund's head and wrestled the fur-lined leather coat from his shoulders. 'What in blazes do you think you're doing?' he growled at them all. 'Have you not seen the rain clouds in the west? Do you not feel the strengthening wind? You should be building a shelter, not wasting time on idiotic games. If the heavens don't open tonight, they will tomorrow.'

Edmund took a mutinous step backwards. 'We were just having fun,' he muttered. 'If it comes to that, why haven't *you* built a shelter?'

Thaddeus made no answer, merely stared from one to the other as if he'd never seen them before. Ian took an uncertain step forward. He felt he should offer comfort but didn't know what to say or why it was needed, and his hesitation meant the opportunity was lost. Thaddeus stooped to retrieve Killer's saddle and harness and headed towards the hobbled horses, quietly cropping the grass some fifty yards distant.

Puzzled, the boys turned to watch him. 'Why is he in such a bad mood?' Peter whispered. 'He should be pleased to have found a wagon.'

'More to the point, where's he going?' murmured Ian as Thaddeus slipped the bridle over Killer's head. 'It'll be pitch-black in an hour. He won't be able to see a thing and he's had nothing to eat. None of us has.'

They waited in silence while Thaddeus buckled the girths, donned the coat and swung into the saddle before walking Killer towards them. He paused beside the wagon to take a chaperon hood from the pile of garments, pulling the soft cloth over his head for warmth before placing the beaver hat on top. Next he selected a pair of leather mittens which were broad enough to take his palm, then he gestured to the pile of torches on the ground. 'Hand them up,' he ordered Olyver, taking them one at a time and balancing them in front of him. 'Now my sword and kitbag.' He looped the weapon over his head and checked the bag to make sure his tinderbox was inside. 'You can die of cold for all I care,' he said, turning Killer's head towards the path that led to Athelhelm. 'But I'll have your hides if one of those barrels gets wet. I haven't broken my back all day to deliver rotten grain to Develish.'

∽

Shamed to action, the boys set about building a shelter inside the woodland. For once, they worked as a team, aware that each was as guilty as the next for failing to think of it for themselves. Edmund cleared the ground beneath four young beech trees which had branches still supple enough to bend. By hacking off the lower ones with the axe, he was able to bind them into those at head height to form a rough square base for a roof. Ian and Olyver cut withies from the osiers along the riverbank to weave into a framework to sit atop the branches, while Peter and Joshua collected bracken, water reeds and sedge to form a thatch.

As darkness fell, Joshua pointed to sparks shooting into the sky above the trees to the west. 'Thaddeus is burning Athelhelm,' he said.

'We're not blind,' Ian snapped irritably.

'Why didn't he take us with him?'

'Because he knew he could do it quicker and better on his own,' said Olyver, kicking the arrows they'd spent the morning fletching and mounting with the iron heads. 'We didn't have to make these. It's just as easy for him to sit on Killer's back and throw burning torches onto the thatch. The rats can't get him if he's astride a horse.'

Peter, crouching on a barrel, twisted another withy into the wattle roof they were weaving. 'He does everything quicker and better on his own. All we do is hold him back.'

'Speak for yourself,' said Edmund, toiling to light a fire with the tinderbox from the inn so that they could see what they were doing.

'I am. It wasn't me who pulled the smithy wall down. Thaddeus could have done it by himself. He only took me along to make me feel useful.'

'He couldn't have burnt Afpedle on his own.'

'You sure about that?' asked Olyver sarcastically. 'He's making a pretty good blaze out of Athelhelm. Peter's right. None of us does a damn thing unless he tells us when and how to do it.'

'He's doing it himself because he knows there are people still alive in the cottages,' Ian retorted. 'It means none of us will have murder on his conscience, so show some gratitude for once.'

'Do you think that's why he lost his temper?'

'It would make me lose mine.'

Thirty-one

Develish, Dorseteshire

HUGH DE COURTESMAIN RETREATED WELL into the shadows when Eleanor emerged from the spinning room and walked to the head of the stairs. She had lost the wild madness he had seen so short a time ago—indeed, she looked as pretty as he'd ever seen her, with her bruises disguised by powder and a blush of rouge on her cheeks—but her inability to recognise the animosity in the room or take anything from the stony silence that greeted her alarmed him. Did she have no understanding of what these people thought of her?

He wondered at her foolishness in facing her accusers in this way. If he had worried the mob would become angry at the mother making excuses for the daughter, how much worse would the mob's resentment be when the daughter tried to excuse herself? He doubted Eleanor had the necessary humility to make an apology.

He watched Lady Anne send Isabella down the steps before turning towards her daughter. 'Where would you have me stand?' she asked. 'Below with our people or here with you?'

'Below.'

'Are you sure, Eleanor? Have you thought wisely about what you wish to say?' She made a gesture of entreaty. 'There will be no turning back from the decision you make now. Once spoken, a word cannot be recalled.'

The girl stared at her with dislike. 'You should have taken your own advice, should you not? When My Lord of Blandeforde hears of the rebellion you've been preaching to these serfs, he'll have you dragged in chains to his dungeons. They will share your fate if they leave this demesne without my permission.' She looked with contempt at the crowd. 'Do you hear what I say?'

No one answered. The only sound was the shuffle of feet as the crowd at the front parted to allow Lady Anne to take her place amongst them. Indeed, Hugh couldn't remember ever hearing such a silence as that which blanketed the room while Eleanor declared herself the rightful mistress of the demesne. There was no hint of apology to Isabella, only disdain for the whole serf class and for the woman who had allowed them to think of Develish as their own. Yet the reaction to her revelation that Lady Anne had finally confessed to usurping the powers of a mother was an even deeper silence.

'Are you too stupid to understand my meaning?' Eleanor demanded angrily. 'Lady Anne is barren but pretended she was not by claiming me as her child. She has lied to you all these years to give herself a position in Develish as mother to Sir Richard's heir. She had no right to take control of the demesne or even act as my guardian once my father was dead.'

She was answered by the rasp of a man clearing his throat. 'You're an ungrateful miss,' growled Will Thurkell, spitting phlegm on the floor. 'There's not many will take a bastard into their house. You should be down on your knees thanking Milady for her charity, not condemning her for saving you from servitude.'

Eleanor's eyes widened in shock, and Hugh wondered if it had occurred to her that she would be labelled a by-blow. 'Do you dare to question that Sir Richard was my father?'

'It makes no difference whether he was or not. I'll not bend my knee to a harlot's daughter.'

'You'll be flogged for insolence if you speak in that way again.'

Will gave a grunt of derision. 'You're mighty uppity for a half-grown girl. I owed you some respect while Lady Anne claimed you—if only for her sake—but you'll get none from me now. She's been a better mother to you than I was father to Thaddeus. I'd sooner bend my knee to the cur I raised than a vicious mongrel who gives herself airs for no reason.'

The murmurs of agreement from the crowd sounded ominous to Hugh's ears and he watched to see how Eleanor would respond. Surely she must realise that without Lady Anne's protection she had made herself vulnerable to these people's anger? It seemed not. She had learnt her behaviour from her father and, whether through madness or stupidity, she appeared to think her world had been unaffected by the coming of the pestilence.

He felt a small pity for her as she raged at being compared with a base-born slave. It wasn't for a cuckold like Will Thurkell to put the daughter of Sir Richard of Develish on a par with the changeling his whore of a wife had tried to pass off as his. She was the daughter of a lady—the sister of My Lord of Foxcote—and could claim status from both her parents.

'My father wanted an heir,' she said, pointing an accusing finger at Lady Anne, 'but this woman couldn't give him one. She acted the part of my mother to cover her own sins. Do you think she'd have kept the circumstances of my birth secret if she could have given Sir Richard a son?'

This time Clara Trueblood spoke. 'By that token, every woman here is barren. Do you see your father's features in any of our children? He forced himself on all of us until Lady Anne came to Develish and took his cruelty upon herself. Mercifully for us, his seed lacked strength, otherwise you would have bastard half-brothers and -sisters throughout the demesne.'

'And all with the heartless nature you've inherited so well,' said Martha Startout in a small, tight voice. 'Your father wasn't satisfied unless he caused women and children pain—just as you like to do yourself, missy.' She studied Eleanor with open dislike. 'I have reason to celebrate this day, despite the hurt you've done my Isabella. It gives me joy that not one drop of Lady Anne's blood runs in your veins. She is too good and kind to have produced a daughter such as you.'

'You will bend your knee to me even so,' Eleanor snapped. 'For I will have Lady Anne burnt as a heretic if you do not. Do you think My Lord of Blandeforde will listen to the whinings of a peasant woman before he listens to the daughter of Sir Richard?'

Could such a threat work? Hugh wondered. It was hard to tell from the guarded expressions of those around him.

Once again, Eleanor's words were greeted with silence and she turned in frustration to Lady Anne. 'I mean what I say. You will burn as a witch if they don't pay me homage. I have only to repeat the sacrilege you spoke in the church, and My Lord of Blandeforde will condemn you to fire. Make these people understand that.'

'They understand you perfectly well, Eleanor. Nothing I can say will make your meaning clearer.'

'Then they will burn with you. It is I who controls their fate, not you.'

With a sigh of boredom, Gyles Startout stepped forward and turned to face the crowd. 'We waste time listening to this nonsense. My Lord of Blandeforde won't be interested in the rantings of a mad girl. His lands are vast and it will take him many months to discover which of his vassal demesnes have survived the pestilence. Our choice is simple. To accept whichever lord he sends to Develish, or to leave before his messengers arrive.'

'What choice will *you* make, Gyles?' called a woman.

'To seek freedom for my family with Lady Anne.'

A chorus of voices rose in agreement as men called out their names and shouted, 'My family also.'

Gyles held up his hand. 'James Buckler told you how it is. The decision about when to leave may be forced on us if Thaddeus and our sons do not return soon. With careful rationing—' He broke off in surprise as John Trueblood darted forward and pushed him to one side.

'Oh, no, you don't,' the man ordered, catching Eleanor's wrist and twisting it behind her back as she reached the bottom of the stairs. 'You've done enough damage for one day.' He plucked the bodkin from her fingers and threw it to the floor before turning to Lady Anne. 'If she's suffering from madness, milady, it's a powerful dangerous madness. She'll kill before long. What are we to do with her?'

'That's for you and my other leading serfs to decide, John. She freed me of responsibility when she renounced me as her mother.'

'Martha and Gyles will insist she answers for the wounds she inflicted on Isabella.'

'And so they should.'

Eleanor tried to wrest herself free from John's grip, kicking out at Lady Anne while she did so. 'This man is little better than a slave,' she hissed. 'Make him unhand me!'

But Lady Anne shook her head. 'You chose this path yourself, Eleanor. You must make the rest of the journey alone.'

Tears of frustration—and fear?—limned the girl's lashes. 'I suppose you planned all this with Thaddeus before he left.'

There was a small hesitation before Lady Anne answered. 'You know better than anyone that I did not, Eleanor. The death of his brother Jacob meant there was no time to plan anything. Have you forgotten so easily the tragedy that befell the Thurkell family? I assure you, I have not.'

It was evident to all that something in Lady Anne's words caused Eleanor to have second thoughts. She ceased her struggles immediately and ordered John Trueblood to return her to the spinning room. When he made no move to obey, she addressed Lady Anne. 'Order him to do it. I don't choose to remain here.'

'That may be so, Eleanor, but you have accusations to answer— and since the spinning room is one of *my* chambers, I've already decided that the women who've been sleeping outside should have it. Your possessions will be removed once a decision has been reached about where to house you.'

Hugh watched the play of expressions on Eleanor's face. They were as simple to read as a painstakingly crafted alphabet on a child's slate. He could almost hear the pendulum ticking in her mind as she counted through her options. All too predictably, she appealed to Lady Anne's sympathies.

'You've been my mother in name these fourteen years. Will you abandon me now?'

'You give me no choice,' Lady Anne said gently. 'I haven't the power to alter the decisions you've made. You must do as the rest of us do and learn to live with them.'

She held John Trueblood's gaze for a moment, as if passing authority to him, and then walked up the stairs to her chamber.

❧

James Buckler and Adam Catchpole stepped in front of Hugh de Courtesmain as he tried to slip quietly out of the front door at the rear of the crowd. It was clear to both that he was looking to absent himself from Eleanor's questioning, although they couldn't know it was because he was afraid Isabella would reveal the part he'd played in placing her in danger. He hoped that if he were out of sight he would also be out of mind.

'Your presence is demanded on the forecourt, sir,' said Buckler amiably, nodding to where Eleanor was screaming her rage at Alleyn and Gyles Startout for marching her out with pinioned arms.

Hugh ran his tongue across his lips. He was even more afraid of what Eleanor would reveal of his whispered conversations with her through the spinning room door. He'd receive no sympathy from these people if she repeated his pledges of loyalty and friendship. 'I have urgent business to discuss with Father Anselm,' he muttered.

'There's nothing so urgent it can't wait an hour, sir. You're the only one amongst us who has some understanding of the law. It's common knowledge you administered justice in Foxcote.'

Hugh's eyes widened in alarm. Eleanor would be provoked into mouthing all manner of beastliness against him if he was forced to play the role of judge. 'You're mistaken. I know nothing of the law. Who told you this falsehood?'

'Sir Richard. He spread the word freely before you came that his new steward wouldn't tolerate thieving. He warned us to account precisely for every bushel of grain we harvested or you would have us punished, telling us you were a righteous zealot who would have a man flogged rather than let him feed his starving family.'

The words of Lady Beatrix's letter to her brother rose in Hugh's memory. 'The law on evasion of taxes is different from other laws,' he answered weakly.

'Then you must do your best with what you have,' Catchpole told him. 'Someone has to make this foolish girl understand she can't behave as she did and expect to get away with it.'

'It's not the place of a steward to stand in judgement on her. Only Lady Anne can do that. The rights of nobles to be tried by their peers is well established.'

'And the young miss will be cock-a-hoop if she can force Milady to do it,' said Buckler, taking Hugh's arm and urging him, none too gently, into movement. 'You play the part of steward prettily enough when the mistress does the work; now show us you can do it for real.'

Hugh pulled against him. 'What are you expecting of me?'

'What your role demands, sir. At the very least, Martha's daughter is owed some justice for the wounds on her breasts and arms. If she doesn't receive it from you, the people of Develish may decide to exact revenge themselves . . . and that will be worse for Lady Eleanor than any punishment you decide to impose.'

'But she won't listen to reason,' Hugh protested, watching the girl's fury at being handled by peasants. 'Anger has overcome her senses.'

'Then don't reason with her,' countered Catchpole. 'You were a witness to her imprisonment of Isabella, were you not? If she refuses to answer the charges Isabella makes against her, you can find her guilty from what you observed yourself.' He saw the resistance in Hugh's face. 'Do you think Thaddeus would refuse to act if he were here? He has no love for Lady Eleanor, but he wouldn't allow her to be attacked by a crowd rather than order her to be detained for a period of time in a serf's hut.'

Hugh's eyes narrowed. 'You seem well enough briefed in how to conduct a trial, Master Catchpole. Why press the role of judge on me if you can do it yourself? Are you more afraid than you'll admit to challenge God's natural order?'

Adam gave an amused shake of his head. 'That is *your* fear, sir. You would rather hide yourself away than give Lady Eleanor reason to accuse you when My Lord of Blandeforde's messengers come.' He prodded the little Frenchman with his finger. 'Are you a mouse or a man? Do the tantrums of a spoilt miss frighten you so much?'

'You asked for the law and I gave it to you. None of us has the right to try Lady Eleanor. Would you have me pretend otherwise?'

'Not if it makes you uncomfortable. It was through courtesy only that we offered you the chance to preside.' Adam nodded to James Buckler. 'Keep a firm grip on him. He'll make himself a laughing-stock if he has to be dragged from the church to give his testimony.'

How often Hugh cursed his foolishness afterwards. It was he who had told Eleanor that power would rest with whoever was clever enough and strong enough to seize it, yet when the chance came he lacked the courage to take it for himself. He could have won admiration if he'd conducted Eleanor's trial with the scrupulous fairness John Trueblood brought to it. Instead, he showed himself to be an unwilling participant, visibly reluctant to commit himself to anything when Trueblood requested him to step forward and give his evidence.

The crowd of serfs had formed a large ring around the fore-court, creating an empty circle at its heart where John Trueblood stood between Eleanor and Isabella—the one restrained by Adam Catchpole and Alleyn Startout, the other supported by the arms of her mother and father. The maid, pale and clearly tired, had told her story in a quiet voice, making no mention of why she had gone to the spinning room, describing only what had happened after she entered. Her one reference to Hugh was when she explained how the steward and Lady Anne had come to rescue her, and how Eleanor had plunged the bodkin into her breast to make her cry out.

The expression on Eleanor's face told Hugh he would not get off so lightly when his turn came, unless he gave her reason to be grateful. The stare she fixed on the Frenchman was full of enmity when James Buckler forced him to take a pace forward and expose himself to her view. Invited by Trueblood to give evidence in support of Isabella's story, Hugh shook his head and said he could not. Yes, he had gone to the spinning room with Lady Anne, but since the chamber was barred to them he couldn't swear on oath that what the maid said was true. He hadn't even known of her presence inside until Lady Eleanor opened the door of her own volition.

John Trueblood frowned. 'Let me understand you,' he murmured when Hugh came to the end of his unhelpful responses. 'You can't say Isabella was a prisoner because the door has no lock and was opened quite easily by Lady Eleanor. You can't say Isabella was badly injured because she had no trouble walking from the room with Lady Anne. You can't say there was blood on her dress because Lady Anne shielded her from your view. And you can't say Lady Eleanor acted with malice because you didn't witness her doing so. Is that correct?'

'Yes.'

'Yet Isabella tells us you were on the other side of the door when Lady Eleanor pushed the bodkin into her breast to make her cry out. Is that not true? Was Isabella lying?'

'I don't recall. I believe Lady Anne had already asked me to step aside by then.'

'And well she might,' the man said bluntly. 'You were of little use to her if you saw no danger in the situation. Isabella told us she was afraid Lady Eleanor had lost her wits. Did you have the same idea when the spinning room door opened?'

'I remember her being a little dishevelled, but I made no decision about the state of her mind.'

Trueblood dismissed him with a wave of his hand and turned to Eleanor, inviting her to answer the charges of imprisonment and bodily harm. She had stood in mutinous silence while Isabella and Hugh had given evidence, but now she allowed her tongue free rein, refusing to recognise the court and castigating slaves for daring to stand in judgement on her.

'Do you deny that you held Isabella captive and wounded her with a bodkin?' Trueblood asked when she finally came to a halt.

'You are beneath me. I will not answer your questions.'

'As you wish. But do you understand that this is your only chance to speak on your own behalf?' He nodded to where Hugh was standing. 'I will ask Master de Courtesmain to plead for you, if you prefer. He seems to have sympathy with your plight.'

'You will do no such thing. I have as much scorn for him as I have for you. He was quick enough to betray my father . . . as was every man here. Blame yourselves for my anger and hatred of the serf class before you blame me.'

'Would you rather we'd all perished of the pestilence, Lady Eleanor?'

'Yes.'

'Yourself, too?'

'It would have been God's will if I had.'

'Then it was God's will that your father died and Isabella's did not, so should you not accuse God of betraying you before you accuse us? Do you think you'd be in this sorry situation, milady, if the Almighty favoured the Devilishes as much as He favours the Startouts?'

Eleanor's eyes, white and wide, told everyone that this was indeed what she feared. Perhaps it also explained her hatred of Gyles's daughter. The comfortable world she had known under her father existed no more. She could storm and threaten as much as she liked, but the God she knew had resided in Develish only while Sir Richard was alive.

A boy's treble voice broke the silence that followed. 'I'll speak for Lady Eleanor if no one else will, Master Trueblood.'

'Step forward.'

Robert Startout pushed his way into the circle and looked hard into Eleanor's eyes. 'Do you wish me to? I owe you this favour for not having me whipped.'

To everyone's surprise, she gave a small nod.

He turned to address the crowd. 'I've been wondering what it's like to be Lady Eleanor. Me, I'd be pretty mad if my father died of the pestilence and no one said they were sorry about it . . . madder still if I found out that Lady Anne wasn't my mother. I don't say that gives her the right to prick Isabella, but I do say it gives her reason to feel angry. *I'd* be angry.' He made a small bow to John Trueblood. 'That's all . . . 'cept I doubt Isabella wants Lady Eleanor punished as badly as my aunt Martha would like.'

გა

As darkness fell, Isabella made her way to the steward's office, where she found Lady Anne writing by candlelight. The woman raised her head to smile at the girl and ask her how she was before gesturing to a stool and urging her to sit. 'I'm sorry Eleanor treated you so badly, Isabella. I should have warned you more strongly to stay away from her.'

'It's not your fault, milady. I knew better than anyone that she was ill-disposed towards me.' She lowered herself to the stool and folded her hands over a square of parchment in her lap.

'Why did you go to her?'

'Master de Courtesmain ordered me. He said the instruction came from you.'

Lady Anne shook her head. 'He lied. I gave no such order.'

'I didn't think you would have done, milady, but he was very insistent.' She gave an apologetic smile. 'I would have come to ask you, but he never left my side.' She paused. 'I still don't understand what purpose he had in sending me to Lady Eleanor . . . unless he wanted her to hurt me.'

'I doubt it was that, Isabella. He was very shocked when he saw what she'd done.'

'Then why?'

'To win her favour. I imagine she asked for you by name, and he hoped that by seeking you out he would be rewarded for his diligence. He's curious about why I had her removed from my chamber. He thinks if he knows the reason it will give him an advantage. Did he try to speak with her again after she took you prisoner?'

Isabella shook her head. 'Only Mistress Trueblood came. Lady Eleanor didn't answer her and wouldn't allow me to either.'

'Where is Lady Eleanor now?'

'Master Trueblood has ordered her to be confined in the hut next to his for fifteen days—one day for each prick she made. It was my cousin Robert's idea. He spoke for her when no one else would, and I was glad that he did.'

'Does the punishment satisfy you?'

Isabella nodded. 'It's better that she's detained away from sharp objects, milady. She's not in her right mind. She caused herself to bleed as often as she did me. I had no wish to see her given a harsher sentence.'

Lady Anne studied the girl's sweet face, which reminded her so powerfully of Abigail's. 'Do you feel sorry for her?'

'I do, milady. She believes herself nothing unless she's acknowledged as the daughter of Sir Richard of Develish. For myself, I would hate to feel so empty.'

'Yet she does nothing to earn her people's respect.'

'She doesn't know how, milady. Sir Richard taught her that a serf who is treated badly will bend his knee more easily than one who is treated well. She made me swear allegiance to her many times to avoid having the bodkin plunged into my eyes.' The girl stared down at the parchment, turning it between her fingers.

'Is there something else you think I should know, Isabella?'

'I fear so, milady, but you will not want to hear it. You should first read this letter which Thaddeus left for me.' She placed it on the desk. 'I beg you to believe that what he says in it is true.'

Lady Anne reached for the parchment with some reluctance, recognising the handwriting and seeing the sentiments expressed in the first line. *My Good Friend, I have never needed your kindness and wisdom more* . . . 'Are you sure, Isabella? I doubt Thaddeus intended me to see this.'

'He will not mind if I do not, milady.'

Lady Anne moved the page closer to the candlelight and scanned the words.

I do what I do to free your brothers and their friends from intrigue, not to ensnare them in more . . . *Protect yourself by saying nothing of what you witnessed this morning with Lady Eleanor* . . .

It was a moment or two before Lady Anne spoke. 'I should have asked you long since what you knew, but I was afraid to hear it.'

'I'm glad you didn't, milady. I wouldn't have wanted to lie to you.'

'Will you tell me now? I have suspected from the beginning that Eleanor was responsible for Jacob's death, and that Thaddeus's companions were involved in some way, so nothing you say will shock me.'

But how wrong she was. Some of Isabella's story related to the scene she had witnessed between Thaddeus and Eleanor on the day he left, but most was drawn from what Eleanor had revealed in the spinning room during the hours of Isabella's imprisonment that afternoon. And it was all so much worse than anything Lady Anne had imagined.

'Was she telling the truth?' she asked Isabella at the end.

'I believe so, milady. She has starved and hurt herself to no purpose. She made me put my hand on her belly and I could feel the swelling. Her thinness means she can still fit into her gowns for the moment, but her condition will become visible soon. She is sorely in need of your help, I think.'

Lady Anne sat on in the office alone after the girl had left, and it was only when the candle flame began to flicker as the wick reached its end that she told herself she must get up and leave. Yet she was too weary to move. The truth she'd wanted from Isabella was who had fathered Eleanor's baby, but it wasn't a question the girl could answer.

All Isabella could do was repeat what Eleanor had told her: that Jacob Thurkell and the five boys who had left with Thaddeus had taken it in turns to violate her inside the church.

⁓

Father Anselm was passed out on the dregs of his mead barrel, and it was several minutes before the persistent knocking on his door penetrated his bleary mind. He would have rolled over and gone back to sleep if he hadn't recognised Lady Anne's voice and seen the light from her lantern shining through the cracks in the oak planking. 'I need you out here in the church, Father. It matters not what state you are in.'

When he didn't reply, she resumed her knocking, an irritating rat-a-tat which caused his head to throb. 'What is so important that it cannot wait for daybreak?' he grumbled.

'I am troubled, sir. Would you deny me confession just because it's dark outside?'

The old man sat up and rubbed his eyes. 'You haven't sought absolution since you became a widow, milady, and you only did so before out of pretence at piety. Why should I believe you want to make peace with your Maker now?'

'It's not for you to decide, Father, only to remember that Jesus said there would be joy in Heaven over one sinner who repented.'

She heard his grunts as he levered himself to his feet, heard the sound of him pissing into his pot and his mutterings of discontent as he told himself it was a trick to tease him from his warm bed. What a dreadful creature he was, Lady Anne thought, as the door opened and the rank odours of urine and stale drunken breath accompanied him into the church. Had her husband really believed that such a man could intercede between him and God? Had Eleanor believed it when she'd hammered on his door and wailed her distress to the whole of Develish?

She walked to the altar and placed her lantern beside the cross, pushing back the hood of her cloak and showing her face. 'You and I have never trusted each other,' she told him. 'You were taught to believe in the religion of the Church, and I was taught that the word of God is written in the Bible. They are not the same. Jesus preached love while the Church preaches only cruelty and fear.'

The priest glared at her. 'This does not sound like confession, milady. Would you add lying to all your other sins?'

'I can mouth a few *mea culpas*, if it makes you happy, Father, but you'll return to your bed the sooner if we forgo such nonsense. God is able to read what is in my heart without the need for you to translate for Him.'

'God can read nothing in a heart that is closed. There is no greater sin than heresy. Do you think I was deaf to what you said to Lady Eleanor in front of this altar?'

Lady Anne shook her head. 'No more than to anything else that happens inside your church.' She held his gaze. 'You seem to pick and choose the sins you condemn, Father. Was my little lie to draw you from your chamber in the middle of the night more heinous than Jacob's murder?'

The old man's brain was too fuddled to pretend ignorance. He stared back at her, but not with an expression that said the idea was new to him. She watched the contortions of his red-veined face as the implications of her words sank in. *If she knew Jacob hadn't died by accident, what else did she know?* 'You are surely mistaken,' he whimpered. 'I understood from Thaddeus that his brother's death was an accident.'

'Did you, Father? Then I owe you an apology. I was sure you knew the truth when so little escapes your attention in and around your church.'

His eyes slid away from hers. 'I know only what Thaddeus told me, milady, and he made no mention of murder.'

'And I'm sure you hope that by refusing to hear Eleanor's confession, you can continue to protest your ignorance.'

'I have refused her nothing.'

'Everyone in Develish knows you have. You may have feigned sleep or absence when she cried to you, but you rebuffed her nonetheless.' She paused. 'I wonder why, when you are bound as a priest to keep the secrets of the confessional and would have had no need to divulge what she said. Did you fear the demands her distress would put upon you?'

He studied her with dislike. 'I wonder you care whether she receives absolution or not. You had nothing good to say about it when you spoke to her beside this altar and made a mockery of her father's devotion to the cross.'

'Sir Richard's devotion was to himself and his appetites.' She reached for the cross. 'He was fortunate his sin didn't show in his face. He retained his beauty through every vile act he committed. As long as you placed this in his hands and recited prayers of penance and forgiveness, he believed himself clean until the next time he transgressed.'

'By God's mercy the same is true for all of us.'

'Not for women like Eva Thurkell,' Lady Anne countered. 'Their sin is apparent to all and visited afterwards upon the wretched children they are unfortunate enough to bear.' She stared at the piece of wood. 'Where was God's mercy when thirteen-year-old Mathilde was in despair over Sir Richard's rape and made to take the blame for his wrongdoing? Can you tell me that, Father?'

The priest looked uncomfortable. 'You use strong words against your husband, but only God knows the truth of what happened.'

'Not so. Mathilde's story was the same as Abigail Startout's five years later. My husband was a man of vile depravity—as you well know, since you forgave his wrongdoing each time.' She searched his drink-sodden eyes. 'How many other such crimes did he bring to you, claiming it was the child's fault for seducing him?'

For a second time, he couldn't meet her gaze. 'You know I cannot tell you.'

'Indeed,' she agreed slowly. 'The secrets of the confessional are as convenient to you as they were to him.' She laid the cross flat on the altar and looked at it for several long seconds. 'Eleanor is with child and has been starving and hurting herself to be rid of it. She blames Thaddeus's companions for her condition, saying they took it in turns to violate her here in God's house. Is that true, Father? You must have seen it if it happened.'

The old man gobbled like a turkey cock, flapping his hands in impotent protest, but whether in shock at Eleanor's pregnancy or denial of his role as a witness Lady Anne couldn't tell.

'I fear you find yourself in an unhappy position,' she went on. 'There seems no doubt she had secret assignations with serf boys in this place. She was here on the night of Jacob's death and admitted as much to Thaddeus before he left. Isabella was in the room when she did so.' She watched the priest's eyes grow large with alarm. 'If what she says is true, many will ask why you did nothing to protect her—worse, allowed her degradation to go on so long. She told Isabella she's missed a third bleed, which means the boys were violating her even before Sir Richard left for Bradmayne.'

He couldn't find words, just worked his mouth in silent shock.

'Be sure that every woman on the demesne will count back the months when the baby is delivered, Father. Do you think any will understand why you didn't feel it necessary to inform her father of what was happening?'

He ran his tongue across his lips. 'You seem to believe I know things I do not, milady.'

She shook her head. 'This is what I believe, Father. I believe there are many secrets Eleanor wants to confide in you . . . but since you know what they are, your heart quails at the thought of hearing them. How much easier to pretend drunken sleep than cope with the turbulence of her emotions since Sir Richard's death. She's never been an easy girl to guide—we both know that—but she's quite impossible now, for her actions are governed by fear of what's growing inside her.'

'You can't hold me responsible,' he cried. 'It's Thaddeus's fault. He should never have brought her here after she destroyed your room. It gave her ideas.'

Lady Anne wondered if he realised how much he'd given away in those three sentences. 'Of course,' she answered calmly. 'She could not have introduced serf boys to my chamber—or even the spinning room—with the ease she brought them here. How desperate she must have been to find someone to blame for her unhappy condition.'

A sigh fluttered from the priest's mouth. 'There was nothing I could do. The sin was Lady Eleanor's. The boys allowed her to flog them in return for a kiss and a fondle, nothing more. When I took her to task for it, she turned the whip on me and began to encourage the boys to spill their seed on the ground. I found it easier to pretend sleep than watch her wickedness.'

'How long did it go on?'

'A month . . . until the boys left with Thaddeus. She was quite shameless in her behaviour.'

'Would you have said as much if Thaddeus had kept them here and she'd accused them of rape?' She went on when he didn't answer. 'He did his best to protect them, but I'm sure Eleanor hopes they won't return, leaving her free to claim whatever gross violation will fit her story. Perhaps you hope it also? Your life will be more congenial if they die, will it not? You can continue to pretend you were deaf and blind to Eleanor's foolish attempts to explain her swollen belly.'

'Blame yourself before you blame me,' the priest snapped. 'Had you cared for her as a mother should, you would not have allowed her the freedom to behave as she did.'

'Then why didn't you tell me about it? Surely you were bound as my priest to chastise me for allowing my husband's child such licence?'

'You wouldn't have welcomed the news any more then than you do now. I prayed it would stop and it did.'

Lady Anne smiled bitterly. 'Indeed—with Jacob Thurkell's murder. Your God has a strange way of answering prayers, Father. Does it please Him to cure one wickedness with another?'

'His ways are a mystery.'

'We can agree on that at least. The biggest mystery is why He ever created a monster like Sir Richard.' She looked down at the cross again. 'How evil does a man have to be to lie with his own daughter . . . and how corrupt does a priest have to be to absolve him of it?'

The old wretch's eyes narrowed to slits. 'The fault is yours,' he spat. 'You gave protection to your precious serfs but none at all to the child you called your own.'

ⵣ

Outside the church, Lady Anne quenched her lantern so that none of the guards would see its light and be curious. So much grief was in her heart that she couldn't hold back her tears, and she lowered her head to let them course freely down her cheeks. The priest was right to say the guilt was hers. After Abigail, she had guarded every young maid in the house against her husband's lechery but had never thought to guard Eleanor. Yet how many times had she watched Sir Richard pull the girl into a tight embrace and run his hands over her slim young body? How many times had she expressed her disapproval to Eleanor only to be accused of jealousy?

It should have occurred to her that Sir Richard would despoil his daughter with as little conscience as he'd despoiled Mathilde and Abigail. Eleanor's love for him had been very great, and her trust so much easier to exploit. He couldn't have resisted taking her for himself. Did it explain why he'd wanted to advance her wedding? Had he come to see that such an unnatural relationship must be ended? Or, worse, had he known that Eleanor was with child and looked to pass it off as Lord Peter's?

From grief she turned to anger, cursing God more roundly than she had ever cursed Him before. Must she always be made responsible for the misery Sir Richard caused? She might have opened her mouth to scream the imprecations aloud had a voice not spoken from beyond the graveyard wall.

It was Gyles. He carried a lantern of his own, half shuttered to keep the light small. 'Are you all right, milady?' he asked, widening the beam and turning it towards her.

Lady Anne drew the hood of her cloak about her face. 'I'm tired, Gyles. The day's events have drained me.'

He heard the tremor in her voice and guessed it was more than tiredness that afflicted her. He understood better than most the pain of losing a daughter. 'Is there something I can do to assist you, milady?'

She surprised him with a soft laugh. 'Not unless you've learnt the trick of turning back time, my friend.'

Thirty-two

LADY ANNE SAT WRITING IN a ledger by candlelight until she was certain all in the house were asleep. Little of what she wrote was true, for this was the manuscript she planned to leave behind for others to find, and it would make no sense to alert My Lord of Blandeforde to the serfs' plans to leave. Instead she described the day as any other—the education of children, the careful counting and preparation of rations and a constant watch for the approach of strangers.

She had recorded every detail of My Lord of Bourne's attack in the sincere hope that he and his men would face retribution, but she had yet to decide how to introduce the pestilence to her story when the time came to leave. It seemed wrong to describe the actions she and Thaddeus had taken to keep it out only to pretend they had failed. What value would such a document have to those who came after if the only conclusion they drew from it was that men, however ingenious, must always bow to God's design in the end?

The hourglass told her it was close to midnight when she finally rose and gathered together what she needed. She took an infusion of angelica, wormwood and pennyroyal leaf from a locked cabinet in the corner, a pile of napkins from a coffer, and then donned her cloak and reached for the lantern. Outside, the air felt cold against her skin. Clouds had been building in the west all day and the strengthening wind foretold approaching rain. Her thoughts were of Thaddeus who would be camped in the open without shelter. Would he agree with what she was about to do, she wondered, when his very existence was a permanent reminder that she played God each time she helped a woman escape childbirth?

How willing the husbands of Develish had been to hear her advice on safeguarding the health of their wives, and how lax they were at following it. A man always put his needs before a woman's. The abbess had taught her this as she instructed her young pupil in the skills of abortion and the secrets of chewing wild carrot seeds to avoid falling with child at all. Lady Anne had used both to save the women of Develish from unwanted pregnancies and would have purged Mathilde also if the poor girl hadn't been too far gone by the time Lady Anne reached Foxcote. Even Mother Maria could not bring on a bleed so late without killing the mother as well as the foetus.

As Lady Anne made her way towards the serf huts on the path to the church, she found herself wishing she could give Eleanor the tincture without telling her what it was. The girl might be grateful for it now, but not in six months' time when her fears were forgotten and she came to realise that other women must have benefited from Lady Anne's knowledge. 'Murderess' would slip as easily from her tongue as 'heretic' if it suited her. But with three bleeds missed, Lady Anne knew she had no choice but to explain what the tincture was. There would be no mistaking an abortive for a sleeping draught. All she could do was pray that Isabella's description was accurate and Eleanor had yet to miss her fourth. Lady Anne had the skills to rid the girl of a June conception but not one that was earlier.

Taking a deep breath to keep her voice level, she paused outside the Truebloods' door. 'Are you there, John?' she whispered, tapping on the wooden panels. 'Will you allow me to speak with Lady Eleanor for five minutes?'

John Trueblood emerged, still dressed in his thick woollen tunic, as if he had only just returned from guarding the wall. 'If milady wishes,' he said, studying her curiously, 'but by rights I should lock you in with her since that is her punishment.'

'Then you must do that,' she agreed. 'I will call when I'm ready to leave.'

He nodded, but the curiosity persisted in his eyes as he took a key from a hook on the wall of his hut and stooped to insert it into the padlock on Eleanor's door. 'She has tired herself out with her tantrums,' he murmured, looking at the girl asleep on the rush matting, 'but you should still be wary, milady. She has more strength in her kicks than most men.'

Lady Anne placed the lantern on the floor as John secured the padlock again, then she knelt and placed her palm over the girl's mouth. 'I've come to help you,' she breathed, placing a finger to her lips when Eleanor's eyes snapped open. 'You must whisper if you don't want your words to be overheard.'

It was hard to tell what Eleanor felt—her expression was more guarded than friendly—but she signalled agreement. 'Are you going to make them release me?' she asked when Lady Anne removed her hand.

The woman shook her head. 'If you want that, you must show remorse for hurting Isabella,' she whispered. 'It's a different kind of release I'm offering you.' She held up the vial containing the infusion. 'This will cleanse you of your baby. You must take half now and half when the sun has risen. There will be pain, and much blood, but you will be well again in a few days.'

The girl's eyes widened in shock.

'Starving yourself won't work, Eleanor, nor will causing your arms to bleed. You need angelica, wormwood and pennyroyal to dislodge the foetus from your womb. I will come again two hours after daybreak to assist you.' She took the napkins from inside her kirtle. 'Use these to staunch the flow if the rush of blood begins before I return.'

'Did Isabella tell you?'

Lady Anne nodded. 'By your wish. You wouldn't have made her feel your belly otherwise.'

'Did she tell you it's her brothers' fault for violating me in the church?'

'She did.'

'Then you know who to blame.'

Lady Anne shook her head. 'You're too advanced,' she whispered, placing her own palm on the girl's midriff. 'Three missed bleeds means you must have conceived before Sir Richard left for Bradmayne, and no serf boy would have dared violate you while he was alive . . . certainly not five of them taking it in turns. He would have ordered them hanged the minute you told him about it.'

The girl smacked the hand away. 'This has nothing to do with my father,' she hissed.

'Would you rather the baby was born, knowing that every woman on the demesne will count back the days and weeks to work out who sired it? If it's healthy and properly formed—which I fear it won't be—no one will mistake it for a serf's child. It will have blonde hair and blue eyes like you and Sir Richard. Did you not think to come to me instead of looking to blame gullible boys for what your father did?'

Eleanor's eyes welled with tears. 'You'd have been angry.'

'With reason. Sir Richard compounded every sin he ever committed by lying with his own daughter.'

'At least he loved me.'

At least he loved me . . . Was this the limit of Eleanor's understanding? With sudden deep weariness, Lady Anne sat back on her heels. 'I said I wouldn't make any more decisions for you, and I won't,' she murmured. 'This tincture is the means by which you can purge yourself, but the choice of whether to take it must be yours.' She shook her head at the girl's expression. 'Be sure you understand the consequences of doing nothing, Eleanor. You will be called worse names than any you have given Eva Thurkell when the baby is born—and harlot will be the kindest.'

The tears flowed freely down Eleanor's cheeks. 'What if it's a boy? He'll be the heir that Develish needs. My Lord of Blandeforde will accept him if you say you gave birth to him. It's what my father would have asked you to do.'

Would he have dared, Lady Anne wondered, knowing how angry she'd have been to learn of his twisted and unnatural love for his daughter? Perhaps. 'Did you tell him you were with child before he left for Bradmayne? Is that why he was so keen to seal your marriage to Lord Peter?'

'The marriage was your desire.'

'No, Eleanor, my choice was to wait another year to see if we could find someone more to your taste. It was Sir Richard who insisted. Had the pestilence not come, you would have been wed by the end of August. I should have guessed he'd done something terrible.'

It seemed Eleanor still felt the need to defend her father. 'It wasn't terrible,' she pleaded. 'It was nice. He loved me so much . . . and I loved him.' She watched Lady Anne closely. 'He said it was your fault. If you'd been a better wife to him, he wouldn't have done it. He made you mistress of his demesne, and you showed him only coldness and dislike in return.'

Lady Anne had heard these words so often they barely registered any more. She placed the vial on the rushes beside the napkins. 'This is the only help I can give you. If you choose not to take it, you must face the world bravely and be honest about who sired your child, for I will not allow you to accuse Thaddeus's companions. I shall insist Father Anselm repeats in public what he told me earlier—that the worst any of them did was spill their seed on the ground. Do you understand?'

'There are other ways to help me,' Eleanor said, clutching at Lady Anne's hand. 'Did you hate Sir Richard so much that you'd sooner kill his baby than let me find a way to keep it? Are you jealous because I might have a son who'll inherit Develish?'

Lady Anne pulled away. 'Cease dreaming of something that can never happen, Eleanor. Without legitimacy, your son will be heir to nothing, in the same position Thaddeus is—worse, if the timing of his birth leads people to believe he was conceived through incest. He will carry his father's sin forever . . . as will you. God's law does not allow a woman to be both mother and sister to her child.'

The girl lowered her gaze. 'I could still say a serf did it. It was almost true. The boys would have violated me if they could— Jacob more than the others. He thought he could threaten me with his silly little knife and looked so surprised when I snatched it away.' She fell into a brief silence. 'Thaddeus spoilt everything by pretending it was an accident. I hoped someone else would find the body . . . someone who was so frightened they'd run screaming through the demesne.'

'Why?'

'You'd have believed me if you'd found me hiding in a corner, and I said I'd killed a boy because he forced himself on me.'

Lady Anne studied the bent head. 'Why didn't you wake me and say it anyway?'

'I didn't know if Jacob was dead. He shouldn't have been. I only pricked him once.'

'And Thaddeus didn't tell you when Isabella took you to the steward's office?'

'No.'

'Then he must have guessed it was you who killed Jacob. I imagine he took the boys away to keep you from accusing them in your place—though he may have suspected something worse after he spoke to Olyver and Edmund. Did you tell any of them you were with child? Could they have guessed by feeling your belly?'

Eleanor's shock was genuine. 'Of *course* not! I hate serfs. It makes me sick to be touched by them.'

A faint smile twisted Lady Anne's mouth. 'Yet you're willing to claim this baby as a serf's if it means you can keep it? Do you think anyone will believe you could love such a misbegotten child or show it the care a mother should?'

'I'll give it to you. No one will question your affection for a serf's baby.'

Lady Anne pushed herself to her feet, recognising that to speak further would achieve nothing. The girl's thinking was very confused if she thought a serf's child could inherit Develish. 'Try to understand that your best release is the purgative in the vial,' she said. 'I'll leave you the lantern so that you can see what you're doing and will attend morning and evening to ensure that nothing goes wrong.' She took a step backwards, preparing to leave, but Eleanor caught at the hem of her kirtle to prevent her.

'Why can't you be as kind to me as you were to Mathilde?'

'What else would you have me do?'

'The same as you did for her. If you tell Develish I'm sick and order me returned to your room, no one will question it. You can say I've lost my wits.' She tried to pull the woman closer, her eyes full of pleading.

Lady Anne shook her head. 'The gift Mathilde wanted was the one I'm giving you, and I would have offered it gladly had I thought it would work. Her misfortune was to be into her fifth month by the time I arrived.'

It took Eleanor a second to understand her meaning. 'I wouldn't have been born.'

'No . . . and the lives of the two women who were forced to play mother to you would have been different.'

As ever, Eleanor interpreted the words in the context of herself. 'You've never been able to see good in me,' she whispered bitterly. 'Why were you able to show fondness for Mathilde but not for me?'

Lady Anne stepped away, pulling her kirtle free of Eleanor's fingers. 'She found my love easier to recognise than you do,' she said, before calling to John Trueblood that she was ready to leave.

ତ୍ୟ

A small figure peeled away from the shadows of a buttress as Lady Anne approached across the forecourt. A beam of light shone briefly on her face as the shutter of a lantern was opened and closed but, with heavy clouds obscuring the moon, it was hard to make out who it was until she heard the voice of Robert Startout. He sounded very frightened. 'Oh, milady, milady,' he stammered. 'My Uncle Gyles has need of you. He sent my mother to your chamber, but you weren't there—and nor could she find you anywhere else.'

She placed her palm against his cheek. 'I'm here now, Robert. Where is your uncle?'

The boy caught her hand and urged her towards the moat. 'Guarding the northern step, milady. Bandits have come across the hills from the south. My father and Master Catchpole say they're circling the valley to come at us on all sides.'

It was a second or two before the import of his words registered with Lady Anne. Her mind was so full of Eleanor's woes that she couldn't conceive of worse troubles elsewhere. Her steps faltered. 'Bandits?'

'Yes, milady. My father guards the eastern step, overlooking the highway, and he saw men in numbers some half-hour since; Master Catchpole likewise from his place on the southern step.' Robert sighed in relief as a shadow moved towards them. 'My uncle can tell you better than I.'

Gyles ducked his head to Lady Anne and placed a comforting hand on Robert's shoulder. 'Don't fret before you need to,' he urged the lad. 'Are you willing to be my messenger again? Then wait by the buttress until you hear my signal. When I whistle, rouse the men and send them to me here. They must bring what weapons they can and find their way without lanterns or candles. Understood?'

Lady Anne waited until the boy was out of earshot. She could barely breathe for the sudden panic that gripped her heart. 'Is this true, Gyles?'

'It is, milady. Alleyn and Adam are certain of what they saw. They've been uncommonly vigilant since a torch flared briefly to life on the road to the south. The light lasted a bare second or two, but it showed a multitude of men beneath it. It speaks of what we've always feared—an army of serfs in search of food.' He put a hand beneath her elbow to steady her. 'Our best help will be rain. They'll not be able to burn us out if God brings a downpour.'

'And if He doesn't?'

'We must fight, though I question whether our people have the heart to kill Englishmen. I worry they'll hesitate if a Dorseteshire voice begs for mercy.' He felt a tremor of shock run through her. 'You need to be brave, milady. Our people will lose heart if they see you afraid.'

He asked too much of her. 'But I *am* afraid,' she whispered. 'Any courage I had is gone. I thought I could play the part of liege lord, but I was wrong. I am quite unable to shoulder the many burdens the position places on me.'

Gyles didn't doubt Eleanor was the cause of Milady's anguish, and he cursed the girl roundly in his head. It seemed the pain she'd visited on Isabella wasn't enough for her. She must destroy the people of Develish too by destroying their mistress. Without care for the impropriety of the gesture, he placed his arm around Lady Anne's waist and drew her close with the same sweet tenderness he showed his daughter.

'I remember when you first came to Develish as a young bride,' he told her gently. 'You were barely older than my Isabella is now. I was on this forecourt, summoned to watch a flogging, and I recall the look in your eye as you stepped from the wagon and saw the poor wretch who was being whipped. I knew then we'd found a friend. Inside two months such brutal flayings had stopped and you'd drawn Sir Richard's ire onto yourself. Will you show a lesser spirit tonight before a ragtag band of thieves?'

Lady Anne raised the hem of her cloak to her eyes. The last man who had held her in such a way had been her father. She took a long tremulous breath and raised her head. 'I will try my best, Gyles. Tell me what you would have me do and I will do it.'

Gyles didn't doubt her, for his faith in her was very great. 'Assist Robert in waking the house and then barricade yourself inside with the women and children. Our men will fight better for knowing their families are under your protection.' He narrowed his eyes to stare across the moat, but the rain clouds were thickening so rapidly there was no seeing the road that led to the village or the land that lay on either side of it. 'You won't know if we've succeeded until dawn breaks, so be ruthless in keeping the door barred. In this darkness, you'll not be able to tell one Dorseteshire serf from another.'

Lady Anne didn't argue with him. He knew as well as she that their men would be no better at telling friend from foe. To fight blindly was madness, yet what else could they do? There was no future for Develish if the walls were breached. She breathed a silent prayer that Alleyn and Adam were wrong, but even that hope was extinguished when a light, as small as a pinprick, appeared in the blackness ahead of them. By its direction, it seemed to be on the edge of the village but, as they watched, it began to move, growing brighter as it came towards them.

'What is that?' she whispered.

'A burning torch, milady.'

'Who carries it?'

Gyles looked at the distorted shapes that eddied and flowed beneath the flickering flame and, with a sigh, he eased away from her and took his bow from his shoulder. He'd left it too late. 'The people we dread, milady. They've circled the valley faster than I expected. I see five or six in this group alone.'

'Why do they alert us to their presence?'

'As a signal to others in the valley that the attack is about to begin.' Gyles looked towards the west, searching for signs of movement on the peasant strips. But the night was impenetrable. 'You must leave,' he said, urging her to move. 'Go. Encourage our men to fight and use your cleverness against these thieves to keep our women and children safe. Even under siege inside the house, a hundred can last well into the spring on the supplies that are left.'

With the hood of her cloak about her face, Lady Anne's expression was hidden from him, but he felt the brush of her fingers against his cheek. 'You are my dearest friend,' she whispered. 'Guard yourself well this night.'

Gyles forced a smile into his voice. 'Be sure of it, milady.'

But as he watched the approaching flame, and the shadows that moiled beneath it, he doubted it was a promise he could keep . . .

W as there ever a night such as this? God raised me from despair to joy and yet, despite His kindness, I feel my spirits lowering again. It is truly said that the darkest hour is just before dawn.

I still tremble at how close Gyles came to putting an arrow through Thaddeus's heart though, in truth, the shadows thrown by the swirling flames of the torch were very strange. It took Robert Startout's sharp young eyes to see a man on foot with his arms outstretched—the reins of a weary charger in one hand and the torch held aloft in the other. I have given him a penny in gratitude but don't doubt he will tease his uncle and father mercilessly for mistaking the horse for bandits.

No blame attaches to them. We are so turned in on ourselves that anything beyond the moat frightens us. In hope, we have looked for messengers to tell us the pestilence has passed. In despair, we have feared that only we survive.

Would I could say that Thaddeus brought us reason to believe in a future outside Develish but the wasteland he described beyond our boundaries is worse than anything I've imagined. To picture a world almost devoid of people is very different from learning it to be a reality. I wonder now what is to become of us.

The rain which has threatened for hours has finally come, but I have never known such a torrent as beats upon the roof and windows. If day has broken, there is precious little easing of the darkness outside. I hear the children stirring in the great hall and fear their anxious minds will believe this unending night is the harbinger of the Black Death.

I wish I could tell them they are wrong.

The
Turn of
Midnight

AUTUMN AND WINTER, 1348

The night of the eleventh day of September, 1348

When the hourglass tilts, midnight will have turned and a new day started. Yet I still can't bring myself to move. Once done, this cannot be undone, and the guilt will be mine. I should have been more of a mother to Eleanor, for I knew better than anyone the vileness of her father's nature. But would she have listened if I'd warned her that his love for her was unnatural? Will she listen now?

I must put an end to indecision. Despite the vicious wounds Eleanor inflicted on her, Isabella Startout came in search of help for her, and the maid's sweet generosity should be my guide. In my heart I know I must act. To do nothing will be to betray the girl I have called daughter all these years.

God forgive me. I can surely bear Eleanor's hatred more easily than she will bear the slur of incest if this misbegotten child is born.

Mea culpa.

One

Develish, Dorseteshire

THE NIGHT SEEMED DARKER WHEN Lady Anne took her leave
of Eleanor and stepped away from the serf's hut. Perhaps she'd
tarried longer than she realised in her attempts to persuade her
daughter to understand the stark choices that faced her. There
was no telling time with the moon hidden by cloud. She pulled
her cloak tighter about herself as protection against the rising
wind and felt her way blindly along the path to the manor house.
Behind her, the church was lost in blackness; ahead of her, the glow
of the six candles she lit each night in the south-facing window of
her chamber was just discernible through the panes overlooking
the forecourt. Their feeble light was all that was visible in the
enshrouding darkness.

Only John Trueblood knew of her visit, for he'd had to open
the padlock on the door of Eleanor's prison. She didn't doubt he
would speak of it to Clara but hoped both would believe that her
sorrow at being disowned by her adopted daughter had compelled
her to come. Certainly, John had seen her sadness when she left;
he'd given her arm a clumsy pat and begged her not to take Lady

553

Eleanor's hate-filled words of that afternoon to heart. Once the girl's strange madness passed, she would know that Milady was her true mother. Lady Anne thanked him for his kindness, but tears clouded her eyes as she made her way back to the house. She doubted Eleanor would ever come to see that an abortive of angelica, wormwood and pennyroyal was a gift of love and not hate.

She had left the girl to administer the purgative herself, saying the choice of what to do must be hers. If Eleanor decided to keep the baby, she must live with the consequences afterwards because Lady Anne could not protect her from gossip once her belly began to swell in earnest. She had warned Eleanor against repeating the lies she'd told Isabella about being raped by serf boys because all would guess the truth as soon as the infant was born. There wasn't a woman in Develish who wouldn't be able to name the real sire when she saw the baby's features and worked out from the date of delivery that Sir Richard, the girl's own father, was still in Develish at the time of conception. Dead he might be, but he still had the power to destroy any chance his daughter might have of an unsullied future.

Lady Anne trod softly as she approached the forecourt, anxious not to be seen coming from the direction of Eleanor's prison, but loose stones shifted beneath her feet and her heart skipped a beat when a beam of light shone briefly on her face as the shutter of a lantern was opened and closed. It was impossible to make out who was holding it until she heard the voice of young Robert Startout. He sounded very frightened. 'Oh, milady, milady,' he stammered. 'My Uncle Gyles has need of you. He sent my mother to your chamber, but you weren't there—and nor could she find you anywhere else.'

She placed her palm against his cheek. 'I'm here now, Robert. Where is your uncle?'

The boy caught her hand and urged her towards the moat. 'Guarding the northern step, milady. Bandits have come across the hills from the south. My father and Master Catchpole say they're circling the valley to come at us on all sides.'

It was a second or two before the import of his words registered with Lady Anne. Her mind was so full of Eleanor's woes that she couldn't conceive of worse troubles elsewhere. Her steps faltered. 'Bandits?'

'Yes, milady. My father guards the eastern step, overlooking the highway, and he saw men in numbers some half-hour since; Master Catchpole likewise from his place on the southern step.' Robert sighed in relief as a shadow moved towards them. 'My uncle can tell you better than I.'

Gyles ducked his head to Lady Anne and placed a comforting hand on Robert's shoulder. 'Don't fret before you need to,' he urged the lad. 'Are you willing to be my messenger again? Then wait by the buttress until you hear my signal. When I whistle, rouse the men in the house and send them to me here. They must bring what weapons they can and find their way without lanterns or candles. Understood?'

Lady Anne waited until the boy was out of earshot. She could barely breathe for the sudden panic that gripped her heart. 'Is this true, Gyles?'

'It is, milady. Alleyn and Adam are certain of what they saw. They've been uncommonly vigilant since a torch flared briefly to life on the road to the south. The light lasted a bare second or two, but it showed a multitude of men beneath it. It speaks of what we've always feared—an army of serfs in search of food.' He put a hand beneath her elbow to steady her. 'Our best help will be rain. They'll not be able to burn us out if God brings a downpour.'

'And if He doesn't?'

'We must fight, though I question whether our people have the will to kill Englishmen. I worry they'll hesitate if a Dorseteshire voice begs for mercy.' He felt a tremor of shock run through her. 'You need to be brave, milady. Our people will lose heart if they see you afraid.'

He asked too much of her. 'But I *am* afraid,' she whispered. 'Any courage I had is gone. I thought I could play the part of liege lord, but I was wrong. I am quite unable to shoulder the many burdens the position places on me.'

Gyles guessed Eleanor's madness was the true cause of Milady's anguish, and he cursed the girl roundly in his head. It seemed the pain she'd visited on his daughter Isabella wasn't enough for her. She must destroy the people of Develish too by destroying their mistress. Without care for the impropriety of the gesture, he placed his arm around Lady Anne's waist and drew her close.

'I remember when you first came to Develish as a young bride,' he told her gently. 'You were barely older than my Isabella is now. I was on this forecourt, summoned to watch a flogging, and I recall the look in your eye as you stepped from the wagon and saw the poor wretch who was being whipped. I knew then we'd found a friend. Inside two months such brutal flayings had stopped and you'd drawn Sir Richard's ire onto yourself. Will you show a lesser spirit tonight before a ragtag band of thieves?'

Lady Anne raised the hem of her cloak to her eyes. The last man who had held her in such a way had been her father. She took a long tremulous breath and raised her head. 'I will try my best, Gyles. Tell me what you would have me do and I will do it.'

Gyles didn't doubt her, for his faith in her was very great. 'Assist Robert in waking the house and then barricade yourself inside with the women and children, milady. Our men will fight better for knowing their families are under your protection.' He narrowed his eyes to stare across the moat, but there was no seeing the road that led to the village nor the land that lay on either side of it. 'You won't know if we've succeeded until dawn breaks, so be ruthless in keeping the door barred. In this darkness, you'll not be able to tell one Dorseteshire voice from another.'

Lady Anne didn't argue with him. He knew as well as she that their men would be no better at telling friend from foe. To fight blindly was madness, yet what else could they do? There was no future for Develish if the walls were breached and the pestilence entered. She breathed a silent prayer that Alleyn and Adam were wrong, but even that hope was extinguished when a light, as small as a pinprick, appeared in the blackness ahead of them. By its direction, it seemed to be on the edge of the village but, as they watched, it began to move, growing brighter as it came towards them.

'What is that?' she whispered.

'A burning torch, milady.'

'Who carries it?'

Gyles looked at the distorted shapes that eddied and flowed beneath the flickering flame and, with a sigh, he eased away from her and took his bow from his shoulder. He'd left it too late. 'The people we dread, milady. They've circled the valley faster than I expected. I see five or six in this group alone.'

'Why do they alert us to their presence?'

'As a signal to others in the valley that the attack is about to begin.' Gyles looked towards the west, searching for signs of movement on the peasant strips. But the night was impenetrable. 'You must leave,' he said. 'Go. Encourage our men to fight and use your cleverness against these thieves to keep our women and children safe. Even under siege inside the house, a hundred can last well into the spring on the supplies that are left.'

With the hood of her cloak about her face, Lady Anne's expression was hidden from him, but he felt the brush of her fingers against his cheek. 'You are my dearest friend,' she whispered. 'Guard yourself well this night.'

Gyles forced a smile into his voice. 'Be sure of it, milady.'

Be sure of it . . . Lady Anne knew him too well to be deceived by such lightness of tone. He was bidding her farewell and a terrible panic overwhelmed her at the thought of trying to protect the people of Develish alone. Was God not content with death from the pestilence that He must set survivors against each other until no human life remained? Where was His love in this terrible world?

A small hand slipped into hers. 'Use some of my strength, milady,' whispered Robert. 'You will fall otherwise. Do you think Thaddeus knows there are bandits in the valley?'

The question was a strange one, for Robert knew well that Thaddeus, whom he greatly admired, had left the demesne two weeks ago. The child's twin cousins and three of their friends had departed with him, but none had returned. 'Have you missed Thaddeus, Robert?'

'Yes, milady, but he's foolish to lead his horse instead of riding it. He'll be attacked more easily on foot. My uncle should call out a warning.'

She squeezed his hand by way of comfort. 'Your uncle will do what is right. He always does.'

'I don't think so, milady, or he'd have done it already. He pretends he can see in the dark, but he can't. My father's the same. Me, I'd tell Thaddeus to stop being such a numbskull. The way he's walking even I could put an arrow through his heart.'

Lady Anne told herself it was fantasy, the imaginings of a frightened child, but she drew him to a halt. 'Look again,' she urged, turning him towards the moat. 'Describe what you see. Is it one man or many?'

'One, milady. He walks with his arms spread wide like Jesus on the cross. In his right hand he holds reins and in his left a torch. I think he worries the flame will frighten the horse. He wears a high hat and a long coat.'

'Can you really make out so much? Are you sure it's Thaddeus?'

'If it's not, it's someone tall who moves like him, milady. Now he's stopped to let the horse crop some grass at the edge of the road . . . and he's staring at the ground the way Thaddeus does when he's thinking.'

Lady Anne yearned to believe him. 'It's a strange hour for him to come. He knows better than any that all in Develish will be asleep.'

'Except the men on the guard steps, milady,' said Robert matter-of-factly. 'If my cousins are dead, Thaddeus will want my uncle to hear of it first.'

The same thought had occurred to Lady Anne. But who to trust when her own sight was better at reading ledgers than seeing into the distance? 'Give me your lantern,' she said with sudden decision, 'and then take your place beside the buttress. I'm putting much faith in you, Robert. If you're wrong and your uncle is right, there will be minutes only to rouse our men to defend the walls.'

'I'm not wrong, milady,' he answered confidently, letting go her hand, 'but don't blame me if there are bandits out there as well.'

∽∾

Gyles lowered his bow when the flickering torchlight showed him his nephew was right. At fifty paces there was no mistaking Thaddeus's height and long, loping stride, never mind he was dressed like a lord in a wide-skirted, fur-lined coat with a beaver hat atop a chaperon hood on his head. 'My age is catching up with me, milady. I mistook the horse for men.'

Lady Anne suppressed a smile. 'I, too, my friend. There's less to fear than we thought.'

'Except bad news,' murmured Gyles. 'He wouldn't come when all are abed if he had something good to impart.'

Lady Anne handed him the closed lantern. 'Should we open it to show him we're here?'

'Not yet, milady. Let's hear what he has to say first.' He raised his voice as Thaddeus approached to within twenty paces of the moat. 'Are you well, Thaddeus?' he called.

A familiar voice came back to them. 'Is that you, Gyles? I am blinded by this torchlight but I feared an arrow through my heart if I approached unannounced.' He stooped to quench the flames in the dirt of the road. 'Are you alone, my friend?'

The careful way he asked the question persuaded Lady Anne to step behind Gyles. She was so slight his body hid hers easily. 'Say you are,' she whispered. 'He'll tell you nothing otherwise.'

'There are guards on the steps,' Gyles replied. 'If you don't want your words overheard, you must come to the moat and keep your voice low. What troubles you?'

Lady Anne heard the stamp of hooves as Thaddeus brought the horse to a halt on the bank, and the rattle of the bridle as it lowered its head to drink. 'First give me news of Develish,' he said. 'Is it as it was when we left? I saw candles in the window of Lady Anne's chamber. Does she look forward to our return?'

'Of course,' answered Gyles in obvious surprise. 'We all do. Why would it be otherwise?'

There was a small hesitation before Thaddeus answered. 'No reason. I promised your sons I would ask is all. They worry that you and Martha are angry because they didn't seek your blessing before they left.'

'I would have refused it if they had.'

'They guessed as much.'

Gyles gave a grunt of amusement. 'You put the fear of God into me by coming at this hour. I thought you were here to tell me they were dead.'

'Far from it. All the boys live and are well. Develish can be proud of them. I could not have asked for braver companions. Their courage in the face of the pestilence has been as great as yours, and we've found plentiful supplies to restore the stocks here. Where people die, animals thrive and grain goes uneaten.'

'Is it bad out there, my friend?'

Lady Anne heard a tired sigh. 'It's a wasteland, Gyles. Death sweeps all before it. I can neither rid myself of its smell nor erase the memories of what it leaves behind. To survive is to know damnation. This night I have walked in Hell.'

The words were so bleak that Gyles opened the shutter of the lantern and held it aloft. Thaddeus had removed his hat and pushed back his hood, and the beam of light shone on his drawn, exhausted face. Seeing him flinch at the brightness, Gyles dipped the beam to the water. 'There was a glow in the sky to the south some five hours ago,' he said. 'I guessed it was Athelhelm being set ablaze. Was that your doing?'

'It was.'

'For what reason?'

'To create safe passage for the boys and two hundred sheep along the highway from Afpedle to Develish. I would have delayed the burning another few days if I could, but the rain is almost upon us and would have made the task impossible.'

It took little imagination for Gyles to read between the lines of what he said. 'Is the pestilence in Athelhelm? Are all infected?'

Thaddeus nodded. 'All those that remained.'

'And the dead lay unburied?'

'Some had been placed in a communal grave but most were abandoned to die inside their huts. The body of a monk who'd been caring for them lay in a doorway, his face eaten by scavengers. I could see no course but to cleanse the village with fire. I called a warning of what I was about to do but none answered or came out.'

'So what troubles you?'

There was a long pause. 'A man begged for mercy even as I prepared to throw a flaming torch onto his thatch. I saw him through his open door. He was lying on rushes and turned his head to look at me. I could have stayed my hand but I didn't.'

'Did he try to rise?'

'No.'

'Then perhaps death was the mercy he wanted.'

'He thought I was the Devil come to burn him. I read it in his eyes.' Thaddeus cursed quietly to himself. 'Pay no heed to me. I promised myself I wouldn't talk of it. You dealt with worse when Sir Richard and your fellow soldiers were dying.'

Gyles recalled how Thaddeus had crossed the moat at night to keep him company while he tended the sick and then buried them. The younger man had always kept his distance but his presence had been a comfort. 'And I was grateful to you for listening to me. A trouble shared is a trouble halved.' Gyles paused. 'Were my sons with you?'

'No. Their consciences were pricked enough by what I asked them to do in Afpedle.' Thaddeus painted a brief picture of the previous fourteen days, detailing the demesnes they'd visited and the supplies of food they'd found. He spoke of finding a wagon and grain at Holcombe and two hundred sheep at Afpedle, but his descriptions of the smell of corruption that lingered over all the demesnes turned the stomachs of his listeners, as did his warnings about infestations of rats in the villages where people had died. 'The stores of grain attract them, and with more food they seem to be breeding faster. I don't know if they're spreading the disease—or how—but we found a handful of survivors in Woodoak who believe they're the carriers. You'd do well to keep a close watch for any that swim the moat.'

'There were rats in Bradmayne.'

'I remember you telling me.' Thaddeus fell silent for a moment to order his thoughts. 'Ian said you're never been bitten by fleas. Is that true?'

'It is.'

'The survivors in Woodoak spoke of how sufferers scratched themselves before they fell sick, and how the skin of the living crawled after touching the dead. Full immersion brought relief, as it did for you in Devil's Brook, and I wonder if the water washed away fleas. Do you recall if Sir Richard or any of your companions complained of itching?'

'They all did. Bradmayne was a filthy place. Fleas and lice were as prevalent as rats. Sir Richard didn't know whether to envy me my thick skin or curse me for escaping my share of the bites. It's a good guess, Thaddeus, but is it true?'

Another weary sigh. 'I don't know, but it's the only explanation I can think of for why the pestilence moves so freely between demesnes. Rats stay close to food but fleas travel with their hosts. Talk it through with Lady Anne. She'll know better than I whether such a thing is possible. We discussed many times how a merchant or pedlar might carry the sickness without succumbing himself.'

Gyles half expected Lady Anne to declare herself, since there was no reason for her to remain hidden. But she didn't. 'Let me summon her so that you can talk it through with her yourself.'

Thaddeus's refusal was immediate. 'There's no time. I must leave again within the hour. I came for horse collars, harness and rope to pull the wagon from Holcombe. I believe we stored all the tackle in Sir Richard's chamber. I see you decided to leave the raft in the water, so can you send across enough for two horses? Also, put your mind to thinking which route we should take out of Holcombe. Do you have a good enough memory of the highways from when you travelled with Sir Richard to say if there's a throughway to Afpedle? It would help if we could herd the sheep and drive the wagon together.'

Gyles pictured the roads in his mind. 'I remember a drovers' lane that leads to the west some five miles down the highway south out of Holcombe, and another a mile or so to the north which comes out above Athelhelm . . . but I wouldn't advise taking either of them. You'll become bogged down in mud when the rain comes. Your best bet would be to haul the wagon to Athelhelm and meet the sheep there. How far is it from your camp?'

'Three thousand paces . . . maybe four . . . but the path along the bank is barely wide enough to take a horse. It won't take the wagon.'

'The river might. It's not deep and has a gravel bottom if memory serves me well. I recall Sir Richard riding along it once and marvelling at the trout swimming ahead of him.' Gyles shrugged. 'The work will be arduous but it'll make your journey a great deal safer than negotiating passage through demesnes you don't know. Would you like my help with the task? I'm sure Milady will grant me leave to accompany you.'

Lady Anne heard a low laugh. 'Nothing would please your sons less, old man. They want the glory for themselves.' Another hesitation. 'Is Milady well?'

'She is, and has promised a celebration to honour you and our sons when you return. She has named you as heroes and lights six candles in your memory every night. You saw them in her window as you came along the highway.'

'I did,' said Thaddeus. 'It's a kind thought, but a foolish one, perhaps, since it speaks of the presence of people here. What of Lady Eleanor? How does she fare?'

Gyles was unsure how much to say until Lady Anne whispered that he should be truthful. 'Not well. She seems to have lost her wits. In the space of a few hours this day, she attacked and wounded my Isabella; declared herself free of Lady Anne, claiming her real mother to be a child under My Lord of Foxcote's protection; and threatened to have us all burnt at the stake for refusing to acknowledge her as the true mistress of Develish. Her greatest rage was for Lady Anne's plan to give us our freedom. She'd rather watch us die of the pestilence than release ourselves from bondage.'

Thaddeus asked how bad Isabella's injuries were. 'I hate to think of her in pain, Gyles.'

'As do we all. She's pale and weak but able to walk. She took fifteen pricks from a bodkin but none was deep. Milady and Martha are caring for her and say she'll be recovered within a week.'

'I'm happy to hear that. Her brothers will be, too. Did Lady Eleanor give a reason for her behaviour?'

'Only mad rantings about Lady Anne usurping power that should have been hers. She seems unable to understand that, by keeping the secret of her birth all these years, it was Lady Anne who gave her legitimacy. Your stepfather pointed it out to her. You wouldn't have recognised him, Thaddeus. He spoke in praise of you, saying he'd rather bend his knee to you than the ungrateful mongrel Lady Anne has raised.'

There was another quiet laugh. 'I recognise very little of what you're telling me, Gyles. How long has Eleanor known that Milady is not her mother?'

'The mistress told her this afternoon in the hopes of curing her madness. Martha says she's been acting strangely since her father died but never with such lunacy as today. She promises to have Milady condemned as a heretic if she's ever given the chance.'

'Has she been confined?'

'In a serf's hut next to John Trueblood. The enclosure has rung all afternoon with her curses and complaints.'

'What form do her complaints take?'

It was Gyles's turn to be amused. 'Whatever comes to mind. Her worst slurs are against the men of the demesne—yourself included. When we're not cowards and thieves, we're base-born slaves with the appetites of dogs.'

'Is there sympathy for her?'

'Only from my daughter and young Robert. They see virtue in her that others don't, never mind Isabella was within her rights to demand a stronger punishment than Robert's suggestion of a day's imprisonment for each prick she made. No one wants her released before her madness passes. She's vicious enough to kill next time, and she'll receive no mercy from me if she harms Isabella again.'

'Then detain her until your twins return. They've grown in courage and resolve through the death and misery they've seen and won't tolerate anger against their sister from such as Lady Eleanor. Make sure she understands that.'

'You ask for the moon. She refuses to listen to anything serfs have to say.'

'Will she listen to Master de Courtesmain?'

'He's afraid of his own shadow. He can barely stand for trembling at the thought of the vengeance the High Sheriff will wreak on us for daring to put Sir Richard's daughter on trial for wounding one so far beneath her as Isabella. You did Milady no service by handing him your position, Thaddeus. John Trueblood would have made a better steward than the two-faced Frenchman.'

'I thought it wiser to keep him at Lady Anne's side. He has a jealous nature and would have caused trouble for anyone else in the position.'

Gyles nodded agreement before changing the subject. 'How long before we see you again?'

'I'll send your sons and the sons of your friends with the sheep from Afpedle in three days' time. They'll need pens on this side of the moat to take the flock, and a shelter for themselves from the rain. Can the men of Develish build so much in so short a time? And will Milady allow them to cross the moat?'

'No reason why not. She gave permission for you to cross when I returned with Sir Richard. Will you be with the boys?'

'No. I'll bring the wagon later when I've worked out how to get it here. You should make them wait two weeks on this side of the moat. I'm as certain as I can be that they don't have the pestilence, but you should still be cautious. They can use the time to slaughter the sheep and send the carcasses across on the raft.'

'Sheep won't be easy to drive through rain. A man should be in charge of such an undertaking. Let me return with you and take the lead.'

There was a brief pause before Thaddeus answered. 'I don't say I'm not tempted, but your sons have worked hard to prove themselves. Don't think of them as boys, Gyles. Greet them as men and you won't be disappointed.' He urged Gyles to make haste to bring him rope, collars and harness, also oats for the horse if there were any to spare. 'People will expect answers if they find me here, and I'm not a great talker. Any one of my companions will tell our story better than I can.'

Gyles made one last attempt to persuade Lady Anne to reveal herself. She'd seemed so keen to speak with Thaddeus when he'd first approached the moat. 'At least let me wake Lady Anne and bring her out alone. She has felt the loss of your counsel very deeply, Thaddeus.'

'And I hers . . . but I want no sweeter reminders of what I'm missing when even your gravelly old chords are tempting me to linger. Assure her of my loyalty when you tell her of this visit, but do not disturb her sleep on my behalf.'

'Is there anything else you'd like me to say?'

'Nothing you can deliver without blushing, old man. I find I'm more attached to Develish than I thought. It's not easy to break the bonds that hold us to the people and places we know.'

ତ୍ୟୋ

Lady Anne walked in Gyles's shadow to the house, slipping through the door first before instructing him to fetch the rope and tackle while she looked for oats. In the kitchen she made a package of bread, moistened with cold potage—all that was left from the night before—and added a precious hard-boiled egg, pickled in brine. Before she tied the corners of the small sacking bag, she hurried to the steward's office, lit a candle and penned a note which she folded and placed across the egg where Thaddeus would find it.

It was hard to know what Gyles made of this quiet visit by night, but Lady Anne thought she understood it. Almost every question Thaddeus asked had been designed to find out if Eleanor had made accusations of rape or murder against his companions, and Lady Anne knew he would not allow them to return if she had. She wished she could share everything with him, for he deserved an explanation of Eleanor's behaviour, but the girl's secret wasn't hers to tell. Instead, she prayed the words she had written would persuade him she had uncovered the truth about Jacob, and that Eleanor would cause him and his companions no more trouble.

Would he appreciate, or even understand, her need of his support? she wondered. She hoped most earnestly that he did, for a heaviness in her heart told her he was undecided whether to cross the moat himself once the sheep and the grain were safely delivered. He'd been so firm in his resistance to seeing her that, despite his words to Gyles, she feared his true intention was indeed to cut his ties with Develish.

ତ୍ୟୋ

My Dear Friend,

I write this letter in haste while Gyles gathers what you need for your journey. I pray you find it and will be comforted by my words when the sun comes up. I believe you removed yourself and the boys in secret to keep the harmony of Develish from being fractured, and I thank you for your kindness in doing so. I regret most deeply the manner of Jacob's passing—the details of which are known to me—but be assured he rests in peace and the problems you foresaw have not arisen. No one questions that his death was an accident or that your enterprise is noble—to seek supplies for Develish.

I envy you your freedom, Dear Friend, and will not take it from you at any price, but remember the hearts that beat for you in Develish. My guess is that you plan to leave again when you have fulfilled your promise to bring us food, but I beg you not to do so in a hurry. It will sadden me terribly if you arrive and depart a second time by night with only a wagon of grain to show you ever returned. Can you even begin to understand how much you've been missed?

You and I have achieved so much together and I believe you find my counsel wise. Please do not vanish again without allowing me to give you the benefit of my thoughts. You and I have long shared dreams of freedom for our people, but they will have little meaning if you are not amongst us when the time comes for us to break the bonds that keep us here. We depend on your strength more than you realise.

Perhaps you believe your life less necessary to the demesne than husbands and fathers like Gyles Startout and John Trueblood? If so, you are wrong. I have much need of you.

Yours in sincerity,
Anne

ख๛

It was an hour before Gyles came looking for Lady Anne in the steward's office to say Thaddeus had departed again. She was sitting by candlelight, drawing up plans to build pens outside the moat, and she smiled when he spoke of his joy on hearing that his sons were well. 'I'm glad for you, Gyles.'

'But now I have more reason to worry for their safety, milady. I informed Thaddeus of My Lord of Bourne's attack on us, and he shocked me by saying that My Lord and his fighting men were in Holcombe two days ago, a bare forty-eight hours after leaving here. He assured me that he and our sons weren't seen, but Develish will suffer badly if he's wrong. Bourne has only to bring the six of them here in chains and you'll be forced to bargain their lives against the two hundred inside the moat.'

Lady Anne's smile died. She had all but forgotten the evil old man in the tumultuous ups and downs of the day, yet she didn't doubt he would avenge himself on Develish if he could. To have his Norman army repelled by English serfs would have dented his pride, and his greed for the gold he believed to be in Develish's treasury would not have diminished. 'We watched him travel north. How could he have reached Holcombe so quickly? We killed four of his horses and injured more.'

'But not his tow-horses, milady. My guess is he did what I advised Thaddeus against and took a drovers' route. They're the shortest links between highways and, without livestock to hinder him and with enough men to keep his wheels turning, his carriage could manage them easily. Being a thief, he'd prefer them. He's less likely to be seen or challenged if he stays off the public roads.'

'But why Holcombe?'

'Thaddeus says it's all but abandoned, milady. He watched it several days ago and believes only serfs remain in the manor house. He saw horses in the fields so I'm guessing My Lord has taken them to replace the ones he lost. Weapons too, since no peasant would have the courage to gainsay him if he demanded them from their master's armoury. I fear our triumph against him was short-lived and it won't be long before we see him again—with or without Thaddeus and our sons.'

'Did you explain that to Thaddeus?'

'I did, and repeated my offer to accompany him, even suggesting we take James Buckler and Adam Catchpole. With more guards, we'll have a better chance of bringing the supplies home safely.'

'How did he answer?'

'He said you wouldn't permit it, milady. The defence of Develish is more important than sheep herding. He's right, of course, but it doesn't stop me worrying.'

'Nor I, Gyles. I hoped this day would end in the happy knowledge that all six are alive, but it seems our anxiety for them must continue a while longer.'

'Thaddeus looks to the weather to protect him, milady. He offered me a wager that Develish serfs and Afpedle sheep will take driving rain more easily than My Lord of Bourne and his men.'

Lady Anne smiled. 'Then I'll pray for a storm.'

Gyles studied her silently for several moments. 'You were quick to step behind me when Thaddeus approached, milady. What made you think he wouldn't speak freely if he knew you were there?'

There was barely a pause before she answered. 'He asked if you were alone. I understood why when he told you about burning Athelhelm. It's not something he'd want anyone else to hear.'

'Was that your impression, milady? I thought he seemed more worried about the welcome our sons would receive.'

Lady Anne placed her elbows on the desk and rested her cheek against her hands. If she confided in anyone, it would be Gyles. He had been her friend and adviser for ten years, and her affection for him and his family ran very deep. But how could she be honest without revealing why Thaddeus had removed his sons from the demesne? Gyles's pride would be much diminished if he learnt of Ian and Olyver's readiness to be whipped by Eleanor in return for a touch of her breasts.

She recalled the words Thaddeus had written in a letter Isabella had insisted on showing her when she came to tell her of Eleanor's pregnancy—*I do what I do to free your brothers and their friends, not to ensnare them in more intrigue*—and the sentiment was surely as true tonight as it had been two weeks ago.

'You must blame me for Thaddeus's caution,' she said. 'I refused him permission to leave during Jacob's funeral because I felt it spoke of a lack of respect for his brother. I imagine he came to discover if I'd made good on my threat to post him and your sons as absconders if they disobeyed me.'

Disbelief showed in Gyles's eyes. 'You're accomplished in many things, milady, but not in telling falsehoods. Perhaps it would be better to inform our people he came for horse collars and to request that sheep pens be built.'

'I'm sure that's wise.'

He made to turn away but changed his mind. 'Have I done something wrong, milady, failed you in some way, that you think I can't be trusted with the truth? If I frightened you with talk of bandits, I most humbly apologise. Young Robert was right to say my sight is not what it was.'

Lady Anne shook her head in immediate denial. 'You're my closest friend and I would trust you with my life.' She searched his face for a moment. 'Let me pose a different conundrum for you. Would you have me tell you the mysteries of your wife's heart if I knew them?'

Gyles pulled a twisted smile. 'I'd not hear anything good about myself if you did.'

'Then it wouldn't be truth—just words said in a moment of irritation—and my betrayal would be the worse for stirring up trouble where none existed.'

He was too clever to accept such an anodyne excuse. 'But what if the trouble were real, milady? Wouldn't it be a greater betrayal to stay quiet when you know that harm may come to others from your silence?'

Lady Anne spread her hands in a small gesture of apology, praying he didn't think she'd known of Eleanor's plan to attack Isabella. 'I'm less accomplished at reading minds than I am at lying, Gyles. If I knew where harm was lurking, be sure I would tell you.'

He gave a small nod then moved to the door, pausing with his hand on the latch. 'Thaddeus asked me to thank you for the package of food. He recognised the way the bundle was tied and knew you must have prepared it. He thanks you, too, for the candles you light in your window each night.'

She smiled again. 'I heard him say they were a foolish idea.'

'He was jesting. I believe he knew them for what they were the moment he saw them—as I should have done the first day you lit them.'

'And what's that, Gyles?'

He eased open the door. 'A sign that it's safe for our sons to come home, milady . . . though I'm puzzled why they or Thaddeus would need such assurance.'

ఆౚ

Two miles down the highway, Thaddeus wished he'd had the sense to bring a pack horse to carry the heavy horse collars that he wore around his shoulders and the tightly coiled ropes and harness that were balanced across his saddle and thighs. However delicately Killer picked his way around the ruts in the road, the collars drew blisters on his neck and the rope jabbed relentlessly against his groin.

The rain, which had begun as a fine drizzle when he left Develish valley, grew in strength the farther south he and Killer travelled, and both were as wet as if they'd taken a swim in the moat by the time they reached the open ground where he and the boys had left the highway a fortnight earlier. He considered looking for shelter under the trees that lined Devil's Brook but doubted he'd ever get himself or the charger moving again. Instead, he gritted his teeth and closed his mind to discomfort, thinking instead about the letter he'd found in Milady's package.

Even while Gyles had been narrating the story of how the serfs of Develish had repelled My Lord of Bourne's attack, Thaddeus had been devouring the bread and the pickled egg. Both tasted the sweeter for being absent from his diet for two weeks, and now the only parts of him that didn't hurt were his half-full belly and the patch of skin on his chest that was covered by the small square of parchment he'd tucked inside his tunic. Without light, he hadn't been able to read what Milady had written but he was sure her words were full of kindness, since she'd had no need to send him a message at all.

Gyles had been careful to hold the lantern at his side as he walked to the front door of the manor house, but Thaddeus's eyes were too well adjusted to the dark to miss the swish of a cloak behind his legs and the deference with which he shepherded a small, slender shadow inside.

He'd felt a brief hurt that Lady Anne had hidden herself from him until he remembered he'd asked Gyles if he was alone. He worried then that it was he who had hurt her by refusing Gyles's offers to fetch her, until the raft brought her package atop the rope.

'I saw you step aside to let her enter the house,' he'd confessed to Gyles as he ate the egg. 'Had I known she was behind you I would have tempered my language about what we've encountered. It wasn't my intention to frighten her.'

'She guessed as much, which is why she hid herself,' Gyles answered. 'But you're wrong to think she frightens easily, Thaddeus. My Lord of Bourne's captain gave a clear indication that the women of Develish, being free of the pestilence, would be as highly prized by his men as gold, so Milady gathered our wives and daughters in the church and armed herself with a dagger in order to kill the first soldier who entered. She knew she would suffer for it, but she intended to fight as fiercely as the men.'

And suffer she would have done, Thaddeus thought now. He could think of no quicker way to break her spirit—and the spirit of her people—than to strip her naked and force her to submit to a relay of soldiers in front of her own serfs. The same would be true if he and the boys were taken prisoner and brought to Develish for a hanging. Gyles had spoken honestly when he said that, for all her strength of mind, Milady would surrender the demesne before she allowed six of her own to be strung from a gallows on the other side of the moat.

Nonetheless, Thaddeus thought Gyles's fears more alarmist than real, for the chances of Bourne finding their camp near the River Pedle were negligible. The greater threat was to Develish, not least because it offered comfort and safety from the storm. If Thaddeus was picturing the joy of being warm, dry and fed inside the great hall, how much more would My Lord and his men be coveting the same?

With sudden impatience, he dismissed Bourne from his mind. It was all too easy to give way to imagined fears when the brain was tired. The more urgent problem was how to move the grain from their camp to Develish. He was taken by Gyles's suggestion of hauling the wagon up the river to Athelhelm, although he worried about the water rising if the downpour continued. He and the horses might keep their feet, but the boys would not. They were too slight and too short in stature.

He recalled his angry denouncing of them the previous night. His mood had darkened after Edmund related the story of Eleanor's birth—a secret known only to Clara until she'd chosen to share it with her son—but he'd lost patience when the boys began to prance about the grass in front of the camp, wearing the clothes and wielding the swords they'd stolen from Holcombe. Their carefree antics were a bitter reminder of the childhood he'd never had, and every frustration he'd ever felt about his own birth had hammered inside his head. But he'd been wrong to lose his temper, and he wished now that he hadn't. They weren't to blame for his terrible sense of betrayal because Milady had allowed him to believe he was the only bastard in Develish.

He fell asleep to the slow, gentle rhythm of Killer's walk, and the beast, unaware of his rider's inattention, continued to feel his way around the ruts and holes in the road. It was what he'd been trained for; rare had been the journey when Sir Richard of Develish was sober enough to see where he was going.

It meant neither was alert to sentries at the end of the drovers' route above Athelhelm, or prepared for the sudden beam of light from a lantern that shone on Thaddeus's face and revealed him as a Develish serf.

Two

Thaddeus's camp on the River Pedle

IAN STARTOUT SAT HUNCHED IN misery, wondering if dawn would ever break. By building a shelter amongst the trees, and positioning their stolen wagon against the side that faced the river, he and his four companions were protected against the worst of the weather, but their inability to light a fire had rendered them blind. Pressed hard against each other in the small space left to them by the twelve large barrels of pilfered grain, they stared sightlessly at nothing, preferring to withdraw into their thoughts than shout above the pounding rain.

Ian's mood was turbulent, swinging between love for Thaddeus and a deep hurt that the man he'd thought of as a friend had left without explanation. Had he not done everything Thaddeus had asked without complaint in their search for supplies? Had he not been the most dutiful and received the fewest rewards? And what should he do if Thaddeus didn't come back? Force these churls to drive sheep through the rain? He hadn't the strength to keep punching their stupid faces when they challenged his orders. The only leader they respected was Thaddeus.

Not one of the boys would have blamed Thaddeus for turning his back on Develish if Edmund's tale about Lady Anne not being mother to Eleanor was true. Any man, bastard-born, would cavil at being forced to live the life of a slave while Sir Richard's daughter, carrying the same stain of illegitimacy, was paraded as a lady. Ian understood well that Thaddeus must have been pained to hear the story from Edmund rather than Lady Anne, but were hurt feelings enough of a reason to cause him to abandon his companions without a word?

Ian's first awareness that night was coming to an end was when he saw the ghostly glimmer of faces in front of the curtain of rain that was running off the shelter's interwoven roof of osiers and fern. As the light strengthened, he saw his own emotions reflected back at him in the eyes of his friends. Wretchedness. Uncertainty. Anxiety. But with the dawn came reason. It made no sense that Thaddeus hadn't returned. He'd worked too hard to locate supplies for Develish to give up on the venture now, and he wouldn't have burdened his conscience with burning Athelhelm if he hadn't intended to herd sheep along the highway that ran through it.

With sudden decision, Ian pushed himself to his feet and began searching through the weapons, clothes and saddles that were piled on top of the grain barrels. They'd tossed everything in when the rain began to fall in earnest, and with the light still too dim to see, he used touch to select what he wanted.

His twin, Olyver, raised his voice to carry above the drumming on the roof. 'Are you planning to look for him?'

'Yes.'

'I'll come with you.'

'Me too,' called the other three boys in unison.

Ian shook his head. 'Just Olyver. If we don't return by nightfall, one of you must ride to Develish tomorrow to tell Lady Anne there's grain here and sheep at Afpedle. The other two must keep the rain off these kegs until help comes.'

'It's not possible,' protested Edmund Trueblood. 'We can keep plugging the roof, but when the ground becomes saturated the water will rise from below.'

'Then think of a way to lift the kegs,' Ian growled. '*Build* something . . . sit with the damned things on your laps, if necessary. Behave like men as Thaddeus expects, and find a solution to the problem instead of saying it can't be done. Develish won't thank us for bringing home mouldy grain.'

Joshua Buckler laid a calming hand on Edmund's arm. 'There are beds at the inn in Holcombe,' he said. 'They're low enough and sturdy enough to make a decent platform if we carry them back.'

Peter Catchpole watched Ian don a second tunic for warmth and then hand another to his brother to do the same. 'You'd better be sure you're doing the right thing,' he warned. 'What if Thaddeus comes back frozen to the bone and finds you gone?'

'Lay him down and warm him up,' retorted Olyver.

'He'll go after you.'

'It's not his job. Get off your own arses to do it.'

'There's no sense in us all dying of cold.'

'Then put your minds to keeping a fire alight and finding food,' Ian told him. 'Whatever happens, we'll need to eat—unless you want to kill Joshua's dogs and swallow them raw.' He selected a leather jerkin and buttoned it across his chest, handing a second to Olyver. 'We'll divide the arrows we made yesterday between us and tie them in bundles across our saddles,' he said, passing his brother a sword and a bow. 'They may not fly straight but they'll look threatening.'

'Where do you think Thaddeus went?' Joshua asked.

'We'll start in Athelhelm and then ride to Afpedle and on to Woodoak. If he comes back without us, follow that path. We'll be somewhere along it.' Ian dragged down a couple of saddles. 'All I know for certain is that he would come looking for us if he thought we were in trouble, so it's only right we do the same for him.'

He glanced at Joshua's hunting hounds, wondering if they'd be able to follow Thaddeus's scent, but he felt Olyver's immediate resistance. Better the twins travel alone than have Joshua's nervousness holding them back was the thought that came to him. He gave a small nod before stringing a sword and bow across his back and reaching for the bundle of arrows.

'Do your best and we'll do the same,' he told the others as he followed his twin into the rain.

They found the horses huddled within the tree line, their flanks running with water. Both boys felt momentary qualms about saddling the two they selected, knowing the animals would develop sores as the hard leather slithered to and fro across sodden fur and rain-softened skin. 'We have to do it,' Olyver shouted. 'We'll get nowhere on foot.'

Ian nodded. 'We should lead them first. There's no point mounting until we reach the highway at Athelhelm. They'll break their legs if they slip on wet grass.'

They didn't speak after that, but as Ian followed behind his brother with the river in spate on one side and dark woodland the other, he wondered if they'd ever been so in tune with each other. He felt the same fears Olyver felt. The light was too dim.

The rain too strong. The level of the river too high. They wouldn't be able to cross the ford at Athelhelm . . . It was strange. They had fought all their lives—refusing to sound alike, behave alike or look alike—yet today he knew every thought that was running through Olyver's head. *Please, God, make me brave.*

෨෬

Neither was prepared for what they found in Athelhelm. The storm had come too soon after Thaddeus had fired the village to reduce everything to ash, and charred bodies lay amongst the ruins. One had struggled to his doorway, lying half in and half out of the entrance, and the boys retched at the hideous, swollen face that lay in the dirt. It was impossible to say if it was black from smoke or the putrid blood of the pestilence, but the sight of the bulging, terrified eyes was the stuff of nightmares.

The relentless rain had caused Devil's Brook to break its banks and a stream of loosened mud and stone was washing towards the ford. Even as Ian and Olyver watched, the arm of a corpse lifted as debris passed beneath it, giving the appearance of life. Each wondered how long it would be before the stream became a flood and washed the bodies away or buried them beneath drifts of earth. Perhaps God had brought this downpour for a reason.

As they'd drawn closer to the village and seen how turbulent the water in the river was becoming where Devil's Brook was feeding into it, they'd left the path and moved through the trees in order to come out on the highway above the village. From that vantage point, they could see that the ford to Afpedle was impassable. If they'd known where safe passage was from crossing it before, it might have been different, but the river had backed up the highway, forming a lake which disguised the curve of the road.

'It would explain why Thaddeus hasn't come back,' called Olyver. 'Maybe he's decided to camp in Afpedle.'

Ian turned to look along the highway to Develish. The visibility was so poor he could barely see to the first bend but he was drawn by the idea that Thaddeus might have returned to their home demesne. Yet why? What was so urgent that he was persuaded to ride in darkness instead of waiting for daylight? And who would know he was there except the men who stood on the guard steps?

'I think he went this way,' he answered, gesturing to his right. 'Father and John Trueblood take turns to watch the approach from the village at night. I'm guessing Thaddeus wanted to speak with one of them privately while the rest of the demesne slept. He'll not take us back if Eleanor's made accusations of rape and murder against us.'

Olyver followed his gaze, questioning whether Thaddeus cared enough for any of his companions to continue protecting them. He'd been in a black mood the previous evening, cursing them roundly for their laziness and tomfoolery. 'What if it's Thaddeus she's accused?' he asked, leading his mount alongside Ian's. 'She hates him enough. Could Father have taken him in charge?'

Ian shook his head. 'He has too much fondness for Thaddeus. He'd have sent him away again. John Trueblood likewise.'

'Then where is he?' Olyver asked reasonably. 'It's not that far to Develish . . . and he'd have to have left before dawn if he didn't want his presence known to everyone.'

Ian put his foot in the stirrup and heaved himself into the saddle. 'Let's find out. He'll cuss the Devil out of us if he's round the next bend, and we'll feel mighty foolish for worrying, but we can't get any wetter than we are already.'

He came to regret that statement when his teeth were chattering with cold. The sun had been up for two hours by then but its light, blocked by dark, heavy clouds was the murky grey of dusk. There was no warmth in it, and the wind sliced easily through his jerkin and double tunic. He kept narrowing his eyes against the stinging rain, searching for movement ahead, but there was nothing to see. He was close to giving up, certain he'd guessed wrongly about Thaddeus's intentions, when Olyver put a restraining hand on his bridle and brought both horses to a halt. He jerked his chin towards the woodland on their right.

'There's something in those trees. Look at the horses' ears. They can hear it.'

Ian canted his head, listening. The sound of a whinny, barely discernible over the wind, was unmistakeable. 'Do you think it's Killer?'

'Bound to be,' said Olyver with decision. 'How many other horses will be out in weather like this?' He slid from his mount. 'We should go on foot.' He adjusted his bow and sword across his shoulder and lifted the bundle of arrows Ian had given him from his saddle. 'Let's pray we don't have to use these.'

They tied their mounts to trees at the edge of the road and crept forward slowly, alert for any noise that would tell them which direction to go, but if a second whinny came, they both missed it. They felt a pounding on the ground more often than they heard anything above the wind and rain. If either had been alone, he would have turned back out of superstitious fear—such strange tremors in the earth weren't normal—but, together, they went on. They could barely see ten yards ahead, so dark was the shade inside the wood, and both gave shouts of alarm as something huge and black rose out of the ground in front of them.

They would have lost all courage if they hadn't heard the rattle of harness and laboured breathing as the creature crashed to earth again. 'Praise be to Mother Mary and all the Blessed Saints!' Ian gasped, before stepping forward and holding out a hand. 'Whoa, boy! Whoa! What's troubling you?'

'Take care he doesn't rear again,' warned Olyver. 'He's scared out of his wits.' He made a gesture to show he was going to approach the animal from the other side. 'He seems to have lost his reins so be ready to catch his head collar. It'll need both our strength to stop him from bolting.'

Perhaps Thaddeus's charger recognised their voices, because his only resistance to being caught was a half-hearted buck as their hands closed on the straps beneath his rolling eyes. Ian ran a soothing palm down his neck, feeling the heat and the trembling under the skin, but it wasn't until he looked at the back legs that he saw why the wretched creature was so frightened. For a brief moment he wondered if the rope bound tightly around the fetlocks was a badly applied hobble, but the tangle of hemp on the forest floor, caught in brambles and fallen branches, told a different story. The horse's rear hooves had become caught in the coils and his attempts to free himself had tightened the noose around his legs.

'What should we do?' Olyver called. 'He's too worked up. The rope's the only thing that's holding him. If we cut him free, he'll run.'

'Not if you go back for our two. He'll calm quicker with his own kind around him.'

'He'll smash your skull if he rears again. Thaddeus didn't call him Killer for nothing.'

'Do you have a better idea?'

'No.'

'Then go.'

All Ian could do was talk to the animal and keep running his hand down the wet neck, ever ready to jump back if Killer made another futile attempt to break free. His eyes were drawn to a breast collar, lying on the forest floor some ten paces behind Killer. The leather bore the Develish crest, much faded from being bleached by the sun, but Ian recognised it as one the serfs used to harness ponies to the plough. He knew then why Thaddeus had returned to the demesne. He'd gone for tack and rope to yoke a number of horses together in order to move the wagon and grain from their camp. He would have called Thaddeus's name if he hadn't been afraid of spooking the horse. And what would shouts achieve anyway? Thaddeus was no coward or weakling. Whatever accident had befallen him, he would have tried to follow Killer's tracks once daylight came.

It was clear to Ian that the horse had been dragging the rope for a distance because the churned-up trail in the leaf mould stretched farther than his eyes could see. Surely Thaddeus could have found it? Surely he would have heard the whinny and the intermittent pounding of the creature's front hooves as Ian and Olyver had done?

If he were able . . .

It seemed Olyver had been thinking along similar lines. 'Something bad must have happened,' he told his twin as he came to a halt with the other two horses.

Ian nodded. 'How should we do this? Killer seems calmer but he's not going to like us touching his back legs. He'll lash out as soon as we cut him free.'

'Do we have a choice?'

'No.'

Olyver's teeth flashed in a grin. 'Your turn then. At least his eyes have stopped rolling.' He tied their two mounts to a tree and stepped forward to take Ian's place at Killer's head. 'We'll need an anchor to stop him running. If you cut a length of rope from the coils on the ground, I'll make a halter to run around the trunk behind me.'

It took longer than Ian hoped. A sword was a poor substitute for a knife when cutting through fibres that were wound so tightly about flesh and bone that there was no give in them. He was mindful of time passing and even more mindful of Killer's hooves. All the while he hoped the clouds would thin, the rain would ease, and the sun would send more light into the forest. But it didn't happen. If anything, the visibility worsened, and with it their chances of finding Thaddeus. As the final strand of hemp tore apart, he rolled aside, shielding his head from lashing kicks as Killer danced away from him.

Olyver placed a foot on the trunk of the tree to brace himself as the horse fought to tear himself free of the halter. 'I'm losing him,' he shouted. 'He's too strong.'

With a groan, Ian scrambled to his feet and caught the end of the rope behind Olyver, wrapping it around his fist and digging his heels into the ground. 'If we find Thaddeus dead, I'll slit the brute's throat myself,' he muttered through gritted teeth.

'Don't tempt fate,' his twin warned as together they reeled the charger in. Once there was enough slack, he secured the rope about the tree and dropped to a squat to draw breath. 'He near scared me to death. I thought he was the Devil rising up.'

Ian walked to where he'd dropped his sword. 'Me too,' he agreed. 'Maybe this darkness is Hell . . . and we just don't know it.'

'I'm hurting too much to be dead.'

Ian followed the trail of rope that Killer had left behind him on the forest floor for twenty yards. 'There's more harness here,' he called back. 'Another breast collar and traces.'

Olyver rose to his feet, stooping to collect the bundle of arrows he'd dropped when they first saw Killer. He split the bundle in two and passed half to Ian as he drew level with him.

After two hundred yards they came across a second set of traces, and it wasn't hard to work out that Thaddeus must have been carrying them, coiled inside the rope, on the pommel of his saddle. Once he fell, the rope had unravelled and become entangled about Killer's legs, sending the creature into a frenzied charge through the trees, dragging the traces and reins behind him.

After another two hundred yards the trail began to dwindle and the twins knew that if Thaddeus wasn't at the end of it their chances of finding him were small. Killer could have travelled a mile with the coil still in place, in any direction, and neither boy was clever enough to follow a track without clear markers.

'Where next?' Ian asked as he cast around for signs of disturbed leaves. 'Do you think we mistook the trail farther back?'

Olyver shook his head. 'We should return to the highway and look for where Killer first bolted into this woodland. Thaddeus is more likely to be there than here.'

Ian couldn't fault his logic but something—instinct?—wouldn't let him give up. He drew his sword and slashed a slice of bark from the far side of the nearest trunk. 'We'll mark every fifth tree,' he said. 'Keep a count. I'll call it a day when you reach a hundred.'

Olyver hadn't reached fifty when the trees began to thin and the light, such as it was, intensified. Either they were heading back to the highway or there was a clearing ahead. He watched Ian draw to a halt and make a damping motion with his hand to urge silence. 'Did you hear that?' he asked, putting his lips to his brother's ear. 'It sounded like a laugh.'

Olyver nodded, tucking his sword into his belt and readying his bow. They didn't need to give each other instructions. They knew it wasn't Thaddeus they'd heard and neither believed that chance could have put strangers so close to where they'd found Killer.

For once the rain was their friend, hiding the sound of snapping twigs under their feet as they crept forward. As the trees grew wider apart, showing an expanse of grass beyond, Olyver spread his hands to suggest they should separate and approach the clearing from different angles. Ian gave a jerk of his chin to signal agreement. Independently, they could move more easily and find better cover behind the thinning trunks, but he swivelled his first and middle fingers between Olyver's eyes and his own to stress the need to keep in visual contact. They must act together or not all.

Ian recognised the wagon in the middle of the clearing as soon as he was close enough to see My Lord of Bourne's crest emblazoned on the side. There was no sign of My Lord or his fighting men, but it was easy to see Thaddeus. He'd been stripped of his clothes and was lying spread-eagled on the grass in front of the wagon, his wrists and ankles bound to stakes which had been driven into the earth. His nakedness, closed eyes and utter immobility told Ian he was dead. No living person could remain so still with freezing rain beating like needles on his exposed skin.

Twenty yards away Olyver was thinking the same. He looked for any flicker of life in Thaddeus and his heart burnt with anger as he made a solemn pledge to kill My Lord of Bourne. From where he was standing, he could see horses hobbled together on the far side of the clearing, but when he followed the tree line to the left and the right, looking for sight of a soldier, he realised it wasn't a clearing at all but some kind of road. The tracks of My Lord of Bourne's wagon, leading from the east, showed clearly in the grass where the wheels had cut into the turf.

He searched the trees around the horses, convinced Bourne's men must be hiding in the woodland, but if they were there he couldn't see them, and the idea entered his mind to run towards Thaddeus and cut him free. Perhaps Ian sensed the thought because he shook his head and held up his hand to signal his twin to be patient. The scene had all the appearance of trap. Yet he wondered who My Lord was expecting. Soldiers from Develish?

He was racking his brain for a plan when a second laugh came from the direction of the wagon. It was followed by the grunt of a voice and he watched the leather canopy open to allow a man to climb out. Ian recognised him as the captain of arms who had ordered his men to burn Develish village a month earlier. He was clad in the fur-trimmed coat that Thaddeus had stolen from the tannery in Holcombe, and he walked to the spread-eagled serf and kicked him in the ribs.

'My Lord grows impatient,' he said. 'Explain the letter you carry from Lady Anne. What is this freedom she speaks of? Do you carry a message of insurrection to the other peasants of Dorset? Is your treachery against God and the King to blame for the pestilence?' He jerked his head towards a couple of horse collars on the ground near the wagon. 'Why were you carrying those? Whose wagon do you plan to steal? Answer me.'

To Ian's eyes the man looked drunk as he launched another kick at Thaddeus's side, staggering slightly when he missed. There was no response at all from their friend, not even the smallest flinch to show he was aware of the other's kicks or even his presence.

'Your refusal to speak makes My Lord the more suspicious. He sees witchcraft behind it. What manner of creature are you with your height and dark skin? Did you think you wouldn't be recognised as the serf who stood with Lady Anne and lied about Develish dying of the pestilence?' He parted his coat and pulled his cock from his britches. 'You seem to find the rain easy enough to bear. Let's see how you like being used as a piss-pot again.'

The bows of the two boys came up in unison but neither had time to unleash his arrow before Thaddeus ripped his hands from the earth and lunged at his tormentor's legs, catching him behind the calves and flipping him backwards. With a tremendous heave, he pulled himself into a sitting position and reached for the stake that bound his right ankle, grasping it with both hands and wrenching it to and fro to loosen it.

On the other side of the clearing, Ian saw a shape emerge from behind an oak. Without hesitation he levelled his arrow at the man's heart and let it fly. He felt a surge of triumph as it flew straight, and he paused only to watch the man drop before feeding a second arrow onto the string and seeing with detachment that Olyver's arrow had also found a mark. He glanced briefly at the squirming body of a soldier on the grass to his right then raised his eyes to scour the woodland for further movement. There had been ten fighting men when Bourne came to Develish to burn it, and a rider on one of the horses that pulled the wagon.

But where were they?

He heard the twang of a string as his twin released a second arrow but Olyver must have missed because Ian caught a movement out of the corner of his eye and turned to see a cloaked figure running at Thaddeus with a drawn sword. He took a breath to calm himself then loosed his own, and watched with satisfaction as the man tumbled to the ground with a hazel whip buried in his thigh.

He had time to see Thaddeus free his left ankle, but it was hard to keep up with events after that. An arrow, shot from a longbow, thudded into the ground at their friend's side and the boys, seeing how defenceless he was, shouted warnings. In doing so, they gave their own positions away and, within seconds, came under attack themselves. Since their only recourse was to crouch in the lee of their trees while arrows ripped through the leaves above them, they had to interpret what happened from what they heard.

Both believed the hideous and prolonged screams that filled the air came from Thaddeus. They told themselves they should do something—move into the clearing, surrender, beg, plead— but their terror was too great. They pictured their own agony when they suffered the same fate, and looked to escape rather than intervene. But how? In the moment Ian realised the rain of arrows had ceased, he looked up to see a man approach through the woodland, bow raised and string drawn taut, frightened eyes darting to left and right.

He was of a similar age to Ian's father and was almost on top of the boy before he saw him. He stared in disbelief at the skinny youth sitting on the ground, his knees drawn up to his chin as if to make himself as small a target as possible. 'You're just a child,' he said in French, lowering his weapon. 'By what madness do you dare attack My Lord of Bourne's army?'

Ian gave a small shrug before stretching his legs to put tension on his bow and rocking backwards to lift it from the ground. The soldier watched in fascinated horror as the tightly bent arc rose horizontally from amongst the leaves, and he had time to curse himself for lowering his guard as a shaft whipped towards his chest from between the boy's feet. He felt the thud as it pierced his ribs and penetrated his lung, and with sudden weariness tried to bring up his own bow to fire back. He'd been wrong to call this youth a child, he thought, as a second shaft caught him in the heart.

Ian had no idea how long he sat looking at the fallen man. A minute? An hour? They were too close to each other. Ian could smell the sweat on his clothes and see the grizzle of grey hair about his jaw. It might have been any of Develish's elders lying there. The noise of screaming from the clearing beat upon his ears, overwhelming him with grief and guilt, and with a sigh he leant to one side and retched on the forest floor. He'd failed in everything, he thought as he rose unsteadily to his feet and forced himself to confront what was happening to Thaddeus.

He couldn't see him. Only two men writhed on the ground, screaming and clutching their bellies, but Thaddeus wasn't one of them. Ian watched their blood, diluted by rain, spread in pink pools across the grass. One wore Thaddeus's fur-lined coat, the other was the soldier with the arrow in his thigh. To their right lay the body of the man Olyver had killed. A flame of hope lit in Ian's breast. Had Thaddeus escaped? He searched to his left for his twin, and the flame became a blaze of joy when he saw Olyver running through the trees towards him.

'Why the hell didn't you show yourself when the longbows stopped?' his brother demanded angrily, jabbing two fingers at Ian's eyes. 'What was all this about if you couldn't be bothered to look at me? I thought you were dead.' He followed Ian's gaze to the crumpled body of the grizzled fighting man. 'Sweet Mary!'

'He could have killed me if he'd wanted to. He lowered his weapon because he thought me a child.'

'Don't feel bad about it,' answered Olyver sternly. 'There's not an ounce of compassion in any of them. You saw what they did to Thaddeus. I thought it was him who was screaming.'

'Me too.' Ian stared around the clearing. 'Where is he?'

'If he has any sense, he's taken to his heels.'

'Maybe we should do the same.'

But neither moved except to make their bows ready to fire again. They shared a conviction that Thaddeus wouldn't run. Ian watched the blood continue to flow from the wounded men, wondering how Thaddeus had injured them so badly until he remembered the stakes that had pinned him to the ground. They'd still been attached to his wrists when he ripped them out, and the points had been sharp. It would be a good and easy revenge to plunge them into an enemy's belly. The pain would be great and the death slow.

'The soldier you hit in the thigh was carrying a sword,' Olyver muttered, 'but it's not there now. Thaddeus must have taken it. Do you think he's gone after the rest? Five are down so there must be six still standing.'

Ian saw that his brother was right. 'Perhaps that's why the archers stopped firing at us,' he said slowly. 'Perhaps they retreated into the wood so he wouldn't be able to see them. This one looked frightened as he came through the trees but it wasn't me he was afraid of.' He paused. 'Maybe we should draw them out again—give Thaddeus a fighting chance.'

'How?'

'By attacking the wagon. Soldiers won't stay hidden if their lord's in danger.' A glint of anticipated triumph lit in Ian's eyes. 'None of his men will fire on us for fear of hitting their master. We can force the surrender of all of them.'

Olyver smiled wryly. 'You've a grand imagination, Twin. You've made him your prisoner before you've even worked out how to do it.'

Ian assessed the distance between them and the wagon. 'It can't be more than thirty paces,' he said. 'I'll lay money I can make that run and put my sword to the old devil's throat before an archer even has time to pick me out.' He laid his bow on the ground, stripping off his jerkin and second tunic to give himself more freedom of movement. He shook his head as Olyver prepared to do the same. 'We can't both go. You're quicker on the draw than I am. Someone needs to bring the fighting men down as they cross the clearing. Shout numbers as they fall.'

'Just don't run in a straight line,' Olyver cautioned. 'You'll take an arrow in the heart if there's an archer behind the flap in the canopy.' He waited while Ian picked up his sword. 'I'll not let you die,' he said with sudden emotion, gripping the other boy's shoulder. 'I'm in no mood to lose a brother today.'

Ian pulled him into a rough embrace. 'And I'm in no mood to lose you or Thaddeus,' he said. 'By God's grace, we'll all three come out of this alive.'

Three

Olyver put more faith in gut feelings than in God. He was so convinced the danger would come from inside the wagon that he trained his arrow on the side of the canopy and loosed it the minute the aperture opened. Ian, running in a curving arc, saw a man slump backwards, pulling the flap aside with his arm, and he had time to bless his brother as he leapt onto a small wooden step and hauled himself inside.

The space was confined and he hadn't thought My Lord of Bourne would have a weapon. He felt the sting of a blade against his cheek before the impetus of his leap slammed him against the old man in the far corner of the seat. His flesh recoiled before the pale eyes that looked into his own. If there was fear in them, Ian didn't see it. My Lord seemed to believe his stare alone could compel obedience.

As if to prove him right, Ian scrambled away along the seat, flicking his eyes over the chests and barrels on the floor and the fighting man who was slumped, groaning, atop a wooden box. He felt blood run from the wound on his face and saw a snarling lapdog on the floor at My Lord's feet. The first lesson his father had taught him in sword practice was never to hesitate, and the advice served him well as My Lord eased his arm away from the side of the wagon. Ian swung his sword in a backhanded arc, slicing through the ermine-trimmed cloak and cutting the flesh of the old man's shoulder.

My Lord's blade clattered to the floor as he gave a gasp of pain, but Ian's attention had already shifted to the wounded soldier. Olyver's arrow had embedded itself in his side and Ian watched as the man grasped the shaft with both hands and pulled it from his body. With more regret than he'd felt for injuring My Lord—this was another who could have been his father—he sprang to his feet and thrust his sword into the man's neck. Gyles had told him that such a cut brought instant death but he hadn't prepared his son for the hot blood that sprayed from the wound when the blade was withdrawn.

With a feeling of nausea, he heaved the man's torso across the sill of the wagon and toppled him to the ground before whipping around to place the point of his sword to My Lord of Bourne's throat. Only the dog showed fight, baring its teeth and yapping ferociously, until Ian kicked it and the yaps turned to whimpers of pain. The dead soldier's gore was everywhere. On Ian, on the canopy walls and on My Lord's face and clothes; and this time the pitiless eyes did show fear. 'A place is reserved for you in Hell,' the old man whispered in French. 'You offend against God's laws by what you do.'

Ian placed his knee on one of the barrels to steady himself. He'd never spoken to a lord in his life, not even Sir Richard of Develish, and he needed to calm himself before he did so. He felt a fizz of excitement in his veins to have taken Bourne prisoner but it was hard to forget the Church's teachings that men such as this owned him body and soul. The only sounds were the beating of the rain on the leather roof and the whimpers of the dog. Even the screams of the men in the clearing had silenced.

He ran his tongue around the inside of his mouth to produce some saliva, tasting blood as he did so. But whether it was his or the dead soldier's he didn't know. 'You should fear Hell more than I do,' he answered in English. 'Your cruelty marks you out for Satan. His evil is written in your face.'

'A murderer dares accuse me of sin?'

'I'm no murderer. You invited attack when you ordered your men to take an innocent traveller prisoner.'

'Your friend is a common thief. No serf wears such clothes or rides such a fine charger. My sentries recognised him immediately as the liar from Develish. Few men are so tall or so dark of skin.'

Above the pounding of the rain, Ian heard a cry from outside. He recognised the voice as Olyver's. 'Seven!' his twin shouted.

'Do you hear that?' he asked, leaning forward to press the blade tighter against the crepey skin of My Lord's neck, smelling the foul odour of his breath and seeing the trembling in his hands. 'You have four men left. Will you speak so arrogantly when none remains?'

'I am in God's hands.'

'As am I.'

'Not so. You condemn yourself by your actions.'

A smile flickered across the boy's face as he rested his sword point on the old man's ermine collar. 'Yet you are nothing without these trappings. Even the lowest slave would mock if you stood naked before him and claimed to be one of God's chosen.' He leant forward to part the cloak with his left hand, revealing a loose-fitting gold-embroidered gown. 'You are fashioned as other men. You bleed as readily. What is it that sets you apart except your robes?'

Bourne's pale eyes glittered angrily. 'I carry the King's warrant and am here on his business. If his armies find me dead when the danger has passed, they will search out every living person within twenty miles of this place and put them to the question with hot irons. You will have their agony on your conscience as your entrails are torn from you, and your limbs broken on the wheel.'

Was he speaking the truth? Ian wondered, trying to recall if My Lord had made mention of riding for the King when he'd come to Develish. The idea made him nervous. What if he and Olyver had been wrong about Thaddeus? What if Thaddeus knew Bourne was a King's man and had fled to save himself? He couldn't deny he was a thief. They were all thieves. Murderers, too, if the men Ian and Olyver were killing bore their orders from the King.

A smile played across My Lord's thin lips as he pushed Ian's blade aside with the edge of a gnarled finger. 'Your hand shakes with terror. You understand now how great your offence is in daring to challenge one so far above you.'

It was true. Ian could feel his courage deserting him. Whatever determination had carried him this far seemed suddenly gone, and he sought desperately for what to do next. His brain, worn out by a sleepless night and the constant battering of the weather, had no answers. His only thought was that if he left My Lord alive, he and Olyver would forfeit their lives for certain; and if he killed him, they might not.

Would he have gone through with it? He didn't know. His heart cringed at the thought of slaughtering an unarmed man, for it would make him a murderer indeed. Yet what choice did he have? A rush of weary tears rose in his eyes when Thaddeus's voice spoke from outside.

'It is I who challenges you, My Lord. The offences you have committed against the innocent people of Dorset will not go unpunished.'

A huge fist reached past Ian, grasping the collar around the old man's neck and pulling him bodily past the boy before flinging him to the ground. No words were exchanged as Thaddeus cut the bonds and stakes from his wrists and ankles and used them to bind his prisoner's hands. His concern was for Ian. 'Are you all right, my friend?'

'I think so,' said the boy, jumping from the wagon. Over Thaddeus's shoulder, he saw Olyver emerge from the trees and begin running towards them. 'What about you?' There wasn't an inch of Thaddeus's body that didn't carry lash marks, bruises or scratches. 'We saw the soldier kicking you.' He stared in fascination at the blood-stained sword in Thaddeus's hand.

'It's nothing to fret about. There are more brambles than trees in this vile forest. Does the cut on your face trouble you?'

'Not yet.'

Thaddeus stabbed his sword into the soft turf to keep it upright before bending to unfasten the jewelled clasp at the neck of My Lord's cloak and pulling the garment off him. 'This will give me some warmth at least. He's a scrawny little brute but there's width in the material.'

'Where are your own clothes?'

'Stolen by this thief and his men. I'll have them back as soon as I strip the corpses.'

Olyver arrived as he wrapped the cloak around himself, repositioning the clasp some six inches lower to allow for his broader shoulders and neck. 'I'll not forget this day or the debt of gratitude I owe you,' he promised them.

'We're not safe yet,' Olyver said urgently. 'By my count there are still four in the trees. They'll not fire on us while we have My Lord of Bourne prisoner, but I see no way to escape with our lives unless we take him with us.'

Thaddeus retrieved his sword and rested the tip against the old man's cheek, watching the rain wash gore and mud from the blade onto the grey skin. Both twins recoiled at the look of hatred in Thaddeus's eyes. 'You give him hope of rescue,' he said. 'Only these two wretches still live.' He nodded to the men who'd been screaming.

'I'm not sure every man I hit is dead,' confessed Olyver.

'Nor I,' said Ian. 'They fell but they may only be injured.'

Thaddeus looked around the clearing. 'How did you make your way here? Did you ride?' They nodded. 'Where did you leave your horses?'

'In the same place we found Killer. Half a mile inside the wood.'

A brief smile lifted Thaddeus's lips. 'Is he injured? He fought harder than I to avoid capture.'

Ian, as keen to depart as Olyver, assured Thaddeus that Killer was frightened but unharmed and begged him to make haste. 'We found the rope and traces you brought from Develish so there's nothing to keep us here,' he said. 'Let's go while we can.'

Olyver nodded. 'Our luck won't last. We'll not explain this easily if travellers come along the highway.'

Thaddeus shook his head. 'I've a score to settle with My Lord of Bourne. Fetch our horses and all the harness you can find and bring them to the edge of the woodland, then stay out of sight until you hear my call. What I choose to do here is no concern of yours.'

Ian flicked a nervous glance at the old man. 'He said he's on the King's business. It will cause trouble if he dies.'

'Only for him,' answered Thaddeus before sending them on their way with a warning to concentrate on their own tasks and ignore his. 'Guard your consciences well,' he said, 'and let me guard mine. You've done nothing this day to earn God's judgement. To kill a man in battle is not a crime.'

His words were meant for My Lord as much as for Ian and Olyver, and he took grim humour from the fear in Bourne's face. Judging by the way the old wretch cowered on the ground, he expected death within seconds.

ం⌀

Five miles north, in the steward's office at Develish, Lady Anne was writing in a ledger by candlelight. The rain was incessant, causing Devil's Brook and the moat around the manor house to overtop their banks. She recorded that the fathers of Thaddeus's young companions were building sheep pens and a shelter on the pastureland outside the enclosure while the rest of her people, consumed with anxiety, were gathered in the great hall. The news that Thaddeus had visited during the night to report that he and his companions had found plentiful supplies of food had been a cause for rejoicing until rumours began that he'd said this unnatural darkness was the beginning of the Black Death.

Gyles Startout, the only person to speak with Thaddeus, did his best to calm the fears, but his eleven-year-old nephew Robert proved more successful. Lady Anne paused in her writing to listen to his treble voice win laughter from the crowd by regaling them with a disrespectful tale of how his uncle's elderly eyes had mistaken a horse on a halter for a crowd of bandits. He embroidered the story wickedly, but few doubted he spoke the truth when he said Thaddeus had come only for collars and rope to pull a wagon of grain from Athelhelm to Develish.

Lady Anne had many reasons to bless the boy's level-headedness, not least his matter-of-fact observation to Gyles that Eleanor should be released from her prison when the rain began in earnest. There wasn't a serf's hut inside the enclosure which was strong enough to survive a storm, as they were built as temporary shelters when news of the pestilence first reached Develish, and the decision was made to bring everyone inside the house. With two hundred crammed into limited space, the serfs had had to sleep in serried rows on the floor of the great hall, and none had argued against Eleanor being placed in Lady Anne's charge. Better the vicious girl be confined to a chamber than allowed to wreak her madness amongst the crowd.

Robert had willingly accepted Milady's request to move amongst the rows and relay her order that no one was to enter her room while Eleanor remained inside it. She asked him how much he'd heard of what Thaddeus had said from his position beside the buttress, and when he answered 'everything', she begged him to keep the words to himself. Talk of the land being wasted and Death sweeping all before it would do nothing to alleviate fear, she explained, and there would be no peace anywhere if all began jumping at shadows because they believed rats and fleas caused the sickness.

But what if Thaddeus was right? Robert had asked. Shouldn't Develish heed his warnings if he'd ridden so far to give them? For answer, Lady Anne had urged him to have faith in the moat.

Water prevented rats from crossing to the enclosure as assuredly as it prevented strangers. Had it not kept them safe so far?

As the laughter in the hall died away, she bent again to the ledger. This was a public record which she planned to leave for others to find. In the early days she had written it only as a history of her people in the hope their names would live after them if all perished from the pestilence, but now it had become a story of survival. She dipped her quill in the ink and inscribed Thaddeus's ideas on how the pestilence was spread, adding two paragraphs of her own at the end.

If we have proved anything in Develish, it is surely that isolation is effective against the sickness. In this we have been helped by the moat. Only Gyles Startout has crossed since we burnt the bridge and cut ourselves off from the world beyond our boundaries. I instructed him to wait fourteen days on the other side to prove himself well before allowing him entry, and when the time came for his return, Thaddeus insisted he swim the water naked to prove to our people that he was free of boils and blackened blood. But I wonder if the discarding of his clothes wasn't as important as his two-week exclusion. Fleas prefer the warmth of garments to the sudden cold of bare skin.

More and more, I wonder if Thaddeus has found the answer to how a healthy man might carry the sickness upon him. Yet it's a strange irony that the person we should thank for our continued protection is the man I married. Sir Richard's desire to be admired by visitors persuaded him to order our people to forgo work on their strips in order to spend a season digging the moat and,

while many were weakened by the exercise, it may be that
they will owe their lives to his conceit.

A stir in the air told her the door had opened and she sensed who her visitor was without having to raise her head. Only one man in Develish felt entitled to intrude upon her without invitation or good reason. At times, she wondered if he thought his persistence in seeking her out would soften her heart towards him. If so, he was wrong. 'You have need of me, Master de Courtesmain?'

The Frenchman bent his neck in exaggerated deference. 'My apologies, milady. I was unaware of your presence here. I assumed you were with Lady Eleanor. She was much in need of your care when John Trueblood passed her to your charge during the night.'

'At least she was able to change into dry clothes. Not all are so fortunate. The men who guarded the walls and now build sheep pens on the other side of the moat have been wet to their skins for hours.'

Annoyed that she wouldn't look at him, Hugh de Courtesmain gave a mild admonishment. 'Peasants are better able to withstand discomfort than a nobleman's daughter, milady.'

Lady Anne laid aside her quill and raised her eyes. 'You've taught me something I didn't know, Master de Courtesmain,' she said dryly. 'I was clearly in error to think Isabella felt pain when Lady Eleanor plunged the bodkin into her breast. By what virtue do serfs feel discomfort less than Sir Richard's daughter? Enlighten me. Do they have thicker skin?'

Hugh de Courtesmain cursed himself for yet again giving this woman cause to mock him. To speak with her was to walk on eggshells. He had been trained to answer to hardened lords who knew the place of serfs, not to credulous widows who treated them as equals. 'I misspoke, milady. I should have said they are more accustomed to discomfort than Lady Eleanor.'

She nodded. 'On that we can agree. But being accustomed to hardship doesn't make it any more bearable. If you believe otherwise, cross the moat on the raft and assist our men in building sheep pens.'

'I'm not tutored in the art of building, milady.'

She smiled slightly. 'Nor I, sir, but I believe I could hold a post steady if required.' She studied him for a moment. 'For an educated man, you are slow to understand that the world is changing, Master de Courtesmain. There will be little call for stewards if the pestilence robs all England of its peasant class. The ability to build and to grow food will far outweigh an ability to read when shelter is needed and mouths want feeding.'

Hugh assumed she was signalling her intent to demote him now that she knew Thurkell was safe, and he eyed her bitterly. It wasn't his fault that her husband had chosen him for steward, nor that he had misjudged who held the power in Develish. 'I deserve better, milady. Had you granted me the same confidence you grant Thurkell, I could have served you better. I have tried these many weeks to prove my loyalty to you. Is it because I'm a Norman that you refuse to trust me?'

She shook her head. 'It's because your mind is closed, Master de Courtesmain. You interpret everything I say in terms of yourself instead of looking for the wider meaning. I sought only to advise you to learn skills while you have the chance. A man of many talents will find more opportunities to succeed when the pestilence passes than one who has few.'

'Perhaps I don't share your view of the future, milady. Should I be criticised for that? God gave me the talent of intelligence and I believe it will serve me well whatever lies ahead.'

Lady Anne held his gaze for a moment before bending to her work again. 'I hope you're right, sir. God could surely not have been so mischievous as to give the same talent to bonded men . . . or, worse, bastard slaves and women.'

Four

The drovers' route above Athelhelm

WHEN THE SERF FROM DEVELISH showed no immediate desire to kill him, My Lord of Bourne struggled to a sitting position and rested his back against a wagon wheel. His brindled lapdog crept from beneath the wagon to lick his face and, as the creature nestled on his lap and the rain drenched them both, he studied Thaddeus fearfully from beneath hooded lids.

The man wasn't human, he thought. Nothing affected him. Not pain, not cold, not lack of sleep. Only a creature of the Devil could take the beatings this serf had done and still find the strength to tear himself free of the earth to smite fighting men. Even his great height singled him out as unnatural. Not a word had passed his lips, yet by some magic he had conjured identical twins to his side. It was rare for such siblings to survive a year when no bonded woman had the milk to sustain two demanding infants. But this Develish pair had grown almost to adulthood. How so, unless through heathen practices and black arts?

Bourne felt no emotion when Thaddeus dispatched the dying by cutting their throats, but he watched in alarm as every corpse was stripped of its garments. The intention was clear: to leave the unclothed bodies above ground for scavengers to devour. If the bones were found, there would be nothing to show what manner of men had died, who they were or which lord they'd served. A shiver ran through him as he recalled the words of the boy who had entered his wagon.

You are nothing without these trappings. Even the lowest slave would mock if you stood naked before him and claimed to be one of God's chosen.

Thaddeus grew more fearsome as he re-dressed himself in the clothes that had been taken from him. All were stained with blood, even the boots, but none so badly as the fur-trimmed coat that carried the captain's gore. To Bourne's troubled imagination, the giant had the look of a warrior who wore Death with indifference. If he had a conscience at all, it would not be troubled by the murder of a frail, unarmed noble.

Thaddeus dropped Bourne's cloak into his lap before tossing all the other garments into the wagon. He followed them with the Develish horse collars he'd been wearing across his shoulders when he was captured, and the soldiers' swords, bows and arrows. As a final act of desecration, he dragged the dead deep into the woodland on either side of the drovers' lane before returning with the livery and weapons of the last four men he'd killed and those of the grizzled fighting man who had died by Ian's hand.

Persuaded his time had come, My Lord found his tongue. 'Will you treat me with the same contempt?' he asked in French.

Thaddeus paused to look at him. 'You have my contempt now,' he replied in the same language. 'What more do you fear?'

'That you'll leave me unburied.'

'What difference will a handful of earth make? You'll become food for worms whether you're above ground or below it.'

'Only the Devil would say such a thing. Is that what you are?'

A faint smile twitched at Thaddeus's mouth. 'Believe it, My Lord. Believe your crimes have found you out and Satan has come to claim you.' He watched the old man's tongue flicker nervously across his lips. 'You don't seem to share your companions' faith in the relic you wear around your neck. Why not? You persuaded your men it would protect them from everything, even the pestilence.'

'How do you know this?'

'Your captain told me of it each time he pulled out his cock. He believed a splinter of wood from the Holy Cross could ward off witchcraft and demons. He must have died wondering why you'd lied to him.'

'Your mockery proves you're of the Devil.'

'Only Develish,' answered Thaddeus. 'The spelling is not the same.' He gestured along the sunken lane. 'Is this a drovers' route? Did it bring you here from Holcombe?' When he received no response, he set off to where the soldiers' horses were tethered at the side of the road.

'Don't go,' Bourne cried in sudden terror, believing he had a better chance of life if he kept this man talking. 'You interest me. I would speak with you longer.'

'Then speak,' said Thaddeus. 'Your voice is not so reedy that I won't hear you. I caught every one of your drunken maunderings with your captain last night.' He paused to glance back. 'Begin with why I found you here when all sensible men have fled the pestilence by heading north.'

Bourne blustered about the King's warrant and God's injunction to the righteous to root out evil. Dorseteshire had brought the pestilence to England and My Lord had a duty to hold her people to account. Unheeding, Thaddeus led the soldiers' chargers two by two to the wagon, linking them with halters to a rail at the back before taking the sturdy tow-horses to the front and hobbling their legs until he was ready to harness them. He refused to answer any questions himself.

'But you insist that *I* explain myself,' Bourne snapped in frustration.

'I insist on nothing,' said Thaddeus, leaning through the leather canopy and pulling a wooden chest towards him. 'If you wish to speak, you may. If you don't, don't.' He studied the padlock and then bent to pull the neck of My Lord's gown apart. A delicate glass vial, contained in gold tracery, hung on a gold chain around the scrawny neck and, beneath it, an iron key on a leather thong. 'I've no wish for your relic,' he said, lifting the thong over the old man's head. 'Splinters come two-a-penny on any carpenter's floor.'

'You blaspheme against the Holy Cross.'

'I question your intelligence. Whoever sold you your sliver of wood must have thanked God for sending him a fool for a customer.'

Thaddeus turned the key in the lock and threw back the lid. Folded parchments, a small writing box with a quill and a stoppered bottle of ink lay on a treasure of coins. He recognised Lady Anne's handwriting on one of the squares, the seal broken, and he opened it to decipher what she'd written.

'Where is mention of treachery or insurrection in this?' he asked, showing the page to My Lord.

'Your mistress speaks of overturning God's social order. There can be no freedom for serfs.'

'The pestilence will free us. Those who survive will be in high demand when there's no one to work the land. Lords and their households will starve if they cannot attract labourers to their demesnes on the promise of payment.'

'You share her heresy.'

'I share her reasoning, as do all Develish serfs. It's incompetent fools who cling to the belief that the world will be unchanged when the pestilence ends.'

The old man's lips thinned. 'Only a sorceress could have kept her people alive so long.'

'Or a saint. You should praise God for His mercy instead of giving the honour to Satan.'

'Now you blaspheme against your Maker. Have you no fear of His anger?'

'None. There can be only one truth if the pestilence was sent by God. To die is a punishment for wickedness, to be spared is a reward for goodness. Since Develish has been spared, what further evidence do you need that Milady is loved in Heaven?'

There was a small silence. 'Do you believe that?'

'I believe what I see and know—that there are wicked amongst the living and good amongst the dead.' Thaddeus reached for another parchment. 'If you're the King's man you'll carry his mandate. Which of these bears his signature? I'll break every seal if I have to.'

Bourne's eyes narrowed angrily. 'For what reason except to damage them? They can mean nothing to you.'

Thaddeus ignored him. He snapped the wax and scanned the document briefly before reading another. 'Would these ever have reached the King?'

In the absence of an answer, he continued to break the seals and read what was written. All were addressed to His Gracious Majesty in French and all bore the names of women with their demesne titles beside them. *Lady Mary of Steynsford . . . Lady Paulann of Herringstone . . . Lady Bernadine of Chetel . . . Lady Katherine of Wolueston . . .* The writing was in the uniform script of a single hand, as if each woman had dictated her thoughts to the same person, and he didn't doubt that person was Bourne. There was desperation in every word. All spoke of the deaths of their husbands and their inability to run their demesnes alone. Some said their stewards had died, others that they'd fled when the pestilence began to wreak havoc amongst the serfs.

> *Your Majesty . . . Have mercy . . . My husband is dead*
> *and his steward gone . . . I have no one to advise me . . .*
> *You leave us destitute by this demand for gold . . . The*
> *pestilence rages across the land . . . There is nowhere to*
> *sell our produce . . . The serfs die in the fields even as they*
> *struggle to bring in the harvest . . . Your people will starve*
> *without money to buy fresh supplies . . . Have mercy . . .*
> *Have mercy . . .*

Thaddeus recalled how often Lady Anne had told him she was unusual in having an education. The only talents most women of her class possessed were skill with embroidery and the ability to manage servants. 'I wonder you bothered to record accurately what these poor ladies dictated,' he murmured. 'Were you not afraid to condemn yourself by your own hand?' He lifted a darker pigmented parchment, the seal of which was already broken. 'The King sends his respects,' he read aloud, 'and directs Bourne to collect revenues on his behalf in Wiltshire.' He ran a finger over the cracks in the vellum. 'The letter is an old one, written long before the pestilence reached our shores.'

My Lord eased his wrists inside their bonds. A nervousness bit at his belly; he'd been mistaken to think a man who could read so fluently was a serf. 'What is your name and status?' he asked. 'You seem to have some learning.'

'Rather more than you, My Lord.'

'May God strike you down for your insolence.'

'And you for yours. Does the King know you traduce his name in order to rob the people of Dorseteshire when your estates are in the neighbouring county of Wiltshire?' Thaddeus held the vellum in the water that streamed off the leather canopy and watched the ink begin to run. 'The demesnes in these parts are the fiefdom of My Lord of Blandeforde. Do you have leave to collect taxes on his behalf?'

'You speak of things you don't understand.'

Thaddeus shut the lid of the chest before relocking it and placing the leather thong around his own neck. 'You shouldn't have kept these letters, My Lord. They tell the tale of your deceit clearly enough. If it was your hand that wrote them, you're doubly condemned as a liar as well as a thief. Only the basest of men would give a woman hope of the King's mercy while leaving her destitute.' He pushed the chest aside and hoisted himself into the wagon.

'You're no less of a thief,' My Lord snapped. 'You plan to steal the gold, do you not?'

Thaddeus ignored him. 'You searched out demesnes where only widows and serfs remained, knowing an army on horseback would frighten them into bringing out their wealth. Lady Anne defeated you but few others dared try, I imagine.' He found collars and harness for the tow-horses beneath the seat and lowered them to the ground. 'How much worse are your crimes than the paltry sins of the Dorseteshire peasants who've died of the pestilence? You should have joined them long since . . . yet I'm guessing the opposite is true, and it's the wretches you've robbed who have perished.' He jumped to the ground with a bundle of traces in his hand. 'Is that why you stay amongst us? To make sure of it? If all are gone, My Lord of Blandeforde and the King will never hear of your thieving.'

Bourne turned his head.

'You were travelling away from the pestilence when you first passed through Develish. How far north did you go? What did you find? Are counties other than Dorseteshire affected?' When no response came, Thaddeus placed his heel on his prisoner's ankle. 'You have no value to me except in what you know,' he said. 'I'll kill you bone by broken bone if you choose silence now.' He began to exert pressure. 'And don't waste time with talk of God's vengeance. Worry more about mine.'

Perhaps Bourne needed to tell his story for, once started, he required little prompting to continue. He had been staying with cousins in the west of the county when a messenger arrived with news that a pestilence was sweeping the land. He was undecided about returning home until a servant died and he saw the putrid colour of her face. The journey back to his own estates in Wiltshire, some sixty miles to the north-east, would be long and perilous, but he believed it was necessary. It was clear to him that Dorseteshire was doomed, more so when travellers and mendicant friars warned with increasing alarm that nowhere was safe. From Melcombe in the south to Shafbury in the north, all were afflicted, and monasteries and grand houses were falling as easily to the sickness as the smallest of hamlets.

At times he used the words 'I have sinned', as if he hoped a sign of contrition would wring sympathy from his persecutor. He excused his actions on weakness. To see a demesne dying and to learn from a desperate woman that there was gold in her husband's coffers was a temptation. Death was written in every face and, since My Lord believed that only the wicked were being punished, it seemed a worse crime to let the money go to waste.

'We refused offers of hospitality,' he said, 'preferring to make camp in the open air. We put our faith in God to protect us.'

'Did you ever reach your own estates?'

My Lord nodded. 'They are as ravaged and desolate as any we saw here. Barely three in ten of my people survives. My foolish wife gave orders that comfort should be offered to the sick, and she brought death to my demesnes—to herself also—by doing so. She was as dull-witted as all her sex.'

'Was there no steward to guide her?'

'He was as dull-witted as she. They listened to the priest who preached salvation through good deeds and kindness, and now all are dead.'

Thaddeus wondered that the old man dared declare his hypocrisy aloud, but he was more interested in why he'd returned to Dorseteshire. He put the question to him, adding, 'Wouldn't it have been wiser to keep heading north, away from the pestilence?'

'It was too far ahead of us already. We heard word at the abbey that it had reached Oxford. The whole country trembles in fear. London has fallen to it in the east and Bristol in the west. The abbot called it a wind of destruction, blowing across the land, and

it seemed more sensible to retreat behind it than run before it.'
The pale eyes studied Thaddeus. 'Your good health suggests I was
right. Has the danger passed here?'

Thaddeus shook his head. 'You owe your life to the way you've
been living and not the capricious nature of wind.' He took
up the collars and traces and walked to the tow-horses. 'Your
saviours have been this wagon and these horses. If you'd had to
pass through afflicted villages on foot—or your conscience had
allowed you to take a woman's hospitality before you stole her
gold—you'd be dead.'

'Why?'

'We found survivors in Woodoak who say the pestilence comes
from rats, and it may be true. None has died in that demesne since
they left their houses to live in the open.' He laid the harnesses
on the ground to untangle them.

'Why do you refuse to see God's hand behind it?'

'Because good people like your wife are dead while you and
I are not,' answered Thaddeus, placing the harness across the
horses' backs.

My Lord watched him attach the traces to the collars before
easing the animals between the shafts and buckling the back straps
and girths. 'Is your plan to kill me even though I've answered
your questions?'

Thaddeus stooped to remove the hobbles. He took hold of
the lead horse's bridle, clicking his tongue to set the animal in
motion. He was afraid the wheels would bind in the wet ground,
but they moved easily enough, and he drew the convoy to a halt
after a few yards. He looked back to see My Lord fallen on the
grass, crying out in terror of the dancing hooves of the horses at
the rear of the coach.

Thaddeus dragged him clear and propped him against the wheel once more. 'Why would I want your life?' he asked, squatting on his haunches to stare into the old man's eyes. 'You're no threat to us. My young friend had it right when he said you're nothing without your trappings. Who will recognise you for a lord when you have no fighting men or servants to vouch for you?' He paused. 'I'll take your wagon and horses because they're a gift sent by God—they'll save me from having to drag my own cart along a riverbed—but I'll not take your life. It's of no value to me. I don't say I wouldn't enjoy stealing your estates in Wiltshire by claiming to be My Lord of Bourne—' a brief humour flickered in his eyes—'but even if only a handful of your people survive, they'll know me for an imposter.'

A look of disquiet appeared on My Lord's face. 'Is this the freedom your mistress spoke of in her letter?' he gasped, struggling to bring his breathing under control. 'The theft of another's birthright?'

'Why not? Do you think a rise in status less tempting than widows' gold? The pestilence makes equals of us all. A clever and resourceful serf can seize whatever opportunities are placed in his way.'

Bourne seemed genuinely shocked, and Thaddeus wondered that he was unable to conceive of a world where the rules he lived by were overturned and abandoned.

'You'll never pass for a noble,' the old man protested, while knowing he was wrong. If any serf was clever and resourceful, it was surely this one.

'I already have.' Thaddeus watched the brindled cur crawl through the grass to resume its place on its master's lap. 'You may keep your dog for company, and I'll leave you your clothes and the use of your hands and feet . . . which is more than you allowed me.'

'I'll die without food or shelter. You'll be no less guilty of murder if you leave me helpless. My death will be forever on your conscience.'

Thaddeus smiled. 'Don't flatter yourself, My Lord. I shall forget you as quickly and easily as you would have forgotten me.'

Bourne dropped his gaze. 'My intention was never to kill you,' he muttered. 'Had you answered my questions, I would have ordered your release.'

Thaddeus pushed himself to his feet, the strain of stretching bruised and stiffening muscles showing in his face. 'Before or after you took your brutish soldiers to Develish with me as your hostage?' he asked, reaching inside the canopy for his sword.

Bourne's mouth dried in fear. 'There was no such plan.'

'I heard you talk of it. You told your captain it would relieve the men's boredom to play cock-sports with witches. Lady Anne's letter appeared to express affection for me so you didn't doubt she'd offer herself and all Develish's young girls in return for my life.'

'It was said in jest. I sought to humour him with a common soldiers' fantasy.'

Thaddeus ran his finger down the edge of the blade, testing for sharpness. 'You succeeded. He liked the idea of using Lady Anne as a vessel for his Norman filth. If memory serves me right, he promised to break her for you first.'

Bourne closed his eyes. 'Your mistress was never in danger. I wouldn't have allowed it.'

'She'd have died before her people because she'd have placed herself between them and your men. She takes her oaths of fealty seriously, unlike you.' Thaddeus rested the blade against the old man's neck. 'Remind me again why my young friend committed an offence by daring to challenge you. I forget the reasons.'

There was a long hesitation. 'You know them well enough. Each person's standing is defined by his birth. You cannot alter what God has ordained.' A sigh fluttered from his lips. 'What do you want from me? Contrition for the privilege my birth gave me?'

Thaddeus smiled slightly. 'I'm not your priest, but if I were, I'd demand a more honest repentance than that.' He lowered the tip of his sword to the ground and put his hand behind the old man's neck to force his head forward. 'Your sin was to abuse your privilege, not to be born to it.' He was surprised at how violently his prisoner fought against his restraining hand.

'Have you no mercy?' Bourne cried, writhing and struggling to avoid the chop of the blade. 'At least give me time to make my peace with God before you strike.'

'I am a man of Develish,' Thaddeus answered. 'My word is my bond.' He cut the sodden ropes that tied his prisoner's hands. 'This is as merciful as I'm prepared to be,' he went on. 'In two or three days, I shall return along the highway with your wagon full of grain. If you're still alive and free of the pestilence, I'll hear your entreaties then.'

Spared one death, My Lord rushed to be spared another. 'I'll not survive that long,' he pleaded. 'The cold and wet are already deep in my bones.'

'In mine also ... and through your fault.' Thaddeus pulled Bourne to his feet and felt the shivers in his hand and arm. With a sigh of irritation, he reached back through the flap in the canopy and pulled tunics and britches from beneath the tabards. 'You'll be warm enough in dead men's clothes,' he said, dropping them to the ground. 'The inner layers will stay dry if you wear your cloak atop them.'

Above the old man's head, he saw the twins appear amongst the trees with Killer and the other two horses. The boys paled at the sight of My Lord on his feet and the sword in Thaddeus's hand, their eyes full of anxiety that they were about to witness a murder. To set their minds at rest, Thaddeus tossed the blade into the wagon.

'Your other choice is to walk to Develish,' he said, retrieving the cloak and handing it to the old man. 'At a steady pace you should make it before nightfall. If you're willing to beg charity from a woman you've wronged, Lady Anne will float warm potage and clothing to you on the raft and allow you the use of a shelter which is being built on this side of the moat. Make no attempt to cross the water and be honest when you explain your presence there. Milady will not believe lies.'

He raised a hand to the boys, calling to them that he was ready to leave, and My Lord followed his gaze, a frightened confusion in his face, as if the reality of his situation was only just beginning to dawn on him. 'Will you do this?' he asked.

'What?'

'Leave me to die.'

'I'm not your keeper, My Lord. What you choose to do once we've gone is your business. If you lack the will to live, no one can help you.'

Trembling fingers gripped his sleeve. 'It's but a few days since my archers fired on Develish. Milady will recognise me and not offer charity.'

'Then die here,' said Thaddeus dispassionately, pulling himself free. 'You'll not be recognised when your bones are found, for no one will know they were yours. Bourne will be written out of history as surely as every poor serf who has died of the pestilence.'

He took up the reins of the tow-horses and motioned to the boys to fall in at the rear with Killer. Having never driven a wagon before, he preferred to lead the convoy on foot rather than attempt to control it from the saddle. Had he been confident of keeping the wheels moving on saturated turf, he would have turned the vehicle and taken the drovers' route to Holcombe, but common sense told him the impacted mud of the highway was the safer course. He shook his head as My Lord tried to mount the step beneath the opening in the canopy.

'Don't make me pull you out again,' he warned. 'I'll snap you across my knee the next time, and your death will be the more painful because of it. Make your way to Develish and say Thaddeus Thurkell sent you. You'll not be judged as harshly by Lady Anne and her people as you will by God.'

The thirteenth day of September, 1348

A strange event happened this afternoon. Gyles Startout summoned me to the moat with news that a cloaked figure was approaching on foot from the village. The traveller had come from the south and his progress up the valley had been slow. I recognised My Lord of Bourne as soon as he was close enough for me to see his face, but he is much diminished from the last time we saw him. He lacks presence, dressed in peasant's britches and without a carriage or fighting men to give him stature.

I had it in my heart to feel sorry for him when I saw how his teeth chattered from the cold. His garments were so drenched by the rain—which continues to fall as heavily as ever—that we could see his bony shape through the many layers of fabric. Quite a crowd gathered to watch him, and I fancy my pity was shared by others, for no one laughed to see him in such distress. He carried a small lapdog, cradled tenderly against his breast, as if he cared more for the animal's welfare than he did for his own.

Whether through fear or cold, he was unable to speak. He stood trembling on the other side of the moat with eyes cast down and his right hand stretched out in entreaty. His arm clearly troubled him, for he was unable to hold the gesture without wincing, but I couldn't tell if the seat of his pain was beneath the tear in his cloak or in the raw injuries about his wrist, which suggested his hands had been bound. He was without a head covering and scabs of dried blood were matted in his white hair, adhering so fast to the strands that the rain had not dislodged them. I looked for a wound on his scalp but could not see one.

He cut a sad and pathetic figure, and even Gyles seemed moved to sympathy. I sent Jenny Buckler for a tunic, britches and Sir Richard's heavy woollen mantle, and asked Clara Trueblood to bring a bowl of hot potage and a jar of liniment. While they were away, I explained to My Lord that we would send the items across on the raft, but that he must not attempt to board it or my archers would fire on him.

If he had thoughts of disobeying, he changed his mind when he saw the intent in the faces of my leading serfs. Even as John Trueblood and Adam Catchpole used poles and ropes to set the raft adrift and control its direction, Gyles Startout and James Buckler raised their bows and sighted their arrows on My Lord's chest. His alarm was so great that I feared he would die of fright before he could warm himself with the soup and clothes.

I gave him leave to use the hut we've built to shelter Thaddeus and his companions, but he is incompetent at performing even basic tasks. Despite our leaving dry kindling, wood and a tinderbox inside the shelter, he was quite unable to set a fire. John Trueblood urged me in a whisper to be thankful, for he didn't doubt My Lord would have set the hut ablaze had he succeeded. However, the old man's inability to warm himself obliged me to send precious fleeces across to bring colour back to his cheeks.

When he found his voice, he thanked me from inside the shelter for my charity towards him. I suggested he extend his thanks to all in Develish, since the homespun he was wearing and the food he was eating were as much my people's as mine. He did so with a show of humility, although it clearly demeaned him to bend his neck to serfs. I asked then why he had come to us without fighting men to protect him, and he answered that Thaddeus Thurkell had sent him, promising food and shelter as long as he made no attempt to cross the moat.

My Lord is unused to having his pronouncements questioned. I believe he hoped we would think that Thaddeus had found him wandering and bereft and had taken pity on him. He showed great reluctance to explain further until I asked who had bound his wrists and what manner of injury had caused blood to clot in his hair.

Few accept as true the story My Lord told us, and we will have to wait for Thaddeus's return to learn it all. My Lord would have us believe that Thaddeus and twin youths used the cover of darkness to take him and his men by surprise while they slept; but since Thaddeus was travelling alone and did not leave Develish until some 3 hours before dawn, this seems unlikely. When and where could he have met the Startout twins in order to plan and launch such an attack before daybreak?

My Lord said their purpose was to steal his wagon and horses, but when I asked him why Thaddeus would endanger himself and his companions for something he already had— namely, a wagon and horses at Holcombe—he had no answer. Nor could he give me a reason for why Thaddeus would spare his life but murder 11 defenceless men in their sleep.

Whatever the truth, it pleases Gyles to know his sons fought alongside Thaddeus—which they surely must have done for Bourne to mention twins—although John Trueblood, Adam Catchpole and James Buckler worry for Edmund, Peter and Joshua. If they live, why were they not with Ian and Olyver?

We are wary of taking My Lord's word on anything. Indeed, had he not arrived in such a parlous state, giving Thaddeus's name as the man who had sent him, we would have dismissed his tale as an old man's fantasy or, worse, a deliberate falsehood to persuade us we're no longer at threat from his soldiers.

He claims to be free of the pestilence and promises to make it known if he begins to feel unwell. It's of little matter whether he does or not. Gyles, who knows the sickness better than *anyone, will see the signs even before My Lord is aware of them. If he dies inside the hut, we will use fire arrows to set it ablaze as soon as the rain ends.*

I pray that end comes soon, for I worry that Thaddeus was overly confident to think he and his companions would survive this storm easily. Cold and damp kill as mercilessly as the pestilence.

Five

Develish, Dorseteshire

ELEANOR WATCHED MY LORD OF Bourne's arrival from the window of Lady Anne's chamber. She knew his face from the first time he came to Develish but little else about him was recognisable. He seemed frail and shrunken and cupped his hands in entreaty more often than he asserted dominance. Indeed, were it not for Lady Anne's courtesy in giving him his title and urging him to accept the only hospitality she could give him, strangers would have said he was a person of no account.

She was still at the window a half-hour later when Lady Anne sought her out. 'He should be raging at you for denying him entry,' she said harshly, her stance rigid and unforgiving. 'He disgraces himself by showing so little spirit.'

Lady Anne stood beside her and watched Bourne, huddled in fleeces in the gloom of the shelter, stroke the little dog in his lap. 'Do you have no pity for him, Eleanor?'

'Why should I?'

'He's alone and afraid. His men are gone and his only comfort is his pet.'

'Does it please you that Thaddeus Thurkell killed them?'

'If he did, it would have been for a reason.'

Eleanor rounded on her, eyes glittering with tears. 'For the same reason you would have me kill Sir Richard's baby? To be rid of a nuisance?'

With a sigh, Lady Anne reached for her hand. 'The choice isn't mine to make, Eleanor. I have given you the means, but the decision on whether to take it must be yours.'

The girl drew back, as if fearing Lady Anne's touch would cause her pain. 'You'll judge me whatever I do,' she said bitterly. 'You forgive Thaddeus Thurkell everything, but never me or my father.'

This time, Lady Anne wouldn't allow her to escape. She reached for Eleanor's hand again and caressed it gently between hers. 'You've committed no fault, daughter, so I've no reason to judge you. It's I who should beg forgiveness of you.'

Eleanor's tears spilled on to her cheeks. 'Why?'

'For failing as a mother. I should have worked harder to earn your love instead of leaving you to seek comfort from your father. You would not be in this unhappy situation if you'd felt able to trust me. Do you think you might be able to trust me now? I beg you to believe, I have always thought of you as my daughter and truly do have only your best interests at heart.'

Perhaps pain was indeed what Eleanor felt, for she snatched her hand away, as if from a burning flame. But the racking sobs that consumed her thereafter suggested her anguish was based in regret; though whether for what might have been or for what she faced now, Lady Anne didn't know.

∽

Pain had featured largely in the decisions Edmund, Joshua and Peter had made that day. Left to find a solution to keeping grain barrels dry inside a shelter with a leaking roof and water rising from the ground, they had opted to take them back to where Thaddeus had found them: the inn at Holcombe. But since Thaddeus was the only one strong enough to lift a hundred-weight barrel on his own, the work was laboured and arduous.

Peter, the most workshy of the three, took every opportunity to scold Joshua for not supporting him the previous day when he'd urged Thaddeus to leave the barrels where they were. It had been hard enough moving the damned things in sunlight; to do it again in a storm was well nigh impossible. Nevertheless, he put his back into the task when Joshua reminded him that the inn had a hearth and enough furniture to keep a fire going for days. The place was a palace compared with their sodden camp, which was close to being submerged by the rising waters of the River Pedle.

The wagon had proved worse than useless, becoming stuck in the sodden sward before they'd loaded a single barrel, and they were forced to do the job by hand. To spread the weight, Edmund fashioned a triangular litter out of hazel whips to allow each to take a corner, but they could only manage one barrel between them and the inn was some two thousand paces from their camp. Peter estimated they'd have to walk more than twenty-four miles to complete the task, twelve with the weight of a barrel and twelve without, but Joshua said it had to be done so there was no point complaining. On each trip they added some of what they'd stolen from the tannery, spreading the wet garments and cloth over the stools and tables in the inn's hall to dry.

When they lowered the last keg to the floor, Peter announced his intention of lighting a fire and stewing the remains of the sheep that Thaddeus had slaughtered two days ago. But Joshua shook his head. 'We must go back to the camp. The others won't know where to find us.'

Edmund agreed. 'There'll be no light at all in a couple of hours. If they're not there already, we'll have to go looking for them.' He took a sword from one of the tables and tucked it into his belt. 'You made the same promises we did,' he reminded Peter, seeing the reluctance on the other boy's face. 'Do I have to fight you to make you honour them?'

Grudgingly, Peter pulled on a second tunic. 'It'll be a waste of energy,' he grumbled, heading for the door. 'We'll not be able to search in semi-darkness.'

He regretted his words when they reached the camp and discovered Ian's pony standing listlessly amongst the trees and the boy unconscious inside the shelter. He lay in a ball on the ground, blue-lipped and pale-skinned, a crusted gash scarring his cheek, and no amount of Joshua's shaking or calling woke him. Yet he seemed to be breathing and a pulse throbbed in his wrist.

'What's wrong with him?' asked Edmund. 'Has the cut robbed him of blood?'

'He's cold,' said Peter, dropping to the ground and manhandling Ian onto his lap so that he could pull him tight against his chest. 'We need to warm him. One of you must kneel on his other side and press up close.'

Joshua obeyed readily but Edmund shook his head. 'We'd do better to carry him back to the inn.'

'There's no time,' countered Peter. 'If Ian's in this state, Olyver will be worse. Sleep like this isn't good. My grandfather never woke from it that winter we had three feet of snow in Develish.'

Watching Peter's efforts to bring colour to Ian's cheeks, Edmund wondered what made him so contrary. There was no telling which tasks he would choose to shirk and which to embrace. Seemingly oblivious to the saturated ground and the rain dripping through the thatch, he put all his energy into ministering to their friend, instructing Joshua to breathe warm air onto the nape of Ian's neck while he did the same to each hand, and urging Edmund to rub the boy's arms and legs in order to heat the sluggish blood. When, finally, a flutter began in Ian's lids, Peter dug his finger and thumb into an earlobe and spoke in a good imitation of Gyles Startout's gravelly voice.

'It's past time to wake, boy . . . We need to find your twin . . . Your mother's tears will never end if Olyver dies . . . Tell me where he is so that we can look for him . . .'

A whisper of sound came from Ian's mouth. 'On the highway.'

'Which part of the highway?'

'Above Athelhelm . . . too much mud.'

Peter urged him to say more, but his speech was slurred and impossible to understand.

Edmund rose to his feet. 'He's given us enough,' he said. 'Joshua and I will head through the woods and hope the dogs can pick up the scent once we reach the road. What about Ian? Can you manage him alone?'

Peter nodded. 'If I can't wake him enough to walk to the inn, I'll lay him across the pony.' He jerked his chin towards the sward where the remaining horses were hobbled. 'You should take one of the others in case you have to do the same with Olyver.'

The advice was good but, without a halter, there was no way to implement it. Nor was it possible to lead a horse along the footpath towards Athelhelm. The river had risen so high the water was lapping inside the tree line. Edmund searched for sizeable pieces of chalk on the sward, handed some to Joshua, took what bearing he could from where he judged the sun should be and then entered the woodland in a direction he hoped would bring them to the road.

'Make crosses on the far side of every tree we pass,' he told his friend. 'That way we can look back and see if we're heading in a straight line. We'll move in circles otherwise.'

After that, they spoke little. Edmund checked behind him constantly to make sure their path was true but, since he had little confidence in his estimate of the sun's position, his greatest fear was that they were travelling due north instead of north-west. His worries grew as the light faded and the chalk marks on the trees became harder to see.

Joshua sensed his anxiety. 'Don't lose heart,' he called. 'I've been counting paces. We've done three thousand so far, which is well short of the two miles we know we have to walk . . . probably more, since we'll be coming out above Athelhelm. The time to fret is when we pass six thousand.'

From then on he spoke the numbers aloud. Edmund found the sound reassuring, though he doubted Joshua had told the truth about counting the first three thousand. He had yet to reach five when a road, awash with water, opened out in front of them.

ରଝ

Ian opened his eyes to see Peter kneeling before a blazing fire inside a great hearth and stirring a cauldron. He had a vague recollection of reaching the camp and finding it empty, but none at all of being brought to a building. His exhausted mind would have lapsed into sleep again had Peter not turned and seen that he was awake.

'Oh, no, you don't!' the boy said firmly, shuffling across on his knees and linking his arm through Ian's to pull him into a sitting position. 'You'll stay awake long enough to eat, then you can sleep as long as you like.' He pulled forward some rushes and wedged them behind Ian's back before returning to the cauldron and ladling some mutton stew into a bowl.

'Where are the others?'

Peter squatted beside him and fed a spoonful of shredded meat into his mouth. 'Looking for Olyver. You woke long enough to tell us where you'd left him. What happened? How did your cheek get sliced?'

But Ian's only interest was the story of My Lord of Bourne's wagon, and Thaddeus's single-minded determination to keep it moving. 'The highway became impassable a half-mile above Athelhelm. Devil's Brook had overrun its banks and the wheels became stuck in ruts filled with silt and debris. I told Thaddeus we should give up and head for the camp but he wouldn't listen.'

'Why not?'

'He said we hadn't come all that way to abandon the wagon on the highway. He persuaded the horses to pull it another few paces by lifting the front and walking backwards, but I swear to God I've never been so scared. He thinks he can do everything . . . and he can't. His face turned grey with the effort. I thought he was going to die.'

Peter offered him another spoonful of meat. 'He needs to succeed. I'm guessing it comes from being called a bastard slave all his life. I'd not accept that title either if I were Thaddeus.'

'He has nothing to prove to us.'

'We're not the ones he wants to impress.'

'Who then?'

Peter thought the question foolish. 'Lady Anne,' he said. 'He'll break his back getting food to Develish if that's what he's told her he'll do. Was it your idea to ride for help or his?'

'Mine. I thought we'd have better luck with six of us moving the wheels. He'll not be happy to see just Edmund and Joshua.'

'He'll be mighty glad to see anyone if he's anything like you when we found you,' Peter retorted bluntly. 'Where did you leave him?'

'By the roadside. Olyver said he'd get him into the wagon but I don't know if he did. They'll be all right, won't they?'

Peter gave a reassuring nod but, in his heart, he doubted it. There was a big difference between the half-hour it had taken him to hoist Ian's limp body across his pony and lead him back to the inn and the much longer time it would take Edmund and Joshua to do the same for Thaddeus and Olyver.

Assuming they found them.

∾

Edmund looked from left to right, but the road was empty in both directions. 'We must separate. I'll head towards Athelhelm and you for Develish. If I don't find Olyver before I reach the village, I'll turn and follow you.'

'And if you do find him?'

'I'll shout. The pack will hear me even if you don't.'

Joshua gestured to the dogs who stood together, hindquarters quivering, muzzles pointing to the left. 'They sense something already. We should both go towards Athelhelm.'

Edmund nodded. 'And we must hurry,' he said, setting off at a run. 'The light's all but gone.'

It was a quarter-mile to the first bend and the pack rounded it well ahead of the boys. With no barks or howls to alert them, and with heads lowered against the driving rain, Edmund and Joshua followed blindly and were amongst the horses at the rear of Bourne's wagon before they knew it. Each thought the same as he jumped away from the stamping hooves and buffeting rumps of the nervously recoiling animals: where there was a wagon, there would be soldiers.

Dry-mouthed, Edmund pulled his sword from his belt and made ready to fight, but Joshua laid a hand on his arm. 'The dogs aren't anxious,' he whispered. 'Look at the mastiff. He recognises someone in the wagon.'

Edmund watched the creature scent the air at the side of the vehicle then rear up on its hind legs, tail wagging, to place its paws on the sill. 'Olyver?'

'More likely Thaddeus. That dog has a real liking for him. I think Olyver's over there.' Joshua pointed some twenty paces along the road to where the rest of the pack was milling around something in the shelter of the trees. 'I see an arm.'

Edmund swore under his breath. Every instinct told him he was entering a trap, but he raised his sword anyway and took an unsteady step forward. He could barely produce a croak as he approached the back of the wagon, demanding that those inside show themselves. He pounded the hilt of his sword against the canopy to inspire fear, but the only response came from the mastiff, who gave an excited whine before dropping to the ground again.

Edmund positioned himself to the side of the opening and used the point of his sword to lift the flap. When nothing happened, he took a deep breath and glanced through the aperture. To his left were clothes, boots, tabards and weapons, piled on top of barrels and chests. To his right lay Thaddeus, curled in a crumpled heap on the floor, his knees drawn tight against his chest and his feet twisted awkwardly beneath the seat. There was no one else.

The pallor of Thaddeus's skin and the blood and gore on his sodden clothes suggested death and, with a sense of dread, Edmund reached beneath the cuff of the fur-lined coat to feel for a pulse. His fingers touched raw flesh where Thaddeus had pulled and strained against his bonds, and he wasn't prepared for the groan that issued from the big man's mouth or the speed and strength with which a vice-like grip fastened on his throat.

'Who are you?' Thaddeus whispered in a grating rasp.

Edmund cast a pleading glance at Joshua as he tried to pull away. 'Edmund Trueblood, son to John and Clara,' he gasped. 'Joshua Buckler is with me. We're here to assist you, Thaddeus. You'll die of cold if you can't rouse yourself. Do as we say and we can lead you to safety.'

When Thaddeus made no answer, Joshua climbed onto the step beside Edmund and reached inside to force Thaddeus's fingers apart. He spoke in the same firm tone that Peter had used with Ian. 'Wake up!' he ordered. 'You must be strong. Olyver lies by the roadside and his need of warmth is more pressing than yours. We can't save you both unless you help yourself. You're too heavy for Edmund and me to lift from this wagon. When we bring you a horse, you must pull yourself onto it. Do you understand?'

Thaddeus half opened his eyes and Joshua was relieved to see recognition in them. 'What of Ian?'

'He's safe,' answered Edmund. 'He told us where to find you. We expected soldiers when we saw the wagon. Should we still?'

'Not unless the dead can walk.'

Perhaps it was fortunate his legs became racked with cramps once Joshua and Edmund succeeded in hauling him to a sitting position. The air turned blue with his blasphemies but the pain restored intelligence. He took a key from around his neck and unlocked a chest at his side, muttering that he cared nothing for the gold but he'd have the letters. One he placed inside his tunic, the others he gave to Joshua, telling him to put them in Killer's saddle pack. He then sent Edmund to help Olyver and instructed Joshua to release Bourne's horses into the woodland. They'd not wander so far they couldn't be found again.

Edmund persuaded himself that Olyver looked no different from Ian, closing his mind to the coldness of his friend's wrist and the absence of a pulse. He knelt at his side, watching the relentless rain fall on the upturned, unresponsive face, and then, with a grunt of effort, hoisted Olyver over his shoulder and rose to his feet. 'Is Thaddeus mounted?' he called to Joshua. 'Do you have Olyver's pony?'

Receiving a yes to both questions, he carried the body across the mud of the road and laid it face down over the pony's saddle before clambering through the canopy to fetch tabards and rope. 'They'll keep him warm,' he said as he draped the tabards over the boy's back and wrapped the rope over him and under the pony's belly to secure them. 'He'll be fine once we get him back to the inn.'

Joshua heard the tremor in his voice and knew he was lying. 'We should head towards Athelhelm,' he answered gently. 'From there, the route through the woodland will be shorter. As long as we keep the river on our right, we can't fail to find our way to Holcombe.'

✺

They left the highway after rounding the bend above Athelhelm, too scared to draw any closer to the turbulent scene that confronted them. A river of mud and stones pounded against what remained of the buildings, and neither had the stomach to dwell too long on the dimly seen shapes that bobbed and rolled in its flow.

Inside the trees, they walked in single file with Joshua at the front, leading Killer. Every so often Edmund moved alongside the charger to put up a hand to keep Thaddeus in the saddle. He took heart from the fact that Thaddeus responded to his prodding, for it suggested he was fighting sleep rather than surrendering to it.

There was so little light in the forest that Joshua allowed the dogs to pick a path. They seemed to understand the need for a track wide enough to take the horses, for only rarely was he brushed by a low-hanging branch. Each time, he held it aside to allow Thaddeus and Killer to pass before alerting Edmund to do the same for the pony carrying Olyver. They spoke little, because the sound of the river would drown their words, but both shed unashamed tears of relief when the pack took them unerringly to the stretch of grassland that led to Holcombe.

As they moved along it, Joshua wondered if it was the snickering of their hobbled horses that had drawn the dogs. The whinnies and snorts grew louder the closer they came to the camp. One of the mastiffs darted forward with a yap of excited acknowledgement, receiving an answering yap in return, and suddenly the woodland was alive with sounds. The swelling crow of a rooster. The contented grunt of pig. Most sweetly, the song of a robin.

Edmund's face cracked into a tired smile when Peter appeared out of the darkness in front of them, his hands cupped in front of his mouth.

'I swear I've never been so bloody pleased to see anyone in my life,' he declared as Peter, the master mimicker of sounds, put a thumb and finger between his lips and the robin's chirrup gave way to the trill of a skylark, ascending into the blue of a summer's day.

⚉

The hall of the inn was sweltering after the weather outside. Peter had stacked the fire high with broken stools and added more as Edmund and Joshua carried Olyver inside and laid him on the floor in front of it. Ian slept peacefully a few paces away, the colour in his face a stark contrast to the deathly white of his twin's.

'I couldn't leave him out there alone,' said Edmund with a break in his voice. 'We all need to say our goodbyes, but Ian most of all. He'd not have forgiven me if I hadn't brought him back.'

Peter pressed his fingers to Olyver's wrist, and like Edmund felt nothing. Milady had taught every serf in Develish how to tell the difference between a strong beat and a weak one, but with Peter's grandfather, she had also searched for a pulse in his neck. He tried the same with Olyver and wondered if he was imagining the intermittent flicker. With sudden decision, he ordered Edmund and Joshua to return outside for Thaddeus while he stripped Olyver of his clothes and dressed him in dry ones. Lady Anne had worked so hard to bring life back to his grandfather, and it had broken Peter's heart when she failed—the old man was his truest friend—but her failure was no excuse not to try as hard for Olyver.

He moved the boy closer to the fire and pulled him into a tight embrace as he'd done with Ian. He watched Edmund and Joshua walk Thaddeus inside with his arms draped across their shoulders, and told them to bring him close to the fire and give him dry clothes. But Thaddeus would only allow them to remove his coat. Even half-asleep, he guarded the square of parchment that was pressed against his chest, unwilling for anyone else to read Lady Anne's words. His awareness improved as the heat of the fire warmed his blood, but not enough to move or speak. He saw Ian lying on the floor and Olyver, white and unmoving in Peter's arms, but he lacked the will to do anything about it.

All the industry came from Peter. While Edmund and Joshua were saying prayers for their dead friend, he was rubbing and pinching Olyver's exposed skin. Every so often a blush of pink appeared beneath his fingers, and he told his friends it was what Milady had looked for in his grandfather. 'I think it means the blood's still flowing in his veins.'

He instructed them to take his place so that he could feed Thaddeus. 'Work as hard as I did,' he told them, filling another bowl from the cauldron of mutton stew. 'Grandfather looked a lot worse, but Milady still thought she could warm him enough to save him.' He carried the bowl to Thaddeus and began feeding him spoonsful of shredded meat and gravy. 'When a body loses heat, it must be warmed from within as well as from without. Milady was very clear about that. When Olyver opens his eyes, we must force him to eat whether he wants to or not.'

The method had worked with Ian, and it seemed to be working with Thaddeus. Joshua and Edmund were alarmed by the violent shivers that suddenly rocked the big man's body. Peter said Ian had reacted the same. A person only shivered when he knew he was cold.

There was no shivering in Olyver; no movement of any kind. If he was breathing at all, his breaths were too shallow to lift his chest. When Edmund said as much, Peter moved to kneel beside Joshua at Olyver's side. 'I once saw Lady Anne bring a newborn to life,' he told them. 'It was a little girl. She lay still and unmoving until Milady blew warming air into her mouth.'

'Which little girl?' asked Edmund.

'My sister. I asked Milady how she'd known to do it and she said it's written in scripture that God formed man from the dust of the earth and breathed life into him. When I told Father Anselm what she'd done, he said only a devil would do such a thing. Do you think he was right?'

Edmund shook his head. 'Your sister wouldn't have lived if God hadn't wanted her to.' He eased his arm beneath Olyver's shoulders to raise him up and the small elevation caused the boy's throat to arch and his lips to part. 'It's a sign,' he said. 'If Lady Anne showed you the way, I believe you should try. It can't be a sin to want to save a friend.'

ᐁᐁ

In a corner of Lady Anne's chamber in Develish a darker scene was unfolding as an infusion of angelica, wormwood and pennyroyal leaf dislodged the foetus from Eleanor's womb. The pains that cramped her belly and the blood that flowed from between her legs would have brought forth screams had Lady Anne not held a hand over her mouth for fear of waking the household. There was so much distrust of the girl that cries of any kind would lead Milady's people to think violence was being done. The door would be forced and all hope of keeping the incestuous pregnancy secret would be gone.

Eleanor lay on a pile of linen napkins to absorb the blood, tears of distress coursing down her cheeks. There was nothing Lady Anne could say to ease her mind. All she could do was change the napkins and lessen Eleanor's pain with birch-leaf oil and white willow bark liniment. Had she thought it would help to say the purgative was working as it should, she would have done so, but the girl needed no reminders that her decision to take the infusion meant a life was being washed away.

Lady Anne had neither looked for, nor wanted, gratitude for her part in this tragic story. It had surprised and moved her, therefore, when she returned to her chamber and Eleanor had thanked her in a tearful whisper for not abandoning her to deal with the miscarriage alone. Lady Anne had expected anger, even accusations that the murder of the foetus was her crime and not Eleanor's; and, in truth, she'd have thought that a rightful penance, for she had held herself to blame from the moment she'd learnt of Eleanor's condition the previous evening. She had protected her servants from her husband's lust but hadn't thought to protect his daughter. Even in her worst imaginings she had never believed Sir Richard so vile that he'd lie with his only child.

When the flow of blood ceased, Lady Anne fetched a bowl of water from a table and washed Eleanor clean before dressing her in a shift and assisting her to the bed. She gave her chamomile and valerian to help her sleep and then returned to the corner to remove all evidence of the aborted birth. She placed one of her shawls on the floor, laid the bloodied napkins on top and tied the corners to form a tight bundle. As she opened the window which overlooked the moat and dropped the shawl into the fast-flowing water, she could only pray it would stay afloat long enough to be carried away from the demesne by Devil's Brook. Too many of the female serfs would recognise the fabric and ask questions if it became snagged on weeds in sight of the house.

She remained where she was, allowing the rain to wet her face. Eleanor would continue to bleed for several days, but the servants would think it was her natural cycle. In time, Lady Anne hoped Eleanor would believe the same, because her life would be happier if she persuaded herself the pregnancy had never happened. When the weather improved, she would be returned to her prison to serve the allotted time of her sentence for harming Isabella—fifteen days in a hut beside John Trueblood's on the path to the church—and her forced absence would allow the serf boys she had hoped to blame for her condition to come home to plaudits for driving two hundred sheep from Afpedle.

Was it wrong to hope for such outcomes? Lady Anne knew the Church would condemn her harshly if she ever confessed to her actions this night, but did God? Was He so set on every misbegotten life being born that innocent youths must be accused of rape to excuse their lord's wickedness? Was Sir Richard's depravity so easily forgiven that his daughter must play both mother and sister to his child?

With a sigh, she closed the window and drew a stool to the side of the bed. She was loath to trouble God with entreaties, believing the duty of solving problems was hers alone, but she had prayed so many prayers these last twenty-four hours. For Eleanor. For Develish. For Thaddeus. For rain. Would it be wrong to add another? She placed her hand over Eleanor's and bent her head.

In nomine Patris et Filii et Spiritus Sancti, may something good come out of this sad and terrible night.

The first week of October, 1348

T haddeus and his companions have been with us 7 days now. The boys came first with 200 sheep from Afpedle. They were delayed by the River Pedle flooding, and had to wait for the water to subside before they could cross the ford at Athelhelm. They stayed long enough to pen the sheep, exchange greetings with their families and speak briefly to My Lord of Bourne before departing again. They returned 2 days later with Thaddeus, bringing My Lord's wagon filled with grain and flour, a column of horses, a pack of hunting dogs, fine clothes, weaponry, jewellery and 2 black cats in wicker cages.

Thaddeus has allowed My Lord the use of the hut and has built a second shelter twenty paces from it for him and his companions. They have used their time to harvest what was left of the beans and vetch after the torrential downpours, and to truss sheep for safe carriage on the raft. 20 of the animals have been slaughtered and preserved, 30 are in the pens behind the church, 50 in the orchard, and some 100 graze the pastureland outside the moat.

Each night, the boys build a fire close to My Lord's hut and regale us with stories of their adventures. The young girls swoon to hear of their heroism, apparently unaware that the tales are growing in the telling! Edmund Trueblood would have us believe there are rats as big as foxes roaming the land, Peter Catchpole that he is able to demolish buildings single-handedly and Joshua Buckler that his hounds are so ferocious they would put an army to rout.

The only story Develish hasn't heard is how Thaddeus and the Startout twins defeated My Lord of Bourne's army. The details are known to me and our leading serfs after Gyles crossed the moat by night to speak with Thaddeus in secret, but Thaddeus has asked us to keep it to ourselves. He believes there is more to be gained by allowing My Lord of Bourne to keep his dignity than making the full extent of his crimes and cruelty known to our people.

A strange friendship has developed between the two, despite the circumstances under which they met. It may have something to do with a treasure chest which Thaddeus removed from the wagon and returned to Lord Bourne, along with a key that hung on a thong around his neck. Neither has any concern that the other may carry the pestilence and, while the youngsters entertain us with their stories, Thaddeus sits with My Lord and shares a meal with him. What they speak of is anyone's guess, but Bourne seems less fearful of us since Thaddeus's arrival.

Six

WHEN A LOW WHISTLE CAME from the peasant strips, Clara Trueblood flicked the shutter on her lantern twice to confirm that it was she who was waiting. She stood at the outside door to the kitchen and heard a gentle ripple as a body slid into the moat and began swimming. Until now, the door had served only to allow the drawing of water for the washing of pots and pans or, on occasion, the dousing of fires when careless maids scattered glowing embers from the hearth, but at Lady Anne's request it was becoming a thoroughfare.

Clara's authority was such that she could do as she pleased in her own domain, and if it pleased her to bar the door to the great hall at night in order to sleep in private once in a while, then so be it. None questioned her on it. Behind her, a candle burnt on the table that ran the length of the kitchen, lending a soft glow to the room, and her broad shoulders shook with suppressed laughter as Thaddeus, naked and dripping, heaved himself across the threshold a few minutes later.

'You'll make Milady swoon,' she said, taking a woollen blanket from the table and wrapping it around his waist, tying the corners tightly to prevent it slipping. 'Could you not have retained your tunic and britches at least?'

Thaddeus's dark face split in a pleasing grin. 'Not without giving Bourne reason to question why I'm dressed in wet clothes when the sun comes up. Did Gyles not ask you to provide something dry for me to wear?'

'He did,' said Clara, sorting through a coffer in the corner. 'The pair of you will turn me into a common laundress before this is over.' She handed him a loose smock and the largest britches she could find. 'You'll be lucky if they fit. I swear you've grown another inch since I last saw you.'

He took the garments gratefully and shrugged the smock over his head before pulling the britches on beneath the blanket. 'You're a good friend, Clara.'

She chuckled. 'If I can tolerate Gyles's wrinkled old frame dripping all over my floor, I can certainly tolerate yours. There'd be no end of questions if naked men began running about the forecourt.' She reached up to button the smock about his neck and then did the same at his wrists. 'We must hide your scars and bruises. If Milady sees them, she'll waste the little time you have searching out liniment to make them better.'

'Is she happy to meet me, Clara? The request was mine, for there's much I should tell her before she gives permission for Bourne to cross, but I've had no word of agreement. I hoped she might send a note with the food on the raft.'

Clara tut-tutted. 'There'd be no quicker way to set tongues wagging. Every woman in the kitchen would have been curious about why she did it. Bourne, too, when it reached the other side,

I don't doubt. Did Gyles not tell you that my lantern would signal her willingness?'

'He did.'

'Then stop fretting, my dear. She's had nought but Master de Courtesmain's counsel these last few weeks and has grown weary of it.' She untied the blanket at his waist and then took up a napkin to dry his hair and beard.

She'd known Thaddeus all his life but he'd always been a mystery to her. Like many of her neighbours, she'd stepped in to curb Will's brutality towards him when he was a child, but he'd never shown gratitude to be spared a beating. Sometimes, Clara had thought he'd welcomed the pain because he needed constant reminders to hate the man who wielded the cudgel; other times, she had wondered if it was simple ignorance of how to express thanks that had kept him dumb.

Silence came more easily to him than speech. Clara still remembered the day he'd wrested the cudgel from Will's hand on the last occasion the man had raised it against him. All who witnessed the scene had expected Thaddeus to take a violent revenge but, instead, and without a word, he had turned his back on Will and carried the cudgel into the wooded hills above Develish. It was never seen again, though gossip said Will had searched long and hard for it.

Clara had little difficulty understanding this incident once Lady Anne made Thaddeus her steward. If anyone could teach a brutalised child that nurtured hate was destructive, it was surely Milady. Some had resented Thaddeus's advancement, claiming Milady had favoured him unfairly through her quiet care and teaching, but Clara, who knew the secret of Eleanor's birth, understood why he'd been singled out. It was not in Lady Anne's nature to ignore the plight of one ill-conceived child while protecting another, though she was fortunate the boy she'd felt obliged to help was Thaddeus.

Even at six years old, when Will first set him to work in the fields, his intelligence had been obvious. It made no matter what task he was given, he had picked it up quickly and performed it well. He was also the only serf in Develish who would never betray Milady's secret support by flaunting his learning, because he would have invited a beating if he had. Nevertheless, as Clara squeezed the water from his hair, and felt him tense against the intimacy, she wondered if he or Lady Anne would ever be able to express their feelings openly. They were two of a kind, each with natures so reserved that neither would presume fondness in the other.

With sudden tenderness, she raised her palm to his cheek and gave it a brief caress before turning away to wring out the napkin. 'Do you think Milady any less excited to hear your stories than the rest of us? We listen to our sons tell theirs each night but have yet to hear yours.'

'I don't have their gift of embroidery, Clara.'

'Perhaps not, but I, for one, would wish to know what magic you've used to turn them into men. I barely recognise them as the surly churls who left Develish with you a month ago.'

Thaddeus moved towards the glowing embers in the kitchen hearth. If he answered honestly, he would have to say he'd removed them from Eleanor's malign influence, but there was another truth which was just as valid. 'I asked them to show courage and they did.'

She smiled. 'You also, Thaddeus? If what the boys say is true, you played a lord in Woodoak in order to save women and young maids from terrible abuse. Did you know it's treasonable to pretend a rank you don't have? Were you not afraid you'd be found out?'

He shook his head. 'It helped that I was riding Sir Richard's charger and had a sword in my hand.'

'Well, you won't need either to persuade Milady. She tells me our sons have convinced her you make a compelling lord. It pleases her greatly to know her teaching hasn't gone to waste.'

ඞ

Clara trod softly past sleeping bodies towards the steward's office. She eased the latch and slipped inside. 'Are you ready, milady?' she whispered. 'We must walk in darkness. If you take my hand, I can lead you.' She saw the same shy hesitation in Lady Anne's face that she'd seen in Thaddeus's and, with a smile of encouragement, she raised her beloved mistress to her feet and drew her soft brown curls about her face. 'Trust your heart, my dear. It hasn't led you false yet.'

ඞ

Hugh de Courtesmain witnessed Lady Anne's entry to the kitchen from the other side of the hall. He had been drawn to descend the stairs when he noticed the glimmer of candlelight beneath the steward's door. Seeing it, he had reasoned it was Milady's steps along the corridor that had woken him, and that she was writing in her private journal. He had always suspected her of keeping one but had never caught her working on it. To wait quietly in the shadows to see if she emerged with it in her hands would at least confirm his belief that she kept it concealed in her chamber.

He wanted to know what secrets it contained, most particularly why Thaddeus Thurkell had removed the serf boys from the demesne. Hugh had never believed the explanation Lady Anne had given, which had painted them as heroes. Their departure had followed too quickly on the death of Thurkell's brother, and Hugh felt certain the two were connected. He didn't doubt either that Lady Eleanor had some involvement, for her rages had become ungovernable in the weeks afterwards. Nonetheless, it was Lady Anne's recently altered attitude towards the girl that intrigued him. From being willing to be disowned by Lady Eleanor, she now held her closer than ever before. But why?

As Clara Trueblood opened the door to the kitchen to usher Lady Anne inside, Hugh saw a tall figure step forward to greet her. It hardly needed the candlelight to tell him it was Thurkell. No other man could have drawn Milady into a secret assignation at the dead of night, and Hugh's heart burnt with jealousy as his hated rival dropped to one knee and pressed a kiss into each of her palms. He turned away as the door began to close again, unable to watch as Lady Anne moved her hands to cradle his face. Such a bitterness grew in Hugh's heart that his only thought was to expose her for the harlot she was.

His eyes now well adjusted to the darkness in the hall, he watched Clara Trueblood place a stool in front of the entrance and seat herself upon it. He was willing to wait as long as was necessary to make his way to the steward's office but estimated a bare quarter-hour passed before the woman's head began to nod. Work and slumber were all serfs knew, and Clara Trueblood was a poor guard of her mistress's honour.

Search as he might, however, Hugh found nothing resembling a private journal in the office. It seemed Milady's industry had been dedicated to working out the sleeping arrangements when Bourne entered the demesne. My Lord was to be given

Sir Richard's chamber, and Hugh and the men who slept in it now were to be relegated to the great hall with the women, children and greybeards. There was no mention of where Thurkell would lay his head.

ॐ

Clara was startled awake by the brush of fingers on her hair. She opened her eyes to see Eleanor standing before her, barefoot and dressed only in a shift. Certain she had come to cause trouble for Lady Anne, Clara rose to her feet and caught the girl's hands in hers. 'There's nothing for you here, Lady Eleanor,' she murmured. 'Return to your mother's chamber. She'll not be happy if you disturb the household.'

Eleanor stared straight ahead, making no attempt to release herself or give a response. Indeed, she seemed oddly content to be held by Clara. A small smile played across her face as if she were remembering a time from infancy when the woman had been her nursemaid. It was clear to Clara that the girl was asleep, and she loosened her grip so as not to rouse her. But how disturbed Eleanor's mind must be, she thought. In daylight, she sought to capture Milady's attention through intemperate rages; at night, she felt impelled to wander through rooms in search of her. It was strange. Stranger still that, in slumber, she had known Milady was not in her bed.

But what to do about it? Keep her here, or take her back upstairs? She chose upstairs. There was no predicting how Eleanor would react if she woke. With a light hand on the girl's back, she guided her around the walls towards the stone steps in the far corner, then circled her arm about Eleanor's waist to assist her in mounting them. It wasn't uncommon for serfs to walk in their sleep. The need to work was so ingrained that some rose from their beds in the dark and headed for the fields with their eyes closed. Most came home of their own accord, others needed guidance, but Clara couldn't remember any being as compliant as Eleanor.

She took care to walk softly down the corridor and ease the latch on Milady's door without a sound, and it was arguable who was the more surprised when she pushed it open and found Hugh de Courtesmain searching through one of the coffers. He looked at her with an expression of horror, and Clara blessed Milady's foresight in continuing to light candles in her window each night until Thaddeus and his companions proved themselves free of the pestilence and crossed the moat. Without their glow, she wouldn't have known of his presence.

She pulled Eleanor close. 'What outrage is this, sir?'

He lowered the lid of the coffer. 'What I do here is no concern of yours, Mistress Trueblood. You overstep the mark by questioning Milady's steward.'

He tried to push past her but she stood her ground and, seeing an easier route, he put his hands on Eleanor to move her aside. Her awakening was violent. Eyes previously glazed and unblinking snapped back to intelligence, and, hissing words of fury to find him in her mother's room, she attacked de Courtesmain with uncontrolled ferocity, slapping and kicking him until he retreated to the far side of the chamber.

He pointed a trembling finger at Clara. 'She's madder than I've ever seen her. Hold her in check before she kills me.'

Clara folded her arms defiantly. 'I see no madness, sir. She acted as any daughter would do to find a man in her mother's chamber. Is it your custom to inspect Milady's garments when she's absent from her room?'

'I was looking for documents.'

'On whose command?'

'I need no command. I am steward of Develish.'

'Not for much longer,' said Clara, drawing Eleanor to her side again and leaving de Courtesmain's exit clear. 'Be gone, sir. You will never serve Develish as well and honestly as Milady and Thaddeus Thurkell do.'

Eleanor clung to Clara, wrapping her arms about the woman's waist and talking in riddles about blood and guilt. Whatever troubles beset her, they clearly filled her with remorse, for Clara didn't doubt the guilt of which she spoke was hers. She whispered *mea culpa* too often to believe otherwise. Unsure of what to do for the best, Clara led her to Lady Anne's bed and lay on it beside her, cradling the girl tight against her side. Within minutes, Eleanor had fallen asleep again, but it was a shallow, disturbed sleep, and any attempt Clara made to move brought forth whimpers and tears.

It seemed safer to stay with her. Dawn could not be far off and Lady Anne knew she must leave the kitchen before the first rays of the sun woke the serfs in the great hall. Better Milady find Clara gone from her stool than Eleanor set off in search of her again. She was as likely to attack Thaddeus as de Courtesmain if she thought the handsome giant was stealing her mother's affections. Thief was the least of what she'd called de Courtesmain, and Clara spent time wondering what documents he'd hoped to find. Whatever they were, he'd have used them to control Milady. His single ambition was to have her listen to him and not her serfs.

She made a gesture of apology when Lady Anne entered the chamber some quarter-hour later. 'I had no choice but to remain, milady. I found Eleanor wandering in her sleep and feared she might do it again if I left.'

She tried to ease the girl away from her, but Lady Anne pulled forward a stool and begged her to remain where she was. 'She'll not wake while you hold her. I allow her to sleep in the bed with me and she only becomes agitated if I move to the table to write in my journal.'

'Would that be what Master de Courtesmain was looking for, milady? I caught him going through your coffer.' Clara described what she'd seen when she opened the door. 'I'm guessing he knew you were absent and took a chance on entering when he saw Lady Eleanor leave. Guilt was written into every bone of him.'

'He fears Thaddeus's return. He doubts he'll keep his place as steward.'

'Nor should he, milady.'

Lady Anne shook her head. 'He'll cause less trouble if he remains in the post. His nature's too frail to want Bourne thinking him a serf.' She watched Eleanor for a moment. 'Did he wake her?'

Clara nodded. 'And reaped a bad reward by doing so.' She told the story with a smile. 'You couldn't have asked for a more dutiful daughter, milady. She cast slurs at him while speaking only good about you, and the praise surprised him, I think.' She paused. 'I, too, if I'm honest. I can't remember the last time she had anything kind to say about you.'

If she hoped Lady Anne might offer an explanation, she was disappointed. Both Milady's expression and answer were carefully controlled. 'I'm the only constant in her life,' she said. 'Her father is lost to her and she doesn't know whom else to trust. Her greatest fear is to lose me as well, I think.'

'She seemed more troubled by guilt than loss, milady. Before she fell asleep, her talk was of blood. I made no sense of it but her remorse was clear. If she said *mea culpa* once, she said it a hundred times.'

Lady Anne placed her elbows on the edge of the bed and rested her chin in her hands. How comforting it would be to confide in Clara and share the burden of Eleanor with another woman. If anyone could understand the tumult of emotions the girl was experiencing, it was surely Clara who had helped other women through the terrible anguish of miscarriage and stillbirth. But to do so would be to reveal everything, and Eleanor's slow steps towards believing that Lady Anne had her best interests at heart would end.

'I let her down at the time of her father's death, Clara. So much changed for her so quickly and I gave no thought to how it might affect her. Her guilt is for wounding Isabella and renouncing me, and she is deeply remorseful for both. By keeping her close, I hope she will learn that my love isn't easily broken.'

Clara wondered if that was the truth. 'Maybe so, milady,' she said bluntly, 'but she'll make you her captive if you allow her to become too dependent on you. You need a man in your bed, not a troubled child whose passions can swing between love and hate in a single moment.'

A glint of mischief danced in Lady Anne's eyes. 'You shock me, Clara. Would you have your liege lady take a serf to bed and destroy any chance Develish has of forging her future?'

Clara smiled. 'I would have a man who loves you, milady.'

'So would I, my dear friend, but a lover would be more appealing and useful if he were a wealthy noble, approved by Blandeforde, who sees merit in freeing his serfs.'

'Does such a man exist, milady?'

'Not yet, but with My Lord of Bourne's help, he might.' She smiled at the puzzlement in Clara's face. 'If he holds to the agreement Thaddeus has made with him, we have a chance of gaining our freedom lawfully.'

'What sort of agreement?' asked Clara suspiciously. 'I'd sooner remain a serf than have you marry that vile old man. No one's more deserving of freedom than you.'

Lady Anne squeezed her fingers affectionately. 'Have faith in Thaddeus,' she said. 'He hasn't supped with the Devil every night to hand him the keys of Develish. I have a request that you may not like, however.'

'You have but to ask, milady.'

'We must forget our grievances against Bourne and show him only respect when he crosses the moat. Will you spread that word amongst our people? Thaddeus has persuaded him he has nothing to fear from educated serfs, and he will know it for certain if he's treated with courtesy.'

∽

Clara gave the instruction the following day, saying it came from Milady, but in private she questioned what sort of agreement Thaddeus had made that allowed Bourne to think his sins forgiven. Many cavilled at showing respect to the Norman who had burnt their homes and attacked their demesne, but Gyles lent his authority to the request, saying nothing would be gained by giving Bourne reason to fear them. When the time came for My Lord to leave, better he went as a friend than an enemy. It would not bode well for Milady or her people if he took unfavourable tales of Develish to Blandeforde.

This argument was accepted, and the old man received a warmer welcome than he might have expected. He chose to wait for Thaddeus and his companions to serve their fourteen days' exclusion before entering with them, and there was so much joy from mothers at the prospect of being able to clasp their sons to their hearts again that he seemed to feel himself included in the happiness. It helped that Thaddeus had instructed his companions to introduce him to their families before accepting their mothers' embraces, and Lady Anne's leading serfs and their wives were more than willing to set the example for others to follow.

When it came to Clara's turn, she bobbed a deep curtsey and said she trusted My Lord was looking forward to the feast Milady had ordered in celebration of his arrival. He declared that he was, urging her graciously to rise, and she wondered if he was really so arrogant that he believed it was *his* arrival Milady wished to salute. Perhaps so, for he accepted Lady Anne's offer of her husband's chamber as his due, together with fine garments from Sir Richard's coffers to replace his homespun tunic and britches.

Dressed in a gown befitting her station—sewn from russet-coloured silk with softly falling skirts and a gold circlet about her waist—Lady Anne allowed him to precede her into the house in recognition of his superior status. Inside, she asked Master de Courtesmain to accompany My Lord to his room and assist him with any requests he might have. Gyles whispered to Thaddeus that he thought it a bad idea to give the Frenchman such free access to Bourne. Who knew what poison he'd whisper in the old man's ear?

Thaddeus placed a comforting hand on Gyles's arm. 'Milady knows what she's doing, my friend. De Courtesmain will find a way to speak with Bourne whatever she does—most likely in the church with Father Anselm's blessing—and Bourne will listen more closely if de Courtesmain claims he's being kept from him.'

'He'll say nothing good about us, Thaddeus.'

'For certain, but Bourne is neither blind nor foolish. He'll learn soon enough that what I've told him about Develish is the truth. De Courtesmain will do himself no favours by trying to persuade him otherwise.'

And as the days passed, this proved to be true. For all the Frenchman's attempts to snare the old man, Bourne showed more willingness to consort with Lady Anne and her people. As often as not, he sat in the great hall, watching Isabella Startout teach the children, taking pleasure in hearing them read aloud from the English translations Lady Anne had made of the parables. Each day, he expressed new wonderment that urchins as young as ten were as fluent in letters as he was himself.

Thaddeus's companions were made uncomfortable by the welcome they received. The young girls swooned over them, begging to hear more of their stories, but they seemed to prefer each other's company and took no advantage of the maids' shameless flirting. As Clara said, Thaddeus's influence over the boys was so strong they broke every heart with their courteous indifference. To Lady Anne's private relief, they showed no interest in Eleanor, seeming more preoccupied by their ambitions to forge a future outside Develish.

For her part, Eleanor was content to avoid them. She spent her days in Lady Anne's chamber and only appeared for an hour or two in the evenings to sit with her mother and My Lord of Bourne. Her demeanour was always appropriate, and her affection for Lady Anne obvious, perhaps because Milady never failed to refer to her as her daughter. Some thought she'd forgiven the girl too readily for her bitter words of hatred; others pointed to Eleanor's unlikely friendship with Robert Startout, which seemed to have had a soothing effect on her temper. Few understood why the eleven-year-old had spoken on Eleanor's behalf at her trial for imprisoning and wounding Isabella, but there was no doubting she paid him more mind than anyone else.

Most days, he visited her in Lady Anne's chamber and, together, they played with the cats that Thaddeus had brought from Holcombe. At Milady's request, Thaddeus had gifted them to Eleanor, and under Robert's guidance, she learnt to love and not fear them. Father Anselm called them the Devil's creatures, but Eleanor saw only good in them and found solace in feeding and nurturing them. And with this first small rebellion against the priest, her self-centred vision of the world, where her place was God-ordained by virtue of her birth, seemed to soften towards an acceptance that earthly life was not as intelligible as her father and the Church had led her to believe.

Thaddeus and his companions built a shelter for themselves in the orchard, preferring to sleep outside as had become their custom. Thaddeus showed no interest in reclaiming his post as steward, speaking courteously to de Courtesmain whenever they met but he drew the man's ire by spending an hour each morning alone with Lady Anne in the office. De Courtesmain's frustration at being barred on these occasions, displayed by an impatient tapping of his foot until the door opened, amused every serf who saw it. He should have been grateful that Milady hadn't stripped him of his duties and title; instead, he sulked and pouted because the counsel of a bastard slave was preferred to his.

His irritation was further inflamed by Lady Anne's willingness to allow Joshua's dogs to roam freely about the compound. When she withdrew her people inside the moat, she had commanded the mongrels from the village to be destroyed in order to preserve food for human consumption. Now she humbly accepted Joshua's argument that that decision had been wrong, agreeing that the curs would have guarded the walls as faithfully as his hounds were doing now. It mattered not that Hugh's irritation had more to do with his fear of dogs than that Milady demeaned herself by admitting error to a serf.

Not that Thurkell's companions behaved like serfs. They conducted themselves well, listening when others spoke and showing consideration to all. Clara was not alone in finding it hard to recognise her son in the respectful young man who offered to perform chores that he'd have thought beneath him a month ago. James Buckler, more used to criticising Joshua for failing at tasks, found himself in awe of his son's ability to control his pack and speak with confidence of acting as Thaddeus's master of hounds. Meanwhile, Peter Catchpole, known for his laziness, astounded his parents and everyone else by his dedication to learning the skills of medicine from Lady Anne. A story circulated that he had brought Olyver Startout back from the dead by breathing warm air into his mouth, and most believed it must be true when Father Anselm went out of his way to warn that such practices were heretical.

De Courtesmain demanded the truth of the story from Isabella Startout. 'I don't doubt you're aiding and abetting your brothers and their friends in the lies they're telling,' he said angrily. 'But to what end? Does Thurkell seek to make himself master here by winning the hearts of the credulous with myths and falsehoods?'

Isabella lowered her head 'All are loyal to Lady Anne, Master de Courtesmain. There's not a person in Develish who would wish to have anyone other than her as their liege lord.'

'Except Thurkell. He makes his ambitions clear.'

Isabella stepped away and her answer was so quiet he wasn't sure he'd heard it correctly. 'But not as clear as you make yours, sir.'

St Andrew's Day, last week of November, 1348

$\mathfrak{I}$t has been agreed. On the first day of January, 1349,
Thaddeus Thurkell, Ian and Olyver Startout, Edmund
Trueblood, Peter Catchpole and Joshua Buckler will escort
My Lord of Bourne to his estates in Wiltshire. They will remain
with him one month in order to secure his property, bring
his surviving bondsmen to live on his principal demesne and
introduce some method to his affairs.

As payment for this service—and in recognition that he
is compromised by the letters he wrote on behalf of the ladies
of Dorseteshire, which will stay with me in Develish—My Lord
has agreed to prepare a scroll, bearing his signature and seal,
introducing the man who carries it as My Lord of Athelstan.
He will recommend Athelstan's honesty and good character to
all he encounters. My Lord is willing to write this falsehood but
has warned Thaddeus it will be no protection if imposture is
suspected. Thaddeus must play the noble at all times if he is to
avoid detection.

I have chosen Athelstan because the title was in my family
until my maternal grandfather died without male issue. His
ring came to me and I have kept it these many years, along

with his crest and lineage. They show descent from Godwin of Wessex, father to King Harold, who was defeated in battle by William of Normandy. It may be that Thaddeus will be more in danger of exposure through claiming royal English blood, but My Lord of Bourne believes the opposite to be true. Few Normans have knowledge of Saxon ancestry, though most are acquainted with their own.

I have taught Thaddeus all I know of my family's history and have inscribed a new lineage, showing him to be descended from an invented younger brother of my grandfather, who departed these shores over half a century ago. I have urged him to say that his grandmother's family is of Spanish-Moorish descent, for this will explain his dark complexion.

My leading serfs, whose sons will accompany him, worry that the pretence will be uncovered, but Thaddeus has persuaded them it's a gamble worth taking. To risk all is to win all. Nevertheless, so much faith is being placed in my belief that land will be cheap once the pestilence passes that I feel a weight of responsibility upon my shoulders. Only God knows if Eleanor's dowry remains where Gyles left it on his journey home with Sir Richard. And only God knows if a base-born slave can pass for a lord and purchase the demesne of his choosing.

☙❧

Christmas Day, 1348

𝕴 shall look back on this day as the happiest of my life. For the first time, the people of Develish were able to celebrate Christ's Nativity together as equals. Father Anselm called us to prayer early so that the long-awaited games could take place at noon. We all laughed as fathers and sons vied for the laurel wreaths, since there was more cheating than competing in each event. Afterwards, we feasted on roasted mutton and warm bread while the children sang to us. How sweet their voices are and how ably Isabella has taught them. My Lord of Bourne has great admiration for her and remarked that she would make a better wife to a lord than most women who are born to the role.

Thaddeus and his companions paraded themselves in the garments I and my seamstresses have stitched for them from the clothes they brought from Holcombe. Thaddeus looked every inch a lord and the boys—who seem to grow in stature with each day that passes—every inch his soldiers. For fun, they invited us all to join them in a merry jig. Neither Thaddeus nor I knew which steps to make, for we are sadly lacking in dancing skills, but Adam Catchpole's rhythmic drumming of a goatskin was so enticing that I could not resist taking Thaddeus's hand. It's my greatest joy that my dear friend's time out of Develish seems to have conquered his shyness.

It can't be wrong to feel such enjoyment, however
ferociously Master de Courtesmain frowned to see us smile!

ᢒᢐ

The first day of January, 1349

So many of our hopes have gone with the convoy that set
off at dawn.

My Lord of Bourne thanked me for the hospitality he has
received in Develish, and gifted me the horses and tackle of his
dead fighting men by way of compensation for my generosity.
It amuses me that he is still unable to look me in the eye when
he speaks to me. Thaddeus says he's shamed by my refusal to
accept a portion of the stolen gold, but I think it more likely that
he continues to suspect me of practising black arts. Women have
been inferior to men so long that it frightens him to see one such
as I managing a demesne.

Perhaps, more simply, he doesn't trust me not to use his
letters against him, though why he thinks I should be the first to
break our bargain is anyone's guess. Unless because I'm a witch!

I have allowed Master de Courtesmain to accompany him
to act as his steward in Wiltshire. Bourne has more need of a
scribe than I, and Develish will benefit from de Courtesmain's
absence since his only ambition seems to be the sowing of

discord. Father Anselm will miss him, since de Courtesmain is his single confidant, but I can't imagine anyone else will regret his departure.

Winter is well set in and I hope it stays with us for several months. If Thaddeus is right about rats and fleas spreading the pestilence, the journey will be safer with the ground frozen. Vermin and parasites dislike the frost and snow as much as we do.

I bid farewell to the fear and misery of 1348 with a gladsome heart and pray most earnestly that my people, Dorseteshire and England will enjoy better fortune in 1349.

1349

Seven

HUGH DE COURTESMAIN HID HIS irritation behind a thin-lipped smile as he watched Thaddeus Thurkell take his leave of the peasants who crowded around him. It was the fifth day of February and past time the slave and his men allowed Bourne's estates to be managed by their rightful steward. But how it galled Hugh to watch the hated giant's departure. Thurkell might be a god for all the adulation being showered upon him. Even after a month of behaving no differently from the serfs who sought to kiss his hand, none of Bourne's people questioned that he was My Lord of Athelstan.

His height, his bearing, his dress and mannered speech, whether in French or English, suggested a person of privilege, and Hugh's heart burnt with envy because he knew he lacked the ability to play such a part himself. Even now, he had a yearning to reveal the imposture, though he doubted these fools would view the harlot-hatched bastard differently if he did. The idea that one lower than they could rise above his station in life was more likely to excite than annoy them. It was only Hugh who felt demeaned by having to bend his neck to an imposter. He would have betrayed Thurkell gladly these last four weeks had he not feared Bourne's anger at the secret of his protégé's birth becoming known. Hugh had worked too hard to ingratiate himself with Bourne to lose his position out of momentary pique.

He comforted himself that his time of being eclipsed by Thurkell was over. In minutes, the slave and his five companions would be gone, and the only commands these serfs would hear then would be Hugh de Courtesmain's. Out of the corner of his eye, he spotted the figure of My Lord of Bourne at the top of the stone stairs, leading to the upper chamber, and he took satisfaction from the look of disquiet on the old man's face as he watched the scene below. Could it be Bourne had finally come to understand the danger of allowing an English serf to gain such ascendancy over his people?

No one who entered the great hall of Bourne would question that the owner's loyalties lay with France. My Lord had spent his wealth on dressing the walls and floor with the finest hangings and most elegant of French furniture, and the sight had warmed Hugh's heart when he first arrived. Even as a young student in Normandy, he had never visited a house so fine. There were tapestries from Arras, armoires and tables from Limousin, stools from the Breton province and a carved oaken throne from Rheims. By comparison, Develish was spare and humble, and Hugh was certain Thurkell couldn't understand the value of what he was looking at until he heard him murmur under his breath to Ian Startout that he saw now why My Lord had felt it necessary to steal from Dorseteshire widows. To My Lord's face, he was less offensive, saying only that serfs could feed as well from a French table as from an English one.

Whether through shame at having his thieving discovered or a genuine belief that treating his people with kindness would bring results, My Lord had given Thurkell leave to introduce Develish practices to his own estate. Hugh had questioned the sense when he saw the group of filthy, undernourished field serfs who assembled in the great hall within an hour of their master's return. Of what use could education be to these cowering shadows? Their community had once numbered over six hundred but a bare hundred and twenty remained, and none looked capable of productive labour. The pestilence had destroyed their families and broken what little spirit they had left.

Hugh had wanted to run at the sight of them, sure they carried the pestilence, but Thurkell, who had first addressed them outside, had accepted their word that a month had passed since anyone had died of it. He had already made enquiries of the servants in the house and all had given the same testimony. The last death had been at the end of November. Since Lady Anne had insisted on only two weeks exclusion to prove a person free of the sickness, he had persuaded Bourne that four weeks was long enough to believe his people, too, were free of it. And he didn't doubt the cold winter was to thank for this blessing.

My Lord's long absence in Dorseteshire, coupled with the death of most of his household, meant his serfs had been without direction for months. Where Hugh would have set them to work immediately to cure them of idleness, Thurkell began by instructing the handful of remaining house servants to prepare food to feed them. He and his companions assisted in the task by butchering five sheep and milling grain on the castle's quern-stones to make flour for bread, and the serfs seemed entranced to see a lord and his squires buckle to tasks usually reserved to bonded men. A ripple of curiosity ran through the assembled mass.

It was a first stirring of life, as if something out of the ordinary was all that was needed to wake them; but what they made of the orders Thurkell gave when their bellies were full was anyone's guess. Most stood with downcast eyes as he listed the tasks he wanted them to perform. Their village must be burnt to kill the vermin in the thatch, and new homes erected in another location. Their habit of defecating and urinating outside dwellings and in woodland would end. Instead, latrines would be dug at a distance from the new village to bury human waste beneath ground to deter scavengers. Great importance would be placed on the cleanliness of bodies and clothes. The women would run a communal laundry and manufacture thin-toothed combs to pick lice and fleas from the heads of all, including their own.

Athelstan understood these ideas might seem strange, but he urged compliance. Spring planting was a good two months away and there was time to complete the building work and grow accustomed to the new rules before the call came to return to the fields. For his part, My Lord of Bourne pledged food and shelter for all and an abandonment of the whip for any but the most serious of crimes.

This last brought looks of disbelief to several faces but only one man dared voice his doubts aloud. Some forty years of age, he stood at the centre of the crowd, his arms laid protectively across the shoulders of children, and he advised his neighbours in an undertone to question everything they were being told. Hugh would have challenged such insolence, but Thurkell saw courage and stepped forward to seize the serf's hand and make him an ally.

Did it gall Hugh now that his assessment had been wrong and Thurkell's right? Not so much as it had galled him to watch Robin Pikeman grow in stature over the weeks that followed. The peasant might never learn the skills of reading and writing, but Thurkell's patronage and Pikeman's own knowledge of his master's demesne won him the ear of My Lord. His fear of Bourne was obvious but, assisted by Thurkell, he found his voice and demonstrated a keen grasp of the difficulties My Lord faced through the loss of so many of his field serfs—not least the inability of one hundred and twenty to farm land that had required six hundred to make profitable before the coming of the pestilence.

He raised other issues which were rightly the preserve of the steward. The necessary redistribution of peasant strips which had become redundant through the deaths of entire families. The support of orphaned sons, too young to work, who were nevertheless heirs to their fathers' land entitlements. The protection of orphaned daughters. A recognition of the rights of the elderly to a share in the fruits of their families' strips whomever was appointed to farm them. The impossibility of selling surplus livestock with markets closed and drovers and merchants too frightened to travel the highways.

Pikeman numbered My Lord's sheep and cattle at well over two thousand beasts and argued that slaughter was essential before predicted births in the spring put an even greater burden on already scarce pastureland. Where the pestilence killed humans, it allowed stock to flourish, and My Lord would lose his flocks and herds to starvation if he continued to allow his ram lambs and bull calves to live.

Bourne studied the serf's gaunt face and frame and asked why he hadn't slaughtered and eaten the animals himself, and

Pikeman reminded him of the edicts he had issued which listed the punishments for thievery. To hide a handful of grain when taxes were being counted earned twenty lashes. To tickle a trout from the river, forty. To steal a sheep from the pastures or a deer from the forests, death.

Perhaps the old man felt shame for his own misdeeds, because he ordered the surplus male animals to be slaughtered and preserved as food for his people before turning to the problem of how to farm the demesne's land without sufficient labour. My Lord of Athelstan had suggested bringing the surviving serfs from his vassal estates to make their homes in Bourne. Did Pikeman foresee difficulties in such an exercise? Would the serfs of Bourne accept strangers in the place of those who had died?

The serf answered that My Lord's people would do as they were ordered whether they liked the new arrangement or not but, encouraged by Thurkell to say how best to create one community from four, he advised that leading men from each of the vassal demesnes should be brought to Bourne first. 'They will know the number and names of those who still live, the size of their present holdings and the rights to which each family is entitled, sire. If they're persuaded that the distribution of plots and strips in Bourne will be fair, they will take that message to their villages.'

'And My Lord's own people?' Thaddeus asked. 'How will they feel about newcomers?'

Pikeman hesitated, clearly questioning how bold he could be. 'To increase each family's portion by a third will ease any tensions, sire. When a man has the ability to grow more food, his fear of hunger decreases and taxes become less onerous. If the vassal demesnes have suffered as badly as we have, there's more than enough land to be generous.' He ducked his head to

Bourne. 'Be assured your people have done their best to till and plant your virgates, sire. We honoured our oaths of fealty even without instruction, for none of us wished you to return and find your own fields uncultivated.'

Hugh thought the churl overreached himself to pretend such work had been done out of loyalty rather than fear of a flogging, but My Lord readily accepted the lie as reason to offer rewards. He instructed Hugh to make preparations for the reallocation and enlargement of the peasant strips, appointed Pikeman overseer of the digging of latrines and the building of the new village and tasked Thurkell with bringing worthy men from the vassal demesnes. All three estates lay on the highway to Sarum, the farthest some thirty miles distant, and Thurkell requested the use of My Lord's carriage to bring the selected serfs from their villages.

At least on this My Lord showed caution. 'Is that necessary? Surely such privilege will convince them they're superior to my own people?'

Thurkell gestured to Pikeman. 'They'll be no stronger or better fed than this man, sire. Even to ride a horse saps energy when the body is unaccustomed to the saddle. To request those from the farthest demesne to walk thirty miles will be to kill them before they arrive.'

Pikeman found the courage to speak without being prompted. 'They'll be more afeared than honoured to travel in your wagon, sire. It makes no matter what reasons they're given for the journey, they'll expect your anger when they arrive.'

'Why?'

'For bringing the pestilence to your demesnes, sire. The priest told us it was God's punishment for sin.'

'The Church teaches us so.'

'Yet my wife was a better person than I am, sire, and my children quite innocent. I should have been taken before them . . . and certainly before the priest.'

Thurkell answered when Bourne stayed silent. 'It wasn't by God's will that your family died, Robin. It was through misfortune. In Develish, where your master took refuge during the autumn, none has fallen to the pestilence. They've kept it at bay by using the same methods I'm asking you and your people to follow. If you rid yourselves of vermin and parasites, you have a goodly chance of survival.'

Pikeman searched his face. 'We've never died of such things before, sire. Why should it be different now?'

'I can't tell you that, my friend. My understanding of the sickness is very limited. I know only what I've seen and heard. You and your fellows must decide for yourselves if the advice I give is good.'

He couched his explanation in words the serf would understand, only falsifying the details that related to his status, claiming cousinship with Lady Anne of Develish as his reason for being on her demesne when news of the pestilence first reached them. He explained the measures Lady Anne had taken to protect her people and then told of how he and his soldiers had ventured out in search of grain and livestock to replenish Develish's dwindling stores as autumn drew in.

෨ඔ

Hugh had first heard the story some three months previously, when he and Develish's leading serfs had been summoned to the church shortly after Lady Anne had given leave for My Lord of Bourne, Thurkell and his companions to cross the moat. My Lord and Lady Anne were seated in the prayer stalls and the tall figure of Thaddeus Thurkell stood by the chancel window, staring towards the land beyond the moat. He seemed more imposing for his near month-long absence and, as always, Hugh resented having to look up to him. God had dealt him a poor hand when He'd made him a head shorter than a bastard-born English slave.

At Lady Anne's invitation, Thurkell had spoken of his journey, neither tempering his language nor sparing his listeners a true picture of what he'd observed. He had described a land almost barren of people. There was evidence that lords and freemen, able to travel at will, had fled north to escape the pestilence while bolder serfs, willing to live by their wits, had seized the opportunity of their lord's absence to abscond; but the size of the plague pits in abandoned villages were testimony to how many had died. He dismissed any suggestion that the sickness was carried on the wind or in the water, since he and the youths who rode with him remained well, and he respectfully challenged Lady Anne's belief that sufferers must pass the infection to others on their breath or through their touch.

Had the disease been confined to Melcombe, where it first appeared, Thurkell would have agreed with her, but the speed with which it had spread made him question whether afflicted travellers could be the carriers. Survivors spoke of the pain sufferers endured from the moment the fever took hold. Boils erupted within hours, and death followed in three to four days. Not even the strongest and most determined of men could have journeyed far enough from Melcombe to cause the whole of Dorseteshire to be wasted in under ten weeks.

In the demesne of Woodoak, where he and his companions had found people still alive, Thurkell had asked how they'd escaped the pestilence. Not one had claimed goodness as a reason, telling Thurkell their beloved priest had been amongst the first to die. Instead they blamed rats, quoting the words of a wise woman—as versed in medicine as Lady Anne—who had devoted herself to nursing the sick on the priest's death. Her reward had been to die of the pestilence herself, but her fellow serfs had followed the instructions she'd given them and none had succumbed since. Burn your houses to rid yourselves of rats, she had urged. Immerse yourselves fully in water to cleanse the feeling of dirt on your skin. Sleep outside in the open air, and build a fire each night to keep vermin away.

Thurkell would have given these warnings little credence had rats been less evident in the demesnes he and his companions visited. The creatures bred faster where peasants had died or fled, leaving easy sources of grain on unharvested strips or in sacks inside abandoned huts. As to how they might pass the pestilence to people, he repeated the descriptions the Woodoak serfs had given of the sick. Some had complained of terrible itching before boils erupted on their necks, and all, including survivors, had spoken of their skin crawling in the presence of the dead and the dying.

Some five days later, while his companions delivered sheep to Develish, Thurkell had returned alone to Woodoak. This time he had asked only about the itching. What had caused it? All cited fleas, having seen the bites on the skin of their dear ones. One spoke of how her small daughter had scratched and clawed at the virulent eruptions on her arms until painful pustules broke out around her neck. The woman was no stranger to fleas and couldn't account for why these eruptions had been so inflamed, but her husband and son, similarly afflicted, had both died within a week of her daughter.

Challenged by My Lord of Bourne to explain if it was rats or fleas that passed the pestilence to humans, Thurkell had argued for both. He knew of no illness that moved from animals to humans, but to stand near a mangy cur was to invite a legful of bites. It was the same when humans shared their living space with rats. As a child, he'd found a dead one in his bedding and the straw around it glistened with escaping fleas as he'd lifted it by the tail. To prevent the infestation spreading, his mother had seized a burning brand from the fire and set his bedding alight. Every serf in Develish had suffered similarly until Lady had instructed them on how to rid their homes of vermin and parasites.

He returned to the question of how the pestilence had spread so quickly through Dorseteshire. If sin wasn't the determiner of death, and sufferers were too weak to travel, then it must be the healthy who carried the sickness. Yet how? It was inconceivable that a man could be ignorant of a rat in his knapsack, but he could carry a flea without knowing it. Thurkell had pulled back his sleeve to show the darkness of his skin. Whether because of its colour or toughness, he was never troubled in the way that the fair-complexioned were. He could journey many miles with a flea in his clothing before losing it to a more palatable, softer-skinned host.

My Lord of Bourne had been party to Thurkell's thoughts during the time they'd spent together outside the moat, yet he still remained wedded to the idea that divine punishment was the reason for the pestilence. Nothing else made sense to him, and he appealed to Lady Anne to explain how a single flea could infect a whole village. She had answered seriously that it wouldn't be just one. Fleas must breed like any other creature, for God had no cause to make them different. If rats grew in numbers when there were ample supplies of grain, then the fleas that lived on the rats would multiply also. She had no explanation for why they had suddenly become deadly to man, but nor could she say why one pox was mild and another fatal, though experience told her it was so.

Lady Anne went on to speak of the ease with which the pestilence had entered Melcombe. There had been rumours of a killing sickness in France even before her husband had died, and it made good logic that it had crossed the sea in a ship. If the source of the infection had been dying sailors, they would have had limited contact with people ashore, but rats, bearing fleas, would have disappeared into the sewers and houses of Melcombe where colonies of their fellows already lived. The same was true of every town and village where waste lay above ground and food was unsecured.

'Are you so convinced of God's hatred for man that you cannot conceive of a different agency being responsible for this sickness?' Lady Anne asked Bourne. 'You're surely not blind to the fact that the moat has kept Develish free both of rats *and* the sickness?'

'Do you always trust what your eyes tell you, milady?'

'I do, sire. Is there a reason why I should not?'

'God's truths are as much invisible as they are visible.'

'The Church would have it so,' she agreed, 'but it's written in Proverbs: *The hearing ear and the seeing eye, the Lord made them both*. And to what purpose would He bestow such wonderful gifts upon us if He didn't intend us to have faith in what they reveal?'

'It's a great arrogance to presume to know the mind of God, milady.'

'Indeed,' she said lightly. 'The bishops took much responsibility upon themselves when they declared sin to be the cause of the pestilence. I grieve deeply for the caring priest of Woodoak who must have breathed his last in terrible distress, wondering how he had erred.'

✇

Hugh had felt tainted by heresy every time Lady Anne questioned the authority of the Church. He experienced the same sense of dread listening to Thurkell assure Robin Pikeman that his family had not been found wanting. It made no matter that he used reason to support his arguments. Hugh had been taught that the Bible could only be read and interpreted by the clergy and to hear a disbeliever dismiss the Church's teachings on sin was to conspire in his blasphemy.

He had struggled long and hard to accept that a Saxon dissenter might have right on her side but, much as he longed to, he could not avoid the truth: that Lady Anne's methods of protecting her people had worked. While all in Develish—sinners to their cores—still lived, the records in Bourne showed that eight-tenths of Bourne's servants and serfs had died.

Robin Pikeman needed little persuasion that something other than wickedness had caused his family's deaths. He even endorsed Thurkell's belief that fleas were the culprit, describing how his eldest son, the first to die, had complained of vexatious itching in the days before he fell to the fever. Nevertheless, he had little confidence that others would agree.

'Most here are persuaded that God intends all men to die, sire, with the worst being kept to last. The youngest still have hope, and may accept that washing will keep them free of the pestilence, but the adults have none. They await death in the belief that their punishment was to endure the loss of those they loved before being taken themselves.'

This bleak prediction touched a chord in Hugh, for he had always feared God's wrath, but Thurkell would have none of it. And neither, it seemed, would Bourne. With My Lord's approval and encouragement, Thurkell tasked himself with restoring the survivors' faith in the future. The following day, he and his companions assisted Pikeman in building the first house on the plot reserved for the new village. They had it finished by nightfall and attracted a crowd of curious watchers when Thurkell asked Pikeman whose home it should be. The serf consulted with his fellows and all nominated a woman who had made herself responsible for orphaned girls under twelve years old.

The day after, they began a second house and, whether drawn to help by the sight of a lord in rolled-up shirtsleeves or fuelled with new energy from the communal meals they were consuming, twenty men joined them in the enterprise, setting to work on multiple buildings. Watching from a distance, Hugh wondered what sedition Thurkell was preaching, for he knew the man well enough to know he wouldn't be arguing in favour of God's social order. Lady Anne had indoctrinated him too well in the profane belief that an accident of birth was the only difference between a noble and a slave.

He suspected more sedition a week later when Thurkell returned from a two-day journey with six greybeards comfortably seated in My Lord of Bourne's carriage. The elders showed none of the fear of punishment that Pikeman had predicted, and Hugh was certain Thurkell and his companions had tutored them in how to behave and speak along the way. They greeted their liege lord gravely and listed the names and ages of those who still lived in his vassal demesnes. Hugh recorded the names in his ledger and, when all were counted, the number of serfs remaining from a population in excess of three thousand a year previously was five hundred and three, some fifty of whom were too young to work.

The elders were unable to say whether their own lords—vassal knights to Bourne—were alive or dead. Each had departed with his household when news came that the sickness had crossed the border between Dorseteshire and Wiltshire. Two were thought to have headed west and the third north, but no word had come from them since. One of the stewards had died, two had fled, and all three priests had perished. There were no bailiffs. Responsibility for My Lord's demesnes had fallen to his bonded men and they had done their best to safeguard his land, livestock and property.

After being shown the demesne by Pikeman, and consulting with him at length, the elders had expressed their willingness to bring their fellows to live and work in Bourne on the same terms that My Lord had agreed with his own serfs. Hugh watched in disbelief as Bourne signed a writ, prepared by Thurkell, which not only granted them extra land but rights of access to education, medicine and a meal of meat every seven days. It was a world in disarray when base-born men, sworn to obedience through their oaths of fealty, could expect rewards in return for their labour.

The next two weeks saw columns of tired humanity and livestock shepherded into Bourne by Thurkell and his companions. Those too old or young to walk rode with caged poultry on open-sided bullock carts while the able-bodied drove their demesnes' sheep, pigs and cattle ahead of them. Secured inside My Lord's covered wagon were the gold reserves, weaponry and fine garments which had been abandoned by his vassal knights in their haste to flee. My Lord, watching the arrival of the first convoy, remarked to Hugh that Thurkell had the air of Moses, leading the Israelites to the Promised Land, and Hugh's heart soured when he saw the description was accurate. The words 'blessed saviour' ran in whispers through each weary throng as Thurkell urged them to rest and eat the food that was brought to them.

Brought back to the present by the weeping of maids at Athelstan's departure, Hugh raised his eyes again to the shadowy figure of the old man, standing half hidden behind a pillar to watch the scenes in the great hall. Did Bourne understand now that the slave was less Moses than Judas? He should. It was a powerful betrayal to persuade a noble he could keep his people's allegiance by rewarding them with kindness, only to take their gratitude to himself.

One young maid clung desperately to Thurkell's hand and begged him to stay. He had found her amongst the remaining house servants, a shy and frightened orphan of some twelve years whom others said had a knowledge of letters. She had learnt the skill from the priest but was fearful of admitting to it until Thurkell praised her for her cleverness and urged My Lord of Bourne to appoint her tutor to the children. He had sat at her side for seven days, helping in the teaching of the young ones, and she had grown in confidence under his guidance. But now she wept and shook with grief, for she had no belief My Lord of Bourne's approval would continue once her protector was gone.

The same apprehension was in every face.

☙❧

Edmund Trueblood turned in his saddle for a last look at the demesne before a bend in the highway hid it from view. The burnt-out remains of the old village lay like an ugly scar on the land but the new houses, some five hundred paces to the west, stood clean and fine as if to prove that life would go on. 'Do you think My Lord cares enough about his people to continue what you've started?' he asked Thaddeus.

'It depends what you mean by caring. He understands the value of their labour well enough.'

'They'll abscond if he doesn't keep his word,' said Peter Catchpole. 'I answered more questions about journeying the roads than I ever did about burying turds or getting rid of fleas. There isn't a lad in Bourne who hasn't thought about slipping away at night to make his fortune as a freeman.'

Olyver Startout nudged his horse to the left to avoid a rut. 'And Thaddeus will be blamed when they do. Master de Courtesmain will make sure of it.'

Peter gave a snort of derision. 'He's a weaselly little fellow. It galls him that even Joshua tops him by a couple of inches now. He puts it down to eating meat. I heard him tell My Lord of Bourne it was a bad idea to add mutton to a serf's diet.'

Joshua grinned. 'How did My Lord reply?'

'Coldly. He advised the steward to count the number of surplus rams and explain what he planned to do with them if they weren't eaten. He's no more enamoured of de Courtesmain than Lady Anne was.'

Edmund glanced at Thaddeus. 'Is that true?'

'For the moment . . . but de Courtesmain's no fool. He'll work his way into the old man's favour in time. My guess is the elders will be blamed for failing to meet My Lord's hopes of the harvest before I'm blamed for absconders.'

'Have you warned them?'

Humour glinted in Thaddeus's dark eyes. 'No need. They've laboured under stewards like de Courtesmain all their lives. I've left him a letter, urging him to make them his allies, but he'll not heed the words. It pleases him to think peasants too ignorant to merit his respect. He'll cite their laziness and stupidity for producing lower yields than he predicts.'

'What if My Lord believes him?'

'He won't. He has a keen understanding of what his land can produce.'

'You shouldn't put so much faith in him,' Peter scolded. 'He has no more liking for his serfs than de Courtesmain has. I saw it in his eyes. He can't stand to be near them.'

'Maybe so, but he's willing to tolerate them as long as his greed's satisfied. He made a bargain with the elders that if his people, working together, can increase the yield on his land by in excess of one-fifth on previous years, he'll award them the profit on the surplus. There's no better spur to persuade men to work. Rightly or wrongly, they all believe they can surpass a fifth quite easily.'

'De Courtesmain will hate you even more if you're right,' said Olyver. 'Did you tell him we were going in search of Eleanor's dowry?'

Thaddeus shook his head. 'It's not his business. I let him believe we're returning to Develish, looting what we can from every deserted demesne we pass. The idea pleased him.'

'Why?'

'He'd rather remember me as a common thief than a serf who passed for a lord. It galled him more than he could bear to have to bend his neck to me.'

'Then you'd better not have signed your letter Athelstan,' Olyver warned, 'or he'll be feeding it to the pigs by now.'

Thaddeus laughed. 'I did not. My intention was to help him, not provoke him. He needs to open his eyes to the future and stop yearning for a past that is gone.' He nodded to the road ahead. 'I suggest you do the same. I don't care how many young maids won your hearts in Bourne, everything we do from hereon in, we do for Develish.'

(THADDEUS THURKELL'S LETTER TO HUGH DE COURTESMAIN)

Honoured Sir,

*I write in the hope that you will see advantage to
yourself in upholding the pledges My Lord of Bourne
has made to his people. He is more receptive than you
realise to the ideas he encountered in Develish, and to
argue against them may cause him to doubt you. He
understands well that the future of his estates depends on
the goodwill of his serfs to work his fields and seeks ways
to encourage their loyalty rather than weaken it.*

*He is persuaded that our world will look different
when the pestilence ends, and I advise you to give some
thought to this yourself. I have tried several times to
engage you on the subject, but your clear resistance to
men being rewarded for their work suggests you believe
that obedience can only be won through the whip. If so,
you are wrong. No whip has been wielded in Develish for
over a decade. Instead, Lady Anne has allowed her people
to share in the profits of their labour, and the yields per
head have been significantly higher, year on year, than
anything Bourne has managed to achieve.*

*Before the pestilence, a nobleman's wealth was
assessed by how many serfs he owned. The greater the
number the more profitable his land. Yet, even by merging
four demesnes into one, My Lord still lacks the workers
to return Bourne to profit. The same will be true of every
landowner in Wiltshire because none will have taken the
measures Lady Anne did to protect her people. I beg you*

to ask yourself how this shortage will be managed except by lords luring their neighbours' serfs away on a promise of payment for work and an end to their oaths of fealty. Should this happen, My Lord of Bourne will look to you to keep his people true to him, and your success in the venture will earn his gratitude.

That task is already begun. Robin Pikeman tells me he and his neighbours dare to believe in a future since My Lord gave his undertakings, and their confidence in him will only increase as their health and strength improves. You may not agree that the dark ages of serfdom are almost over, Master de Courtesmain, but you must surely accept that every landowner, including My Lord of Bourne, will welcome skilled workers who declare themselves free and willing to work for a small imbursement. No questions will be asked about the truth of the claims when fields need planting and crops harvesting.

I urge you most strongly to put aside your doubts and suspicions of the English peasant class and seek allies amongst the elders. Not one is your enemy unless you choose to make him so. Robin Pikeman has the ear of all and will be an honest adviser on how to draw the best from My Lord's people. Robin's family is buried in Bourne and he has made himself responsible for the many young boys who've been orphaned by the pestilence. He and they will have no cause to leave unless the pledges they've been given are abandoned.

Our paths are unlikely to cross again, Master de Courtesmain, since our loyalties lie in separate directions, but please accept my sincere hope that you enjoy good fortune in the weeks, months and years ahead.

Your obedient servant,
Thaddeus Thurkell

FEBRUARY, 1349

Eight

Pedle Hinton

THEY RODE TWO DAYS TOWARDS the south-west, sleeping in woodland by night and taking to the road again when the sun came up. The weather had been cold for weeks but a change in the wind on the second night presaged snow. By mid-morning of the third day, they shivered under an icy blast from the east which snatched at breath and bit at exposed skin. The youths drew their chaperon hoods about their faces and looked warily to their left, where leaden clouds were building in the sky. Thaddeus took a firmer hold on the pack pony he was leading and urged his companions to pick up the pace while the going was good. There would be no steering their horses clear of ruts and holes when the roads were blanketed with snow.

He kept to himself that he was beginning to question whether they were on the right highway. It was one thing to memorise a list of landmarks, described to him more than a month ago by Gyles Startout in Develish, quite another to recognise them now. He was confident they'd ridden the Shafbury to Sherborne road because milestones along the way had told him so, but he was deeply concerned he'd chosen the wrong crossroads to turn south towards Pedle Hinton. *You'll know it by an oak tree which stands at the north-east corner*, Gyles had said. *It's as wide as it's tall and casts such deep shade that nothing grows within twenty paces of it.*

But had Thaddeus been right to assume the burnt and blasted trunk of a once-great tree was the landmark Gyles had meant? It was three years since Gyles had ridden this road from the north as part of Sir Richard's retinue, and a bolt of lightning could well have cleaved the mightiest oak in the meantime, but there was little else to recognise along the way. If milestones had ever existed, they'd been long hidden by encroaching foliage.

Ian drew alongside as Thaddeus slowed before a shallow ford. 'We'll have to make camp soon,' he said, gesturing to the sky. 'The snow's almost upon us.'

Thaddeus nodded.

Ian looked to some woodland on their right. 'Wouldn't here be a good place? There's water close by and no one to see us.'

Thaddeus ignored him to stare up the incline ahead. 'Your father spoke of a ford in the valley before Pedle Hinton. He said the highway would veer to the south-west on the other side of the river.'

Ian followed his gaze. 'We've crossed several fords already and the road has continued south or south-west each time.'

'Mm.' Thaddeus turned to study the advancing line of cloud. 'We've another hour yet. We'll strike camp when we've breasted the hill.'

'It'll be harder to build a shelter if we leave it too late,' Ian warned.

'Then make haste,' said Thaddeus, clicking his tongue to set Killer going again. 'We'll need dry kindling if we want a fire tonight.'

The snow began to fall when they were halfway up the incline, soft flakes that melted as they came to rest on the chaperon hoods and woollen coats. Before long, the boys felt the icy water penetrate through the fabric to their skin and watched in growing dismay as a wispy veil of white began to shroud the road and the hedgerows. Joshua, bringing up the rear with his pack of dogs padding miserably at his horse's heels, muttered that the poor beasts would die of cold if they didn't find shelter soon.

Thaddeus, fifty paces ahead, halted on the breast of the hill to lean forward in his saddle and stare through the falling snow at the valley below. Gyles had said he would know Pedle Hinton by the way the manor house was situated and built. Standing on a bend of the River Pedle, the structure had the appearance of a cross with an elongated entrance porch on one side of the great hall, a kitchen and buttery on the other and part of a church showing behind it. The village would be clustered to the right of the highway with a hunting forest to the east and vast acres of cleared land to the west.

He scratched his beard thoughtfully as he waited for his companions to draw level. The swirling flakes were nigh impenetrable, but he thought he could make out the walls of a large building some thousand paces distant. He gestured into the valley when Ian and Edmund drew level. 'What do you see?' he asked.

Ian narrowed his eyes. 'Not much,' he admitted. 'Ask Edmund. He has the best sight for distance.'

Edmund linked his hands across his face like a visor and studied the valley through a slit between his fingers. 'There's a river behind the tree line on the southernmost boundary. I see a gap where the highway crosses it to the left of what must once have been a manor house. The walls still stand but half the roof has gone. There's a church behind it.'

'What shape is the house?'

'Long and thin with protrusions on both sides.'

'Like a cross?'

'Yes. There's cleared land to the right but I can't tell which are peasant strips and which pastures. There's the remains of a village beside the road and a mound about a hundred paces beyond.' He dropped his hands. 'It's huge. If anyone's still alive here, it'll be the poor wretch who buried the bodies.'

They'd come to recognise that a feature common to all demesnes was the bank of earth that spoke of a mass burial site. 'The pestilence was in Pedle Hinton even before Sir Richard reached it,' said Thaddeus. 'Gyles told us some forty had died in the week before they arrived.' He aped Edmund's trick with his fingers. 'I wonder what caused the roof to collapse.'

'Flames,' said Ian. 'Maybe the gravedigger went mad and set fire to everything. The village too. Burning seems to be the only way to cleanse a place.'

By then, the other four boys were lined up beside them. 'Are we there?' Peter asked hopefully. 'Does it look right this time?'

Thaddeus nodded. 'As close as anything we've seen.' He gathered up his reins. 'We'll know for certain when we've crossed the river. There should be a track into the forest some quarter-mile beyond which was wide enough to take Sir Richard's wagon.'

Joshua glanced at his shivering dogs. 'What if we find the track but not the wagon?'

'Worry more that we will,' said Thaddeus unsympathetically. 'When Sir Richard abandoned it, there were five dead bodies inside. I doubt they've been removed.'

The snow fell relentlessly as they pushed on to the river, but if Thaddeus felt the biting wind through his sodden clothes he didn't show it. The boys consulted in whispers about encouraging him to look for shelter before the river, but none voiced the idea aloud. They all knew what his answer would be. *Do as you like. I'm not your keeper.* And the last they would see of him was when he was swallowed by the blizzard.

He had warned them often enough that they must accept his decisions or be left behind, but even Ian, his most loyal supporter, questioned the sense of continuing. The purpose of their journey was to recover a chest of gold—Lady Eleanor's unpaid dowry—which the twins' father had left in woodland outside Pedle Hinton some seven months previously. He had given Thaddeus directions on how to find it, but neither believed it would still be there. Half a year was a long time to abandon a coffer of coins, unprotected, on a forest floor.

Most of what Ian knew of his father's journey home with Sir Richard had come from his mother. She gave him answers in return for a promise that he wouldn't pester Gyles for explanations. Better he be allowed to forget, she said, than relive his anguish in nightmares. Yet it was a strangely misdirected anguish. For reasons Ian didn't understand, his father felt he should have died along with his companions and started out of sleep with shouts against God's injustice. Sometimes, he muttered prayers for the men Sir Richard had chosen to forsake, feverish but still alive, inside his wagon on a woodland track.

There was no honour in Sir Richard. He had discarded his men with as little care as he took the pestilence into Pedle Hinton. His intent was to secure a bed for the night, but he feared the doors being closed to him if there was any suspicion he'd been in contact with the pestilence. By then, just three of his retinue of eleven remained—his captain of arms, his bailiff and Gyles—and he ordered them to say they'd come from Develish, where all were well. To his host, he feigned good health, blaming the flush of fever in his cheeks on a surfeit of ale, and upon learning that forty of My Lord's field serfs were already dead, had shamelessly requested My Lord to bar the rest from his house for fear they would pass the sickness to his guest.

Martha said it was right and just that God had condemned so venal a man to die. Not content with infecting Pedle Hinton, he had ordered Gyles to drive the wagon, the dying soldiers and surplus horses to Develish, threatening him with a flogging if he failed. She had kinder words for the captain of arms and bailiff, who were as feverish as their master the next morning. Too weak to do anything but support Sir Richard in his saddle, they had begged Gyles's pardon for leaving him to manage such an impossible task alone. There was no way of turning a heavily laden wagon in the narrow confines of a woodland track without assistance.

Gyles wouldn't have done it even if he'd been able; he'd rather be flogged for disobedience than take a killing disease to Develish. He told Martha of his relief to find the five soldiers dead, for it was easier to turn his back on corpses than it would have been to watch men suffer in the stinking Hell the vehicle had become. The stench of suppurating boils and putrid blood, made worse by the heat of the sun, had attracted blowflies, and the horses hobbled around it were near driven mad by their bites and stings. He had cut the horses free to find water and pasture. There was no better way to excuse his failure to drive a pestilence-ridden vehicle to Develish than to lack the means to pull it.

His mind and flesh recoiled against climbing amongst the stiffening bodies to remove Lady Eleanor's dowry, but he baulked at allowing thieves to enrich themselves at Develish's expense. He gave the dead what dignity he could by closing their eyes and folding their hands, and took some comfort from the peacefulness of their faces. Had the chest been lighter and more manageable, he might have been tempted to carry it home across his saddle, but he was as wary of displaying it too openly along the highway as leaving it in the wagon. Instead, certain he couldn't escape the pestilence himself, he chose to hide it in the woodland, pledging himself to live long enough to pass the secret of where he'd left it to Lady Anne, the one person he trusted to use Develish's wealth to benefit her people before herself.

Martha believed it was this unselfishness that had persuaded God to spare Gyles. For the same reason, she had faith that God would have kept the gold hidden from thieves. Neither conviction was shared by Thaddeus, who rarely saw God's hand in anything, and yet he continued on, seemingly oblivious to the cold and the wet. His obstinacy made sense when they reached the river. On either side the banks were pushing into the stream as plants and rushes bent under a weight of snow, causing the waters to narrow and run fast across the slabs of stone that had been laid on the bed to provide secure footing to wheeled vehicles. The crossing looked dangerous now and would surely be impassable by the morning.

Thaddeus chose to dismount and wade through the freezing flow ahead of his horses, advising his companions to do the same. 'You'll not get far if your animal slips on the stones,' he said, removing his boots. 'Better a few moments of discomfort than a mount with a broken leg.'

'A few *moments*?' Ian echoed sarcastically, sliding from his saddle and tugging at his own boots. 'We've been in discomfort for *hours*.'

'Not for much longer. The track we're looking for is ahead on the left.'

'Assuming this is Pedle Hinton.'

'Assuming that,' Thaddeus agreed dispassionately as he felt for safe passage with bare feet.

ᏯᎶ

They located Sir Richard's covered wagon some two hundred paces inside the forest, half drawn into the trees at the edge of the track. Thaddeus halted twenty yards short of it, and motioned to the others to do the same. He was as surprised as the boys to see it there, wondering why the Pedle Hinton serfs hadn't made use of it long since. There was enough oak in the structure to make a multitude of stools.

'Could the dead soldiers have frightened them off?' said Edmund.

Thaddeus shook his head. 'They'd buried forty of their own already, and all in the same state. Why cavil at another five? It speaks more to the wagon never being found than it does to fear of corpses.'

Olyver glanced back down the track. 'It's not that far from the demesne. Women and children out looking for firewood couldn't have missed it.'

'If they were well enough,' answered Thaddeus thoughtfully. 'Perhaps the village was worse afflicted than Gyles realised. The sick wouldn't have had the strength to walk a mile.'

He examined the woodland to the left. The trees were largely ash and oak, and, though leafless, their tight canopies offered good protection from the falling snow. He gestured towards a high-domed, wide-branched oak which had a sizeable stretch of dry ground beneath it. 'We'll camp there tonight,' he said, easing himself from Killer's back and lifting off the leather saddlebags which had been crafted for him in Develish. He tossed them into the shelter of a low-growing hazel then unbuckled the girth and divested the animal of its saddle and harness. 'You have spare clothes in your own bags,' he told the boys as he looped a rope halter about the horse's neck and muzzle before stripping the pack pony of its burdens. 'Take off anything wet and dress in dry tunics and britches before you go looking for firewood. You'll warm up soon enough if you put some effort into your search.'

Olyver lowered his own saddle beside Thaddeus's and replaced the reins with a halter. 'What will you be doing?'

Thaddeus waited while the others did the same and then took charge of the halters. 'Feeding and watering these poor brutes. There was meadowland to the south of the river. I'll hobble them there.'

They watched him walk the horses down the track.

'Doesn't he feel the cold?' asked Edmund.

'He shuts his mind to it,' said Ian. 'He says a person can withstand anything if he forgets how much he's hurting and applies himself to what he has to do.'

They put the doctrine to the test in the collection of firewood, but the promised warmth never came. The frosts of winter had permeated the forest floor and nothing was dry enough to take a flame, not even leaves. The twins began paring away the damp outer layers of fallen branches to reach the unsaturated wood inside, but Edmund said they'd have more success if they looked in the wagon. Sir Richard had never travelled anywhere without chests of clothes, barrels of brandy and hessian sacks full of sweetmeats. All and any would be dry as long as they were still there.

Ian couldn't fault his logic. The wheels had kept the base from sucking water from the ground and the leather canopy had prevented rain and snow coming in from above. Nevertheless . . . 'Have you forgotten what's in there and how they died?' he asked.

'They'll be bones by now.'

'With fleas in their clothes.'

'Not to mention rats,' murmured Olyver. 'There could be a whole colony of them feasting on Sir Richard's sweetmeats.'

Edmund selected a six-foot long branch from the stack of firewood and trimmed it to form a sharp-pointed stave. 'There's no harm looking if we keep our distance. Most of the studs holding the roof to the sill seem to have rotted.'

He approached the side of the wagon and used the pointed end of the stave to jab at the head of a carved wooden peg to the left of the opening flap. Protruding some two inches clear of the side, the peg served the double purpose of anchoring the main canopy to the sill and providing a knob for the loop of rope that fastened the flap closed. He remembered his father saying that Sir Richard would come to regret not choosing English oak for his embossed dowels but, even so, he was surprised at how few strikes were needed to knock the head from its shaft.

Ian joined him a few moments later with a stave of his own, and between them they fractured enough of the studs to prise the canopy away from the side of the wagon. When the vehicle had been in constant use the wax coating which had kept the leather stiff was regularly renewed but, after being at the mercy of the elements for more than half a year, the fabric had become soft and pliable. Together, Edmund and Ian hooked their staves beneath the edges and flipped the cover up and over the wooden hoops that formed the supports.

'Mary Mother of God!' said Peter in disgust, staring at the tangle of half-chewed bones and ripped and stained livery on the floor. 'What happened to them?'

'Scavengers,' said Edmund, pointing to a wide, splintered gap at the base of the far wall. 'Probably badgers . . . they're the only ones strong enough to claw through wood.' He turned to the stack of boxes and barrels at the front, raising his stave to point at a smaller cask atop the pile. 'That looks like a brandy keg. Will it start our fire?'

'Should do,' said Joshua. 'You can set fire to brandy. My mother saw it done in the kitchen once.'

'We'll have to hook it out,' said Olyver, kicking the stack of firewood apart and choosing a branch with a strong lateral spur at one end. He positioned the spur behind the keg and flicked it to the ground, but the ease with which he did it and the way it bounced told them it was empty. Joshua said it was probably for the best, since his mother had described the brandy flames as blue and unnatural. He took the branch from Olyver and skimmed a rag-topped torch some twenty paces clear of the wagon.

'What do you think?' he asked the others, walking across to examine it. 'Is it safe to touch? Do you see any fleas? Will it light?'

'Should do,' said Ian. 'There's still resin in the rags.' With sudden decision, he stooped to pick up the torch and told Olyver to roll the keg towards the oak tree. 'Who cares? We'll die of cold before we ever catch the pestilence if we can't make a fire.'

Thaddeus returned with a dead sheep across his shoulders; he'd culled it from a flock in the meadow where he'd left the horses. He made a strange sight with his wide-skirted coat turned white by snow and his dark eyebrows and beard glittering with frozen flakes. As he passed the wagon, he paused to look inside and then heaved the sheep to the ground and changed out of his sodden clothes, remarking idly that more steam than heat seemed to be coming from the boys' niggardly blaze.

'Blame the logs,' Ian told him, patiently paring wet bark from a branch.

'We'd do better to burn the wagon except none of us fancies eating food cooked on dead men's bones,' said Edmund.

'It's the chests and barrels we want,' said Olyver, 'but there's no way of getting them over the sill without climbing in, and none of us wants to do that in case the pestilence is still inside.'

'Mm.' Thaddeus knelt to open one of the sacks from the pack pony. He removed an axe and a coil of rope. 'It'll be easier with the side removed.'

Rather than chop against the grain of the planks, he chose to strike through the mitred joints that held the sideboard to the front and tailgates, but cold and weariness caused him to miss his aim as often as find it. Edmund took the axe from him. 'You're not made of iron,' he said gruffly. 'Take what heat you can from the fire and watch us do it.'

Given permission to destroy, the boys set to with a will. When enough of the sideboard had come away at both ends, they inserted the rope behind it and used their combined strength to tear it free of the joints which held it to the bottom. Thereafter they threw loops behind the chests and barrels that were stacked at the front beneath the driver's perch and pulled them to the ground. The three barrels, all with broaching taps, had once held wine or ale. As he used Olyver's branch to bowl them towards the fire, Peter said he hoped the soldiers had drunk them dry. Death would be easier to face if the brain was numbed.

Still wary of touching anything, Edmund used the axe blade to prise open the metal clasps that held the lids of the chests closed. Some, which had contained dried food or sweetmeats judging by the dusting of detritus on their bottoms, were empty; others were packed with articles of clothing that had once belonged to Sir Richard. Certain they were flea-ridden, Ian and Olyver scooped out shirts, gowns and hose on the points of the staves and tossed them into the rear of the wagon before pushing the chests ahead of them.

Joshua kicked the damp wood off the embers of the brandy keg and relit the torch. He motioned to Peter to push one of the barrels onto the glowing cinders and then held the torch to the staves to encourage flames. 'Be ready with the next when it takes,' he told Peter. 'Once we have a goodly blaze, we can start feeding the damp firewood into the mix. We need the fire to last the night not burn itself out in an hour.'

'More like seven nights,' Thaddeus corrected as he ran the blade of his knife down the belly and breast of the sheep which he'd strung by its back legs from a branch of the oak tree. 'The last time we saw snow like this it fell for three days and lay on the ground a week. I doubt we'll see Develish tomorrow.'

'We'll not keep anything alight that long,' said Peter.

Thaddeus nodded. 'We'll look for shelter in the church or manor house tomorrow.' He grasped the top left edge of the fleece in one hand and used the side of the other to chop at the membrane between the skin and the meat, pulling the coat away in one piece. 'Our first task come daybreak will be to look for the gold.'

Ian was performing the same actions as Thaddeus on the right-hand side of the carcass. 'How?' he asked.

'Your father built a cairn on the other side of the track. We begin with four hundred paces due south.'

'I didn't see a cairn.'

Thaddeus gave a grunt of amusement. 'It's a bare foot high and he didn't bargain for snow. I could just about make it out when we arrived but not when I came back. We wouldn't have found it if the wagon hadn't been here.'

Ian eased the rest of the skin from the carcass then crouched to slice through the spine and sinews at the neck. 'Or you hadn't forced us to keep going.'

'That too.'

Peter levered another barrel onto the flames. 'It'll all be for nothing if the gold's been stolen.'

'Let's hope it hasn't.' Thaddeus took the skin from Ian and laid it fleece down on the ground beneath the carcass before using his blade to split the sheep's belly and breast to allow the still-warm entrails to drop. 'I'll have the skin back when your hounds have done feeding,' he told Joshua. 'I want something dry to sit on while the mutton's roasting.'

Joshua knelt to cut away the liver, heart and lungs. 'What about the rest of us?'

'Get your own,' Thaddeus said unfeelingly. 'There are plenty more sheep in the meadow.'

They settled for the wagon's sideboard, laying it on the ground across the fire from Thaddeus. There was some debate about whether fleas might be hiding in the joints between the planks until Thaddeus said they could never have survived half a year. Fleas lived on animals and humans, he said, not on wood. If it were otherwise, My Lord of Bourne's furniture would have given them the pestilence.

The air grew colder as the night lengthened, yet despite filling their bellies with half-raw sheep, none of them slept. The sound of the wind in the trees dropped but the snow continued to fall in eerie silence, and the fire became increasingly difficult to keep alight. By dawn the tangled livery inside the wagon was hidden by a clean white shroud, and a two-foot drift covered the track beyond it. Peter glanced nervously at the translucent sheet that covered their oak and said it wouldn't be long before the branches sagged under its weight.

Thaddeus nodded. He was on his feet, moving the packs, harness and saddles against the trunk of the tree. 'We'll need the horses to carry these,' he said. 'We'll come back when the weather improves.' The damp clothes of yesterday were frozen stiff, but he told the boys to shake and pummel them to loosen the ice crystals and then pull them over what they were wearing. 'With luck the inner layer will stay warm long enough to reach the manor house. Bring your weapons and tools but nothing else.'

If they thought this meant he was planning to make shelter a priority, they were quickly disappointed. He stamped out the embers of the fire and used the tip of his sword to draw lines in the ash. 'Gyles used the sun as a guide,' he explained. 'Due south, four hundred paces . . . due east, five hundred paces . . . and due south again, one thousand paces. At each change of direction, he placed a ring of stones beneath a tree.' He drew circles around the points where his lines moved at right-angles to each other. 'Here and here . . . and another halfway down the long stretch.' He touched the tip to the centre of the last line. 'We need to find the rings to have any hope of locating the chest.'

'Why should that be difficult?' asked Edmund.

'We can't predict due south with the sun obscured,' said Thaddeus, marking another line which veered away from the first he'd drawn. 'If we stray west . . . like this . . . we could spend all day looking for the first ring of stones.'

'Wouldn't it be more sensible to make the search when we return for our packs?' suggested Olyver. 'Won't the sun come out when a thaw sets in?'

'More likely the snow will turn to rain and cover the ground with ice,' said Peter. 'That's what happened after grandfather died.'

'Do you have a plan?' Ian asked Thaddeus.

Thaddeus nodded. 'We know south lies beyond your father's cairn.' He placed the tip of his sword at the point that indicated the cairn and drew six lines radiating away from it. 'Edmund is the same height as Gyles. If he takes one of the centre lines and counts off four hundred paces, and the rest of us angle away from him, the chances are good that the first ring of stones will lie somewhere between the six of us when he calls to us to stop. I'll take the outermost line towards the west and work my way east. The rest of you stay put until I reach you.'

The task was easier imagined than performed. Thaddeus insisted on looking beneath every tree for twenty paces on either side of the median in the lengthy gaps between the boys and, all too predictably, he found the stones in the last stretch to be searched. They were more obvious than he'd expected, a foot-wide ring of lightly coloured flints, placed on dark earth in the cleft between the twisting, muscular roots of an ash tree, and he blessed Gyles for his common sense. It was surely no accident that he'd chosen a spot which was protected from drifting leaves.

'You should have let me work in from this side,' said Ian, who had taken the outermost line to the east and had cursed freely about boredom and cold by the time he was allowed to move. 'We'd have found it sooner if you had.'

'Now that we know what we're looking for, you can,' said Thaddeus. He stood sideways to the tree, raised his left arm to point towards where he believed the wagon to be and squared his right to indicate due east. 'Edmund, follow this line for five hundred paces, and the rest do as we did before. Don't skimp on searching,' he warned Ian. 'We'll none of us thank you if we have to return to your father's cairn and start again.'

Whether by chance or through Edmund's accuracy in judging direction, the second and third rings were within thirty paces of where he halted. Thaddeus asked how he was managing to keep his line so true, and he said he didn't know. He was simply choosing the most direct route through the trees to be sure of walking the measured distance.

Olyver said his father would have done the same. 'He told our mother the chest weighed a tonne . . . and he'd have cursed to Hell and back if he'd kept bumping into trees with a load like that on his shoulder.'

A smile creased Thaddeus's dark face. 'He'll have cursed anyway, trees or not. The chest is carpentered from three-inch-thick oak and contains four hundred gold nobles. It required two men to lift it into the wagon.'

'*Four hundred*?' Peter echoed in amazement. 'No wonder you're so keen to retrieve it.'

'And Gyles to hide it, since it was earned by the sweat of Develish serfs. We'll spread out as before for the last five hundred paces. We've not come this far to go awry at the end.' He turned to

Ian. 'We're looking for a fallen tree. Your father pushed the coffer into a space beneath the trunk where it forms an arch with the torn-up roots. Seven months ago the tree was rotten to its core and it may have broken apart since, so be sure to search under every piece of sizeable deadwood you encounter.'

As Ian dutifully turned every log, he listened for shouts of excitement from the other end of the line. When none came, he wondered what Thaddeus would do if they failed to find the gold. The woodland canopy was protecting them from the worst of the snow, but in parts, where tall, slender birches had taken the place of oak and ash, the flakes fell freely through the thinner branches and the ground beneath them was deeply carpeted. He began to fear that the mile-long walk to the manor house was already impassable. Joshua expressed similar worries when Ian released him to join the search, muttering that his dogs would die of exhaustion if Thaddeus expected them to breast drifts three feet high.

By the time they reached Peter, he was jumping up and down and swinging his arms in a vain attempt to keep warm. 'You've been bloody ages,' he growled, motioning behind him. 'There's a fallen tree with its roots still attached about thirty paces back. It's pretty much buried by snow but it's worth a look. I'm thinking your father's paces probably shortened as he grew tired.'

Ian removed his bow, scabbard and arrows and propped their tips together to form a pyramid, denoting Peter's spot so they could find it again. 'I'll wring your neck if you're right,' he snapped crossly. 'We'd be halfway to the manor house by now if you'd left a marker and made the search yourself.'

Nevertheless, he planted a hearty kiss on Peter's cheek when a small amount of scrabbling through windblown leaves and a scattering of snow exposed a carved wooden chest with its padlock intact.

໐໐

Four miles to the east, Eleanor was watching the falling snow through the window of the steward's office. In her arms, she cradled one of her cats as tenderly as a baby, planting kisses on its head and rubbing her cheek against its soft fur. As ever, the soft, rumbling purr that answered her honest love brought a sweet smile to her face.

She had only the dimmest memories of the last time snow had fallen on Develish and she was entranced by its prettiness. The land was white as far as the eye could see and the unsightly remains of the burnt-out village were softened and cleansed. She drew Lady Anne's attention to a group of men on the other side of the moat who were moving three abreast across the pastureland.

'What are they doing?' she asked.

Lady Anne left her desk to stand beside her. 'Tramping a path to the sheep.' She pointed to where the flock was huddled against some wattle fencing. 'Do you see how the snow is beginning to bank over them? We must move them now or they'll be smothered.'

'Why don't they move themselves?'

'They believe they're safe. It's their nature to stay together.'

'Where will the men take them?'

Lady Anne turned her towards where Gyles Startout, John Trueblood and James Buckler were enlarging the shelter My Lord of Bourne had used. 'They've taken the timber from the serfs' huts in the orchard to build a low-roofed barn.'

'Where will the serfs sleep?'

'In the house. No one can live outside while this cold spell endures.'

With unexpected tenderness, Eleanor slipped her arm around Lady Anne's waist. 'You must be worried for Thaddeus,' she said gently. 'You told me he will have left Bourne a week ago but his journey home seems overly long.'

'I expect his work in Bourne has delayed him.'

'I hope that's true, Mama. Robert is greatly worried for him. He says he and his companions could freeze to death if they've become trapped in the snow without a fire to warm them.'

For once, Lady Anne believed Eleanor's concern was sincere. Certainly, her soft embrace seemed kindly-meant. 'Robert frets unnecessarily,' she answered with a light laugh to disguise her own fears. 'Thaddeus is more of a wolf . . . and they thrive in weather like this.'

Nine

Evidence that the great hall of Pedle Hinton had been destroyed by fire was seen in the soot-blackened walls and the charred rafters that had once supported a timber roof. The heavy oak doors of the entrance porch stood wide open, revealing a pristine covering of snow lying like a downy coverlet on the floor. Here and there, undulating folds suggested something buried, but Thaddeus ignored his companions' superstitious mutterings about corpses as he walked through the porchway to look towards the southern end of the house which retained its roof.

A set of stone steps in the farthest corner led to upper chambers which opened off a railed gallery, and two doors in the supporting wall below to lower ones. He looked for footprints in the snow but couldn't see any. If people still lived here, they hadn't left their quarters last night or this morning. He called out a greeting. 'My Lord of Athelstan and five of his fighting men ask hospitality of My Lord of Pedle Hinton. We are free of the pestilence but need shelter from the blizzard. Does anyone hear me?'

Perhaps it was only an echo of his own voice, but he had a strong sense that he'd been answered. He stood listening, his hand reaching for the sword that hung at his side. Ian and Olyver did the same, motioning to Joshua to send his dogs forward. At the rear, Edmund and Peter, who were carrying the chest of gold between them, lowered it to the ground and lifted their strung bows over their heads.

'Try again,' urged Joshua. 'The pack will tell us soon enough if you get a response.'

The dogs reacted even before the words had left Thaddeus's mouth, racing for the stairs and bounding up them two at a time, giving vent to mournful howls as they paced the gallery and sniffed at doors. Joshua prepared to follow, but Thaddeus caught his arm. 'Summon them back,' he said. 'Whoever's up there must think the hounds of Hell have arrived.'

Joshua gave a piercing whistle. 'What will you do?'

'Try to coax our hosts into revealing themselves. If they're from Pedle Hinton, they're more entitled to be here than we are, and if they're not—' Thaddeus unsheathed his sword—'we'll have to agree temporary rights of tenure.' He beckoned the other boys forward and motioned to the doors at the end of the hall beneath the gallery. 'See if those rooms are occupied, but let the dogs enter first.'

He trod quietly up the steps and looked along the landing. Four chambers opened off it but there was nothing to tell him whether one or all were occupied, since there were only paw prints in the dusting of snow on the floor. He moved softly to the first door and placed his ear to the planking, waiting through the sound of Joshua's warnings outside a room below and the wrench of rusted hinges as Ian forced entry. In the hush that followed, he heard a child's whimper and the whispered tones of women, urging silence.

He walked on light feet to the other doors, listening outside each for several minutes. From downstairs, the intermittent conversation of the boys was clearly audible, yet there was no reaction to it inside these chambers. He positioned himself to the right of the first door and used his sword hilt to tap lightly against the wood. 'I am My Lord of Athelstan, cousin to your near neighbour Lady Anne of Develish and related through marriage to Sir Richard, her deceased husband. Be assured that I and my men mean you no harm. If one amongst you remembers Sir Richard from his visits or knows anything of Develish, then ask me questions so that I may prove my truthfulness.'

There was some whispering before the tremulous voice of an elderly man spoke. 'Sir Richard was sick the last time he was here. Did he die of the pestilence?'

'Yes. Three days after leaving Pedle Hinton. Lady Anne worried that he brought the pestilence to you, but Gyles Startout, who rode with him, told us you'd buried forty of your own in the week before they arrived.'

'I know Gyles. Is he well?'

'He is, as are all in Develish. Only Sir Richard and his Norman fighting men are gone. Gyles's twin sons, Ian and Olyver, form part of my retinue. Two of the voices you hear downstairs are theirs.' He paused to allow time for a reply, but none came. 'How many are you? We will assist you if we can.'

'We do well enough on our own, My Lord. Pay heed to your affairs and leave us to ours.'

There was a whispered altercation before a woman spoke. 'We are eighteen, sire. One elder, seven women and ten children.

We have lived in this chamber since bandits fired the village and a malign wind carried burning thatch to the roof of the great hall. We thought the whole house would be razed, but God saw fit to leave us this part as shelter.'

'When was that?'

'I can't tell you, sire, for we have lost count of the sun's rising and setting. Three weeks and more, I think. We stay together for warmth but grow weaker as each day passes.'

'When did the last of your neighbours die of the pestilence?'

'Before Christmas, sire. We are all that is left, though we don't know why God has spared us. We are much in need of assistance.'

Briefly, Thaddeus closed his eyes. He knew full well what he would find when he opened the door, for he had seen starvation in the hollow faces of the peasants of Woodoak and Bourne. He reached for the latch. 'Do I have your permission to enter, mistress? Lady Anne judges a person free of the pestilence after two weeks. Were she here, she would tell you it's time to embrace life.'

⁊

There was no understanding people like this, Ian thought, as he took an adult woman from Thaddeus's arms and carried her down the steps to where Edmund had lit a fire in the largest of the ground-floor rooms. She had so little flesh on her bones that she weighed as lightly as a child and only the grime on her face gave her skin some colour. He placed her carefully on the floor, afraid of breaking her, and her eyes filled with tears as she thanked him. He smiled and spoke comforting words but, in truth, his mind rebelled against her stupidity. By what reasoning did anyone choose death from hunger when there were sheep aplenty in the fields beyond the house?

He, Olyver and Thaddeus had caught and slaughtered two ram lambs within a hundred paces of the front door, and Joshua had found the means to cook them simply by putting his shoulder to the door of the kitchen. Little of the roof remained, but shelves around the walls were piled with iron cauldrons, pewter plates and earthenware tankards. A heavy oak table, miraculously unscathed, stood in the centre. Once swept of snow, Joshua used it to butcher the carcasses while Edmund and Peter, having looted every room of furniture to make fire, dug out a mighty stack of wood beside the kitchen's outer door and brought the logs inside to dry.

The first to be brought downstairs in Thaddeus's strong arms had been a shrivelled greybeard who took deference as his due. He seated himself on a pile of rushes and gestured towards the floor each time Thaddeus, Ian or Olyver appeared with another wraithlike figure clasped against their chests, apparently believing that women and children must always sit beneath him. He was more alarmed than grateful to see his master's furniture being broken up for firewood.

'We'll suffer for this,' he warned the women as Ian fed the legs of a stool into the blaze to keep Joshua's cauldron of diced mutton at a rolling simmer. 'They compound theft with wilful destruction by what they do.'

Olyver entered the room and placed a barely alive toddler in the lap of the woman Ian had carried. He was as impatient with these people's foolishness as his twin. 'Whose judgement do you fear?' he asked the old man. 'If God's, you can escape sin by allowing me to return you to the upper chamber without food.'

'The offences have been committed. You have made us party to your crimes whether we like it or not. Removing ourselves will make no difference.'

Olyver gave an involuntary laugh. 'You have a strange way of reasoning, sir. Do you think God doesn't know who the true culprits are? Why should He punish the innocent when My Lord of Athelstan and his men are willing and able to take the blame upon themselves?'

Thaddeus paused at the bottom of the stairs. Cradled in his arms was the last to be rescued, a woman of some thirty years with sunken eyes and transparent skin. It was she who had spoken to him through the door, and she who had insisted on the old man going first, using the opportunity of his absence to urge the women and children to pay heed only to My Lord of Athelstan. Together they listened to the exchange between the twins and the elder.

'I am acquainted with your father,' the old man told the youths severely. 'He would not approve of your behaviour.'

'You're mistaken,' answered Ian, kneeling to touch the cold, pale cheek of the toddler. 'Gyles Startout would endure an eternity in Hell before he let a babe such as this die from lack of warmth and nourishment . . . as will his sons, if that is to be our punishment.'

'Then accept God's judgement when you appear before Him.'

'We will do so gladly if this little one survives.'

'He will not. His only salvation was freedom from sin. Ours also. Now God will punish us all for your misdeeds. Boils will break out on our necks and our bodies turn black—and you will bear our suffering on your conscience along with your other crimes.'

A young maid began to weep.

'You must take me in, sire,' begged the woman in Thaddeus's arms, plucking urgently at his sleeve. 'They will crawl from the fire and eat nothing if he continues. He has a powerful hold over them.'

'Yet you seem ready to defy him. Could you not have done so sooner?'

'Not on my own, sire. He is my father.'

Thaddeus needed no further explanation. In a social order created and governed by men, women learnt obedience early. 'What is your name, mistress?'

'Alice Bartram, sire.'

'And your father's?'

'Harold Talbot, sire. He is persuaded God means us all to die. If you know differently and have the words to change his mind, I beg you to use them.'

With a nod, Thaddeus carried her into the room and sat her amongst the women and children. He dropped to one knee in front of the old man. 'Why do you deny yourself food and warmth, Master Talbot? Is the sin of self-killing not greater than the sin of theft?'

'If God wants me to live, I will.'

'He has saved you from the pestilence and placed these seventeen women and children in your charge. What more proof do you need that He wishes you to keep serving Him on earth?'

'We serve Him best by following his commandments. To prolong our lives through theft and wanton destruction will invite punishment. We are judged by the manner of our living not by the span of our years.'

Thaddeus was reminded of his stepfather, whose mind, once set, was impossible to change. 'Then you have a fine advantage over the rest of us,' he said lightly. 'We could all wish a half-century of enjoyment before being asked to account for ourselves.'

Harold's eyes glittered angrily. 'The older we are the harder we are tested,' he snapped. 'Innocents such as these—' he gestured dismissively to the toddler—'have places reserved for them in Heaven. Old men such as I have to earn our redemption through privation and suffering.'

A cynical smile flickered briefly at the corner of Thaddeus's mouth. It was a shameless tyranny that exploited weakness for its own benefit. 'I doubt redemption comes through the wilful neglect of children, sir.' He turned to the women. 'Without a priest to guide you, you must decide for yourselves what God expects of you. If you truly believe you'll be judged more harshly for stealing a sheep than leaving a little one to die, then do nothing; if you do *not* believe it, you must act.'

Ian, seeing the way the women dropped their eyes, worried that Thaddeus had pushed them too far too fast. Even men needed courage to gainsay an elder, and there was no spark of resistance in any of the faces before him.

A breath of time passed before Alice raised her head. She addressed Thaddeus. 'We grieve for our families and long to see them again, My Lord. All were lost to the pestilence, but my father assures us that the youngest and least sullied will be waiting for us in Heaven. He urges us to keep pure hearts so that we may join them. It makes death more welcome to believe we can once again clasp our newborns to our breasts.'

Thaddeus wondered if even Lady Anne could have said so much in so few words. He knew now how the old man had gained a hold over her companions' minds—grief for lost children never went away—but he had little idea how to loosen it. To urge them to live the life they had rather than yearn for an uncertain Heaven would be to take all hope away. He looked to Ian and Olyver for inspiration.

'Our father, Gyles Startout, would tell you all your family will be waiting for you, mistress,' said Ian. 'He heard the confessions of dying soldiers because there was no priest to do it, and he found only good in them. He has no belief that God caused their suffering in order to send them to Hell.'

The old man stirred. 'They were punished for the sins of all mankind, as were my grandchildren. It was the same when the Flood covered the earth and caused every living thing to perish. God saw that His creations were evil and corrupt, and He repented of making them. Only Noah, a man without blame, was saved.'

Tears wet Alice's lashes. Again, she addressed Thaddeus. 'Our priest told us this before he breathed his last, sire. He thought it would comfort us to know our families paid the price for others' sins and not their own.'

'When did he die, mistress?'

'Some six weeks after the pestilence arrived, sire.'

'Did he tend the sick?'

'Every hour of every day. We mourned his passing deeply.'

Thaddeus nodded. 'We hear the same story everywhere we go. God's servants die early.' He took her hand in his. 'Why do you think that is?'

He felt a trembling in her fingers, as if his touch made her uneasy. 'To keep their suffering short, sire. The greatest anguish is to watch others endure terrible pain, knowing you can do nothing to help them.'

'To believe that is to believe that Christ's agony on the cross was less than His mother's pain to watch it. Is that not a heresy, mistress?'

Alice glanced nervously towards her father. 'We try only to make sense of why a good man died early, My Lord.'

Thaddeus reached for her other hand to encourage her to look only at him. 'In Develish, where Lady Anne protects her serfs by refusing entry to strangers until they prove themselves free of the pestilence, every man, woman and child still lives. Here, where no such measures were taken, eighteen remain. Your priest died because he honoured his vows. He gave himself unstintingly to those who needed him and he caught the sickness through his closeness with them.'

She took so long to answer that her father spoke into the silence. 'He utters the Devil's words. You'll not escape Hell if you heed him, daughter.'

Alice ran her tongue across her dry lips. 'I nursed my husband and all my children, sire, but they died and I lived. How can that be if the sickness is caught through closeness?'

Ian held his breath, praying that Thaddeus wouldn't talk about rats or fleas. Precious few in Bourne had believed him, only following his rules on cleanliness because they were rewarded with food for their obedience. To expect this woman, so steeped in submission to her father and the Church, to understand a strange, new reasoning would be to lose her.

'In the same way that you didn't catch the sneezes every time your husband had them, or the pox from your children. Not all fall to every sickness.' Thaddeus nodded to Ian and Olyver. 'These twins' father nursed Sir Richard and two of his fellow soldiers as they lay dying, and remains healthy to this day, yet he rejects any idea that God singled him out for favour. He knows his flaws too well to believe himself more deserving of life than those who have perished.'

'But does God not ordain everything, My Lord? How else was I spared the sneezes except by His mercy?'

A smile lit Thaddeus's eyes. 'If I knew that, mistress, we could be free of them forever.' He paused. 'I have few answers except to remind you that Jesus gave us only two commandments: *Love the Lord your God with all your heart and your neighbour as yourself.*' He released her hands to cup his palm under the chin of the toddler. 'This is your neighbour. If you abandon him, you abandon God.'

ᙇᙇ

It was another two days before the snow stopped falling. By then, the church had become a stable for horses and the great hall a pen for as many sheep as Thaddeus and his companions had been able to shepherd through the blizzard. All were in need of fodder. On the first morning of clear skies, Edmund, Joshua, Peter and the twins located a barn stacked with hay on the edge of the pastureland, and used wooden spades from a shed beside the manor house to dig through the drift in front of the double doors.

They stood for several minutes, contemplating the sheaves that were piled inside and the two pitchforks impaled in the ground on either side of the doorway. The pack's lack of interest suggested there was nothing to find, but Joshua said dogs responded to movement as much as scent. If rats had burrowed into the hay to sleep through the winter, they'd emerge as soon as the sheaves were disturbed. Fleas too.

Edmund, always the most reluctant to encounter rats, gave a groan of anguish before seizing a pitchfork and using it to stab a sheaf. 'Bloody well set your animals on to anything that twitches or I'll wring their necks myself,' he warned Joshua, as he slung the bundle onto the snow behind them. 'I'm damned if I'll catch the pestilence to keep Pedle Hinton serfs alive.'

He made a fine show of proving differently, Ian thought with amusement, as he watched his friend make deeper inroads into the stack. But whether Edmund wanted to keep sheep alive for the sake of the women or the toddler was anyone's guess. He'd become the women's favourite after patiently coaxing the infant to open his eyes and take nourishment, and there was no question he enjoyed their praise. They said his voice and face must resemble the child's father's, for the little boy responded more to him than to anyone else—so much so that he would only eat if Edmund cradled him in his lap and fed him from his plate.

Thaddeus asked the child's name and how old he was, but none of the women knew. He'd been found wandering the village one morning in November, but no one could say if he was from Pedle Hinton or had become detached from a family fleeing north to escape the pestilence. From his size, he was believed to be some two years old, but he couldn't tell them his name. Before the pestilence, Pedle Hinton field serfs had numbered above five hundred, and toddlers had been hard to distinguish when some families ran to eight or ten children, with half being lost in the first three years of life. Alice thought he might be a Blount, the last of whom was believed to have perished in the week before he was discovered, but the other women were doubtful. He hadn't the look of John Blount and they couldn't recall Jeanne binding a suckling babe to her breast in order to work the fields in any of the previous eight seasons.

Out of curiosity, the following morning Thaddeus searched the church for the parish register after he and his companions had hobbled their horses in the nave. He found it in the priest's quarters, beneath the dead man's blood-and-pus-stained stole, which he flicked to the floor with the point of his sword, along with the wooden cross that lay on top. He bent his head in apology to the altar before he left, as much for turning God's house into a stable as for his affront to the crucifix. He harboured no heresies against Christ, only against the Church which claimed to speak for Him.

That afternoon, by the light of the fire, he traced the Blount family's history in the register. The last child to be born to John and Jeanne had been a son in the winter of 1346, but his early death was recorded six months later. In the eleven years before, Jeanne had given birth to nine babies, only three of whom had survived long enough to see the pestilence. The priest had recorded their deaths before he, too, had succumbed.

Since sons were valued more highly than daughters, Thaddeus found it hard to believe the toddler had been abandoned by fleeing serfs, and he combed the register for every boy born between the summer of 1346 and the spring of 1347. Eight had died within a year of their births, leaving sixteen unaccounted for. He read their names and the names of their parents aloud. In most cases, particularly where peasant strips adjoined or huts were close, one or other of the women was able to say with certainty that the whole family had perished, including babes in arms. But the fate of four was unknown.

'I heard it told that Tom Halfpenny chose to abscond and take his wife and son with him,' said Alice. 'They were young and had more courage than the rest of us.'

'Jacob Cooper did the same after his daughter perished,' another woman said. 'He and Molly swore an oath that they'd not let any more of their children suffer and were gone by the morning.'

Harold Talbot, somewhat mellowed by taking food into his belly, nodded. 'By my guess, upwards of fifty of the younger men absconded,' he told Thaddeus. 'They promised to come back for their families when they'd found shelter elsewhere, but none ever has. It may be that this child belongs to one of them.'

Thaddeus ran his finger down the page. 'We're left with two. William Fulcher and Godfrey Lovell.'

Edmund raised his head. 'My grandfather was Godfrey Trueblood and my grandmother was Meg Lovell. That can't be chance, can it?'

Thaddeus turned back pages to find the births of Godfrey Lovell's parents and grandparents. Every so often, he saw surnames he recognised from Develish and he wondered how many of the demesne's daughters had married into Pedle Hinton. The stories of so many families were written in these simple inscriptions of births, marriages and deaths, and yet the knowledge was lost when there was no one to read them. With patient cross-referencing, he traced Godfrey Lovell's lineage to the birth of his grandfather, Robert Lovell, and from there, three pages earlier, learnt the name of Robert's older sister, Meg.

He gave a bark of satisfaction. 'I can tell you for certain when I've checked the Develish ledger,' he told Edmund, 'but it looks as if your grandmother was sister to this little fellow's grandfather. She must have moved to Develish on her marriage.' He read out the entries for both births. 'Godfrey Lovell is your cousin.'

෨෨

Alice looked down from the gallery as the young men in My Lord of Athelstan's entourage untied the sheaves and dropped the hay in loose piles amongst the flock. They were very assured in what they were doing. Peter Catchpole turned a lame ewe on her back and used his knife to dig a stone from between the cloves of her hoof while the twins moved from sheep to sheep, running their fingers around faces and ears, searching for ticks. Through the open door of the kitchen, she saw Edmund and Joshua filling My Lord of Pedle Hinton's embossed metal piss-pots with snow before holding them over six-inch-wide candles to melt the crystals to water. She made a silent prayer that her father wasn't watching as they carried the costly vessels into the great hall and placed them in front of the animals as drinking troughs.

When she'd first seen the youths, she hadn't doubted their status was above hers. True, they looked younger than the fighting men she'd seen in the past, but their weapons, their manner of speech and their coats and liveries, though saturated, had given them the bearing of freemen. Seeing them now, dressed in tunics and britches and showing more knowledge of how to manage stock than any Pedle Hinton soldier ever had, she wasn't so sure. Certainly, her father believed them to be serfs, whispering constantly in her ear that Gyles Startout was as low-born as he.

She turned to watch Thaddeus sort through scrolls on the shelves in My Lord of Pedle Hinton's chamber. Most he returned to their places with only the briefest of glances, a few he placed on the floor at his feet. Feeling her gaze upon him, he looked towards her with a smile. 'What troubles you, mistress?'

A flush of embarrassment stained her cheeks. How churlish she would seem to question this man when his presence had brought so much hope and strength. And yet she was fearful. 'You must not think me ungrateful, sire. Two days ago, I could barely stand, and I wept to see little Godfrey fade when the last of the dried plums were gone. It filled me with happiness to hear him laugh this morning.' She searched his face, her own creased with anxiety.

'Say what is in your heart, Alice. The truth will not offend me.'

She took a breath to steady herself. 'My father tells me Gyles Startout is as base-born as we and that his sons can be no different, sire. To accept the food they give us will not serve for excuse when a new lord comes.'

Thaddeus interpreted her words as best he could. 'You think it better to say you took food from a noble?'

'We are obligated to obey the commands of those above us, sire.'

He studied her with amusement. 'You've come a long way, Alice. When we first met, you were afraid of God; now your mind is troubled only by the imagined arrival of a man who doesn't exist.' He nodded towards the burnt-out roof. 'Which lord is so foolish that he'll pay the taxes of inheritance to acquire a demesne without labourers? Who will repair this house and rebuild the village? Who will plough the fields and harvest the corn?'

Alice shook her head in bewilderment. Such thoughts had never occurred to her.

'No landowner in England will have the men to work his estates once the pestilence has passed,' Thaddeus went on, bending to lift a scroll from the floor. 'This letter was sent to My Lord of Pedle Hinton from a cousin in Normandy.' He unfurled the vellum. 'It's dated Christmas, 1347—some six months before the pestilence entered Melcombe—and speaks of towns and villages in France and Italy being laid waste by a killing disease. In his own estates, this man had already lost one-third of his serfs and expected to lose another third before summer. He finishes by saying he'll be reduced to penury if that happens.'

He watched Alice's expression move from bewilderment through shock to anger. 'We thought only Dorseteshire had sinned,' she said. 'My Lord of Pedle Hinton raged at us for bringing God's wrath to the county, and the priest ordered us to beg his forgiveness before we asked God for His. Neither said Normandy was afflicted.'

'Would it have made a difference if they had?'

'For certain, sire. It filled us with terror to think we were alone in our suffering. My poor husband died not knowing what wickedness Dorseteshire had committed.' She dashed a tear from her eye with the back of her hand. 'The master was cruel to berate us. If he knew that France had fallen to the sickness, he should have made plans to protect us, the same way My Lady of Develish did.'

'I doubt he had Lady Anne's courage, Alice. It takes strength and bravery to defy the Church. If Milady had believed what His Grace the bishop told her, the story of Develish would have been different.'

'Why did she not believe it, sire?'

Thaddeus answered honestly. 'She was raised by nuns who taught her to follow the teachings of Jesus. It makes her the kindest and most considerate of mistresses. Since she sees no fault in her people, she cannot accept that God does either, and strives to keep them safe because her faith tells her that this is what she must do.'

'Do her serfs follow the teachings of Jesus, sire?'

'They try, Alice.'

'Then that is why God has spared them, sire. They have more goodness than the rest of us.'

Thaddeus laughed as he dropped the scroll to the floor and took another from the shelf. 'I have high hopes of you, mistress,' he teased. 'A minute past, you were quibbling about taking food from Develish thieves, now you raise them to the level of saints. You'll be stealing yourself in another two days, if you believe the cause virtuous enough.'

The last day of February, 1349

*T*haddeus has returned with yet more plundered sheep. He has put them to graze on the common land, which is bare of snow now that the thaw has come.

   He and his companions surprised us by emerging from the woodland where the footpath from Pedle Hinton enters Develish. We had been searching the highway to the north and south for days, never expecting them to come along the track. They were herding the flock ahead of them, using Joshua's dogs to confine stragglers, and we heard the animals' plaintive bleating before we saw them. Gyles summoned me to watch as the column of sheep issued from the trees, followed by a motley army of women and children on horseback, and Thaddeus and his companions on foot.

   Edmund Trueblood appeared first, bearing a tiny boy on his shoulders and leading his horse with 3 young maids in the saddle. The Startout twins, Peter Catchpole and Joshua Buckler followed, each with 2 or 3 frail-looking passengers on their mounts, while at the rear came Thaddeus, guiding a heavily laden pack pony with one hand and, with the other, his charger with a greybeard and woman upon its back. I counted 18 extra souls and asked Gyles where they could have come from. He guessed Pedle Hinton, for he recognised the greybeard as an elder who goes by the name of Harold Talbot.

And so it proved. Thaddeus called out their circumstances from across the moat and, with the agreement of my people, I have given permission for them to remain in Develish once they have served their fortnight's exclusion. Thaddeus believes some may have kinship with our serfs and has given me their names so that I may search our registers. Certainly, John and Clara Trueblood have no doubt that Edmund's small charge is part of their family, for he has the look of Edmund at the same age. They have pledged to raise the child as their own, and I don't doubt others will be as generous.

Thaddeus and his men (they are too well grown now to be called boys) have cleaned one end of the open-sided barn and strung fleeces in the gaps between the upright posts to provide shelter for the Pedle Hinton serfs. Our sheep still have use of the other end and will add warmth from their bodies at night. It is hardly the most inviting of welcomes to our demesne, but the 2-week exclusion has served us well until now. For themselves, Thaddeus and his men use the hut they built when Bourne was here.

I have sent clean clothes and warm broth across on the raft, and in return Thaddeus delivered our chest of gold and a coffer of scrolls from Pedle Hinton. In a private letter atop the documents, he drew my attention to the warnings Pedle Hinton received from France—but did not heed—about the progress of the pestilence. He urged me to study one vellum in particular, dated August, 1348, which he found with its seal intact. This suggested to Thaddeus, as it does to me, that My Lord and his steward never saw it, being dead before it arrived.

The letter was scribed by a French monk who charged himself with informing My Lord of Pedle Hinton that his cousin, a bishop of Normandy, had relinquished his life after days of intense suffering. I record the second paragraph here to remind myself that the rules we follow are wise:

'In his dying breath, His Grace implored that I request all in his family to protect themselves against this pestilence. His greatest fear was that none will survive and a proud name will be lost. Be comforted that you will do no wrong by closing your doors to sufferers since His Holiness, Pope Clement of Avignon, has granted remission of sins to all who die a painful death. Such benevolence will allow those you exclude to enjoy eternity. Nonetheless, His Grace's wish was that you embrace life, and he asked that you pray daily for his soul, avoid contact with the sick and pledge yourself to the service of God.'

There is much to read in the words of this unknown bishop, not least his belated realisation that it might be possible to survive the pestilence. I am left to wonder why he didn't come to this reasoning earlier and why His Holiness thought it kinder to remit sins—a fact which is known only to a handful of French clerics, I imagine—than offer wise advice on avoidance.

☙❧

The fourth day of March, 1349. Midnight

Thaddeus and his companions will leave again at dawn, and I am sad to have had only one chance to talk with my gentle giant. Clara allowed us the use of her kitchen for a snatched hour once all were asleep, but our meeting was bittersweet, being too short and taken up with business. We both issued warnings as often as we exchanged expressions of tenderness.

Thaddeus worries that Harold Talbot will cause disharmony when I allow him into our enclosure, and urges me to assist his daughter, Alice Bartram, in the management of him. The old man's mind has gone, causing him to dwell on the sins of others, and he makes his accusations with such force and anger that even Thaddeus's companions find them unsettling.

In return, I worry that My Lord of Blandeforde's steward will know Athelstan for an imposter. Thaddeus tells me his plan is to travel to Blandeforde in April, and I am already concerned for him and his companions. The steward's name is Jacques d'Amiens and I have never met a man so clever or so knowledgeable about his master's demesnes. In the time I've lived in Develish, he has come several times to oversee the collection of taxes, and I am deeply afraid he may have seen my dear friend performing ad opus work inside the moat. If he did, he will recognise him and know him for a serf. Thaddeus's appearance is too distinctive not to have been noticed.

Thaddeus pays little heed to these fears, for he has no understanding of how eyes are drawn to him because of the tallness of his frame, the darkness of his skin and the fineness of his features. I have begged him to avoid all contact with the steward but he refuses to humour me. He says, quite rightly, that he cannot secure a future for our people without talking to the person who controls My Lord of Blandeforde's affairs.

Thaddeus has written a long report of all that happened in Bourne, begging me to read it to our people once he and his companions have left. It seems the youths have lost their taste for storytelling, having learnt the last time that there is always a clamour for more. I wonder if they finally understand why Gyles was so reluctant to speak of his final journey with Sir Richard. After all, some things are best kept to oneself.

Thaddeus and his companions will ride first to Dorchester and Melcombe to discover how many still live in those towns. From there, they will travel to the west, charting the deserted demesnes along the way, and then to the east for the same purpose. They expect to arrive in Blandeforde in the second week of April, and Thaddeus hopes their knowledge of how south Dorseteshire fares, along with news of France and Italy from the Pedle Hinton letters, will stand them in good stead when they arrive.

This eve, the raft carried their newly laundered liveries, together with half the gold nobles from Eleanor's dowry. Our leather workers have created 6 separate saddle packs so that the weight of the coins can be spread evenly between 6 riders. The packs have been stitched in such a way that the coins stand in a series of columns inside them and the slimness of the design should allow them to escape notice beneath the bulkier packs above them. I pray this is so, for it will be a tragedy indeed if bandits believe they see something worth stealing.

Thaddeus is so determined to prove himself a worthy match for me by purchasing a demesne of his own, he's quite foolhardy enough to give his life in defence of gold.

Ten

Develish, Dorseteshire

CLARA TRUEBLOOD HAD WITNESSED MANY things in her kitchen but never a wild-haired old man pushing a young maid to the floor and raising her skirts to beat her naked buttocks with a wooden paddle. She thrust through the crowd of startled servants and seized Harold Talbot's wrist before he could land another blow. 'What is the meaning of this?' she demanded.

He turned his fury on her. 'You dare lay hands on an elder?'

'I dare and I will. You have no authority here, Master Talbot. By what right do you chastise one of my helpers?'

'By God's right. She profaned against one superior to her.'

Clara nodded to the girl to stand up. She was half-sister to Thaddeus and had yet to turn eleven. 'Is this true, May? Did you speak ill of Lady Anne?'

The girl shook her head.

'Who then?'

She wriggled her shoulders. 'Father Anselm . . . but I said only what others say.'

'Which is?'

'No one wants to clean his chamber because he lives like a pig.'

Clara turned her face so that Harold Talbot wouldn't see the smile that twitched at the corners of her mouth. She received more complaints about the drunken priest's dirty habits than anything else, and had heard rather worse slurs than 'pig' used to describe him. Some days, when she was feeling kind, she left the kitchen in another's charge and did the job of cleaning his quarters herself, if only to give some respite to the younger servants. It was one thing to empty the old brute's semen-filled piss-pot, quite another to run the gauntlet of his groping fingers. She had a sense that Harold Talbot was cut from the same cloth, since he had been overly keen to raise little May's skirts in order to give her a beating.

She resisted his attempts to free himself. 'Calm yourself, sir. This is my kitchen and you are an uninvited guest.'

He slapped her face. 'Where is your respect? I don't take orders from women.'

Clara, bigger and stronger than he was, caught his other wrist and twisted both arms behind him. 'You are in Develish, sir, where customs are different from Pedle Hinton.' She picked out thirteen-year-old Isabella Startout, who was standing near the doorway to the great hall. 'Oblige me by fetching Milady, Isabella. She will know better than I how to judge the rights and wrongs of this. Be sure to explain the situation to her. I wouldn't want her to be unprepared for what she finds.'

Isabella gave a nod of understanding before darting from the room. It was minutes only before she returned with Lady Anne, and Clara was relieved to see that her mistress seemed fully aware of why she had Harold Talbot under restraint. She spoke gently to him, but her words were intended for everyone.

'Do you know me, sir? We met two days ago when I welcomed you to Develish as your new liege lord.'

The old man spat on the floor. 'My Lord has been dead these many months. His wife also.'

'Indeed. Pedle Hinton suffered cruelly from the pestilence. Only you and a handful of women and children remain from the hundreds who once lived there.'

He stared at the faces around him. 'I see many in this room alone.'

'But all are strangers to you, Master Talbot, for this is Develish and not Pedle Hinton. Will you allow me to take you to your daughter, so that she can tell you again why you are here? I believe weariness has caused you to forget the journey you made to reach us.'

He frowned in confusion. 'My daughters are lost to me.'

'Not all, sir. One still lives. Her name is Alice. You will know her when you see her.'

He gave a baffled nod, and Lady Anne signed to Clara to release him. The woman did so, but remained ready to seize him again if he raised his hand to her mistress. She had more knowledge than most of the anger that accompanied the scrambled wits of age, for her grandmother had suffered the same debility.

'Shall I come with you, milady?' she asked.

'I believe we can manage on our own,' Lady Anne answered, putting her hand beneath Harold's elbow. 'It's but a few steps to the great hall, where Alice awaits us. It would be a kindness to make Master Talbot a bowl of chamomile tea with an infusion of valerian. He is much in need of rest, I think.'

'Isabella will bring it to you promptly, milady.'

Clara watched them make their way through the door and then took a jar of dried chamomile and a vial of valerian tincture from a high shelf on the wall behind her. 'You've nothing to feel anxious about,' she told May Thurkell as she spooned petals into an earthenware bowl and added a ladleful of water from the boiling cauldron on the fire. 'Milady finds no fault in you.'

'Are you sure, Mistress Trueblood?' the girl asked tearfully. 'I thought her kinder to Master Talbot than to me.'

'He's old and his mind has wandered. She sought to lessen his rage not provoke it further.' Clara strained the liquid into a second bowl and poured in the vial of valerian. 'He'll give us no more trouble today, as this tea will send him to sleep, but you must take care to avoid him tomorrow.' She beckoned Isabella forward. 'You also,' she said, handing her the dish. 'He's not so confused that he won't remember the prettiness of both your faces.'

Isabella knew Clara was right when she saw how the old man leered at her as she entered the hall. His daughter stood beside him and he seemed less confused than in the kitchen. He was telling Lady Anne he'd been a man of importance in Pedle Hinton.

Milady smiled as she took the bowl from Isabella. 'We must find you some quarters suitable to your status, sir. It's not fitting for an elder to sleep in this hall with children and servants.'

'I had a fine house in Pedle Hinton.'

'And you shall have the same in Develish. Alice tells me you're a man of devotion and, from recollection, we have an empty dwelling on the path to the church. You will be neighbour to one of my leading advisers and able to make confession at times of your own choosing.' She turned to Isabella. 'Will you ask your mother to help you make the hut comfortable, child? Master Talbot will sleep more soundly on a good bed of rushes. A handful from each of the rolls in my chamber should suffice.'

⊗⊘

Martha Startout tut-tutted loudly as she and Isabella swept dusty remains from the empty shelter and laid new straw on the floor. 'The women will resent having their mattresses depleted for the sake of a vicious old man.'

'They'll complain more if he pulls up their daughters' skirts in the middle of the night,' said Isabella.

Martha straightened the rushes and stood back. 'Thaddeus was wrong to bring him here. Not one of the Pedle Hinton women can control him—certainly not Alice, who flinches every time he approaches her.'

'It's not her fault, Mama. She has told me some of her story and it makes me glad I wasn't born in Pedle Hinton. It sounds a cruel place.'

'How so?'

'Girls and women were treated as slaves. All Alice has ever been shown is that men are above her.'

'Develish was no different before Milady came.'

'That doesn't make it right, Mama.'

'I don't say it does, but pity won't help them. The best lesson Lady Anne taught me was to learn to speak up for myself. She was a year older than you when she married Sir Richard, but she refused to back down before any man.' A smile lit her eyes. 'She took your father to task in a way I would never have dared, never mind he was more than twice her age.'

Isabella eyed her curiously. 'What had he done?'

'Demanded food after eighteen hours' toil in the fields.'

'And that was wrong?'

Martha laughed. 'Milady thought so. She pointed to the cauldron of meat she'd prepared and instructed him to serve himself, saying that only the most selfish and uncaring of men would expect the mother of newborn twins to act as his slave.' She shook her head, remembering. 'It was but a month since the boys had been delivered, and your sister Abigail was yet to reach her second birthday. I had scarce enough milk to feed one baby, let alone two, and without Lady Anne's help, I could not have managed. She came each day to care for the babies while I worked in the kitchen, and even persuaded other women still in milk to act as wet nurses at the end of their long days.' She touched her finger to Isabella's chin. 'Best of all, by staying late that eve, she showed me your father wasn't the monster I thought he was.'

Isabella struggled to believe Martha had ever seen Gyles in such a light. 'How?'

'He begged her to tell him what else he could do to ensure his wife and his children's welfare and, such was her understanding of his position, she insisted on speaking to him outside so that all in the village would hear.' She saw her daughter's puzzlement. 'He was a man,' she explained. 'His duties were to honour his oath to his lord, plant and grow crops, and govern his household according to custom and law. To tend one twin while the other fed at my breast or prepare a meal to give me time to sleep were tasks reserved to women. Milady attracted much criticism for forcing a proud man to demean himself, but she freed Gyles of blame.'

'Did Father feel demeaned?'

Martha shook her head. 'It made good sense to him that a husband should tend his wife and children as carefully as he tended his master's stock. Your brothers were the first set of twins ever to live beyond six months in Develish and Gyles has sung Milady's praises ever since.' She gestured towards the door. 'We should go. There'll be no advantage to anyone if Master Talbot falls asleep in the house.'

Isabella followed. 'Develish is lucky Milady passed her wisdom to Father,' she remarked thoughtfully. 'If she'd chastised a man like Master Talbot, he'd have turned the demesne against her.'

'He still might,' said Martha sourly. 'There'll be no keeping him in that hut unless she orders John Trueblood to padlock the door.'

 birds

Father Anselm made no attempt to hide his suspicion as Lady Anne closed the church door and joined him at the altar where he was lighting candles for Vespers. There was too much distrust between them for her to have an amiable reason to seek him out. He gave a token nod of his head. 'Milady.'

'Father,' she answered courteously.

He waited for her to state her business but, as ever, she teased him with silence. 'Is there some service I can perform for you?' he asked.

'I've come in that hope, sir.' She watched him offer a spill to a wick but his hand trembled so much that the two never met. She took the spill from him and held the flame to the wick herself. 'Clara tells me you're out of mead. Is she right?'

He made no answer.

'We have a goodly store of wine at the house which has remained untouched since Sir Richard's death. I'll have some sent to you. My husband's tremors were never so bad as when he was forced to abstain from drinking because the carter was late in bringing fresh supplies.' She lit the remaining candles and then blew out the taper.

The priest put need before pride. 'Milady is kind.'

She pulled a wry smile. 'Don't be too keen to thank me, Father. You have yet to hear my request.'

He cursed himself for not guessing she would set a trap. 'Does the wine depend on my agreement, milady?'

She shook her head. 'I give you that with the same willingness I have given you tinctures in the past to cure the aches in your bones. I have no wish to see you suffer. The disputes between us have been over matters of conscience, never medicine.'

Father Anselm doubted heresy could be dismissed so easily, but he was willing to accept that wine was a medicine. 'I have always recognised that your skill in healing is superior to mine. I told Sir Richard of it many times.'

Lady Anne answered with a laugh. 'For which I had little reason to thank you. My husband found a new ailment each day to bring to my attention. Had he been less ready to accept a vial of tinted water as a cure, I might have encouraged him to bedevil with you with even more requests for confession and absolution.'

The priest bridled. 'And I would have offered both gladly as my duty demanded,' he snapped. 'You will not deny, I hope, that in matters concerning the rites and rituals of the Church I have superiority.'

'I will not, sir. You stand alone in your knowledge of procedure.'

Strangely, her words seemed to trouble him. He turned to the altar and fluttered a finger to his forehead to make the sign of the cross. 'So Thurkell would have us believe. I pray hourly that he is mistaken.'

It was a moment before Lady Anne understood his meaning, and she reached out an instinctive hand in sympathy. 'Forgive me,' she said. 'I should have asked myself long since how Thaddeus's talk of priests and monks dying might affect you. You're so much a part of Develish's community that I forget you belong to the wider one of the Church. It must have distressed you greatly to hear of the deaths of your brothers.'

He seemed glad to take her hand. 'I am more afraid than distressed, milady.'

She studied him with surprise, as much for the tight, needy grasp of his fingers as for the dread in his voice. 'What is it you fear?' she asked.

'That I shall be the only priest to survive. I haven't the ability to carry so much responsibility alone.'

Lady Anne wondered that so bleak a vision of the future had never occurred to her. She had little trouble imagining the sense of isolation and loneliness he must be feeling, because she felt it herself. She sought for an answer that would comfort. 'God never tests us so hard that we fail, Father. Perhaps His purpose for you—and for everyone who survives the pestilence—is to be a witness for those who have died. Their names will be written out of history if we allow ourselves to forget.'

Her words seemed to alarm him more. 'I've witnessed nothing,' he cried, snatching his hand away to tremble through another sign of the cross. 'You've kept all suffering from Develish's door . . . even your husband's.'

'But isn't that something to celebrate?' she asked in perplexity. 'I could wish all demesnes had done the same. The lives of so many have been lost unnecessarily for want of a little thought.'

The priest rounded on her angrily. 'It's not for you to decide which death is necessary and which is not. You raise yourself above God when you make such statements.'

Lady Anne gave a weary shake of her head. 'That was not my intention,' she answered quietly. 'If I have offended you, I am sorry.'

'Your offence is against God.'

'Then I beg His pardon even more humbly than I beg yours. He watches over us with more kindness than we deserve. Are you able to bear witness to that at least?'

The old man's mouth worked in furious denial. 'I am not. God has been absent from this place since you came here. Master de Courtesmain saw it and so do I.' Spittle formed along his lips. 'You have encouraged your people to break every commandment, and so infected are they by your profanity that none sees the need for confession or absolution. Would you have me speak of that? Or *worse*—' his spittle sprayed the air—'describe how your lover, a slave, parades as a noble, steals at will, and even brings demons into our midst in the shape of cats?'

Lady Anne turned away, unwilling to be drawn into any more argument. 'You must state the truth as you understand it, Father,' she said. 'That's all any of us can do. I'll have the wine sent to you shortly but be wise in how much you consume each night. The supply is limited.'

He watched her small figure disappear into the shadows beyond the candlelight. 'You had a request of me.'

There was a pause in her steps. 'It's of no matter. You gave me your answer when you spoke of your knowledge of rite and ritual.'

He heard the sound of the latch being raised and Lady Anne's voice speaking softly to people outside. She must have given them leave to enter, for her words were followed by the whisper of feet across the rush-strewn floor. He recognised the faces of the Pedle Hinton serfs, whom he'd watched cross the moat, and frowned from one to the other in puzzlement. 'What brings you here?' he asked.

'Vespers, Father,' said Alice Bartram. 'It's six months and more since we've attended a service.'

'Or seen a priest,' said another woman, dropping to her knees and reaching for Father Anselm's hands. 'We beg you most earnestly to hear our confessions.'

Harold Talbot stepped from their midst and searched Father Anselm's face. 'I don't know this man,' he said, turning to his daughter. 'Where is Father Jean?'

'He died of the pestilence and is buried in Pedle Hinton,' said Alice. 'We are in Develish now and this is their priest.' She made a gesture of pleading to Father Anselm. 'He will take solace from your chanting of the psalms, sir. Please begin—and pay no mind if he interrupts. He is excitable from having spent the day in sleep. He means no offence by it.'

Offence. The word rang like a condemnation in Father Anselm's ears, and he wondered if he'd been wrong to distrust Lady Anne's motives. 'Why did you wait outside?' he asked.

'Milady advised us that your custom is to use Vespers for private communion between yourself and God, sir. She wanted to be sure you were happy to include us. My father knows all the psalms, having learnt them word by word from Father Jean. He will assist in their recitation if you allow it.'

Father Anselm retreated to the altar to support himself. In drink he had some memory of the Vespers' chants, but sober he had none. He ran a trembling hand over the surface of the table as if a miracle might suddenly produce his Bible and catechism, for he had no recollection of where they were or when he had last used them. He felt the brush of a cloak against his arm.

'You will do Master Talbot a great kindness if you allow him to lead the service, Father,' said Lady Anne. 'He asks for under-standing of mistakes, being less proficient in the language of the Church than you.' Under cover of her cloak, she took her own Bible from the pocket of her kirtle and slipped it onto the altar. 'He wishes to begin with Psalm One Hundred and Nine.' She opened the book at a marked page and read aloud in Latin: '*My God, whom I praise, do not remain silent, for people who are wicked and deceitful have opened their mouths against me.*'

From behind them, the old man took up the verse in the same language. '*They have spoken against me with lying tongues and surround me with hatred. They attack me without cause and repay my friendship with loathing. I am a man of prayer, my God. Appoint someone evil to oppose my enemy. Let an accuser stand at his right hand. When he is tried, let him be found guilty. Let his days be few. Let his wife become a widow, and his children wandering beggars, driven from their ruined homes.*'

When Father Anselm failed to respond, Lady Anne placed a finger beside the text to show him where they were. '*May no one extend kindness to my enemy or take pity on his fatherless children,*' he read in tremulous tones. '*May his descendants be cut off, their names blotted out from the next generation. May the sins of his mother never be forgiven. May knowledge of his family be erased from the earth . . .*'

He faltered to a halt and, in the silence that followed, Harold drew breath to start again. With a sigh, Father Anselm turned towards him. 'Do you have any understanding of what you are saying, my son? Did your priest in Pedle Hinton ever give you these words in English?'

'He did.'

'Do you take comfort from them?'

Harold studied Father Anselm with suspicion. 'All men of prayer do. We imperil our souls when we forget that God should be feared. His wrath is terrible against the unrighteous.'

This time Father Anselm's hesitation went on so long that Lady Anne found herself regretting his sobriety. If she'd had the foresight to send a flagon of wine an hour before Vespers, he would be looking on Harold as a man of virtue and reciting Psalm 109 without a qualm. As it was, he seemed lost in indecision. She lifted the Bible from the altar and stepped forward to read for him, but he stayed her with a surprisingly firm hand.

'There's no fear of God in Develish and no place for this psalm in our church,' he told Harold. 'The Lord blesses us with love and kindness and we do our best to repay Him by sharing what we have with each other. Milady urges her people to entreat that all men are spared, be they God-fearing or not, for we have no wish that anyone should suffer death and misery. Were you so surrounded by enemies in Pedle Hinton that you like to be reminded of their suffering through these bitter words of hatred?'

'It's God's choice if I am. The words are His.'

Father Anselm shook his head. 'They are a man's, spoken in malice against those who disagree with him. Do you repeat them because your own heart is full of malice?'

Anger flared in Harold's eyes. 'The Bible is the word of God. What manner of priest are you that you don't know that?'

'A poor one, my son, for I am ignorant of how God answered this man's demands for retribution. Was it Father Jean's belief that rage and resentment are rewarded? For myself, I know only that God sent His son to take our sins upon His shoulders and teach us to forgive one another—and that simple message of love couldn't be more distant from the brutal vengeance requested in this psalm.'

Harold seemed so baffled by the question that Alice answered for him. 'The bishop sent word that the pestilence was a punishment for ungodliness, sir, and My Lord of Pedle Hinton ordered Father Jean to read the psalm each Vespers as warning that everything predicted in it would come to pass if we forgot our prayers and strayed from the path of righteousness. We thought him correct until we came to Develish.' She glanced shyly at Lady Anne. 'Now we're unsure what to believe except that the people here are blessed in their mistress.'

Perhaps Father Anselm was as confused as Harold, for he sank to his knees before the altar and buried his head in his hands.

EASTER, 1349

Eleven

Blandeforde, Dorseteshire

THADDEUS SAT ASTRIDE KILLER ON the ridge of a small hill and gazed down on Blandeforde. Gyles had described this place as a busy market town which drew its importance from standing at a bridge across the River Stour, but while the settlement was larger than many Thaddeus and his companions had seen, there was no greater evidence of people. They could see handfuls lingering at corners or moving about the streets, but not enough to indicate a once-thriving community. As ever, Thaddeus was struck by their lethargy. Even those who appeared to be walking with purpose lacked urgency, as if they had long since accepted that the struggle for life was more trouble than it was worth.

Ian adjusted his reins as his horse sidled sideways out of boredom at being forced to stand still for so long. 'Do you suppose they know tomorrow's a feast day?' he asked. 'Perhaps all their priests have perished and they think we're still in Lent?'

Thaddeus shook his head. 'There's not a man or woman in England who doesn't know that Easter falls on the Sunday after the first full moon of spring. The skies have been clear this last week. They'll have seen it shining in the heavens just as we did.'

The swelling moon had been their signal to ride north, for Thaddeus had hoped their arrival would spark less interest amidst the joy and celebration of Christ's resurrection. Easter was a day for parades and hearty eating after six long weeks of fasting, and he had expected to find Blandeforde readying itself for the festivities. In Develish, the Saturday eve was taken up with the slaughter of lambs for roasting and the final stitching of new apparel for the parade. But there was no such industry here.

'They'll be like the survivors in Melcombe,' said Peter. 'We didn't find one who thought there was cause to rejoice.'

'Nor anywhere else,' added Joshua. 'They're all just waiting for death.'

Thaddeus couldn't disagree with either statement. They had travelled the coastline for a month, seeking knowledge, but they could have ended their journey in Melcombe had they realised the people's sense of despair there was shared by everyone else. By night they had camped outside the port; by day they had ridden the streets to gain what information they could. It was hard to come by. The pestilence had so overwhelmed the town that no one could say how many had died. Even when they were directed to a town elder, a man of authority, he proved as ignorant as the beggars who inhabited the gutters. So many had fled when the pestilence first struck, there was no knowing who had perished and who had survived.

From Melcombe they had headed west along the coast to Lyme Regis, riding through deserted or barely inhabited demesnes along the way. Thaddeus spoke to all he met, offering what help and advice he could, but he had no answers to the three questions he was most commonly asked. Does God punish us by keeping us alive? Will our liege lord ever return? Does the King know of our troubles? All he could say with certainty was that, whether through flight or death, Dorseteshire was almost empty of people.

The truth of this statement was driven home to them when they returned along the highway to Dorchester—once the most prosperous market town in south Dorseteshire. They found it all but deserted, with shops and taverns closed, doors daubed with crosses and only the odd movement at windows to suggest that anyone still lived there. Thaddeus would have turned north towards Blandeforde then had the sea held less fascination for him. He told his companions he wanted to discover if there was another port to the east, but he showed no hurry to find it, choosing bridleways that hugged the crooked coastline as often as he returned to the straighter highway that ran inland.

The youths had no complaints. A man could believe he was free indeed when he stood on a rocky height and stared across an ocean. Some days the water was a turgid grey, but on clear afternoons, when a spring sun shone in the heavens, it mirrored the blueness above and there was no saying where the water ended and the sky began. Their favourite camping spots were on pebble beaches where small rivers had cut through the cliffs to empty into the sea. Driftwood made easy fires and the rhythmic sound of the waves lapping along the shore brought a deep and restful sleep.

They grew accustomed to the mournful cries of seagulls but never to the numbers and size of the birds. As big as buzzards, they ruled the sea and the shore, watching the travellers from pale eyes. Thaddeus thought they must live on fish, but Joshua said he'd seen a dozen pecking flesh off a dead sheep outside Melcombe.

Only Peter had any liking for them, mimicking their calls with the same ease he mimicked blackbirds and larks.

They took most pleasure from discovering a stretch of golden sand which ended in a mighty bay, dotted with tree-covered islands. Because the entrance was narrow—a quarter-mile cleft between two arms of land—the waters of the bay were as calm as an inland lake and the youths shook their heads in wonder at the beauty of the scene. How dreary Develish seemed by comparison. Half-a-dozen sailing ships rode at anchor down the centre, but all seemed as carelessly forgotten as the fishing boats that lay tilted on their sides along the banks. Edmund's long sight picked out a settlement far away on the other side, but Thaddeus guessed the only way to reach it was by the highway. There were too many marshy inlets where brooks and rivers were feeding into the bay for horses to find an easy path around the shoreline.

He gladly gave in to his companions' pleas to spend the night on the beach, being as entranced as they by the softness of the sand and the white-frothed spume that rolled across it. They returned the way they'd come, looking for a sheltered spot amongst the trees that grew along the promontory. Thaddeus chose to remove his boots and lead Killer through the shallow waves. He was fascinated by the pull of sand beneath his feet each time the water receded and only became aware that a fishing boat was drifting towards the shore behind him when Ian called a warning.

He turned to watch a greybeard and a youngster using their oars to try to push the vessel back into deeper water. He called out to them, asking where they were headed, and the greybeard pointed back to the mouth of the bay, saying the current had carried them past it. The craft was too heavy for a tired old man and his grandson to handle alone when all their effort had gone into hauling in nets full of fish. Without thought for whether either had fleas, and pausing only to remove his coat and jerkin, Thaddeus released Killer and waded towards them, putting his shoulder to the planking at the bow. As the boat began to turn, he moved to the stern to push it into deeper water and then called for a rope.

'The water's shallow enough for me to tow you to the end of the headland, but from there you must manage on your own.'

The greybeard had no doubts that his finely apparelled rescuer was a man of status and he expressed his gratitude humbly, promising My Lord a parcel of mackerel as reward for his help. Thaddeus said he would be as happy with information, and the talkative old man gave him all he required. Thaddeus learnt that the settlement on the far side of the bay was called Poole, with another to the west named Warham, which stood between the mouths of the River Pedle and the River Frome. More than half the inhabitants of both towns had died or fled, and fishing had become harder with only the weakest left to handle the boats and nets.

'The boy and I have done well this day, but our catch would have become food for gulls if the tide had stranded us on the beach. God was kind to send us a man so tall to push us clear. Do you not fear drowning, sire?'

Thaddeus laughed as the waves lapped around his chest. 'Not yet, my friend. Tell me about these fish you've caught. Do they taste the same as river fish?'

'Better. The salt water gives them flavour.'

'And they're called mackerel?'

'They are.'

'And the birds are gulls? I've not encountered them before either.'

The greybeard found that hard to believe. 'You have the look of a foreigner, sire. How did you come here if not by sea?'

Thaddeus made a mental note to watch his words more carefully when he spoke with Blandeforde's steward. 'I came as an infant and have no memory of the journey,' he lied. 'Since then I've lived in the north.' He ran some of the rope through his fingers to allow the craft to move farther from the shore as the end of the headland approached. 'Do many foreigners come to this bay?'

'They used to, but we've seen none since September. Word has it that all Europe has perished.'

'Not all. There'll be some like you who've survived. They'll take to their ships again once the pestilence passes.'

He was answered with a hollow laugh. 'There's few here believe it will, sire. If we don't die today, we'll die tomorrow. What makes you think differently?'

'Common sense. When did the last person succumb to it in Poole?'

'I've not heard of any deaths since Christmas.'

'Then, God willing, the towns along the coast have seen the end of it already, for we've been told the same story in Melcombe and Lyme Regis.' Thaddeus halted. 'You must make ready to take the rope and begin rowing, my friend. I cannot take you beyond this point.'

'A moment longer, My Lord. The boy wraps fish in sacking and will throw them when you've tossed the rope.' The old man's eyes regarded Thaddeus thoughtfully. 'You seem more trusting than most that you'll survive, sire. What practices do you follow to avoid it?'

Thaddeus recalled Ian's injunctions to avoid talk of rats and fleas. It was one thing to give people hope that the pestilence had run its course but quite another to invite derision. 'I come from a country where cleanliness is valued,' he said instead. 'We bury our waste and do not tolerate vermin or parasites in our houses or on our persons. Such customs keep us healthy.'

'Would that be one of the Moorish lands of Africa, sire? We've had ships from there in the past and all the sailors have your height and dark skin. They have more kindness and courtesy than most and are a goodly sight cleaner. Many's the time I've watched them cover their mouths and noses to protect themselves from English stink.'

Africa . . . 'Do you know the names of these lands?'

'Only Egypt.'

'Because her people visit here or because your priest has taught you about Moses?'

'Both. Their ships sail from a town called Alexandria. It's said to be very fine.'

Thaddeus nodded to the youngster, who was showing him that the parcel of fish was ready. He coiled the end of the rope and threw it towards the greybeard before catching the sacking bundle in return. 'Stay well,' he said, raising his hand in farewell.

The old man chuckled. 'If you were from a land in Africa, you would do this,' he said, leaning his head forward and touching the fingers of his right hand to his forehead.

Thaddeus mimicked the gesture. 'I thank you for the fish.'

The old man took up his oar. 'And you for your help, sire. Thanks be to God, we'll all eat well tonight.'

Thaddeus retreated to the shore and watched them angle into the bay before returning along the sand to where Ian was holding Killer. His teeth chattered uncontrollably as he stripped off his dripping clothes and pulled spare ones from his saddle pack, but his eyes were alight with good humour as he did it.

'What did the fishermen say to make you so cheerful?' asked Ian.

'He told me something I didn't know.' Thaddeus re-dressed himself and knelt to undo the sacking. 'These are called mackerel,' he said, revealing twelve silvery-blue fish. 'They'll make a welcome change from mutton.'

There was never any shortage of sheep. Everywhere they went, flocks were multiplying as ewes gave birth to spring lambs and pastures recovered from the frosts of winter. But these days only Joshua's dogs showed excitement to see yet another carcass being butchered. Despite the height and bulk that plentiful meat had added to the previously slender frames of Thaddeus's companions, they grumbled endlessly about the boredom of their diet. Even so, faced with only two mackerel apiece after a long day's riding, the ram Joshua had been carrying across his horse's withers was turned into stew anyway.

They made a fire in the sand, using driftwood and fallen branches from the woodland, and watched the sun turn brilliant red as it dipped towards the horizon and sent a blazing trail across the sea. The mackerel was roasted on a woven lattice of pliable green saplings and the scent from the bubbling skin was irresistible, as was the tender oily flesh when they came to pick it from the bones. Ian licked his fingers after swallowing the last morsel.

'What else did the greybeard tell you?' he asked Thaddeus. 'I don't say the taste of mackerel isn't enough to make any man smile but just learning its name wouldn't.'

Thaddeus pondered for a moment, wondering how much to reveal about himself and the questions that had plagued him most of his life. 'He told me something about the man who sired me. I've never been able to picture him before.'

'How do you see him now?' asked Peter.

'As a clean, courteous, dark-skinned Moor from a land in Africa . . . perhaps even a town called Alexandria in Egypt.' A small laugh escaped his mouth. 'I have no idea what or where Africa is, but a father from there sounds sweeter to my ears than "passing gypsy".'

'He'll be a man of importance, whoever he is,' said Joshua. 'You're too clever to have a dunce for a sire.'

Peter nodded. 'My guess would be a wealthy merchant who journeyed to England to sell silks and tapestries.'

'Or a lord,' countered Edmund. 'Why settle for less if you can have more?'

Thaddeus shook his head. 'It's a private comfort only and not something any of us should dwell upon,' he warned. 'If I'm to pass for Athelstan, my title must have come from my father and my Moorish blood from my mother. Take care to remember that in Blandeforde and never mention Eva. We'll none of us fare well if my imposture is discovered.'

෨෧

Ian recalled those words as they looked down on the town. The prospect of entering it had been such a distant idea when they set out, and so easily put from mind during their travels along the coastline, that he'd given no heed to whether or not he was ready. Thaddeus might feel confident about being questioned by the steward, but the same wasn't true of his companions. To pass as a fighting man before a fisherman was very different from upholding the pretence before My Lord of Blandeforde's proctor. Nor, in truth, did any of them understand why it was necessary. What did Thaddeus hope to learn from the steward that he couldn't as easily discover from the townsfolk?

Olyver, picking up on his twin's thoughts, shifted in his saddle. 'Why is it so important to go there?' he asked Thaddeus. 'Can't you tell just by looking that we'll hear nothing new?'

'I doubt we'll be allowed in,' said Edmund, pointing to the far end of the bridge. 'I see a group of men in livery who look like guards. I'd guess they're there to turn back all who come from this direction.'

Thaddeus nodded. He, too, had seen the men. 'We might be able to use them to our advantage,' he said thoughtfully.

'How?'

'By persuading them to fetch the steward to us. He'll be less alarming out here than inside Blandeforde.'

'What is it you want from him anyway?' asked Peter. 'And don't say "news", because that's the excuse you give for everyone you speak to.'

Thaddeus thought it only fair to answer honestly, since his companions would take the consequences alongside him if he failed. 'I want his agreement to Athelstan's purchase of Pedle Hinton for two hundred nobles. Unless the steward's a fool, he'll jump at the chance to replenish his master's coffers in return for a derelict demesne and a half-ruined house.'

'Are you serious?'

'Very serious.'

'How will it help Develish to buy another demesne? You've always said our future will be in a town where we can earn our living as freemen.'

'But not lawfully. Wouldn't you rather gain your liberty in Develish first and then choose the future you want?' He smiled at Peter's puzzlement. 'Milady and I look to turn Develish into a demesne like Holcombe, where every man is free to earn his living as he chooses. His rent will be in coin from the trade he pursues, and a proportion will be rendered as taxes to Blandeforde.'

'What does Pedle Hinton have to do with that?' Edmund asked.

'If Athelstan is granted title to a derelict demesne, and succeeds in remitting taxes at the required time, Milady believes Blandeforde will look more favourably on his request to partner Pedle Hinton with Develish. Once both demesnes are under Athelstan's governance, all serfs will have the right to buy themselves out of bondage—as long as they have the money.'

Olyver grinned. 'Is that why we've been stealing dead men's gold these last few weeks?'

'It is.'

'Does Milady know?'

Thaddeus shook his head. 'She's too honest to do what Bourne did. Fortunately for you and your families, I am not.'

'But why not just offer for Develish?' asked Joshua.

'Because it was in Blandeforde that Bourne heard rumours of everyone still being alive there, and if he picked up on those stories, then be sure the steward has also. He'll be wary of granting anyone title to a lucrative demesne, let alone an unknown noble whose lineage shows he's related to Sir Richard's widow. I look to allay his suspicions not raise them.'

Peter groaned. 'It won't work. He'll know us for imposters.'

'Only if you show timidity. Play the part of a fighting man and you'll be taken for one. Even stewards believe what their eyes tell them.'

'Why didn't you explain all this before?' asked Ian.

Thaddeus's dark face split in smile. 'Because you'd have bedevilled me with your doubts these last few weeks.' He nodded to a large stone building which stood on pastureland inside the western loop of the river, some five hundred paces from the nearest habitation. 'Is that a house or a monastery?' he asked Edmund.

'What's the difference?'

'Does it have a belltower?'

Edmund shook his head. 'There's a church behind that does, but not the house.'

'Are you thinking it's where My Lord of Blandeforde lives?' asked Ian.

'When he's at home.' Thaddeus cast a last glance across the town. 'There's nowhere else imposing enough for a man of his wealth.' He shortened his reins and touched his heels to Killer's flanks to set him back on the highway. 'Let's see if the guards let us pass.'

They descended the slope into the valley at a walk, with Joshua and his dogs at Thaddeus's side and the others riding two by two behind. The white-and-gold crest of Athelstan, stitched by Lady Anne and her seamstresses onto the cloth beneath Killer's saddle and the breasts of the youths' crimson tabards, showed up well in the late-afternoon light, but it was greeted with blank looks from the men at the northern end of the bridge. They knew every lord's emblem for miles around but this wasn't one they recognised.

Thaddeus brought Killer to a halt when he was halfway across the cobbled bridge and leant his arms on the pommel of his saddle to study the five men who guarded the exit. He made an impressive figure with his great height, his jet-black charger and seven large hunting dogs quivering at his side. 'I come to speak with Blandeforde,' he called in French. 'Lord Bourne of Wiltshire said I'd receive a warm welcome here. Was he wrong?'

Their leader answered in the same language. 'Wiltshire's to the north. Why do you approach from the south?'

'Eight weeks have passed since I was in Bourne. In that time, I've journeyed through Dorseteshire to discover if there's any truth to the reports that all in the south have perished.'

'What have you found?'

'Nothing that I choose to share with you. Is your lord in residence?'

'He left for his estates in the west last summer. The steward governs in his place.'

'Is he as ill-mannered as the men he commands?'

'We are here to prevent strangers crossing the bridge. There's no requirement to pretend a welcome that doesn't exist.'

Thaddeus looked to his left and picked out a stretch of woodland some half-mile to the west across cleared land. 'My men and I will camp there overnight. You may tell the steward that Athelstan has news of Blandeforde's vassal demesnes. If he wishes to hear it, he must seek us out before the light fades. I take no responsibility for my dogs once darkness falls.'

He nudged Killer into a turn, instructing Ian to lead them out across the cleared land. The guard shouted that he hadn't meant to be disrespectful. The town had seen all sorts, demanding refuge and bringing the pestilence with them. Had he known he was speaking to My Lord of Athelstan, he would have sent a runner to fetch the steward. He would do so now if My Lord was willing to wait. The sun was a bare two hours from setting and it made better sense to converse at the bridge. Thaddeus ignored him.

'Why didn't you answer?' asked Joshua when they were clear of the cobbles.

'Because leaving makes the point better. Stewards wait on lords not lords on stewards.'

'He only showed interest when you said you were Athelstan.'

Thaddeus nodded. 'I noticed.'

'Do you think the steward will come to the camp?'

'Not in person, but I'll wager he'll be curious enough to send spies.'

ळल

They came when the soft grey of twilight had drained colour from the grass and trees, and the flames of the fire shone bright in the gathering gloom. The dogs heard them long before Thaddeus and his companions did, leaping to their feet with throaty growls and pointing their muzzles along the line of trees that bordered the cleared land between the camp and the highway. With an encouraging smile, and certain that his voice would carry in the stillness of the night, Thaddeus ordered his men to arm themselves.

'But keep the pack close until we know who these visitors are, Buckler. The steward won't thank us if his envoys are mauled in mistake for bandits.'

For himself, he remained where he was, seated on a bed of bracken with his back supported by his saddle and his legs stretched out in front of him. On his lap was a slim wooden box crafted by John Trueblood, which, when closed, contained vellum and writing implements, and when open served as a desk. As he'd been doing for the last hour, he continued to write on the page in front of him, dipping his quill into the inkwell at his side and forming his letters by the light of the fire.

'Three men have walked from the woodland, sire,' called Ian. 'They're still some fifty paces away but they're not wearing livery. What is your command?'

'Hold your bows level until they prove themselves. No one of good intent creeps through trees when he can more easily approach across pastureland.'

'They hold their hands high to show they're unarmed, sire.'

'Ask their names and what service they perform for My Lord of Blandeforde. I'll not accept beard-trimmers, cooks or pot-emptiers.'

'We are Joseph Spend of the guild of wheelwrights, Paul Cooper of the guild of barrel makers and Andrew Tench of the guild of wool merchants,' cried one. 'We come at the request of My Lord of Blandeforde's steward.'

Thaddeus lodged his quill in the inkwell and raised his head to look at them. 'Take ten paces away from the trees and thirty towards me,' he instructed. 'My soldiers will range themselves in front of you while my dogs search the woodland for others who may be hiding.' He gave a nod to Joshua. 'Wait until they reach their places and then send the hounds about their business.'

The men, trembling visibly, advanced a bare three steps before a shadowy figure stepped from between the trees some twenty paces away. He made a small bow. 'I am Jacques d'Amiens, steward to My Lord of Blandeforde, sire,' he said in French. 'There are no others. These three men and I came alone.'

Thaddeus studied him with interest. He was somewhat as Lady Anne had described him, of middle height and middle build, but there was no sign of the birthmark—a port-wine stain on his nose and right cheek—that Lady Anne had said was his most distinguishing feature. Whoever this man was, he was not who he was claiming to be.

Nevertheless, Thaddeus gave a small nod of acknowledgement before telling Joshua that his instructions for the dogs remained unchanged. 'You must forgive my suspicious nature, Master d'Amiens,' he answered in the same language, 'but it's an unusual Norman who chooses unarmed Englishmen to protect him when he could as easily have brought the guards from the bridge. You still have time to order them from the trees. My men and I wish them no harm but I can't say the same for my mastiffs.'

Whatever command the man gave was too low for Thaddeus to hear, but four armed soldiers appeared from the trees behind him. 'We live in difficult times, My Lord. All men are wise to be wary of strangers.'

'Indeed.' Thaddeus turned to watch the guildsmen's hesitant approach. 'These poor fellows look ready to die of fright,' he murmured. 'Are they here of their own free will or under threat?'

'Your dogs unsettle them, My Lord.'

Thaddeus ordered Joshua to take the pack twenty paces onto the pastureland before beckoning the guildsmen closer. 'We'll do well to keep the fire between us,' he told them. 'You don't look as if you're carrying the pestilence but I'm reluctant to risk my life on it.'

'Does God not protect you, My Lord?'

'Without doubt, but I do my best to assist Him.' He pointed to a pile of saddle packs. 'Bring forward three of those if you care to sit. Do you find French easy to understand or would you prefer that we speak in English?'

It seemed they needed the imposter's permission both to seat themselves and express a preference for English, and Thaddeus wondered who the man was and what his purpose was in bringing them. The guildsmen's anxiety remained strong even with the dogs at a distance, and he sensed they'd been given a task they didn't want to perform. The imposter elected to stand apart with his guards, watching without comment as Ian positioned himself and his remaining men behind Thaddeus. None held weapons in their hands but Ian took quiet satisfaction from the unease in the faces of the two younger soldiers.

The only change Thaddeus made to his position was to sit a little straighter by easing his saddle more firmly into the small of his back. He asked the guildsmen to repeat their names and tell him about their families, showing sympathy when they listed their numbers of dead.

'Our guilds are as badly affected, My Lord,' said Joseph Spend. 'I am one of but two wheelwrights who remain, and Master Cooper and Master Tench are the only barrel maker and wool merchant left in Blandeforde.'

'How many departed before the pestilence arrived?'

'We don't know, sire. The town was so filled with people heading north there's no saying how many of our own went with them. Will they have found safety? Is the north more favoured by God than the south?'

'I've seen nothing on my travels to tell me so. Wiltshire's as badly affected as Dorseteshire, and as long ago as last September, we heard that the sickness had reached Oxford. I fear all England will have fallen to it before the year is out.'

'Is there good news, My Lord?'

'Some first glimmerings, perhaps.' Thaddeus selected a parchment from a small stack at his side and held it up for them to see. 'These are the towns and villages along the coast of Dorseteshire where my men and I found people still living. In each place, we were told that no one has died since Christmas. Does Blandeforde fare the same or worse?'

There was a short silence before the barrel maker spoke. 'The last burial was eight weeks ago, sire. Should we take that as a sign of hope?'

Thaddeus wondered why the man found it so hard to meet his eye. 'I can think of no reason not to, Master Cooper. A full season without death in those communities first afflicted suggests to me that the pestilence may have run its course. It's surely something to celebrate that the same seems to be happening here.'

The imposter stirred. 'You speak as if the pestilence is no different from the pox or the ague, My Lord. Is that your belief?'

Thaddeus watched Andrew Tench, the wool merchant, give the faintest shake of his head. He took it for a warning, though why a Blandeforde freeman should side with a stranger against the man who had brought him here, he didn't know.

'There's no likeness at all between the pestilence and the pox, Master d'Amiens,' he answered. 'The one gives rise to virulent boils which kill in three days, and the other to a red rash that fades after two weeks. Have you not seen sufferers yourself?'

'My apologies, sire. I should have made my meaning clearer. We live in ignorance here in Blandeforde and any information you can give us about the pestilence would be welcome. To describe it as an infection that must inevitably run its course is to suggest it's a disease like the common pox. I'd be interested to hear what led you to that belief.'

If Thaddeus believed anything, it was that knowledge shared was knowledge gained, but he hardly needed the clear alarm in Tench's face to avoid an honest answer. 'You're asking if I know God's mind, sir, but I'm as ignorant of His plan for us as you are. I take comfort from the knowledge that no one has died in Melcombe in the last four months, but I can't give a reason for it. Only priests know why some are more deserving of life than others.'

'Did you consult with the clergy in Melcombe?'

'There were none to be found. An elder told us the last to die was a Franciscan monk who tended sufferers into autumn and then fell to the sickness himself. The same was true everywhere we went.'

'Here too. All the clergy in the town have been taken, and there are many who question why—these three guildsmen amongst them. They came in the hope you'd have answers, My Lord.'

Thaddeus ran a thoughtful hand around his beard. 'Can your own priest not help them? I presume he still lives since you spoke only of those in the town dying.'

'His duties to the household keep him occupied.'

Thaddeus smiled slightly. 'Then you and My Lord of Blandeforde's servants are more fortunate than your fellows in the town.' He shifted his attention to Tench. 'Does the household fare better than you and your neighbours?' he asked.

'We believe so, sire, but it's a long time since we saw any of the servants. We've heard of only four dying since the pestilence came.'

Thaddeus allowed his surprise to show. 'Out of how many?'

'Above one hundred, sire. Father Aristide hears the confessions of all and recites the liturgy of the hours from Matins to Compline so that the house is sanctified by prayer and absolution. The town accepts that this is why so few have succumbed.'

But not you and your friends, thought Thaddeus, while pondering Tench's use of the word 'accept'. Had he chosen it deliberately? 'Truths have to be explained before people can believe them. Why do you not seek answers from whomever told you of Father Aristide's cleansing rituals?'

'It was a young maid, sire. She was sent from the house to seek solace from her mother and father, and was in great despair to find they had perished. She had the early signs of the pestilence and died some five days later. Her anguish at being judged more wicked than the rest of the household was matched by her despair to find that every member of her family was dead.'

Thaddeus leant forward to stare into the fire as an excuse to lower his gaze. The man posing as d'Amiens was ignorant of the expressions on the guildsmen's faces because their backs were towards him, but for Thaddeus to respond to their intense stares with even a nod to show he fully understood what he was hearing would be to reveal the same to the imposter. There were too many conflicting tensions at play, and Thaddeus had little grasp of any of them. Had d'Amiens died and this man seized control? Did the guards on the bridge serve some purpose other than to keep the pestilence out?

The only thing he was sure of was that the imposter was inviting him to challenge the Church's position on the pestilence. But why? What possible reason could he have to suspect a lord he had never met of dissent? And why accuse Athelstan of a heresy he clearly shared? There was surely only one interpretation of the maid's tale: that My Lord of Blándeforde's household had isolated itself from the rest of the town, expelling any who showed signs of fever, while claiming to be protected by prayers and absolution.

Thaddeus took a slender branch from a stack at his side and fed the tip into the fire. 'Word has come from France that Pope Clement grants absolution to all who die of the pestilence,' he told the guildsmen. 'Had the young servant known that, her anguish for herself and her family would have been lessened.' He raised his head. 'Does the closure of the bridge prevent such news reaching you?' he asked Spend.

Spend shook his head. 'There have been no messengers in months, My Lord. The guards make no difference.'

'How long have they been there?'

'A matter of days only, sire. The steward looks to deter thieves from entering the town while the Easter festivities take place. Pickings will be easy while all attention is on the parade.'

A faint smile curved Thaddeus's mouth. 'You have reason to thank him. Only the pestilence is less welcome than a thief.'

Twelve

IAN HAD BLESSED THADDEUS EACH time he'd answered a question wisely but now, hearing the edge to his friend's voice, he became nervous that Thaddeus's patience was wearing thin. In his mind, he begged him not to abandon restraint. There was too much strangeness in the air and Ian, with no reason to doubt that the steward was who he said he was, had even less understanding of why that should be than Thaddeus.

Perhaps Thaddeus picked up on Ian's silent urgings because he took up his quill and wrote the signature of Athelstan at the bottom of the parchment page before raising his head to look at the imposter. 'I've documented what my men and I discovered in the demesnes we believe to be Blandeforde's, Master d'Amiens. Some are abandoned and derelict. Some retain small groups of serfs and servants whom God has chosen to spare. They are without guidance because their lords, priests and stewards have died or fled.' He retrieved the branch from the fire and used its smouldering tip to melt sealing wax on to the page beneath his signature before pressing his ring into the soft surface. 'If

Blandeforde returns, I suggest you prepare him for the news that there'll be no tax receipts this year. If he does not, you must account to the King yourself.'

The man seemed amused. 'You expect me to take your word on this, My Lord? You and I are strangers to each other. What assurances can you give me that what you say is true?'

Thaddeus rolled the parchment between his hands and then secured the edge with a second seal. 'None. The choice of whether to believe me is yours. I tasked myself only with passing on what I've learnt. Tomorrow we ride for Sarum so that I can render the same service to His Grace the Lord Bishop. He may not be aware how many of his clergy have died or that tithes will go unpaid.'

There was a brief hesitation. 'Is His Grace expecting you?'

Thaddeus shook his head. 'No more than you were.'

'Why should he grant you an audience?'

'For the same reason you've chosen to speak to me, Master d'Amiens. I'm the messenger who gives information to those who want to hear it.'

'On whose authority do you act?'

Thaddeus smiled. 'God's . . . as do we all.' He tossed the scroll across the fire to Andrew Tench and settled back against the saddle. 'Be good enough to hand the parchment to the steward as you leave, Master Tench,' he murmured, closing his eyes. 'I believe our business is concluded.'

The guildsmen rose to their feet immediately but the imposter clenched his hands in irritation. 'I have more questions, sire.'

'I'm sure you do, Master d'Amiens,' came the lazy response. 'Every person we meet has questions. Put them to your priest. I don't doubt he'll be able to answer them better than I can.' He made a gesture of dismissal. 'Take the path across the cleared land. My soldiers can shield you from the pack in the open, but not if you're hidden by trees.'

Ian, recognising that these words were as much for him as d'Amiens, called to Buckler that the visitors were leaving under escort. 'My Lord asks that you hold the hounds steady until we've passed. Once we're clear, send them to search the woodland.' He stepped around the fire and motioned to the steward and his guards to join the guildsmen. 'My men and I will accompany you the first two hundred paces, sir. I suggest you make speed in order to reach the bridge before the light goes.'

Edmund, Peter and Olyver moved to join him and together they shepherded the eight men away from the fire. Thaddeus remained where he was, pretending sleep, but from beneath his apparently closed lids he was watching for movement in the darkened woodland. It may have been imagination but he fancied he saw a shift in the shadows amongst the trees. But were they retreating or coming forward?

Unhurriedly, he rose to his feet, stretching to his full height before stooping to take a torch from beside the pile of parchments. He heard Joshua approach with the dogs as he held the resin-soaked hemp to the flames of the fire. 'We'll be following the pack, Buckler. The steward brought more men than he admitted to. I want to know why.'

Joshua searched his face for guidance. 'I can't believe the steward would lie, My Lord.'

'He's done nothing else since he arrived.' Thaddeus raised the torch in his left hand and drew his sword from his sheath with his right. 'Come,' he said, crossing the space to the trees. 'Let's see what the dogs unearth.'

Joshua couldn't tell what Thaddeus's expectations were, but if he hoped to flush men from the woodland with words, he was disappointed. Nothing stirred. Joshua watched him advance through the trees, swinging the torch slowly from side to side until the beam settled on a well-trodden path, running east to west. He nodded understanding when Thaddeus levelled the tip of his sword towards it. On quiet feet, he led the pack across leaf mulch to the impacted track and knelt to point the muzzle of his best wolfhound in the direction of the highway.

The animal set off at a rapid pace with the others falling in behind, and Joshua muttered that they were probably following a deer's scent. But Thaddeus shook his head. In the flames of the torch, he could see where boots had trampled over clusters of the bluebells which grew in profusion beside the track, flattening leaves and breaking stems. Beckoning to Joshua to keep up, he strode fast behind the dogs, holding the torch high to light the gloom.

They were almost at the highway when a discordance of barks and throaty growls split the air. Joshua made a vain attempt to catch at the skirts of Thaddeus's coat in the hope of encouraging caution, but the black-haired giant was beyond his reach. Without even the briefest break of stride, Thaddeus stepped boldly onto the road, showing neither care nor fear of what might be waiting for him.

ᘒᘔ

At two hundred paces, Ian ordered his companions to halt and allow the eight Blandeforde men to continue alone. 'My respects, sirs,' he said in French. 'We wish your town a joyful Easter and pray that you will have good fortune in the coming months.'

The imposter gave a dry laugh. 'Your lord has taught you well. *Too* well. I've yet to meet a Norman soldier who speaks so eloquently. Is your twin as fluent?'

Ian held his gaze for a moment before turning to the guildsmen and speaking in English. 'May God go with you, sirs. We will wait here until you're safely across the river.'

Peter, Edmund and Olyver formed a line beside him and stood in silence as the column moved away. By then the light was so dim that it wasn't long before all eight were swallowed by darkness. 'Maybe we should have accompanied them to the bridge,' Edmund muttered in an undertone. 'There's nothing to stop them doubling back along the highway.'

'They'll do that anyway if they have a mind to it,' said Peter reasonably. 'Watching them cross won't prevent it. They'll wait an hour or two on the other side and then creep over again.'

Olyver stood with his arms folded, trying to pick out the fleece collar on Andrew Tench's cloak, but even that was invisible. 'What did the steward say that troubled you?' he asked Ian. 'I felt your worry.'

'He spoke of my twin.'

'So?'

'How did he know I had one? It was dusk when he arrived and you and I look less alike now than we've ever done. He might have taken us for brothers, but never twins.'

Pensively, Olyver scratched at the stubble around his jaw. From a young age he and his brother had sought to look different. Since riding with Thaddeus, however, they had turned their quest for difference into a sport to amuse their companions. The longer Ian's hair grew in the manner of Thaddeus's, the shorter Olyver cut his to resemble the shaven look of their father. The more Olyver nurtured and darkened his beard and moustache with charcoal, the sharper Ian kept his knife in order to scrape his face clean. Close to in daylight, a stranger might see the identical shape and colour of their eyes. But at night? And at ten paces distant?

'It must have been a guess,' he said slowly. 'Who could have told him? The only people who know about us are in Develish.'

'You're forgetting Bourne,' murmured Peter. 'There wasn't a person in the demesne who didn't know you were twins. The girls kept asking you to stand together because they'd never seen grown ones before.' He paused. 'It can't be far from here. I remember the elder in Melcombe telling Thaddeus that Blandeforde was only half a day's ride from the Wiltshire border.'

Ian would have answered that it was My Lord who'd been most intrigued by their twinship, but he was distracted by the distant barking of dogs. The sound seemed to be coming from the highway and he turned to look in that direction. As he listened, the barking turned to whimpering and, with a sense of terrible foreboding, he drew his sword and began to run.

෴

Joshua remained hidden inside the tree line, frozen by fear and indecision when he saw that there were other lights than Thaddeus's. Even as he watched, more sprang to life and his dogs whimpered and cringed as burning flames were thrust into their faces. It seemed to Joshua that soldiers were everywhere. Some six stood abreast across the highway to bar escape to the south and a dozen more lined the verges on either side. All had their swords drawn with the tips pointing at Thaddeus, who had walked so carelessly into their trap.

If the big man was aware of the danger he was in, he didn't show it. Sheathing his own sword, he knelt to quench his torch in the dust of the road and then drew the dogs to him with a click of his fingers. As he ran his hands around their muzzles to calm them, he was looking at a cloaked figure in the centre of the highway some fifteen paces distant. Joshua followed his gaze and felt a thrill of horror as the man lowered his hood to reveal a disfiguring stain across his nose and right cheek. So pale was the rest of his skin that the splash of livid colour appeared black, and Joshua's immediate thought was that he must have the pestilence.

Thaddeus gave a nod of acknowledgement. 'My respects, Master d'Amiens,' he said in French.

'Sir.'

With a smile, Thaddeus rose to his feet and gestured to the soldiers. 'Whom do I have to thank for this honour guard?'

'Yourself. I thought you'd have more sense than to pursue me.'

'You pay me too much credit, Master d'Amiens. I'm not so sharp-sighted that I knew it was you I was following. I took you for a thief.' He tapped a finger against his cheek. 'I only know you now because of your birthmark.'

'Who told you of it?'

'My Lord of Bourne. He passed through Blandeforde some months ago.'

D'Amiens gave an indifferent shrug. 'We've had a hundred lords use our town as a staging post these last two seasons. What marks Bourne out that I should recall him?'

'Nothing at all,' said Thaddeus with amusement. 'Dressed in tunic and britches, he could easily pass for a serf. Few have the good and bad fortune to be as recognisable as you, Master d'Amiens.'

The man's lips thinned in a sardonic smile. 'Or *you*, Master Thurkell. We are both known by the unusual colour of our skins.'

Terrified, Joshua shrank deeper into shadow. He had feared this moment from the day Thaddeus had ridden into Woodoak and allowed a handful of serfs to believe he was a lord. Thaddeus broke every law by doing so—not least the laws of treason against the King—and Joshua cursed him for ever believing that Lady Anne's invented lineage and My Lord of Bourne's letter of accreditation could provide protection. He watched in anguish as the steward instructed Thurkell to step away from the dogs and surrender his weapon.

Thaddeus answered with a laugh. 'How long have you believed yourself the equal of lords, Master d'Amiens?'

'You're no lord, sir. You're a slave posing as one.'

'Then show me the warrant that accuses me of such. I would know who signed it and what his status is. You can't be so ignorant of the law that you'd arrest Athelstan on your own recognisance.' He shook his head scornfully when d'Amiens made no answer. 'You're a fool, sir. Acting for your absent lord doesn't give you licence to behave without due process.' He glanced towards the soldiers. 'Which of you is captain of arms?'

'I am, sire,' said one, stepping forward.

'Then escort me back to my camp before Master d'Amiens' hubris leads you and your men to further sedition. Your duty to your lord is to uphold the King's justice not traduce it on the twisted fancies of an ambitious steward.'

Without pausing to see if the captain would obey, he approached the two soldiers who were guarding the entrance to the track and instructed them to lower their swords and move aside. They did so, but whether out of fear of a man whose height was so much greater than theirs or because the captain gave a curt nod, Joshua couldn't tell. He watched in relief as the dogs responded to the clicking of Thaddeus's fingers, but he was at a loss as to whether to show himself when the captain followed behind with a torch. Was it better or worse that these people believed Thaddeus was alone?

His indecision meant he heard d'Amiens' muttered instruction to the two soldiers nearest to him.

'Find the priest's guest and bring him to me. He's a wretched creature but I don't doubt he's telling the truth.'

໑

Ian, who had crossed the cleared land at an angle to reach the highway where the woodland began, saw a glow of light through the tree trunks. He came to an abrupt halt, dropping to one knee and placing his hand over his mouth to mute his laboured breathing. Close behind, Edmund did the same.

They could tell from the way the flames moved from side to side that they were looking at torches but neither could judge how distant they were. Ian counted eight, Edmund ten, and both knew there must be a throng of men on the road. To draw closer in order to see if Thaddeus and Joshua were amongst them, Ian pointed towards the tree line and then flattened and lowered his hand to urge Edmund to keep low, but he'd barely given the signal when they heard the sound of running feet on the road. Together, they dropped to the ground, faces pressed to the grass, and through half-closed lids watched two liveried soldiers, the foremost bearing a torch, hasten past them towards the bridge. Ian turned his head to the left to watch their progress, Edmund looked to his right, where he thought he'd glimpsed the intermittent flicker of a light inside the woodland.

It took only a second or two of searching to find it again. It was a single flame, and he couldn't see who carried it, but he was ready to wager that soldiers were involved. He pulled himself forward on his elbows and pressed his mouth to Ian's ear. 'Someone's heading towards our camp,' he said. 'Perhaps several. If they're armed, we should go back to help Peter and Olyver defend it.'

'Where are they?'

'Behind you to your right.' Edmund drew away and pushed himself into a crouch, raising his arm to show the direction. 'There,' he whispered. 'Do you see the flame?'

Ian nodded. 'They're too far ahead. We'll not reach the camp before them.'

'Then let's cut through the trees and follow. They'll not be expecting an attack from behind.'

A stream of quiet curses issued from Ian's mouth as he rose to his feet. 'I *knew* it was a bad idea to come here,' he muttered.

ଚ୨

Joshua was thinking the same as he slipped through the trees behind Thaddeus and the men who accompanied him. The captain had instructed another three to fall in behind as he followed Thaddeus onto the path, and not one had sheathed his sword. Joshua kept close enough for the torchlight to show him the silhouettes of trunks but not so close that the dogs would detect his presence. While they remained at Thaddeus's heels, the soldiers hung back, but Joshua trembled at what might happen if the pack deserted him. He appeared quite blind to the danger he was in, engaging in light-hearted chitchat with seemingly little concern for his safety.

With no wind inside the woodland to carry Thaddeus's words away, Joshua heard them easily. He asked the soldiers their names, where they came from and how long they'd been in My Lord of Blandeforde's service but, receiving no answers, he glanced over his shoulder to address the captain directly, allowing a note of sympathy to enter his voice.

'You must worry for your family in France, captain. I've met many mercenaries who long for news that never comes. All fear they'll die in England without ever knowing the fate of those they love. Is it a wife or a mother who holds a place in your heart?'

Perhaps it was surprise that this man understood another's anguish that prompted the captain to reply. 'A mother and two sisters, sire. I haven't seen or heard from them in over a year.'

'I feel for you, my friend, but it's truly said that while there's life there's hope. Keep faith that God blesses your women as surely as He blesses you.'

'I try, sire—we all do—but it's not easy.'

'At least you're fortunate in your priest. His understanding of God seems greater than his brothers' in the town, since he is alive and they are dead.'

'The town priests gave their time to tending the sick, sire. Father Aristide gives his to prayer and absolution. By such means he keeps the household alive.'

'He deserves much praise for it. It's an onerous task to hear a hundred confessions each day while finding time to recite the liturgy of the hours.'

'I doubt any man could do so much, sire. We are summoned to the great hall each morning so that Father Aristide can absolve us with a blessing. His Holiness the Pope sent word last autumn that sins can be pardoned without the need for confession.'

Thaddeus slowed. 'Were the town priests dead when this news came? I wonder they took such care of the sick if they knew that general absolution was all that was needed to keep the pestilence at bay.'

'There's more sin in the town than in My Lord's household, sire. Thieving and fornication are rife, and merchants worship money more than they do God. A priest can only protect the pure of heart.'

Joshua prayed most earnestly that Thaddeus would let these statements pass. To challenge the Church's teachings in front of men carrying swords would be madness.

'Indeed. Some transgressions demand a more profound penance than can be gained from a blessing. Was the little maid who was forced from the house a thief and a fornicator? Her depravity must have been great to merit such a punishment.'

There was a long pause before the captain answered. 'The punishment was God's, sire.'

'How so?'

'He afflicted her with the pestilence.'

'What age was she?'

'A child still. Perhaps ten or eleven.'

'Were you acquainted with her?'

'She came with the women who brought food each night to our barracks. We called her Little Sparrow because she was timid and shy, but we were greatly deceived by her. Satan uses many guises to lure men from the path of righteousness.'

Thaddeus came to an abrupt halt and turned to look at the captain. 'Then she was wicked indeed,' he said with such sarcasm that Joshua couldn't believe all four of the fighting men didn't hear it. 'What vile sins did she persuade you to commit? Was her timidity enough to lure you into bedding her?'

The three soldiers drew level with their captain and one raised his sword. The tip was only a wrist's length from Thaddeus's throat. 'If you're the slave the steward says you are, I'll have your hide for that. There's not a man here would have tarnished the maid. You malign *her* when you malign us.'

Thaddeus's reach was so long and his reactions so fast that he'd seized the blade in a gauntleted fist and snapped it across his knee even before the other was aware it was gone. 'Your anger's misplaced,' he said, tossing the pieces into the undergrowth at the side of the track. 'Blame your captain for saying she was touched by Satan before you blame me for asking how Satan manifested Himself.'

'He repeats only what the priest said when he ordered her expulsion.'

'Who was tasked with it?'

'We were.'

'Did she resist?'

The man shook his head. 'She accepted that she was damned.'

A look of contempt crossed Thaddeus's face. 'Then take responsibility for the guilt you feel,' he said coldly, 'and be grateful to the thieves and fornicators in the town who took her in and cared for her. She died in wretchedness because she believed herself too wicked to live, but at least she knew kindness at the end.' He turned to the captain. 'Keep your men under better control. I'll do more than break the weapon of the next to threaten me.'

'Philippe was provoked by what you said, sire. He had a great fondness for Little Sparrow, who reminded him of his sister.' The captain gestured to the other two soldiers to sheathe their swords. 'Why do you say in one moment that we are fortunate in our priest and then judge us harshly for obeying his orders?'

'I make no judgement on your obedience. You and the rest of the household stay alive by following his instructions, do you not? It's your willingness to accept his reasons that angers me.'

'I don't understand, sire.'

With a shrug, Thaddeus began walking again. 'It's an offence against God to call an innocent ten-year-old a creature of Satan.'

☙☙

Ian put an arm around Joshua's chest and clamped a hand across his mouth to keep him from shouting out. Their paths had converged some fifty paces from the camp, and Joshua, intent on listening to Thaddeus's dangerously honest answers to the soldiers, had neither seen nor heard Ian and Edmund's approach. He ceased struggling when he heard Ian's voice in his ear. 'Is Thaddeus their prisoner?'

'Not yet,' he whispered when Ian removed his hand. 'He's looking to win them to his side.'

'How?'

'In the worst way possible. He's telling them their priest's a liar and a fraud.'

☙☙

Olyver and Peter fed arrows onto their strings, raised their bows and sighted along the shafts. They stood before the fire, their left shoulders towards the woodland, their right hands holding steady against their cheeks. The only movement either of them made was a fractional adjustment of their bows to the left when the sound of voices amongst the trees seemed to shift direction.

Thaddeus was the first to emerge and he nodded approval when he saw their readiness. Briefly, his gaze roamed around the rest of the campsite, looking for Ian, Edmund and Joshua, but he made no comment when he didn't find them. He moved to stand beside Olyver, clicking his fingers to persuade the dogs to follow him, and raised a hand in acknowledgement to the captain and three soldiers who remained within the trees.

'I thank you for your safe escort, captain, and wish you and your men well.'

'The steward will expect us to stay with you, sire. Will you ask your soldiers to lower their weapons?'

Thaddeus shook his head. 'The steward is your master not mine, my friend. He has no authority here. You may go of your own free will or I will ask my men to accompany you.'

'We are four and they are two, sire. The odds are not in your favour.'

Ian's voice spoke from behind them. 'You're in error, sir. The odds have always been in My Lord's favour. Had he given the signal we would have felled you in the woods.'

Ᏼ

Thaddeus listened to Joshua and Ian's stories as he knelt to replace the parchments and writing implements in his travel desk, but he didn't need Ian's account of the imposter's mention of twins or Joshua's repeating of d'Amiens' reference to the priest's guest to tell him it was time to leave. He'd guessed from the moment the guards on the bridge responded to the name of Athelstan that he was testing his luck, but he'd known it for certain when the guildsmen signalled their unease.

He refused to waste time, debating over who had betrayed them, and shook his head when Peter asked if he should stamp out the fire. 'We'll build it up. The steward will see its glow from the highway and the longer it burns the better start we'll get.'

'But in which direction?' asked Olyver. 'We'll not find a path to the south through these woods in the dark—and even if we do, there's no knowing where we'll come out. What if the steward's set a second block on the road a mile farther down? We'll ride straight into it.'

Thaddeus nodded. With the bridge to the north and the highway to the east and south, their only way out was to the west. But at night in the forest they were as likely to veer south as maintain the direction they wanted. He pictured the loop of river that he'd studied earlier that day, recalling how it had run west from the bridge for some five hundred paces before curving towards the north.

'We'll hug this tree line to the river,' he said, 'and then make our way along the bank. Providing we follow the water course, we'll come to another highway eventually. This bridge can't be the only crossing.'

'It could be miles away,' said Edmund.

'It could,' Thaddeus agreed, 'and we'll be doing it on foot. We need to move quietly. Lead your horses on rope halters and store your reins and stirrups in your saddle packs. The night's so still, the rattle of harness will give us away.'

'Who's to hear us?' asked Joshua.

'Anyone with the wit to work out which way we've headed.' Thaddeus rose to his feet with a sigh. 'I've led you into a trap and for that I am deeply sorry. If we're fortunate, the flames of the fire will persuade the steward we're still here; otherwise, he'll send men who know the forest paths to cut us off somewhere along the riverbank.' He glanced from one anxious face to the other. 'Should that happen, I want your promise that you'll leave me to deal with the threat alone.'

'None of us can promise that,' said Ian.

'You can and you will, for we carry the fate of Develish in our hands as well our own.' He held out his palm. 'Give me your pledges. Free of restraint, you have a better chance of helping me than if I'm forced to watch as each of you is broken on the wheel.'

Easter Day, 1349

Harold Talbot lost his temper again today. This time his wrath was directed at our parade from the church as Father Anselm led us through the vegetable garden and orchard before shepherding us into the great hall for our Easter banquet. Before the pestilence, women and maids would spend weeks stitching new apparel for themselves and their families in honour of Christ's rising, but with fabric in short supply they chose instead to bedeck old clothes with brightly coloured woollen sashes and tassels. The children hopped and skipped to set their ribbons fluttering and the sight was pleasing to all except Harold.

I've never known a man so keen to embrace misery. If he'd had his way, every person in Develish would have worn hair shirts and beaten themselves with flagellants' whips as penance for Christ's crucifixion instead of walking together in celebration of His resurrection. Alice tells me his temper has grown worse since age scrambled his wits, but in truth I suspect he's always been angry. On the rare occasions when his mind is untroubled, he shows himself to be a person of intelligence, and I can't help feeling his frustrations would have been lessened if he'd received an education.

As ever, it was Eva Thurkell who soothed him. There's no accounting for why he responds so readily to her voice and touch, but she wins our admiration each time she succeeds in quieting him. Alice says Eva's fair prettiness reminds him of his youngest daughter, but I wonder if it wasn't Eva's staying of Will's hand when he sought to punish Harold for raising little May's skirt that won the old man's heart. Whatever the reason, it pleases me that Eva has gained in confidence from being able to do something that no one else can.

I thought my eyes deceived me yesterday when I watched her inscribe her name on a slate with Isabella's help. She took so much satisfaction from the task that her face was wreathed in smiles, and for once they didn't disappear when she became aware of my presence. She tells me she is determined to master the names of all her family before Thaddeus returns, and I wonder whether her previous resistance to acquiring new skills was driven by fear of mockery if she failed.

She asked if I thought Thaddeus and his companions were safe, and I said I was sure they were. But it wasn't an honest answer. This last week my nights have been troubled by dreams of Jacques d'Amiens. It may only be because Thaddeus said he would enter Blandeforde during the Easter celebrations, but my sense of foreboding is very great.

Thirteen

Develish, Dorseteshire

GYLES HAD REASON TO BLESS the Easter festivities as he released the raft from its moorings and let it drift on long ropes towards the centre of the moat. By Lady Anne's command, the day of revelry, sport and feasting had ended with watered wine being shared by all as the sun began to set; and now, at close to midnight, every person in Develish was deeply asleep, except for the men who stood on the guard steps.

The bank was narrow beneath the defensive wall that surrounded the manor house enclosure but, even in the miserly light of a shrouded moon, Gyles was sure-footed enough to keep his balance. The raft moved with the current from Devil's Brook and needed little effort to assist it on its way. He heard Adam Catchpole's whispered acknowledgement as he passed beneath the western guard step and then, five hundred paces later, felt the touch of his brother Alleyn's hand on his shoulder to tell him he'd reached the southern step behind the church.

Neither he nor Alleyn spoke, for fear of alerting Father Anselm to their presence. This part of the moat was the least visible to anyone inside the enclosure, but they had no wish to make the irascible priest a witness to what they were doing. Gyles dug his heels into the moist grass of the bank and pulled on the ropes to draw the raft in, allowing the hemp to drop in coils at his feet. He heard the soft thud as John Trueblood eased himself over the wall and dropped to the ground beside him and then the rub of cloak against homespun kirtle as Alleyn swung Lady Anne across the parapet and lowered her into John's waiting arms.

Without a word, Gyles took the heavy leather bag that his brother handed down to him. He placed it on the raft and assisted John and Milady aboard before running the ropes through his hands to allow the vessel to drift towards the far bank. He watched a shadowy figure step from behind a clump of alders to catch the coils which John threw from the front and then raised his hand in acknowledgement when Edmund turned to signal that the raft was firmly moored to one of the alder's trunks. He forgave John's intemperate clasping of his son to his chest as soon as he stepped ashore—he would have done the same had one of his twins returned—but he prayed most earnestly that Edmund was free of the pestilence.

The boy had shown himself to James Buckler some hour after the sun had passed its zenith. James, standing guard on the southern step, had been staring towards the woodland that bordered the cleared land to the south when the edge of his vision caught movement amongst the dried brown stems of vetch on a peasant strip some fifty paces from the moat. He thought it was a fox until he shifted his gaze towards the rustling plants and saw that it was a man. He lay flat on the ground, his britches and tunic so close in colour to the dead vetch that it would have been hard to make him out were his head not raised and his face visible. When he was sure he had James's attention, the man placed a finger to his lips to urge silence and then rose to his knees. It was arguable which surprised James more—that the 'man' was fifteen-year-old Edmund Trueblood or that he had made his way across a quarter-mile of open land without being seen.

James needed no prompting to hoist himself across the wall and slither down to the bank below. The mere fact that Edmund was alone suggested he had bad news to impart, and the fewer who heard it the better. He beckoned the boy to approach the far bank and urged him to keep his voice low. The Easter feast had yet to end but there would be some, already replete, who preferred to walk outside than stay in the great hall. Edmund, seemingly more aware than James of how his unexpected arrival might impact on Develish, positioned himself beside a small copse of alders, scanning above the wall for listeners and ready to duck out of sight should he see one. He spoke in short, clear sentences to be sure he was understood.

Thaddeus had been taken prisoner outside Blandeforde the previous night by the steward, Master d'Amiens. His companions had escaped by following the River Stour, and were safe. They had camped overnight at a distance from Blandeforde, and Edmund had ridden south at dawn to consult with Lady Anne. She was the only person clever enough to advise them on how best to help Thaddeus. Should Edmund fail to return by noon tomorrow, his friends would act as they saw fit. Would Lady Anne come to the moat so that Edmund could speak with her? It would be wiser if she came after dark so that they could talk freely. He would wait amongst the alders for her answer.

Despite the grimness of the message, James's first emotion was admiration for Edmund's courage and good sense. The lad must have ridden hard to reach Develish so soon, yet rather than cause alarm, he'd taken the time to leave the highway and circle around the valley from the north in order to approach the only guard step that wasn't in constant view of the house. Such a feat was beyond most men. He raised a hand in agreement, motioning Edmund to take some rest inside the copse, then pulled himself back over the wall and went in search of Gyles. Together they sought out Lady Anne.

They found her in the steward's office, taking time for herself while the great hall was cleared of the feast before being made ready for skittles and horseshoe throwing. She was writing in her journal and looked up with a smile when Gyles and James entered, but the smile died when she heard what they had to say. Nevertheless, they were surprised at how calmly she took the news, showing more concern for Edmund than for Thaddeus. Was the boy frightened? she asked James. Did he look in need of food? Should she come now to speak with him?

James shook his head to all the questions, describing Edmund's demeanour as composed and strong. 'He's a credit to Thaddeus's teaching, milady. He'll wait as long as he must to hear your advice—though I'm sure he'll be glad of something to eat if we can find a way to send it across.'

Lady Anne glanced again at what she'd been writing. 'Did he say why the imposture failed?'

'No, milady. Only what I've already told you. Shall I tell him you'll speak to him?'

She hesitated for several long seconds. 'I've long feared this moment would come, and I've made a hundred plans for how to respond when it did. Yet even at my most hopeful, I didn't expect to hear within hours that Thaddeus was arrested. At best,

I thought a month would pass before we learnt of it. At worst a year.' She turned to Gyles. 'Is it possible to float the raft to the southern step once darkness has fallen?'

'I see no reason why not, milady. What do you have in mind?'

ை

The ghostly shapes on the other side of the moat were quickly swallowed by darkness as they moved out onto the peasant strips, and with a sigh Gyles bound the ropes about his waist and hunkered down for a long vigil. Every so often, he heard the shuffle of boots on stone above him as his brother shifted position, but otherwise the only sound to accompany his thoughts was the soft ripple of water through the grass at the edge of the bank.

Who was to say that Lady Anne's decision was wrong? Certainly not he. He couldn't remember a time when he'd had reason to think her ideas misguided or foolish. His fellows on her council had urged him strongly to use his influence to make her think again, for they all knew she was acting with her heart and not her head, but Gyles had refused. He couldn't agree that Thaddeus's life was worth sacrificing for the good of all; and nor, he believed, would his sons or their friends. Nonetheless, he had raised no objections to one or all of the other fathers arguing their case.

He heard John's quiet call from the far bank sooner than he expected. 'Make ready, Gyles. I've freed the moorings on this side.'

Gyles rose to his feet and pulled on the sodden ropes to draw the raft back. 'I'm sorry, my friend,' he said with sincerity, as he reached out a hand to help the other ashore.

John gave a dispirited shrug. 'You were right and I was wrong. Neither listened to reason.'

'Did Milady honour her promise to order the boys home?'

'She did, and more forcefully than I thought she would. Edmund seemed taken aback that she would even issue such a command. He told her he'd come for advice, not to be ordered to forsake his leader.'

'How did Milady reply?'

'She asked him to hear my arguments before he heard hers, but Edmund said he and his friends would rather suffer the same fate as Thaddeus than play the part of traitors.'

'It's a fine impulse, John.'

'Maybe so, but you know as well as I that Lady Anne is allowing her feelings for Thaddeus to cloud her judgement.'

Gyles handed him one of the ropes. 'I'll need your help to tow the raft back to its mooring position beneath the northern step. We'll be going against the current.'

John stared at him in frustration. 'Why does her foolishness not concern you? There'll be no future for Develish without her.'

Gyles lifted the sodden hemp to his shoulder and prepared to take up the slack. 'She'll be lost to us anyway if Thaddeus denounces her. Which he will. No man's strong enough to stay silent while his legs and arms are broken on the wheel. Pray God Milady reaches Blandeforde before that happens. All Develish will be condemned otherwise.'

෨෨

Edmund led Lady Anne through the peasant strips to where he'd left the horses in a grassy clearing amongst the trees that bordered Devil's Brook. To assist her across the rough ground, he held his right forearm rigid so that she could rest her palm on it while in his left hand he carried the heavy leather bag. He spoke only to warn her of ruts and tangled vetch, being too shy to voice his opinions on anything else, and she blessed his silence because it allowed her to fix her mind on staying upright in the darkness. It wasn't part of her plan to make the poor boy regret her company even before they'd started.

He launched into words when the hobbled horses snickered at their approach, apologising for only being able to give her Killer to ride. 'The twins thought you might permit their father to help us, milady. If we'd thought you'd make the journey, I'd have brought one of the ponies.'

She smiled. 'I'm grateful you had the foresight to bring any mount at all, Edmund. I don't say you won't have to lead me—and that I shan't complain royally of soreness before we ever reach Blandeforde—but I'm sure Killer will make the journey less wearisome than if I had to do it on foot.'

'I can lift you into the saddle so that you can sit sideways, milady. If you hold hard to the pommel, you'll find Killer's gait smooth enough at a walk.'

She shook her head. 'We need to travel faster than that, Edmund, at least when daylight comes. I shall ride astride.'

'Do you know how, milady?'

'My father taught me when I was very young.'

She asked him to place the leather bag on the ground and knelt to undo the straps. 'I've brought food for you. James Buckler tells me you must have been on the road since dawn.' She handed him a package of bread and cold meat left over from the Easter banquet. 'It was thoughtful of you to make your way around the valley to approach from the south, Edmund. A lesser man would have caused panic by riding at full tilt down the road from the village.'

Had it not been so dark, she would have seen that her compliment caused a flush of pleasure to colour his cheeks. 'It wouldn't have helped Thaddeus to spread panic, milady,' he said gruffly, tearing at the meat with his teeth. 'He told us to keep cool heads before he ordered us to abandon him.'

'When did that happen?'

'Around midnight, milady.' He described the events leading up to Thaddeus's capture and the pledge they'd given him to avoid being taken themselves. 'He handed me Killer's reins when Joshua's dogs became restless. Shortly afterwards we saw torches moving along the riverbank towards us. Thaddeus sent us into the forest, and he went on alone to meet the guards.'

Lady Anne laid some folded garments on the ground beside her. 'Did you see him being taken?'

Edmund nodded. 'They surrounded him the same way they did on the highway. He gave them his sword, and the captain asked where his men were. He said we were with the horses at the camp, looking to keep the steward's attention while he escaped along the river.'

She drew a sash from the bag. 'And they believed him?'

'They must have done. No one came looking for us in the wood, though they'll know he lied if they raided the camp later.'

'What happened next?'

'The guards took Thaddeus back the way they'd come and we continued to follow the river. We came to a ford after about five hours. We waited there for dawn to break, and I left as soon as it was light enough to see the road.'

Lady Anne replaced all the garments in the bag except for the sash and one folded item of clothing. 'Did you know where you were?'

'Only when I saw the first milestone, milady. It told me I was on the highway from Shafbury to Dorchester—the same one

Develish is on. I couldn't believe my luck. Do you think it means God doesn't want Thaddeus to die?'

She stood with a smile. 'I'm sure it does. Will you be so kind as to turn your back so that I can pull on these britches and tie the hem of my kirtle about my waist? We'll make better progress if I'm not hampered by skirts.'

৫৩

Confident that the night was dark enough for them not to be seen from the house, Edmund led Lady Anne through Devil's Brook and across the pastureland to the highway north. He chose to go on foot, leading both horses, and she seemed happy to accept that their pace must be careful and slow while the moon was obscured. He was glad to see that she sat straight in her saddle once he'd adjusted the stirrups, but his doubts about taking her with him were very great.

His companions expected to see Gyles Startout, and he knew they'd react as he'd done to having Milady wished upon them instead. Edmund had hidden his own disappointment well to her face, but it swelled and grew in his heart as he walked ahead of her. What good was a woman when they needed an experienced fighting man? How much time would they waste attending to her needs? How uncomfortable would she make them feel when she discovered how rough and hard it was to live in the open air and learnt that men behaved coarsely when they were alone?

From disappointment, he moved to anger, for he felt he'd been given no choice but to assume responsibility for her after she'd announced her intention of accompanying him. He should have been able to appeal to his father, but John had been too intent on persuading him to obey her first command to bring his companions home. He'd lectured his son about common sense and obligation to Develish, and the right moment never came for Edmund to say that he and his friends wanted Gyles and not Lady Anne.

Perhaps Lady Anne guessed at his conflict, for she spoke once they'd breasted the hill out of Develish valley. 'Did Thaddeus suggest how you might rescue him, Edmund?'

'No, milady, but we made some plans of our own while we waited for daylight.'

'Bold ones, I'm sure.'

'Bold enough, milady.'

A smile entered her voice. 'Your fathers feared as much. They know how courageous you are. Thaddeus also. Tell me how he persuaded you to give him your pledge when your more natural instinct was to remain at his side.'

'He said we'd have a better chance of helping him if we were free, milady, though, in truth, I think he was more worried about what the steward might do to us.'

'With good reason,' she answered. 'There's no quicker way to force the truth from a man than to put his friends to the torture in front of him.'

'We'd not have confessed to anything easily, milady . . . and nor will Thaddeus.'

'I know that.'

He waited for her to say more and, when she didn't, he spoke more curtly than he should. 'What plans do *you* have to rescue him, milady?'

'Only one, Edmund. To enter Blandeforde this day and demand that he's tried for the crimes he's said to have committed.'

∞

They made faster progress once the sun was above the horizon. Better able to see the road ahead, Edmund mounted his own horse and led Killer at a fast trot. He called to Lady Anne to relax into the saddle and allow herself to rise and fall with the charger's extended gait, but the strain in her face when they were within a half-mile of the ford told him the ride had been an uncomfortable one. He slowed to a walk.

'We're nearly there, milady. Would you like time to compose yourself?'

She summoned a smile. 'Will your friends think less of me if I arrive on foot?'

'I'm afraid they might, milady. They're hoping to see the twins' father.'

'Then I must endeavour to play the part of an experienced horsewoman. Will you be so kind as to pass me the reins, Edmund? I shall be greatly obliged if you stay at my side and keep Killer from bolting. I shall look very undignified if he throws me by the wayside.'

Edmund could only admire her fortitude when they reached the ford and his companions emerged from the woodland to greet them. He well remembered his own blisters and bruises the first time he rode any distance, and he wondered that Milady was so able to dismiss hers. She accepted his help in dismounting and took his arm gratefully as he led her towards where his fellows had made their camp; but not once did she stumble or show distress at the looks of despair on the faces that greeted her.

∞

The sun had been up a bare hour when the peace of Develish was rent by high-pitched screams. Clara Trueblood, organising work in the kitchen, clapped a hand to her chest in shock. 'Mercy me!' she cried to the other servants. 'What in heaven's name is going on?'

'It'll be Harold Talbot up to his tricks again,' said one of the women.

Clara looked for Eva Thurkell. 'Come,' she said, hurrying her through the door to the great hall. 'You're all that stands between him and instant death. I'll smother the old brute myself if we find him molesting a child.'

But whatever the trouble was, it was happening elsewhere, for they were greeted with looks of puzzlement from the serfs in the hall. Most were tying their rush mattresses into neat rolls, making them ready to stack along the walls, and all had paused to listen to the screams. Some crossed themselves for fear the Devil was nigh; others looked towards the stairs which led to the upper storey, as if to say the sound was coming from above.

This was proved true when the screams gave way to thumps that drummed on the wooden ceiling. Seizing Eva's hand, Clara shouldered her way through the crowd, instructing mothers to take their children outside and men to follow her to the stairs. She had no idea what the confusion of sounds represented, but they spoke of violence and seemed to be coming from Lady Anne's chamber. Her first instinct was that Harold Talbot had lost complete leave of his senses and was attacking Eleanor; her second that Eleanor had lost leave of hers and was venting her rage on Milady. In either case, she didn't doubt that murder was being done.

She and Eva were halfway up the stone steps when the thudding ceased and a great hush fell on the hall. They heard the sound of running feet along the walled-in corridor that linked the rooms, and even Clara's stout heart quailed at the thought of who might appear. None expected to see Isabella Startout.

She cried out in relief when she saw Clara. 'Oh, Mistress Trueblood, Lady Eleanor is much in need of help and I don't know what to do for her. I fear she's dying.'

'Is Lady Anne with her?'

Isabella shook her head. 'She must be in the church, but it'll take too long for her to come.' She descended the steps and tugged at Clara's free hand. 'Please make haste. Lady Eleanor will perish for certain if we do nothing.'

Clara paused only to send one of the men in search of Lady Anne and then, together with Eva, ran with Isabella to the chamber. They found Eleanor, pale and limp upon the ground, blood and froth oozing from the side of her mouth. There was no one else in the room.

Clara knelt to place her palm on the girl's chest. 'She's still breathing,' she said, 'and I can feel the beat of her heart. What caused this foam and blood to come from her mouth? Did you strike her, Isabella? We heard screams and then a terrible thudding on the floor.'

'It was none of my doing, Mistress Trueblood. I was in the spinning room when the cries began and I was sorely afraid the voice was Milady's. I crept to this door and pushed it wide but all I could see was Lady Eleanor flinging herself about the floor and banging her head and heels on the planks. She's so pale. What should we do for her?'

Eva Thurkell knelt on Eleanor's other side and used the hem of her kirtle to wipe the blood and foam from the girl's mouth. 'Nothing,' she said. 'She has bitten her tongue is all and the pallor comes from her swoon. It won't last long. There was a boy on my last demesne who suffered the same.'

'What made him do it?' asked Clara.

'The priest said it was heat in his brain. He was an excitable child—keen to dance and play one moment, angry the next. He fell and twitched most often when he was thwarted. He always slept afterwards. Lady Eleanor will do the same.'

'Was he able to speak when he came out of the swoon?'

Eva nodded. 'It was as if it had never happened. See? Lady Eleanor's lids are beginning to flutter. I expect she'll ask us why she's on the floor and what we're doing here.'

Clara answered as well as she could when Eleanor did precisely that. 'You swooned, milady. Isabella summoned us to help you. I've sent for your mother. She'll be with us shortly.'

Eleanor stared at her in confusion. 'Where is she?'

'In the church, milady.'

'Is she in her coffin?'

Clara's surprise was obvious. 'Of course not. Whatever made you think such a thing?'

Eleanor turned on her side, unable to fight sleep. 'Her silk gown is gone,' she slurred. 'I thought she must have died . . .'

As her voice faded to nothing, Clara turned to Isabella with an enquiring frown. 'What did she mean?'

Isabella was equally puzzled until she saw that the lid of a small chest in the corner was open. She walked across to look inside. 'It's quite empty,' she said.

Clara motioned to Eva to lift Eleanor's legs while she placed her hands beneath the girl's arms. 'What did you expect to find?'

With an anxious expression, Isabella watched them carry the inert body to the bed. 'The embroidered blue gown that Lady Anne stitched for her wedding day. It's her finest and most beautiful. Lady Eleanor has tried many times to persuade her to wear it but she always refuses. She says it would be a shame to reduce it to tatters before it's needed.'

'You're talking in riddles,' Clara declared bluntly, as she placed a feather pillow beneath Eleanor's head. 'What does a missing gown have to do with death?'

Isabella clasped her hands together. 'Everything,' she said. 'Milady told Lady Eleanor she was keeping it for her burial.'

ॐ

Eleanor watched Isabella through half-closed lids for several minutes. She thought it was Lady Anne perched on a stool before the tapestry frame, making tiny French knots in a pattern of fleurs-de-lis, because the maid sat in silhouette against the bright spring sun which shone through the latticed windows. Her soft brown curls were tumbled about her face as she leant over her work, just as Lady Anne did, and Eleanor felt a surge of relief that her earlier anguish had been misplaced.

Her last clear memory was of screaming in terror when she believed her mother dead, but she realised now that she must have been mistaken. There was some other reason for Lady Anne's possessions to be missing and her bed not to have been slept in. Eleanor had no recollection of how she came to be in the bed herself, or when Lady Anne had returned to the chamber, but she took comfort from her presence. Her grief at the thought of losing her had been very great.

She had so many apologies still to make to Lady Anne, but anxiety had kept her mute, for she feared seeing reproach in Lady Anne's eyes if she talked of things best forgotten. Eleanor's greatest shame was that she'd believed her father's lies about Milady. Robert said it wasn't her fault—Sir Richard had twisted her mind for his own purposes—but Eleanor guessed the boy only said this to lessen her feelings of guilt. Robert would never accept another's judgement on a person without questioning whether it was true. He proved it every day through his continued friendship with her, despite being told by others that he should open his eyes and remember that the acorn didn't fall far from the tree. Eleanor was Sir Richard's daughter and no amount of teaching could change her vicious nature.

Eleanor took comfort from Robert's scornful rejection of such ideas. Even the numbskulls who mouthed them were capable of learning from their mistakes, and the same was true of Eleanor. Look how far she'd come already through learning her letters with his and Lady Anne's help. Before Sir Richard's death, she had thought reading and writing beneath her; now she was striving hard to become as proficient as Robert. And what of the cats? Her father would have ordered them killed but Eleanor preferred to love and nurture them. Did these choices not suggest she was more like Lady Anne than Sir Richard? All Eleanor needed was the courage to embrace her mother and trust that nothing she confessed would be betrayed or greeted with disapproval.

Sleep might have taken her again had Isabella not turned to look at her. This time there was no mistaking the girl for the woman, and Eleanor's eyes widened in shock. Fearing more screams, Isabella rose from her stool and came to kneel beside her. 'Try to be calm, Lady Eleanor. You will bring on another swoon if you allow yourself to fret.' She took a cloth from a bowl of water and wrung it out to press the cool fabric against Eleanor's brow.

'Your tongue may hurt where you bit it but, when you're able to sit up, I have medicine that will soothe the pain.'

Her words made no sense to Eleanor until she tried to form a response. Her lacerated tongue rubbed against her teeth and the pain was such that her shock gave way to tears. With a sigh of concern, Isabella replaced the cloth in the bowl and reached her hands beneath Eleanor's arms to pull her upright. She plumped the pillow and urged Eleanor to shuffle backwards while she tucked the coverlet about her legs.

'The medicine is salt, Lady Eleanor. I will add it to a beaker of water and you must keep the brine in your mouth for as long as you are able before spitting it out. If you swallow it, you will be sick. Do you understand?' Receiving a nod, she took a spoonful of salt from a wooden box on the table beside the bed, stirred it into some warm water and then held the beaker to Eleanor's lips. 'The longer you hold it, the more easily you will be able to speak afterwards,' she said, placing a clay bowl in Eleanor's lap for the spit. 'When you're ready, you may ask as many questions as you like. I will answer each as best I can.'

Eleanor did as she was bid but it took three doses of brine before the stinging was numbed enough for her to speak. All the while she felt Isabella's strength and wondered how the girl had grown so much in half a year. Gone was the timid maid who been the victim of Eleanor's tantrums since she was eight years old, and in her place stood a composed and confident young woman who seemed as adept as Lady Anne at alleviating suffering. Her prettiness was startling yet, far from feeling jealousy, Eleanor knew only regret for the careless disregard she'd had for Isabella in the past.

She spat the last of the brine into the bowl. 'You shouldn't be alone with me,' she managed. 'Lady Anne made me promise to keep ten paces between us at all times.'

'And so you have, milady. I choose to be here, which is what I shall tell your mother if she asks.'

'Do you still think of her as my mother?'

'I find it hard not to, milady. She's always loved you as a daughter and treated you as such.' Isabella took the bowl from Eleanor's lap and placed it on the table. 'Would it please you better if I called her your guardian?'

Eleanor shook her head. 'I have no wish to deny her a second time.' She stared at her hands. 'I remember being frightened to discover that her gown was gone . . . also her comb and her hand mirror . . . but I don't recall anything else. Why did I bite my tongue? And who put me in this bed?'

Isabella pulled forward her stool and described the seizure Eleanor had suffered. 'Eva Thurkell says it's nothing to worry about, milady. It was just a faint. She says fear for your mother made your brain overheat.'

'You said I was throwing myself about the floor.'

'A boy on Mistress Thurkell's last demesne did the same, which is how she knows so much about it. He always recovered afterwards.'

'How often did it happen to him?'

'Hardly at all,' Isabella lied, 'and only when he became over-excited. He was very young and liked to dance and shout.'

'I remember screaming.'

Isabella nodded. 'That will have been the cause, milady.'

When Eleanor made no response, Isabella wondered if she believed this excuse or was looking to blame others for her strange condition. In truth, it was hardly a convincing explanation. Isabella couldn't count the number of times Eleanor had thrown tantrums and screaming rages in the past without ever dropping in a swoon afterwards.

Eleanor reached for Isabella's hand and raised it to her cheek. 'I was afraid,' she whispered. 'My mother gives me an hour each morning to teach me my letters, but when I awoke at dawn she wasn't here. I listened to the sounds of people rising in the house, thinking she'd been called away, but when the sun had been up for some time and she hadn't returned, I decided to read our book alone to show her how much I've improved. It's the record she makes of Develish's history. She brings it to this chamber at the end of each day and places it beside her pillow—but I couldn't see it, and nor did her pillow look as if it had been used.'

'And that frightened you, milady?'

'Not so much as finding that everything personal to her was missing. Her washing cloth, her comb, even the small jar of rouge that she kept for when my father had guests. I became truly frightened when I opened the chest that holds her wedding gown and slippers. I have such dread of her dying, for she is all I have left in the world.'

Isabella's warm heart was moved. She understood now why Eleanor had thought Lady Anne had passed to the next life. Everything she'd mentioned spoke of preparation for the coffin. A cloth to wash the body. A comb to draw the hair about the face. Rouge to give colour to dead skin. A gown to be worn for burial.

She took both of Eleanor's hands in her own to warm them. 'She's not dead, milady. She rides to Blandeforde with Edmund Trueblood in the hope of freeing Thaddeus Thurkell from imprisonment. If she fails, he will likely be hanged for imposture.'

Fourteen

Blandeforde, Dorseteshire

THADDEUS SNAPPED AWAKE WHEN THE first grey fingers of dawn lifted the gloom inside his prison. He looked to see where the light was entering and saw an unglazed slit in the wall to his right. He guessed he was in a storeroom for ale because the air smelt strongly of fermented grain and yeast, yet his brief glimpse of the chamber in the flames from his guards' torches the night before had shown it to be empty of barrels. The only piece of furniture had been a narrow bench against one wall, and when the door slammed shut, plunging him into darkness, he had stretched himself along it, preferring the discomfort of unforgiving wood to the risk of disturbing rats amongst the litter of straw on the floor.

He'd been confined the first night to a six-foot-square cell in the soldiers' barracks outside. Shackled and chained to a bar on the wall, he'd been able to squat on the floor, but not lie down, and he viewed the bench as an improvement. He still wore the shackles on his wrists but, since they weren't tethered to anything, he could tolerate their discomfort more easily. No explanation had been offered for his removal from the barracks, but he guessed his guards' increasing friendliness had had something to do with it.

The steward could have wished for a better day to incarcerate a felon than Easter Sunday, for the Church banned the meting out of punishment on the anniversary of Christ's resurrection. It was a time of giving, and in that spirit, Thaddeus's guards had taken him into the main chamber of the barracks and allowed him food and water and the use of their piss-pot. He'd had little trouble engaging with them. His ease of manner, fluency in their language and genuine gratitude for their charity won him sympathetic ears. He listened to their histories and told them some of his own—his descent from Godwin of Wessex, the marriage of his grandfather to a Moorish princess and his rearing in Spain—and, by evening, many were questioning whether the steward had been right to arrest him. Given more time, he had hoped to induce the captain to accept his parole and remove his shackles, but his abrupt transfer to the house had put an end to familiarity.

His sleep on the wooden bench had been restful. In childhood, he'd passed many a wakeful night worrying about the morrow but, as he grew, he'd come to understand the futility of so much squandered energy. The blows of Will Thurkell's cudgel across his shoulders were no less raw for imagining them in advance. The trick of closing down his thoughts had been hard to master but, once learnt, it had stood him in good stead. Even pain became bearable when the mind was able to free itself from the body.

This wasn't to say he hadn't dwelt for some time on Hugh de Courtesmain. The Frenchman had been in the great hall when Thaddeus had been brought through the imposing entranceway the previous night. The signs of Easter Sunday's festivity lingered in the air—the redolent scent of roasted lamb, the sourer smell of ale and wine—but none of the household was in evidence. Jacques d'Amiens had sat alone at the head of a long table, the livid stain across his nose and cheek enhanced by the light of torches in sconces around the walls, his fingers playing with a garland of spring flowers on the surface in front of him.

He had made Thaddeus a mocking bow and then summoned de Courtesmain from the shadows behind a pillar. The shock in the Frenchman's eyes to be forced to confront the man he'd accused was very great, and Thaddeus had felt a small pity for him. It was one thing to traduce an enemy in his absence, quite another to do it to his face. For himself, he showed only indifference when de Courtesmain confirmed him as Thurkell, but in truth his relief had been huge to discover that his betrayer was the duplicitous Frenchman and not Bourne. It would have been harder to brand a peer of the realm as a liar, particularly one for whom he had developed a liking, than a hired steward who seemed unable to remain in post.

As the light strengthened outside, Thaddeus rose from the bench and moved to the window. His view was restricted by the narrowness of the slit, but he could tell he was on the northern façade of the house because he could see the roofs of the town in the distance. He had a clear picture of the lie of the building, thanks to his study of it from the hillside two days before, and knew the entranceway opened on to a forecourt on the southern-facing side. If he wanted to escape, that would be the easiest exit to find, but the idea wasn't a serious one and he didn't linger on it. He knew from his counting of the guards in the soldiers' barracks that d'Amiens had in excess of fifty armed men guarding his lord's estate, and to attempt to evade them all would be fruitless.

The air was filled with the sound of the dawn chorus and Thaddeus's gaze was drawn to a group of sparrows pecking for seeds in the grass beyond the window. There was no telling them apart, and he wondered what it was about the human face that made each so recognisable. All had eyes, noses, mouths and hair, and the position of these features never varied, yet no one who had acquaintanceship with a person mistook him for another.

Would he be believed if he denied he'd ever met Hugh de Courtesmain?

෨෬

Only Edmund, who'd had time to think about it, listened with any enthusiasm to Lady Anne's plan to rescue Thaddeus. The others stared despondently at their hands and questioned how entering the lion's den could achieve anything but their own and Lady Anne's arrest. She placed too much trust in Master d'Amiens' willingness to obey the law and even more in her belief that Thaddeus would never admit that his claim to the title of Athelstan was fraudulent.

She sat cross-legged on a bracken bed, sharing the cold remains of some mutton stew with Edmund, attending patiently while the youths explained that her idea wouldn't work. Each in turn tried to persuade her that she would risk her own safety if she presented herself as Thaddeus's advocate and demanded he be tried according to law.

Ian Startout spoke for them all. 'You'll be condemned as a perjurer alongside him, milady, and he won't want that. He has too much regard for you to see you suffer the same fate as him.'

She had heard the same arguments from their fathers. 'I can only be accused of perjury if he denies being Athelstan before we arrive,' she said lightly. 'Do you have so little faith in him that you believe he might?'

'If he thinks it will help Develish, he will, milady.'

She laid aside her plate. 'Then we have nothing to worry about, for he knows it won't. Every serf on the demesne will be punished if the steward believes they knew of the deceit.'

'You more than anyone, milady.'

She shook her head. 'Master d'Amiens' authority extends only to the serfs and tenants on his lord's estates. He may convict a base-born man of criminality in Blandeforde's absence but not a person of noble birth.' She rested her soft gaze on their anxious faces. 'Thaddeus is as knowledgeable of the law as Master d'Amiens. As long as he insists on his right to be tried by his peers, the steward cannot act against him.'

'But what if it's My Lord of Bourne who accuses him, milady?'

Lady Anne leant forward to unbuckle the leather bag that Edmund had placed in front of her. 'He'll wish he'd held his tongue,' she said, showing them the letters from Dorset widows. 'I'll not spare him if he's broken the pledge he made to me in Develish.'

☙❧

Thaddeus's prison was the last chamber at the end of a long corridor. The five guards who escorted him from it blocked his view of the other rooms they passed, but he guessed that, like his, they were used for storage. Ahead was a kitchen. The door stood slightly ajar and Thaddeus heard the clatter of pots and crockery before he was shepherded to the right and through an archway into the great hall. The room was quite empty. If servants slept in it, they had long since risen and placed their bedding rolls out of sight.

Thaddeus wondered if he was being kept from their sight when the guards marched him to the front entranceway and took him outside. Were this Develish, the hall and forecourt would be humming with industry, but here there was none. The house and grounds seemed deserted, and he began to think it was by design that the only people he'd seen since his arrival were Norman fighting men. Yet why? What had the steward to fear from his English servants? And why had it taken the man so long to decide on what to do with him? By the sun, which was casting the shadows of trees across the forecourt, he estimated the time to be some four hours after dawn.

They turned right out of the doorway, and the captain of the guard ordered him to relieve himself in a sewage channel which ran from the western end of the house to the river. Thaddeus made a play of viewing it with disgust, even though he recalled being taken over it twice in darkness. His nose had told him it was there even if the night had obscured it. 'Is cleanliness unknown in this godforsaken place that you ask a guest to soil his boots on other men's excrement?'

'It's this or nothing, sire. Be grateful for the chance. You'll take a flogging from the priest if you foul yourself inside his church.'

Thaddeus had already noticed the tower, sheltering amongst trees some two hundred paces farther to the west. He could also see a nearer building, which he guessed was the guard house where he'd spent the previous day. He could have wished to return to it, since he doubted the priest's company would be as congenial as the soldiers'. 'He should worry more about the filth you trample on his floor. God asks more of men than that they behave like pigs.' He nodded to a small, planked bridge which carried a path across the channel. 'Is that the route we'll take?'

'It is.'

'Then allow me to stop on it and perform the function there. I have more respect for my Maker than to carry the stench of this place into his house.'

It was hard to say what the younger guards made of him. He was a full head taller than they were and, though his age was no greater than theirs, his thick black beard made him look closer to thirty than twenty. They'd abandoned any thought of trying to restrain him after he'd prised the captain's fingers off his arm in the chamber. He was willing to accompany them, he said, if only to find out why he'd been confined all night in a stinking storeroom, but he had an aversion to being touched. The pain on the captain's face as the bones of his palm were crushed in a giant fist persuaded the others to keep their distance.

'Your lord and priest lack education,' he murmured as he rebuttoned himself and stepped from the bridge, gathering the chain into his hands again. 'It's the habit of animals to pollute their ground and water in this way. I expect to find such foolishness in towns where land is limited, but not in a demesne like this.'

One soldier eyed him curiously. 'What other method is there?'

'The Bible tells us to bury our excrement.' Thaddeus gestured to the grassland around them. 'In a single day, a dozen men could dig a large enough pit to take the waste of the whole household for a year. Open sewers attract vermin. Do you enjoy the thought of your food being defiled by rats which carry other men's faeces on their fur?'

The soldier shrugged. 'We don't see many. The steward has a hatred of them and orders their nests destroyed. Rumour has it he found rats in his bed when he was a child and has had a fear of them ever since. The same with mice.'

'His instincts serve him well,' said Thaddeus mildly. 'You'd be wise to follow his example.' He glanced along the channel towards the river. 'He should worry as much about polluted water. To bathe in sewage is worse than not bathing at all.'

'We do neither.'

Thaddeus gave a grunt of amusement. 'Indeed. The reek of sour sweat blowing off your clothes would fell an ox.' He continued along the path. 'Come. I'm interested in meeting your priest. It's an unchristian nature that condemns a shy little sparrow to Hell because she had the misfortune to fall ill of the pestilence.'

◈

The church was twice the size of Develish's, and it was a moment before Thaddeus's eyes were well enough adjusted to the gloom to see the figure of a man before the unlit altar. He wore a long black vestment with a cowl pulled over his head and he seemed to be struggling to set fire to the char in a tinderbox. The impatient click of flint on fire-steel echoed loudly in the vaulted chamber. He half turned at the sound of approaching steps.

'Are you practised in the use of a tinderbox, Thurkell? I seem unable to strike a spark this morning.'

The voice was the imposter's, and his question so blatant a trick that it would have brought a smile to Thaddeus's face had he been a mere observer to this piece of mummery. Instead, he looked about the church, showing more interest in the murals on the wall than the man at the altar. He understood now why the guildsmen had been so uneasy two nights before. They'd been brave to voice any thoughts at all in front of a priest who condemned townsfolk as fornicators and thieves, let alone caution Thaddeus to be wary of him.

The captain stepped in front of him to catch his attention. 'Father Aristide addresses you, sire,' he said.

Thaddeus frowned. 'He does? Then I'm confused. Do names count for nothing in Blandeforde? Is this not the person who told me he was Jacques d'Amiens? Was he lying to me then or do you lie to me now?' When he received no answer, he raised a manacled wrist to point at a silk-robed depiction of St Nicholas, carrying the Christ child across a river upon his shoulder. 'Would that be the face of Lord Blandeforde? I see the shadow of an older image behind it, so the figure must have been painted recently. Is the likeness a true one?'

'It is, sire.'

'How strange. For myself, I would hesitate to display my arrogance so openly.' He turned to address the priest. 'I came for explanations. Begin with why I've been brought to this church under restraint.'

'You know the reason.'

'I do not, unless Blandeforde treats all his guests in the same way. Is he touched in the mind that he imagines himself to be a richly robed saint while demanding penance from visitors?'

'It's God who demands penance from you.'

'Perhaps so, but only He knows how much.'

The priest stared at him for a moment before instructing the captain to take his men outside. When the door had closed behind them, he pushed back his cowl and beckoned Thaddeus to approach the altar. 'Let's be done with pretence,' he encouraged. 'There's no escape from the trials that await you. The steward is set on punishing you as an example to others. He fears rebellion across his master's vassal demesnes if every base-born serf thinks he can feign nobility.'

Thaddeus took the flint and the fire-steel from the altar. 'If you speak of your pretence at being a priest, then I agree,' he said, striking sparks onto the char cloth and blowing on the embers to encourage a flame. 'On my reckoning, you've missed the hour of Terce by sixty minutes.' He held a splint to the flame.

'You're foolish to mock. Be grateful for this chance to purge your sins while you can still speak.'

Thaddeus lit each candle in turn. 'Who offers me this chance?'

'I do.'

Thaddeus pinched the end of the splint between his fingers and studied the man's face through the drift of smoke that rose from it. 'Any deceiver can don a priest's vestments. Who vouches for you? Certainly not the guildsmen who referred to you as the steward two nights ago.'

'You heard the captain address me by name five minutes ago.'

'I've no more reason to believe him than I have you. Why would God have spared Father Aristide when every other priest in Blandeforde is dead? What marks him out for saintliness? Does he honour his vows to comfort the dying with more sincerity than his fellows?'

He was surprised at how easily the other was provoked when he saw a flush of anger rise in Aristide's cheeks. Or was it shame? Whichever, Thaddeus took heart from the display of emotion, since he didn't doubt the priest had been tasked with teasing a confession from him. A man who couldn't be riled would be harder to manage than one who rose to every bait, yet he questioned why a confession was necessary if Hugh de Courtesmain's allegations of imposture were believed.

'You accuse Blandeforde of arrogance but yours is worse,' Aristide snapped. 'Pride will be your downfall. You think you can speak and act with impunity, but your crimes are so numerous God will have His vengeance—if not in this life, then in the next.'

Thaddeus shifted his gaze to the south-facing chancel window. Through the panes he could see the graveyard, and beyond, the river. He wondered what his chances were of shaking off the guards and swimming to the far bank. Since none bathed, he doubted they'd learnt the skill of staying afloat, but he knew he'd fare no better, dressed as he was in the full regalia of a lord and carrying the weight of shackles. 'What crimes do you say I've committed?' he asked.

'Murder . . . thievery . . . imposture . . . heresy. You embraced Satan when you denied the authority of the Church.'

Thaddeus gave an involuntary laugh. 'Then it's a mystery I've avoided God's vengeance for so long.' He glanced back when the priest made no answer. 'What crimes did the young maid commit to warrant His wrath? The fighting men called her Little Sparrow because of her shyness, but I find it hard to imagine that a timid, illiterate child was guilty of anything as venal as heresy.'

'She judged herself to be wicked when the signs of the pestilence first appeared on her neck.'

The guards had told a different story but Thaddeus let the falsehood pass. 'Did Father Aristide offer comfort and absolution? He will have known from her confessions that her view of herself was flawed.'

'No priest can decide a person's worth. Only God sees into our hearts.'

'Indeed . . . yet it's hard to understand why He found so little worth in the clergy of Blandeforde that He allowed them to perish along with those they tended. Is that not the puzzle the guildsmen wanted explaining?' A glint of irony appeared in Thaddeus's dark eyes. 'How would Father Aristide have answered them had he been there?'

This time there was no mistaking anger for shame. The priest slammed his fist upon the altar, causing the candle flames to flicker. 'You're a slave . . . the bastard son of a harlot . . . incubus to a black-hearted woman who stole her husband's demesne by denying him access to it. And you dare accuse *Aristide* of perfidy?'

Perfidy . . . It was an interesting choice of word. 'I imagine he accuses himself,' Thaddeus murmured, placing his hand on the wooden cross at the centre of the altar to steady it. 'There are kinder ways to separate the sick from the healthy than to persuade an innocent maid she's too evil to live amongst righteous people.'

'She left of her own free will.'

'I doubt that.' He repeated the thoughts he'd shared with the soldiers in the woodland. 'A ten-year-old would have been fearful even to seek solace from her family after being told the town was full of thieves and fornicators. God was merciful to allow her to live long enough to learn she'd been sold a bag of lies. She received more kindness and charity in five days from sinners than she ever did here.'

'You speak from ignorance.'

'Maybe so, but her story's no different from others I've heard. Do you think you're alone in shunning those you suspect of having the pestilence? Or that sufferers don't feel anguish to die in wretched abandonment?'

Aristide's face darkened. 'You must know this better than I, for you condemned your sworn lord to die in such a way.'

Thaddeus allowed a frown of puzzlement to crease his brow. 'Now *you* speak from ignorance. What is it you fear? That your lies about absolution and cleansing rituals will be exposed?' He turned back to the window when the priest made no answer. 'The steward should have ordered a hospital built on the cleared land beyond the river,' he said, nodding to the trees on the other side. 'More of the townsfolk might have survived had the sick been given care away from their families and neighbours. It won't please Blandeforde to find that his paying tenants have perished while his unproductive household lives. What use will a hundred servants be to him when the King demands his taxes and the Church her tithes?'

'God will provide.'

'I pray you're right,' Thaddeus responded dryly, 'for I doubt many cooks know how to drive a furrow through compacted earth.'

Behind him, he heard the sound of the door to the priest's chamber creak open, followed by the scuff of boots across the rushes on the church floor. He made out two sets of steps—the first determined and strong, the second faltering—and it didn't require much guesswork to tell him the bolder tread was Jacques d'Amiens' and the weaker Hugh de Courtesmain's.

If this was to be his trial, he thought, his chances of escaping justice were slim. It wouldn't matter how cleverly he tied Hugh de Courtesmain in knots, or how poorly the Frenchman gave his evidence, the zealous steward and self-righteous priest would find Athelstan guilty.

ର୍ଚ

Ian explained to Lady Anne that there were only two ways to Blandeforde: to return along the riverbank, or to ride down the Shafbury to Dorchester highway in the hope Edumund was right that a crossroad he'd seen some mile to the south would take them to the Blandeforde road. The riverbank, being completely encroached by forest, would have to be walked and might take upwards of five hours; the highway could be done on horseback at greater speed, making their arrival earlier. Lady Anne chose horseback.

'If we had time to spare, I would prefer to go on foot,' she said with a wry smile, 'but since we do not, I beg you to ignore my groans and sighs. I had forgotten how painful it is to sit astride a horse.'

'There's no shame in groaning, milady,' said Peter. 'We all cursed mightily the first time we rode any distance.'

Ian looked towards the saddlebags which were piled beneath a tree. 'You might be more comfortable if you're willing to sit across one of our laps, milady,' he said. 'We can fashion a cushion out of Thaddeus's clothes to give you a softer seat, and as long as you hold tight to the horse's mane, you'll not slide so much.'

'I'd hate to be a trouble, Ian.'

'You won't be, milady,' he answered gruffly. 'In any case, Thaddeus will have our hides if he thinks we haven't looked after you properly.'

'Not to mention that you'll be too weary argue his case if you're as sore as we were the day we left Develish,' Peter said. He clapped Edmund on the back. 'You should choose this fellow. He's the strongest of us all except Thaddeus.'

Joshua nodded agreement. 'And the most accomplished rider, milady. He'll give you more support than we can.'

'And see the ruts in the road sooner,' added Olyver. 'It wasn't by accident that we chose him to bring the news of Thaddeus's arrest to you.'

Lady Anne had to take a breath to quell the sudden emotion that rose in her throat. It was one thing to dream of giving her people the chance of freedom, quite another to have the worth of the idea proved through results. These five conducted themselves so well they were quite unrecognisable as the unformed serf boys who'd departed Develish with Thaddeus the previous summer. 'It would be a great kindness if you felt able to oblige me, Edmund.'

Edmund ducked his head in a bow. 'It will be my pleasure, milady. If I had half Ian's cleverness, I'd have thought of it myself before we left the demesne.'

Lady Anne expressed confidence in Ian's saddle-pack cushion, though in truth she viewed it with considerable alarm, since there was no way of attaching it to Edmund's saddle. Both youths seemed to think it was enough to empty one bag, fill the other with soft, woollen clothes, and then lay the central strap and flattened bag along the saddle. Edmund mounted to sit astride the strap, settling the cushion over the pommel and into his lap and then invited Ian to jump Milady backwards into his arms. She was so small and slight that he caught her with ease and placed her to sit sideways in front of him with her legs across his thigh.

'You'll feel more secure if you hold the horse's mane in your right hand and grip my belt at the back with your left,' he said, steering her arm around his waist. 'It's the way your husband used to take Lady Eleanor around the demesne when she was younger.'

'I'd forgotten,' she answered, forbearing to add: *but only at a slow walk*. Sir Richard's riding skills had been so poor, and his fear of Eleanor wriggling so great, that he'd been afraid of falling himself. And for once Lady Anne had sympathy with him. 'What of my bag?' she asked, closing her mind to the dangers of being tossed to the ground at speed.

Ian lifted the packs of gold from behind Edmund's saddle to lighten his mount's load. 'I'll attach it with this and Thaddeus's writing desk to Killer's back, milady,' he said, stepping aside and instructing Edmund to set off. 'We'll follow when we've struck camp. Wait for us at the crossroad if we don't catch up with you sooner.'

Was there ever such a ride? It was surely sinful for a woman of Lady Anne's years to experience such excitement in the arms of a boy half her age. Even more sinful to wish that the arms had been Thaddeus's. Yet she felt every exhilarating moment as Edmund spurred his mount from walk to trot to canter. He steered one-handed, wrapping his left arm about her waist to hold her tight against him, and as her fear of falling lessened, she gave way to the thrill of moving at speed.

She recalled something Thaddeus had written in one of his accounts about his first journey out of Develish. It was a description of the fear and elation he'd felt at riding a bolting horse with ravening hounds at its heels.

It's good to be afraid. In that quarter-hour dash, I felt more alive than I'd done in the twenty years that went before.

ଏ୬

Thaddeus acknowledged Hugh de Courtesmain with a nod, running his gaze over the other's peasant clothes. 'You seem much diminished from the last time I saw you, sir. I thought you set for life as steward at Bourne.'

Hugh cast a look of triumph towards the priest, as if to say Thurkell's acknowledgement of him proved his accusations. 'It's you who wears shackles. Not I.'

'Indeed. God tests us all. I pray Bourne and his people are well, and that it's not through fear of the pestilence returning that you left your post.'

'They are well.'

'I'm glad to hear it. Did you ignore my advice to work with My Lord and not against him?'

'I was unable to work with him at all. He found his serfs' company more congenial than mine and refused to listen to anything I said.'

A gleam of humour sparked in Thaddeus's dark eyes. 'You should have been more careful, Master de Courtesmain. Ambition is never served well by the spreading of falsehoods. Have you not learnt that by now?'

D'Amiens stirred impatiently. 'Enough. It's your deceit that's in question not this man's.' He moved to the altar and placed several rolls of parchment in front of the cross, selecting one to read before handing it to Thaddeus. 'Do you recognise this letter? De Courtesmain tells me you left it for him to find when you departed Bourne. It's signed Thaddeus Thurkell. How so when you're now calling yourself My Lord of Athelstan?'

Thaddeus scanned the words to remind himself of what he'd written. 'I remember it well,' he agreed. 'I wrote it in friendship to try to help de Courtesmain keep his position. I doubted he had the ability to stay long in Bourne's good graces—' he replaced the scroll on the altar—'and I was right.'

'Why is it signed Thaddeus Thurkell?'

Thaddeus shrugged. 'It's the name by which de Courtesmain knew me when he first came to Develish. He grew embittered when he learnt my true status. I thought he'd take Thurkell's advice more readily than Athelstan's.'

'You call the preaching of heresy and insurrection "advice"?'

'I was merely repeating what Bourne believes,' Thaddeus answered. 'Blandeforde too, in all probability. There won't be a landowner anywhere who isn't counting the cost of the pestilence to his revenues and working out how best to manage the serfs who remain to him. Bourne chose to bring his together on one demesne and offer them rewards for increased production. Will you accuse *him* of heresy and insurrection? He seeks only to protect the land the King gave him, and the position and responsibilities bestowed on him by God.'

D'Amiens eyed him thoughtfully. 'Explain why you went by a different name in Develish from the one you're claiming now.'

Thaddeus nodded to the priest. 'For the same reason this man called himself Jacques d'Amiens when he came to my camp. It suited my purpose for the brief time I was there.'

The answer seemed to throw d'Amiens. He turned to Hugh de Courtesmain with a frown. 'You said Thurkell was born in Develish.'

'He was . . . to a harlot called Eva. She was already with child when she arrived in Develish and looked to pass the infant off as her husband's once they were wed. I heard the story from Lady Eleanor who had no reason to lie.'

'How do you answer that?' d'Amiens asked Thaddeus.

'With the contempt it deserves. De Courtesmain's stay in Develish was briefer than mine and he was greatly disliked. Every person in Develish had reason to lie to him.'

'Not Lady Eleanor,' Hugh cried. 'She took me as her confidant and begged me to escort her from the demesne after Sir Richard died.'

'Only because her mother told her you'd refuse. Lady Eleanor wanted to see for herself how far your hypocrisy went. You changed your loyalties so quickly it was hard to keep up with them.'

Hugh turned a haggard gaze on the steward. 'He twists the girl's feelings as falsely as he twists my words. Her hatred for her mother and the Develish serfs was nothing compared to the hatred she had for this—' he pointed a trembling finger at Thaddeus—'*slave*.'

'You surprise me,' d'Amiens said dryly. 'If Lady Eleanor is like other young women, I would have thought the opposite to be true. Whoever this man is, he is not without charm.' He ran the back of his thumb down the stain on his nose as if to point up his own deficiencies. 'What purpose took you to Develish?' he asked Thaddeus.

'I can't tell you that. I gave my pledge never to speak of it.'

'You will make me doubt you if you don't.'

'Then do so. The matter was a private one. Would you have me betray a confidence because a duplicitous steward puts ambition before allegiance to those who employ him?'

'Who can release you from the pledge?'

'My cousin, Lady Anne of Develish.'

'He lies,' protested Hugh. 'There's no familial relationship between them. He took the woman for his whore on her husband's death.'

With a sigh, Thaddeus slammed his elbow into the Frenchman's throat. 'Next time you slur Milady so vilely, I'll have your liver,' he murmured, watching in idle curiosity as de Courtesmain toppled backwards to the floor, gasping for breath. 'You were never deserving of the kindness she showed you.'

Fifteen

ISABELLA SOUGHT OUT HER FATHER and begged him to come to Lady Anne's chamber to speak with Lady Eleanor. 'She's in great distress, Papa, and through my fault. I told her of Thaddeus's arrest and now she fears her mother will be condemned alongside him. I've tried to explain that Milady's in no danger from the Blandeforde steward but she doesn't believe me. She may understand it better if it comes from you.'

Gyles was on the forecourt, having just made his rounds of the boundary wall. 'I'm not the person to do it,' he said. 'You must ask John Trueblood. We all agreed he should govern the demesne in Milady's absence.'

She caught his hand. 'But you told me he tried to stop Milady leaving, Papa, and I fear it will make Lady Eleanor's distress worse if Master Trueblood agrees Milady should never have gone.'

Gyles squeezed her fingers by way of comfort. 'How real is her concern? Is it truly for her mother . . . or only for herself?'

'It seems real to me, Papa. She talked about Lady Anne leaving a letter but she was crying so much I didn't really understand her meaning. I think it has something to do with Master de Courtesmain. She believes her mother will be burnt because Master de Courtesmain was in the great hall when she accused her of heresy.'

Gyles made what he could of these confused ideas. 'Come,' he said, drawing her towards the house. 'We'll talk to the girl together. I'm sure I can persuade her that she worries unnecessarily. It's My Lord of Blandeforde's steward Milady expects to confront, not de Courtesmain.'

But he wondered if he was right after he'd heard what Eleanor had to say. They found her standing at the window of Lady Anne's chamber with a parchment in her hands. Through tears, she told Gyles her mother had written it the afternoon before. 'She placed it atop the gowns in my coffer and I asked her what it was and why she had put it there. She said it was a letter to me which I would be able to read for myself when I was practised enough.'

'She teased Isabella in the same way, milady,' Gyles said gently. 'It's her way of persuading her pupils to work harder at their alphabets. Can you make sense of it?'

Eleanor shook her head. 'There are too many words I've never seen before though she taught me to know the name de Courtesmain, and I see that here.' She stared down at the script. 'I think she wrote it this way so that I wouldn't know what it said before she left.'

Gyles was sure she was right and wondered if Lady Anne had hoped Eleanor would ask for help in deciphering it. 'Will you permit Isabella to read it to you, milady? I'll wait outside while she does. You can be sure she'll not repeat the contents to anyone else unless you give her leave.'

The girl raised anguished eyes. 'What if Mother blames me?'

'For what, milady?'

'Revealing so much to Master de Courtesmain. I said many cruel things about her and he'll remember them all.'

Gyles shook his head. 'She'll not blame you for that, Lady Eleanor. Herself, perhaps, because she knew he wasn't to be trusted, but never you. The words will be kind. Let Isabella read them to you.'

༺༻

My Dear Eleanor,

I worry that my departure will frighten you but beg that you put your trust and faith in our people. They accept you fully as my daughter and will protect you until my return. Have confidence that you will see me again before the week is out.

You have asked me several times about the dreams that have disturbed my sleep this past week. I did not give you an answer, for I knew it would trouble you to learn about them, but I do so now. The images I see are of My Lord of Blandeforde's steward and Hugh de Courtesmain. The steward sits in judgement while de Courtesmain accuses every man, woman and child in Develish of treason and heresy.

I know not if these visions were God-sent, Eleanor, but I do believe I would be wrong to ignore them since hearing of Thaddeus's arrest. It seems his imposture was discovered even before he entered Blandeforde, and that speaks to betrayal by one who carries deep resentments against both him and Develish.

Dear Daughter, only Master de Courtesmain fits that description. Can you understand why I must try to prevent him speaking against Thaddeus and our people? There will be no future for anyone in Develish, yourself included, if all are punished for decisions that I—and I alone—have made.

Be strong and brave, and know that I love you.

> *Your Affectionate Mother,*
> *Anne*

ର୍ତ୍ତ

The sun was still an hour from noon when the column of horses neared the hill from where Thaddeus and his companions had looked down on Blandeforde two days before. Ian, at the head, slowed to a walk to allow the others to draw level with him. 'We're almost there, milady,' he said, signalling a halt. 'When we top that crest, we'll be in sight of the bridge. You said there were preparations you needed to make before we present ourselves.'

She glanced towards the woodland on their left. 'Which can be done inside the privacy of those trees if one of you is kind enough to carry my bag and give me a goatskin of water.'

Ian performed the service for her and, when he returned, he instructed his companions to brush the dust of the road from their liveries and hair and use their own goatskins of water to moisten their cloths and wash their faces. 'We'll let Milady down if we look like paupers,' he told them.

'What's she doing?' asked Peter.

'You'll see.'

It was a quarter-hour before Lady Anne emerged again from the trees and asked Ian to be kind enough to retrieve the bag. She smiled at the look of astonishment on the youth's faces. 'The guards on the bridge won't give us passage if they think me a peasant,' she said.

'You look like a queen, milady,' said Joshua.

'Thank you, Joshua, but a real queen would have a carriage. Can you think of a way to convey me to Blandeforde in a fitting manner? Much as I've enjoyed riding with Edmund, it's hardly seemly for a liege lady to sit across a soldier's lap.'

∞

Ian could only guess at what the guards on the bridge made of their approach. Even when My Lord of Bourne was in Develish, she had never been so finely adorned as she was now, sitting sideways on Killer's saddle. To see her arrayed in blue silk, with gold around her neck and on her fingers, was to be reminded of how high her status really was. Even so, he worried that appearance alone wouldn't be enough to convince the guards to let them pass. Thaddeus had looked every inch a lord and had been denied.

Their progress down the hill was necessarily slow, for Lady Anne's position was too precarious for anything faster than a walk. Ian and Olyver rode at her side, controlling Killer with thin rope halters through the metal loops of his bit strap, while Edmund and Peter followed close behind. At the rear, some ten paces back, came Joshua with the dogs and the pack horses, giving a sense of greater numbers than there were. By the time they reached the bridge, Ian took some relief from the fact that the attention of every guard was fixed on Lady Anne.

He was conscious that the crests on his and his companions' tabards were Athelstan's when they should have been Develish's. Conscious, too, that, even if the guards were different from those two days ago, they would know from what their fellows had told them that Lady Anne's entourage was the same as Thaddeus's. He'd worried about embroiling her in trouble before she ever reached the steward; but when he'd voiced his concerns, she had begged him not to worry, saying her peril would be greater if she rode alone.

Ian discovered the truth of this when they were some two-thirds across the bridge and he could see the way the guards were leering at her. One was moving the circled forefinger and thumb of his right hand up and down the middle finger of his left, another was rubbing his rod within his britches. Perhaps Lady Anne felt his anger for she urged him in a whisper to pay no heed, but he was offended enough on her behalf to act on impulse. The men were ranged at the end of the bridge some fifteen yards distant and, with a command to Olyver to hold fast to Killer, he let drop his rope and spurred his mount from a walk to a canter. The charge was so rapid and unexpected that the line of guards fragmented without a sword or bow being drawn.

Olyver watched his twin wrestle the animal to a halt on the road as the soldiers scattered in disarray towards the riverbank. 'By rights he should be flat on his back on the ground,' he murmured, clicking his tongue to set Killer moving again. 'Only a mad man rides his horse at speed over cobbles.'

'Or a brave one,' Lady Anne said.

Olyver grinned. 'Thaddeus would tell you they're one and the same, milady.'

੭੧੦

The steward took another parchment from the altar and handed it to Thaddeus. 'What is this, if not further evidence of imposture?'

Thaddeus unrolled it and recognised it immediately as a page from the Develish parish register. It was a record of births and deaths in 1328 and towards the bottom he saw his own name. *A sun, Thades, was bor this 2 week of June, 1328, to Wil and Ev Thkell.* The script was poorly formed and the words ill-spelt, and he knew them to be Father Anselm's because it wasn't until Sir Richard's violation of Abigail Startout some decade later that Lady Anne had taken charge of the register. Her anger against the priest for supporting Sir Richard's claim that an unformed maid, yet to reach her eleventh year, was above fourteen and known to have experience of men was so great that she had forbade him from ever recording the lives of her serfs again.

Each page of parchment was held inside the wooden covers of the ledger by leather thongs, threaded through holes on the left-hand side, and he saw the careful snips de Courtesmain had made to allow him to withdraw this page without its removal being obvious. Such planning spoke of the Frenchman's intent to unmask Thaddeus, and by entanglement Lady Anne, even before he knew he would be going to Bourne. There hadn't been time between Lady Anne giving him permission to leave, and his departure three hours later, to extract and hide documents in the chest of clothes he took with him.

Thaddeus scanned the scroll. 'Why should a list of names and dates in a hand I don't recognise suggest imposture? The letters are so poorly drawn and the words so illiterate I would hazard a guess the scribe sought to disguise his own style. Where do you say it comes from?'

D'Amiens watched Hugh de Courtesmain struggle to his feet. 'From the Develish parish record, if this man is to be believed.'

'I've seen that record. It's a detailed history, kept by Lady Anne. She was taught the art of inscription by nuns and has a fine hand which looks nothing like this.'

'It's rare for a lady to have such a skill.'

'Milady is a rare woman, Master d'Amiens. As you should know since you've met her.'

'You credit me with too much knowledge. I've never had the pleasure of speaking with her. She always stood in the shadow of her husband, ready to prompt him with answers that would satisfy me.' D'Amiens turned to Hugh. 'Explain why the document is so flawed.'

'At the time of Thurkell's birth, the scribe was Father Anselm,' muttered Hugh. 'Lady Anne discharged him from the responsibility some ten years ago. The reason why is unknown to me, but she holds the priest in great animosity . . . and he her.'

With a shrug, Thaddeus handed the page back to d'Amiens. 'Anselm must have lived well beyond his natural span for his hand to have been trembling so badly more than two decades ago. What age does de Courtesmain say he's claiming?'

Hugh stared at him with loathing. 'You know the cause as well as I,' he snapped. 'The priest is an inebriate. His office weighs heavily on him because of his mistress's rejection of the Church and the heretical beliefs she teaches her people.'

Thaddeus's eyes creased with amusement. 'You should rehearse your history before you assign yet more villainy to Lady Anne, Master de Courtesmain. Whatever ailed Father Anselm when he

was appointed to the benefice of Develish could not have origi-
nated with her. He was in position a good eight years before
Sir Richard brought her to the demesne as a bride of fourteen.'

There was a lengthy silence which was finally broken by Father
Aristide. 'This man offers other documents to prove you're a
base-born serf. Will you deny them all?'

It was a foolish question. 'What else would you have me do?
Admit de Courtesmain tells the truth? At least acknowledge that
my age alone rules me out of being a serf called Thurkell. My years
are thirty but, if this man lives, he has yet to pass twenty-one.'

The priest gave an uneasy shrug. 'De Courtesmain has less
reason to lie than you. He gains nothing by what he does.'

Thaddeus smiled slightly. 'I doubt you're wise to disappoint
him so early, Father. Treachery looks more enticing when it's
rewarded with thirty pieces of silver.'

☙

Ian hadn't counted on people leaving their houses to watch Lady
Anne's passage. He was used to riding through towns which
seemed deserted, with only the odd glimpse of faces at open doors
and unshuttered windows to show that anyone had survived. To
say the streets of Blandeforde were thronged would be an exag-
geration, but enough were drawn by the sight of a richly gowned
lady to give a sense of numbers.

For Lady Anne, it was her first experience of the despair most
felt to still be alive. She saw the early signs of starvation in the
hollow eyes of children who had been left to fend for themselves
on the deaths of their parents, and the seeming lack of purpose
in men who stood listlessly at corners, barely speaking with each
other. More particularly, she was struck by the empty expressions

of widows who stood alone and bereft before houses that had once been filled with laughter. It was as if the women had turned in on themselves, so consumed by their own woes that they barely noticed the trials and tribulations of others. She asked Ian why this should be. Would they not benefit from taking the orphans into their homes?

'You would think so,' he answered, 'but we see the same everywhere we go. Thaddeus says it's because their priests are dead and there's no one to guide them. When men are without answers—worse, believe the pestilence will take us all in the end—women lose their resolve. It's hard to make decisions for yourself when your life has been lived in obedience to others.'

Lady Anne looked ahead to where a cluster of men was gathered outside a church. 'What of the three guildsmen who were at your camp two nights ago?' she asked Ian. 'Are they not leaders here?'

He shook his head to say he didn't know.

'Do you remember their names?'

'The one who talked the most was called Andrew Tench, milady. He said he was a wool merchant.'

She nodded to the group by the church. 'Will you halt us there and ask for him to be brought to me? It's surely right to offer hope if we can.'

Ian kept to himself that Thaddeus had tried the same many times and had learnt that it took days of persuasion to convince survivors to embrace life. A person on his own, such as the fisherman or Robin Pikeman might listen to a quarter-hour of reasoned sense, but a company of more than two rarely did. It was as if their minds were so firmly set on death that resistance to hearing good news was strengthened in proportion to their numbers.

He was surprised, therefore, when his request that Master Tench be summoned to speak with Lady Anne of Develish was greeted with warmth. A young urchin was dispatched and an old man dropped to one knee. 'We've heard stories of Develish from travellers who've passed through our town, milady. They say the village is deserted but a multitude of men and women in peasant clothing are alive inside the moat. It leads us to wonder if their lord seeks to protect his serfs from the pestilence.'

Ian answered when Lady Anne hesitated. 'The lord of Develish is this lady,' he said. 'The responsibility for her husband's demesne fell to her when Sir Richard died away from home, and, yes, she has sought from the beginning to protect all her people—be they nobles, freemen or serfs.'

'We could wish our own lord as generous.'

'Is he here?' asked Lady Anne, wondering if Bourne's captain of arms had led her false the previous autumn by saying Blandeforde had left for his estates in the west.

'He is not, milady. He abandoned us when news of the pestilence first arrived.'

'Who acts on his behalf?'

'The steward, Master d'Amiens, who takes his instructions from the priest.'

Lady Anne saw discomfort in the faces of the younger men around him, as if they felt he'd been more honest than he should. 'Would that be My Lord of Blandeforde's confessor? Why did he leave him behind?'

The greybeard made to spit on the ground but thought better of it when the hand of one of his companions gripped his shoulder. 'Father Aristide would make any journey burdensome, milady.'

There was a bustle of movement behind him as a man of middle years with a sheepskin collar about his cloak pushed through the small crowd and presented himself to Lady Anne with a bow. 'You summoned me, milady. I am your obedient servant, Andrew Tench. How may I be of service to you?'

He had a pleasant, if careworn, face and she dipped her own head in acknowledgement. 'I sought rather to be of service to you and the people of your town, sir. I see children looking hungry, men without purpose standing at corners, and women, alone and sad, in doorways. Is there a reason why all feel so lost and desolate?'

'Each one of us has had to watch our families die before our eyes, milady.'

'And for that I am deeply sorry, Master Tench. The pestilence is a cruel disease.' She glanced from one man to the next. 'God cries out in pain each time another innocent dies . . . as all of you will have done to see your beloved wives and children perish. But is that cause to turn your backs on the widows and orphans of your neighbours?'

They shuffled their feet as if the question had been put to them before. 'Master Tench has argued the same, milady, as have I,' said the greybeard, pushing himself upright, 'but these fellows—' he gestured towards the crowd—'would rather debate issues of property than the welfare of women and children.'

Tench placed a calming hand on the older man's arm. 'Many of us would willingly take the needy into our homes, milady— God knows we are all in want of companionship—but none can agree on how to do it. The man who offers his home to a widow, rich in property, will double his wealth overnight if she agrees to tie her assets to his. Orphaned sons of successful merchants are as prized.'

Lady Anne nodded understanding. 'For the value of their inheritances.'

'Yes, milady.'

'It's a great problem,' she said thoughtfully.

Tench nodded. 'Master Slater and I—' he indicated the greybeard—'have proposed drawing lots, but most resist the idea for fear of picking badly. Concern about the pestilence remains strong and few wish to invite it into their homes through ill chance. It's but eight weeks since the last sufferer was buried.'

Lady Anne had heard this from Edmund when she'd asked him to repeat as much as he could remember of Thaddeus's conversation with the guildsmen. 'Eight weeks is a long time, Master Tench. Did my cousin Athelstan not tell you that towns to the south have been without deaths since Christmas? God willing, we can dare to hope that Dorseteshire's suffering is almost over.'

He looked startled. 'My Lord is your cousin, milady?'

'He is, sir, and has travelled the land, seeking and dispersing news so that all who survive may know they're not alone. I trust he gave you reasons to believe in a future free of the pestilence. His men tell me you spoke with him two nights ago.'

Tench stared at her in horror. 'We did our best to warn him, milady.'

Her kind eyes smiled into his. 'About what, Master Tench?'

'The fate that awaited him, milady.'

The greybeard gave a grunt of impatience. 'There's no sense mouthing riddles,' he said. 'Milady wouldn't be here if she didn't know of the arrest.' He raised his gaze to Lady Anne's. 'If it's information you seek, I can tell you the little we know. The steward's guards brought your cousin through the town in chains two nights ago after three of our people were ordered to meet him. The priest told them he was an absconding serf, looking to pass for a lord, and tasked them with unmasking him. He thought an English peasant would speak more openly with men of his own kind.'

Lady Anne pretended surprise. 'How strange. Whatever gave the priest such ideas?'

The greybeard shook his head to say he didn't know.

She turned to Tench. 'Was my cousin easily mistaken for a serf?'

'Not at all, milady. I doubt I've ever seen so fine a noble. Father Aristide feigned the role of steward in order to question him on matters of heresy, but I heard nothing untoward in what My Lord said.'

'Then why does the Father accuse him of imposture?'

'We don't know, milady, unless the allegation was made by the Frenchman who entered the town from the north some dozen days ago. He demanded to be taken to Master d'Amiens, claiming to be a messenger, but since none is allowed to approach My Lord's house, we could only point out the direction he should take.'

'Was he on horseback?'

'No, milady, he came on foot. Had he not declared himself a messenger, we would not have taken him for one. He shrank from us, calling us filthy and unclean, and jumped at every shadow, believing they were rats.'

The greybeard gave a grunt of contempt. 'I've never seen such a pitiful creature. Mind, he must have had a good tale to tell, because the steward stationed guards on the bridge after speaking with him.' He glanced towards the river. 'It's a pity he didn't have the sense to do it months ago. More might have survived if the bridge had been closed when news of the pestilence first reached us.'

Once again, Lady Anne saw disquiet in the faces of those around him, as if they feared his intemperate speech would reach d'Amiens' ears. 'Was the messenger of small stature with dark hair and thin features . . . aged some thirty years?'

'He was, milady.'

She gave silent thanks to God for her dreams. 'Then all is explained,' she said. 'I know this man and he is not to be trusted. He uses deceit to win positions of favour, and I don't doubt he hopes to do the same here.' She glanced from one face to another in the group. 'Good sirs, am I right to understand from Master Tench's words that there is little communication between you and your lord's household?'

'You are, milady,' called a man from the back. 'The steward looks to the priest to keep the house cleansed of sin and has barred entry to the townsfolk for fear they'll bring their wicked-ness with them.'

Andrew Tench pointed to the church behind him, where several parchments were nailed to the door. 'Guards come from time to time to post these writs, milady, but we see no one else.'

'What sort of writs?'

'Reminders of when our rents and taxes are due, milady. Most were able to pay last quarter day but, without commerce, none will have the wherewithal on the next. The town tax is the most onerous, for it remains unchanged despite there being fewer to pay it. We've tried to send warning of this to the steward but have had no reply. He reserves his care for My Lord's servants.'

Lady Anne doubted that. She thought it more likely d'Amiens' care was for himself, since he had a better chance of saving his own skin if he kept the household free of the pestilence. She asked to see the most recent writ, and it was torn from the door and passed forward to Master Tench, who prepared to read the words aloud. She would have allowed him to do so had Olyver not seen benefit in earning the crowd's respect. With a smile, he leant down and took the parchment from Tench's hands, saying Lady Anne would prefer to read it for herself.

She did so, and her expression when she'd finished was pensive. 'Do you commonly pay taxes in grain and foodstuffs?' she asked Tench. 'It's the practice on demesnes, but I would have thought coinage or silver a more normal currency in towns.'

'We pay in any way we can, milady. Some were grateful that the guards were ordered to seize grain from the communal store in lieu of silver last quarter day.'

'We think the steward uses it to feed the household,' said the greybeard. 'If so, he's stealing from us. We keep the grain for selling not for eating.'

'There's no one to buy it,' called the man at the back. 'You know this, Master Slater. It's months since merchants came from outside. Better we keep our silver than grain we can't use.'

The greybeard gave a grunt of impatience. 'It's time you took thought for the future, Miller. You'll change your mind when your own stores run out. Not one of us will be greedy for silver when we've nothing to eat.'

Andrew Tench nodded. 'It's these concerns we wish to raise with the steward, milady.'

She placed the writ on her lap. 'I will do my best on your behalf when I speak with him,' she said, 'though I fear he'll pay as little heed to me as to you. Men who close their eyes to the troubles of others usually close their ears as firmly.'

A wry expression crossed Tench's face. 'Do you accuse us of the same thing, milady?'

'I do, sir. The town needs leadership but you waste your time squabbling.'

The man at the back raised his voice again. 'The last of our council died before Christmas. Since then we've been without elders because none can agree on who should take the authority.'

Lady Anne smiled slightly. 'Then I despair of you, Master Miller. Do you think Develish could have survived the pestilence if my people were as mean-spirited as the men of Blandeforde? It takes courage and generosity to keep a community alive. Are those qualities absent here?'

'We ask only for a fair distribution of property,' he answered irritably. 'If you know of a way to achieve that, then tell us.'

He reminded Lady Anne of Will Thurkell, who was always first to complain that his share of food was smaller than his neighbour's. Yet the looks of approval on the faces of those around him whenever he spoke suggested he had a following. 'Explain what you mean by fair, sir, and I will do my best to oblige you.'

'Wealthy widows should go to poor men, impoverished widows to the rich. By such methods, all will be equal.'

'And what do the widows say? Does the woman who's worked hard to help grow her dead husband's wealth agree that it should go to a man too lazy and profligate to accumulate anything?'

Her words were greeted with a scowl. 'Do you accuse me of laziness?'

'I accuse you of nothing, sir, for I don't know you.' She paused. 'I merely question your interpretation of fairness. Where's the justice in bartering women and children like cattle so that envious men can feel the equal of their more successful neighbours?'

Miller shrugged. 'I can barely sustain myself. How do you expect me to feed more mouths on the little I have?'

'I don't,' Lady Anne answered lightly. 'If what you tell me is true, you're in no position to welcome anyone into your house. My advice would be that only the men who can afford to be generous should put their names forward.'

'Thereby enriching themselves further. How is that fair?'

'You're as free as any man here to do the same, sir. In Develish even those with the least share what they have with others.' She dropped her gaze to his midriff. 'You have a handsome girth, so could it be you have more in your cupboards than you pretend?' A ripple of amusement ran through the crowd and she shifted her gaze back to Tench and the greybeard. 'Your idea of drawing lots is a good one, but I would urge you to ask the widows and orphans to make the pick. Since God will be guiding their hands, no one can begrudge the choices they make.'

There was a short silence before the greybeard gave a throaty chuckle. 'You have a fine way of solving problems, milady. Now tell us how to choose leaders. I warrant you'll not find that as easy.'

She laughed. 'I warrant you're right, Master Slater, since you all seem more intent on fighting than advancing the cause of your people.'

'That's the truth of it,' he agreed. 'Even so, there are some amongst us who would appreciate your thoughts. You've spoken more sense in a quarter-hour than I've heard in months. What would you advise?'

She looked around the group, which had more than doubled in size since she and her companions had first halted. 'Choose one man and task him with picking the rest. You will argue less over a single name than you do over several.'

'Many will vie for such authority,' called Miller.

'Then be wise in whom you select. For myself, I would want the man who finds most fault in the steward and the priest, for it would give me confidence that his loyalty lies with the town and not the house.'

'There's only one who fits that description,' he answered. 'You'd choose Jeremiah Slater, never mind he loves to berate us for our failings.'

Lady Anne nodded to Ian that it was time to leave. 'I would, sir . . . and afterwards, were I Master Slater, I would choose you. You have a good mind and a loud voice and, if you're willing to lay your grievances aside, you'll make a fine leader. There are other ways for men to prove themselves than by swelling their coffers with widows' gold.'

'But none so tempting.' He stared hard at her for a moment and then, as if his mind was suddenly made up, he shouldered his way forward to stand beside Tench and the greybeard. 'Come,' he called to the crowd. 'If Milady is willing to express our concerns to the steward then the least we can do is walk with her to the gates of the house.'

*I, Hugh de Courtesmain, steward to Lady Anne of Develish,
swear by Our Lord Jesus Christ that everything written
here is true. Should I die of the pestilence—and this vellum
be found—I beg that whoever reads it will take it to My Lord
of Blandeforde or His Grace the Bishop of Sarum and ask
that prayers be said for my soul. Be confident that Hugh de
Courtesmain is innocent of all wrongdoing and stands alone
amongst the inhabitants of Develish in remaining true to the
Church and the King.*

*I write this record without Lady Anne's knowledge or
permission, for it is she who must answer for what has been
done here when the pestilence has passed. Her heresies are
numerous and she infects her people with them, inciting serfs
to break their oaths of allegiance and conduct themselves as
freemen. Even the priest fails to discharge his duties as he
should, cowering inside his room through fear of the evil that
surrounds him.*

*The King's taxes and the Church's tithes have been
squandered on feeding a multitude of base-born men and
women who have taken refuge in their lord's house. They treat
it as their own and assume entitlement to everything inside.*

My unhappy situation—being bound to Develish through promises I made to Sir Richard before his death—forces me to hold my tongue over each new sacrilege committed, but the truth of what my pen writes cannot be silenced.

Develish is well named. If God be present here, I do not see Him.

The worst of men goes by the name of Thaddeus Thurkell. He was born a slave and is shameless in his overturning of God's social order, taking powers to himself by virtue of the unnatural favours the widow of his liege lord bestows on him. Lady Anne debases herself and her class by making herself his whore.

Thurkell is a common thief and bandit, acting outside the laws of the Church and the King. In early September, he roamed the countryside with five companions, destroying villages at will and stealing whatever he could find. There is no sin or crime this man will not commit in service to himself and the woman he calls Mistress. He is a confessed thief and liar and, unless I miss my guess, a murderer also. It is beyond comprehension that all in the villages he has burnt were dead, yet neither he nor his companions show repentance. Instead they boast of their exploits, looking to receive admiration from the people who crowd about them wherever they go.

Along with 200 sheep and a wagon full of grain, he has delivered a Norman hostage, My Lord of Bourne, to Develish.

My Lord's age and infirmity make him quite unable to
withstand the many terrors inflicted upon him by Thurkell.
In return for his life and freedom, he has agreed to falsify
a letter of accreditation, naming the man who bears it as
My Lord of Athelstan.

Thurkell and his band plan to leave Develish on the first
day of 1349, arrayed in finery once belonging to Sir Richard.
Milady makes no secret of her approval of these men, labouring
long hours with her seamstresses to stitch fine apparel for
them. Since everything they wear or carry will be embossed
with the crest of Athelstan, it is clear that Thurkell's intention
is to pretend nobility in order to steal more easily from the
unfortunates he and his men encounter.

Every person in Develish is complicit in the deceit—even the
children. The intent of all is to free themselves from bondage,
and Thurkell goes with their blessing to find the means to
achieve this ambition. My guess is he plans to win the confidence
of lords and freemen in order to cheat them out of their gold.

The crest and title have been bestowed on him by Lady
Anne of Develish, who claims descent from Godwin of Wessex,
father to the usurper Harold who was defeated in battle by
the rightful King, William of Normandy. In wickedness and
complicity in his crimes, she has permitted a base-born slave to

claim royal English blood through a designation lost when her maternal grandfather died without male issue.

Let these words of mine be shouted across the country if I am not alive to testify to them when the pestilence has passed.

The man who calls himself Athelstan was born Thaddeus Thurkell, the bastard son of a Develish harlot, reared in bondage without land or property to call his own. He may be recognised through the quickness of his mind, the tallness of his build, the darkness of his skin, the blackness of his hair and the heresy in his heart. He is twenty years of age but has the look of a man ten years older. He is well educated, and reads and writes as fluently as any scribe.

In nomine Patris et Filii et Spiritus Sancti

Sixteen

THE SEVEN REMAINING SCROLLS CONTAINED de Courtesmain's record of his stay in Develish. D'Amiens took them one by one from the altar and allowed Thaddeus time to read them, and since Thaddeus saw merit in stalling for as long as he could, he lingered long over each parchment. In themselves they proved nothing, since they were written in de Courtesmain's own hand, but they made compelling reading. The angriest, denouncing Thaddeus as a thief and a murderer, had clearly been written in Develish; but from the differences of ink and vellum, Thaddeus guessed the others had been composed in Bourne.

It was hard to say what de Courtesmain's purpose had been in writing them because their tone was so bitter and vengeful they read more like a rambling reassurance to the writer that he was a good man amongst heathens than a well-constructed accusation. He painted himself throughout as an honest, God-fearing innocent, obliged to live amongst heretics for half a year, and called on God to witness his innocence as often as he condemned Lady Anne and Thurkell for their guilt. Indeed, so strong were his protestations of continued dedication to the Church that Thaddeus wondered if, in truth, he hadn't been trying to quell a voice of dissent in his own head.

He couldn't fault the Frenchman's memory. Every Develish secret was laid bare—from Lady Anne's encouragement to her serfs to bid for freedom through to Eleanor's revelation that Milady was not her mother—and, though Thaddeus toyed with dismissing it all as the workings of an imaginative mind, he knew the steward and priest would not believe him. No one could invent so elaborate a story and transcribe it in such detail to the page.

Thaddeus passed the last scroll back to d'Amiens without comment.

'Well?' the steward demanded. 'Is all this true?'

'As true as your priest's claim that he keeps the household free of the pestilence through the cleansing of sin.'

'What other truth is there?'

'That you and he are using the same methods Lady Anne employs. First, strive to keep the pestilence out by closing your gates, and then be ready to remove any who succumb. Milady would have taken Develish sufferers outside the moat and cared for them herself, but you and this man—' he glanced towards the priest—'chose to banish yours for wickedness.' He smiled cynically. 'Which truth do you prefer, Master d'Amiens?'

'It's not a case of preference. If the Church cites wickedness as the cause of the pestilence, who am I to argue differently?' The steward placed the scroll with the others on the altar. 'Tell me how Master de Courtesmain's account is flawed.'

Thaddeus glanced towards the Frenchman. His only recourse was to keep discrediting him. 'In his depiction of himself. Had he mentioned his many deceits, you would struggle to believe anything he said.'

'Name one.'

'His constant switching of allegiance. It was hard to know from one day to the next where his loyalties lay. It made him greatly distrusted by the people.'

De Courtesmain appealed to the steward. 'They had a hatred of Normans,' he cried. 'Sir Richard and Lady Eleanor felt their dislike as much as I did.'

Thaddeus gave an involuntary laugh. 'You're an ungrateful fellow,' he said. 'You were given the chance to leave after Sir Richard died. Why didn't you take it, if Develish was the Hell you portray in your writings?'

'The pestilence was at the gates.'

'You know it was not. We saw people moving north for several weeks afterwards. You were free to go whenever you wanted, yet you describe yourself as a prisoner.' Thaddeus looked back to the steward. 'He had more faith in Milady's ability to keep the pestilence at bay than he did in God's mercy. He's greatly afeared his sins will find him out.'

'Isn't the same true of all men?' asked d'Amiens.

'You tell me, sir. Do you not have confidence in Father Aristide's cleansing rituals?' His lips twitched into another cynical smile. 'I can't blame you if you don't. His inability to strike a spark suggests it's a long time since these altar candles were lit.' He caught the priest's hand as the man made to slap him. 'You and Master de Courtesmain are two of a kind,' he murmured. 'You both look to save your own lives at the expense of others. Do you fear becoming as low as he when your deceits are revealed?'

With relentless pressure, he twisted the priest's arm behind his back and forced him to his knees. The steward moved to intervene but Thaddeus shook his head in warning. 'Nothing would please me more than to wrap my chains around your neck, Master d'Amiens. Be sure de Courtesmain won't come to your assistance. He's more frightened of my anger than he is of yours. He knows I have little patience with hypocrites.'

'You'll compel me to summon the guards.'

'Oblige me by doing so. I'd rather deal with honest men than cowardly liars who pretend a piety they don't have.'

It seemed d'Amiens was as easily provoked as the priest. 'You'd be in your shroud if I had some recollection of you,' he snapped. 'De Courtesmain tells me you've been doing *ad opus* work in Develish for more than a decade, but I have no memory of seeing you there. Be grateful for that. Were it otherwise, I'd have known you for a common serf and ordered the skin flayed from your bones.'

With feigned impatience, Thaddeus released the priest's hand and thrust him away. 'I'm wearied of this nonsense. If it's the truth you want, put de Courtesmain to the question. He'll refute his claims on the mere threat of pain.' He cast a scornful look at the Frenchman. 'He can barely stand for trembling at the lies he's told.'

The sudden thoughtfulness in the steward's expression suggested this ploy might work, but the creak of the church door distracted him. He narrowed his eyes at the captain of the guard who eased through the opening. 'What do you want?' he demanded.

'Lady Anne of Develish is at the gate, sir. She's accompanied by men from the town and is requesting entry. I need your orders.'

A slow smile spread across d'Amiens' face as the captain's words registered with him. 'How fortuitous,' he murmured, turning to

Thaddeus. 'God must be as eager as I to see you released from your pledge. Will Milady's story be the same as yours, I wonder?'

‿◌‿

Ian felt his twin's nervousness as they approached to within a hundred yards of My Lord of Blandeforde's walled enclosure. *This was madness.* On horseback, they could see above the gates, and both were intimidated by the extent of the enclosed land. A bend in the long driveway hid most of the house from their view, but enough of the eastern wall and roof was visible to suggest immense grandeur.

The trembling of Lady Anne's hands on the reins told Ian she was as nervous and he asked her in a whisper if she would like him to bring the column to a halt. She shook her head and answered from a dry mouth that the men of Blandeforde would withdraw their support if they thought her afraid. Ian knew this to be true because the closer they came to the gates, the more the crowd began to drag its heels. Even Master Slater's brow creased with uncertainty at the sight of archers with raised bows on the steps to either side of the barred entrance.

What to do?

Out of the corner of his eye, Ian watched Olyver remove a wooden beaker from the pack that was slung across the saddle in front of him and fill it from the goatskin of water that hung on the other side. He used movements so small they might have been taken for a need to adjust his horse's breast collar, and when he passed the cup quietly to Lady Anne no one noticed. As she sipped from it gratefully, Ian turned in his saddle to beckon Edmund, Peter and Joshua forward.

'Milady asks that we range ourselves in front of these brave townsmen to give them protection,' he called. 'Buckler, ride beside me with the dogs and pack horses. Trueblood and Catchpole, take up positions on the other side. As far as she is able, Milady promises to shield and safeguard all who walk with her.'

At thirty paces, one of the archers ordered the column to halt. 'State your business,' he called in French.

Lady Anne instructed Ian and Olyver to take her closer. She answered in the same language in a clear, untroubled voice. 'My business is with the steward,' she said. 'Send word that Lady Anne of Develish awaits him at the gate.'

'He'll not come for a woman. He answers only to God and My Lord of Blandeforde.'

'Is Master d'Amiens dead?'

'He is not. Why would you ask such a question?'

'Common soldiers don't normally make decisions for stewards.'

'We have our orders.'

'You do indeed,' she said boldly. 'Send word that Lady Anne of Develish awaits Master d'Amiens at the gate.' She gestured to the crowd behind her. 'Be assured neither I nor these men will leave until I've spoken with him.'

It was a good quarter-hour before a liveried captain climbed up next to the archer and instructed Milady to enter alone. She refused, reiterating her request that the steward be brought to her. After another quarter-hour, the captain returned with new orders. If her entourage dismounted and left their horses and weapons outside, they would be allowed to accompany her. She refused again.

The captain shook his head. 'I urge you not to try Master d'Amiens' patience further, milady. It's only out of courtesy to your dead husband's status that he agrees to see you at all.'

She smiled slightly. 'My request is a reasonable one, captain. Before I enter, I ask that the steward presents himself in person so that I can be assured he lives and has true charge of his master's estates.'

'You have my word that he does, milady.'

'Does your word count for more than the men of Blandeforde's, sir? They tell me they haven't seen Master d'Amiens in months. Writs, purporting to be his, are posted by soldiers and all attempts to contact him are met with silence. What should I make of that?'

'Whatever you choose, milady. You've been given the terms on which you may enter. If you accept them, I will open the gates. If you do not, they will remain closed.'

She bent her head in a mocking bow. 'Thank you, sir. I believe that tells me all I need to know.' She twisted around to address the crowd of men behind her, continuing to speak in French so that the captain would understand her. 'You'll find no leadership here. I'll return with you to the town and then ride to Sarum to inform His Grace the bishop that the steward is dead and the house overrun by Norman fighting men. His Grace will know better than I how to reach My Lord of Blandeforde with the news. Meanwhile, I urge you to withhold your taxes for they will surely be stolen by these mercenaries.'

Ian heard a few voices call out for her to speak in English but Master Slater quickly hushed them. ''Er woords be for the Franky gaeky,' he said in Dorset brogue. 'She wan 'en affrighted enow to faetch the stoörd.'

But it seemed the captain was more distressed than afraid. 'Have you not come for your cousin, milady? I felt certain you had. Will you abandon him?'

Both his words and his tone surprised Lady Anne, for they seemed to imply some sympathy with Thaddeus. 'I can't bargain with Norman thieves, sir. However small the ransom you demand for Athelstan's release, it will be above anything Develish can afford. My only recourse is to seek help from the bishop.'

'You malign me and my fighting men unfairly, milady. None of this is our doing.'

'Then bring Master d'Amiens to the gate, sir. I have only to see him for my doubts to be resolved. His appearance is not one that's easily forgotten.'

ତ୍ୟୁ

Thaddeus was thinking the same as he watched d'Amiens rage against the captain. The split nature of the steward's face—more pronounced in anger as blood suffused the livid stain—seemed to mirror his character. His moods swung from light to dark in the blink of an eye. All his earlier triumph in the church to hear that Lady Anne was at the gate had now given way to fury. Yet there was no accounting for the wrath he was unleashing on the unfortunate wretch who stood before him, unless he believed his own authority was strengthened by it.

And perhaps it was. The young guards who'd been ordered to bring Thaddeus to the great hall halted him inside the entranceway, hunching their shoulders and staring at the floor as if fearful of being seen to have sympathy with their captain. For a brief moment, Thaddeus thought about returning outside. With everyone's attention elsewhere, he could walk clear across the forecourt before his absence was noticed. Yet what would it achieve except a few moments of amusement for himself and a torrent of abuse against his guards? There was more to be gained by earning their gratitude than causing them trouble.

D'Amiens seemed most exercised by the captain's inability to implement simple orders. He was a poor, weak-spirited creature. Only a coward would quail before a woman. She was a widow without rights. Blandeforde's terms of entry, as decided by his steward, must always prevail over hers. It mattered nothing that she had townsmen at her side. Were his soldiers incapable of firing arrows?

Thaddeus advanced into the hall with a laugh. 'You attack the wrong person, Master d'Amiens,' he said, lowering himself into the same carved chair the steward had used two nights previously. 'It's hardly your captain's fault that Lady Anne refuses your terms.' He placed his chains on the table. 'Were I less encumbered with iron, I would refuse them also. You have no authority over either of us.'

D'Amiens rounded on him in fury. 'In your case, that is yet to be demonstrated,' he spat. 'As for her, she can only ever be a supplicant in My Lord of Blandeforde's house. Should he choose to grant her a new husband, she will gain status through the marriage, but until then she is subject to my governance as proctor in My Lord's absence.'

Thaddeus felt moved to agree with him, since he had no wish to embroil Lady Anne in his troubles. And yet . . . Just the knowledge of her presence had lightened his heart. 'Perhaps you aren't as knowledgeable as you think you are,' he said mildly. 'Milady draws her status from her father and not her dead husband.' He switched his gaze to the captain. 'What reason does she give for refusing the steward's terms?'

The man turned to him in relief. 'She requests that Master d'Amiens present himself in person to prove he's alive, sire. He so rarely leaves the house that the men of the town are persuaded he's dead.'

'They lie for their own reasons,' said d'Amiens coldly.

Thaddeus doubted that. He thought it more likely the falsehood was Lady Anne's. 'Why do you object to the request?' he asked. 'You demand a great deal of the lady to expect her to enter an armed compound without knowing what awaits her.'

'She's bold enough. The captain tells me she rides on horseback with upwards of fifty men around her . . . and not a chaperone in sight.' A faint smile touched d'Amiens' lips. 'Master de Courtesmain's accusations of harlotry become more credible.'

Thaddeus eased himself back in the chair and placed his feet on the bench that ran lengthways down the table. 'You'll live to regret those words,' he murmured, closing his eyes. 'If the men of Blandeforde don't make you pay for your ill-considered judgements, be sure I will.'

৶৶

There was an audible gasp of surprise—and not a little fear—as the gates swung open to reveal the captain and Master d'Amiens standing some twenty paces back. A dozen guards with drawn bows were ranged at their sides.

Ian and Olyver made to raise their own bows, but Lady Anne stretched out her hands to prevent them. 'I cannot believe Norman soldiers are any more desirous of shedding English blood than we theirs,' she said in French, praying most earnestly that she hadn't misread the captain's sympathy. 'God would not have allowed us to survive the pestilence if He intended us to kill each other.'

She dipped her head to d'Amiens. 'I'm pleased to see you looking so well, sir, but saddened that you feel the need to threaten us. We come in peace, not enmity.'

'You bring too many men with you for me to believe that, milady.'

This time she answered in English. 'But most are your people, Master d'Amiens. What reason do you have to fear them? None is armed. They seek only to explain their difficulties to you.'

He responded in the same language. 'We live in perilous times, milady, and from what I've learnt of Develish, you know this better than I. I'm told you defend your demesne with even more fierceness than I defend My Lord's.'

'But never against those I'm pledged to protect, Master d'Amiens,' she said in French. 'The vows of allegiance that bind me to my people are as sacred as those that bind them to me. Would My Lord of Blandeforde say differently? He's a person of great nobility and honour, so I can't believe he would ever ask his captain to order the murder of defenceless men.'

Her words unsettled the guards, and a brief irritation glimmered in d'Amiens' eyes as he instructed them to lower their weapons. He wished he'd paid more heed to Thurkell's assessment of this woman. Dressed in finery, and at the head of a crowd, she bore little resemblance to the timid wife he'd glimpsed on occasion in Develish. 'My Lord would say you attempt to embellish your importance with such statements, milady. You take unwarranted authority to yourself when you claim oaths that were given and received by your husband as your own.'

She smiled and reverted back to English. 'Do you not believe in honouring your lord's pledges, sir?'

'We are talking about you, milady.'

'Yet our positions are similar, are they not? Through the death or absence of our lords, we have both had responsibility thrust upon us. With God's help, I can say I am comfortable with the choices I've made. Is the same true of you?'

D'Amiens felt forced to answer in the same language, since she was so clearly talking to the men behind her. 'It wasn't God who instructed you to bar your husband from his demesne and seize power from his lawful steward, milady,' he snapped. 'Such actions are treasonable. My Lord of Blandeforde would have dealt with you harshly had de Courtesmain brought the news sooner.'

Lady Anne was relieved to have the steward confirm that de Courtesmain was the informer, though it would help her even more to know he'd come for himself and not for Bourne. 'He was free to do so at any time, but he had a greater fear of the pestilence than he did of me,' she said mildly. 'Treasonable or not, he preferred my protection to the danger of riding the roads. What gives him the courage to brave them now?'

D'Amiens shook his head as if to say he didn't know.

'The last I heard he was steward to Bourne.'

'You heard right, milady.'

'Yet these men—' she gestured behind her—'tell me he entered the town on foot. How so? Was Bourne not gracious enough to give him a horse?'

'It would seem not.' D'Amiens shook his head at the flicker of interest in her eyes. 'If you hope to make something out of it, you'll be disappointed, milady. De Courtesmain's disagreements with Bourne are small compared with the faults he finds in you and the man you call "cousin".'

'I don't doubt it. His grudges grow larger the longer he's away from the source. In Develish his complaints were against Foxcote.

In a week or two, his enemy will be Bourne. I have it in my heart to feel sorry for him. He finds it easier to blame his failings on others than on himself.'

'You'll not be so sympathetic when you see his evidence, milady. He has a page from the Develish register to demonstrate that what he says is true.'

She answered with a low laugh. 'Only *one*, Master d'Amiens? How selective he is in the lies he wishes to promote. I trust you'll allow me to question him on them.'

'As long as you accept my terms. Weapons and horses must be left outside the gate, and only you and your men may enter. I will not tolerate a foolish attempt at rescue if de Courtesmain's accusations are proven.'

'And who will decide that? You?'

'I stand for My Lord of Blandeforde in his absence.'

'In your own mind, perhaps, but not in mine. God demands that a lord deals fairly with all men, not just those they favour.' She lifted the parchment from her lap. 'This is the writ you ordered posted on the church door before last quarter day. Do you recall how it begins? Let me remind you. *Notwithstanding loss of life, the town will remit the same amount in tax as heretofore. The penalty for failure will be harsh.* You go on to list the weight of corn you demand in place of silver.' She raised her head. 'How do you record such payments, sir? As grain or coin?'

He frowned. 'I don't understand you, milady.'

'I'm sure you do, Master d'Amiens. Blandeforde is a King's treasurer. If the sovereign's share of the town's tax is recorded as grain, you will have a granary within the compound to store it. Does such a building exist?'

D'Amiens made no response, but Lady Anne saw the captain give a small shake of his head.

'Then you will have recorded the share in coin after using My Lord's private funds to purchase the grain for the household. I know of no law which forbids such a transaction, but the exchange must be documented so that all, including the King, are persuaded a fair price has been paid and the town's tax faithfully accounted. Will you send for the coffer that holds those monies and the ledger that shows how they were transferred? If all is as it should be, I will have confidence that you are capable of judging fairly between an English noble and a Norman steward.'

Ian thought how clever Lady Anne was to avoid vague accusations of dishonesty in favour of a detail that could be demonstrated. He watched conflicting emotions cross d'Amiens' face. Uncertainty. Disbelief. Calculation. The steward seemed to be struggling with the idea that a woman might be his equal in intelligence, and foolishly decided that she couldn't be. He shook his head impatiently. 'You waste my time with this nonsense. Do you think keeping track of My Lord's revenues is as easy as counting kirtles?'

'For your sake, I hope not, Master d'Amiens. Your pride will suffer badly if you lose your place to a chambermaid.'

A ripple of laughter ran through the crowd, and d'Amiens turned angrily to the captain, ordering him to ready his guard.

With a grunt of displeasure, Master Slater pushed himself through the gap between Ian's and Joshua's horses. 'Do you hold the freemen of Blandeforde in the same contempt as you hold Lady Anne of Develish?' he demanded. 'Our skill with accounting is easily the match of yours, for we trade daily and keep clear records of all we take. You inspected our ledgers often enough before the pestilence, now let us inspect yours, sir. Milady's not alone in questioning your honesty.'

Ian always wondered afterwards what would have happened if the captain had given different orders when the crowd, encouraged by Miller, flowed around the horses to align themselves with Slater. It may have been fear of being overrun that persuaded him to instruct his men to stand aside and allow the column through, but the small nod of respect he gave Lady Anne seemed to tell a different story.

☽☾

The sound of horses' hooves crunching on gravel, and the murmur of many voices, reached the men in the great hall. The priest, newly arrived with de Courtesmain, showed alarm, while the guards merely looked towards the doors with curiosity. It didn't seem to occur to them that a crowd might represent a threat, but it certainly did to Aristide. He rose to his feet from his position at the other end of the table from Thaddeus, and moved hastily up the room, de Courtesmain scurrying behind him. Thaddeus took satisfaction from the fear in their faces.

He studied Aristide with amusement. 'Who frightens you more?' he asked as the man drew close. 'The gentle lady loved by God or the unarmed townsfolk who accompany her?'

'None is cleansed. They carry the seeds of the pestilence within them.'

With a lazy smile, Thaddeus pushed himself from the chair and stepped out to confront him. 'Then why am I here? You know full well that my sins haven't been cleansed. I'd cut out my tongue before I'd confess to a priest such as you.'

'Get out of my way!'

Thaddeus took his chain in his hands and jerked it tight. 'I will not. You owe your lord's steward and his fighting men a better loyalty than to run at the first sign of trouble. They want to believe that God is on their side, not hiding away with a cringing liar for company.'

Aristide turned to the guards. 'This man is in your charge. Remove him from my path.'

But none responded. Perhaps they feared an elbow in their throats or, more simply, saw that obedience was unnecessary. Even as the priest spoke, their captain appeared in the open doorway and called for Father Aristide to join the steward on the forecourt. 'Master d'Amiens asks that you hold a Mass in the open air for the men of the town, Father. There are many who long to hear God's word and feel His presence amongst them again.'

Thaddeus lowered his hands. 'He's cleverer than I thought,' he said with a laugh. 'There's no safer way to soothe unsettled minds than through prayer. Be sure to preach love, Father. The steward won't have reason to thank you otherwise.'

Seventeen

As he listened to the priest recite his well-rehearsed homily, Thaddeus thought of the adage *A person's nature never changes.* A deceiver remains a deceiver; a generous heart remains generous. Even had Aristide wanted to preach God's love, he couldn't have done it, because instilling fear was the only way he knew to maintain his authority. Wrath and hellfire would always slip more easily off his tongue than forgiveness and redemption.

Too frightened to venture far onto the forecourt, he intoned his prayers and exhortations from inside the arched entranceway, and the vaulted ceiling caused his voice to echo back into the great hall. De Courtesmain sat with bent head and praying hands to Thaddeus's left, the guards to his right. All copied de Courtesmain's stance of piety, and Thaddeus watched their faces as they listened to words and phrases they must have heard a hundred times before. Wickedness had brought the pestilence to Blandeforde. Judgement Day was upon them. Absolution was the only salvation.

The young soldier whose sword he'd broken on Saturday night was closest to him, and he fancied the youth seemed more reluctant than his fellows to pretend devotion. Was he too sensible to believe in Little Sparrow's wickedness? And what of de Courtesmain? Where was *his* sense? Had his time in Develish taught him so little that he was happier to believe absolution more effective in keeping the household free of the pestilence than the killing of rats and the barring of gates?

To his left, he saw movement in the shadows around the archway to the kitchen and guessed servants were creeping from their work to listen. He wondered how many more were gathered about windows, and whether fathers, uncles, brothers and cousins were recognised amongst the crowd on the forecourt. If so, were any persuaded by the priest's strident condemnation of thievery and fornication as the twin devils that blighted the town? Did they truly think their men so lost to honesty and decency that they would indulge in such pursuits while the pestilence raged around them?

Perhaps. Oft-repeated doctrines burrowed all too easily into minds when other ideas were suppressed. Thaddeus found himself hoping a challenge would come from the men in the crowd— surely some must resent the slurs—but, if any tried, their voices were lost amongst the chanted responses, and he feared they were as easily swayed as the servants. Each man might know himself to be guiltless but, since he couldn't speak for others, Aristide would succeed in sowing the same doubts and suspicions through the town as he had in the house.

The young soldier leant towards him. 'Why do you shake your head?' he whispered. 'Do you doubt the truth of what the Father says?'

Thaddeus searched his face. 'His certainty surprises me. I wasn't aware he'd ever taken confession in the town.'

'He hasn't.'

'Yet he seems to know their sins. I wonder how.'

'He must have heard them from the Blandeforde priests before they died.'

Thaddeus smiled slightly. 'By committing a sin himself? It's a grave transgression to break the seal of the confessional. He would have expected to die as they did.'

The young man eyed him curiously. 'But there must be a reason why so many in the town have perished.'

'Indeed. And why, by contrast, so many in the household survive. It's a great puzzle.'

'Do you have the answer to it?'

Thaddeus turned to look at de Courtesmain. He was too tense to be at prayer. Every sinew in his body was straining to hear their whispered conversation. Thaddeus spoke louder. 'Ask this man. He knows the truth as well as anyone. Am I not right, Master de Courtesmain?'

A tremor of violent emotion ran through the Frenchman's body. 'Are you so lost to God that you think it right to disturb a man during Mass?'

Thaddeus smiled. 'My apologies. You were so insistent on staying inside that I thought you felt a show of devotion unnecessary. Is it Lady Anne you're trying to avoid? Perhaps you fear her censure? If so, your worries are groundless. She has never judged you unfairly.'

'You lie,' Hugh snapped. 'She judged me even before I arrived in Develish. No one who came from Foxcote would ever be acceptable to her.'

Thaddeus saw that the other guards were listening. 'Not true. She was unhappy to read what Lady Beatrix wrote about your zealotry in flogging serfs, but she made no other judgement. It was your sly manner and many deceits once you were in Develish that caused her to distrust you. You made the error of thinking all women as vicious and scheming as Lady Beatrix and failed to recognise that Milady is different.'

It seemed prayer was less enticing than self-justification, for Hugh dropped his hands to the table. 'She pretended timidity and dressed in homespun. How could a stranger to Develish know it was she and not her husband who ran the demesne?'

'Would you have behaved differently if you'd been told? Did you think it possible that a woman might be your equal in intelligence?'

'She goes against God's natural order by what she does. All should know their place.'

A smile creased Thaddeus's eyes. 'Do you know yours, sir? You switch loyalties so fast it's hard to keep up with you. Last June you were pledged to Sir Richard, in July to Lady Anne and by January to My Lord of Bourne. Should I assume now that you're sworn to Blandeforde? What price has Master d'Amiens demanded in return? Does your allegiance come cheaper each time you bend your neck to a new master?'

Hugh clenched his fists. 'Blame yourself for your imposture before you blame me for exposing it. I speak only the truth.'

'My friend here will be glad to hear it,' Thaddeus murmured, gesturing to the guard. 'He asks why so many have died in the town and so few in the house. Will you give him the answer?'

Such an anger consumed Hugh that he could barely control himself. 'The priest is right to call you the Devil,' he spat. 'I'll not speak your heresies. They corrupt all who hear them.'

He seemed unaware that their audience was growing. Figures were emerging from the shadows behind him as servants crept forward to hear their words above the priest's intoning of the Credo. *Crucifixus etiam pro nobis sub Pontio Pilato, passus et sepultus est, et resurrexit tertia die, secundum Scripturas, et ascendit in caelum, sedet ad dexteram Patris.*

Thaddeus made the sign of the cross. 'Where is the heresy in describing how Lady Anne has protected her people from the pestilence?' he asked mildly. 'Do you doubt God blesses Develish when not a single person there has died of it?'

'You cite God when it pleases you—not otherwise.'

'As do all men, even Father Aristide when he sees wickednesses that don't exist.' Thaddeus turned his head to look at the servants. 'He's taught these people to fear God instead of reminding them of His love. They should know He weeps as surely as they do over every innocent life that is lost.'

The young guard spoke into the silence that followed. 'How can you know the dead were innocent?'

'For the same reason you do, my friend. Our sins are more numerous than Little Sparrow's can ever have been.'

'Would she have lived if she'd been in Develish?'

'I believe so.'

'Why?'

'Milady is skilled in medicine and has taught her people that the best way to cure a disease is never to catch it. The merit of this lesson has been proved many times in Develish. The sick are treated in a hospital away from the village, and by such means illnesses rarely spread.' He paused to see if the guards and the servants understood him. They seemed to. 'When news of the pestilence first reached Develish, Milady reversed the method by secluding the healthy. She withdrew her people inside her moat and barred entry to all others, thereby keeping the sickness out.'

Confiteor unum baptisma in remissionem peccatorum et expecto resurrectionem mortuorum et vitam venturi saeculi.

'And all still live?'

'They do.'

'Was it for the same reason that Master d'Amiens ordered the gates barred here and forbade entry to townsmen?'

'Yes.'

A woman stirred. 'I helped Little Sparrow over the wall one night so that she might visit her mother in the town. It was forbidden to do such a thing but it broke my heart to see her cry. She loved her mother so much and missed her so greatly. Should I blame myself that she died? I thought her too sweet and innocent ever to warrant God's punishment.'

Thaddeus glanced from one to the other. 'Did you all view her in the same way?'

They nodded.

'Then believe in her goodness and know that God loved her as much as He loves you.' He turned back to the woman. 'Don't blame yourself, mistress. If you were persuaded wickedness was the cause of the pestilence, you had no reason to think an act of kindness would cause her death.'

'There were many who wanted to care for her when she fell to the fever,' said another, 'but the priest wouldn't allow it.'

'She was forced out as the three before her were,' said a man. 'Would Lady Anne have done the same had any succumbed in Develish?'

'There would have been no forcing,' Thaddeus answered. 'All were agreed that, for the good of the demesne, sufferers would take themselves willingly across the moat to spend their last days in the hospital. There was no other way to protect the healthy.'

'Are you saying the priest was right to do what he did?' asked the guard.

Thaddeus glanced towards the entranceway. 'He was . . . though his reasons were less than honest. He had no cause to berate the maid and none to berate the townsmen now. They've shown mercy to every sufferer who's come to Blandeforde and their compassion has cost them dear. Any grief you feel for Little Sparrow is far surpassed by theirs for their dead families.'

Whatever he'd hoped to provoke by his statements, it wasn't that Hugh de Courtesmain would pull out a knife and plunge it into the flesh of his shoulder. Thaddeus took the stab for a punch until de Courtesmain rose to his feet with screams of 'heretic' and 'corrupter', and began chopping down at him with a bloodied blade. The assault was so fierce, and Thaddeus so unprepared for it, that he took several more blows in his arm and shoulder before, with a grunt of pain, he thrust himself out of his chair. All was confusion. The Frenchman's cries were overlaid by shouts from the guards and panicked wailing from the maids, and the only thing Thaddeus could think to do was block de Courtesmain's next strike with his left hand.

It may have been a second only that he stared into de Courtesmain's eyes as the steel drove through his palm. It felt longer. He clamped his right hand over the Frenchman's wrist to prevent him withdrawing the weapon, and he had time to wonder if the frenzied creature was acting for himself or the priest. The priest, he thought, when de Courtesmain loosened his grip in order to pull himself free and an embossed cross, much smeared with gore, was revealed on the dagger's haft.

Thaddeus watched dispassionately as the guards wrestled de Courtesmain to the ground and then resumed his seat, placing the edge of his hand on the table. 'Will you be kind enough to bring me a bowl of heated water and some salt, mistress?' he asked the woman who'd spoken first. 'Also clean, boiled rags for binding. The wound will mend faster with a little care.'

She stared at the four-inch blade piercing his palm, and the blood dripping onto the table, then raised her eyes to his, clearly wondering if she would be right to help him. Whatever she saw seemed to persuade her. 'I will, sire,' she said with a nod, beckoning to three young maids to accompany her. 'Whatever the reason for your wounds and shackles, I wouldn't want you thinking My Lord's household less charitable than his town.'

⚭

Lady Anne had taken Ian's advice to remain mounted during the Mass, which meant they remained at the rear of the crowd, close to where the driveway entered the forecourt. To descend would have put them on the same level as the men of the town, and while none seemed to be showing signs of the pestilence, there was no knowing if they were hiding fevers or carrying fleas. Ian had fewer qualms about entering the house. Like Thaddeus, he took the barricaded gate and the guildsmen's tale of the young maid's expulsion to mean the steward had used the same measures as Lady Anne to keep the pestilence out. Even so, he kept a constant watch for rats.

Lady Anne was more interested in the steward and the priest. She sat with bent head, apparently at prayer, watching them from beneath her lashes. Both gave every indication that they knew the pestilence was caught and not imposed by God. D'Amiens stood well apart from the kneeling crowd on the other side of the forecourt, surrounded by the guards who'd kept the townsmen at a distance as they'd shepherded him up the driveway. The priest remained within the arched porchway, ready to retreat at the first sign of trouble.

She wondered if she'd ever seen a man so nervous. He found every reason to maintain a good space between himself and the crowd, ordering them to their knees at the centre of the forecourt and making it clear at the outset that, without unleavened bread, there could be no Eucharist. All he could offer was the liturgy and a blessing. He chastised the men for their impatience and urged them to leave and return the following day, when the servants had had time to prepare the proper repast; but Master Slater called out that they'd take what Father Aristide could give them now rather than gamble on the morrow. The irony in his tone told everyone they would wait through eternity before the priest found the courage to draw close enough to place bread into their mouths.

Lady Anne's reaction to the homily was similar to Thaddeus's. Though spoken in heavily accented English, she thought it sounded rehearsed, as if Father Aristide had delivered it every day since the pestilence first entered Blandeforde; but, unlike Thaddeus, she saw the impact his accusations of fornication and thievery had on his listeners. They eyed each other in puzzlement, as if to ask where such ideas had come from and, were it not for the ingrained respect they had for the Mass, she felt sure one or more would have asked the question aloud. Certainly, the restless movements of Master Miller and his supporters suggested they were far from pleased to be charged with sins they hadn't committed.

The priest raised his voice at the end of the Credo to remind the crowd of his authority. 'I believe in one Holy, Catholic and

Apostolic Church. I confess one baptism for the remission of sins, and I look for the resurrection of the dead, and the life of the world to come. Amen.' He stood in silence for several long moments as the kneeling men crossed themselves and then began the bidding prayers.

Only Joshua was close enough to hear the shouting in the great hall. Before the Mass began, he'd steered his horse and the pack ponies towards a tethering rail which was attached to the sill of a window to the right of the entranceway. He was too curious not to look inside as he leant forward to loop the ponies' halters around the bar. The sun outside was very bright and the gloom of the interior very dark, but he felt certain he could make out Thaddeus seated at the end of a long table.

Dimness and distance obscured the man's features, but he appeared a head taller than those around him. He seemed at ease and Joshua wondered sourly why they'd wasted so much energy on him since the chances were he'd already convinced the steward he was Athelstan. He willed Thaddeus to look in his direction, but his friend's interest was fixed on the priest in the entranceway.

Joshua's position left him exposed to the eyes of the townsmen, and he felt obliged to pretend a greater devotion than his companions, who were behind them. He lowered his head and closed his eyes but, being deeply weary after two anxiety-filled nights, the dreary drone of the priest's sermonising sent him to sleep. He couldn't say what woke him unless it was his dogs' restlessness. They were ranged as a pack slightly in front of his mount, hindquarters quivering and muzzles pointing towards the entranceway.

His immediate assumption was that the priest's decision to advance onto the forecourt was unsettling them. His black cope fluttered around him as he walked and his chants grew louder and more strident. For those in front of him, the sound of his voice drowned out all others, but Joshua distinctly heard the wailing cries of women from inside the house. He turned in alarm towards the window, but the sun was reflecting off the panes and there was no seeing through them. He guessed there were other cries he couldn't hear when one of the mastiffs began to inch forward with growls rumbling in his throat.

Joshua hadn't time to debate the rights and wrongs of what he did. He flung himself from his saddle, drew his sword and ordered the pack on. He might resent this one dog's annoying loyalty to Thaddeus, but he was no more inclined than the animal to stand idly by if his friend was in trouble. As he ran towards the entranceway, he saw the guards around the steward reach for their bows, but he was well inside before any had nocked their arrows.

There was such a confusion of people in the hall that the dogs ran hither and thither, barking ferociously. Joshua saw women and maids scattering in terror towards the walls, while a group of liveried men seemed to be struggling with a prisoner. He thought he recognised him as Hugh de Courtesmain but scarce gave him a glance, for his eyes were fixed firmly on the manacled figure at the end of the table. With a command to his dogs to come to heel, he strode down the room and positioned himself at Thaddeus's side, stationing the pack around him.

'Your mastiff sensed you were in trouble, My Lord, and he would seem to have been right.' He looked at the knife through Thaddeus's hand and the seeping gashes in his coat. 'Did the guards do this?'

'No, Buckler. They've shown me only courtesy. You may lower your sword. No harm will come to us from them, though you have my permission to set the pack on de Courtesmain if he slips their clutches.'

Joshua stared at the Frenchman for a moment. 'They'd make short work of him, sire. There's not enough flesh on him to satisfy one dog, let alone seven. Should I pull the knife from your hand?'

'Not yet, my young friend. It's all that's staunching the flow. I've been promised water and bandages by a kindly servant.'

'You're bleeding from other places, My Lord, and those wounds might be as bad. We should remove your coat so that Lady Anne can tend to you. She is outside and will know better than servants what to do.'

A faint smile lifted Thaddeus's mouth. 'Indeed, but even she will have to remove my shackles first.' He watched the doors darken as the captain and several fighting men entered the hall with swords raised. 'Place your weapons on the table and step away from me,' he murmured. 'Let them see you're not a threat. There's no reason for any more blood to be spilt.'

∾

Lady Anne placed a warning hand on Ian's wrist as half the men surrounding the steward set off in pursuit of Joshua. 'Do nothing,' she whispered. 'To fight would be madness. Thaddeus will be saying the same to Joshua.'

'What if he can't, milady? Joshua wouldn't have entered unless he thought him in danger. They could both be in trouble.'

'Then they must help each other. I will not allow you to imperil the lives of the townsmen by acting foolishly. I gave a pledge of peace and will not break it.'

She said no more and Ian sensed rebellion coming from his twin as the dreary Latin ritual continued. *Why had she refused the steward's orders for them to disarm if she wasn't prepared to let them fight?* Perhaps the question was his own, for he felt the same frustration. But he also knew the answer. No lord would have accepted orders from a man of lower status. For Lady Anne to obey d'Amiens would have been to acknowledge that his rank was above hers, and she would have lost the townsmen's respect.

But was their respect worth having, Ian wondered, as he watched the dutiful crowd respond to every prompt the priest gave? Not one seemed to wonder why he had advanced onto the forecourt and raised his voice. To Ian it was obvious that some noise had erupted inside the house which the priest was trying to hide. But what? Had Thaddeus called for help? Was Joshua expecting his friends to follow him? Ian knew he hadn't imagined the barking of the dogs afterwards.

He observed the captain emerge from the entranceway, relieved to see that his sword was sheathed and his livery unruffled. Nevertheless, the man appeared a reluctant bearer of news as he whispered a hesitant explanation into the steward's ear. Whatever he said was met with anger. D'Amiens' eyes narrowed to slits before he whispered a command and then dismissed the captain with an abrupt nod.

'Keep faith,' Lady Anne breathed as the captain set off at a run towards the western end of the building. 'If anyone is dead or dying, the steward would have ordered him brought outside to the priest. They both hold too fast to Church ritual to deny a man the last rites.'

'What if you're wrong?' whispered Olyver.

'Better two die than fifty.'

In her own way she was as ruthless as Thaddeus, Ian thought, and he wondered if she would react as coldly if he challenged her decision. 'As Athelstan's men, we should be at his side, milady. A lord's soldiers are pledged to protect him. The steward must be wondering why only Joshua has gone to his master's aid.'

'Did you honour your pledge two nights ago?'

Ian shifted uncomfortably. 'You know we did not, milady. Thaddeus wouldn't allow it.'

'And wouldn't now. It's not force that can release him, only persuasion.' She nodded to the far corner of the house. 'I see the captain returning. Can you make out what he has in his hand?'

'A ring of keys, milady.'

'How strange,' she murmured. 'I wonder what purpose they have if they're kept outside.'

❧

The captain refused to approach until Joshua and his dogs had retreated ten paces. 'I need your parole, sire,' he told Thaddeus. 'The steward won't allow me to release you from your chains unless you make your pledge before witnesses. Speak loud enough for the servants to hear.'

Thaddeus glanced towards the assembled household. 'You are the captain's witnesses that I give my parole gladly and will make no attempt to escape.' He turned back. 'Will that suffice? In truth, I'm too tired even to stand at the moment.'

The captain tut-tutted as he used one of the keys to unscrew the metal bar that held the manacle in place on Thaddeus's left hand. 'I hope you don't blame my men, sire. They thought he was slapping you until they saw the knife.'

'I also. Take care not to touch it. I doubt the pain will be so easily borne if the blade moves.'

The captain eased off the hoop of the shackle and dropped it onto Thaddeus's lap. 'It can't stay there forever, sire,' he said, moving around the chair to unlock the other manacle. 'Would you have me draw it for you?'

'No thank you, my friend. I'll do it myself when the servants bring me the means to cleanse and bind it. What keeps them so long?'

A woman stepped forward. 'You asked for clean, boiled rags, My Lord.'

'Is that an unusual request?'

'It is, sire. We have no store of clean rags. Mistress Wilde is scrubbing a threadbare kirtle with tallow soap in order to cut it into strips for boiling. She begs your pardon for the time it is taking.'

'And I hers for putting her to the trouble.' Thaddeus thought for a moment. 'Is my charger outside, Buckler?' he asked.

'He is, My Lord. He carries Lady Anne.'

'Then perhaps the captain will allow you to retrieve the packs from behind the saddle. There are some linen braies inside which I know to be clean since I've yet to find a use for them.' He smiled at the ripple of laughter that ran through the women at this mention of undergarments. 'You would pity me if you knew of the folds linen braies form inside my britches when I'm riding. They rub most severely.'

'My Lord says the same, sire,' called a man. 'He too refuses to wear them, never mind how much Milady begs him to follow the customs of the King and his court.'

'Milady would beg even harder if she had to launder his britches,' said a woman's voice.

The jest brought laughter from all the servants, but there was a tinge of wildness to their merriment which seemed to speak less to humour than the release of long pent-up emotions. Thaddeus beckoned Joshua forward as the sound rippled on. 'Will you permit my man to go?' he asked the captain. 'This blade will be harder to pull the longer it stays in place and I need clean wadding to stem the flow of blood.'

The captain gathered the chain and shackles into a pile on the table. 'I'll have to accompany him, My Lord. The steward won't allow him to approach your cousin alone. There's no knowing how she'll react if he speaks to her of what's happened here.'

'She'll learn soon enough.'

'Maybe so, sire, but Master d'Amiens won't want her inciting the townsmen. He fears the admiration they seem to have for her. We live in strange times. Such people wouldn't normally accept the leadership of a woman.'

Eighteen

JOSHUA KEPT TO HIMSELF THAT he'd moved all the bags from Killer to one of the pack ponies before the descent into Blandeforde. This might be his only chance to pass information to Lady Anne and he had no intention of foregoing it. Yet the plan looked like coming to nought when the captain noticed there was nothing before or behind Milady's saddle. He stood with Joshua inside the vaulted porch, waiting for the priest to end a prayer, and even with her skirts draping her mount's loins, she was too slight and small to hide the absence of bulky leather packs. When he asked for an explanation, Joshua explained in a whisper that My Lord's bags had been shared amongst his fighting men in order to give Milady a more comfortable ride. He gestured towards Edmund and Peter, positioned some fifteen paces behind Lady Anne, as the carriers.

This information pleased the captain. He instructed Joshua to follow him down the great hall and through the archway to the kitchen. It was uninhabited except for Mistress Wilde and the maid servants who bobbed worried curtsies when they came in, only to resume their scrubbing in relief when nothing was said about their tardiness. The captain opened a door and ushered Joshua outside.

'We're at the eastern end of the house, and your two companions are well to the rear of the crowd. We'll not be seen by the townsmen if we approach from this direction. You understand there's to be no conversation. Your single task is to retrieve your master's packs.'

Joshua stared at the ground for a moment, wondering whether it was better to defy the man now or later. He raised his eyes to look directly into the captain's. 'I understand those are *your* wishes, sir, but My Lord gave no such instructions, and his is the only authority I recognise.'

The man sighed. 'Then I can't let you fetch the packs. My orders are to keep Milady from Athelstan until the steward's had time to question her.'

'How does my speaking with my companions break that command?'

'He looks to catch Milady in a lie and will believe you're delivering a message from Athelstan if he sees you talking with any in her entourage.'

Joshua hid his curiosity well, but his thoughts were racing. 'I have no message to give except that My Lord has been wounded,' he said slowly. 'Is that the news Master d'Amiens hopes to keep secret?'

'The wounds don't interest him—only what was said in the church. He gave the order to keep them apart when he first learnt of Lady Anne's arrival. It has to do with a pledge your master made to Milady. Only she can release him from it.'

Joshua made a good pretence at puzzlement. 'Then you have nothing to fear. Such secrets are never shared with fighting men.

I seek only to repeat My Lord's request that no more blood is to be shed. What fault would the steward find in that?'

'None if he knew what you were saying.'

'Then where's the harm? You can tell him afterwards that that is all I said.'

'He'll not believe me unless Milady's story conflicts with your lord's.'

Joshua measured the distance between him and Edmund. Twenty paces? Thirty paces? 'He needn't see me at all if you shield me from his view as we cross the forecourt,' he said reasonably. 'I'll be well hidden once I'm between the horses.'

The captain gave a grunt of derision. 'And how do I achieve that? We're of a similar height, and my girth is not so large that it will cover yours.'

Joshua glanced into the kitchen. 'A group of four women in skirts would hide me as long as I walk in a crouch at their side. Has Mistress Wilde the authority to offer cordial to Lady Anne? It would be what hospitality demands for anyone who's ridden as far as she has this day.'

'Mass is being said.'

'All the more reason to show a small act of charity.' Joshua searched the other's face. 'If you have no sympathy for Milady's weariness, at least find some for My Lord. He was more than fair to excuse your guards from blame in his wounding. You owe him a debt of gratitude for that at least.'

With a shrug, the captain stepped back into the kitchen. 'But not you,' he warned. 'Remember that when the steward orders your arrest.' He paused. 'You'd be wise to take off your tabard. You might pass for a servant in tunic and britches.'

၄၀

Well to the rear of the crowd, Edmund had felt no obligation to feign interest in the Mass. Instead, he'd spent his time studying the house and the land around it. From where he was positioned, he could see both the guards' quarters and the church tower and, though he didn't know what function the smaller building performed, he made a good guess when the captain hurried towards it and two liveried men opened the door to him. After a brief conversation, another appeared in the opening with a ring of keys in his hand.

It was a small step to connect the keys with imprisonment. Edmund recalled an occasion from his childhood when Peter's father, the Develish blacksmith, had forged and hammered iron manacles into hinges for the latrine door after Sir Richard issued an edict that they were never to be used again for the purpose of punishing serfs. Few believed Sir Richard had known what he was signing, but everyone took pleasure in watching the hoops being converted to better use.

Had the captain returned with chains as well as keys, Edmund would have believed they were intended for Joshua, but keys alone suggested unlocking rather than locking. And the thought occurred to him that Joshua and his dogs had somehow effected Thaddeus's release. If the irritating churl had said once that his dogs were worth an army, he'd said it a hundred times, and Edmund pictured him strutting like a cockerel as d'Amiens' guards trembled before ferocious teeth. He watched the entranceway to see who emerged, though in truth he couldn't decide whether he wanted to see Joshua come out in triumph or with his tail between his legs.

A quarter-hour passed before he caught the flutter of women's skirts out of the corner of his eye. He looked to his right and saw a strange procession make its way from the side of the house towards him and Peter. A matronly servant, carrying a silver goblet, was at the head and three young maids, clutching flagons and bonbons, followed close behind. They approached so close to Peter's mount that the animal became restless and Edmund had only the briefest impression of a figure slipping from their midst as Peter laid a soothing hand on his horse's neck.

'Face forward and say nothing,' whispered Joshua, dropping to a crouch between him and Peter. 'All will come to nought if the steward knows I'm here.'

Edmund did as he was bid, watching the servants move in front of Lady Anne's and the twins' horses. Across the heads of the crowd, he saw that d'Amiens' gaze was upon them and, while the steward frowned at their offering of cordial to Milady, he made no move to prevent it. Perhaps he feared the townsmen's reaction if he denied her refreshment. She was most gracious in her acceptance, winning smiles and curtsies from the women.

'I have messages,' Joshua breathed next. 'Thaddeus is wounded but not dying. His attacker was Master de Courtesmain. The guards seem to have a liking for Thaddeus because his shackles have been removed. The servants, too, since they wish to tend his cuts. Thaddeus has told them all that he wants no more blood to be shed and this has increased their sympathy for him. Lady Anne should play on that while remaining wary of the steward. He looks to catch her in a lie by questioning her before she has a chance to speak with Thaddeus. I am told by the captain that the issue concerns a pledge Thaddeus made to Milady and from which only she can release him. But I'm guessing Thaddeus fabricated the story and Milady will be as ignorant as I of what this pledge concerns.'

Edmund leant forward to adjust his horse's noseband. 'Why did the Frenchman attack Thaddeus?'

'I don't know; perhaps anger that the guards are treating him as a lord. De Courtesmain's own status seems much reduced since we last saw him.'

Edmund watched the matron gather the maids together again. 'Make ready,' he muttered. 'The servants are returning. Stay sharp, my friend.'

'You, too,' came the whispered response before Joshua's stooping figure was hidden once again amidst the swirl and rustle of skirts.

The next Edmund saw of him was when he and the captain came out through the entranceway. Joshua, fully dressed again in livery, hurried to the pack ponies to remove Thaddeus's crested leather bags and then hastened back inside the house. The captain turned to follow, but not before dropping to one knee and crossing himself as the priest began the absolution.

Deus, Pater misericordiarum, qui per mortem et resurrectionem Filii . . .

Edmund nudged his mount towards Peter's. 'How do we close the gap between us and Lady Anne without making the steward suspicious?' he murmured. 'We must give her the messages before the service ends. There may not be a chance afterwards.'

Peter nodded. 'A spooked horse won't raise suspicions,' he said, studying the fifteen-yard distance. Without warning, he slid his left boot from his stirrup and drove a sharp kick into the soft flesh between the chest and foreleg of Edward's mount.

Idiot, thought Edmund, as the animal skittered sideways instead of forwards. It took all his skill to turn the creature's head and dance it broadside on towards the rear of Ian's horse while making a pretence of trying to calm it.

The nervous scraping of hooves infected Killer, and Ian turned with an angry order for Edmund to bring his horse under control before Milady was thrown. Edmund made to obey but his handling of the reins was so inept that the animal was alongside Ian's before he had enough command to drop from the saddle. He ducked beneath its neck to make a clumsy bow of apology to Lady Anne and then, with his back to the steward, took hold of its nose collar and ran a soothing hand down its shoulder.

'Can you hear me, milady?' he whispered.

ତ୍ୟ

Thaddeus locked his gaze with Hugh de Courtesmain's as he gripped the haft of the knife and pulled the four-inch blade through his palm. He needed the other's hatred to act as a spur because he knew before he began that the pain would be severe. Yet no amount of imagining had told him how severe. The rawness of the wound, dulled by the length of time he'd kept his hand rigid and unmoving on the table, blazed to life again as the steel ripped through already clotting blood. He was unaware of how pale he became as his mind reacted in shock to this second slicing of tender flesh but he made no sound as he placed the knife on the table and clenched his fist around a balled linen braie to stop the flow of blood. He took satisfaction from the disbelief in de Courtesmain's eyes. If he'd achieved nothing else, he'd demonstrated to the Frenchman that, in a battle of wills between them, his was the stronger.

He allowed Joshua to ease the left sleeve of his coat down his arm and then do the same with his embroidered jerkin. Beneath, the white fabric of the shirt showed seven saturated tears on the upper arm and shoulder where the blade had penetrated. Thaddeus shook his head when Joshua urged him to draw his arm from that sleeve as well. 'Let's wait for Mistress Wilde and her bandages. The wounds are no more than pinpricks thanks to the thickness of my coat and jerkin.' He stirred the knife with his right hand. 'Did you steal this or was it given to you?' he asked de Courtesmain. 'I see that the haft is embossed with a cross.'

When De Courtesmain remained silent, the captain, who was standing to Thaddeus's right, ordered him to speak.

'I'll not answer questions from a slave.'

'You'll wear these if you don't,' said the captain coolly, jerking his chin at the shackles on the table. 'My Lord's not alone in wanting answers. You involved my men in your madness when you attacked their prisoner.'

'They should have remembered what he was when they chose to sit at the table with him. A prisoner should know his place and so should the men who guard him.'

The captain eyed him thoughtfully for a moment. 'You're strangely arrogant for a would-be murderer,' he murmured, leaning forward to push the shackles and keys across the table. 'But you're right to remind me that a prisoner should know his place.' He beckoned to the young guard to pick them up. 'Wrap the chain around a pillar before you secure the manacles.'

From outside came the blessing. *Benedicat vos omnipotens Deus, Pater et Filius et Spiritus Sanctus.*

ഐ

Lady Anne watched the townsmen rise to their feet and clasp each other's hands in friendship. How clever d'Amiens had been to call a Mass, she thought. Knees might be sore and creaking after an hour at prayer on hard ground, but animosities and grievances were forgotten in the spirit of forgiveness that came with absolution and blessing. Several of the men glanced towards the sun, recalling tasks that needed performing, then turned towards the driveway in preparation for departure. Even if she knew the words that might persuade them to stay, she doubted the wisdom of introducing a woman's voice into the solemn quiet that possessed them. The respect they'd shown her in the town would not be replicated if she assumed the right to speak in a place which, however briefly, had served them as a church.

The priest understood this well, for he remained where he was, head bent in prayer and hands folded about the bejewelled cross that he wore on a chain around his neck. Lady Anne wondered if he'd sought permission from his bishop to adorn himself with such a showy ornament or if the idea had been his. Either way, his continued communion with God prolonged the townsmen's sense that the forecourt was a holy place and deterred any from approaching him. Seeing this, d'Amiens did the same, closing his eyes and pressing his palms together beneath his lowered chin, and within minutes the men at the margins of the crowd began to disperse, their appetite for confrontation dispelled as they walked past Lady Anne and Thaddeus's companions towards the driveway.

'If the rest leave, we must go with them,' murmured Lady Anne. 'To stay will be to accept the power of the priest, and through him the governance of Church law. Do you understand?'

'Yes, milady,' said Ian, Olyver and Edmund in unison.

'Then make ready. My hope is the steward is eager enough to speak with me to request that we stay; I can make better terms with him than with the priest.'

'But what if he doesn't, milady?' Ian asked anxiously. 'Who will tend Thaddeus's wounds?'

'He must manage them himself.'

'What of Joshua?'

'He must stay with Thaddeus. There'll be no bargaining either's release from a position of weakness.'

She took Miller and his supporters as her guide. When they began to stray from the forecourt, she instructed Ian to follow. He paused only to beckon Peter forward and order him and Edmund to retrieve Joshua's horse and the pack ponies before nodding to Olyver to draw Killer into a turn. The dirt road was behind them, and they had barely circled their mounts to face it when a guard hurried across the gravel to address Lady Anne.

'The steward forbids your departure, milady.'

'Has he ordered you to make me your prisoner?'

'I'm ordered to prevent you leaving, milady.'

'Then you have my sympathies,' she said. 'I trust he will be understanding of your failure.'

The man reached nervously for his sword but thought better of it when Ian shook his head. 'Only a fool starts a war for no reason,' he murmured, listening to the stamp of hooves as Edmund and Peter came up behind them. 'Be good enough to step aside. You'll not survive a trampling from eight horses.'

The guard retreated in front of them, creating enough of a delay for d'Amiens and the remaining guards to make their way around the forecourt and form a line across the driveway. By doing so, they split the townsmen into two groups, with Miller and his supporters on one side and the rest on the other. Ian wondered whether this was by accident or design. Did the steward hope to intimidate those confined with Lady Anne? If so, he prayed that

Miller, yet to round the bend in the road, would look back to see what was happening.

D'Amiens sketched a small bow. 'Why this sudden urge to depart, milady?' he asked in French. 'Was the Mass not to your liking?'

She answered in English, her voice carrying well in the still air. 'It was hardly a Mass, Master d'Amiens. In Develish, our priest would not deny supplicants the Eucharist for want of unleavened bread.'

'Father Aristide is obedient to the teachings of Christ, milady.'

She smiled. 'Yet I don't recall Jesus telling us what form the bread should take. All the gospels use the same words. *He took bread and when He had given thanks, He brake it and gave it to them, saying, "This is my body which is given for you."* Is Father Aristide's Bible different from mine that he thinks yeasted bread forbidden?'

D'Amiens refused to be drawn. 'I asked about your sudden urge to depart, milady. It's but two hours since you were demanding entrance. What has changed?'

'My hope that you can ever be an honest judge, sir. You led me to believe you would bring out your ledgers for inspection, but instead you summoned the priest to denounce the townsmen as wicked. For what reason unless to divert attention from your own guilt?'

D'Amiens watched the crowd turn their heads to listen more closely. 'Most seemed comforted by the Mass, milady,' he said in French. 'Only you appear troubled by it. Could it be you heard your own sins mentioned by the priest?'

She searched his face for a moment and then pressed her right palm to her breast. 'I don't know what might lead you to make such an accusation, Master d'Amiens,' she answered in English, 'but I can swear, hand on heart and with Almighty God as my witness, that I have never committed the sins of fornication and thievery. I would go further, and say I am grievously offended that you would cast such slurs against me.'

A murmur came from the crowd, and Ian glanced round to see Slater step forward. 'I, too, am offended,' he said, pressing his own palm to his chest. 'And will likewise swear before Almighty God that I am innocent of what the priest accuses me. My wife, now dead, is the only woman I have loved, and stealing has never tempted me.'

The voices of his fellows rose in agreement as hand after hand thumped against chests, and their cries of innocence brought Miller and his supporters hurrying back. They skirted around the guards and lined themselves beside the greybeard, assuming the same stance of right palm to left breast.

'If fornication and thievery brought the pestilence to Blandeforde,' Miller called, 'then the culprits must be here and not in the town. Father Aristide blames us unfairly.'

Andrew Tench moved forward to join their rank. 'Our priests knew our weaknesses better than he, and they rarely sermonised about mortal sin even before the pestilence came.'

'They were good men all,' said Slater. 'Before they died, they begged us to hold to the path of righteousness, and we have tried to do so. No man here would claim to know another's secrets, but we can all speak of the kindness and care our town has shown the many sufferers who have sought sanctuary over the last half-year. Have you and My Lord's household been as generous, Master d'Amiens? Has the priest?'

D'Amiens stared hard at him as if committing his face to memory. 'You stray into heresy with such questions. Only God knows why the house is blessed and the town condemned.' He raised his voice. 'Am I not right, Father Aristide?'

When no answer came, all turned to look for the black-robed figure. But he was gone, and his absence gave Slater courage.

'Where's the heresy in asking how many sufferers you've tended?' he asked d'Amiens. 'We don't question God's plan for us, only why you sent your sick to us instead of caring for them yourselves. We know of four you expelled but none that you've kept and cared for.'

'None was expelled. They left of their own free will.'

The lie was so blatant—as evidenced by the discomfort of the guards—that a silence followed. It fell to Lady Anne, who had heard the story of the little maid from Edmund, to break it, but rather than challenge d'Amiens on his falsehood, she questioned his judgement.

'Did you not have a duty to stop them?' she asked. 'I cannot believe My Lord of Blandeforde would have wanted more sufferers inflicted on his town when they had taken in so many already.'

D'Amiens eyed her with dislike. 'Do not to try my patience too far,' he said in French. 'You delude yourself if you think can incite these men to support you against my guards.'

'I wouldn't ask it of them,' she answered in the same language. 'I have more care for their lives than you do. Your guards also. I wish harm to no man. Yourself included.'

He gave a contemptuous laugh. 'We can all speak brave words from the back of a horse, milady. If lives matter so much to you, descend and stand amongst the townsmen. Your presence on the ground is their best protection, for I'll not order my soldiers to make war on Lady Anne of Develish.'

'You may come to regret that promise, Master d'Amiens.'

He shook his head. 'You haven't kept your people free of the pestilence all these months to act the fool now. Cease your stirring and encourage this rabble to return to their homes. I give my word that you and Thurkell will receive a fair hearing.'

Lady Anne held his gaze for a moment and then turned to Ian. 'Oblige me by assisting me from my saddle,' she said in English. 'I have more faith that Master d'Amiens' guards will honour his first pledge than I do that he will uphold his second.'

Ian's resistance was obvious. 'Are you sure, milady? I doubt the men of Blandeforde would expect you to act as their shield.'

She nodded. 'In Develish, we set fourteen days as the period of exclusion for a man to prove he was well. Here, eight weeks have passed without a death. Do you ask me to show less friendship to these worthy people than to My Lord of Bourne or the serfs of Pedle Hinton?'

Ian nudged his mount backwards and passed his reins to Peter before swinging himself to the ground. 'No, milady,' he said, reaching up to support her dismount. 'My Lord of Athelstan would say the same. Will you allow me the privilege of accompanying you?'

Nineteen

GYLES STARTOUT BROUGHT HIS SMALL convoy to a halt as they breasted the hill above Blandeforde. To his right rode his brother Alleyn, to his left James Buckler. All wore threadbare tabards with the crest of Sir Richard of Develish, these being the only garments left in Develish that might lift them above the level of serfs. The livery looked well enough from a distance but Gyles didn't doubt the moth-eaten fabric would invite derision at close quarters. He had no greater hopes that their mounts, stolen from Holcombe by Lord Bourne, would strike a more commanding appearance. Two seasons on the pastureland by the moat had left them unbrushed and unkempt, giving them more the air of carthorses than chargers.

They certainly hadn't made for a comfortable journey. So long unridden, they had responded poorly to their bits and, with no time to soften the saddle leather with oil and tallow, all three men had suffered. It led Gyles to wonder if Lady Anne could possibly have reached Blandeforde. Was she capable of riding so far when even he, the most experienced horseman, winced with every unexpected lurch in his brute's uneven gait? The only sounds that had come from James and Alleyn's mouths had been full-throated oaths, and both gave sighs of relief as the town came into sight below them.

By the sun, Gyles estimated it was an hour past noon, and he questioned again whether Lady Anne could be ahead of them. She may have had an eight-hour start on him and his companions, having left Develish at midnight, but they had ridden at a fast gallop and her lack of horsemanship would have kept her to a slow walk until dawn. He cursed himself for not insisting that John ask sensible questions of his son instead of spending his time berating the youth about misplaced loyalty. If Gyles knew where Edmund had left his companions, he would have a better idea of Lady Anne's progress.

James Buckler stood in his stirrups to relieve the pressure on his aching groin. 'What's worrying you?' he asked.

'That we've arrived before Lady Anne. I've known her fifteen years but I've never seen her on horseback. She told me she'd manage with Edmund's help but . . .' He shook his head.

'You think she's given up?'

'There's a good chance.'

Alleyn was studying the verge to the left of the highway. 'Horses have stopped here recently,' he said. 'Do you see how the grass has been trampled? I'm guessing they were allowed to graze while their riders looked down on Blandeforde. Who else could it be but Lady Anne and your sons?'

'The steward's fighting men?' suggested Gyles. 'For all we know they've been scouring the countryside since Thaddeus was arrested.'

There was a thoughtful silence, broken by James Buckler. 'Then what are we doing here?' he asked. 'You could have foreseen all this before we left Develish.'

'I felt I had to try.'

'For Lady Eleanor's sake?'

'Isabella's, too. Her pleas were as heartfelt.' Gyles glanced at Alleyn. 'I even had your Robert joining in.'

'The lad's in search of adventure. He'd have taken my place if you'd permitted it.'

Gyles shook his head. 'It's more than that. He fears Eleanor will harm herself if anything happens to Lady Anne. Both he and Isabella say she'll blame herself if Milady is taken in charge for heresy.'

'With good cause,' said James. 'She should have had more sense than to denounce Lady Anne in front of de Courtesmain.'

'Would you have her kill herself over it now? Robert assures me that's what she'll do if harm comes to Lady Anne through her fault.'

James nodded to the leather knapsack behind Gyles's saddle. 'Will the documents you're carrying prevent that?'

'Isabella believes so—as long as it's Master de Courtesmain who betrays us and I can place them in Lady Anne's hands before she's obliged to answer to him.'

'Hence your fussing over whether she's behind or ahead of us.'

Gyles nodded. 'She must read them first. They'll serve no purpose at all if her dreams were misguided and it's Bourne who informs against Thaddeus.'

James grinned. 'You never think anything she does misguided.'

'There's always a first time.'

'But not today,' Alleyn murmured, jerking his chin towards the right-hand edge of the highway. 'That pile of turd looks like dog excrement to me.' He turned his gaze on Blandeforde. 'You must have more faith, brother—if not in Lady Anne, then in God and your sons. The boys will have found a way to make the journey easier for her, and God loves her too much to lead her wrong now.'

ɷ

The town appeared empty of life. There were no guards on the bridge and no people in the streets. Gyles was reminded of riding through Dorchester in the early days of the pestilence, when a pall of death had hung over the streets, but he didn't have that same sense here. There were too many signs of recent industry— broached barrels of ale outside tavern doors, the scent of newly baked bread, sheep carcasses hanging from a beam outside a shop.

He knew Blandeforde well from visits he'd made in the past as part of Sir Richard's retinue, and needed no directions on how to find the manor house. Nevertheless, as they neared the turning which led to it he had a growing fear that they were riding towards a flogging. Or worse.

The whip had been banned in Develish for a decade and a half, but he could still remember when Sir Richard had insisted on every serf being summoned to watch a fellow's skin being flayed. Lady Anne's arrival had brought an end to such punishment but the sport had remained common in neighbouring demesnes. Countless times Gyles had been forced to witness a public scourging while lords laid wagers on how many lashes a serf could endure. His darkest memory was of watching a youth hanged for absconding. Thin and undersized, he had dangled at the end of a rope, his legs twitching through more than three hundred beats of a drum before he breathed his last. The spoils had gone to Sir Richard for guessing that the boy's puny weight would keep him from strangling sooner.

'You should prepare yourselves,' he told James and Alleyn. 'I can think of only one reason why bread has been baked but the streets are empty. The people have been ordered to the house. I pray the steward wants their attendance at a trial, though I fear it's more likely they've been summoned to witness a punishment.'

He led them on to the approach road and urged his mount to a trot. Even from two hundred yards, he could see guards along the walls, but his attention was drawn to the throng of women and children blocking the entrance. He guessed the gates must have been closed against them and wondered why. Had the steward ordered a penance so terrible that only men were able to stomach it? The thought alarmed him, and he nudged his horse to a canter, calling on James and Alleyn to do the same. The clatter of hooves on the road caused the crowd to turn and then scurry to the verges, and Gyles saw with relief that he'd guessed wrongly. The gates stood wide with nothing to impede their progress except a straggle of townsmen on the driveway beyond.

If he'd learnt anything from riding with Sir Richard, it was that Norman soldiers had more proficiency with dice than weapons. Few took the trouble to train once they realised how easily Dorseteshire folk were intimidated. There was no call to draw bows or swords when a charging horse or a flailing whip served the purpose better. At fifty yards, he saw that the guards on the walls to either side of the entrance were of an age with his twins, and he gambled they'd had little practice at firing on a moving target. With a shout to the crowd to stand clear, he took his mount to a gallop, and stretched himself along the animal's neck.

The townsmen on the driveway scattered as he thundered through the pillars with James and Alleyn close on his heels, and only when the bend in the driveway was too close for comfort did he straighten and pull hard on his reins. He took a few deep breaths. 'Compose yourselves as best you can,' he told his companions, straightening his tabard and settling his bow across his shoulder. 'Once around that corner, you will be judged by the way you display yourselves. Recall how well Thaddeus has taught our sons and you'll not go wrong.'

James held his finger to his lips. 'Someone comes,' he murmured, giving a small jerk of his head to the rear.

Gyles glanced behind him and then wheeled his horse to face the approaching townsmen. There were ten or twelve, the same who had been making their way towards the gates before the horses set them running.

'I know your crest,' said one. 'I wove it into a tapestry for Sir Richard of Develish three years back. If it's Milady you seek, you'll find her on the forecourt.'

'Thank you, sir. Has she been there long?'

'As long as the Mass lasted. An hour and a half perhaps.'

Gyles took what he could from these answers. 'Does your priest always hold Mass in the open?'

Another man answered. 'He's the steward's priest and had but one reason to sermonise outside: he fears being close to us. Mind, he absolved us of our sins, and that's a gift we haven't had in nigh on half a year.' He eyed Gyles curiously. 'The soldiers who accompany Milady wear a different crest. How so?'

'Their lord is Athelstan, cousin to Lady Anne. His men rode to Develish to inform her of his arrest.'

'She spoke of him in the town. It seems the steward has made an error by taking him in charge.'

'He has,' said Gyles, tapping the pack behind his saddle. 'And I bring the documents to prove it.' He studied the upturned faces. 'Were you summoned here for a trial or just a Mass?'

'Neither,' said the first man. 'We joined our fellow townsmen when Matthew Miller called on us to escort Lady Anne.'

'There are more of you?'

'Many more . . . and all still on the forecourt with your mistress. We have tasks to perform or would have remained with them.'

'Why do the women and children wait at the gate?'

The man shrugged. 'Entry has been forbidden for many months now. We're only here ourselves because of Milady's determination to gain access.'

Gyles's weathered face creased in a smile. 'She has a powerful way with her. I don't doubt the steward is already regretting the permission.' He pulled on his left rein and nudged his horse into motion again. 'I bid you farewell, sirs. May God go with you.'

He expected to hear the response 'And with you', but it seemed the men were regretting their early departure. As he led James and Alleyn at a walk towards the bend, the group chose to follow, their curiosity stronger than their need to work.

&

Thaddeus was grateful the servants had the same curiosity. Those who were closest to the windows called out descriptions of what they were seeing, and together they painted a clear picture of the battle for authority between Lady Anne and d'Amiens. Thaddeus had little difficulty interpreting Milady's actions, or indeed the steward's, but he found it harder to understand Aristide's. A maid, peering to her right, spoke of him hastening across the bridge to the church, and Thaddeus wondered what was taking him there. He had no need to retrieve de Courtesmain's scrolls, which lay on the table where the steward had tossed them before venturing out to confront Lady Anne.

The news that three mounted men in livery with a dozen townsmen behind them had rounded the bend in the driveway prompted the captain to move to the window. He clearly knew the Develish crest, because he asked Thaddeus if they could expect more of Lady Anne's men to join her. And why had these not accompanied her this morning rather than place her in the care of Athelstan's troop?

'I'm as ignorant as you of what's been happening in Develish this day,' said Thaddeus lightly, turning his hand in the bowl of warm briny water that Mistress Wilde had brought him. 'You'll get better answers by going outside and addressing these incomers directly.'

'To do that, I must trust you to hold to your parole, sire. Your master of hounds knows his way to the kitchen and the woodland beyond, and for all I know there are more of Lady Anne's people at the bottom of the driveway.'

'Then take him and the dogs with you. I cannot escape the guards and servants alone.' Thaddeus glanced at the matronly woman who hovered at his side with a salver of boiled rags. 'And nor would I wish to while Mistress Wilde shows me such kindness.'

Joshua ducked his head in a small bow. 'I would prefer to remain at your side, My Lord.'

Thaddeus looked deep into his eyes. 'You will serve a better purpose if you help the captain make sense of Develish speech,

Buckler. I wager these incomers will try to befuddle him with brogue. They did the same often enough with Master de Courtesmain, which is why he's so confused about my status.'

He couldn't tell if Joshua grasped his full meaning, but de Courtesmain certainly did, and Thaddeus counted the Frenchman's angry reaction a victory. For a quarter-hour, the hall had been subjected to his mummery of martyrdom: a sinking to his knees as he was chained to a pillar, the mouthing of prayers and his calling on God to chastise heretics. But it seemed he had too much conceit to allow Thaddeus's slur against his intellect to go unchallenged.

'Are there any lies you won't tell?' he hissed in French. 'Your precious whore has taught her people too well to have them grunt like pigs. Even the harlot you call mother knows how to fashion speech that can be understood.'

Thaddeus studied him with amusement. 'Take care whom you offend, Master de Courtesmain. You'll not be shown kindness by Dorseteshire folk if you call them pigs.'

'Tha' be the truth,' said Mistress Wilde with disgust. 'I zee but woone grunting hog here an' 'e be a Franky. The stoöard shoulda roped him in a sty avore he let him into My Lord's home to snabble his food an' spread his pwoison.' She stared de Courtesmain down as the servants in the hall greeted her brogue with laughter. 'Your soul is full of malice,' she finished in French. 'Good people will always hide their thoughts from you.'

໑ଚ

Gyles halted his convoy thirty paces short of where d'Amiens and his guards had formed a line across the driveway. He was content to wait until he was noticed, but realised quickly that the wait might be a long one. The attention of all was directed at Lady Anne, who walked amongst a large crowd of men on the forecourt, taking each by the hand and listening gravely as they told her their names and numbered their dead. At her sides were his twin sons, Ian and Olyver.

Away to Gyles's left, on the grassland close to the river's edge, Edmund Trueblood and Peter Catchpole were bent to the task of hobbling eight horses. Ahead, a dozen guards stumbled from the guard house, shrugging on tabards and pulling fingers through sleep-tousled hair. There was no sign of Thaddeus or Joshua.

Gyles thought it a strangely peaceful scene. For more than a decade, he had watched Milady use kindness and reason to quell the anger in men's hearts, but he marvelled that she had the courage to walk alone amongst so many strangers. Few lords would dare. He was reminded of some lines from Isaiah which Milady was fond of quoting. *And the wolf will dwell with the lamb, and the leopard will lie down with the kid. And the calf and the young lion and the fatling together; and a little boy will lead them.* She said it was a foretelling of the coming of Christ, but was it blasphemous to think it spoke of her as well? She displayed more honest love for people than was ever shown by men of the Church.

As if Gyles's thoughts had summoned him, the black-robed figure of the priest emerged from the woodland near the guard house. He seemed weighed down with care, or perhaps by the bag he cradled in his arms, but his rage at the sluggishness of the half-awake soldiers was clear. He struck the nearest across his face when the man was slow to buckle on his sword belt.

'The priest prepares an army,' whispered Alleyn behind him.

Gyles nodded. 'I see him. He looks to make himself their captain and they're not comfortable with it.'

'They're obeying him nonetheless.'

But not willingly, Gyles thought, casting about for the man who should be in charge.

'To your right,' murmured James. 'My son brings company.'

Joshua gave no indication that he recognised any in the convoy as he walked with the captain from the kitchen quarters. He called his pack to heel and addressed Gyles in French. 'I am Buckler, master of hounds to My Lord of Athelstan. This officer is captain of arms to My Lord of Blandeforde's steward. From the crest you wear, he believes you to be from Develish and has asked me to help him understand your speech.' He made a small bow to the captain. 'Will you allow me to explain that in words which are easier for them to understand?'

'As long as you don't play me false.'

Joshua nodded to the small group of townsmen. 'These men will tell you if I do. It's only Normans like Master de Courtesmain who find the brogue hard to understand.' He turned his attention back to Gyles. 'Our big woone a-got the likin' o' this man an' all the maëdes, an' our laëdy a-got the trust o' the v'ok vrom the town. Our Franky stoöard a-got the likin' o' none. The big woone a-told all that the Franky be zo baffled by our zpeech that 'e knows nowt o' truth in Develish. This be why 'e is so mistaëken abou' the big woone's naëme 'n status. Do 'e unnerstan'?'

'Ees,' answered Gyles with a nod. 'But I mun speak wi' the cap'n mysel'. Tell 'im I know Frankish.'

Joshua turned to his escort. 'This man speaks French and is ready to answer any question you have for him, sir.'

Gyles spoke before the captain could. 'I'm the same rank as you, sir, and am willing to give you any information you require, but I believe your own men's need of you is more urgent.' He gestured over the heads of the crowd. 'A dozen approach with swords at the ready and all look nervous. They appear to be under instruction from a priest who walks in their midst. Unless you share his blood lust, I suggest you free them from his command.' He stretched down a hand as a stream of curses issued from the other's mouth. 'Assist him up behind me, Buckler. Together, we'll reach them quicker than if he goes by foot.'

ᘒᘓ

Peter straightened from hobbling Killer and looked up to see a horse emerge from between the trees that lined the driveway and race at speed across the grass between the forecourt and the river. He barely had time to register that two men were astride it before it came to a quivering halt some twenty paces from a troop of armed soldiers. With no idea who the riders were, or where they had come from, he took them to be as much of a threat as the soldiers and cupped his hands about his mouth to give the warning cry of a fox—a sharp screech that burst upon the air. When he saw he had Ian's attention, he extended his arms, palms together, pointing in the direction Ian should look.

Ian turned in time to watch the captain leap to the ground and confront soldiers with drawn swords, but he was more interested in the crest of Sir Richard, which was emblazoned on the back of the rider's tabard. He knew from the way the man sat his horse that this was his father and, startled, he glanced towards d'Amiens, wondering what he made of Gyles's sudden appearance. But there was nothing to read in the steward's face.

'He's undecided what to do,' murmured Olyver in Ian's ear. 'He's asking himself how many more Develish men have come and whether he still has his captain's loyalty.'

Ian watched the captain pull his men forcibly from around the priest, ordering them angrily to sheathe their swords and form a line at his side. It was strange, made stranger by Lady Anne's soft, untroubled voice continuing to greet the townsmen as if nothing out of the ordinary was happening. Yet there was such a froth of anticipation in the air that Ian was sure every person on the forecourt knew something was amiss.

He chose to be unresponsive himself, watching impassively as the captain sent his men back to the guard house and took on the duty of escorting the priest himself. He pretended indifference when his father fell in behind them, and gave only a small nod of greeting to Edmund and Peter who returned, unbidden across the grass, to range themselves alongside him and Olyver. All the while, he studied d'Amiens out of the corner of his eye, certain he would not abide by his promise to keep from waging war on Lady Anne of Develish.

'Step clear of the crowd and make ready to face towards the driveway,' he whispered to his companions. 'We must be first to our bows when the steward instructs his guards to prepare theirs. Loose one arrow into the ground at his feet and aim the second at his heart.'

৩৫

The captain watched in disbelief as Athelstan's men ringed the steward's feet with shafts and nocked and aimed a second arrow even as his own men were struggling to find the string with their first. Two of the guards made a half-hearted attempt to block him as he strode around the forecourt, but he cursed them angrily and ordered them back into line. Their expressions of relief gave him momentary pause, but he was more intent on preventing further shafts from being released.

'What madness is this?' he demanded, planting himself squarely in front of Ian. 'Do you forget that Milady has pledged herself to peace?'

'I do not,' said Ian, taking a step to the side in order to keep d'Amiens in his sights, 'but your argument is with the steward. He questions your reasons for depriving the priest of his guard and seeks to prevent you doing the same with his. He ordered your men to take you in charge.'

'He speaks false,' said d'Amiens coldly. 'Recall your oath to protect your lord and be sure you understand where the real threat lies. These men are Develish serfs who wear livery to mask their banditry and thieving. They are here with the single purpose of forcing the release of the one who calls himself Athelstan. If you aid their attempts at rescue, you will give succour to felons.'

The captain stared at the ground for a moment and then appealed to Lady Anne, who stood a few paces behind Ian. 'Master d'Amiens is correct to remind me that I am bound by oath to protect my lord—or, in his absence, the steward who stands for him. If you value peace, milady, instruct these archers to lower their weapons.'

She shook her head regretfully. 'I cannot, sir, for they answer to Athelstan. You should know their leader speaks the truth, however. Master d'Amiens was the first to offer threat.' She held his gaze. 'It needs only for you to give your surety that it won't happen again. There can be no conflict if both sides are pledged to peace.'

The captain's lips twisted in a wry smile. 'And how do I give such surety, milady? I am a captain who is obliged to obey whatever instructions his lord's representative gives him.'

'Except when they're foolish,' she said with an answering smile. 'If the purpose of these soldiers was to release my cousin by force, they would have made Master d'Amiens their prisoner and bargained his freedom against their master's. The guards on either side of him would be dead and he would have a knife at his throat.' She paused. 'You have authority over your men, sir. I beg you to use it wisely. Athelstan's people ask only that he be allowed to prove his title free of duress and in the hearing of honest men.'

∽

Thaddeus had dressed his hand himself, placing small wads of boiled rag, steeped in brine, on either side of the wound and binding a long strip of the kirtle tightly about his palm to hold them in place. As the maids at the window reported the captain mounting behind a Develish man and riding at speed across the grass, he allowed Mistress Wilde to tie off the ends and help him ease his left arm from the sleeve of his shirt. He forbade her on the grounds of decency from removing the garment completely and refused her suggestion that they leave the great hall so that she might tend his wounds in private. Now was not the time to absent himself if what the maids at the window were describing was true.

Mistress Wilde sucked her teeth to see the blood begin to flow again as the scabs came away with his shirt sleeve, but in truth the blade hadn't penetrated far. Thaddeus urged her to clean the cuts with salted water before she bound them, thanking her kindly when she'd finished. She seemed unused to gratitude and her cheeks flushed rosy red as she assisted him back into his clothing. She asked if it was the custom where he came from to cleanse and treat open wounds in such a way and he answered that it was.

'And where would that be, sire?'

Thaddeus stared at de Courtesmain as he answered. 'My mother's family came from a town called Alexandria in Africa. It was she who taught me the value of salt in the cleansing of wounds.'

Angry spittle formed on the Frenchman's lips at this barefaced lie, but any retort he made was lost beneath a cry from the window that the steward had seized the captain and was threatening him with his own sword. The guards who remained in the great hall looked at each other in alarm and then turned their anxious faces to Thaddeus, looking to him for instruction.

With a sigh, he rose to his feet, taking the dagger from the table and dropping it into the pocket of his coat. 'She also taught me that men make poor decisions when they're afraid,' he murmured, ducking his head to Mistress Wilde before beckoning the guards to accompany him. 'I believe we'll serve peace better by going outside,' he said. 'The steward's quarrel is with me, not with your captain.'

The younger guard gestured towards the archway. 'Would the better route not be through the kitchen, sire? We'll likely meet the priest if we go by the front door and he'll not let you pass if he can prevent it.'

Thaddeus gave an approving nod. 'Lead on and I'll follow.'

Twenty

Ian doubted he and his companions could maintain tension on their strings for much longer. With the captain's body shielding the steward's, they had aimed their arrows at the guards on either side to warn them against entering the fray, but the effort was taking its toll. As each second passed, Ian felt his fingers loosen and his arms tremble under the strain of holding them at shoulder height.

A stillness had fallen on the forecourt as this new threat unfolded, broken only by Joshua and his dogs emerging from the trees that lined the driveway and crossing the grass to join his friends. He commanded the pack to form up in front of them and nocked an arrow in his own bow. His presence gave Ian heart, but in truth he could see no way out of the impasse except surrender. Neither Lady Anne nor the townsmen would tolerate the killing of defenceless guards or the death of the captain who had permitted them to enter the compound. Perhaps Olyver read his thoughts, for he urged him to hold fast.

'I see movement on the driveway,' he whispered.

And so it seemed did Joshua, for he gave a low whistle to set his dogs moving forward, hackles raised and growls rumbling in their throats. It mattered not that this was a trick like any other, performed in return for titbits; so loud were their snarls and so alarming their lowered heads and stalking tread that the attention of every guard in the line was fixed on them. D'Amiens ordered Ian to call them off or bear responsibility for the captain's life.

'You're mighty keen on killing innocent men, sir,' Alleyn Startout said in French, seizing the steward's sword arm from behind and forcing it away from the captain. He cracked d'Amiens wrist across his knee to dislodge the weapon and watched in satisfaction as it clattered to the ground.

James Buckler prised the steward's other arm from the captain's throat and twisted it behind his back. 'Your servant, sir,' he said to the captain in the same language. 'My Lord of Athelstan follows with his guards and a dozen townsmen. He asked me to tell you that he continues to honour his parole.'

The captain took a moment to regain his balance. The dogs had dropped to their bellies on a second whistle from Joshua, but Ian and his companions still kept the tension on their bows. 'Did he give orders for his men to stand down?'

'As long as you give the surety Milady asked for,' said Alleyn. 'He believes you think conflict as senseless as she does.'

'I do,' said the captain grimly, stooping to retrieve his sword. 'As would My Lord of Blandeforde were he here.' He replaced the weapon in its sheath. 'You have my surety,' he told Ian. 'Now oblige me by honouring Milady's pledge of peace.'

'Gladly, sir,' said Ian, lowering his bow and ordering his companions to do the same. He nodded towards the driveway beyond. 'My Lord approaches now.'

The captain turned to watch Thaddeus and his guards cover the last few paces. 'Will you order these men to release the steward, My Lord?' he asked. 'I have no authority to hold him, and nor do you or Milady.'

'Indeed.' Thaddeus motioned James and Alleyn to step away. 'I trust it's only your pride that's hurt, Master d'Amiens.'

'Your men were wrong to threaten me.'

'I could say the same about de Courtesmain.'

'Your wounding was none of my doing.'

'I don't doubt you, sir. It's the priest who holds the power here.' Thaddeus took the dagger from his pocket and balanced it on his bandaged left palm. 'I believe this is Aristide's. De Courtesmain was easily persuaded to wield it on his behalf.'

D'Amiens stared uneasily at the stained blade and the bloodied gashes in Thaddeus's left sleeve. 'You blame the Father unfairly. The intent to harm was clearly de Courtesmain's. He believes you to be a bastard serf from Develish so attacked your sinister side—the side that denotes illegitimacy.'

Thaddeus shook his head in amusement before flicking the knife into the air and catching it neatly in his right hand. 'De Courtesmain's thoughts are never so fanciful. He was simply obeying the priest's command to prevent me speaking to the household of how the pestilence can be avoided. Your confessor fears having his duplicity exposed. Withal, he's a poor judge of character. Whatever de Courtesmain's faults, he hasn't the stomach for murder . . . with or without a promise of absolution.'

D'Amiens chose to answer with bluster. He rounded on the captain. 'This man is a prisoner,' he snapped. 'Why is it he who's in possession of this weapon and not you or one of his guards?'

'It transfixed his palm from side to side, sir. He waited a half-hour before he could withdraw it.'

'Why did you not take it from him then?'

'It wasn't necessary, sir. My Lord had already given me his parole.'

'His status is yet to be determined.'

The captain shrugged. 'Then determine it, Master d'Amiens, and allow us all to resume our lives in peace. There'll be no need for violence once every grievance is resolved.'

'This man has been the cause of the violence and will provoke more once he's shown to be an imposter.'

'Not while my surety stands, sir. Worry more for yourself if his accuser is found to be a liar. You and the priest took much on faith when you chose to believe a stranger's stories of heresy and insurrection in Develish. My Lord of Blandeforde would have demanded stronger proof before he arrested a fellow noble who posed no threat to him.'

ᘓᕽᘔ

The closest and most interested observer of that day's happenings was Matthew Miller. Despite his name, his trade was woodworking and there had been precious little call for his services these past two seasons. Lack of work had pushed him into idleness, and lack of revenue had made him resentful of those who had put money aside when times were good. To be witness to something out of the ordinary—more, to be given a sense of purpose and a belief in the future by a woman he'd never met—had raised his spirits higher than they'd been in months.

He prided himself on knowing a deceiver just by looking at him—perhaps because he wasn't above a little duplicity himself when a customer was too green to know the value of what he was purchasing—and he had the feeling that none of the men who rode with or for Lady Anne was what he pretended to be. Yet he couldn't place their class. They gave themselves too much licence to be peasants or mercenaries. The timid hesitancy of the Norman guards was in stark contrast to the Doreseteshire men's confident threatening and disarming of the steward.

Out of the corner of his eye, Miller saw the mounted soldier, who had taken the captain at speed across the grass, pen the priest inside the angle made by the entranceway and the house. Ahead, he watched the approach of Athelstan. Andrew Tench had said he'd never seen so fine a noble, and Miller agreed. Athelstan's height set him above the men around him and the calmness of his manner gave him authority. He appeared as unaffected by d'Amiens calling him a bastard serf as he was to have had a knife pierce his palm.

Yet Miller questioned whether lords were ever so forbearing of discomfort and insolence. Over the years, he'd watched many pass through the town and he remembered them more for their angry complaining and petulance than their patience. But there was no doubting the captain's belief in the man's nobility. Had his words to the steward not made that clear, the respect he showed Athelstan certainly did.

Jeremiah Slater, too, seemed persuaded, though Miller guessed his sudden intervention was inspired by some hastily whispered words from Lady Anne when the steward ordered the captain to send Athelstan under guard to the church and to escort Milady to his office.

The greybeard stepped forward and raised his voice. 'Begging your pardon, sir,' he called to d'Amiens, 'but there are many on this forecourt who would wish to hear the reasons for this man being taken in charge. The guildsmen who accompanied the priest on Saturday night found no fault in him. Why do you?'

'You will know the explanation once his status has been determined.'

'By whom, sir? And on whose word? We can all see the gore on his sleeve and can guess he's been badly injured. Is his attacker the same who accuses him of imposture? If so, he has the right in law to demand justice for himself first. The claims against him will stand for nothing if a jury decides his accuser had murderous intent.'

A murmur of agreement rippled through the crowd of townsmen and Miller watched angry blood suffuse the paler skin in d'Amiens' face. But what offended him more? Miller wondered. To have his decisions challenged, or to see people he'd forsaken for so long speak with a single voice? Lady Anne had said it took courage and generosity to keep a community alive, and Miller saw that Jeremiah Slater had both. The greybeard showed more courage than younger men by once again drawing the steward's attention to himself.

'My friend speaks with knowledge, for he has served as a juryman in the manor court,' Miller said, thrusting forward to stand with Slater. 'All the townsmen here can claim a similar knowledge because of their obligation to attend—and some have seen it from the other side. You know this, Master d'Amiens, for it's your duty to preside over the court and mete out fines for late payment of taxes.' He gestured towards Thaddeus. 'This man is entitled to be heard before twelve good men who will bring fairness and reason to their verdicts.'

'But not in the manor court, which deals only with infractions against Blandeforde by-laws,' d'Amiens snapped. 'I remember you well, Miller. Your infringements have been many, and more often concern false description of goods than late payment of taxes.'

Miller laughed. 'Hardly infringements, sir, since I never lost those cases. A bowl is a bowl whether it costs a groat or a farthing. It's not the vendor's fault if the purchaser's a fool.' He gestured again to Thaddeus. 'Have you not laid the same charge against this man? There can be no falser description of goods than a bastard serf claiming the title of Athelstan and cousinship with Lady Anne of Develish. Why deny him the manor court when you were so generous in allowing me the use of it?'

'There are other issues involved.'

'But none so difficult that a jury of free townsmen can't decide them. You've insulted our intelligence once, sir. Will you do so again? We are as able to understand argument as we are to read ledgers.'

'Which you've still to show us,' called Andrew Tench. 'The convening of the manor court will give you that opportunity.'

Voices cried out in approval, and the captain stirred uneasily, perhaps worried that the fragile peace was about to be broken. Thaddeus laid a calming hand on his arm and addressed d'Amiens.

'We both know my arrest was unlawful,' he said without animosity, 'and were I able to lay my grievances before a jury of my peers—as is my right—I would do so gladly. Nevertheless, I have no quarrel with the good men of Blandeforde deciding my truthfulness. Do you hesitate to summon the court out of fear of having to answer questions yourself, Master d'Amiens? Or is it the priest who decides such matters?'

D'Amiens frowned at him, but whether in perplexity or dislike it was hard to say. 'The court building is in the town and we heard a half-year ago that all the officers were dead. There's been no manor court since, because verdicts reached by jurymen, not approved by officers, are deemed null and void. Is that your wish, Thurkell? To waste time arguing your case before men who lack the authority to free you?'

Thaddeus gave a grunt of amusement. 'You give away your powers too easily, Master d'Amiens.' He turned to Slater and Miller. 'I'm in your hands, good sirs. Are you elders of this town? If so, I believe you have the necessary standing to select jurymen.'

'We are, sire,' said Miller without hesitation. 'Master Slater is leader of our council and I am one of its members.'

'Andrew Tench also,' said Slater, beckoning the man forward. 'In addition, Roger Wright—' he pointed to one of the men beyond Thaddeus—'and Mark Summerlee.' He nodded towards his right. 'We all have knowledge of the manor court, sire, and, with respect to Master d'Amiens, he is mistaken on how jurymen are selected. It used to be that the officers picked the names until rumours began that favourable verdicts could be bought with money. Thereafter, My Lord of Blandeforde decreed that the choice should be made by lot.'

Roger Wright, the man behind Thaddeus, spoke up. 'You should know, too, that there's no requirement for the court to sit in the town building, Master d'Amiens. I've attended three trials in the great hall here, and my father spoke of several being held on this forecourt. Your predecessor thought it right that as many as possible should be allowed to witness the workings of the law, and the courtroom holds a bare forty.'

Andrew Tench raised his hand. 'As steward and presiding officer, you have but to call us to order and the court is convened,' he said. 'Your captain of arms can serve as bailiff and I as clerk of the rolls. I have a better script than most and will need but the use of a table, quill and parchment to make a true record of what is said. In addition, a Bible to take the oaths of truth. My Lord of Blandeforde summoned us in such a way five years ago and no questions were raised about the legality of the verdicts.'

Briefly, d'Amiens closed his eyes as if to shut out the townsmen's words. 'Do you have no care for Milady's people?' he asked Thaddeus. 'You may save yourself by these means but not them. De Courtesmain accuses the whole demesne of crimes.'

'Indeed. He glories in vaunting his self-proclaimed virtue . . . much like your priest.' Thaddeus turned the dagger in his fingers and then dropped it back into his pocket. 'The serfs of Develish will have nothing to answer for once de Courtesmain's lies are exposed. The truth will release them from suspicion, as it will me.'

'Then you can have no objection to my hearing what Milady has to say first. I will assemble the court here in one hour, and she may sit with me in the steward's office until that time comes. The delay will allow the servants to carry tables and benches outside, and the townsmen to draw lots.' D'Amiens dropped his head in a small bow to Lady Anne. 'Is that acceptable to you, milady?'

There was no hesitation in her reply. 'Quite acceptable, Master d'Amiens, but my journey was long and tiring, and I would beg the courtesy of a moment or two in private with a maid first. May I ask for the kindly matron who brought me cordial? I will need a chaperone when I'm in your office and would have more confidence in an older woman.'

D'Amiens' mouth twisted. 'You seem to have managed without a protectress so far, milady.'

'I haven't needed one,' she answered lightly. 'Apart from my husband, you're the only man who's ever invited me to enter his chamber unaccompanied.'

He scowled ferociously as the forecourt erupted in laughter. 'I was referring to your travelling alone with soldiers, milady.'

'I didn't doubt it, sir, but in truth I couldn't have asked for more chivalrous companions. They have learnt their respect and courtesy from their lord.' She turned to Thaddeus. 'I wish we were meeting again under happier circumstances, cousin, but be assured I shall not reveal the details of our pledge unless you have done so already.'

Thaddeus bent forward, touching his fingers to his forehead in order to hide the relief in his eyes. He had no idea how Milady had come by this knowledge, but he blessed her cleverness in raising it. 'I have not, dear friend. The pledge between us was a sacred one and only you have the right to speak of it.' He raised his head. 'Nevertheless, I would urge you to keep your counsel. Blandeforde's proxy has no better right than de Courtesmain to know my reasons for entering Develish last spring in the guise of a peasant called Thurkell.'

She was as adept at hiding understanding as he was. 'Is it but a year that has passed? So much has happened since that it seems longer.' She switched her attention back to d'Amiens. 'Shall we proceed, sir? I would hate to keep these good townsmen from their work longer than is necessary.'

ꙮ

Once inside the privacy of a chamber, Lady Anne took Mistress Wilde's hands in hers and searched her eyes. The woman must have some sympathy for Thaddeus, she thought, or she wouldn't have lent herself to Joshua's passing of a message to Edmund.

'Did my cousin speak of me to you, mistress?'

'He did, milady, and most highly. Everyone in the household has learnt of your care for your serfs and how you have saved them from the pestilence.'

Everything about her reminded Lady Anne of Clara Trueblood—her stocky stature, her smiling, plump-cheeked face, the straightforward way she spoke—and she followed her instinct that the woman would not betray her to the steward.

'I need your help, Mistress Wilde, but we have a short time only before I must present myself for questioning,' she said.

'What would have you me do, milady?'

'Tell me all you can about Master de Courtesmain. What does the household gossip say about him? How and where does he pass his days? Have promises been made to him in return for accusing my cousin? What happened here this morning? Why did I see him chained to a pillar in the great hall?' She gave a small laugh. 'But all this must be told in the few minutes it takes for me to use a chamber pot and rearrange my gown.'

Mistress Wilde laughed in return. 'There's no need to trouble yourself in that regard, milady. The steward's arse is so tight it takes him a quarter-hour to pass a turd. I'll remind him of that if he chafes at your tardiness.'

She shepherded Lady Anne towards a low chair with a hole in the seat and a chamber pot beneath it, and then brought forward a bowl of water, some cloths and a hairbrush, which she placed on a stool beside the seat. All the while she talked of what she knew. The priest had allowed the Frenchman through the gates some dozen days earlier when a guard reported a messenger speaking of heretical practices in My Lord of Blandeforde's vassal demesnes. A maid had overheard a later conversation between the priest and the steward which suggested the heresy concerned the illegal freeing of serfs. The Frenchman had remained seven days in the church before being given a room inside the house. He had shown great distrust of the servants and had been overly arrogant in the demanding of washing water and victuals.

On the evening of Easter Saturday, a messenger had come from the bridge to report the arrival of one who called himself Athelstan. Shortly afterwards, the priest, the steward and some twenty guards had proceeded down the driveway with flaming torches. The priest was clothed in the steward's attire and the steward was hiding his disfigured face inside the hood of his cloak.

As to what happened during the rest of that night or on Easter Sunday, Mistress Wilde couldn't say. Being head of the kitchen, her task had been to prepare the Easter feast. A rumour said that a prisoner was lodged in the guard house, awaiting trial once the Holy Day had passed; another that he was brought to the house after dark to prevent him corrupting the guards. Both rumours may have been true, because the servants were banned from showing themselves in the great hall or on the forecourt from nightfall on Sunday for fear they, too, would become corrupted by the prisoner's lies and blandishments.

The first Mistress Wilde knew of that morning's happenings was the steward's ranting at his captain of arms for showing cowardice before a woman. So loud was his voice that it could be heard in the kitchen and she had been curious enough to peep through the archway. Imagine her surprise when a tall, handsome man, laden with shackles, had come through the entranceway and chastised the steward for his intemperate speech, saying it wasn't the captain's fault if Lady Anne of Develish had refused his terms.

She spoke of Thaddeus with respect, describing him as calm and unafraid even when the Frenchman attacked him for saying that wickedness wasn't the cause of the pestilence. In truth, few of the servants had thought it was, since there were many more spiteful and cruel folk in their midst than the four who had succumbed. She added that few believed either that the town was as steeped in sin as Father Arisitide claimed.

'Most of us have family there . . . or *had*,' she said, laying aside the brush with which she'd neatened Lady Anne's hair. 'We've never been allowed to know their fate, or the fate of those the priest expelled, but it's hard to think of any of them so wicked that God would want them dead.' She assisted Lady Anne to her feet and knelt to arrange the folds of her gown.

'What reason does Father Aristide give for so few in the house-hold dying?'

'His daily reciting of the liturgy of the hours and the giving of general absolution, milady. By such means he sanctifies the land inside the wall and cleanses us all of our wickedness.'

'Does he sleep in the church?'

Mistress Wilde shook her head. 'The tower's cold and he likes his comforts too much.'

'Was My Lord of Athelstan told of the cleansing rituals?'

'I believe so, milady, for he said Father Aristide has been less than honest in his explanations about why the house remains free of the pestilence.' She stood with a grunt of satisfaction. 'You are truly beautiful. No one would think you'd made a journey this day.'

Lady Anne pulled a wry smile. 'I could wish my tired wits as easily refreshed, Mistress Wilde. I'll need a sharp mind if I'm to avoid the traps the steward and priest set for me.'

The matron chuckled. 'You'll be more at ease than they, milady. The priest's knowledge of women is limited to the confessional, and the steward's to chastising us for wastage. They'll not know how to handle one such as you.'

Lady Anne reached for the woman's hands again. 'I have asked that you stay with me as my chaperone. Do you feel able to do that? I have no wish to cause difficulties between you and Master d'Amiens, but your presence would give me confidence that what he says is truthful. He will surely hesitate to speak falsehoods before a member of the household.'

Mistress Wilde gave her fingers a tight squeeze. 'It'll not cause difficulties, milady. He has too much need of me in the kitchen.' Her eyes gleamed with sudden mischief. 'And if he or the Father wander from the truth, I'll let you know by crossing my wrists in front of my kirtle. It's past time some light was shed on the secrets of this house.'

ତ୦

The priest stood in a corner of the office and the steward behind the desk with his back to the window. Both faces were in shade, and Lady Anne wondered if this was deliberate when d'Amiens invited her to sit on a stool which was placed in such a way that she must look towards the light. With a smile, she requested Mistress Wilde to move the stool into the corner on the other side of the window from the priest, begging the steward's pardon for obliging him to turn around.

'I'm sure you're better able to stare into the sun than I am, Master d'Amiens,' she said, settling herself on the stool and giving a nod of acknowledgement to Aristide. 'How may I help you, sirs?'

The priest spoke first. 'Master de Courtesmain has brought us alarming tales of Develish, milady. He speaks of an abandonment of God, thievery and murder by a serf called Thurkell, and bonded men and women claiming to be the equal of lords. He reserves his worst accusation for you, saying you practise heresy.'

'How very strange of him.'

'These are serious charges, milady,' said d'Amiens.

'Indeed,' she answered gravely. 'As serious as the charges Sir Richard made against you some five years since, when you miswrote Develish's taxes. It was fortunate our steward of the time noticed the error before you departed. Sir Richard would have been obliged to raise the matter with My Lord of Blandeforde otherwise.'

'It was a small mistake in calculation, milady.'

'Hardly small, sir. By recollection you left twenty gold nobles out of your addition. Sir Richard would have ordered you flogged for thievery had I not persuaded him that error was more likely than deceit. He was quite convinced you planned to pocket the nobles yourself.'

D'Amiens eyed her with dislike. The knowledge he had of her now told him it was she who had seen the inaccuracy and sent her husband to rage against him. 'There was no deceit, milady.'

'Of course there wasn't,' she agreed. 'No one else thought as badly of you as Sir Richard did. I felt for you that his intemperate language meant we only saw your deputies thereafter.'

There was a short silence.

'I see no comparison between de Courtesmain's accusations and the false one that was levelled against Jacques d'Amiens,' the priest said then.

'You would if you'd ever been accused of a crime you hadn't committed, Father. Master d'Amiens was deeply distressed to have Sir Richard call him a thief.'

'What reason would de Courtesmain have to make up such tales?'

Lady Anne gave a whisper of a laugh. 'How else could he gain entry here? He was a stranger without place or position. What better way to ensure a welcome than to tell a compelling story about one of Blandeforde's vassal demesnes.' She glanced at d'Amiens. 'The bigger mystery is how he persuaded you he wasn't carrying the pestilence. In Develish, we insist on fourteen days' exclusion before we allow people across the moat.'

'He was confined to the church for a week. The Father took him his food and spoke to him through the door.'

'That must have frightened the household.'

'Why? They had no contact with him.'

Lady Anne showed surprise. 'Do they know that contact is dangerous? I thought they were persuaded that absolution and the liturgy of the hours keeps them safe. To have Father Aristide shut from his church for seven days, and the cleansing rituals abandoned, must have worried them.'

The priest stirred angrily. 'These are insignificant matters beside the godlessness of Develish,' he snapped, gesturing to some scrolls on the desk. 'The details are written here, inscribed by de Courtesmain. Your priest has been silenced, your serfs promised freedom and your daughter declared illegitimate so that you and the son of a Develish harlot can govern the demesne together.'

'You make me quite faint with these words, Father. Master de Courtesmain lived amongst us for eight months and I never once guessed his mind was so disturbed. If you'll allow Mistress Wilde to fetch my bag from outside, I can show you the steward's ledger from Develish which tells the true story of my demesne.'

'As written by you and Thurkell.'

She shook her head. 'There are many hands, for the record dates back twenty years. The most recent are mine, Athelstan's and de Courtesmain's. You will recognise your informant's in the pages he composed. He was eager to make what contribution he could to Develish's survival while he was amongst us, and it saddens me greatly that he maligns us now in order to win favour here.' She turned to Mistress Wilde. 'Oblige me by asking my captain of arms to give you the bag that contains the ledger, mistress. You will know him by his closely cropped hair and the Develish crest he wears. I don't doubt Master d'Amiens and Father Aristide will agree to wait on the other side of the door during your absence.'

Mistress Wilde gave them no choice, stepping behind the desk and using her broad body to urge them ahead of her. Once outside, she closed the latch securely behind her, bobbed a respectful curtsey and then hurried toward the entranceway. Her mind was spinning with what she'd heard. *Master d'Amiens a thief . . . the liturgy of the hours a lie . . . Develish a godless Hell.* Was any of it true? she wondered, searching the forecourt for Milady's captain of arms. She picked him out immediately, for he stood apart from the crowd with two others, each wearing the same crest on his tabard and holding his horse by its reins.

They were deep in conversation but broke off as she approached. 'Are you Milady's captain, sir?' she asked Gyles.

'I am, mistress.'

'She asks that you give me the bag that contains the ledger. She wishes the priest and steward to see it so they know she speaks the truth.'

Gyles glanced towards the river. 'My Lord of Athelstan's men have charge of it,' he said, nodding to where Ian and his companions stood with their horses. 'I can accompany you on foot or fetch it more speedily by riding. Which would you prefer?'

Mistress Wilde laughed. 'Speed, sir. I'm a slow walker and Milady's too wearied from her journey to endure the company of Master d'Amiens and Father Aristide for long.'

Gyles swung into his saddle. 'If you have Milady's trust, you have ours,' he said, nodding to James and Alleyn. 'Tell my men how she fares. We worry that she has no protection inside the house.'

As he left, Mistress Wilde looked to James. 'There's no cause for worry,' she assured him. 'Milady may be tired but her mind is strong. I believe the steward and priest feel more menaced by her than she by them.'

'It's Master de Courtesmain we fear, mistress. It seems he's already attacked My Lord of Athelstan. We cannot allow the same to happen to Lady Anne. Where is he now? What news do you have of him? Are his accusations believed?'

She needed little prompting to repeat what she knew. For herself, she thought Milady was right to say the Frenchman's mind was disturbed and his claims against Develish merely designed to win him a position in Blandeforde, but it was clear the priest believed them. She asked the men if anything de Courtesmain said was true, and because they spoke with Doreseteshire accents, she gladly accepted their denials. The day would end poorly if it was Lady Anne who was lying and not the malicious Frenchman.

Twenty-one

WHEN D'AMIENS RE-ENTERED THE OFFICE, he looked at the scrolls on the desk before he looked at Lady Anne. If any had been unfurled and read, it wasn't obvious, though he saw humour in her eyes when he raised his gaze to hers. There had been time enough for her to scan them all, and he chided himself for not removing them. He handed her an advantage each time he under-valued her character and intelligence.

Mistress Wilde placed the bag at Lady Anne's feet. 'Your captain sends his compliments, milady, and trusts that all is as it should be. He's concerned that the loose scrolls may have been crushed by the weight of the ledger.'

Lady Anne smiled her gratitude. 'I'm sure he worries un-necessarily,' she said. 'Will you oblige me by turning away, sirs?' she asked d'Amiens and Aristide. 'There are garments personal to a lady in here and it wouldn't be seemly for you to see them. It will take but a moment to retrieve the documents from the bottom.'

They did as she asked but, even so, she was careful to use the flap of the bag to obscure the contents once she'd unbuckled it.

She had no more desire for them to glimpse the britches she'd worn than Gyles's 'loose scrolls' of which she was ignorant. There were two of them lying atop her woollen cloak and she moved them to her lap before pulling out the ledger and placing it above the scrolls. She let the flap drop again and thanked the steward for his patience.

She handed him the ledger. 'You'll find Sir Richard's and my own lineage inscribed at the front, Master d'Amiens. Athelstan is shown as my cousin through direct descent from my grandfather's brother. It gives his date of birth as one year before mine. If you'd rather study the record in private, I'm happy to wait in the chamber Mistress Wilde found for me.'

'That won't be necessary, milady. I'll have queries as I read and you'll be better able to answer them if you remain.' He nodded to the scrolls in her lap. 'What are they?'

Lady Anne unrolled the first and recognised the shaky, ill-formed script as Father Anselm's. 'This is written by my priest and is addressed to His Grace of Sarum. And this—' she unrolled the next and saw that, though the letter was signed with Eleanor's childish hand, the writing was Isabella Startout's—'is from my daughter, Lady Eleanor. It, too, is addressed to His Grace of Sarum.'

'Why is neither sealed?'

'Wax is precious in Develish, sir. We reserve what little we have for the making of altar candles.'

Father Aristide gave a snort of disbelief. 'You lie. I watched Thurkell seal a parchment with wax two nights ago.'

She smiled slightly. 'Would that be when you were claiming to be the steward, Father? The townsmen tell me their fellows found it unnerving to have you speak so many lies about yourself.' She paused. 'If by Thurkell you mean Athelstan, he left Develish with

My Lord of Bourne and Master de Courtesmain on the first day of January—some three and a half months since. I imagine any wax he uses comes from Bourne.'

'You have answers for everything, milady,' said d'Amiens.

'You will find more in the ledger, sir.'

But not the ones you want, she thought, as they bent their heads to the pages. There was no mention of Thaddeus entering the demesne last spring in the guise of a peasant or explanation for why he would do such a thing. She could guess he'd devised the idea of a 'pledge' to avoid having to give a reason himself and had then cursed mightily to hear that the person who could release him from his promise was at the gate. But where did that leave her? What possible reason could Milady of Develish have had to ask her cousin to pose as a peasant before her husband and his new steward?

Every story she and Thaddeus had composed had been designed to convince d'Amiens of Athelstan's nobility. Not once had they thought to invent explanations for why he might have feigned being a serf in front of de Courtesmain. She understood why he'd had no choice but to admit knowledge of the Frenchman— de Courtesmain's descriptions in his scrolls were so precise that anyone would recognise Thurkell in Athelstan—but she had no idea what to do about it without knowing what else Thaddeus had claimed. Had he said all in Develish believed him a serf? And why would he not have declared himself after Sir Richard's death?

With an inward sigh, she lowered her gaze to Eleanor's letter. It was a fickle irony that in order to defend Thaddeus against one accusation of imposture she must prove him capable of maintaining another.

⚭

Easter Monday, 1349

Your Most Reverend Grace,

I am Eleanor of Develish, daughter to Sir Richard (now deceased) and his widow Lady Anne. I pray that you are well and that this letter reaches you, for I am greatly troubled in mind over the whereabouts and fate of my beloved mother and her cousin My Lord of Athelstan.

News reached us yesterday in the midst of our joyous celebrations of Christ's resurrection that My Lord of Athelstan had been taken prisoner in Blandeforde. This alarming message was brought by one of his fighting men who spoke of accusations of imposture being made against My Lord. The soldier could not say who the accuser was, but Lady Anne knows of only one person who would level such charges against her cousin. He goes by the name of Hugh de Courtesmain and holds deep grudges against My Lord of Athelstan.

Honoured Sir, I beg you to believe that Master de Courtesmain is not to be trusted. He came to Develish at the behest of my father, who believed he would make a loyal and able steward. This proved to be untrue. Master de Courtesmain was so afeared for himself when Sir Richard died of the pestilence that he handed government to my mother and reduced himself to the class of peasant in order to escape responsibility.

It was by God's mercy that our cousin, Athelstan, was on a visit from Spain when this happened, for he was able to assist Lady Anne in the management of Sir Richard's estate. Being much travelled, he has more knowledge of the world than she, and his different customs and ease of manner endeared him greatly to my father's people in our time of trouble. Together, he and Lady Anne used their wisdom to keep Develish safe, and this caused jealousy and resentment in Master de Courtesmain who saw that he'd been foolish to relinquish his authority so hastily.

Lady Anne has journeyed to Blandeforde to demand My Lord of Athelstan's release but I have grave concerns for her safety. We had word that My Lord of Blandeforde travelled west last year and I do not know who governs in his place. Whoever that person is, I fear Master de Courtesmain has filled his head with falsehoods, and the blame for that is mine. I am more childish than a girl of fourteen years should be and, out of scorn for his cowardice, teased Master de Courtesmain daily with stories that were not true. To my shame, I laughed to see his expressions, for his jealous nature led him to believe the most foolish absurdities.

If you be willing, I beg you to send an envoy to Blandeforde to discover what is happening there. I have such dread that my ill-considered teasing of a man too craven to honour his pledge to my father has led to terrible error. In true contrition, I have performed every penance Father Anselm has asked of me for my falsehoods, but only you have the power to redeem my intemperate words. My Lord of Athelstan is ill-versed in English law, and, being but a woman, my mother may not be given a hearing.

I entreat you to believe that Almighty God blessed Develish twice when He gave charge of the demesne to

Lady Anne and ordained that My Lord of Athelstan was at hand to help her. In great humility and obedience to God, and assisted by the prayers of our priest Father Anselm, they have protected my father's people and welcomed those from other demesnes who have come seeking sanctuary. My Lord of Bourne from Wiltshire was one such and will testify to the truth of what I write.

Your most contrite and humble servant,
In nomine Patris et Filii et Spiritus Sancti
Eleanor of Develish

❧

Lady Anne saw more than Isabella's hand in the letter. The cleverness of the ideas and phrasing were surely hers, for Eleanor would never have thought to write of de Courtesmain looking 'to escape responsibility' or Thaddeus having 'different customs' and being 'ill-versed in English law'. Perhaps Isabella had helped, too, in the construction of Father Anselm's letter for, though the hand was his, the expressions of praise were quite foreign to his nature, and she wondered if Gyles and Clara had had the foresight to soften his mood with drink before he began—or, more simply, Gyles had threatened to oust him from his comfortable quarters in the church.

She watched d'Amiens flick through the pages of the ledger, reading some but ignoring most, and it was clear to her that he was searching for the crimes and heresies that de Courtesmain had listed by date in his scrolls. He wouldn't find them, for they were in her private journal, buried at the bottom of a coffer in her chamber. Nevertheless, she knew there was mention of Thaddeus Thurkell in this ledger, often in her own hand.

After a quarter-hour, d'Amiens raised his head. 'This tells me nothing except that Develish's days are filled with tedium. The only pages of interest are those that refer to Thaddeus Thurkell.'

'Would those be the ones written by Master de Courtesmain?' she asked calmly. 'He cuts his quill very fine so his hand is distinctive. You will know it from his scrolls.'

'Why does he not refer to Thurkell as Athelstan?'

'Because Thurkell is the name by which he knew him.' Lady Anne lifted Father Anselm's letter from her lap and offered it to him. 'This may help you understand. It's addressed to His Grace of Sarum but, since it's unsealed, I see no reason why you shouldn't read it.'

'The date is today's. How did you come by it?'

'Father Anselm entrusted it to my captain of arms. Should I and Athelstan be denied justice here, he will ride with it to Sarum.'

෨෯

Easter Monday, 1349

Most Reverend Sir,

> *I am Anselm of Develish. If this letter reaches you, I beg you to pray for me as I pray for you each morning and night. With God's blessing we will both survive the pestilence.*
> *This letter will accompany one from Lady Eleanor of Develish, who beseeches you on her knees to intercede on behalf of Lady Anne, her beloved mother, and Lord Athelstan, her admired cousin. Since time is pressing, I will not repeat the reasons for her request, which she has*

set out well enough, but will say only that I lend my pleas to hers out of a sincere belief that the light of God shines strongly in the two persons she entreats you to help.

Lady Anne is a noblewoman of great love and kindness who has striven to honour her deceased husband's pledge to protect his people. She has done so in humility, following St Francis's example of wearing simple homespun and sharing all she has with her serfs so that they might better understand how beloved they are by God. In this endeavour, she has had the support of My Lord of Athelstan, whose presence has been a source of hope and belief in God and the future. He, too, adopts the ways of St Francis, taking a simple name, choosing humbleness over extravagance and paying heed to all men, regardless of their class.

It is a cause for joy that none in Develish has died of the pestilence since Sir Richard passed. Yesterday, as we celebrated His glorious resurrection, every voice was raised in praise and gratitude to Christ Our Lord. He has shown us nothing but love and we repay Him a thousandfold in the care we have for each other.

Honoured sir, I commit Lady Anne and My Lord of Athelstan to your mercy and beg that you respond to Lady Eleanor's entreaties.

> Your humble servant,
> In nomine Patris et Filii et Spiritus Sancti
> Anselm

❧

D'Amiens laid the letter aside and examined the page from the Develish register of births. 'The hand is the same,' he said, placing both before Aristide. 'But the thinking and spelling in one is better controlled than the other.'

Aristide took the page of births and deaths from d'Amiens and handed it to Lady Anne. 'How do you explain this, milady? It was written by your priest, was it not?'

She looked at it and nodded. 'Did Master de Courtesmain steal it from us? How very unkind of him. He should have given more thought to families who might want reminding of when their parents and grandparents died.'

'I'm more interested in the birth of Thaddeus Thurkell, milady.'

Lady Anne read the words aloud. '*A sun, Thades, was bor this second week of June, thirteen twenty-eight, to Wil and Ev Thkell.*' She laid the vellum in her lap. 'Poor Eva. It was all too common for children to die early before I arrived in Develish. Did de Courtesmain not think to search for the notification of death? He must surely have questioned why Athelstan looks so much older than a serf born twenty years ago.'

There was a brief hesitation before the priest spoke again. 'Why should he? Thurkell was alive.'

'My *cousin* was alive, Father. Several serfs offered to lend him a name but he chose Thaddeus Thurkell when Eva begged him to take her firstborn's. It pleased her, I think. She loves to picture her lost son as tall and fine as Athelstan.'

'It makes no sense,' the priest snapped. 'Why would a noble pose as a serf? There's no quicker way to incite rebellion than to give such people a sense of importance.'

'Your husband wouldn't have allowed it,' said d'Amiens. 'He had a great hatred of the peasant class.'

Lady Anne smiled. 'He had a hatred of many things, sir. Myself most of all.'

D'Amiens had no doubt then that she had read the scrolls. She wouldn't have admitted Sir Richard's dislike of her had de Courtesmain not revealed it. 'That doesn't answer Father Aristide's question, milady.'

'Perhaps not,' she agreed, 'but it may answer yours. Sir Richard would not have given my cousin entry had he known who he was. He cut me off from my family when we married so that he could do as he pleased with both me and my dowry.'

'You had no rights in the marriage, milady. Few women do.'

'Indeed. He often called me the lowest of his serfs. It's fortunate I can read and write and that kinder stewards than de Courtesmain enabled me to send and receive letters in secret. My situation would have been unbearable otherwise.'

The priest was shocked. 'You abused your husband's trust? The vows of matrimony bound you by sacred oath to honour and obey him.'

Lady Anne nodded. 'And I learnt sympathy for his serfs because of it, Father. Our plights were similar.'

She found an unexpected ally in Mistress Wilde who gave an involuntary laugh. 'Milady of Blandeforde says the same. We're no different, you and I, except in the way we dress, she tells me. We both have to run when the master calls.'

D'Amiens ignored her. 'Do you wish us to understand that you invited your cousin to enter Develish as a peasant in order to deceive your husband, milady?'

'Not so much to deceive as to be invisible,' she answered mildly. 'Had he been noticed by Sir Richard and forced to give a name, you could rightly accuse him of deception . . . but it never happened. Sir Richard had better recognition of his horses than his people.'

'Develish is not so big that a stranger wouldn't stand out, particularly one as distinctive as Athelstan. The steward and bailiff must have seen him. And why would the priest turn a blind eye to the imposture? He owed a duty to be honest with his lord just as you did.'

Lady Anne nodded. 'And so he would have been had Sir Richard asked him directly who the newcomer was. The bailiff also. I made no request of anyone in Develish to tell lies to Sir Richard, only to give a welcome to Athelstan while he was amongst us. None saw harm in it, for they all knew they wouldn't be questioned. Sir Richard was absent from the demesne more often than he was in it, and Athelstan slept in our hospital which my husband never visited. The chances of them meeting were very small.'

'What of the steward?'

'He'd been dead three months. We were awaiting the arrival of de Courtesmain from Foxcote.'

'Explain.'

Lady Anne sighed. 'I doubt you'll understand the reasons if I do, sir, any more than you understand why Milady of Blandeforde likens herself to a servant.'

'There's no avoiding an explanation, milady. If Athelstan is who you say he is, then I'm willing to accept Sir Richard was never told falsehoods about him. But de Courtesmain certainly was. In both his written and spoken word, he affirms that my prisoner is a bastard serf called Thaddeus Thurkell who was born and raised in Develish. How so unless the whole demesne was in league to mislead him?'

Lady Anne lifted Eleanor's letter from her lap and placed it on the desk. 'It was only my daughter who led him false, sir. He sought to ingratiate himself with her after Sir Richard died and she despised him for it. You may blame me and Athelstan for not correcting the misconception but, as God is my witness, de Courtesmain never once asked if the man he believed to be Thurkell was a serf. Had he done so, all Develish would have told him no.'

Grudgingly, d'Amiens read the second letter. 'Why should I believe this? Your daughter will always take your side.'

Lady Anne wondered if he realised how much he was accepting with these words when de Courtesmain had dedicated an entire scroll to Eleanor's hatred and denunciation of her mother. 'I could as easily ask why you believe de Courtesmain, Master d'Amiens.'

'I haven't said I do, milady, but he accuses you and Thurkell of conspiring with others to win freedom for the serfs of Develish. Do you expect me, as Blandeforde's proctor, to ignore such an allegation when every man, woman and child in Develish is as bound to My Lord through sacred oath as they were to his vassal Sir Richard?'

She shook her head. 'I would not, but nor would I expect you to act on such an allegation without first questioning the honesty of the man who makes it. Does his attack on Athelstan not tell you he has great dislike of my cousin and give you cause to wonder whether truth or bitterness drives him?'

When d'Amiens made no response, Father Aristide stepped forward to place a hand on his arm. 'It's easily established, my son,' he said. 'Fetch de Courtesmain here and allow him to make his accusations to Milady. God will tell us which of the two is the perjurer.'

❦

Mistress Wilde wondered at Lady Anne's calmness when the steward returned with de Courtesmain, freed of his shackles. For herself, she was alarmed to be in a small room with him, unchained and unguarded. She took comfort from the knowledge that his weapon had been removed by My Lord of Athelstan, but her comfort was short-lived when the priest untied a hessian roll on the desk to reveal a large bejewelled cross and silver-bound Bible. In the hands of a lunatic, either was heavy enough to crush a skull.

In her mind, she was urging Milady to protest against the steward bringing so dangerous a man into her presence, but Lady Anne did the opposite. She greeted Master de Courtesmain with a gentle nod of welcome and asked how he fared. 'It saddens me to see you here, sir. I had hoped you would find contentment in Bourne.'

How strangely he looked at her, Mistress Wilde thought. Had she thought it possible, she would have said there was a yearning for Milady in his eyes. 'Thurkell destroyed that chance, milady. He turned Bourne against me.'

She shook her head. 'It was he who gave you the chance. Bourne was unpersuaded of your abilities until Athelstan spoke in praise of you. We both had every expectation you would make a success of the post.'

'You wanted rid of me, milady.'

'Not I, sir. I would have preferred you to remain in Develish. We had need of your cleverness these last three months. Our numbers have swelled with starving serfs from Pedle Hinton, and there's too little room for so many. It's been hard to find places for them to sleep.'

'Did you make use of the church, milady? I said many times that upwards of forty could sleep there in comfort.'

She smiled. 'I remembered, and Father Anselm has been most generous in allowing us the benefit of it. He takes particular care of an elder called Harold Talbot whose wits have become scattered through age. Harold addresses us all with titles from his last demesne. I am Milady of Pedle Hinton and Father Anselm is Father Jean. Were you still with us, you would have to answer to Master Marron, whom Harold assures me is quite the best steward in Dorseteshire.'

D'Amiens saw all too well what she was doing: using smiles and honeyed tones to weaken de Courtesmain's resolve. 'Marron has been dead a decade,' he said coldly. 'He was gone even before I became steward here.'

Lady Anne's eyes lit with amusement. 'Indeed. Poor Harold's confusion is very great. He believes his daughter to be his wife, and the head of our kitchen, who chastises him regularly for taking more food than he should, to be his mother—never mind she's fifteen years his junior. We answer to whatever he wants to call us for fear of upsetting him. A name is not so important that I cannot be Milady of Pedle Hinton when the need arises.'

D'Amiens made an ironic bow. 'Cleverly done, milady. Now tell us why it was necessary to keep Athelstan's name and status from de Courtesmain.'

Before she could answer, the priest advanced with the cross and the Bible. 'Kneel and place your hands on these as you swear before Almighty God that you will speak only the truth. Know that both have been blessed by the Holy Father and are as infallible as he at discovering error. Do not imperil your soul by seeking to deceive us.'

Lady Anne did as she was bid, bowing her head and saying the words aloud while begging God in her mind to forgive her. Had the cross and Bible been made from simpler, humbler materials, her conscience might have pricked her more, but she found it as hard to see Christ's love in richly ornate jewels and silver as she did in Father Aristide's thin, judgemental face. In any case, if it was indeed a mortal sin to give a fatherless child a name and family he could be proud of, her soul had been lost to her the day she inscribed Athelstan's lineage.

She placed herself on the stool again. 'Master de Courtesmain came to Develish while Sir Richard was still alive,' she said. 'Had he been made aware of Athelstan's status then, he would have informed my husband. His gratitude at being raised from bailiff in Foxcote to steward in Develish made him intensely loyal to his new master.'

'As was his duty,' said d'Amiens.

'Indeed, and I had no wish to make his position more difficult by revealing a secret he didn't need to know.'

'How was it difficult?'

'Sir Richard employed him for the single purpose of increasing the levy on Develish serfs in order to raise his personal share by another tenth. I believe Master de Courtesmain found that order troubling.'

'He should. My Lord of Blandeforde has a great dislike of extortion.' D'Amiens glanced at de Courtesmain. 'Was that made known to you by Sir Richard?'

Hugh ran his tongue across his lips. 'It was not, sir.'

D'Amiens eyed him for a moment and then instructed the priest to have him swear to the truth as Lady Anne had done. To Mistress Wilde, de Courtesmain's oath sounded false and insincere, being delivered in the same self-righteous tone with which he'd condemned Athelstan's heresy. Perhaps d'Amiens agreed, because he turned again to Lady Anne for answers.

'What other reason might he have had for finding the order troubling?'

Lady Anne's soft gaze held Hugh's for a moment. 'Sir Richard's sister wrote from Foxcote of Master de Courtesmain's zealotry in whipping serfs who could not or would not pay upwards of three-quarters of what they grew. Since my husband was illiterate, I was obliged to read the letter to him and saw how eager he was to acquire such a person. It made me distrustful of Master de Courtesmain before he arrived, though I came to understand later that he had felt debased by the vile regime in Foxcote and had no wish to repeat it in Develish.'

'Is this true, Master de Courtesmain?'

Hugh closed his eyes as if in agony. 'It grieved me greatly that Sir Richard thought I was willing to bring Foxcote's cruelty to Develish. I tried to make him understand that one half of a bounteous demesne's yield would always exceed three-quarters of one that struggled through death and hunger, but his knowledge of letters and numbers was so poor that such thinking was beyond him.'

'Are you a heretic, sir?'

'By no means,' Hugh cried, his eyes rolling in terror.

'Yet throughout your scrolls you accuse Milady and Thurkell of dissent for speaking ill of Sir Richard. How is it different when you do it?'

'I sought only to explain why his orders troubled me. My loyalty to him was never in question. The same cannot be said of Milady and Thurkell, who refused him entry when he returned from Bradmayne.'

'You were his steward. Why did you not override Milady's order and grant him admittance?'

'The serfs conspired against me. Had I tried, they would have prevented me.'

'There was nothing to stop you crossing the moat and informing Sir Richard of his people's insurrection. You wrote of Thurkell offering the raft to anyone who feared his master's anger. Why did you not take advantage of that offer yourself if you were as loyal as you claim?'

'Thurkell would have stopped me.'

'Is that true, milady?'

Lady Anne shook her head. 'Master de Courtesmain was free to leave whenever he chose. I offered him the chance to return to Foxcote after Sir Richard's death but he refused. He preferred to remain in Develish until My Lord of Bourne offered him the position of steward on his estates, which, being larger and wealthier, suited his ambitions better. I imagine he hopes to find a post here now that Bourne has let him go.'

Time passed as d'Amiens stared at one then the other, assessing their credibility. Perhaps the little Frenchman's obvious discomfort to be in Lady Anne's presence tilted the balance, for he seemed suddenly to make up his mind.

'You and Athelstan both spoke of a pledge, milady. If you give me the reasons for it, and I find them acceptable, I'll be more inclined to believe you than de Courtesmain. He has only a page from a register and self-inscribed scrolls to support his story. You have a ledger—in some places written by him—testimony from your priest and daughter, and the clear loyalty of eight fighting men to support yours. Explain why you asked your cousin to live in Develish as a peasant so that I might better reach a judgement.'

'The fighting men are her serfs,' protested Hugh. 'Their word cannot be trusted.'

'But yours *can*, sir?' Lady Anne asked. 'That was never my experience while you were living in Develish.' She turned to d'Amiens. 'I'm within my rights to refuse your request and ask the men of the town to make the judgement. Athelstan has already agreed to accept their verdict.'

'If that's your choice, all Blandeforde will learn your business, milady.'

She smiled. 'They will anyway. Once shared, a secret becomes yet another piece of gossip.' She pressed her fingers to her eyes for a moment and then dropped her hands to her lap. 'My husband was incapable of managing Develish, Master d'Amiens. You may have guessed this from your visits, though I doubt you knew it was I and not the stewards who managed in his stead. Sir Richard was quite ignorant of my involvement. He believed it was his stewards who made the decisions.'

'But they were yours?'

She nodded. 'For the most part, and always with the stewards' agreement. Before de Courtesmain, they were English freemen who saw sense in helping serfs increase their yields through improved health and the teaching of better work practices, because it made their job of collecting the King's taxes and the Church's tithes easier.' She paused. 'Sir Richard was never content with his portion, even though it always surpassed his neighbours who'd been granted larger demesnes. He pestered every steward to increase his personal levy on his people. Each resisted for the reasons Master de Courtesmain gave you, but when I read Lady

Beatrix's letter, I feared he'd finally found a man who would not. It was for this reason I asked Athelstan to come to Develish.'

'To do what?'

'Protect me from my husband when he learnt I was trying to help his serfs buy themselves out of bondage. To lose at dice was enough provocation for Sir Richard to strike me. To lose control of his people would have caused my death, I think.'

D'Amiens eyed her thoughtfully. Perhaps he was recalling Sir Richard's intemperate rage at the missing twenty nobles. 'De Courtesmain accuses you of worse. He says your plan is to take your serfs out of Develish, leaving false evidence that all have died of the pestilence, so that they can live elsewhere and gain their liberty for nothing.'

Lady Anne gave a small shrug. 'If such a plan existed, I wouldn't be here,' she answered. 'Where's the sense in telling you that all in Develish live if, in truth, I want you to believe us dead?'

'Master de Courtesmain tells a chilling tale of you inciting your people to break their oaths of fealty and your daughter denouncing you as a heretic because of it. Is he lying?'

She glanced at Hugh. 'Would you have me make such cruel allegations against you, sir?' she asked him. 'You cannot deny you tried to gain entry to Lady Eleanor's chamber when you knew her to be unchaperoned. By recollection, you told her I had lost my authority, that the serfs were in control of the demesne and only you could protect her from them. Your falsehoods caused her great distress, Master de Courtesmain.'

'Well?' d'Amiens demanded when de Courtesmain stayed silent.

'She twists everything—just as Thurkell did in the church this morning.' De Courtesmain's hands writhed in front of his chest. 'She was planning her serfs' freedom long before the pestilence came. I read in the records that more than just Sir Richard's grain was being sold to visiting merchants in the two years prior.'

'How is that unlawful?' Lady Anne asked. 'Every serf has the right to buy his way out of bondage if he can save enough gold to satisfy his lord. They all knew it would take time, but each man made a judgement on how much he would need to feed his family and sold the surplus. Where's the blame in that? No one was cheated.'

De Courtesmain levelled a trembling finger at her. 'You did it without Sir Richard's knowledge.'

She feigned a soft laugh. 'I did everything without his knowledge, Master de Courtesmain. Had I not, he would have employed a man such as you a decade ago and, together, you would have brought Develish to her knees.'

'You malign me, milady. I argued against the increased levy.'

'Not after he threatened to dismiss you. Sir Richard was so inflamed everyone in the great hall heard the exchange between you. You had to raise your own voice to plead forgiveness and promise to implement faithfully every order he gave you in future.'

Hugh shifted uncomfortably. Too much of what he'd said and done when Sir Richard was alive had been witnessed, and little of it spoke to his credit. 'Sir Richard was not a reasonable man, milady. His rages were alarming.'

'They were,' she agreed. 'Consider yourself blessed that you endured but one and that his death meant you were released from your pledge of obedience. Having surrendered to him once, you could not have resisted his instruction to falsify our yields to My Lord of Blandeforde.' She held his gaze. 'Did you write of that in your scrolls, Master de Courtesmain? Or do you reserve your enmity only for Athelstan? You had evidence of my husband's dishonesty but none at all of my cousin's.'

De Courtesmain stared at her in disbelief. 'He called himself Thaddeus Thurkell and dressed in peasant clothes, milady.'

'Is that what offends you?' she asked gently. 'That he allowed you to think him beneath you? You thought the same of me while Sir Richard lived, believing my fondness for homespun kirtles was evidence of a weak and timid nature. I remember your shock when you discovered how wrong you were.'

He spread his hands in entreaty. 'I believed what I was told, milady. Had you taken me into your confidence when I arrived, all would have been different. Did I not offer you my allegiance on the day you told me Sir Richard had died?'

'You did, sir.'

'Why did you not tell me then who Thurkell was?'

Lady Anne allowed a wry smile to play across her lips. 'You were too afraid of the pestilence to listen to anything I or Athelstan said, sir. When you weren't accusing us of heresy and wickedness, you were wailing that pustules were growing on your neck. There wasn't a moment in the day when you were able to forget your terror long enough to show you had command of yourself.'

'Your lack of fear made mine worse,' he cried. 'I worried that you had no understanding of what you were doing.'

'Yet Athelstan and I did our best to explain it to you. We even asked your advice, and you had no solutions to offer other than constant penance from my people. You found fault in all of us . . . but my serfs most of all. You made your dislike of them so clear I had no desire to give you further cause to distrust them by revealing they'd stayed silent about Athelstan while Sir Richard was alive.'

'But he was the one I distrusted, milady,' Hugh protested. 'I thought such confidence unnatural in a slave and questioned why you were so willing to take his advice. Had you informed me he was of noble birth my concerns would have vanished.'

This time her laugh was genuine. 'Come, sir,' she said with eyes full of amusement. 'You're far too clever to be so ignorant about yourself. I told you at Christmas who Athelstan was and you could barely speak for rage. You were able to tolerate his clever mind and handsome looks while you thought him a slave, but to learn he was superior to you in every way made your jealousy ungovernable.'

Hugh's anguished silence said more than any words could have done.

Twenty-two

ONCE THE JURORS HAD BEEN selected, a table set up for Andrew Tench to act as clerk and benches arranged across the forecourt for seating, Matthew Miller approached Gyles, Alleyn and James. Close up, his sharp eyes noticed the threadbare appearance of their liveries and the shaggy, ungroomed look of their horses, and he saw a passing resemblance between one of the men and Athelstan's master of hounds. Had d'Amiens been right to call them Develish serfs? he wondered. Might he also be right about Athelstan?

'You should intercede with the captain on behalf of Milady's cousin,' he told Gyles. 'He's been standing for well over an hour and his face looks markedly paler than when I first saw him. He's not far off collapse unless I miss my guess.'

Gyles had the same concern but, since soldiers could only serve one master, he nodded towards the river. 'You must raise the matter with his men, sir.'

'He'll drop before I reach them.' Miller gave his ear a thoughtful scratch. 'Mind, he's a rare sort of noble. Any other would have swooned long since from the pain of a knife through his hand.'

'His forebears on his mother's side were Moors,' Gyles said. 'There'll not be another like him outside Spain.'

'How is he related to Lady Anne?'

'Through his grandfather, who was brother to hers.'

Was that the truth? Miller wondered. Perhaps. It was hard to imagine a serf-woman producing such a giant of a man. 'He's struggling nonetheless. If the steward doesn't call the court together shortly, he'll not have the wits to argue his case.'

Gyles had expressed similar worries to Alleyn. They were all troubled by the length of time Milady had been with the steward because none could think of a benign reason why d'Amiens would extend her detention. Yet how to act when they hadn't the authority to enter the house and demand her release? 'What do you suggest, sir? I doubt My Lord will agree to sit on a bench if it means placing himself in a lower position than the people who accuse him.'

'Demand that My Lord of Blandeforde's chair be brought out. It's a hefty carved throne and your man will not lose stature by resting in it.'

Your man . . . ? 'Such a demand would come better from you, sir. You have more acquaintanceship with the captain than I. He'll pay closer heed to your worries for My Lord's welfare than he will to mine.'

Miller shook his head impatiently. 'You make a mistake by distancing yourselves,' he warned. 'Nothing suits d'Amiens better than to rule through division. He has Milady where he wants her, My Lord too weak to stand, and you and these others—' he gestured to where Ian and his companions stood by the river —'split by a furlong of grass. Do you think your mistress so able she can win this case alone?'

Alleyn was staring towards the entranceway. 'She seems to have persuaded the steward,' he murmured.

Miller turned to watch d'Amiens escort Lady Anne onto the forecourt. Her hand rested lightly on his forearm and they stood for several moments, talking quietly together while servants brought out three armed chairs. Hovering at her other side was a formidable-looking matron who seemed to be daring every man on the forecourt to test her ability to protect her adopted mistress. When the chairs arrived, d'Amiens made an extravagant bow to Milady before helping her to settle in the one to the left. He then called the captain to bring Athelstan forward.

Miller suppressed a laugh as the two men crossed the open ground. 'I wouldn't have believed it if I hadn't seen it with my own eyes,' he muttered as d'Amiens lowered his head in respect to Athelstan and begged him to take the chair on the right. 'You're mighty fortunate in your liege lady, though I pray to God there are no more like her. The world is unsettled enough by the pestilence. We'll lose our way completely if women become our masters.'

'Or find it more easily,' James Buckler countered dryly. 'Your numbers would not be so depleted if you'd had Lady Anne as your guide these last twelve months.'

❧

Miller's belief that the eight fighting men were Develish serfs was confirmed by Lady Anne after d'Amiens declared himself satisfied that Athelstan's nobility had been proved. She rose with the assistance of the matron but, despite her clear weariness, her small figure stood strong and firm throughout her speech. She believed the townsmen would better understand the earlier confusion over Athelstan's status if she explained why some of her serfs had been given the liberty of freemen, for she wanted no lingering doubts about her demesne's honour and virtue. Miller expected a tale for the gullible, but she spoke so simply of her people's commitment to her and each other that he found himself greatly moved.

The trappings of nobility had meant nothing when the pestilence arrived at Develish's gate, she said. Fine gowns and embroidered jerkins gave no protection to the wearers, and both she and her cousin had felt it wrong to make a distinction between themselves and the serfs. If the lowest born were willing to share all they had with their masters, then it ill behoved those of higher birth to set themselves apart. For this reason, all in Develish had worn homespun, eaten their meals together and shared the tasks. Only Sir Richard of Develish's steward, Master de Courtesmain, who had come to the demesne as a stranger a bare few weeks before the pestilence struck, had resisted, seemingly out of a belief that to keep company with serfs was demeaning.

She singled out her captain of arms, Gyles Startout, for the greatest praise. Born a serf, he had been elevated to fighting man a decade previously by her husband, and it was he who had brought his master home and given Develish early news of the plague's virulence. The lone survivor of Sir Richard's ill-fated journey to Bradmayne, Gyles had been as determined as she and Athelstan to prevent the sickness entering their compound. To that end, he had tended and buried his master alone and then remained outside the moat for fourteen days, ready to accept whatever fate God had ordained for him.

Her soft eyes searched out Gyles as she spoke and the grizzled serf's face flushed with pleasure as he bent his knee to her. For a brief moment afterwards, her gaze locked with Matthew Miller's and the sweetness of her smile disarmed him. He had no doubt then that she had spoken the truth when she said she and her cousin had made themselves the equals of underlings. In Miller's whole life, he had never felt the warm acceptance that her smile of recognition bestowed on him.

She went on to speak of how the road north had filled with desperate people looking to flee the pestilence, drawing a comparison with the numbers who had passed through Blandeforde. She and Athelstan were happy for the demesne's fields to be raided for food but not to allow strangers carrying the pestilence into the compound. To that end, Athelstan and Gyles Startout had trained every male serf in the use of weapons so that they might defend the moat should the need arise. By God's grace, they'd only had to do it once.

A voice called out, asking if they'd triumphed, and Lady Anne smiled, saying they had. She believed that Develish now had some of the best archers in Dorseteshire, and the most proficient were the five who rode with Athelstan. He had chosen them to travel with him when he left the demesne to learn what was happening in the world outside. It had needed men of courage to make the journey, and it was a source of pride to her that Athelstan had found them amongst her serfs.

'Why did he have no fighting men of his own?' the same voice called.

'For the reason you heard before,' she answered. 'He came to Develish in the guise of a serf. A retinue would have proclaimed him as a noble.'

'Why didn't he want that?' called another.

'He knew my husband would have prevented my speaking with him if he'd known of his presence.'

A clamour of further questions rose on the air—Miller's louder than most—and Gyles felt his heart sink. What possible explanation could Milady give that would appease sceptical freemen? For himself, he thought she was only making this speech to help Thaddeus understand what she'd told the steward, but the big man's quickly veiled look of disquiet suggested he, too, thought she had backed herself into a corner. Certainly, neither he nor Gyles expected the doughty matron to rescue her.

Mistress Wilde glared at the crowd and then harangued them in Dorseteshire brogue. It was better *she* satisfy their vulgar curiosity than that Milady be obliged to do it, she declared. The poor soul had been forced to endure much from her brutal husband, not least his disdain for her Saxon lineage. Were English men so much less able than English women to understand the pain of being taken from their families and made to suffer under a Norman yoke? It was no wonder she had sympathy for her serfs, whose treatment at the hands of their master had been as vile as hers. Did the men of Blandeforde not ask themselves why Sir Richard had brought a vicious criminal to govern his estates? If de Courtesmain thought nothing of a driving a blade into the arm and hand of My Lord of Athelstan, consider the punishments he would have inflicted on Milady's people if they had been unable to meet her husband's demands for a higher levy on their crops. Praise God for her kindness in trying to protect them, and praise God for sending Athelstan to protect Milady.

She directed her last remark at Jeremiah Slater. 'Your life 'a not bin zo eazy you canna unnerstan 'ow badly hurt a wife is from a beäten or 'ow close they serfs are to starvin when en crop is ta'en.'

'I unnerstan it well,' he answered. 'What be the reason for the Franky's haëtred o' milor'?'

Mistress Wilde tapped her heart. 'Jalousie.'

She went on to tell the townsmen what de Courtesmain had said when he withdrew his accusations against Athelstan. He took no fault to himself, blaming Milady and her serfs for allowing him to believe that Athelstan was inferior to him. It made no matter that he should have guessed so unusual a man could never be a serf. To be tricked had caused him heartache and grief, for he felt he had done nothing to merit their mockery. He admitted trying to turn Milady's daughter and her people against her after Athelstan's departure, but only to restore himself to his rightful position as steward. Bereft of Athelstan's support, and with her serfs in revolt, she would have leant on de Courtesmain as she should have done from the start.

Jeremiah Slater looked amused. 'Be he smitten wi' 'er?'

'He be.'

'He mus be blin' to 'issel'.'

Just witless, said Mistress Wilde dismissively. Despite all he had said and done, he had still fallen to his knees before Milady, begging her forgiveness and pleading with her to allow him to return to Develish.

⁄✺⁊

From where they were standing, Ian and his companions felt a deep discomfort to see de Courtesmain dragged in chains from the house to face trial for his attack on Thaddeus. They could tell from the respect d'Amiens showed Milady when he brought her outside that she must have prevailed, but they questioned whether that victory should be at the expense of the Frenchman.

'He was a fool to stab Thaddeus,' said Peter. 'It wouldn't be happening otherwise.'

'Except Thaddeus probably drove him to it,' muttered Edmund. 'He can be mighty provoking when he has a mind to it.'

The same thoughts were in Gyles's mind. He had no liking for de Courtesmain, whose duplicitous ways had been the cause of Isabella's wounding by Lady Eleanor, but he had no wish to see the snivelling creature flogged. Far more lies had been told and written against him than any he had conceived. Alleyn and James showed their unease in the guilty shifting of their feet, and Gyles was grateful Miller had joined the townsmen on the benches and wasn't close enough to feel their discomfort.

Gyles wouldn't have recognised de Courtesmain in the sad appearance the little Frenchman presented now. Gone was the well-oiled hair, clean-shaven face and prettiness of dress, and in their place were straggled locks, a scruffy beard and peasant clothes. Runnels of tears glistened on his cheeks and he clasped a small wooden cross between his shackled hands as if to show penitence. Behind him walked the priest, his face harsh and unsmiling.

There was a blood lust in the air if the caterwauls that came from the back of the crowd were any guide. Perhaps floggings appealed to these men, or they'd grown bored with the interminable wait for something to happen. For once, Gyles felt himself disappointed in Milady, who watched without emotion as de Courtesmain was forced to his knees in the centre of the forecourt. And what of Thaddeus? Was he untroubled by his conscience?

It seemed not. With a brief nod to Lady Anne, as if to acknowledge an agreement between them, he rose lazily to his feet and asked d'Amiens' permission to address the court. His pallor was less marked from sitting for a quarter-hour, and he made an impressive figure, towering as he did over every seated person on the forecourt. He stood for a moment or two in silence, and then bent his head in respect to the assembled men, touching his fingers to his forehead as he had to Lady Anne.

'I am your humble servant, sirs. Should a time arise when one or more of you has need of my help, you have but to ask.' He smiled to see their surprise. 'Not all traditions are the same. That part of me which is Moorish requires me to repay kindness with kindness, and I offer you my services gladly in return for the courtesy you've shown me.' He paused to collect his thoughts. 'I count myself fortunate that I was raised in the customs of two traditions, because both have taught me wisdom. The giving of charity is common to each, but I have yet to meet a person, English or Moor, who is as steeped in human kindness as Lady Anne of Develish.'

He turned to bend his knee to her. 'God was gracious when he permitted your letter to reach me, cousin. We have written to each other many times down the years, but you had never before asked for my help. I bless God that you did and that He allowed me to make the journey in advance of the pestilence. It was my honour to help you defend your people against this terrible disease, and a greater honour to take your message of hope to the men and women of Dorseteshire. From what I have witnessed in my travels these past months, I believe the worst has passed, and through God's grace we can all begin to dream of a future.'

He faced the crowd again, walking forward to stand in front of de Courtesmain's kneeling figure. 'English justice demands that this man be punished for the crime he has committed against me. Do any of the jurymen doubt that he wounded me most gravely?'

'We do not, sire,' called their foreman. 'But we will hear his explanation if he has one.'

The priest placed his hand on de Courtesmain's head. 'It's an offence against God to attack a noble,' he declared loudly. 'There is no excuse. The prisoner has expressed penitence and will accept his punishment.'

Thaddeus smiled slightly. 'He thought me a serf, Father. Should we condemn him for being wrong?'

'He believed what he wanted to believe.'

'As did you.' Thaddeus produced the dagger from his pocket. 'Is this yours? It has the cross of Christ on its haft, though I question how de Courtesmain came by it.'

Aristide's eyes narrowed. 'Would you have me divulge the secrets of the confessional? I say again, the prisoner has expressed penitence and will accept his punishment.'

'Yet I'm curious to know why he didn't attack me inside the church. He had good reason after I knocked him to the ground. If the knife had been in his possession then, would he not have used it to defend himself?'

Aristide stepped past de Courtesmain to speak in an undertone. 'Desist now,' he hissed. 'Your position is not so secure that you can question a priest.'

Thaddeus's answer wasn't loud enough to carry to the townsmen. 'I saw your fear when the captain brought news of Milady's arrival. You knew I'd reveal your deceits if she gained me a public hearing.' He dropped the knife to the ground between them. 'You may have need of it when the people of Blandeforde learn how shamelessly you saved your own skin at the expense of theirs. They won't thank you for accusing them of wickedness when the closing of the bridge was all that was needed to keep their families from dying.'

The priest's hatred was powerful. 'You're everything de Courtesmain claims you to be.'

'And he somewhat wiser than I painted him. He'd have used the blade sooner and with more passion if he'd thought your promises of a position here would be kept.' Thaddeus reached down to place his hand under de Courtesmain's elbow and raise him to his feet, looking beyond Aristide to the crowd. 'I beg a further kindness of you, my friends,' he called. 'The priest tells me this man's mind is so disturbed he has no understanding of what he's done. Allow me to sentence him according to Moorish justice. It's against our custom to take vengeance on the helpless without offering mercy first.'

'What form would the sentence take?' asked the foreman of the jury.

'The court must order him to recompense me through service. He will be without rights or home to call his own until I judge his penance to be over.'

'You would make him your slave?'

'Or offer him to another. Moorish tradition demands that debts be paid, be they debts of honour or dishonour, and it's the entitlement of the victim to decide who should benefit from the reparation. By such means even monetary obligations are met.'

'Do you choose to offer him to another?'

'Only to one who has shown me kindness.' He touched his forehead to Jeremiah Slater. 'Do you request him, sir?'

The greybeard gave a surprised laugh. 'He'll be of no use to me if his wits have gone.'

'Nor to anyone else,' said Miller. 'He'll likely kill the man who takes him in. You should worry about that yourself, My Lord. If he's attacked you once, he'll do it again.'

'Then his life will be forfeit, for I will not be so merciful a second time.' Thaddeus looked towards the jury. 'What is your decision, sirs? Will you allow Moorish justice to prevail?'

They whispered amongst themselves for several minutes before the foreman signalled agreement, and Thaddeus made the now-familiar gesture of touching his forehead in respect. Lady Anne wondered where he had learnt it and why it was so effective at disarming hostility. He performed the obeisance with such easy grace that he might have been born to it, and she marvelled at how quickly the simple courtesy won the townsmen's trust. None seemed to doubt he'd been raised a Moor or that the customs he cited were genuine.

Clearly, d'Amiens saw danger in allowing Athelstan's influence to grow, for his quickness in accepting the jurymen's decision verged on the unseemly. He instructed Andrew Tench to draw up an order, binding de Courtesmain to Athelstan's service, and then commanded the captain to escort My Lord and his prisoner to the riverbank, where his men awaited him.

'You'll be keen to depart, sire,' he said, bending his neck. 'I regret my error in arresting you but entreat you to believe that the decision was made in good faith. As proctor to My Lord of Blandeforde, I am bound by duty to investigate all and every allegation that is laid before me.'

Lady Anne hid her dismay as Thaddeus turned towards him with disdain in his eyes, afeared that her friend was about to overplay his hand and jeopardise their escape. They had both told too many falsehoods to continue this mummery further. Nevertheless, it was arguable whether she or d'Amiens was the more surprised by his response.

'You have stolen two days of my life, Master d'Amiens. Will you hear my terms of reparation before the worthy men of Blandeforde or would you rather accompany me to the river and discuss them as we walk?'

ᴏ⁷ᴏ

There was a lengthy silence while every person on the forecourt turned to watch the procession make its way across the stretch of grass. Athelstan walked with the steward; the captain led de Courtesmain by his chains. Finding herself forsaken, Lady Anne folded her hands in her lap and retained what composure she could by pretending interest in the ground at her feet. She was quite bereft of ideas on what to say or do, and only the stalwart bulk of Mistress Wilde behind her chair gave her any sense of protection.

The priest's animosity was so strong she could feel it from where he was standing, but whether his anger was directed at her or Thaddeus she couldn't tell. Whichever, he would not stay silent with her at his mercy, exposed and abandoned in front of the crowd, and she doubted she had the strength to keep fighting him, for her sleepless night and painful journey had taken their toll. The sound of footsteps on the forecourt caused her to turn her head, and a surge of relief rose in her heart to see Gyles and Alleyn approach. They paused to bow in unison and then took up position on either side of her chair, staring solemnly at Aristide.

'Is this another fanciful Moorish custom?' he demanded in French of Lady Anne. 'The menacing of priests?'

She studied him curiously. Was it Thaddeus's acts of obeisance that had angered him? she wondered. Could it be that his pride was offended because he hadn't received one himself? 'I doubt their intention is to discomfort you, Father,' she answered. 'They follow the English custom of standing guard to their liege lord.'

He shook his fist at her. 'You are not their liege lord, milady, and serfs have no right to enter a manor court. Will you instruct them to withdraw or must I?'

Gyles took a step forward to place himself between the two. 'If you give such an order it will not be obeyed, Father,' he said in French. 'I have no wish to challenge your authority, but I will if I deem it necessary. Milady's safety is all that concerns me.'

Aristide pointed towards the guards who stood around the forecourt. 'These soldiers will take you in charge if you resist.'

Gyles placed his hand on the bow which lay diagonally across his chest. 'Then be it on your head if the captain's peace is broken, sir.'

Jeremiah Slater pushed himself to his feet. He, too, spoke in French. 'You make trouble where there is none, Father,' he said irritably. 'I know of no by-law that precludes serfs from the manor court. If such an injunction existed, the steward would have barred Mistress Wilde's attendance.' He turned to address his fellows, reverting to English. 'I'm minded to follow My Lord of Athelstan's example and demand reparation for the losses we've endured. It impresses me as a better custom than anything the Church or French law offers us. How think the rest of you?'

Had she been a distant observer to the heated discussion that followed, Lady Anne would have found it amusing to watch this group of men argue the merits of invented Moorish customs with the priest. As it was, she was at the heart of it, with the townsmen begging her to support them as fervently as she had supported her people. To avoid antagonising the priest, she reminded them that the court was still in session and that, as an invited guest, her words carried no authority. The men of Blandeforde must decide and argue the case for themselves.

After her fourth such careful response, Aristide accused her of inciting heresy. 'Why do you encourage these thoughts instead of condemning them? Where is your responsibility?'

She bent her head in apology. 'Forgive me, Father. I thought you believed the views of a woman to be of no account. Would you have me answer as a liege lord who is bound by duty to support her King and the Church?'

His lips thinned. 'Not if your ambition is to add to this mockery. The Moors are a heathen race and should be exposed as such.'

'My only knowledge of them comes from Athelstan, and he is far from heathen. Nevertheless, I will do my best to assist you.' She rose to her feet. 'Good sirs, Father Aristide sees heresy in your ideas and urges you to abandon them. I would ask only that you bring reason to your thinking. For each of you, your greatest loss has been the death of your wife and children. I hear the sorrow in your voices when you say you wish God had taken you and not them.'

'We all feel that, milady,' said Slater.

'As does every man and woman in Doreseteshire who has suffered similarly,' she answered gently. 'You are not alone in looking for someone to blame for your grief. But who should that person be? And how much will you demand from him? One noble? Ten? A thousand? What price do you put on the lives of your families?'

'More than any man can pay.'

'Then talk of monetary reparation is foolish, is it not? Your hearts will mend sooner with kindly companions than bags of uncaring gold. You can insist Master d'Amiens choose widows for you as payment for your wives, but are you not better able to manage these affairs yourselves?'

Slater and most of the crowd expressed agreement, but Miller was less easily placated. 'The steward should have given us the same protection he gave the household, milady. How is it right that freemen were left to die while servants were helped to live? I, for one, demand reparation for that.'

'In what form, Master Miller? My cousin has told you that the custom of the Moors is to repay in kind. Would you have Mistress Wilde lose her life because she obeyed the steward's orders?'

His mouth twisted in a sour smile. 'I would have the men responsible pay. And if reparation must be made in kind, there are countless dead in a pit—the little servant girl from here amongst them—who were tossed in without ceremony after the last of our priests died.' He looked at Aristide. 'It's past due they were disinterred and reburied with their names recorded and the proper rites performed—and the priest and the steward are the men to do it.'

Aristide ignored him to address Lady Anne. 'I barely understand his speech,' he said in French. 'You must make the answers for me.'

She thought he'd understood perfectly well. Nevertheless . . . 'It's a poor vengeance that comes back to bite you, Master Miller,' she said. 'I doubt it's wise to unearth the dead when the town has been free of the pestilence for eight weeks.'

'You think we'll catch it from corpses?'

'It's not something I would risk in Develish.'

'Nor I in Blandeforde,' said Slater firmly. 'The dead will rest peacefully enough if Father Aristide consecrates the pit and the land around it. As to their names, Master d'Amiens can supply them from his own register once a census has been taken of the living.'

Miller gave a grunt of disgust when the townsmen voiced agreement yet again. 'You're overly quick to give up on your losses. If reparation is what we want, we must demand it.'

'Then offer sensible ideas,' called a voice from the back.

'Perhaps Milady has a suggestion,' said Andrew Tench. 'She knows the custom better than we, for her cousin will have explained it to her.'

But Lady Anne was drained of both strength and answers. She placed a trembling hand on the arm of her chair to steady herself, and it fell to Gyles to answer for her. 'You would do better to put your questions to My Lord,' he said, nodding towards the grass beyond the forecourt. 'Unless I miss my guess, he and Master d'Amiens are returning.'

Twenty-three

James Buckler, standing with the horses, didn't need Gyles's hard stare and fractional movement of his head towards Thaddeus to know he must act. He'd heard the exchanges on the forecourt and could see as well as his friend that Milady was too fatigued to continue. Yet he doubted Thaddeus was in any better condition to offer solutions. What had seemed like a good idea to save tender Develish consciences was set to become a millstone around their necks.

With quick, practised movements, he hobbled his mount and then attached the halters of the others to its breast collar before stepping away to stand in Thaddeus and d'Amiens' path. Five paces back walked the captain, carrying the manacles he'd removed from de Courtesmain, and behind him came Ian and Edmund, leading a pony with leather bags slung across its withers. James recognised them as those that carried Lady Eleanor's dowry and, praying they presaged good fortune, he forced himself to bend his knee to Thaddeus.

The bandage on Thaddeus's hand was soaked with blood and his face had paled again, but the brief flicker of humour in his eyes said he understood James's reluctance. James had barely been able to show deference to Sir Richard, and to bow before a man he'd known from birth as a bastard changeling was an even greater humiliation. Thaddeus gestured for him to rise. 'You have a message for me?'

'Milady of Develish requests your assistance when your business with the steward is concluded, sire. The townsmen have questions about the Moorish custom of reparation and, being most wearied from her journey and the events of this day, she believes you will answer them better than she can.'

He watched Thaddeus take his left hand in his right and dig his thumb and forefinger into the bandage around his wound. Was it any surprise the bandage was wet with blood if this was the way he was staying alert? The pain must have been severe, but his voice gave no indication of it when he addressed the steward. 'How long will it take to prepare the writs of transfer, Master d'Amiens?'

'Not above an hour, My Lord. The wording is standard and needs but the name of the holder to be changed. I foresee no difficulties as long as the gold reaches the required weight.'

'It will. My men will carry the bags inside and watch as you weigh the amounts. When the documents are ready, bring them to the forecourt so that I may sign them.' He smiled to see d'Amiens' immediate resistance. 'It's never wise to let grievances fester, sir. The townsmen's anger will be harder to appease if you oblige them to wait for Blandeforde's return. You've suffered nothing by honouring your debt to me—indeed, most would say you've gained by it through the added revenue to Blandeforde's coffers—so why fear accord with your own people?'

D'Amiens searched out Matthew Miller. 'Some will break their side of the bargain as soon as it's made.'

'I'm sure they believe the same about you, sir. It's a sad world where trust is in such short supply. Aren't you grieved that a woman finds it easier to win the townsmen's respect than you or the priest? Even with my limited understanding of English customs, that would seem unusual. How do you account for it?'

'You said it yourself, sire. Milady is a rare woman.'

'So rare that she was willing to take the hand of every man on the forecourt. Will you do likewise if I find a way to soothe their sense of injustice? You will win their confidence if you do.'

'Milady was foolhardy.'

'Or wise enough to recognise that two months without a death means the pestilence has passed. If she believes the time has come to abandon fear and embrace the future, should you not also?'

D'Amiens watched irritably as Thaddeus strode towards the forecourt and then, with a muttered command to the captain, he beckoned Ian and Edmund to follow him to the house. As they left, he said crossly that the sooner they finished their business the better he'd be pleased.

The remark won sympathy from James. He may not have known it, but he was as beset by dread as his son had been the first time Thaddeus had claimed to be a noble. So much could still go wrong, yet Thaddeus seemed determined to test God's patience. The wiser course would surely have been to distance himself and Milady from the crowd, but, instead, he lowered himself to his chair and engaged with them.

The captain moved to stand beside James. 'My Lord is powerfully persuasive,' he said, watching Thaddeus touch his forehead to Aristide. 'He'll have the priest reconciled to Moorish customs before he's done.' He motioned towards the guard house. 'Will you accompany me, sir? Master d'Amiens has granted My Lord the use of a carriage and horses so that Milady may return home tonight. The stabling is beyond the house and there are three wagons to choose from. I will order my men to assist you in preparing one.'

James looked at the sun. 'There's scarce three hours of light left.'

'My Lord intends to travel with torches.' A teasing smile lit the captain's eyes. 'Having sampled it himself, he believes Milady will find the highway less arduous than Master d'Amiens' hospitality.'

৶৩

Olyver shrugged when Peter asked what they were supposed to do with de Courtesmain. The Frenchman lay curled on the grass, sobbing like a child, and nothing he said was intelligible.

'What's he afraid of?' asked Joshua.

'Develish's anger?' suggested Olyver.

'More likely being abandoned along the way,' said Peter. 'He'll have nothing if Thaddeus decides to set him loose two miles outside Blandeforde.' He knelt to shake de Courtesmain's shoulder. 'You must cease your crying, sir. You shame yourself by it.'

A whisper reached his ear. 'I am already shamed.'

'Maybe so, but none of us has slept enough to have patience with your whining. You're wrong if you think it'll win Milady's or Athelstan's sympathy. They'll respect you more if you take your punishment bravely.'

'I'm lower than a serf.'

'Only because you behaved like a weasel.' Peter grasped the neck of the Frenchman's tunic and hauled him to his feet. 'What do you say to me taking him out ahead of time and talking some sense into him?' he asked Olyver. 'Milady shouldn't have to deal with him in this state.'

'Where will you go?'

'Along the highway.' Peter set to unbuckling the second pack pony's harness. 'He can use this for a mount. The other will be able to carry the load once its rid of the gold. If you haven't caught up with me before the light fades, which you won't with a wagon in tow, I'll make camp near the road's edge. You'll likely see my fire before I see your torches.'

Olyver helped him lift the load to the ground. 'Then make yourself useful while you wait for us,' he said, loosening the knot that held the cauldron and a bag of butchered mutton before attaching them to Peter's saddle. 'I'll not be the only one slitting my throat if I don't see food this night.'

'These, too,' added Joshua, removing a sack of beans and another of dried fruit. 'You can wear them around your neck the way we've had to,' he told de Courtesmain, stringing the rope across his shoulders. 'Peter won't welcome your company, but I don't doubt he'd rather listen to your grudges than have you cause Milady further irritation here.'

Olyver stooped to lace his hands beneath de Courtesmain's foot. 'You should count yourself lucky that God saw fit to inflict you upon us,' he said severely. 'You'd have died long since if He hadn't sent you to Develish.'

❧

The crowd of women and children at the gate had dispersed, leaving only a handful of youths to witness Peter and de Courtesmain's departure. Two or three walked with them, agog with curiosity to know what was happening. Peter answered their questions honestly but shook his head in disgust when they expressed disappointment to hear there'd be no flogging.

'Is that what you've been waiting for?' he asked.

'There's nothing else to do.'

Peter instructed Hugh to take a firm hold of the pony's mane and led him at a fast trot to the end of the approach road. From there, he slowed to a walk. They received curious glances from the women they passed in the streets but none was emboldened enough to speak. He expected to find guards on the bridge, and advised Hugh to speak and act like a freeman if he didn't want to be returned to the steward as an absconder, but the road was empty and they crossed without trouble.

As they made their way up the gentle incline of the hill, Hugh found his voice. 'Do you plan to kill me?'

Peter glanced at him. 'Why would I want to?'

'To spare Milady further worry. I can't speak of what I know if I'm dead.'

'You've already spoken,' said Peter. 'What use would your death be now? The time to kill you was before you entered Blandeforde. I don't say I wouldn't have been tempted. We'd all have been saved a lot of trouble if you'd met with an accident on the road from Bourne.'

'Others may believe me.'

'Not while you're bonded to Athelstan, they won't. No one will hear you unless he gives you permission to speak. Be grateful he kept you alive. You know from the lashes you inflicted on the serfs of Foxcote that you'd not have survived. We had word before you ever reached Develish that five of the men you scourged died from having their skin torn from their ribs.'

Hugh closed his eyes. 'I did what I was commanded to do.'

Peter thought of the numerous times Thaddeus had chastised his companions for blaming their faults on others instead of taking responsibility themselves. 'Is that your defence for every bad act you commit? "Someone else made me do it." I'll wager you blame God for your misfortunes as often as you blame men.'

'I fear His wrath too much to chastise Him.'

'Then I'd not wish to live a second in your shoes, Master de Courtesmain. You must struggle with terror every day. An angry God's as hard to please as an angry lord.'

A flicker of irritation flared in Hugh's heart. 'What knowledge do you have of either? Develish serfs are ignorant of the meaning of wrath or fear.'

Peter gave a grunt of amusement. 'As were you while you lived amongst us. Was that not more pleasurable than where you find yourself now?'

It was a moment before Hugh could produce the words. 'I fear returning to Develish.'

'Because you're a traitor or because you're a slave?'

'Both,' came the whispered reply. 'I'll be a figure of hatred and mockery through what I've done. It would be a kindness to end my life now.'

Peter led him over the breast of the hill. 'You give up too easily, Master de Courtesmain. If the steward honours his promise to grant Athelstan title to Pedle Hinton, you'll be making your home there rather than Develish.' He saw relief enter de Courtesmain's face. 'You won't be so keen when you see it,' he warned. 'The village is destroyed and the roof of the house half-burnt. Your hands will grow calluses cutting timber and mixing daub before they ever lift a pen again.'

The rest of their conversation took place beside a fire while Peter cooked mutton and watched the highway for approaching torches. For his part, Hugh felt compelled to keep revisiting his sins of omission and commission, and the confessions he made to Peter were more honest than any he'd made to a priest. His greatest wretchedness was to lose his status, but Peter advised him to cease fretting about an order made in Blandeforde. Milady and Athelstan would never reduce a man to slavery. They had striven too long to win freedom for their people to take a backward step now.

'You must learn new skills and work with the rest of us to promote the good of all,' he told Hugh. 'When Milady and Athelstan succeed in their plans to turn Develish and Pedle Hinton into communities of freemen and merchants, you'll profit along with the rest of us. If you cling to your one talent, you'll be left behind.'

Lady Anne had said the same on the morning of the great storm, and Hugh had dismissed the idea as fanciful. But he saw that she and Peter were right when the glimmer of torchlight appeared on the highway. As the convoy approached, there was no mistaking Thurkell astride his black charger. He rode between the Startout twins, both holding flares above their heads. On their flanks, Joshua and Edmund steered their mounts with their knees to leave their hands free to operate the bows they were carrying; ahead of them loped the dogs, questing to and fro across the road to sniff out miscreants amongst the trees.

Had they been strangers, Hugh would have taken them for what they appeared to be, a lord and his fighting men, and to cling to the comforting idea that they were serfs—and therefore beneath him—would be as foolish as Peter had warned. Even the older Develish men who followed with Milady's wagon rode with assurance, and Hugh's cheeks heated to recall how he had disparaged them to her, saying none had the wisdom or ability to sit on her council.

Panic engulfed him as they drew closer, and such strong pains struck at his chest that he thought he was dying. He prayed he was. Dead, he would not have to take their derision or search in vain for ways to atone. It was a mystery to him now that he had been so unable to accept that the education which had benefited him might also benefit those whom the Church had ruled beneath him.

He felt Peter's hand grip his arm and heard the youth's call of welcome to Thurkell.

'You're a sight for sore eyes,' came the laughing retort. 'I'm told you have a veritable feast for us.' As the charger brought him level, he gave a nod to Hugh. 'I trust I find you well, Master de Courtesmain.'

Hugh felt tears prick behind his eyes. 'You do, sire.'

Thaddeus swung from his saddle. 'I'm glad to hear it. You were in safe hands with Peter.' He passed his reins to Ian. 'Let me speak with Milady. If she's happy to spend the night in the open, I say we make camp here. For myself, I haven't the energy to travel to Develish this night.'

※

As the flames of the fire flickered across the smiling faces of the people around it, Hugh was reminded of when Lady Anne had danced with her serfs to celebrate their victory over Bourne's archers. He had condemned her for it, believing she was endangering her daughter and him by lowering herself to their level. To offer friendship to base-born people was to encourage rebellion, and he'd feared that he and Lady Eleanor, being Normans, would become the butts of their hatred.

He wished now that he had followed her advice and sought closeness with these men. Lady Anne had lost no respect through her care for them. Indeed, their admiration for her showed in everything they said and did. When she stepped from the carriage, taking Thurkell's hand to steady herself, she was dressed once again in homespun, and Hugh had felt an absurd relief to see the simple kirtle. It made his own peasant tunic and britches less noticeable amidst the Athelstan and Develish liveries.

Behind her had come Mistress Wilde, her face wreathed in shy smiles as Thurkell assisted her to the ground. Her belief that he was Athelstan was reinforced by the Develish men's constant use of his title, and Hugh saw that they found it easy to do. Whatever the truth of his birth, there was little doubt they accepted him as a worthy leader beside Milady.

Mistress Wilde was presented as Lady Anne's chaperone for the journey, but when the woman spoke of her excitement to spend a few days in Develish before returning home, Hugh guessed that Milady's reason for bringing her was to remove any lingering uncertainties d'Amiens might have about Thurkell's status. The people of Develish were as committed to upholding the imposture as every man here, and Mistress Wilde would take her belief in his nobility back to Blandeforde. It seemed she was also the bearer of clean rags to re-dress Thurkell's wounds, and Hugh was grateful to Peter for drawing him away while that task was performed.

'We'll serve a better purpose collecting wood,' he said, beckoning to Edmund to bring a torch. After a hundred paces, he asked Edmund if Athelstan had succeeded.

The other youth grinned. 'He did. In return for a pledge of fealty to Blandeforde, Athelstan bears writs granting him vassal status over Pedle Hinton.'

'Will they hold?'

'No reason why not. D'Amiens wanted the gold more than he wanted a demesne devoid of people. Ian said he warned Athelstan he'd give him no quarter if the estate failed in its tax obligations.'

'How did My Lord answer?'

'He advised d'Amiens to concern himself with his own affairs. He was fortunate to have Athelstan's gold to plug the holes in Blandeforde's revenue today, but the shortfalls will increase if the townsmen can't find the confidence to reopen the markets and resume trading. He's persuaded d'Amiens to meet with their council and hear their ideas. It seems they're proposing to hold markets outside their boundaries until they're sure the pestilence has passed.'

'Will that help?'

'Athelstan believes so. Their greatest fear is to allow sufferers into the town again. He's advised all to keep their distance and toss their money onto the ground rather than touch hands. If customers and visiting merchants do the same, confidence will grow on both sides.'

'What else did he say?'

'That he and Milady will set an example by sending their surplus stock to Blandeforde as soon as the markets open. Where Develish and Pedle Hinton lead, others will follow. The townsmen cheered him, but he told us afterwards that it will benefit us as well as them. D'Amiens will be reassured that both demesnes can submit taxes if he sees us trading regularly in Blandeforde.'

Peter saw Hugh shake his head. 'You don't agree, Master de Courtesmain?'

'If the dead are as numerous as Athelstan says, there won't be enough hungry mouths to fetch a good price on meat. To satisfy d'Amiens, he'll need to show another source of wealth.'

'What do you suggest?'

'That he brings in reserves of gold from his Spanish demesnes as soon as foreign ships make entry to England's harbours again. A receipt, properly set out and signed by a ship's captain, will be all that is needed to convince d'Amiens the transaction took place.'

Edmund exchanged a glance with Peter, neither sure what de Courtesmain meant by this. That he believed Athelstan had reserves of gold or that a receipt could be easily forged? Both could see the merit of forgery to explain the wealth they'd plundered from abandoned demesnes this last month. Their biggest haul had come from Bradmayne. For all his professed need of Lady Eleanor's dowry, My Lord of Bradmayne had still left a sizeable fortune behind in his treasury. It should have been stolen by bandits, since the demesne was deserted, but as Thaddeus had said, he and his companions seemed to be the only bandits left in south Dorseteshire.

The fruits of their labour were buried deep in a sand dune over-looking the sea near Poole. Used carefully and wisely, Thaddeus believed there was enough dead men's gold to rebuild Pedle Hinton and set all in Develish on the path to freedom. Nevertheless, he had yet to find a way to excuse his thieving. Certainly, the idea of forging receipts hadn't occurred to him.

'Do you think ships will return soon, Master de Courtesmain?' Edmund asked.

Hugh wondered afterwards if that was the moment he chose to embrace change, or if the desire to do so hadn't been with him from the moment a chattel wife took control of Develish. 'My Lord of Bourne thought so,' he answered. 'I prepared several receipts for him in expectation of trade resuming before too long. He thought it wise to divide his stolen gold across several ships, and I still remember the names I gave the vessels. Will Athelstan be interested to learn them? His own transactions might carry more credence if another lord has used the same ships.'

Peter gave a friendly nod. 'Be sure he will,' he said.

⨍

As the meal was eaten, Hugh kept his head lowered for fear of meeting Lady Anne's or Thurkell's gaze. He had little confidence that Peter spoke for either of them, and believed it was a matter of time only before one or both forced him to account for his actions. He feared that time had come when Thurkell laid aside his plate and asked Ian to bring his writing desk. He opened the lid and revealed the scrolls Hugh had taken to Blandeforde. He handed Lady Anne the page from the Develish register. 'This is part of your people's history and belongs to you, milady.'

Lady Anne took a moment to read it again and then leant forward to feed the cracked vellum into the fire. 'A small part only,' she said, 'and since there's no way of threading it back into the ledger, it will be lost to us anyway. Better it adds to our warmth than crumbles to dust through neglect.'

Thaddeus watched a lick of flame destroy the evidence of his birth and then raised his eyes to Hugh's. 'The rest are yours, sir, even the letter I left for you in Bourne. Master d'Amiens had no interest in keeping them so I asked for their return. Do you wish to retain them or shall we allow cleansing fire to do its work? I suggest we'll build a better future on new foundations than ones that have become twisted over time.'

Hugh was too nervous to answer. Was he included in this future, he wondered, or did Thurkell speak only for the people of Develish? If the man's intention was to cast him aside, would he not do better to keep the scrolls and threaten to use them as Lady Anne had threatened to use Bourne's letters?

'Perhaps Master de Courtesmain will find the decision easier if you burn the writ of slavery first,' Lady Anne advised quietly.

'Indeed.' Thaddeus lifted the writ and passed it to Peter. 'Allow Master de Courtesmain to reassure himself it's the correct document and then place it in the flames. Blandeforde's seal at the bottom should help it burn.'

Hugh took the page from Peter in trembling hands and ran his tongue around his mouth to produce some words. 'I wounded you badly and had malice in my heart when I did it. What punishment will you demand of me in place of this?'

With a sigh of impatience, as if despairing of Hugh's ability to understand anything, Peter seized back the parchment and thrust it into the fire. 'If it's pain you seek, you'll find it soon enough by working without complaint at whatever you're asked to do,' he said sternly. 'I wasn't jesting when I said your hands will grow calluses cutting timber before they ever lift a pen again.' He stood to retrieve the scrolls from Thaddeus's writing desk. 'All Athelstan asks is whether you wish to make your future with us or forge it alone. There's few would offer you the choice after the trouble you've caused, but Athelstan does. What's your decision?'

'I would join you,' Hugh whispered.

Peter tossed the scrolls into the flames and resumed his seat, tapping the Frenchman's shoulder by way of welcome. 'You'll likely change your mind after you've eaten Joshua's stew five nights in a row, but that's a penance we all have to pay.'

When the laughter subsided, the conversation turned to the ending of Develish's isolation. Thurkell said that there was no knowing how the rest of England fared but he believed it would be safe for Lady Anne to cross the moat on the morrow. She agreed so readily that Hugh knew she must have come to the same decision herself. Perhaps her journey to Blandeforde had been all that was needed to confirm what she and Thurkell had believed all along: that the pestilence would end as surely as the pox or the flux. Hugh wondered that he had been so unwilling to see the soundness of their arguments when even a priest like Aristide had preferred reason over the teachings of the Church.

Lady Anne promised Mistress Wilde a fine celebration, and the woman's plump face was wreathed in smiles to be invited as an equal. It seemed, however, that Thurkell would not be part of the festivities because he gave instructions on where the convoy would divide the following day. Lady Anne, Mistress Wilde and Milady's men would take the highway to Develish, while he and his, together with Master de Courtesmain, would ride to Pedle Hinton. With God's grace, he hoped to invite Milady and her daughter for a visit in the summer, when the forget-me-nots were in full bloom and the beginnings of a fine new demesne were underway.

Hugh felt Lady Anne's gaze upon him. 'Do you look forward to helping My Lord rebuild Pedle Hinton, Master de Courtesmain?' she asked.

Tongue-tied by nerves again, he could only nod.

'I shall ask the women of Develish to stay with me to till and plant our fields, and the men to cross the hills to assist in Pedle Hinton. Master Miller and several more have already promised to make the journey from Blandeforde, and My Lord hopes to attract others in return for wages. He looks to create a community of freemen who can use their wits and skills to improve their lives and the lives of their children. When the time comes, he will need a person knowledgeable in figures to keep a tally of their earnings. Would you be comfortable in such a post, Master de Courtesmain?'

Hugh stared at his hands so that he wouldn't have to look at her. His greatest regret was that he had accepted her illiterate husband's view of her instead of deciding her character for himself. 'I doubt you and My Lord would be right to trust my judgement, milady. I have been wrong about everything.'

'Not everything,' she answered gently. 'Your only real error was to believe that God judges a man by his birth and not by his deeds.'

❧

When the moon was three hours from midnight, Gyles Startout lit a torch from the fire and instructed the men to follow him into the woodland in search of bracken for beds. He invited Mistress Wilde to accompany them, raising her forcefully to her feet with his free hand cupped beneath her elbow when she expressed reluctance to leave the warmth of the flames. Alleyn moved to assist him, marching her unceremoniously into the trees while telling her amiably that she must make herself responsible for Milady's mattress in the wagon.

She wrestled herself free after a hundred paces and glared indignantly at the amused faces around her. 'If your purpose is malign, be sure I shall scream,' she warned. 'Lady Anne will be shocked if her chaperone is ill-treated by men she trusts and will send My Lord to rescue me.'

Gyles raised his hand in apology. 'Forgive us, mistress. Our hearts are pure and our purpose good. It's many weeks since My Lord and Milady were able to speak in private. They will welcome some time alone, I think.'

She made a pretence of patting down her cloak to restore some dignity. 'You had but to say. Are they close as cousins? I sense a strong bond between them.'

'Their cousinship is distant but their friendship close. There is admiration and respect on both sides.'

'Grown stronger since her husband's death, I don't doubt. Neither was free to express regard while Sir Richard lived.'

'Indeed . . . and have had little opportunity since.'

Mistress Wilde heard the wry note in Gyles's voice, and looked from one man to the other. Sudden understanding appeared in her eyes. 'Do you hope for more than expressions of regard? A betrothal perhaps?' A laugh rumbled in her throat when none of them answered. 'Go look for bracken and let God do His work,' she said, shooing them away. 'If ever a union was ordained, it was surely this one.'

Develish, the evening of the fifteenth day of April, 1349

We received such a welcome when we returned this noon that I wept for the gladness our people displayed. So loud were the cheers from across the moat that it was several minutes before Gyles could announce that our time of exclusion is over and Athelstan has been granted title to Pedle Hinton. At the forefront of the crowd was Eleanor, clasping the hands of Isabella and Robert as naturally as if they were her brother and sister, and I cannot recall ever seeing her so happy. It was a sweet moment when I stepped from the raft and she allowed me to embrace her as a mother; sweeter still when she begged me to accept the embraces of our serfs.

I have promised to give an account of our time in Blandeforde when we assemble to eat, though I doubt it will be necessary. Clara Trueblood has invited Mistress Wilde to the kitchen, claiming quite shamelessly that she needs a woman of experience to help in the preparation of the meal. From the noisy gasps of astonishment which echo through the great hall, Mistress Wilde's rendering of the tale is more enthralling than mine can ever be. Who, except Thaddeus, will understand that the most exciting of yesterday's events was to ride at speed along a deserted highway?

I have no fear that our people will reveal the truth about Athelstan. They and I have talked it through many times and none resents Thaddeus's assumption of nobility. All have confidence that his single purpose is to secure their freedom and future prosperity, not least Will and Eva. It's 3 months since he pledged to support them in idleness if they maintained the fiction, and Will has been counting his good fortune ever since. He tells me now that he always had confidence the son he raised would succeed in acquiring a demesne of his own!

It matters not if the name Thaddeus is used by accident. Mistress Wilde is so enchanted by Athelstan's Moorish ways and thoughtful courtesy that she is quite persuaded he encouraged all to call him Thaddeus while he lived as a serf. Gyles, Alleyn and James have tasked themselves with spreading the story that Athelstan entered Develish last spring as a peasant, and as long as enough repeat it, Mistress Wilde will confirm that truth to d'Amiens upon her return to Blandeforde. I don't doubt he will question her thoroughly, for a man such as he does not abandon his suspicions lightly.

I cannot say what caused de Courtesmain to fall to his knees and beg me to forgive his errors and lies but we would not have escaped so easily if he hadn't. In truth, I had expected him to hold even more strongly to his accusations after d'Amiens threatened him with a flogging, and I am sure the

priest expected the same, because he was most put out when
de Courtesmain chose retraction instead. Mistress Wilde assures
me God stepped in to prick de Courtesmain's conscience, but I
think it more likely de Courtesmain looked to prick mine. If so,
he's fortunate Thaddeus is able to read my thoughts and found a
convincing reason to spare his attacker.

I pray de Courtesmain has the sense to bury his animosities
and work with Thaddeus in Pedle Hinton. Gyles says he'll have
little choice, since the only audience for his whispered poison
in the next few weeks will be Ian, Olyver, Edmund, Joshua and
Peter, and not one of them will waver in loyalty to the man
who is taking them from bondage to freedom. I don't doubt for
a moment that Gyles is correct. His sons and their friends are
as worthy as their fathers and wholly committed to the path
Thaddeus has chosen for them.

Dear Gyles. He has been my kindest and most generous
supporter since I came to Develish. Mistress Wilde tells me I
have him to thank for allowing me some moments alone with
Thaddeus last night. How precious they were, for it is many
weeks since my beautiful Moor last held me in his arms. Then,
we could only dream that a day might come when a vassal
widow might marry a bastard slave, but now we dare to hope
that the dream will be realised. Thaddeus tells me he finds his
Moorish part easier to play than his noble English part, but in

truth he plays both with such ease that God must surely have
intended him to be Athelstan.

It will be a few months yet before Pedle Hinton is restored
and My Lord of Athelstan in a position to ask permission from
Blandeforde to unite his demesne with Develish. That time will
allow me to help Eleanor make peace with herself so that she
gains in confidence and her mind becomes calm. I worry less
than Clara and Isabella about her seizure because her character
is not as frail as they believe. She needs only to understand that
love is not diminished through being shared, and I see evidence
of that lesson already being learnt through her nurturing of the
cats and the happiness her friendship with Robert brings her.
I even dare to hope that it won't be long before Isabella, too,
becomes a loved and trusted confidante.

Robert tells me it was he who helped Father Anselm
compose his letter, by keeping the old man's tankard replenished
with wine. He says the more the Father drank the better
his ideas and handwriting became! I can believe the second
claim but not the first. The sweet praise could only have come
from Robert. He assures me that his ambition now is to be a
merchant and not a fighting man, but I've made a small wager
with his father that he will reach even greater heights. He has
the same cleverness and thirst for knowledge as Thaddeus and

Isabella at the same age, and it will not be long before he has
learnt all that I can teach him.

I bless God daily for the bonds of affection that have held us
together and brought us through the pestilence. To be loved and
honoured for who we are, and not what our status represents, is
surely the lesson He wanted us to learn when he sent His son to
live as a carpenter and not as a king.

The future will be bright indeed when even the humblest
are given the chance to prove their worth.

In nomine Patris et Filii et Spiritus Sanctus